THE COMPLETE ILLUSTRATED NOVELS OF

Jane Austen

VOLUME 1

THE COMPLETE ILLUSTRATED NOVELS OF

Jane Austen

VOLUME 1

PRIDE AND PREJUDICE

MANSFIELD PARK

PERSUASION

Illustrated by
Hugh Thomson

CHANCELLOR
PRESS

Pride and Prejudice first appeared in Great Britain
in 1813
Mansfield Park first appeared in Great Britain
in 1814
Persuasion first appeared in Great Britain
in 1818

This collected edition published in Great Britain 1985
by Chancellor Press
an imprint of Reed Consumer Books Limited
Michelin House, 81 Fulham Road, London SW3 6RB
and Auckland, Melbourne, Singapore and Toronto

Reprinted 1993

ISBN 1 85152 418 5

A CIP catalogue record for this book is available at
the British Library

Printed in the Slovak Republic
50639

Contents

PRIDE AND PREJUDICE
7

MANSFIELD PARK
305

PERSUASION
651

Pride and Prejudice

He came down to see the place

CHAPTER ONE

IT IS A TRUTH UNIVERSALLY ACKNOWLEDGED, that a single man in possession of a good fortune, must be in want of a wife.

However little known the feelings or views of such a man may be on his first entering a neighbourhood, this truth is so well fixed in the minds of the surrounding families, that he is considered as the rightful property of some one or other of their daughters.

'My dear Mr Bennet,' said his lady to him one day, 'have you heard that Netherfield Park is let at last?'

Mr Bennet replied that he had not.

'But it is,' returned she; 'for Mrs Long has just been here, and she told me all about it.'

Mr Bennet made no answer.

'Do not you want to know who has taken it?' cried his wife impatiently.

'*You* want to tell me, and I have no objection to hearing it.'

This was invitation enough.

'Why, my dear, you must know, Mrs Long says that Netherfield is taken by a young man of large fortune from the north of England; that he came down on Monday in a chaise and four to see the place, and was so much delighted with it that he agreed with Mr Morris immediately; that he is to take possession before Michaelmas, and some of his servants are to be in the house by the end of next week.'

'What is his name?'

'Bingley.'

'Is he married or single?'

'Oh! single, my dear, to be sure! A single man of large fortune; four or five thousand a year. What a fine thing for our girls!'

'How so? how can it affect them?'

'My dear Mr Bennet,' replied his wife, 'how can you be so tiresome! You must know that I am thinking of his marrying one of them.'

'Is that his design in settling here?'

'Design! nonsense, how can you talk so! But it is very likely that he *may* fall in love with one of them, and therefore you must visit him as soon as he comes.'

'I see no occasion for that. You and the girls may go, or you may send them by themselves, which perhaps will be still better, for as you are as handsome as any of them, Mr Bingley might like you the best of the party.'

'My dear, you flatter me. I certainly *have* had my share of beauty, but I do not pretend to be any thing extraordinary now. When a woman has five grown up daughters, she ought to give over thinking of her own beauty.'

'In such cases, a woman has not often much beauty to think of.'

'But, my dear, you must indeed go and see Mr Bingley when he comes into the neighbourhood.'

'It is more than I engage for, I assure you.'

'But consider your daughters. Only think what an establishment it would be for one of them. Sir William and Lady Lucas are determined to go, merely on that account, for in general you know they visit no new comers. Indeed you must go, for it will be impossible for *us* to visit him, if you do not.'

'You are over scrupulous surely. I dare say Mr Bingley will be very glad to see you; and I will send a few lines by you to assure him of my hearty consent to his marrying which ever he chuses of the girls; though I must throw in a good word for my little Lizzy.'

'I desire you will do no such thing. Lizzy is not a bit better than the others; and I am sure she is not half so handsome as Jane, nor half so good humoured as Lydia. But you are always giving *her* the preference.'

'They have none of them much to recommend them,' replied he; 'they are all silly and ignorant like other girls; but Lizzy has something more of quickness than her sisters.'

'Mr Bennet, how can you abuse your own children in such a way? You take delight in vexing me. You have no compassion on my poor nerves.'

'You mistake me, my dear. I have a high respect for your nerves. They are my old friends. I have heard you mention them with consideration these twenty years at least.'

'Ah! you do not know what I suffer.'

'But I hope you will get over it, and live to see many young men of four thousand a year come into the neighbourhood.'

'It will be no use to us, if twenty such should come since you will not visit them.'

'Depend upon it, my dear, that when there are twenty, I will visit them all.'

Mr Bennet was so odd a mixture of quick parts, sarcastic humour, reserve, and caprice, that the experience of three and twenty years had been insufficient to make his wife understand his character. *Her* mind was less difficult to develope. She was a woman of mean understanding, little information, and uncertain temper. When she was discontented she fancied herself nervous. The business of her life was to get her daughters married; its solace was visiting and news.

Mr and Mrs Bennet

'I hope Mr Bingley will like it'

CHAPTER TWO

MR BENNET WAS AMONG THE EARLIEST of those who waited on Mr Bingley. He had always intended to visit him, though to the last always assuring his wife that he should not go; and till the evening after the visit was paid, she had no knowledge of it. It was then disclosed in the following manner. Observing his second daughter employed in trimming a hat, he suddenly addressed her with,

'I hope Mr Bingley will like it Lizzy.'

'We are not in a way to know *what* Mr Bingley likes,' said her mother resentfully, 'since we are not to visit.'

'But you forget, mama,' said Elizabeth, 'that we shall meet him at the assemblies, and that Mrs Long has promised to introduce him.'

'I do not believe Mrs Long will do any such thing. She has two nieces of her own. She is a selfish, hypocritical woman, and I have no opinion of her.'

'No more have I,' said Mr Bennet; 'and I am glad to find that you do not depend on her serving you.'

Mrs Bennet deigned not to make any reply; but unable to contain herself, began scolding one of her daughters.

'Don't keep coughing so, Kitty, for heaven's sake! Have a little compassion on my nerves. You tear them to pieces.'

'Kitty has no discretion in her coughs,' said her father; 'she times them ill.'

'I do not cough for my own amusement,' replied Kitty fretfully.

'When is your next ball to be, Lizzy?'

'To-morrow fortnight.'

'Aye, so it is,' cried her mother, 'and Mrs Long does not come back till the day before; so, it will be impossible for her to introduce him, for she will not know him herself.'

'Then, my dear, you may have the advantage of your friend, and introduce Mr Bingley to *her*.'

'Impossible, Mr Bennet, impossible, when I am not acquainted with him myself; how can you be so teazing?'

'I honour your circumspection. A fortnight's acquaintance is certainly very little. One cannot know what a man really is by the end of a fortnight. But if *we* do not venture, somebody else will; and after all, Mrs Long and her nieces must stand their chance; and therefore, as she will think it an act of kindness, if you decline the office, I will take it on myself.'

The girls stared at their father. Mrs Bennet said only, 'Nonsense, nonsense!'

'What can be the meaning of that emphatic exclamation?' cried he. 'Do you consider the forms of introduction, and the stress that is laid on them, as nonsense? I cannot quite agree with you *there*. What say you, Mary? for you are a young lady of deep reflection I know, and read great books, and make extracts.'

Mary wished to say something very sensible, but knew not how.

'While Mary is adjusting her ideas,' he continued, 'let us return to Mr Bingley.'

'I am sick of Mr Bingley,' cried his wife.

'I am sorry to hear *that*; but why did not you tell me so before? If I had known as much this morning, I certainly would not have called on him. It is very unlucky; but as I have actually paid the visit, we cannot escape the acquaintance now.'

The astonishment of the ladies was just what he wished; that of Mrs Bennet perhaps surpassing the rest; though when the first tumult of joy was over, she began to declare that it was what she had expected all the while.

'How good it was in you, my dear Mr Bennet! But I knew I should persuade you at last. I was sure you loved your girls too well to neglect such an acquaintance. Well, how pleased I am! and it is such a good joke, too, that you should have gone this morning, and never said a word about it till now.'

'Now, Kitty, you may cough as much as you chuse,' said Mr Bennet; and, as he spoke, he left the room, fatigued with the raptures of his wife.

'What an excellent father you have, girls,' said she, when the door was shut. 'I do not know how you will ever make him amends for his kindness; or me either, for that matter. At our time of life, it is not so pleasant I can tell you, to be making new acquaintances every day; but for your sakes, we would do any thing. Lydia, my love, though you *are* the youngest, I dare say Mr Bingley will dance with you at the next ball.'

'Oh!' said Lydia stoutly, 'I am not afraid; for though I *am* the youngest, I'm the tallest.'

The rest of the evening was spent in conjecturing how soon he would return Mr Bennet's visit, and determining when they should ask him to dinner.

'I'm the tallest'

He rode a black horse

CHAPTER THREE

NOT ALL THAT MRS BENNET, HOWEVER, with the assistance of her five daughters, could ask on the subject was sufficient to draw from her husband any satisfactory description of Mr Bingley. They attacked him in various ways; with barefaced questions, ingenious suppositions, and distant surmises; but he eluded the skill of them all; and they were at last obliged to accept the second-hand intelligence of their neighbour Lady Lucas. Her report was highly favourable. Sir William had been delighted with him. He was quite young, wonderfully handsome, extremely agreeable, and to crown the whole, he meant to be at the next assembly with a large party. Nothing could be more delightful! To be fond of dancing was a certain step towards falling in love; and very lively hopes of Mr Bingley's heart were entertained.

'If I can but see one of my daughters happily settled at Netherfield,' said Mrs Bennet to her husband, 'and all the others equally well married, I shall have nothing to wish for.'

In a few days Mr Bingley returned Mr Bennet's visit, and sat about ten minutes with him in his library. He had entertained hopes of being admitted to a sight of the young ladies, of whose beauty he had heard much; but he saw only the father. The ladies were somewhat more fortunate, for they had the advantage of ascertaining from an upper window, that he wore a blue coat and rode a black horse.

An invitation to dinner was soon afterwards despatched; and already had Mrs Bennet planned the courses that were to do credit to her housekeeping, when an answer arrived which deferred it all. Mr Bingley was obliged to be in town the following day, and consequently unable to accept the honour of their invitation, &c. Mrs Bennet was quite disconcerted. She could not imagine what business he could have in town so soon after his arrival in Hertfordshire; and she began to fear that he might be always flying about from one place to another, and never settled at Netherfield as he ought to be. Lady Lucas quieted her fears a little by starting the idea of his being gone to London only to get a large party for the ball; and a report soon followed that Mr Bingley was to bring twelve ladies and seven gentlemen with him to the assembly. The girls grieved over such a number of ladies; but were comforted the day before the ball by hearing, that instead of twelve, he had brought only six with him from London, his five sisters and a cousin. And when the party entered the assembly room, it consisted of only five altogether; Mr Bingley, his two sisters, the husband of the eldest, and another young man.

Mr Bingley was good looking and gentlemanlike; he had a pleasant countenance, and easy, unaffected manners. His sisters were fine women, with an air of decided fashion. His brother-in-law, Mr Hurst, merely looked the gentleman; but his friend Mr Darcy soon drew the attention of the room by his fine, tall person, handsome features, noble mien; and the report which was in general circulation within five minutes after his entrance, of his having ten thousand a year. The gentleman pronounced him to be a fine figure of a man, the ladies declared he was much handsomer than Mr Bingley, and he was looked at with great admiration for about half the evening, till his manners gave a disgust which turned the tide of his popularity; for he was discovered to be proud, to be above his company, and above being pleased; and not all his large estate in Derbyshire could then save him from having a most forbidding, disagreeable countenance, and being unworthy to be compared with his friend.

Mr Bingley had soon made himself acquainted with all the principal people in the room; he was lively and unreserved, danced every dance, was angry that the ball closed so early, and talked of giving one himself at Netherfield. Such amiable qualities must speak for themselves. What a contrast between him and his friend! Mr Darcy danced only once with Mrs

When the party entered

Hurst and once with Miss Bingley, declined being introduced to any other lady, and spent the rest of the evening in walking about the room, speaking occasionally to one of his own party. His character was decided. He was the proudest, most disagreeable man in the world, and every body hoped that he would never come there again. Amongst the most violent against him was Mrs Bennet, whose dislike of his general behaviour, was sharpened into particular resentment, by his having slighted one of her daughters.

Elizabeth Bennet had been obliged, by the scarcity of gentlemen, to sit down for two dances; and during part of that time, Mr Darcy had been standing near enough for her to overhear a conversation between him and Mr Bingley, who came from the dance for a few minutes, to press his friend to join it.

'Come, Darcy,' said he, 'I must have you dance. I hate to see you standing about by yourself in this stupid manner. You had much better dance.'

'I certainly shall not. You know how I detest it, unless I am particularly acquainted with my partner. At such an assembly as this, it would be insupportable. Your sisters are engaged, and there is not another woman in the room, whom it would not be a punishment to me to stand up with.'

'I would not be so fastidious as you are,' cried Bingley, 'for a kingdom! Upon my honour, I never met with so many pleasant girls in my life, as I have this evening; and there are several of them you see uncommonly pretty.'

'*You* are dancing with the only handsome girl in the room,' said Mr Darcy, looking at the eldest Miss Bennet.

'Oh! she is the most beautiful creature I ever beheld! But there is one of her sisters sitting down just behind you, who is very pretty, and I dare say, very agreeable. Do let me ask my partner to introduce you.'

'Which do you mean?' and turning round, he looked for a moment at

'She is tolerable'

Elizabeth, till catching her eye, he withdrew his own and coldly said, 'She is tolerable; but not handsome enough to tempt *me*; and I am in no humour at present to give consequence to young ladies who are slighted by other men. You had better return to your partner and enjoy her smiles, for you are wasting your time with me.'

Mr Bingley followed his advice. Mr Darcy walked off; and Elizabeth remained with no very cordial feelings towards him. She told the story however with great spirit among her friends; for she had a lively, playful disposition, which delighted in any thing ridiculous.

The evening altogether passed off pleasantly to the whole family. Mrs Bennet had seen her eldest daughter much admired by the Netherfield party. Mr Bingley had danced with her twice, and she had been distinguished by his sisters. Jane was as much gratified by this, as her mother could be, though in a quieter way. Elizabeth felt Jane's pleasure. Mary had heard herself mentioned to Miss Bingley as the most accomplished girl in the neighbourhood; and Catherine and Lydia had been fortunate enough to be never without partners, which was all that they had yet learnt to care for at a ball. They returned therefore in good spirits to Longbourn, the village where they lived, and of which they were the principal inhabitants. They found Mr Bennet still up. With a book he was regardless of time; and on the present occasion he had a good deal of curiosity as to the event of an evening which had raised such splendid expectations. He had rather hoped that all his wife's views on the stranger would be disappointed; but he soon found that he had a very different story to hear.

'Oh! my dear Mr Bennet,' as she entered the room, 'we have had a most delightful evening, a most excellent ball. I wish you had been there. Jane was so admired, nothing could be like it. Every body said how well she looked; and Mr Bingley thought her quite beautiful, and danced with her twice. Only think of *that* my dear; he actually danced with her twice; and she was the only creature in the room that he asked a second time. First of all, he asked Miss Lucas. I was so vexed to see him stand up with her; but, however, he did not admire her at all; indeed, nobody can, you know; and he seemed quite struck with Jane as she was going down the dance. So, he enquired who she was, and got introduced, and asked her for the two next. Then, the two third he danced with Miss King, and the two fourth with Maria Lucas, and the two fifth with Jane again, and the two sixth with Lizzy, and the Boulanger –'

'If he had had any compassion for *me*,' cried her husband impatiently, 'he would not have danced half so much! For God's sake, say no more of his partners. Oh! that he had sprained his ankle in the first dance!'

'Oh! my dear,' continued Mrs Bennet, 'I am quite delighted with him. He is so excessively handsome! and his sisters are charming women. I never in my life saw any thing more elegant than their dresses. I dare say the lace upon Mrs Hurst's gown –'

Here she was interrupted again. Mr Bennet protested against any description of finery. She was therefore obliged to seek another branch of the subject, and related, with much bitterness of spirit and some exaggeration, the shocking rudeness of Mr Darcy.

'But I can assure you,' she added, 'that Lizzy does not lose much by not suiting *his* fancy; for he is a most disagreeable, horrid man, not at all worth pleasing. So high and so conceited that there was no enduring him! He walked here, and he walked there, fancying himself so very great! Not handsome enough to dance with! I wish you had been there, my dear, to have given him one of your set downs. I quite detest the man.'

CHAPTER FOUR

WHEN JANE AND ELIZABETH WERE alone, the former, who had been cautious in her praise of Mr Bingley before, expressed to her sister how very much she admired him.

'He is just what a young man ought to be,' said she, 'sensible, good humoured, lively; and I never saw such happy manners! – so much ease, with such perfect good breeding!'

'He is also handsome,' replied Elizabeth, 'which a young man ought likewise to be, if he possibly can. His character is thereby complete.'

'I was very much flattered by his asking me to dance a second time. I did not expect such a compliment.'

'Did not you? *I* did for you. But that is one great difference between us. Compliments always take *you* by surprise, and *me* never. What could be more natural than his asking you again? He could not help seeing that you were about five times as pretty as every other woman in the room. No thanks to his gallantry for that. Well, he certainly is very agreeable, and I give you leave to like him. You have liked many a stupider person.'

'Dear Lizzy!'

'Oh! you are a great deal too apt you know, to like people in general. You never see a fault in any body. All the world are good and agreeable in your eyes. I never heard you speak ill of a human being in my life.'

'I would wish not to be hasty in censuring any one; but I always speak what I think.'

'I know you do; and it is *that* which makes the wonder. With *your* good sense, to be so honestly blind to the follies and nonsense of others!

Affectation of candour is common enough; – one meets it every where. But to be candid without ostentation or design – to take the good of every body's character and make it still better, and say nothing of the bad – belongs to you alone. And so, you like this man's sisters too, do you? Their manners are not equal to his.'

'Certainly not; at first. But they are very pleasing women when you converse with them. Miss Bingley is to live with her brother and keep his house; and I am much mistaken if we shall not find a very charming neighbour in her.'

Elizabeth listened in silence, but was not convinced; their behaviour at the assembly had not been calculated to please in general; and with more quickness of observation and less pliancy of temper than her sister, and with a judgment too unassailed by any attention to herself, she was very little disposed to approve them. They were in fact very fine ladies; not deficient in good humour when they were pleased, nor in the power of being agreeable where they chose it; but proud and conceited. They were rather handsome, had been educated in one of the first private seminaries in town, had a fortune of twenty thousand pounds, were in the habit of spending more than they ought, and of associating with people of rank; and were therefore in every respect entitled to think well of themselves, and meanly of others. They were of a respectable family in the north of England; a circumstance more deeply impressed on their memories than that their brother's fortune and their own had been acquired by trade.

Mr Bingley inherited property to the amount of nearly an hundred thousand pounds from his father, who had intended to purchase an estate, but did not live to do it. – Mr Bingley intended it likewise, and sometimes made choice of his county; but as he was now provided with a good house and the liberty of a manor, it was doubtful to many of those who best knew the easiness of his temper, whether he might not spend the remainder of his days at Netherfield, and leave the next generation to purchase.

His sisters were very anxious for his having an estate of his own; but though he was now established only as a tenant, Miss Bingley was by no means unwilling to preside at his table, nor was Mrs Hurst, who had married a man of more fashion than fortune, less disposed to consider his house as her home when it suited her. Mr Bingley had not been of age two years, when he was tempted by an accidental recommendation to look at Netherfield House. He did look at it and into it for half an hour, was pleased with the situation and the principal rooms, satisfied with what the owner said in its praise, and took it immediately.

Between him and Darcy there was a very steady friendship, in spite of a great opposition of character. – Bingley was endeared to Darcy by the easiness, openness, ductility of his temper, though no disposition could offer a greater contrast to his own, and though with his own he never appeared dissatisfied. On the strength of Darcy's regard Bingley had the firmest reliance, and of his judgment the highest opinion. In understanding Darcy was the superior. Bingley was by no means deficient, but Darcy was clever. He was at the same time haughty, reserved, and fastidious, and his manners, though well bred, were not inviting. In that respect his friend had greatly the advantage. Bingley was sure of being liked wherever he appeared, Darcy was continually giving offence.

The manner in which they spoke of the Meryton assembly was sufficiently characteristic. Bingley had never met with pleasanter people or prettier girls in his life; everybody had been most kind and attentive to him, there had been no formality, no stiffness, he had soon felt acquainted with all the room; and as to Miss Bennet, he could not conceive an angel more beautiful. Darcy, on the contrary, had seen a collection of people in whom there was little beauty and no fashion; for none of whom he had felt the smallest interest, and from none received either attention or pleasure. Miss Bennet he acknowledged to be pretty, but she smiled too much.

Mrs Hurst and her sister allowed it to be so – but still they admired her and liked her, and pronounced her to be a sweet girl, and one whom they should not object to know more of. Miss Bennet was therefore established as a sweet girl, and their brother felt authorised by such commendation to think of her as he chose.

CHAPTER FIVE

WITHIN A SHORT WALK OF LONGBOURN lived a family with whom the Bennets were particularly intimate. Sir William Lucas had been formerly in trade in Meryton, where he had made a tolerable fortune and risen to the honour of knighthood by an address to the King, during his mayoralty. The distinction had perhaps been felt too strongly. It had given him a disgust to his business and to his residence in a small market town; and quitting them both, he had removed with his family to a house about a mile from Meryton, denominated from that period Lucas Lodge, where he could think with pleasure of his own importance, and unshackled by business, occupy himself solely in being civil to all the world. For though elated by his rank, it did not render him supercilious; on the contrary, he was all attention to every body. By nature inoffensive, friendly and obliging, his presentation at St James's had made him courteous.

Lady Lucas was a very good kind of woman, not too clever to be a valuable neighbour to Mrs Bennet. – They had several children. The eldest of them, a sensible, intelligent young woman, about twenty-seven, was Elizabeth's intimate friend.

That the Miss Lucases and the Miss Bennets should meet to talk over a ball was absolutely necessary; and the morning after the assembly brought the former to Longbourn to hear and to communicate.

'*You* began the evening well, Charlotte,' said Mrs Bennet with civil self-command to Miss Lucas. '*You* were Mr Bingley's first choice.'

'Yes; – but he seemed to like his second better.'

'Oh! – you mean Jane, I suppose – because he danced with her twice. To be sure that *did* seem as if he admired her – indeed I rather believe he *did* – I heard something about it – but I hardly know what – something about Mr Robinson.'

'Perhaps you mean what I overheard between him and Mr Robinson; did not I mention it to you? Mr Robinson's asking him how he liked our Meryton assemblies, and whether he did not think there were a great many pretty women in the room, and *which* he thought the prettiest? and his answering immediately to the last question – Oh! the eldest Miss Bennet beyond a doubt, there cannot be two opinions on that point.'

'Upon my word! – Well, that was very decided indeed – that does seem as if – but however, it may all come to nothing you know.'

'*My* overhearings were more to the purpose than *yours*, Eliza,' said Charlotte. 'Mr Darcy is not so well worth listening to as his friend, is he? – Poor Eliza! – to be only just *tolerable*.'

'I beg you would not put it into Lizzy's head to be vexed by his ill-treatment; for he is such a disagreeable man that it would be quite a misfortune to be liked by him. Mrs Long told me last night that he sat close to her for half an hour without once opening his lips.'

'Are you quite sure, Ma'am? – is not there a little mistake?' said Jane. – 'I certainly saw Mr Darcy speaking to her.'

'Aye – because she asked him at last how he liked Netherfield, and he could not help answering her; – but she said he seemed very angry at being spoke to.'

'Miss Bingley told me,' said Jane, 'that he never speaks much unless among his intimate acquaintance. With *them* he is remarkably agreeable.'

'I do not believe a word of it, my dear. If he had been so very agreeable he would have talked to Mrs Long. But I can guess how it was; every body says that he is ate up with pride, and I dare say he had heard somehow that Mrs Long does not keep a carriage, and had come to the ball in a hack chaise.'

'I do not mind his not talking to Mrs Long,' said Miss Lucas, 'but I wish he had danced with Eliza.'

'Without once opening his lips'

'Another time, Lizzy,' said her mother, 'I would not dance with *him*, if I were you.'

'I believe, Ma'am, I may safely promise you *never* to dance with him.'

'His pride,' said Miss Lucas, 'does not offend *me* so much as pride often does, because there is an excuse for it. One cannot wonder that so very a fine young man, with family, fortune, every thing in his favour, should think highly of himself. If I may so express it, he has a *right* to be proud.'

'That is very true,' replied Elizabeth, 'and I could easily forgive *his* pride, if he had not mortified *mine*.'

'Pride,' observed Mary, who piqued herself upon the solidity of her reflections, 'is a very common failing I believe. By all that I have ever read, I am convinced that it is very common indeed, that human nature is particularly prone to it, and that there are very few of us who do not cherish a feeling of self-complacency on the score of some quality or other, real or imaginary. Vanity and pride are different things, though the words are often used synonymously. A person may be proud without being vain.

Pride relates more to our opinion of ourselves, vanity to what we would have others think of us.'

'If I were as rich as Mr Darcy,' cried a young Lucas who came with his sisters, 'I should not care how proud I was. I would keep a pack of foxhounds, and drink a bottle of wine every day.'

'Then you would drink a great deal more than you ought,' said Mrs Bennet; 'and if I were to see you at it I should take away your bottle directly.'

The boy protested that she should not; she continued to declare that she would, and the argument ended only with the visit.

CHAPTER SIX

THE LADIES OF LONGBOURN SOON WAITED on those of Netherfield. The visit was returned in due form. Miss Bennet's pleasing manners grew on the good will of Mrs Hurst and Miss Bingley; and though the mother was found to be intolerable and the younger sisters not worth speaking to, a wish of being better acquainted with *them*, was expressed towards the two eldest. By Jane this attention was received with the greatest pleasure; but Elizabeth still saw superciliousness in their treatment of every body, hardly excepting even her sister, and could not like them; though their kindness to Jane, such as it was, had a value as arising in all probability from the influence of their brother's admiration. It was generally evident whenever they met, that he *did* admire her; and to *her* it was equally evident that Jane was yielding to the preference which she had begun to entertain for him from the first, and was in a way to be very much in love; but she considered with pleasure that it was not likely to be discovered by the world in general, since Jane united with great strength of feeling, a composure of temper and a uniform cheerfulness of manner, which would guard her from the suspicions of the impertinent. She mentioned this to her friend Miss Lucas.

'It may perhaps be pleasant,' replied Charlotte, 'to be able to impose on the public in such a case; but it is sometimes a disadvantage to be so very guarded. If a woman conceals her affection with the same skill from the object of it, she may lose the opportunity of fixing him, and it will then be but poor consolation to believe the world equally in the dark. There is so much of gratitude or vanity in almost every attachment, that it is not safe to leave any to itself. We can all *begin* freely – a slight preference is natural enough; but there are very few of us who have heart enough to be really in love without encouragement. In nine cases out of ten, a woman had better shew *more* affection than she feels. Bingley likes your sister undoubtedly; but he may never do more than like her, if she does not help him on.'

'But she does help him on, as much as her nature will allow. If *I* can perceive her regard for him, he must be a simpleton indeed not to discover it too.'

'Remember, Eliza, that he does not know Jane's disposition as you do.'

'But if a woman is partial to a man, and does not endeavour to conceal it, he must find it out.'

'Perhaps he must, if he sees enough of her. But though Bingley and Jane meet tolerably often, it is never for many hours together; and as they always see each other in large mixed parties, it is impossible that every moment should be employed in conversing together. Jane should therefore make the most of every half hour in which she can command his attention. When she is secure of him, there will be leisure for falling in love as much as she chuses.'

'Your plan is a good one,' replied Elizabeth, 'where nothing is in question but the desire of being well married; and if I were determined to get a rich husband, or any husband, I dare say I should adopt it. But these are not Jane's feelings; she is not acting by design. As yet, she cannot even be certain of the degree of her own regard, nor of its reasonableness. She has known him only a fortnight. She danced four dances with him at Meryton; she saw him one morning at his own house, and has since dined in company with him four times. This is not quite enough to make her understand his character.'

'Not as you represent it. Had she merely *dined* with him, she might only have discovered whether he had a good appetite; but you must remember that four evenings have been also spent together – and four evenings may do a great deal.'

'Yes; these four evenings have enabled them to ascertain that they both like Vingt-un better than Commerce; but with respect to any other leading characteristic, I do not imagine that much has been unfolded.'

'Well,' said Charlotte, 'I wish Jane success with all my heart; and if she were married to him tomorrow, I should think she had as good a chance of happiness, as if she were to be studying his character for a twelve-month. Happiness in marriage is entirely a matter of chance. If the dispositions of the parties are ever so well known to each other, or ever so similar beforehand, it does not advance their felicity in the least. They always continue to grow sufficiently unlike afterwards to have their share of vexation; and it is better to know as little as possible of the defects of the person with whom you are to pass your life.'

'You make me laugh, Charlotte; but it is not sound. You know it is not sound, and that you would never act in this way yourself.'

Occupied in observing Mr Bingley's attentions to her sister, Elizabeth was far from suspecting that she was herself becoming an object of some interest in the eyes of his friend. Mr Darcy had at first scarcely allowed her to be pretty; he had looked at her without admiration at the ball; and when they next met, he looked at her only to criticise. But no sooner had he made it clear to himself and his friends that she had hardly a good feature in her face, than he began to find it was rendered uncommonly intelligent by the beautiful expression of her dark eyes. To this discovery succeeded some others equally mortifying. Though he had detected with a critical eye more than one failure of perfect symmetry in her form, he was forced to acknowledge her figure to be light and pleasing; and in spite of his asserting that her manners were not those of the fashionable world, he was caught by their easy playfulness. Of this she was perfectly unaware; – to her he was only the man who made himself agreeable no where, and who had not thought her handsome enough to dance with.

He began to wish to know more of her, and as a step towards conversing with her himself, attended to her conversation with others. His doing so drew her notice. It was at Sir William Lucas's, where a large party were assembled.

'What does Mr Darcy mean,' said she to Charlotte, 'by listening to my conversation with Colonel Forster?'

The entreaties of several

'That is a question which Mr Darcy only can answer.'

'But if he does it any more I shall certainly let him know that I see what he is about. He has a very satirical eye, and if I do not begin by being impertinent myself, I shall soon grow afraid of him.'

On his approaching them soon afterwards, though without seeming to have any intention of speaking, Miss Lucas defied her friend to mention such a subject to him, which immediately provoking Elizabeth to do it, she turned to him and said,

'Did not you think, Mr Darcy, that I expressed myself uncommonly well just now, when I was teazing Colonel Forster to give us a ball at Maryton?'

'With great energy; – but it is a subject which always makes a lady energetic.'

'You are severe on us.'

'It will be *her* turn soon to be teazed,' said Miss Lucas. 'I am going to open the instrument, Eliza, and you know what follows.'

'You are a very strange creature by way of a friend! – always wanting me to play and sing before any body and every body! – If my vanity had taken a musical turn, you would have been invaluable, but as it is, I would really rather not sit down before those who must be in the habit of hearing the very best performers.' On Miss Lucas's persevering, however, she added, 'Very well; if it must be so, it must.' And gravely glancing at Mr Darcy. 'There is a fine old saying, which every body here is of course familiar with – "Keep your breath to cool your porridge," – and I shall keep mine to swell my song.'

Her performance was pleasing, though by no means capital. After a song or two, and before she could reply to the entreaties of several that she would sing again, she was eagerly succeeded at the instrument by her sister Mary, who having, in consequence of being the only plain one in the family, worked hard for knowledge and accomplishments, was always impatient for display.

Mary had neither genius nor taste; and though vanity had given her application, it had given her likewise a pedantic air and conceited manner, which would have injured a higher degree of excellence than she had reached. Elizabeth, easy and unaffected, had been listened to with much more pleasure, though not playing half so well; and Mary, at the end of a long concerto, was glad to purchase praise and gratitude by Scotch and Irish airs, at the request of her younger sisters, who with some of the Lucases and two or three officers joined eagerly in dancing at one end of the room.

Mr Darcy stood near them in silent indignation at such a mode of passing the evening, to the exclusion of all conversation, and was too much engrossed by his own thoughts to perceive that Sir William Lucas was his neighbour, till Sir William thus began.

'What a charming amusement for young people this is, Mr Darcy! – There is nothing like dancing after all. – I consider it as one of the first refinements of polished societies.'

'Certainly, Sir; – and it has the advantage also of being in vogue amongst the less polished societies of the world. – Every savage can dance.'

Sir William only smiled. 'Your friend performs delightfully;' he continued after a pause, on seeing Bingley join the group; – 'and I doubt not that you are an adept in the science yourself, Mr Darcy.'

'You saw me dance at Meryton, I believe, Sir.'

'Yes, indeed, and received no inconsiderable pleasure from the sight. Do you often dance at St James's?'

'Never, sir.'

'Do you not think it would be a proper compliment to the place?'

'It is a compliment which I never pay to any place if I can avoid it.'

'You have a house in town, I conclude?'

Mr Darcy bowed.

'I had once some thoughts of fixing in town myself – for I am fond of superior society; but I did not feel quite certain that the air of London would agree with Lady Lucas.'

He paused in hopes of an answer; but his companion was not disposed to make any; and Elizabeth at that instant moving towards them, he was struck with the notion of doing a very gallant thing, and called out to her,

'My dear Miss Eliza, why are not you dancing? – Mr Darcy, you must allow me to present this young lady to you as a very desirable partner. – You cannot refuse to dance, I am sure, when so much beauty is before you.' And taking her hand, he would have given it to Mr Darcy, who though extremely surprised, was not unwilling to receive it, when she instantly drew back, and said with some discomposure to Sir William,

'Indeed, Sir, I have not the least intention of dancing. – I entreat you not to suppose that I moved this way in order to beg for a partner.'

Mr Darcy with grave propriety requested to be allowed the honour of her hand; but in vain. Elizabeth was determined; nor did Sir William at all shake her purpose by his attempt at persuasion.

'You excel so much in the dance, Miss Eliza, that it is cruel to deny me the happiness of seeing you; and though this gentleman dislikes the amusement in general, he can have no objection, I am sure, to oblige us for one half hour.'

'Mr Darcy is all politeness,' said Elizabeth, smiling.

'He is indeed – but considering the inducement, my dear Miss Eliza, we cannot wonder at his complaisance; for who would object to such a partner?'

Elizabeth looked archly, and turned away. Her resistance had not injured her with the gentleman, and he was thinking of her with some complacency, when thus accosted by Miss Bingley.

'I can guess the subject of your reverie.'

'I should imagine not.'

'You are considering how insupportable it would be to pass many evenings in this manner – in such society; and indeed I am quite of your opinion. I was never more annoyed! The insipidity and yet the noise; the nothingness and yet the self-importance of all these people! – What would I give to hear your strictures on them!'

'Your conjecture is totally wrong, I assure you. My mind was more agreeably engaged. I have been meditating on the very great pleasure which a pair of fine eyes in the face of a pretty woman can bestow.'

Miss Bingley immediately fixed her eyes on his face, and desired he would tell her what lady had the credit of inspiring such reflections. Mr Darcy replied with great intrepidity,

'Miss Elizabeth Bennet.'

'Miss Elizabeth Bennet!' repeated Miss Bingley. 'I am all astonishment. How long has she been such a favourite? – and pray when am I to wish you joy?'

'That is exactly the question which I expected you to ask. A lady's imagination is very rapid; it jumps from admiration to love, from love to matrimony in a moment. I knew you would be wishing me joy.'

'Nay, if you are so serious about it, I shall consider the matter as absolutely settled. You will have a charming mother-in-law, indeed, and of course she will be always at Pemberley with you.'

He listened to her with perfect indifference, while she chose to entertain herself in this manner, and as his composure convinced her that all was safe, her wit flowed long.

A note for Miss Bennet

CHAPTER SEVEN

MR BENNET'S PROPERTY CONSISTED ALMOST entirely in an estate of two thousand a year, which, unfortunately for his daughters, was entailed in default of heirs male, on a distant relation; and their mother's fortune, though ample for her situation in life, could but ill supply the deficiency of his. Her father had been an attorney in Meryton, and had left her four thousand pounds.

She had a sister married to a Mr Philips, who had been a clerk to their father, and succeeded him in the business, and a brother settled in London in a respectable line of trade.

The village of Longbourn was only one mile from Meryton; a most convenient distance for the young ladies, who were usually tempted thither three or four times a week, to pay their duty to their aunt and to a milliner's shop just over the way. The two youngest of the family, Catherine and Lydia, were particularly frequent in these attentions; their minds were more vacant than their sisters', and when nothing better offered, a walk to Meryton was necessary to amuse their morning hours and furnish conversation for the evening; and however bare of news the country in general might be, they always contrived to learn some from their aunt. At present, indeed, they were well supplied both with news and happiness by the recent arrival of a militia regiment in the neighbourhood; it was to remain the whole winter, and Meryton was the head quarters.

Their visits to Mrs Philips were now productive of the most interesting intelligence. Every day added something to their knowledge of the officers' names and connections. Their lodgings were not long a secret, and at length they began to know the officers themselves. Mr Philips visited them all, and this opened to his nieces a source of felicity unknown before. They could talk of nothing but officers; and Mr Bingley's large fortune, the mention of which gave animation to their mother, was worthless in their eyes when opposed to the regimentals of an ensign.

After listening one morning to their effusions on this subject, Mr Bennet coolly observed,

'From all that I can collect by your manner of talking, you must be two of the silliest girls in the country. I have suspected it some time, but I am now convinced.'

Catherine was disconcerted, and made no answer; but Lydia, with perfect indifference, continued to express her admiration of Captain Carter, and her hope of seeing him in the course of the day, as he was going the next morning to London.

'I am astonished, my dear,' said Mrs Bennet, 'that you should be so ready to think your own children silly. If I wished to think slightingly of any body's children, it should not be of my own however.'

'If my children are silly I must hope to be always sensible of it.'

'Yes – but as it happens, they are all of them very clever.'

'This is the only point, I flatter myself, on which we do not agree. I had hoped that our sentiments coincided in every particular, but I must so far differ from you as to think our two youngest daughters uncommonly foolish.'

'My dear Mr Bennet, you must not expect such girls to have the sense of their father and mother. – When they get to our age I dare say they will not think about officers any more than we do. I remember the time when I liked a red coat myself very well – and indeed so I do still at my heart; and if a smart young colonel, with five or six thousand a year, should want one of my girls, I shall not say nay to him; and I thought Colonel Forster looked very becoming the other night at Sir William's in his regimentals.'

'Mama,' cried Lydia, 'my aunt says that Colonel Forster and Captain Carter do not go so often to Miss Watson's as they did when they first came; she sees them now very often standing in Clarke's library.'

Mrs Bennet was prevented replying by the entrance of the footman with a note for Miss Bennet; it came from Netherfield, and the servant waited for an answer. Mrs Bennet's eyes sparkled with pleasure and she was eagerly calling out, while her daughter read,

'Well, Jane, who is it from? what is it about? what does he say? Well Jane, make haste and tell us; make haste, my love.'

'It is from Miss Bingley,' said Jane, and then read it aloud.

'MY DEAR FRIEND,

'If you are not so compassionate as to dine to-day with Louisa and me, we shall be in danger of hating each other for the rest of our lives, for a whole day's tête-à-tête between two women can never end without a quarrel. Come as soon as you can on the receipt of this. My brother and the gentlemen are to dine with the officers. Your ever,

'CAROLINE BINGLEY.'

'With the officers!' cried Lydia. 'I wonder my aunt did not tell us of that.'

'Dining out,' said Mrs Bennet, 'that is very unlucky.'

'Can I have the carriage?' said Jane.

'No, my dear, you had better go on horseback, because it seems likely to rain; and then you must stay all night.'

Cheerful prognostics

'That would be a good scheme,' said Elizabeth, 'if you were sure that they would not offer to send her home.'

'Oh! but the gentlemen will have Mr Bingley's chaise to go to Meryton; and the Hursts have no horses to theirs.'

'I had much rather go in the coach.'

'But, my dear, your father cannot spare the horses, I am sure. They are wanted in the farm Mr Bennet, are not they?'

'They are wanted in the farm much oftener than I can get them.'

'But if you have got them to-day,' said Elizabeth, 'my mother's purpose will be answered.'

She did at last extort from her father an acknowledgment that the horses were engaged. Jane was therefore obliged to go on horseback, and her mother attended her to the door with many cheerful prognostics of a bad day. Her hopes were answered; Jane had not been gone long before it rained hard. Her sisters were uneasy for her, but her mother was delighted. The rain continued the whole evening without intermission; Jane certainly could not come back.

'This was a lucky idea of mine, indeed!' said Mrs Bennet, more than once, as if the credit of making it rain were all her own. Till the next morning, however, she was not aware of all the felicity of her contrivance. Breakfast was scarcely over when a servant from Netherfield brought the following note for Elizabeth:

'My Dearest Lizzy,

'I find myself very unwell this morning, which, I suppose, is to be imputed to my getting wet through yesterday. My kind friends will not hear of my returning home till I am better. They insist also on my seeing Mr Jones – therefore do not be alarmed if you should hear of his having been to me – and excepting a sore-throat and head-ache there is not much the matter with me.

'Yours, &c.'

'Well, my dear,' said Mr Bennet, when Elizabeth had read the note aloud, 'if your daughter should have a dangerous fit of illness, if she should die, it would be a comfort to know that it was all in pursuit of Mr Bingley, and under your orders.'

'Oh! I am not at all afraid of her dying. People do not die of little trifling colds. She will be taken good care of. As long as she stays there, it is all very well. I would go and see her, if I could have the carriage.'

Elizabeth, feeling really anxious, was determined to go to her, though the carriage was not to be had; and as she was no horse-woman, walking was her only alternative. She declared her resolution.

'How can you be so silly,' cried her mother, 'as to think of such a thing, in all this dirt! You will not be fit to be seen when you get there.'

'I shall be very fit to see Jane – which is all I want.'

'Is this a hint to me, Lizzy,' said her father, 'to send for the horses?'

'No, indeed. I do not wish to avoid the walk. The distance is nothing, when one has a motive; only three miles. I shall be back by dinner.'

'I admire the activity of your benevolence,' observed Mary, 'but every impulse of feeling should be guided by reason; and, in my opinion, exertion should always be in proportion to what is required.'

'We will go as far as Meryton with you,' said Catherine and Lydia. – Elizabeth accepted their company, and the three young ladies set off together.

'If we make haste,' said Lydia, as they walked along, 'perhaps we may see something of Captain Carter before he goes.'

In Meryton they parted; the two youngest repaired to the lodgings of one of the officers' wives, and Elizabeth continued her walk alone, crossing field after field at a quick pace, jumping over stiles and springing over puddles with impatient activity, and finding herself at last within view of the house, with weary ancles, dirty stockings, and a face glowing with the warmth of exercise.

She was shewn into the breakfast-parlour, where all but Jane were assembled, and where her appearance created but a great deal of surprise. – That she should have walked three miles so early in the day, in such dirty weather, and by herself, was almost incredible to Mrs Hurst and Miss Bingley; and Elizabeth was convinced that they held her in contempt for it. She was received, however, very politely by them; and in their brother's manners there was something better than politeness; there was good humour and kindness. – Mr Darcy said very little, and Mr Hurst nothing at all. The former was divided between admiration of the brilliancy which exercise had given to her complexion, and doubt as to the occasion's justifying her coming so far alone. The latter was thinking only of his breakfast.

Her enquiries after her sister were not very favourably answered. Miss Bennet had slept ill, and though up, was very feverish and not well enough to leave her room. Elizabeth was glad to be taken to her immediately; and Jane, who had only been withheld by the fear of giving alarm or inconvenience, from expressing in her note how much she longed for such a visit, was delighted at her entrance. She was not equal, however, to much conversation, and when Miss Bingley left them together, could attempt little beside expressions of gratitude for the extraordinary kindness she was treated with. Elizabeth silently attended her.

When breakfast was over, they were joined by the sisters; and Elizabeth began to like them herself, when she saw how much affection and solicitude they shewed for Jane. The apothecary came, and having examined his patient, said, as might be supposed, that she had caught a violent cold, and that they must endeavour to get the better of it; advised her to return to bed, and promised her some draughts. The advice was followed readily, for the feverish symptoms increased, and her head ached acutely. Elizabeth did not quit her room for a moment, nor were the other ladies often absent; the gentlemen being out, they had in fact nothing to do elsewhere.

When the clock struck three, Elizabeth felt that she must go; and very unwillingly said so. Miss Bingley offered her the carriage, and she only wanted a little pressing to accept it, when Jane testified such concern in parting with her, that Miss Bingley was obliged to convert the offer of the chaise into an invitation to remain at Netherfield for the present. Elizabeth most thankfully consented, and a servant was dispatched to Longbourn to acquaint the family with her stay, and bring back a supply of clothes.

The apothecary came

'Covering a screen'

CHAPTER EIGHT

AT FIVE O'CLOCK THE TWO LADIES retired to dress, and at half past six Elizabeth was summoned to dinner. To the civil enquiries which then poured in, and amongst which she had the pleasure of distinguishing the much superior solicitude of Mr Bingley's, she could not make a very favourable answer. Jane was by no means better. The sisters, on hearing this, repeated three or four times how much they were grieved, how shocking it was to have a bad cold, and how excessively they disliked being ill themselves; and then thought no more of the matter: and their indifference towards Jane when not immediately before them, restored Elizabeth to the enjoyment of all her original dislike.

Their brother, indeed, was the only one of the party whom she could regard with any complacency. His anxiety for Jane was evident, and his attentions to herself most pleasing, and they prevented her feeling herself so much an intruder as she believed she was considered by the others. She had very little notice from any but him. Miss Bingley was engrossed by Mr Darcy, her sister scarcely less so; and as for Mr Hurst, by whom Elizabeth sat, he was an indolent man, who lived only to eat, drink, and play at cards, who when he found her prefer a plain dish to a ragout, had nothing to say to her.

When dinner was over, she returned directly to Jane, and Miss Bingley began abusing her as soon as she was out of the room. Her manners were pronounced to be very bad indeed, a mixture of pride and impertinence; and she had no conversation, no stile, no taste, no beauty. Mrs Hurst thought the same, and added,

'She has nothing, in short, to recommend her, but being an excellent walker. I shall never forget her appearance this morning. She really looked almost wild.'

'She did indeed, Louisa. I could hardly keep my countenance. Very nonsensical to come at all! Why must *she* be scampering about the country, because her sister has a cold? Her hair so untidy, so blowsy!'

'Yes, and her petticoat; I hope you saw her petticoat, six inches deep in mud, I am absolutely certain; and the gown which had been let down to hide it, not doing its office.'

'Your picture may be very exact, Louisa,' said Bingley; 'but this was all lost upon me. I thought Miss Elizabeth Bennet looked remarkably well, when she came into the room this morning. Her dirty petticoat quite escaped my notice.'

'*You* observed it, Mr Darcy, I am sure,' said Miss Bingley; 'and I am inclined to think that you would not wish to see *your sister* make such an exhibition.'

'Certainly not.'

'To walk three miles, or four miles, or five miles, or whatever it is, above her ancles in dirt, and alone, quite alone! what could she mean by it? It seems to me to shew an abominable sort of conceited independence, a most country town indifference to decorum.'

'It shews an affection for her sister that is very pleasing,' said Bingley.

'I am afraid, Mr Darcy,' observed Miss Bingley, in a half whisper, 'that this adventure has rather affected your admiration of her fine eyes.'

'Not at all,' he replied; 'they were brightened by the exercise.' – A short pause followed this speech, and Mrs Hurst began again.

'I have an excessive regard for Jane Bennet, she is really a very sweet girl, and I wish with all my heart she were well settled. But with such a father and mother, and such low connections, I am afraid there is no chance of it.'

'I think I have heard you say, that their uncle is an attorney in Meryton.'

'Yes; and they have another, who lives somewhere near Cheapside.'

'That is capital,' added her sister, and they both laughed heartily.

'If they had uncles enough to fill *all* Cheapside,' cried Bingley, 'it would not make them one jot less agreeable.'

'But it must very materially lessen their chance of marrying men of any consideration in the world,' replied Darcy.

To this speech Bingley made no answer; but his sisters gave it their hearty assent, and indulged their mirth for some time at the expense of their dear friend's vulgar relations.

With a renewal of tenderness, however, they repaired to her room on leaving the dining-parlour, and sat with her till summoned to coffee. She was still very poorly, and Elizabeth would not quit her at all, till late in the evening, when she had the comfort of seeing her asleep, and when it appeared to her rather right than pleasant that she should go down stairs herself. On entering the drawing-room she found the whole party at loo, and was immediately invited to join them; but suspecting them to be playing high she declined it, and making her sister the excuse, said she would amuse herself for the short time she could stay below with a book. Mr Hurst looked at her with astonishment.

'Do you prefer reading to cards?' said he; 'that is rather singular.'

'Miss Eliza Bennet,' said Miss Bingley, 'despises cards. She is a great reader and has no pleasure in anything else.'

'I deserve neither such praise nor such censure,' cried Elizabeth; 'I am *not* a great reader, and I have pleasure in many things.'

'In nursing your sister I am sure you have pleasure,' said Bingley; 'and I hope it will soon be increased by seeing her quite well.'

Elizabeth thanked him from her heart, and then walked towards a table where a few books were lying. He immediately offered to fetch her others; all that his library afforded.

'And I wish my collection were larger for your benefit and my own credit; but I am an idle fellow, and though I have not many, I have more than I ever look into.'

Elizabeth assured him that she could suit herself perfectly with those in the room.

'I am astonished,' said Miss Bingley, 'that my father should have left so small a collection of books. – What a delightful library you have at Pemberley, Mr Darcy!'

'It ought to be good,' he replied, 'it has been the work of many generations.'

'And then you have added so much to it yourself, you are always buying books.'

'I cannot comprehend the neglect of a family library in such days as these.'

'Neglect! I am sure you neglect nothing that can add to the beauties of that noble place. Charles, when you build *your* house, I wish it may be half as delightful as Pemberley.'

'I wish it may.'

'But I would really advise you to make your purchase in that neighbourhood, and take Pemberley for a kind of model. There is not a finer county in England than Derbyshire.'

'With all my heart; I will buy Pemberley itself if Darcy will sell it.'

'I am talking of possibilities, Charles.'

'Upon my word, Caroline, I should think it more possible to get Pemberley by purchase than by imitation.'

Elizabeth was so much caught by what passed, as to leave her very little attention for her book; and soon laying it wholly aside, she drew near the card-table, and stationed herself between Mr Bingley and his eldest sister, to observe the game.

'Is Miss Darcy much grown since the spring?' said Miss Bingley; 'will she be as tall as I am?'

'I think she will. She is now about Miss Elizabeth Bennet's height or rather taller.'

'How I long to see her again! I never met with anybody who delighted me so much. Such a countenance, such manners! and so extremely accomplished for her age! Her performance on the piano-forte is exquisite.'

'It is amazing to me,' said Bingley, 'how young ladies can have patience to be so very accomplished, as they all are.'

'All young ladies accomplished! My dear Charles, what do you mean?'

'Yes, all of them, I think. They all paint tables, cover skreens and net purses. I scarcely know any one who cannot do all this, and I am sure I never heard a young lady spoken of for the first time, without being informed that she was very accomplished.'

'Your list of the common extent of accomplishments,' said Darcy, 'has too much truth. The word is applied to many a woman who deserves it no otherwise than by netting a purse, or covering a skreen. But I am very far from agreeing with you in your estimation of ladies in general. I cannot boast of knowing more than half a dozen, in the whole range of my acquaintance, that are really accomplished.'

'Nor I, I am sure,' said Miss Bingley.

'Then,' observed Elizabeth, 'you must comprehend a great deal in your idea of an accomplished woman.'

'Yes; I do comprehend a great deal in it.'

'Oh! certainly,' cried his faithful assistant, 'no one can be really esteemed accomplished, who does not greatly surpass what is usually met with. A woman must have a thorough knowledge of music, singing, drawing, dancing, and the modern languages, to deserve the word; and besides all this, she must possess a certain something in her air and manner of walking, the tone of her voice, her address and expressions, or the word will be but half deserved.'

'All this she must possess,' added Darcy, 'and to all this she must yet add something more substantial, in the improvement of her mind by extensive reading.'

'I am no longer surprised at your knowing *only* six accomplished women. I rather wonder now at your knowing *any*.'

'Are you so severe upon your own sex, as to doubt the possibility of all this?'

'I never saw such a woman. I never saw such capacity, and taste, and application, and elegance, as you describe, united.'

Mrs Hurst and Miss Bingley both cried out against the injustice of her implied doubt, and were both protesting that they knew many women who answered this description, when Mr Hurst called them to order, with bitter complaints of their inattention to what was going forward. As all conversation was thereby at an end, Elizabeth soon afterwards left the room.

'Eliza Bennet,' said Miss Bingley, when the door was closed on her, 'is one of those young ladies who seek to recommend themselves to the other sex, by undervaluing their own; and with many men, I dare say, it succeeds. But, in my opinion, it is a paltry device, a very mean art.'

'Undoubtedly,' replied Darcy, to whom this remark was chiefly addressed, 'there is meanness in *all* the arts which ladies sometimes condescend to employ for captivation. Whatever bears affinity to cunning is despicable.'

Miss Bingley was not so entirely satisfied with this reply as to continue the subject.

Elizabeth joined them again only to say that her sister was worse, and that she could not leave her. Bingley urged Mr Jones's being sent for immediately; while his sisters, convinced that no country advice could be of any service, recommended an express to town for one of the most eminent physicians. This, she would not hear of; but she was not so unwilling to comply with their brother's proposal; and it was settled that Mr Jones should be sent for early in the morning, if Miss Bennet were not decidedly better. Bingley was quite uncomfortable; his sisters declared that they were miserable. They solaced their wretchedness, however, by duets after supper, while he could find no better relief to his feelings than by giving his housekeeper directions that every possible attention might be paid to the sick lady and her sister.

Mrs Bennet and her two youngest girls

CHAPTER NINE

ELIZABETH PASSED THE CHIEF OF THE night in her sister's room, and in the morning had the pleasure of being able to send a tolerable answer to the enquiries which she very early received from Mr Bingley by a housemaid, and some time afterwards from the two elegant ladies who waited on his sisters. In spite of this amendment, however, she requested to have a note sent to Longbourn, desiring her mother to visit Jane, and form her own judgment of her situation. The note was immediately dispatched, and its contents as quickly complied with. Mrs Bennet, accompanied by her two youngest girls, reached Netherfield soon after the family breakfast.

Had she found Jane in any apparent danger, Mrs Bennet would have been very miserable; but being satisfied on seeing her that her illness was not alarming, she had no wish of her recovering immediately, as her restoration to health would probably remove her from Netherfield. She would not listen therefore to her daughter's proposal of being carried home; neither did the apothecary, who arrived about the same time, think it at all advisable. After sitting a little while with Jane, on Miss Bingley's appearance and invitation, the mother and three daughters all attended her into the breakfast parlour. Bingley met them with hopes that Mrs Bennet had not found Miss Bennet worse than she expected.

'Indeed I have, Sir,' was her answer. 'She is a great deal too ill to be moved. Mr Jones says we must not think of moving her. We must trespass a little longer on your kindness.'

'Removed!' cried Bingley. 'It must not be thought of. My sister, I am sure, will not hear of her removal.'

'You may depend upon it, Madam,' said Miss Bingley, with cold civility, 'that Miss Bennet shall receive every possible attention while she remains with us.'

Mrs Bennet was profuse in her acknowledgments.

'I am sure,' she added, 'if it was not for such good friends I do not know what would become of her, for she is very ill indeed, and suffers a vast deal, though with the greatest patience in the world, which is always the way with her, for she has, without exception, the sweetest temper I ever met with. I often tell my other girls they are nothing to *her*. You have a sweet room here, Mr Bingley, and a charming prospect over that gravel walk. I do not know a place in the country that is equal to Netherfield. You will not think of quitting it in a hurry I hope, though you have but a short lease.'

'Whatever I do is done in a hurry,' replied he; 'and therefore if I should resolve to quit Netherfield, I should probably be off in five minutes. At present, however, I consider myself as quite fixed here.'

'That is exactly what I should have supposed of you,' said Elizabeth.

'You begin to comprehend me, do you?' cried he, turning towards her.

'Oh! yes – I understand you perfectly.'

'I wish I might take this for a compliment; but to be so easily seen through I am afraid is pitiful.'

'That is as it happens. It does not necessarily follow that a deep, intricate character is more or less estimable than such a one as yours.'

'Lizzy,' cried her mother, 'remember where you are, and do not run on in the wild manner that you are suffered to do at home.'

'I did not know before,' continued Bingley immediately, 'that you were a studier of character. It must be an amusing study.'

'Yes; but intricate characters are the *most* amusing. They have at least that advantage.'

'The country,' said Darcy, 'can in general supply but few subjects for such a study. In a country neighbourhood you move in a very confined and unvarying society.'

'But people themselves alter so much, that there is something new to be observed in them for ever.'

'Yes, indeed,' cried Mrs Bennet, offended by his manner of mentioning a country neighbourhood. 'I assure you there is quite as much of *that* going on in the country as in town.'

Every body was surprised; and Darcy, after looking at her for a moment, turned silently away. Mrs Bennet, who fancied she had gained a complete victory over him, continued her triumph.

'I cannot see that London has any great advantage over the country for my part, except the shops and public places. The country is a vast deal pleasanter, is not it, Mr Bingley?'

'When I am in the country,' he replied, 'I never wish to leave it; and when I am in town it is pretty much the same. They have each their advantages, and I can be equally happy in either.'

'Aye – that is because you have the right disposition. But that gentleman,' looking at Darcy, 'seemed to think the country was nothing at all.'

'Indeed, Mama, you are mistaken,' said Elizabeth, blushing for her mother. 'You quite mistook Mr Darcy. He only meant that there were not such a variety of people to be met with in the country as in town, which you must acknowledge to be true.'

'Certainly, my dear, nobody said there were; but as to not meeting with many people in this neighbourhod, I believe there are few neighbourhoods larger. I know we dine with four and twenty families.'

Nothing but concern for Elizabeth could enable Bingley to keep his countenance. His sister was less delicate, and directed her eye towards Mr Darcy with a very expressive smile. Elizabeth, for the sake of saying something that might turn her mother's thoughts, now asked her if Charlotte Lucas had been at Longbourn since *her* coming away.

'Yes, she called yesterday with her father. What an agreeable man Sir William is, Mr Bingley – is not he? so much the man of fashion! so genteel and so easy! – He has always something to say to every body. – *That* is my idea of good breeding; and those persons who fancy themselves very important and never open their mouths, quite mistake the matter.'

'Did Charlotte dine with you?'

'No, she would go home. I fancy she was wanted about the mince pies. For my part, Mr Bingley, *I* always keep servants that can do their own work; *my* daughters are brought up differently. But every body is to judge for themselves, and the Lucases are very good sort of girls, I assure. It is a pity they are not handsome! Not that *I* think Charlotte so *very* plain – but then she is our particular friend.'

'She seems a very pleasant young woman,' said Bingley.

'Oh! dear, yes; – but you must own she is very plain. Lady Lucas herself has often said so, and envied me Jane's beauty. I do not like to boast of my own child, but to be sure, Jane – one does not often see any body better looking. It is what every body says. I do not trust my own partiality. When she was only fifteen, there was a gentleman at my brother Gardiner's in town, so much in love with her, that my sister-in-law was sure he would make her an offer before we came away. But however he did not. Perhaps he thought her too young. However, he wrote some verses on her, and very pretty they were.'

'And so ended his affection,' said Elizabeth impatiently. 'There has been many a one, I fancy, overcome in the same way. I wonder who first discovered the efficacy of poetry in driving away love!'

'I have been used to consider poetry as the *food* of love,' said Darcy.

'Of a fine, stout, healthy love it may. Every thing nourishes what is strong already. But if it be only a slight, thin sort of inclination, I am convinced that one good sonnet will starve it entirely away.'

Darcy only smiled; and the general pause which ensued made Elizabeth tremble lest her mother should be exposing herself again. She longed to speak, but could think of nothing to say; and after a short silence Mrs Bennet began repeating her thanks to Mr Bingley for his kindness to Jane, with an apology for troubling him also with Lizzy. Mr Bingley was unaffectedly civil in his answer, and forced his younger sister to be civil also, and say what the occasion required. She performed her part indeed without much graciousness, but Mrs Bennet was satisfied, and soon afterwards ordered her carriage. Upon this signal, the youngest of her daughters put herself forward. The two girls had been whispering to each other during the whole visit, and the result of it was, that the youngest should tax Mr Bingley with having promised on his first coming into the country to give a ball at Netherfield.

Lydia was a stout, well-grown girl of fifteen, with a fine complexion and good-humoured countenance; a favourite with her mother, whose affection had brought her into public at an early age. She had high animal spirits, and a sort of natural self-consequence, which the attentions of the officers, to whom her uncle's good dinners and her own easy manners recommended her, had increased into assurance. She was very equal therefore to address Mr Bingley on the subject of the ball, and abruptly reminded him of his promise; adding, that it would be the most shameful thing in the world if he did not keep it. His answer to this sudden attack was delightful to their mother's ear.

'I am perfectly ready, I assure you, to keep my engagement; and when your sister is recovered, you shall if you please name the very day of the ball. But you would not wish to be dancing while she is ill.'

Lydia declared herself satisfied. 'Oh! yes – it would be much better to wait till Jane was well, and by that time most likely Captain Carter would be at Meryton again. And when you have given *your* ball,' she added, 'I shall insist on their giving one also. I shall tell Colonel Forster it will be quite a shame if he does not.'

Mrs Bennet and her daughters then departed, and Elizabeth returned instantly to Jane, leaving her own and her relations' behaviour to the remarks of the two ladies and Mr Darcy; the latter of whom, however, could not be prevailed on to join in their censure of *her*, in spite of all Miss Bingley's witticisms on *fine eyes*.

CHAPTER TEN

THE DAY PASSED MUCH AS THE DAY before had done. Mrs Hurst and Miss Bingley had spent some hours of the morning with the invalid, who continued, though slowly, to mend; and in the evening Elizabeth joined their party in the drawing-room. The loo table, however, did not appear. Mr Darcy was writing, and Miss Bingley, seated near him, was watching the progress of his letter, and repeatedly calling off his attention by messages to his sister. Mr Hurst and Mr Bingley were at piquet, and Mrs Hurst was observing their game.

Elizabeth took up some needlework, and was sufficiently amused in attending to what passed between Darcy and his companion. The perpetual commendations of the lady either on his hand-writing, or on the evenness of his lines, or on the length of his letter, with the perfect unconcern with which her praises were received, formed a curious dialogue, and was exactly in unison with her opinion of each.

'How delighted Miss Darcy will be to receive such a letter!'

He made no answer.

'You write uncommonly fast.'

'You are mistaken. I write rather slowly.'

'How many letters you must have occasion to write in the course of the year! Letters of business too! How odious I should think them!'

'It is fortunate, then, that they fall to my lot instead of to yours.'

'Pray tell your sister that I long to see her.'

'I have already told her so once, by your desire.'

'I am afraid you do not like your pen. Let me mend it for you. I mend pens remarkably well.'

'Thank you – but I always mend my own.'

'How can you contrive to write so even?'

He was silent.

'Tell your sister I am delighted to hear of her improvement on the harp, and pray let her know that I am quite in raptures with her beautiful little design for a table, and I think it infinitely superior to Miss Grantley's.'

'Will you give me leave to defer your raptures till I write again? – At present I have not room to do them justice.'

'Oh! it is of no consequence. I shall see her in January. But do you always write such charming long letters to her, Mr Darcy?'

'They are generally long; but whether always charming, it is not for me to determine.'

'It is a rule with me, that a person who can write a long letter, with ease, cannot write ill.'

'That will not do for a compliment to Darcy, Caroline,' cried her brother – 'because he does *not* write with ease. He studies too much for words of four syllables. – Do not you, Darcy?'

'My stile of writing is very different from yours.'

'Oh!' cried Miss Bingley, 'Charles writes in the most careless way imaginable. He leaves out half his words, and blots the rest.'

'My ideas flow so rapidly that I have not time to express them – by which means my letters sometimes convey no ideas at all to my correspondents.'

'Your humility, Mr Bingley,' said Elizabeth, 'must disarm reproof.'

'Nothing is more deceitful,' said Darcy, 'than the appearance of humility. It is often only carelessness of opinion, and sometimes an indirect boast.'

'And which of the two do you call *my* little recent piece of modesty?'

'The indirect boast; – for you are really proud of your defects in writing, because you consider them as proceeding from a rapidity of thought and carelessness of execution, which if not estimable, you think at least highly interesting. The power of doing any thing with quickness is always much prized by the possessor, and often without any attention to the imperfection of the performance. When you told Mrs Bennet this morning that if you ever resolved on quitting Netherfield you should be gone in five minutes, you meant it to be a sort of panegyric, of compliment to yourself – and yet what is there so very laudable in a precipitance which must leave very necessary business undone, and can be of no real advantage to yourself or any one else?'

'Nay,' cried Bingley, 'this is too much, to remember at night all the foolish things that were said in the morning. And yet, upon my honour, I believed what I said of myself to be true, and I believe it at this moment. At least, therefore, I did not assume the character of needless precipitance merely to shew off before the ladies.'

'I dare say you believed it; but I am by no means convinced that you would be gone with such celerity. Your conduct would be quite as dependant on chance as that of any man I know; and if, as you were mounting your horse, a friend were to say, "Bingley, you had better stay till next week," you would probably do it, you would probably not go – and, at another word, might stay a month.'

'You have only proved by this,' cried Elizabeth, 'that Mr Bingley did not do justice to his own disposition. You have shewn him off now much more than he did himself.'

'I am exceedingly gratified,' said Bingley, 'by your converting what my friend says into a compliment on the sweetness of my temper. But I am afraid you are giving it a turn which that gentleman did by no means intend; for he would certainly think the better of me, if under such a circumstance I were to give a flat denial, and ride off as fast as I could.'

'Would Mr Darcy then consider the rashness of your original intention as atoned for by your obstinacy in adhering to it?'

'Upon my word I cannot exactly explain the matter, Darcy must speak for himself.'

'You expect me to account for opinions which you chuse to call mine, but which I have never acknowledged. Allowing the case, however, to stand according to your representation, you must remember, Miss Bennet, that the friend who is supposed to desire his return to the house, and the delay of his plan, has merely desired it, asked it without offering one argument in favour of its propriety.'

'To yield readily – easily – to the *persuasion* of a friend is no merit with you.'

'To yield without conviction is no compliment to the understanding of either.'

'You appear to me, Mr Darcy, to allow nothing for the influence of friendship and affection. A regard for the requester would often make one readily yield to a request, without waiting for arguments to reason one into it. I am not particularly speaking of such a case as you have supposed about Mr Bingley. We may as well wait, perhaps, till the circumstance occurs, before we discuss the discretion of his behaviour thereupon. But in general and ordinary cases between friend and friend, where one of them is desired by the other to change a resolution of no very great moment, should you think ill of that person for complying with the desire, without waiting to be argued into it?'

'Will it not be advisable, before we proceed on this subject, to arrange with rather more precision the degree of importance which is to appertain to this request, as well as the degree of intimacy subsisting between the parties?'

'By all means,' cried Bingley; 'let us hear all the particulars, not forgetting their comparative height and size; for that will have more weight in the argument, Miss Bennet, than you may be aware of. I assure you that if Darcy were not such a great tall fellow, in comparison with myself, I should not pay him half so much deference. I declare I do not know a more aweful object than Darcy, on particular occasions, and in particular places; at his own house especially, and of a Sunday evening when he has nothing to do.'

Mr Darcy smiled; but Elizabeth thought she could perceive that he was rather offended; and therefore checked her laugh. Miss Bingley warmly resented the indignity he had received, in an expostulation with her brother for talking such nonsense.

'I see your design, Bingley,' said his friend. – 'You dislike an argument, and want to silence this.'

'Perhaps I do. Arguments are too much like disputes. If you and Miss Bennet will defer yours till I am out of the room, I shall be very thankful; and then you may say whatever you like of me.'

'What you ask,' said Elizabeth, 'is no sacrifice on my side; and Mr Darcy had much better finish his letter.'

Mr Darcy took her advice, and did finish his letter.

When that business was over, he applied to Miss Bingley and Elizabeth for the indulgence of some music. Miss Bingley moved with alacrity to the piano-forte, and after a polite request that Elizabeth would lead the way, which the other as politely and more earnestly negatived, she seated herself.

Mrs Hurst sang with her sister, and while they were thus employed Elizabeth could not help observing as she turned over some music books that lay on the instrument, how frequently Mr Darcy's eyes were fixed on her. She hardly new how to suppose that she could be an object of admiration to so great a man; and yet that he should look at her because he disliked her, was still more strange. She could only imagine however at last, that she drew his notice because there was a something about her more wrong and reprehensible, according to his ideas of right, than in any other person present. The supposition did not pain her. She liked him too little to care for his approbation.

After playing some Italian songs, Miss Bingley varied the charm by a lively Scotch air; and soon afterwards Mr Darcy, drawing near Elizabeth, said to her —

'Do not you feel a great inclination, Miss Bennet, to seize such an opportunity of dancing a reel?'

She smiled, but made no answer. He repeated the question, with some surprise at her silence.

'Oh!' said she, 'I heard you before; but I could not immediately determine what to say in reply. You wanted me, I know, to say "Yes," that you might have the pleasure of despising my taste; but I always delight in overthrowing those kind of schemes, and cheating a person of their premeditated contempt. I have therefore made up my mind to tell you, that I do not want to dance a reel at all – and now despise me if you dare.'

'Indeed I do not dare.'

Elizabeth, having rather expected to affront him, was amazed at his gallantry; but there was a mixture of sweetness and archness in her manner which made it difficult for her to affront anybody; and Darcy had never been so bewitched by any woman as he was by her. He really believed, that were it not for the inferiority of her connections, he should be in some danger.

Miss Bingley saw, or suspected enough to be jealous; and her great anxiety for the recovery of her dear friend Jane, received some assistance from her desire of getting rid of Elizabeth.

She often tried to provoke Darcy into disliking her guest, by talking of their supposed marriage, and planning his happiness in such an alliance.

'I hope,' said she, as they were walking together in the shrubbery the next day, 'you will give your mother-in-law a few hints, when this desirable event takes place, as to the advantage of holding her tongue; and if you can compass it, do cure the younger girls of running after the officers. – And, if I may mention so delicate a subject, endeavour to check that little something, bordering on conceit and impertinence, which your lady possesses.'

'Have you any thing else to propose for my domestic felicity?'

'No, no; stay where you are'

'Oh! yes. – Do let the portraits of your uncle and aunt Philips be placed in the gallery at Pemberley. Put them next to your great uncle the judge. They are in the same profession, you know; only in different lines. As for your Elizabeth's picture, you must not attempt to have it taken, for what painter could do justice to those beautiful eyes?'

'It would not be easy, indeed, to catch their expressions, but their colour and shape, and the eye-lashes, so remarkably fine, might be copied.'

At that moment they were met from another walk, by Mrs Hurst and Elizabeth herself.

'I did not know that you intended to walk,' said Miss Bingley, in some confusion, lest they had been overheard.

'You used us abominably ill,' answered Mrs Hurst, 'in running away without telling us that you were coming out.'

Then taking the disengaged arm of Mr Darcy, she left Elizabeth to walk by herself. The path just admitted three. Mr Darcy felt their rudeness and immediately said, –

'This walk is not wide enough for our party. We had better go into the avenue.'

But Elizabeth, who had not the least inclination to remain with them, laughingly answered,

'No no; stay where you are. – You are charmingly group'd, and appear to uncommon advantage. The picturesque would be spoilt by admitting a fourth. Good bye.'

She then ran gaily off, rejoicing as she rambled about, in the hope of being at home again in a day òr two. Jane was already so much recovered as to intend leaving her room for a couple of hours that evening.

Piling up the fire

CHAPTER ELEVEN

WHEN THE LADIES REMOVED AFTER dinner, Elizabeth ran up to her sister, and seeing her well guarded from cold, attended her into the drawing-room; where she was welcomed by her two friends with many professions of pleasure; and Elizabeth had never seen them so agreeable as they were during the hour which passed before the gentlemen appeared. Their powers of conversation were considerable. They could describe an entertainment with accuracy, relate an anecdote with humour, and laugh at their acquaintance with spirit.

But when the gentlemen entered, Jane was no longer the first object. Miss Bingley's eyes were instantly turned towards Darcy, and she had something to say to him before he had advanced many steps. He addressed himself directly to Miss Bennet, with a polite congratulation; Mr Hurst also made her a slight bow, and said he was 'very glad'; but diffuseness and warmth remained for Bingley's salutation. He was full of joy and attention. The first half hour was spent in piling up the fire, lest she should suffer from the change of room; and she removed at his desire to the other side of the fire-place, that she might be farther from the door. He then sat down by her, and talked scarcely to any one else. Elizabeth, at work in the opposite corner, saw it all with great delight.

When tea was over, Mr Hurst reminded his sister-in-law of the card-table – but in vain. She had obtained private intelligence that Mr Darcy did not wish for cards; and Mr Hurst soon found even his open petition rejected. She assured him that no one intended to play, and the silence of the whole party on the subject, seemed to justify her. Mr Hurst had therefore nothing to do, but to stretch himself on one of the sophas and go to sleep. Darcy took up a book; Miss Bingley did the same; and Mrs Hurst, principally occupied in playing with her bracelets and rings, joined now and then in her brother's conversation with Miss Bennet.

Miss Bingley's attention was quite as much engaged in watching Mr Darcy's progress through *his* book, as in reading her own; and she was perpetually either making some inquiry, or looking at his page. She could not win him, however, to any conversation; he merely answered her question, and read on. At length, quite exhausted by the attempt to be amused with her own book, which she had only chosen because it was the second volume of his, she gave a great yawn and said, 'How pleasant it is to spend an evening in this way! I declare after all there is no enjoyment like reading! How much sooner one tires of any thing than of a book! – When I have a house of my own, I shall be miserable if I have not an excellent library.'

No one made any reply. She then yawned again, threw aside her book, and cast her eyes round the room in quest of some amusement; when hearing her brother mentioning a ball to Miss Bennet, she turned suddenly towards him and said,

'By the bye, Charles, are you really serious in meditating a dance at Netherfield? – I would advise you, before you determine on it, to consult the wishes of the present party; I am much mistaken if there are not some among us to whom a ball would be rather a punishment than a pleasure.'

'If you mean Darcy,' cried her brother, 'he may go to bed, if he chuses, before it begins – but as for the ball, it is quite a settled thing; and as soon as Nicholls has made white soup enough I shall send round my cards.'

'I should like balls infinitely better,' she replied, 'if they were carried on in a different manner; but there is something insufferably tedious in the usual process of such a meeting. It would surely be much more rational if conversation instead of dancing made the order of the day.'

'Much more rational, my dear Caroline, I dare say but it would not be near so much like a ball.'

Miss Bingley made no answer; and soon afterwards got up and walked about the room. Her figure was elegant, and she walked well; – but Darcy, at whom it was all aimed, was still inflexibly studious. In the desperation of her feelings she resolved on one effort more; and, turning to Elizabeth, said,

'Miss Eliza Bennet, let me persuade you to follow my example, and take a turn about the room. – I assure you it is very refreshing after sitting so long in one attitude.'

Elizabeth was surprised, but agreed to it immediately. Miss Bingley succeeded no less in the real object of her civility; Mr Darcy looked up. He was as much awake to the novelty of attention in that quarter as Elizabeth herself could be, and unconsciously closed his book. He was directly invited to join their party, but he declined it, observing, that he could imagine but two motives for their chusing to walk up and down the room together, with either of which motives his joining them would interfere. 'What could he mean? she was dying to know what could be his meaning' – and asked Elizabeth whether she could at all understand him?

'Not at all,' was her answer; 'but depend upon it, he means to be severe on us, and our surest way of disappointing him, will be to ask nothing about it.'

Miss Bingley, however, was incapable of disappointing Mr Darcy in any thing, and persevered therefore in requiring an explanation of his two motives.

'I have not the smallest objection to explaining them,' said he, as soon as she allowed him to speak. 'You either chuse this method of passing the evening because you are in each other's confidence and have secret affairs to discuss, or because you are conscious that your figures appear to the greatest advantage in walking; – if the first, I should be completely in your way; – and if the second, I can admire you much better as I sit by the fire.'

'Oh! shocking?' cried Miss Bingley. 'I never heard any thing so abominable. How shall we punish him for such a speech?'

'Nothing so easy, if you have but the inclination,' said Elizabeth. 'We can all plague and punish one another. Teaze him – laugh at him. – Intimate as you are, you must know how it is to be done.'

'But upon my honour I do *not*. I do assure you that my intimacy has not yet taught me *that*. Teaze calmness of temper and presence of mind! No, no – I feel he may defy us there. And as to laughter, we will not expose ourselves, if you please, by attempting to laugh without a subject. Mr Darcy may hug himself.'

'Mr Darcy is not to be laughed at!' cried Elizabeth. 'That is an uncommon advantage, and uncommon I hope it will continue, for it would be a great loss to *me* to have many such acquaintance. I dearly love a laugh.'

'Miss Bingley,' said he, 'has given me credit for more than can be. The wisest and the best of men, nay, the wisest and best of their actions, may be rendered ridiculous by a person whose first object in life is a joke.'

'Certainly,' replied Elizabeth – 'there are such people, but I hope I am not one of *them*. I hope I never ridicule what is wise or good. Follies and nonsense, whims and inconsistencies *do* divert me, I own, and I laugh at them whenever I can. – But these, I suppose, are precisely what you are without.'

'Perhaps that is not possible for any one. But it has been the study of my life to avoid those weaknesses which often expose a strong understanding to ridicule.'

'Such as vanity and pride.'

'Yes, vanity is a weakness indeed. But pride – where there is a real superiority of mind, pride will be always under good regulation.'

Elizabeth turned away to hide a smile.

'Your examination of Mr Darcy is over, I presume,' said Miss Bingley; – 'and pray what is the result?'

'I am perfectly convinced by it that Mr Darcy has no defect. He owns it himself without disguise.'

'No' – said Darcy, 'I have made no such pretension. I have faults enough, but they are not, I hope, of understanding. My temper I dare not vouch for. – It is I believe too little yielding – certainly too little for the convenience of the world. I cannot forget the follies and vices of others so soon as I ought, nor their offences against myself. My feelings are not puffed about with every attempt to move them. My temper would perhaps be called resentful. – My good opinion once lost is lost for ever.'

'*That* is a failing indeed!' – cried Elizabeth. 'Implacable resentment *is* a shade in a character. But you have chosen your fault well. – I really cannot *laugh* at it. You are safe from me.'

'There is, I believe, in every disposition a tendency to some particular evil, a natural defect, which not even the best education can overcome.'

'And *your* defect is a propensity to hate every body.'

'And yours,' he replied with a smile, 'is wilfully to misunderstand them.'

'Do let us have a little music,' – cried Miss Bingley, tired of a conversation in which she had no share. – 'Louisa, you will not mind my waking Mr Hurst.'

Her sister made not the smallest objection, and the piano-forte was opened, and Darcy, after a few moments recollection, was not sorry for it. He began to feel the danger of paying Elizabeth too much attention.

CHAPTER TWELVE

IN CONSEQUENCE OF AN AGREEMENT BETWEEN the sisters, Elizabeth wrote the next morning to her mother, to beg that the carriage might be sent for them in the course of the day. But Mrs Bennet, who had calculated on her daughters remaining at Netherfield till the following Tuesday, which would exactly finish Jane's week, could not bring herself to receive them with pleasure before. Her answer, therefore, was not propitious, at least not to Elizabeth's wishes, for she was impatient to get home. Mrs Bennet sent them word that they could not possibly have the carriage before Tuesday; and in her postscript it was added, that if Mr Bingley and his sister pressed them to stay longer, she could spare them very well. – Against staying longer, however, Elizabeth was positively resolved – nor did she much expect it would be asked; and fearful, on the contrary, as being considered as intruding themselves needlessly long, she urged Jane to borrow Mr Bingley's carriage immediately, and at length it was settled that their original design of leaving Netherfield that morning should be mentioned, and the request made.

The communication excited many professions of concern; and enough was said of wishing them to stay at least till the following day to work on Jane; and till the morrow, their going was deferred. Miss Bingley was then sorry that she had proposed the delay, for her jealousy and dislike of one sister much exceeded her affection for the other.

The master of the house heard with real sorrow that they were to go so soon, and repeatedly tried to persuade Miss Bennet that it would not be safe for her – that she was not enough recovered; but Jane was firm where she felt herself to be right.

To Mr Darcy it was welcome intelligence – Elizabeth had been at Netherfield long enough. She attracted him more than he liked – and Miss Bingley was uncivil to *her*, and more teazing than usual to himself. He wisely resolved to be particularly careful that no sign of admiration should *now* escape him, nothing that could elevate her with the hope of influencing his felicity; sensible that if such an idea had been suggested, his behaviour during the last day must have material weight in confirming or crushing it. Steady to his purpose, he scarcely spoke ten words to her through the whole of Saturday, and though they were at one time left by themselves for half an hour, he adhered most conscientiously to his book, and would not even look at her.

On Sunday, after morning service, the separation, so agreeable to almost all, took place. Miss Bingley's civility to Elizabeth increased at last very rapidly, as well as her affection for Jane; and when they parted, after assuring the latter of the pleasure it would always give her to see her either at Longbourn or Netherfield, and embracing her most tenderly, she even shook hands with the former. – Elizabeth took leave of the whole party in the liveliest spirits.

They were not welcomed home very cordially by their mother. Mrs Bennet wondered at their coming, and thought them very wrong to give so much trouble, and was sure Jane would have caught cold again. – But their father, though very laconic in his expressions of pleasure, was really glad to see them; he had felt their importance in the family circle. The evening conversation, when they were all assembled, had lost much of its animation, and almost all its sense, by the absence of Jane and Elizabeth.

They found Mary, as usual, deep in the study of thorough bass and human nature; and had some new extracts to admire, and some new observations of thread-bare morality to listen to. Catherine and Lydia had information for them of a different sort. Much had been done, and much had been said in the regiment since the preceding Wednesday; several of the officers had dined lately with their uncle, a private had been flogged, and it had actually been hinted that Colonel Forster was going to be married.

CHAPTER THIRTEEN

'I HOPE, MY DEAR,' SAID MR BENNET to his wife, as they were at breakfast the next morning, 'that you have ordered a good dinner to-day, because I have reason to expect an addition to our family party.'

'Who do you mean, my dear? I know of nobody that is coming I am sure, unless Charlotte Lucas should happen to call in, and I hope *my* dinners are good enough for her. I do not believe she often sees such at home.'

'The person of whom I speak, is a gentleman and a stranger.' Mrs Bennet's eyes sparkled. – 'A gentleman and a stranger! It is Mr Bingley I am sure. Why Jane – you never dropt a word of this; you sly thing! Well, I am sure I shall be extremely glad to see Mr Bingley. – But – good lord! how unlucky! there is not a bit of fish to be got to-day. Lydia, my love, ring the bell. I must speak to Hill, this moment.'

'It is *not* Mr Bingley,' said her husband; 'it is a person whom I never saw in the whole course of my life.'

This roused a general astonishment; and he had the pleasure of being eagerly questioned by his wife and five daughters at once.

After amusing himself some time with their curiosity, he thus explained. 'About a month ago I received this letter, and about a fortnight ago I answered it, for I thought it a case of some delicacy, and required early attention. It is from my cousin, Mr Collins, who, when I am dead, may turn you all out of this house as soon as he pleases.'

'Oh! my dear,' cried his wife, 'I cannot bear to hear that mentioned. Pray do not talk of that odious man. I do think it is the hardest thing in the world, that your estate should be entailed away from your own children; and I am sure if I had been you, I should have tried long ago to do something or other about it.'

Jane and Elizabeth attempted to explain to her the nature of an entail.

They had often attempted it before, but it was a subject on which Mrs Bennet was beyond the reach of reason; and she continued to rail bitterly against the cruelty of settling an estate away from a family of five daughters, in favour of a man whom nobody cared anything about.

'It certainly is a most iniquitous affair,' said Mr Bennet, 'and nothing can clear Mr Collins from the guilt of inheriting Longbourn. But if you will listen to his letter, you may perhaps be a little softened by his manner of expressing himself.'

'No, that I am sure I shall not; and I think it was very impertinent of him to write to you at all, and very hypocritical. I hate such false friends. Why could not he keep on quarrelling with you, as his father did before him?'

'Why, indeed, he does seem to have some filial scruples on that head, as you will hear.'

Hunsford, near Westerham, Kent.
15th October.

DEAR SIR,

The disagreement subsisting between yourself and my late honoured father, always gave me much uneasiness, and since I have had the misfortune to lose him, I have frequently wished to heal the breach; but for some time I was kept back by my own doubts, fearing lest it might seem disrespectful to his memory for me to be on good terms with any one, with whom it had always pleased him to be at variance. – 'There, Mrs Bennet.' – *My mind however is now made up on the subject, for having received ordination at Easter, I have been so fortunate as to be distinguished by the patronage of the Right Honourable Lady Catherine de Bourgh, widow of Sir Lewis de Bourgh, whose bounty and beneficence has preferred me to the valuable rectory of this parish, where it shall be my earnest endeavour to demean myself with grateful respect towards her Ladyship, and be ever ready to perform those rites and ceremonies which are instituted by the Church of England. As a clergyman, moreover, I feel it my duty to promote and establish the blessing of peace in all families within the reach of my influence; and on these grounds I flatter myself that my present overtures of good-will are highly commendable, and that the circumstance of my being next in the entail of Longbourn estate, will be kindly overlooked on your side, and not lead you to reject the offered olive branch. I cannot be otherwise than concerned at being the means of injuring your amiable daughters, and beg leave to apologise for it, as well as to assure you of my readiness to make them every possible amends, – but of this hereafter. If you should have no objection to receive me into your house, I propose myself the satisfaction of waiting on you and your family, Monday, November 18th, by four o'clock, and shall probably trespass on your hospitality till the Saturday se'night following, which I can do without any inconvenience, as Lady*

Catherine is far from objecting to my occasional absence on a Sunday, provided that some other clergyman is engaged to do the duty of the day. I remain, dear sir, with respectful compliments to your lady and daughters, your well-wisher and friend.

WILLIAM COLLINS

'At four o'clock, therefore, we may expect this peace-making gentleman,' said Mr Bennet, as he folded up the letter. 'He seems to be a most conscientious and polite young man, upon my word; and I doubt not will prove a valuable acquaintance, especially if Lady Catherine should be so indulgent as to let him come to us again.'

'There is some sense in what he says about the girls however; and if he is disposed to make them any amends, I shall not be the person to discourage him.'

'Though it is difficult,' said Jane, 'to guess in what way he can mean to make us the atonement he thinks our due, the wish is certainly to his credit.'

Elizabeth was chiefly struck with his extraordinary deference for Lady Catherine, and his kind intention of christening, marrying, and burying his parishioners whenever it were required.

'He must be an oddity, I think,' said she. 'I cannot make him out. – There is something very pompous in his stile. – And what can he mean by apologizing for being next in the entail? – We cannot suppose he would help it, if he could. – Can he be a sensible man, sir?'

'No, my dear; I think not. I have great hopes of finding him quite the reverse. There is a mixture of servility and self-importance in his letter, which promises well. I am impatient to see him.'

'In point of composition,' said Mary, 'his letter does not seem defective. The idea of the olive branch perhaps is not wholly new, yet I think it is well expressed.'

To Catherine and Lydia, neither the letter nor its writer were in any degree interesting. It was next to impossible that their cousin should come in a scarlet coat, and it was now some weeks since they had received pleasure from the society of a man in any other colour. As for their mother, Mr Collins's letter had done away much of her ill-will, and she was preparing to see him with a degree of composure, which astonished her husband and daughters.

Mr Collins was punctual to his time, and was received with great politeness by the whole family. Mr Bennet indeed said little; but the ladies were ready enough to talk, and Mr Collins seemed neither in need of encouragement, nor inclined to be silent himself. He was a tall, heavy looking young man of five and twenty. His air was grave and stately, and his manners were very formal. He had not been long seated before he complimented Mrs Bennet on having so fine a family of daughters, said he had heard much of their beauty, but that, in this instance, fame had fallen short of the truth; and added, that he did not doubt her seeing them all in due time well disposed of in marriage. This gallantry was not much to the taste of some of his hearers, but Mrs Bennet, who quarrelled with no compliments, answered most readily,

'You are very kind, sir, I am sure; and I wish with all my heart it may prove so; for else they will be destitute enough. Things are settled so oddly.'

'You allude perhaps to the entail of this estate.'

'Ah! sir, I do indeed. It is a grevious affair to my poor girls, you must confess. Not that I mean to find fault with *you*, for such things I know are all chance in this world. There is no knowing how estates will go when once they come to be entailed.'

'I am very sensible, madam, of the hardship to my fair cousins, – and could say much on the subject, but that I am cautious of appearing forward and precipitate. But I can assure the young ladies that I come prepared to admire them. At present I will not say more, but perhaps when we are better acquainted –'

He was interrupted by a summons to dinner; and the girls smiled on each other. They were not the only objects of Mr Collins's admiration. The hall, the dining-room, and all its furniture were examined and praised; and his commendation of every thing would have touched Mrs Bennet's heart, but for the mortifying supposition of his viewing it all as his own future property. The dinner too in its turn was highly admired; and he begged to know to which of his fair cousins, the excellence of its cookery was owing. But here he was set right by Mrs Bennet, who assured him with some asperity that they were very well able to keep a good cook, and that her daughters had nothing to do in the kitchen. He begged pardon for having displeased her. In a softened tone she declared herself not at all offended; but he continued to apologise for about a quarter of an hour.

CHAPTER FOURTEEN

DURING DINNER, MR BENNET SCARCELY spoke at all; but when the servants were withdrawn, he thought it time to have some conversation with his guest, and therefore started a subject in which he expected him to shine, by observing that he seemed very fortunate in his patroness. Lady Catherine de Bourgh's attention to his wishes, and consideration for his comfort, appeared very remarkable. Mr Bennet could not have chosen better. Mr

Collins was eloquent in her praise. The subject elevated him to more than usual solemnity of manner, and with a most important aspect he protested that he had never in his life witnessed such behaviour in a person of rank – such affability and condescension, as he had himself experienced from Lady Catherine. She had been graciously pleased to approve of both the discourses, which he had already had the honour of preaching before her. She had also asked him twice to dine at Rosings; and had sent for him only the Saturday before, to make up her pool of quadrille in the evening. Lady Catherine was reckoned proud by many people he knew, but *he* had never seen any thing but affability in her. She had always spoken to him as she would to any other gentleman; she made not the smallest objection to his in the society of the neighbourhood, nor to his leaving his parish occasionally for a week or two, to visit his relations. She had even condescended to advise him to marry as soon as he could, provided he chose with discretion; and had once paid him a visit in his humble parsonage; where she had perfectly approved all the alterations he had been making, and had even vouchsafed to suggest some herself, – some shelves in the closets up stairs.

'That is all very proper and civil, I am sure,' said Mrs Bennet, 'and I dare say she is a very agreeable woman. It is a pity that great ladies in general are not more like her. Does she live near you, sir?'

'The garden in which stands my humble abode, is separated only by a lane from Rosings Park, her ladyship's residence.'

'I think you said she was a widow, sir? has she any family?'

'She has only one daughter, the heiress of Rosings, and of very extensive property.'

'Ah!' cried Mrs Bennet, shaking her head, 'then she is better off than many girls. And what sort of young lady is she? is she handsome?'

'She is a most charming young lady indeed. Lady Catherine herself says that in point of true beauty, Miss de Bourgh is far superior to the handsomest of her sex; because there is that in her features which marks the young woman of distinguished birth. She is unfortunately of a sickly constitution, which has prevented her making that progress in many accomplishments, which she could not otherwise have failed of; as I am informed by the lady who superintended her education, and who still resides with them. But she is perfectly amiable, and often condescends to drive by my humble abode in her little phaeton and ponies.'

'Has she been presented? I do not remember her name among the ladies at court.'

'Her indifferent state of health unhappily prevents her being in town; and by that means, as I told Lady Catherine myself one day, has deprived the British court of its brightest ornament. Her ladyship seemed pleased with the idea, and you may imagine that I am happy on every occasion to offer

Protested that he never read novels

those little delicate compliments which are always acceptable to ladies. I have more than once observed to Lady Catherine, that her charming daughter seemed born to be a duchess, and that the most elevated rank, instead of giving her consequence, would be adorned by her. – These are the kind of little things which please her ladyship, and it is a sort of attention which I conceive myself peculiarly bound to pay.'

'You judge very properly,' said Mr Bennet, 'and it is happy for you that you possess the talent of flattering with delicacy. May I ask whether these pleasing attentions proceed from the impulse of the moment, or are the result of previous study?'

'They arise chiefly from what is passing at the time, and though I sometimes amuse myself with suggesting and arranging such little elegant compliments as may be adapted to ordinary occasions, I always wish to give them as unstudied an air as possible.'

Mr Bennet's expectations were fully answered. His cousin was as absurd as he had hoped, and he listened to him with the keenest enjoyment, maintaining at the same time the most resolute composure of countenance, and except in an occasional glance at Elizabeth, requiring no partner in his pleasure.

By tea-time however the dose had been enough, and Mr Bennet was glad to take his guest into the drawing-room again, and when tea was over, glad to invite him to read aloud to the ladies. Mr Collins readily assented, and a book was produced; but on beholding it, (for every thing announced it to be from a circulating library,) he started back, and begging pardon, protested that he never read novels. – Kitty stared at him, and Lydia exclaimed. – Other books were produced, and after some deliberation he chose Fordyce's Sermons. Lydia gaped as he opened the volume, and before he had, with very monotonous solemnity, read three pages, she interrupted him with,

'Do you know, mama, that my uncle Philips talks of turning away Richard, and if he does, Colonel Forster will hire him. My aunt told me so herself on Saturday. I shall walk to Meryton to-morrow to hear more about it, and to ask when Mr Denny comes back from town.'

Lydia was bid by her two eldest sisters to hold her tongue; but Mr Collins, much offended, laid aside his book, and said,

'I have often observed how little young ladies are interested by books of a serious stamp, though written solely for their benefit. It amazes me, I confess; – for certainly, there can be nothing so advantageous to them as instruction. But I will no longer importune my young cousin.'

Then turning to Mr Bennet, he offered himself as his antagonist at backgammon. Mr Bennet accepted the challenge, observing that he acted very wisely in leaving the girls to their own trifling amusements. Mrs Bennet and her daughters apologized most civilly for Lydia's interruption, and promised that it should not occur again, if he would resume his book; but Mr Collins, after assuring them that he bore his young cousin no ill will, and should never resent her behaviour as any affront, seated himself at another table with Mr Bennet, and prepared for backgammon.

CHAPTER FIFTEEN

MR COLLINS WAS NOT A SENSIBLE man, and the deficiency of nature had been but little assisted by education or society; the greatest part of his life having been spent under the guidance of an illiterate and miserly father; and though he belonged to one of the universities, he had merely kept the necessary terms, without forming at it any useful acquaintance. The subjection in which his father had brought him up, had given him originally great humility of manner, but it was now a good deal counteracted by the self-conceit of a weak head, living in retirement, and the consequential feelings of early and unexpected prosperity. A fortunate chance had recommended him to Lady Catherine de Bourgh when the living of Hunsford was vacant; and the respect which he felt for her high rank, and his veneration for her as his patroness, mingling with a very good opinion of himself, of his authority as a clergyman, and his rights as a rector, made him altogether a mixture of pride and obsequiousness, self-importance and humility.

Having now a good house and very sufficient income, he intended to marry; and in seeking a reconciliation with the Longbourn family he had a wife in view, as he meant to chuse one of the daughters, if he found them as handsome and amiable as they were represented by common report. This was his plan of amends – of atonement – for inheriting their father's estate; and he thought it an excellent one, full of eligibility and suitableness, and excessively generous and disinterested on his own part.

His plan did not vary on seeing them. – Miss Bennet's lovely face confirmed his views, and established all his strictest notions of what was due to seniority; and for the first evening *she* was his settled choice. The next morning, however, made an alteration; for in a quarter of an hour's tête-à-tête with Mrs Bennet before breakfast, a conversation beginning with his parsonage-house, and leading naturally to the avowal of his hopes, that a mistress for it might be found at Longbourn, produced from her, amid very complaisant smiles and general encouragement, a caution against the very Jane he had fixed on. – 'As to her *younger* daughters she could not take upon her to say – she could not positively answer – but she did not *know* of any prepossession; – her *eldest* daughter, she must just mention – she felt incumbent on her to hint, was likely to be very soon engaged.'

Mr Collins had only to change from Jane to Elizabeth – and it was soon done – done while Mrs Bennet was stirring the fire. Elizabeth, equally next to Jane in birth and beauty, succeeded her of course.

Mrs Bennet treasured up the hint, and trusted that she might soon have two daughters married; and the man whom she could not bear to speak of the day before, was now high in her good graces.

Lydia's intention of walking to Meryton was not forgotten; every sister except Mary agreed to go with her; and Mr Collins was to attend them, at the request of Mr Bennet, who was most anxious to get rid of him, and have his library to himself; for thither Mr Collins had followed him after breakfast, and there he would continue, nominally engaged with one of the largest folios in the collection, but really talking to Mr Bennet, with little cessation, of his house and garden at Hunsford. Such doings discomposed Mr Bennet exceedingly. In his library he had been always sure of leisure and tranquillity; and though prepared, as he told Elizabeth, to meet with folly and conceit in every other room in the house, he was used to be free from them there; his civility, therefore, was most prompt in inviting Mr Collins to join his daughters in their walk; and Mr Collins, being in fact much better fitted for a walker than a reader, was extremely well pleased to close his large book, and go.

In pompous nothings on his side, and civil assents on that of his cousins, their time passed till they entered Meryton. The attention of the younger ones was then no longer to be gained by *him*. Their eyes were immediately wandering up in the street in quest of the officers, and nothing less than a very smart bonnet indeed, or a really new muslin in a shop window, could recall them.

But the attention of every young lady was soon caught by a young man, whom they had never seen before, of most gentlemanlike appearance, walking with an officer on the other side of the way. The officer was the very Mr Denny, concerning whose return from London Lydia came to enquire, and he bowed as they passed. All were struck with the stranger's air, all wondered who he could be, and Kitty and Lydia, determined if possible to find out, led the way across the street, under pretence of wanting something in an opposite shop, and fortunately had just gained the pavement when the two gentlemen turning back had reached the same spot. Mr Denny addressed them directly, and entreated permission to introduce his friend, Mr Wickham, who had returned with him the day before from town, and he was happy to say had accepted a commission in their corps. This was exactly as it should be; for the young man wanted only regimentals to make him completely charming. His appearance was greatly in his favour; he had all the best part of beauty, a fine countenance, a good figure, and very pleasing address. The introduction was followed up on his side by a happy readiness of conversation – a readiness at the same time perfectly correct and unassuming; and the whole party were still standing and talking together very agreeably, when the sound of horses drew their notice, and Darcy and Bingley were seen riding down the street. On distinguishing the ladies of the group, the two gentlemen came directly towards them, and began the usual civilities. Bingley was the principal spokesman, and Miss Bennet the principal object. He was then, he said, on his way to Longbourn on purpose to enquire after her. Mr Darcy corroborated it with a bow, and was beginning to determine not to fix his eyes on Elizabeth, when they were suddenly arrested by the sight of the stranger, and Elizabeth happening to see the countenance of both as they looked at each other, was all astonishment at the effect of the meeting. Both changed colour, one looked white, the other red. Mr Wickham, after a few moments, touched his hat – a salutation which Mr Darcy just deigned to return. What could be the meaning of it? – It was impossible to imagine; it was impossible not to long to know.

In another minute Mr Bingley, but without seeming to have noticed what passed, took leave and rode on with his friend.

Mr Denny and Mr Wickham walked with the young ladies to the door of Mr Philip's house, and then made their bows, in spite of Miss Lydia's pressing entreaties that they would come in, and even in spite of Mrs Philips' throwing up the parlour window, and loudly seconding the invitation.

Mrs Philips was always glad to see her nieces, and the two eldest, from their recent absence, were particularly welcome, and she was eagerly expressing her surprise at their sudden return home, which, as their own carriage had not fetched them, she should have known nothing about, if she had not happened to see Mr Jones's shop boy in the street, who had told her that they were not to send any more draughts to Netherfield because the Miss Bennets were come away, when her civility was claimed towards Mr Collins by Jane's introduction of him. She received him with her very best politeness, which he returned with as much more, apologising for his intrusion, without any previous acquaintance with her, which he could not help flattering himself however might be justified by his relationship to the young ladies who introduced him to her notice. Mrs Philips was quite awed by such an excess of good breeding; but her contemplation of one stranger was soon put an end to by exclamations and inquiries about the other, of whom, however, she could only tell her nieces what they already knew, that Mr Denny had brought him from London, and that he was to have a lieutenant's commission in the –shire. She had been watching him the last hour, she said, as he walked up and down the street, and had Mr Wickham appeared Kitty and Lydia would certainly have continued the occupation, but unluckily no one passed the windows now except a few of the officers, who in comparison with the stranger, were become 'stupid, disagreeable fellows'. Some of them were to dine with the Philipses the next day, and their aunt promised to make her husband call on Mr Wickham, and give him an invitation also, if the family from Longbourn would come in the evening. This was agreed to, and Mrs Philips protested that they would have a nice comfortable noisy game of lottery tickets, and a little bit of hot supper afterwards. The prospect of such delights was very cheering, and they parted in mutual good spirits. Mr Collins repeated his apologies in quitting the room, and was assured with unwearying civility that they were perfectly needless.

As they walked home, Elizabeth related to Jane what she had seen pass between the two gentlemen; but though Jane would have defended either or both, had they appeared to be wrong, she could no more explain such behaviour than her sister.

Mr Collins on his return highly gratified Mrs Bennet by admiring Mrs Philips's manners and politeness. He protested that except Lady Catherine and her daughter, he had never seen a more elegant woman; for she had not only received him with the utmost civility, but had even pointedly included him in her invitation for the next evening, although utterly unknown to her before. Something he supposed might be attributed to his connection with them, but yet he had never met with so much attention in the whole course of his life.

CHAPTER SIXTEEN

AS NO OBJECTION WAS MADE TO THE young people's engagement with their aunt, and all Mr Collins's scruples of leaving Mr and Mrs Bennet for a single evening during his visit were most steadily resisted, the coach conveyed him and his five cousins at a suitable hour to Meryton; and the girls had the pleasure of hearing, as they entered the drawing-room, that Mr Wickham had accepted their uncle's invitation, and was then in the house.

When this information was given, and they had all taken their seats, Mr Collins was at leisure to look around him and admire, and he was so much struck with the size and furniture of the apartment, that he declared he might almost have supposed himself in the smaller summer breakfast parlour at Rosings; a comparison that did not at first convey much gratification; but when Mrs Philips understood from him what Rosings was, and who was its proprietor, when she had listened to the description of only one of Lady Catherine's drawing-rooms, and found that the chimney-piece alone had cost eight hundred pounds, she felt all the force of the compliment, and would hardly have resented a comparison with the housekeeper's room.

In describing to her all the grandeur of Lady Catherine and her mansion, with occasional digressions in praise of his own humble abode, and the improvements it was receiving, he was happily employed until the gentlemen joined them; and he found in Mrs Philips a very attentive listener, whose opinion of his consequence increased with what she heard, and who was resolving to retail it all among her neighbours as soon as she could. To the girls, who could not listen to their cousin, and who had nothing to do but wish for an instrument, and examine their own indifferent imitations of china on the mantelpiece, the interval of waiting appeared very long. It was over at last however. The gentlemen did approach; and when Mr Wickham walked into the room, Elizabeth felt that she had neither been seeing him before, nor thinking of him since, with the smallest degree of unreasonable admiration. The officers of the –shire were in general a very creditable, gentlemanlike set, and the best of them were of

The officers of the —shire

the present party; but Mr Wickham was as far beyond them all in person, countenance, air, and walk, as *they* were superior to the broad-faced stuffy uncle Philips, breathing port wine, who followed them into the room.

Mr Wickham was the happy man towards whom almost every female eye was turned, and Elizabeth was the happy woman by whom he finally seated himself; and the agreeable manner in which he immediately fell into conversation, though it was only on its being a wet night, and on the probability of a rainy season, made her feel that the commonest, dullest, most threadbare topic might be rendered interesting by the skill of the speaker.

With such rivals for the notice of the fair, as Mr Wickham and the officers, Mr Collins seemed likely to sink into insignificance; to the young ladies he certainly was nothing; but he had still at intervals a kind listener in Mrs Philips, and was, by her watchfulness, most abundantly supplied with coffee and muffin.

When the card tables were placed, he had an opportunity of obliging her in return, by sitting down to whist.

'I know little of the game, at present,' said he, 'but I shall be glad to improve myself, for in my situation of life –' Mrs Philips was very thankful of his compliance, but could not wait for his reason.

Mr Wickham did not play at whist, and with ready delight was he received at the other table between Elizabeth and Lydia. At first there seemed danger of Lydia's engrossing him entirely, for she was a most determined talker; but being likewise extremely fond of lottery tickets, she soon grew too much interested in the game, too eager in making bets and exclaiming after prizes, to have attention for any one in particular. Allowing for the common demands of the game, Mr Wickham was therefore at leisure to talk to Elizabeth, and she was very willing to hear him, though what she chiefly wished to hear she could not hope to be told, the history of his acquaintance with Mr Darcy. She dared not even mention that gentleman. Her curiosity however was unexpectedly relieved. Mr Wickham began the subject himself. He inquired how far Netherfield was from Meryton; and, after receiving her answer, asked in an hesitating manner how long Mr Darcy had been staying there.

'About a month,' said Elizabeth; and then, unwilling to let the subject drop, added, 'He is a man of very large property in Derbyshire, I understand.'

'Yes,' replied Wickham; – 'his estate there is a noble one. A clear ten thousand per annum. You could not have met with a person more capable of giving you certain information on that head than myself – for I have been connected with his family in a particular manner from my infancy.'

Elizabeth could not but look surprised.

'You may well be surprised, Miss Bennet, at such an assertion, after seeing, as you probably might, the very cold manner of our meeting yesterday. – Are you much acquainted with Mr Darcy?'

'As much as I ever wish to be,' cried Elizabeth warmly, – 'I have spent four days in the same house with him, and I think him very disagreeable.'

'I have no right to give *my* opinion,' said Wickham, 'as to his being agreeable or otherwise. I am not qualified to form one. I have known him too long and too well to be a fair judge. It is impossible for *me* to be impartial. But I believe your opinion of him would in general astonish – and perhaps you would not express it quite so strongly anywhere else. – Here you are in your own family.'

'Upon my word I say no more *here* than I might say in any house in the neighbourhood, except Netherfield. He is not at all liked in Hertfordshire. Every body is disgusted with his pride. You will not find him more favourably spoken of by any one.'

'I cannot pretend to be sorry,' said Wickham, after a short interruption, 'that he or that any man should not be estimated beyond their deserts; but with *him* I believe it does not often happen. The world is blinded by his fortune and consequence, or frightened by his high and imposing manners, and sees him only as he chuses to be seen.'

'I should take him, even on *my* slight acquaintance, to be an ill-tempered man.' Wickham only shook his head.

'I wonder,' said he, at the next opportunity of speaking, 'whether he is likely to be in this country much longer.'

'I do not at all know; but I *heard* nothing of his going away when I was at Netherfield. I hope your plans in favour of the –shire will not be affected by his being in the neighbourhood.'

'Oh! no – it is not for *me* to be driven away by Mr Darcy. If *he* wishes to avoid seeing *me*, he must go. We are not on friendly terms, and it always gives me pain to meet him, but I have no reason for avoiding *him* but what I might proclaim to all the world; a sense of very great ill usage, and most painful regrets at his being what he is. His father, Miss Bennet, the late Mr Darcy, was one of the best men that ever breathed, and the truest friend I ever had; and I can never be in company with this Mr Darcy without being grieved to the soul by a thousand tender recollections. His behaviour to myself has been scandalous; but I verily believe I could forgive him any thing and every thing, rather than his disappointing the hopes and disgracing the memory of his father.'

Elizabeth found the interest of the subject increase, and listened with all her heart; but the delicacy of it prevented farther enquiry.

Mr Wickham began to speak on more general topics, Meryton, the neighbourhood, the society, appearing highly pleased with all that he had yet seen, and speaking of the latter especially, with gentle but very intelligible gallantry.

'It was the prospect of constant society, and good society,' he added, 'which was my chief inducement to enter the –shire. I knew it to be a most respectable, agreeable corps, and my friend Denny tempted me farther by his account of their present quarters, and the very great attentions and excellent acquaintance Meryton had procured them. Society, I own, is necessary to me. I have been a disappointed man, and my spirits will not bear solitude. I *must* have employment and society. A military life is not what I was intended for, but circumstances have now made it eligible. The church *ought* to have been my profession – I was brought up for the church and I should at this time have been in possession of a most valuable living, had it pleased the gentleman we were speaking of just now.'

'Indeed!'

'Yes – the late Mr Darcy bequeathed me the next presentation of the best living in his gift. He was my godfather, and excessively attached to me. I cannot do justice to his kindness. He meant to provide for me amply, and thought he had done it; but when the living fell, it was given elsewhere.'

'Good heavens!' cried Elizabeth; 'but how could *that* be? – How could his will be disregarded? – Why did not you seek legal redress?'

'There was just such an informality in the terms of the bequest as to give me no hope from law. A man of honour could not have doubted the intention, but Mr Darcy chose to doubt it – or to treat it as a merely conditional recommendation, and to assert that I had forfeited all claim to it by extravagance, imprudence, in short any thing or nothing. Certain it is, that the living became vacant two years ago, exactly as I was of an age to hold it, and that it was given to another man; and no less certain is it, that I cannot accuse myself of having really done any thing to deserve to lose it. I have a warm, unguarded temper, and I may perhaps have sometimes spoken my opinion *of* him, and *to* him, too freely. I can recall nothing worse. But the fact is, that we are very different sort of men, and that he hates me.'

'This is quite shocking! – He deserves to be publicly disgraced.'

'Some time or other he *will* be – but it shall not be by *me*. Till I can forget his father, I can never defy or expose *him*.'

Elizabeth honoured him for such feelings, and thought him handsomer than ever as he expressed them.

'But what,' said she, after a pause, 'can have been his motive? – what can have induced him to behave so cruelly?'

'A thorough, determined dislike of me – a dislike which I cannot but attribute in some measure to jealousy. Had the late Mr Darcy liked me less, his son might have borne with me better; but his father's uncommon attachment to me, irritated him I believe very early in life. He had not a temper to bear the sort of competition in which we stood – the sort of preference which was often given me.'

'I had not thought Mr Darcy so bad as this – though I have never liked him, I had not thought so very ill of him – I had supposed him to be despising his fellow-creatures in general, but did not suspect him of descending to such malicious revenge, such injustice, such inhumanity as this!'

After a few minutes reflection, however, she continued, 'I *do* remember his boasting one day, at Netherfield, of the implacability of his resentments, of his having an unforgiving temper. His disposition must be dreadful.'

'I will not trust myself on the subject,' replied Wickham, '*I* can hardly be just to him.'

Elizabeth was again deep in thought, and after a time exclaimed, 'To treat in such a manner, the godson, the friend, the favourite of his father!' – She could have added, 'A young man too, like *you*, whose very countenance may vouch for your being amiable' – but she contented herself with 'And one, too, who had probably been his own companion from childhood, connected together, as I think you said, in the closest manner!'

'We were born in the same parish, within the same park, the greatest part of our youth was passed together; inmates of the same house, sharing the same amusements, objects of the same parental care. *My* father began life in the profession which your uncle, Mr Philips, appears to do so much credit to – but he gave up every thing to be of use to the late Mr Darcy, and devoted all his time to the care of the Pemberley property. He was most highly esteemed by Mr Darcy, a most intimate, confidential friend. Mr Darcy often acknowledged himself to be under the greatest obligations to my father's active superintendance, and when immediately before my father's death, Mr Darcy gave him a voluntary promise of providing for me, I am convinced that he felt it to be as much of a debt of gratitude to *him*, as of affection to myself.'

'How strange!' cried Elizabeth. 'How abominable! – I wonder that the very pride of this Mr Darcy has not made him just to you! – If from no better motive, that he should not have been too proud to be dishonest, – for dishonesty I must call it.'

'It *is* wonderful,' – replied Wickham, – 'for almost all his actions may be traced to pride; – and pride has often been his best friend. It has connected him nearer with virtue than any other feeling. But we are none of us consistent; and in his behaviour to me, there were stronger impulses even than pride.'

'Can such abominable pride as his, have ever done him good?'

'Yes. It has often led him to be liberal and generous, – to give his money freely, to display hospitality, to assist his tenants, and relieve the poor. Family pride, and *filial* pride, for he is very proud of what his father was, have done this. Not to appear to disgrace his family, to degenerate from the popular qualities, or lose the influence of the Pemberley House, is a powerful motive. He has also *brotherly* pride, which with *some* brotherly affection, makes him a very kind and careful guardian of his sister; and you will hear him generally cried up as the most attentive and best of brothers.'

'What sort of a girl is Miss Darcy?'

He shook his head. – 'I wish I could call her amiable. It gives me pain to speak ill of a Darcy. But she is too much like her brother, – very, very proud. – As a child, she was affectionate and pleasing, and extremely fond of me; and I have devoted hours and hours to her amusement. But she is nothing to me now. She is a handsome girl, about fifteen or sixteen, and I understand highly accomplished. Since her father's death, her home has been London, where a lady lives with her, and superintends her education.'

After many pauses and many trials of other subjects, Elizabeth could not help reverting once more to the first, and saying,

'I am astonished at his intimacy with Mr Bingley! How can Mr Bingley, who seems good humour itself, and is, I really believe, truly amiable, be in friendship with such a man? How can they suit each other? – Do you know Mr Bingley?'

'Not at all.'

'He is a sweet tempered, amiable, charming man. He cannot know what Mr Darcy is.'

'Probably not; – but Mr Darcy can please where he chuses. He does not want abilities. He can be a conversible companion if he thinks it worth his while. Among those who are at all his equals in consequence, he is a very different man from what he is to the less prosperous. His pride never deserts him; but with the rich, he is liberal-minded, just, sincere, rational, honourable, and perhaps agreeable, – allowing something for fortune and figure.'

The whist party soon afterwards breaking up, the players gathered round the other table, and Mr Collins took his station between his cousin Elizabeth and Mrs Philips. – The usual inquiries as to his success were made by the latter. It had not been very great; he had lost every point; but when Mrs Philips began to express her concern thereupon, he assured her with much earnest gravity that it was not of the least importance, that he considered the money as a mere trifle, and begged she would not make herself uneasy.

'I know very well, madam,' said he, 'that when persons sit down to a card table, they must take their chance of these things, – and happily I am not in such circumstances as to make five shillings any object. There are undoubtedly many who could not say the same, but thanks to Lady Catherine de Bourgh, I am removed far beyond the necessity of regarding little matters.'

Mr Wickham's attention was caught; and after observing Mr Collins for a few moments, he asked Elizabeth in a low voice whether her relation were very intimately acquainted with the family of de Bourgh.

'Lady Catherine de Bourgh,' she replied, 'has very lately given him a living. I hardly know how Mr Collins was first introduced to her notice, but he certainly has not known her long.'

'You know of course that Lady Catherine de Bourgh and Lady Anne Darcy were sisters; consequently that she is aunt to the present Mr Darcy.'

'No, indeed, I did not. – I knew nothing at all of Lady Catherine's connections. I never heard of her existence till the day before yesterday.'

'Her daughter, Miss de Bourgh, will have a very large fortune, and it is believed that she and her cousin will unite the two estates.'

This information made Elizabeth smile, as she thought of poor Miss Bingley. Vain indeed must be all her attentions, vain and useless her affection for his sister and her praise of himself, if he were already self-destined to another.

'Mr Collins,' said she, 'speaks highly both of Lady Catherine and her daughter; but from some particulars that he has related of her ladyship, I suspect his gratitude misleads him, and that in spite of her being his patroness, she is an arrogant, conceited woman.'

'I believe her to be both in a great degree,' replied Wickham; 'I have not seen her for many years, but I very well remember that I never liked her, and that her manners were dictatorial and insolent. She has the reputation of being remarkably sensible and clever; but I rather believe she derives part of her abilities from her rank and fortune, part from her authoritative manner, and the rest from the pride of her nephew, who chuses that every one connected with him should have an understanding of the first class.'

Elizabeth allowed that he had given a very rational account of it, and they continued talking together with mutual satisfaction till supper put an end to cards; and gave the rest of the ladies their share of Mr Wickham's attentions. There could be no conversation in the noise of Mrs Philips's supper party, but his manners recommended him to every body. Whatever he said, was said well; and whatever he did, done gracefully. Elizabeth went away with her head full of him. She could think of nothing but of Mr Wickham, and of what he had told her, all the way home; but there was not time for her even to mention his name as they went, for neither Lydia nor Mr Collins were once silent. Lydia talked incessantly of lottery tickets, of the fish she had lost and the fish she had won, and Mr Collins, in describing the civility of Mr and Mrs Philips, protesting that he did not in the least regard his losses at whist, enumerating all the dishes at supper, and repeatedly fearing that he crouded his cousins, had more to say than he could well manage before the carriage stopped at Longbourn House.

Delighted to see their dear friend again

CHAPTER SEVENTEEN

ELIZABETH RELATED TO JANE THE NEXT day, what had passed between Mr Wickham and herself. Jane listened with astonishment and concern; – she knew not how to believe that Mr Darcy could be so unworthy of Mr Bingley's regard; and yet, it was not in her nature to question the veracity of a young man of such amiable appearance as Wickham. – The possibility of his having really endured such unkindness, was enough to interest all her tender feelings; and nothing therefore remained to be done, but to think well of them both, to defend the conduct of each, and throw into the account of accident or mistake, whatever could not be otherwise explained.

'They have both,' said she, 'been deceived, I dare say, in some way or other, of which we can form no idea. Interested people have perhaps misrepresented each to the other. It is, in short, impossible for us to conjecture the causes or circumstances which may have alienated them, without actual blame on either side.'

'Very true, indeed; – and now, my dear Jane, what have you got to say in behalf of the interested people who have probably been concerned in the business? – Do clear *them* too, or we shall be obliged to think ill of somebody.'

'Laugh as much as you chuse, but you will not laugh me out of my opinion. My dearest Lizzy, do but consider in what a disgraceful light it places Mr Darcy, to be treating his father's favourite in such a manner, – one, whom his father had promised to provide for. – It is impossible. No man of common humanity, no man who had any value for his character, could be capable of it. Can his most intimate friends be so excessively deceived in him? oh! no.'

'I can much more easily believe Mr Bingley's being imposed on, than that Mr Wickham should invent such a history of himself as he gave me last night; names, facts, every thing mentioned without ceremony. – If it be not so, let Mr Darcy contradict it. Besides, there was truth in his looks.'

'It is difficult indeed – it is distressing. – One does not know what to think.'

'I beg your pardon; – one knows exactly what to think.'

But Jane could think with certainty on only one point, – that Mr Bingley, if he *had been* imposed on, would have much to suffer when the affair became public.

The two young ladies were summoned from the shrubbery where this conversation passed, by the arrival of some of the very persons of whom they had been speaking; Mr Bingley and his sisters came to give their personal invitation for the long expected ball at Netherfield, which was fixed for the following Tuesday. The two ladies were delighted to see their dear friend again, called it an age since they had met, and repeatedly asked what she had been doing with herself since their separation. To the rest of the family they paid little attention; avoiding Mrs Bennet as much as possible, saying not much to Elizabeth, and nothing at all to the others. They were soon gone again, rising from their seats with an activity which took their brother by surprise, and hurrying off as if eager to escape from Mrs Bennet's civilities.

The prospect of the Netherfield ball was extremely agreeable to every female of the family. Mrs Bennet chose to consider it as given in compliment to her eldest daughter, and was particularly flattered by receiving the invitation from Mr Bingley himself, instead of a ceremonious card. Jane pictured to herself a happy evening in the society of her two friends, and the attentions of their brother; and Elizabeth thought with pleasure of dancing a great deal with Mr Wickham, and of seeing a confirmation of every thing in Mr Darcy's looks and behaviour. The happiness anticipated by Catherine and Lydia, depended less on any single event, or any particular person, for though they each, like Elizabeth, meant to dance half the evening with Mr Wickham, he was by no means the only partner who could satisfy them, and a ball was at any rate, a ball. And even Mary could assure her family that she had no disinclination for it.

'While I can have my mornings to myself,' said she, 'it is enough. – I think it no sacrifice to join occasionally in evening engagements. Society has claims on us all; and I profess myself one of those who consider intervals of recreation and amusement as desirable for every body.'

Elizabeth's spirits were so high on the occasion, that though she did not often speak unnecessarily to Mr Collins, she could not help asking him whether he intended to accept Mr Bingley's invitation, and if he did, whether he would think it proper to join in the evening's amusement; and she was rather surprised to find that he entertained no scruple whatever on that head, and was very far from dreading a rebuke either from the Archbishop, or Lady Catherine de Bourgh, by venturing to dance.

'I am by no means of opinion, I assure you,' said he, 'that a ball of this kind, given by a young man of character, to respectable people, can have any evil tendency; and I am so far from objecting to dancing myself that I shall hope to be honoured with the hands of all my fair cousins in the course of the evening, and I take this opportunity of soliciting yours, Miss Elizabeth, for the two first dances especially, – a preference which I trust my cousin Jane will attribute to the right cause, and not to any disrespect for her.'

Elizabeth felt herself completely taken in. She had fully proposed being engaged by Wickham for those very dances: – and to have Mr Collins instead! her liveliness had been never worse timed. There was no help for it however. Mr Wickham's happiness and her own was per force delayed a little longer, and Mr Collins's proposal accepted with as good a grace as she could. She was not the better pleased with his gallantry, from the idea it suggested of something more. – It now first struck her, that *she* was selected from among her sisters as worthy of being the mistress of Hunsford Parsonage, and of assisting to form a quadrille table at Rosings, in the absence of more eligible visitors. The idea soon reached to conviction, as she observed his increasing civilities toward herself, and heard his frequent attempt at a compliment on her wit and vivacity; and though more astonished than gratified herself, by this effect of her charms, it was not long before her mother gave her to understand that the probability of their marriage was exceedingly agreeable to *her*. Elizabeth however did not chuse to take the hint, being well aware that a serious dispute must be the consequence of any reply. Mr Collins might never make the offer, and till he did, it was useless to quarrel about him.

If there had not been a Netherfield ball to prepare for and talk of, the younger Miss Bennets would have been in a pitiable state at this time, for from the day of the invitation, to the day of the ball, there was such a succession of rain as prevented their walking to Meryton once. No aunt, no officers, no news could be sought after; – the very shoe-roses for Netherfield were got by proxy. Even Elizabeth might have found some trial of her patience in weather, which totally suspended the improvement of her acquaintance with Mr Wickham; and nothing less than a dance on Tuesday, could have made such a Friday, Saturday, Sunday and Monday, endurable to Kitty and Lydia.

CHAPTER EIGHTEEN

TILL ELIZABETH ENTERED THE DRAWING-ROOM at Netherfield and looked in vain for Mr Wickham among the cluster of red coats there assembled, a doubt of his being present had never occurred to her. The certainty of meeting him had not been checked by any of those recollections that might not unreasonably have alarmed her. She had dressed with more than usual care, and prepared in the highest spirits for the conquest of all that remained unsubdued of his heart, trusting that it was not more than might be won in the course of the evening. But in an instant arose the dreadful suspicion of his being purposely omitted for Mr Darcy's pleasure in the Bingleys' invitation to the officers; and though this was not exactly the case, the absolute fact of his absence was pronounced by his friend Mr Denny, to whom Lydia eagerly applied, and who told them that Wickham had been obliged to go to town on business the day before, and was not yet returned; adding, with a significant smile,

'I do not imagine his business would have called him away just now, if he had not wished to avoid a certain gentleman here.'

This part of his intelligence, though unheard by Lydia, was caught by Elizabeth, and as it assured her that Darcy was not less answerable for Wickham's absence than if her first surmise had been just, every feeling of displeasure against the former was so sharpened by immediate disappointment, that she could hardly reply with tolerable civility to the polite inquiries which he directly afterwards approached to make. – Attention, forbearance, patience with Darcy, was injury to Wickham. She was resolved against any sort of conversation with him, and turned away with a degree of ill humour, which she could not wholly surmount even in speaking to Mr Bingley, whose blind partiality provoked her.

But Elizabeth was not formed for ill-humour; and though every prospect of her own was destroyed for the evening, it could not dwell long on her spirits; and having told all her griefs to Charlotte Lucas, whom she had not seen for a week, she was soon able to make a voluntary transition to the oddities of her cousin, and to point him out to her particular notice. The two first dances, however, brought a return of distress; they were dances of mortification. Mr Collins, awkward and solemn, apologising instead of attending, and often moving wrong without being aware of it, gave her all the shame and misery which a disagreeable partner for a couple of dances can give. The moment of her release from him was ecstasy.

She danced next with an officer, and had the refreshment of talking of Wickham, and of hearing that he was universally liked. When those dances were over she returned to Charlotte Lucas, and was in conversation with her, when she found herself suddenly addressed by Mr Darcy, who took her so much by surprise in his application for her hand, that, without knowing what she did, she accepted him. He walked away again immediately, and she was left to fret over her own want of presence of mind; Charlotte tried to console her.

'I dare say you will find him very agreeable.'

'Heaven forbid! – *That* would be the greatest misfortune of all! – To find a man agreeable whom one is determined to hate! – Do not wish me such an evil.'

When the dancing recommenced, however, and Darcy approached to claim her hand, Charlotte could not help cautioning her in a whisper not to be a simpleton and allow her fancy for Wickham to make her appear unpleasant in the eyes of a man of ten times his consequence. Elizabeth made no answer, and took her place in the set, amazed at the dignity to which she was arrived in being allowed to stand opposite to Mr Darcy, and reading in her neighbours' looks their equal amazement in beholding it. They stood for some time without speaking a word; and she began to imagine that their silence was to last through the two dances, and at first was resolved not to break it; till suddenly fancying that it would be the greater punishment to her partner to oblige him to talk, she made some slight observation on the dance. He replied, and was again silent. After a pause of some minutes she addressed him a second time with

'It is *your* turn to say something now, Mr Darcy. – *I* talked about the dance, and *you* ought to make some kind of remark on the size of the room, or the number of couples.'

He smiled, and assured her that whatever she wished him to say should be said.

'Very well. – That reply will do for the present. – Perhaps by and bye I may observe that private balls are much pleasanter than public ones. – But *now* we may be silent.'

'Do you talk by rule then, while you are dancing?'

'Sometimes. One must speak a little, you know. It would look odd to be entirely silent for half an hour together, and yet for the advantage of *some*, conversation ought to be so arranged as that they may have the trouble of saying as little as possible.'

'Are you consulting your own feelings in the present case, or do you imagine that you are gratifying mine?'

'Both,' replied Elizabeth archly; 'for I have always seen a great similarity in the turn of our minds. – We are each of an unsocial, taciturn disposition, unwilling to speak, unless we expect to say something that will amaze the whole room, and be handed down to posterity with all the eclat of a proverb.'

'This is no very striking resemblance of your own character, I am sure,' said he. 'How near it may be to *mine*, I cannot pretend to say. – *You* think it a faithful portrait undoubtedly.'

'I must not decide on my own performance.'

He made no answer, and they were again silent till they had gone down the dance, when he asked her if she and her sisters did not very often walk to Meryton. She answered in the affirmative, and, unable to resist the temptation, added, 'When you met us there the other day, we had just been forming a new acquaintance.'

The effect was immediate. A deeper shade of hauteur overspread his features, but he said not a word, and Elizabeth, though blaming herself for her own weakness, could not go on. At length Darcy spoke, and in a constrained manner said,

'Mr Wickham is blessed with such happy manners as may ensure his *making* friends – whether he may be equally capable of *retaining* them, is less certain.'

'He has been so unlucky as to lose *your* friendship,' replied Elizabeth with emphasis, 'and in a manner which he is likely to suffer from all his life.'

Darcy made no answer, and seemed desirous of changing the subject. At that moment Sir William Lucas appeared close to them, meaning to pass through the set to the other side of the room; but on perceiving Mr Darcy he stopt with a bow of superior courtesy to compliment him on his dancing and his partner.

'I have been most highly gratified indeed, my dear Sir. Such very superior dancing is not often seen. It is evident that you belong to the first circles. Allow me to say, however, that your fair partner does not disgrace you, and that I must hope to have this pleasure often repeated, especially when a certain desirable event, my dear Miss Eliza, (glancing at her sister and Bingley,) shall take place. What congratulations will then flow in! I appeal to Mr Darcy: – but let me not interrupt you, Sir. – You will not

'Such very superior dancing is not often seen'

thank me for detaining you from the bewitching converse of that young lady, whose bright eyes are also upbraiding me.'

The latter part of his address was scarcely heard by Darcy; but Sir William's allusion to his friend seemed to strike him forcibly, and his eyes were directed with a very serious expression towards Bingley and Jane, who were dancing together. Recovering himself, however, shortly, he turned to his partner, and said,

'Sir William's interruption has made me forget what we were talking of.'

'I do not think we were speaking at all. Sir William could not have interrupted any two people in the room who had less to say for themselves. – We have tried two or three subjects already without success, and what we are to talk of next I cannot imagine.'

'What think you of books?' said he, smiling.

'Books – Oh! no. – I am sure we never read the same, or not with the same feelings.'

'I am sorry you think so; but if that be the case, there can at least be no want of subject. – We may compare our different opinions.'

'No – I cannot talk of books in a ball-room; my head is always full of something else.'

'The *present* always occupies you in such scenes – does it?' said he, with a look of doubt.

'Yes, always,' she replied, without knowing what she said, for her thoughts had wandered far from the subject, as soon afterwards appeared by her suddenly exclaiming, 'I remember hearing you once say, Mr Darcy, that you hardly ever forgave, that your resentment once created was unappeasable. You are very cautious, I suppose, as to its *being created*.'

'I am,' said he, with a firm voice.

'And never allow yourself to be blinded by prejudice?'

'I hope not.'

'It is particularly incumbent on those who never change their opinion, to be secure of judging properly at first.'

'May I ask to what these questions tend?'

'Merely to the illustration of *your* character,' said she, endeavouring to shake off her gravity. 'I am trying to make it out.'

'And what is your success?'

She shook her head. 'I do not get on at all. I hear such different accounts of you as puzzle me exceedingly.'

'I can readily believe,' answered he gravely, 'that report may vary greatly with respect to me; and I could wish, Miss Bennet, that you were not to sketch my character at the present moment, as there is reason to fear that the performance would reflect no credit on either.'

'But if I do not take your likeness now, I may never have another opportunity.'

'I would by no means suspend any pleasure of yours,' he coldly replied. She said no more, and they went down the other dance and parted in silence; on each side dissatisfied, though not to an equal degree, for in Darcy's breast there was a tolerable powerful feeling towards her, which soon procured her pardon, and directed all his anger against another.

They had not long separated when Miss Bingley came towards her, and with an expression of civil disdain thus accosted her,

'So, Miss Eliza, I hear you are quite delighted with George Wickham! – Your sister has been talking to me about him, and asking me a thousand questions; and I find that the young man forgot to tell you, among his other communications, that he was the son of old Wickham, the late Mr Darcy's steward. Let me recommend you, however, as a friend, not to give implicit confidence to all his assertions; for as to Mr Darcy's using him ill, it is perfectly false; for, on the contrary, he has been always remarkably kind to him, though George Wickham has treated Mr Darcy in a most infamous manner. I do not know the particulars, but I know very well that Mr Darcy is not in the least to blame, that he cannot bear to hear George Wickham mentioned, and that though my brother thought he could not well avoid including him in his invitation to the officers, he was excessively glad to find that he had taken himself out of the way. His coming into the country at all, is a most insolent thing indeed, and I wonder how he could presume to do it. I pity you, Miss Eliza, for this discovery of your favourite's guilt; but really considering his descent, one could not expect much better.'

'His guilt and his descent appear by your account to be the same,' said Elizabeth angrily; 'for I have heard you accuse him of nothing worse than of being the son of Mr Darcy's steward, and of *that*, I can assure you, he informed me himself.'

'I beg your pardon,' replied Miss Bingley, turning away with a sneer. 'Excuse my interference. – It was kindly meant.'

'Insolent girl!' said Elizabeth to herself. – 'You are much mistaken if you expect to influence me by such a paltry attack as this. I see nothing in it but your own wilful ignorance and the malice of Mr Darcy.' She then sought her eldest sister, who had undertaken to make inquiries on the same subject of Bingley. Jane met her with a smile of such sweet complacency, a glow of such happy expression, as sufficiently marked how well she was satisfied with the occurrences of the evening. – Elizabeth instantly read her feelings, and at that moment solicitude for Wickham, resentment against his enemies, and every thing else gave way before the hope of Jane's being in the fairest way for happiness.

'I want to know,' said she, with a countenance no less smiling than her sister's, 'what you have learnt about Mr Wickham. But perhaps you have been too pleasantly engaged to think of any third person; in which case you may be sure of my pardon.'

'No,' replied Jane, 'I have not forgotten him; but I have nothing satisfactory to tell you. Mr Bingley does not know the whole of his history, and is quite ignorant of the circumstances which have principally offended Mr Darcy; but he will vouch for the good conduct, the probity and honour of his friend, and is perfectly convinced that Mr Wickham has deserved much less attention from Mr Darcy than he has received; and I am sorry to say that by his account as well as his sister's, Mr Wickham is by no means a respectable young man. I am afraid he has been very imprudent, and has deserved to lose Mr Darcy's regard.'

'Mr Bingley does not know Mr Wickham himself?'

'No; he never saw him till the other morning at Meryton.'

'This account then is what he has received from Mr Darcy. I am perfectly satisfied. But what does he say of the living?'

'He does not exactly recollect the circumstances, though he has heard them from Mr Darcy more than once, but he believes that it was left to him *conditionally* only.'

'I have not a doubt of Mr Bingley's sincerity,' said Elizabeth warmly; 'but you must excuse my not being convinced by assurances only. Mr Bingley's defence of his friend was a very able one I dare say, but since he is unacquainted with several parts of the story, and has learnt the rest from that friend himself, I shall venture still to think of both gentlemen as I did before.'

She then changed the discourse to one more gratifying to each, and on which there could be no difference of sentiment. Elizabeth listened with delight to the happy, though modest hopes which Jane entertained of Bingley's regard, and said all in her power to heighten her confidence in it. On their being joined by Mr Bingley himself, Elizabeth withdrew to Miss Lucas; to whose inquiry after the pleasantness of her last partner she had scarcely replied, before Mr Collins came up to them and told her with great exultation that he had just been so fortunate as to make a most important discovery.

'I have found out,' said he, 'by a singular accident, that there is now in the room a near relation of my patroness. I happened to overhear the gentleman himself mentioning to the young lady who does the honours of this house the names of his cousin Miss de Bourgh, and of her mother Lady Catherine. How wonderfully these sort of things occur! Who would have thought of my meeting with – perhaps – a nephew of Lady Catherine de Bourgh in this assembly! – I am most thankful that the discovery is made in time for me to pay my respects to him, which I am now going to do, and trust he will excuse my not having done it before. My total ignorance of the connection must plead my apology.'

'You are not going to introduce yourself to Mr Darcy?'

'Indeed I am. I shall intreat his pardon for not having done it earlier. I believe him to be Lady Catherine's *nephew*. It will be in my power to assure him that her ladyship was quite well yesterday se'nnight.'

Elizabeth tried hard to dissuade him from such a scheme; assuring him that Mr Darcy would consider his addressing him without introduction as an impertinent freedom, rather than a compliment to his aunt; that it was not in the least necessary there should be any notice on either side, and that if it were, it must belong to Mr Darcy, the superior in consequence, to begin the acquaintance. – Mr Collins listened to her with the determined air of following his own inclination, and when she ceased speaking, replied thus,

'My dear Miss Elizabeth, I have the highest opinion in the world of your excellent judgment in all matters within the scope of your understanding, but permit me to say that there must be a wide difference between the established forms of ceremony amongst the laity, and those which regulate the clergy; for give me leave to observe that I consider the clerical office as equal in point of dignity with the highest rank in the kingdom – provided that a proper humility of behaviour is at the same time maintained. You must therefore allow me to follow the dictates of my conscience on this occasion, which leads me to perform what I look on as a point of duty. Pardon me for neglecting to profit by your advice, which on every other subject shall be my constant guide, though in the case before us I consider myself more fitted by education and habitual study to decide on what is right than a young lady like yourself.' And with a low bow he left her to attack Mr Darcy, whose reception of his advances she eagerly watched, and whose astonishment at being so addressed was very evident. Her cousin prefaced his speech with a solemn bow, and though she could not hear a word of it, she felt as if hearing it all, and saw in the motion of his lips the words 'apology,' 'Hunsford' and 'Lady Catherine de Bourgh.' – It vexed her to see him expose himself to such a man. Mr Darcy was eyeing him with unrestrained wonder, and when at last Mr Collins allowed him time to speak, replied with an air of distant civility. Mr Collins, however, was not discouraged from speaking again, and Mr Darcy's contempt seemed abundantly increasing with the length of his second speech, and at the end of it he only made him a slight bow, and moved another way. Mr Collins then turned to Elizabeth.

'I have no reason, I assure you,' said he, 'to be dissatisfied with my reception. Mr Darcy seemed much pleased with the attention. He answered me with the utmost civility, and even paid me the compliment of saying, that he was so well convinced of Lady Catherine's discernment as to be certain she could never bestow a favour unworthily. It was really a very handsome thought. Upon the whole, I am much pleased with him.'

As Elizabeth had no longer any interest of her own to pursue, she turned her attention almost entirely on her sister and Mr Bingley, and the train of agreeable reflections which her observations gave birth to, made her perhaps almost as happy as Jane. She saw her in idea settled in that very house in all the felicity which a marriage of true affection could bestow; and she felt capable under such circumstances, of endeavouring even to like Bingley's two sisters. Her mother's thoughts she plainly saw were bent the same way, and she determined not to venture near her, lest she might hear too much. When they sat down to supper, therefore, she considered it a most unlucky perverseness which placed them within one of each other; and deeply was she vexed to find that her mother was talking to that one person (Lady Lucas) freely, openly, and of nothing else but of her expectation that Jane would be soon married to Mr Bingley. – It was an animating subject, and Mrs Bennet seemed incapable of fatigue while enumerating the advantages of the match. His being such a charming young man, and so rich, and living but three miles from them, were the first points of self-congratulation; and then it was such a comfort to think how fond the two sisters were of Jane, and to be certain that they must desire the connection as much as she could do. It was, moreover, such a promising thing for her younger daughters, as Jane's marrying so greatly must throw them in the way of other rich men; and lastly, it was so pleasant at her time of life to be able to consign her single daughters to the care of their sister, that she might not be obliged to go into company more than she liked. It was necessary to make this circumstance a matter of pleasure, because on such occasions it is the etiquette; but no one was less likely than Mrs Bennet to find comfort in staying at home at any period of her life. She concluded with many good wishes that Lady Lucas might soon be equally fortunate, though evidently and triumphantly believing there was no chance of it.

In vain did Elizabeth endeavour to check the rapidity of her mother's words, or persuade her to describe her felicity in a less audible whisper; for to her inexpressible vexation, she could perceive that the chief of it was overheard by Mr Darcy, who sat opposite to them. Her mother only scolded her for being nonsensical.

'What is Mr Darcy to me, pray, that I should be afraid of him? I am sure we owe him no such particular civility as to be obliged to say nothing *he* may not like to hear.'

'For heaven's sake, madam, speak lower. – What advantage can it be to you to offend Mr Darcy? – You will never recommend yourself to his friend by so doing.'

Nothing that she could say, however, had any influence. Her mother would talk of her views in the same intelligible tone. Elizabeth blushed and blushed again with shame and vexation. She could not help frequently glancing her eye at Mr Darcy, though every glance convinced her of what she dreaded; for though he was not always looking at her mother, she was convinced that his attention was invariably fixed by her. The expression of his face changed gradually from indignant contempt to a composed and steady gravity.

At length however Mrs Bennet had no more to say; and Lady Lucas, who had been long yawning at the repetition of delights which she saw no likelihood of sharing, was left to the comforts of cold ham and chicken. Elizabeth now began to revive. But not long was the interval of tranquillity; for when supper was over, singing was talked of, and she had the mortification of seeing Mary, after very little entreaty, preparing to oblige the company. By many significant looks and silent entreaties, did she endeavour to prevent such a proof of complaisance, – but in vain; Mary would not understand them; such an opportunity of exhibiting was delightful to her, and she began her song. Elizabeth's eyes were fixed on her with most painful sensations; and she watched her progress through the several stanzas with an impatience which was very ill rewarded at their close; for Mary, on receiving amongst the thanks of the table, the hint of a hope that she might be prevailed on to favour them again, after the pause of half a minute began another. Mary's powers were by no means fitted for such a display; her voice was weak, and her manner affected. – Elizabeth was in agonies. She looked at Jane, to see how she bore it; but Jane was very composedly talking to Bingley. She looked at his two sisters, and saw them making signs of derision at each other, and at Darcy, who continued however impenetrably grave. She looked at her father to entreat his interference, lest Mary should be singing all night. He took the hint, and when Mary had finished her second song, said aloud,

'That will do extremely well, child. You have delighted us long enough. Let the other young ladies have time to exhibit.'

Mary, though pretending not to hear, was somewhat disconcerted; and Elizabeth sorry for her, and sorry for her father's speech, was afraid her anxiety had done no good. – Others of the party were now applied to.

'If I,' said Mr Collins, 'were so fortunate as to be able to sing, I should have great pleasure, I am sure, in obliging the company with an air; for I consider music as a very innocent diversion, and perfectly compatible with the profession of a clergyman. – I do not mean however to assert that we can be justified in devoting too much of our time to music, for there are certainly other things to be attended to. The rector of a parish has much to do. – In the first place, he must make such an agreement for tythes as may be beneficial to himself and not offensive to his patron. He must write his own sermons; and the time that remains will not be too much for his parish duties, and the care and improvement of his dwelling, which he cannot be excused from making as comfortable as possible. And I do not think it of light importance that he should have attentive and conciliatory manners towards every body, especially towards those to whom he owes his preferment. I cannot acquit him of that duty; not could I think well of the man who should omit an occasion of testifying his respect towards any body connected with the family.' And with a bow to Mr Darcy, he concluded his speech, which had been spoken so loud as to be heard by half the room. – Many stared. – Many smiled; but no one looked more amused than Mr Bennet himself, while his wife seriously commended Mr Collins for having spoken so sensibly, and observed in a half-whisper to Lady Lucas, that he was a remarkably clever, good kind of young man.

To Elizabeth it appeared, that had her family made an agreement to expose themselves as much as they could during the evening, it would have been impossible for them to play their parts with more spirit, or finer success; and happy did she think it for Bingley and her sister that some of the exhibition had escaped his notice, and that his feelings were not of a sort to be much distressed by the folly which he must have witnessed. That his two sisters and Mr Darcy, however, should have such an opportunity of ridiculing her relations was bad enough, and she could not determine whether the silent contempt of the gentleman, or the insolent smiles of the ladies, were more intolerable.

The rest of the evening brought her little amusement. She was teased by Mr Collins, who continued most perseveringly by her side, and though he could not prevail with her to dance with him again, put it out of her power to dance with others. In vain did she entreat him to stand up with somebody else, and offer to introduce him to any young lady in the room. He assured her that as to dancing, he was perfectly indifferent to it; that his chief object was by delicate attentions to recommend himself to her, and that he should therefore make a point of remaining close to her the whole evening. There was no arguing upon such a project. She owed her greatest relief to her friend Miss Lucas, who often joined them, and good-naturedly engaged Mr Collins's conversation to herself.

She was at least free from the offence of Mr Darcy's farther notice; though often standing within a very short distance of her, quite disengaged, he never came near enough to speak. She felt it to be the probable consequence of her allusions to Mr Wickham, and rejoiced in it.

The Longbourn party were the last of all the company to depart; and by a manoeuvre of Mrs Bennet had to wait for their carriages a quarter of an hour after every body else was gone, which gave them time to see how heartily they were wished away by some of the family. Mrs Hurst and her sister scarcely opened their mouths except to complain of fatigue, and were evidently impatient to have the house to themselves. They repulsed every attempt of Mrs Bennet at conversation, and by so doing, threw a langour over the whole party, which was very little relieved by the long speeches of Mr Collins, who was complimenting Mr Bingley and his sisters on the elegance of their entertainment, and the hospitality and politeness which had marked their behaviour to their guests. Darcy said nothing at all. Mr Bennet, in equal silence, was enjoying the scene. Mr Bingley and Jane were standing together, a little detached from the rest, and talked only to each other. Elizabeth preserved as steady a silence as either Mrs Hurst or Miss Bingley; and even Lydia was too much fatigued to utter more than the occasional exclamation of 'Lord, how tired I am!' accompanied by a violent yawn.

When at length they arose to take leave, Mrs Bennet was most pressingly civil in her hope of seeing the whole family soon at Longbourn; and adressed herself particularly to Mr Bingley, to assure him how happy he would make them, by eating a family dinner with them at any time, without the ceremony of a formal invitation. Bingley was all grateful pleasure, and he readily engaged for taking the earliest opportunity of waiting on her, after his return from London, whither he was obliged to go the next day for a short time.

Mrs Bennet was perfectly satisfied; and quitted the house under the delightful persuasion that, allowing for the necessary preparations of settlements, new carriages and wedding clothes, she should undoubtedly see her daughter settled at Netherfield, in the course of three or four months. Of having another daughter married to Mr Collins, she thought with equal certainty, and with considerable, though not equal, pleasure. Elizabeth was the least dear to her of all her children; and though the man and the match were quite good enough for *her*, the worth of each was eclipsed by Mr Bingley and Netherfield.

'To assure you in the most animated language'

CHAPTER NINETEEN

THE NEXT DAY OPENED A NEW SCENE at Longbourn. Mr Collins made his declaration in form. Having resolved to do it without loss of time, as his leave of absence extended only to the following Saturday, and having no feelings of diffidence to make it distressing to himself even at the moment, he set about it in a very orderly manner, with all the observances which he supposed a regular part of the business. On finding Mrs Bennet, Elizabeth, and one of the younger girls together, soon after breakfast, he addressed the mother in these words,

'May I hope, Madam, for your interest with your fair daughter Elizabeth, when I solicit for the honour of a private audience with her in the course of this morning?'

Before Elizabeth had time for any thing but a blush of surprise, Mrs Bennet instantly answered,

'Oh dear! – Yes – certainly. – I am sure Lizzy will be very happy – I am sure she can have no objection. – Come, Kitty, I want you up stairs.' And gathering her work together, she was hastening away, when Elizabeth called out,

'Dear Ma'am, do not go. – I beg you will not go. – Mr Collins must excuse me. – He can have nothing to say to me that any body need not hear. I am going away myself.'

'No, no, nonsense, Lizzy. – I desire you will stay where you are.' – And upon Elizabeth's seeming really, with vexed and embarrassed looks, about to escape, she added, 'Lizzy, I *insist* upon your staying and hearing Mr Collins.'

Elizabeth would not oppose such an injunction – and a moment's consideration making her also sensible that it would be wisest to get it over as soon and as quietly as possible, she sat down again, and tried to conceal by incessant employment the feelings which were divided between distress and diversion. Mrs Bennet and Kitty walked off, and as soon as they were gone Mr Collins began.

'Believe me, my dear Miss Elizabeth, that your modesty, so far from doing you any disservice, rather adds to your other perfections. You would have been less amiable in my eyes had there *not* been this little unwillingness; but allow me to assure you that I have your respected mother's permission for this address. You can hardly doubt the purport of my discourse, however your natural delicacy may lead you to dissemble; my attentions have been too marked to be mistaken. Almost as soon as I entered the house I singled you out as the companion of my future life. But before I am run away with by my feelings on this subject, perhaps it will be advisable for me to state my reasons for marrying – and moreover for coming into Hertfordshire with the design of selecting a wife, as I certainly did.'

The idea of Mr Collins, with all his solemn composure, being run away with by his feelings, made Elizabeth so near laughing that she could not use the short pause he allowed in any attempt to stop him farther, and he continued:

'My reasons for marrying are, first, that I think it a right thing for every clergyman in easy circumstances (like myself) to set the example of matrimony in his parish. Secondly, that I am convinced it will add very greatly to my happiness; and thirdly – which perhaps I ought to have mentioned earlier, that it is the particular advice and recommendation of the very noble lady whom I have the honour of calling patroness. Twice has she condescended to give me her opinion (unasked too!) on this subject; and it was but the very Saturday night before I left Hunsford – between our pools at quadrille, while Mrs Jenkinson was arranging Miss de Bourgh's foot-stool, that she said, "Mr Collins, you must marry. A clergyman like you must marry. – Chuse properly, chuse a gentlewoman for *my* sake; and for your *own*, let her be an active, useful sort of person, not brought up high, but able to make a small income go a good way. This is my advice. Find such a woman as soon as you can, bring her to Hunsford, and I will visit her." Allow me, by the way to observe, my fair cousin, that I do not reckon the notice and kindness of Lady Catherine de Bourgh as among the least of the advantages in my power to offer. You will find her manners beyond any thing I can describe; and your wit and vivacity I think must be acceptable to her, especially when tempered with the silence and respect which her rank will inevitably excite. Thus much for my general intention in favour of matrimony; it remains to be told why my views were directed to Longbourn instead of my own neighbourhood, where I assure you there are many amiable young women. But the fact is, that being, as I am, to inherit this estate after the death of your honoured father, (who, however, may live many years longer), I could not satisfy myself without resolving to chuse a wife from among his daughters, that the loss to them might be as little as possible, when the melancholy event takes place – which, however, as I have already said, may not be for several years. This has been my motive, my fair cousin, and I flatter myself it will not sink me in your esteem. And now nothing remains for me but to assure you in the most animated language of the violence of my affection. To fortune I am perfectly indifferent, and shall make no demand of that nature on your father, since I am well aware that it could not be complied with; and that one thousand pounds in the 4 per cents. which will not be yours till after your mother's decease, is all that you may ever be entitled to. On that head, therefore, I shall be uniformly silent; and you may assure yourself that no ungenerous reproach shall ever pass my lips when we are married.'

It was absolutely necessary to interrupt him now.

'You are too hasty, Sir,' she cried. 'You forget that I have made no answer. Let me do it without farther loss of time. Accept my thanks for the compliment you are paying me. I am very sensible of the honour of your proposals, but it is impossible for me to do otherwise than decline them.'

'I am not now to learn,' replied Mr Collins, with a formal wave of the hand, 'that it is usual with young ladies to reject the addresses of the man whom they secretly mean to accept, when he first applies for their favour;

and that sometimes the refusal is repeated a second or even a third time. I am therefore by no means discouraged by what you have just said, and shall hope to lead you to the altar ere long.'

'Upon my word, Sir,' cried Elizabeth, 'your hope is rather an extraordinary one after my declaration. I do assure you that I am not one of those young ladies (if such young ladies there are) who are so daring as to risk their happiness on the chance of being asked a second time. I am perfectly serious in my refusal. – You could not make *me* happy, and I am convinced that I am the last woman in the world who would make *you* so. – Nay, were your friend Lady Catherine to know me, I am persuaded she would find me in every respect ill qualified for the situation.'

'Were it certain that Lady Catherine would think so,' said Mr Collins very gravely – 'but I cannot imagine that her ladyship would at all disapprove of you. And you may be certain that when I have the honour of seeing her again I shall speak in the highest terms of your modesty, economy, and other amiable qualifications.'

'Indeed, Mr Collins, all praise of me will be unnecessary. You must give me leave to judge for myself, and pay me the compliment of believing what I say. I wish you very happy and very rich, and by refusing your hand, do all in my power to prevent your being otherwise. In making me the offer, you must have satisfied the delicacy of your feelings with regard to my family, and may take possession of Longbourn estate whenever it falls, without any self-reproach. This matter may be considered, therefore, as finally settled.' And rising as she thus spoke, she would have quitted the room, had not Mr Collins thus addressed her.

'When I do myself the honour of speaking to you next in this subject I shall hope to receive a more favourable answer than you have now given me; though I am far from accusing you of cruelty at present, because I know it to be the established custom of your sex to reject a man on the first application, and perhaps you have even now said as much to encourage my suit as would be consistent with the true delicacy of the female character.'

'Really, Mr Collins,' cried Elizabeth with some warmth, 'you puzzle me exceedingly. If what I have hitherto said can appear to you in the form of encouragement, I know not how to express my refusal in such a way as may convince you of its being one.'

'You must give me leave to flatter myself, my dear cousin, that your refusal of my addresses is merely words of course. My reasons for believing it are briefly these: – It does not appear to me that my hand is unworthy your acceptance, or that the establishment I can offer would be any other than highly desirable. My situation in life, my connections with the family of de Bourgh, and my relationship to your own, are circumstances highly in my favour; and you should take it into farther consideration that in spite of your manifold attractions, it is by no means certain that another offer of marriage may ever be made you. Your portion is unhappily so small that it will in all likelihood undo the effects of your loveliness and amiable qualifications. As I must therefore conclude that you are not serious in your rejection of me, I shall chuse to attribute it to your wish of increasing my love by suspense, according to the usual practice of elegant females.'

'I do assure you, Sir, that I have no pretension whatever to that kind of elegance which consists in tormenting a respectable man. I would rather be paid the compliment of being believed. I thank you again and again for the honour you have done me in your proposals, but to accept them is absolutely impossible. My feelings in every respect forbid it. Can I speak plainer? Do not consider me now as an elegant female intending to plague you, but as a rational creature speaking the truth from her heart.'

'You are uniformly charming!' cried he, with an air of awkward gallantry; 'and I am persuaded that when sanctioned by the express authority of both your excellent parents, my proposals will not fail of being acceptable.'

To such perseverance in wilful self-deception Elizabeth would make no reply, and immediately and in silence withdrew; determined, if he persisted in considering her repeated refusals as flattering encouragement, to apply to her father, whose negative might be uttered in such a manner as must be decisive, and whose behaviour at least could not be mistaken for the affectation and coquetry of an elegant female.

CHAPTER TWENTY

MR COLLINS WAS NOT LEFT LONG to the silent contemplation of his successful love; for Mrs Bennet, having dawdled about in the vestibule to watch for the end of the conference, no sooner saw Elizabeth open the door and with quick step pass her towards the staircase, than she entered the breakfast-room, and congratulated both him and herself in warm terms on the happy prospect of their nearer connection. Mr Collins received and returned these felicitations with equal pleasure, and then proceeded to relate the particulars of their interview, with the result of which he trusted he had every reason to be satisfied, since the refusal which his cousin had steadfastly given him would naturally flow from her bashful modesty and the genuine delicacy of her character.

This information, however, startled Mrs Bennet; – she would have been glad to be equally satisfied that her daughter had meant to encourage him by protesting against his proposals, but she dared not to believe it, and could not help saying so.

'But depend upon it, Mr Collins,' she added, 'that Lizzy shall be brought to reason. I will speak to her about it myself directly. She is a very headstrong foolish girl, and does not know her own interest; but I will *make* her know it.'

'Pardon me for interrupting you, Madam,' cried Mr Collins; 'but if she is really headstrong and foolish, I know not whether she would altogether be a very desirable wife to a man in my situation, who naturally looks for happiness in the marriage state. If therefore she actually persists in rejecting my suit, perhaps it were better not to force her into accepting me, because if liable to such defects of temper, she could not contribute much to my felicity.'

'Sir, you quite misunderstand me,' said Mrs Bennet, alarmed. 'Lizzy is only headstrong in such matters as these. In every thing else she is as good natured a girl as ever lived. I will go directly to Mr Bennet, and we shall very soon settle it with her, I am sure.'

She would not give him time to reply, but hurrying instantly to her husband, called out as she entered the library,

'Oh! Mr Bennet, you are wanted immediately; we are all in an uproar. You must come and make Lizzy marry Mr Collins, for she vows she will not have him, and if you do not make haste he will change his mind and not have *her*.'

Mr Bennet raised his eyes from his book as she entered, and fixed them on her face with a calm unconcern which was not in the least altered by her communication.

'I have not the pleasure of understanding you,' said he, when she had finished her speech. 'Of what are you talking?'

'Of Mr Collins and Lizzy. Lizzy declares she will not have Mr Collins, and Mr Collins begins to say that he will not have Lizzy.'

'And what am I to do on the occasion? – It seems an hopeless business.'

'Speak to Lizzy about it yourself. Tell her that you insist upon her marrying him.'

'Let her be called down. She shall hear my opinion.'

Mrs Bennet rang the bell, and Miss Elizabeth was summoned to the library.

'Come here, child,' cried her father as she appeared. 'I have sent for you on an affair of importance. I understand that Mr Collins has made you an offer of marriage. Is it true?' Elizabeth replied that it was. 'Very well – and this offer of marriage you have refused?'

'I have, Sir.'

'Very well. We now come to the point. Your mother insists upon your accepting it. Is not it so, Mrs Bennet?'

'Yes, or I will never see her again.'

'An unhappy alternative is before you, Elizabeth. From this day you must be a stranger to one of your parents. – Your mother will never see you again if you do *not* marry Mr Collins, and I will never see you again if you *do*.'

Elizabeth could not but smile at such a conclusion of such a beginning; but Mrs Bennet, who had persuaded herself that her husband regarded the affair as she wished, was excessively disappointed.

'What do you mean, Mr Bennet, by talking in this way. You promised me to *insist* upon her marrying him.'

'My dear,' replied her husband. 'I have two small favours to request. First, that you will allow me the free use of my understanding on the present occasion; and secondly, of my room. I shall be glad to have the library to myself as soon as may be.'

Not yet, however, in spite of her disappointment in her husband, did Mrs Bennet give up the point. She talked to Elizabeth again and again; coaxed and threatened her by turns. She endeavoured to secure Jane in his interest, but Jane with all possible mildness declined interfering; – and Elizabeth sometimes with real earnestness and sometimes with playful gaiety replied to her attacks. Though her manner varied however, her determination never did.

Mr Collins, meanwhile, was meditating in solitude on what had passed. He thought too well of himself to comprehend on what motives his cousin could refuse him; and though his pride was hurt, he suffered in no other way. His regard for her was quite imaginary; and the possibility of her deserving her mother's reproach prevented his feeling any regret.

While the family were in this confusion, Charlotte Lucas came to spend the day with them. She was met in the vestibule by Lydia, who, flying to her, cried in a half whisper, 'I am glad you are come, for there is such fun here! – What do you think has happened this morning? – Mr Collins has made an offer to Lizzy, and she will not have him.'

Charlotte had hardly time to answer, before they were joined by Kitty, who came to tell the same news, and no sooner had they entered the breakfast-room, where Mrs Bennet was alone, than she likewise began on the subject, calling on Miss Lucas for her compassion, and entreating her to persuade her friend Lizzy to comply with the wishes of all her family. 'Pray do, my dear Miss Lucas,' she added in a melancholy tone, 'for nobody is on my side, nobody takes part with me, I am cruelly used, nobody feels for my poor nerves.'

Charlotte's reply was spared by the entrance of Jane and Elizabeth.

'Aye, there she comes,' continued Mrs Bennet, 'looking as unconcerned as may be, and caring no more for us than if we were at York, provided she

They entered the breakfast-room

can have her own way. But I tell you what, Miss Lizzy, if you take it into your head to go on refusing every offer of marriage in this way, you will never get a husband at all – and I am sure I do not know who is to maintain you when your father is dead. – *I* shall not be able to keep you – and so I warn you. – I have done with you from this very day. – I told you in the library, you know, that I should never speak to you again, and you will find me as good as my word. I have no pleasure in talking to undutiful children. – Not that I have much pleasure indeed in talking to any body. People who suffer as I do from nervous complaints can have no great inclination for talking. Nobody can tell what I suffer! – But it is always so. Those who do not complain are never pitied.'

Her daughters listened in silence to this effusion, sensible that any attempt to reason with or sooth her would only increase the irritation. She talked on, therefore, without interruption from any of them till they were joined by Mr Collins, who entered with an air more stately than usual, and on perceiving whom, she said to the girls,

'Now, I do insist upon it, that you, all of you, hold your tongues, and let Mr Collins and me have a little conversation together.'

Elizabeth passed quietly out of the room, Jane and Kitty followed, but Lydia stood her ground, determined to hear all she could; and Charlotte, detained first by the civility of Mr Collins, whose inquiries after herself and all her family were very minute, and then by a little curiosity, satisfied herself with walking to the window and pretending not to hear. In a doleful voice Mrs Bennet thus began the projected conversation. – 'Oh! Mr Collins!' –

'My dear Madam,' replied he, 'let us be for ever silent on this point. Far be it from me,' he presently continued in a voice that marked his displeasure, 'to resent the behaviour of your daughter. Resignation to inevitable evils is the duty of us all; the peculiar duty of a young man who has been so fortunate as I have been in early preferment; and I trust I am resigned. Perhaps not the less so from feeling a doubt of my positive happiness had my fair cousin honoured me with her hand; for I have often observed that resignation is never so perfect as when the blessing denied begins to lose somewhat of its value in our estimation. You will not, I hope, consider me as shewing any disrespect to your family, my dear Madam, by thus withdrawing my pretensions to your daughter's favour, without having paid yourself and Mr Bennet the compliment of requesting you to interpose your authority in my behalf. My conduct may I fear be objectionable in having accepted my dismission from your daughter's lips instead of your own. But we are all liable to error. I have certainly meant well through the whole affair. My object has been to secure an amiable companion for myself, with due consideration for the advantage of all your family, and if my *manner* has been at all reprehensible, I here beg leave to apologise.'

CHAPTER TWENTY ONE

THE DISCUSSION OF MR COLLINS'S offer was now nearly at an end, and Elizabeth had only to suffer from the uncomfortable feelings necessarily attending it, and occasionally from some peevish allusion of her mother. As for the gentleman himself, *his* feelings were chiefly expressed, not by embarrassment, or dejection, or by trying to avoid her, but by stiffness of manner and resentful silence. He scarcely ever spoke to her, and the assiduous attentions which he had been so sensible of himself, were transferred for the rest of the day to Miss Lucas, whose civility in listening to him, was a seasonable relief to them all, and especially to her friend.

The morrow produced no abatement of Mrs Bennet's ill humour or ill health. Mr Collins was also in the same state of angry pride. Elizabeth had hoped that his resentment might shorten his visit, but his plan did not appear in the least affected by it. He was always to have gone on Saturday, and to Saturday he still meant to stay.

After breakfast, the girls walked to Meryton to inquire if Mr Wickham were returned, and to lament over his absence from the Netherfield ball. He joined them on their entering the town and attended them to their aunt's where his regret and vexation, and the concern of every body was well talked over. – To Elizabeth, however, he voluntarily acknowledged that the necessity of his absence *had* been self imposed.

'I found,' said he, 'as the time drew near, that I had better not meet Mr Darcy; – that to be in the same room, the same party with him for so many hours together, might be more than I could bear, and that scenes might arise unpleasant to more than myself.'

She highly approved his forbearance, and they had leisure for a full discussion of it, and for all the commendation which they civilly bestowed on each other, as Wickham and another officer walked back with them to Longbourn, and during the walk, he particularly attended to her. His accompanying them was a double advantage; she felt all the compliment it offered to herself, and it was most acceptable as an occasion of introducing him to her father and mother.

Soon after their return, a letter was delivered to Miss Bennet; it came from Netherfield, and was opened immediately. The envelope contained a sheet of elegant, little, hot pressed paper, well covered with a lady's fair, flowing hand; and Elizabeth saw her sister's countenance change as she read it, and saw her dwelling intently on some particular passages. Jane recollected herself soon, and putting the letter away, tried to join with her usual cheerfulness in the general conversation; but Elizabeth felt an anxiety on the subject which drew off her attention even from Wickham; and no sooner had he and his companion taken leave, than a glance from Jane invited her to follow her up stairs. When they had gained their own room, Jane taking out the letter said,

Walked back with them

'This is from Caroline Bingley; what it contains, has surprised me a good deal. The whole party have left Netherfield by this time, and are on their way to town; and without any intention of coming back again. You shall hear what she says.'

She then read the first sentence aloud, which comprised the information of their having just resolved to follow their brother to town directly, and of their meaning to dine that day in Grosvenor Street, where Mr Hurst had a house. The next was in these words. 'I do not pretend to regret any thing I shall leave in Hertfordshire, except your society, my dearest friend; but we will hope at some future period, to enjoy many returns of the delightful intercourse we have known, and in the mean while may lessen the pain of separation by a very frequent and most unreserved correspondence. I depend on you for that.' To these high flown expressions, Elizabeth listened with all the insensibility of distrust; and though the suddenness of their removal surprised her, she saw nothing in it really to lament; it was not to be supposed that their absence from Netherfield would prevent Mr Bingley's being there; and as to the loss of their society, she was persuaded that Jane must soon cease to regard it, in the enjoyment of his.

'It is unlucky,' she said, after a short pause, 'that you should not be able to see your friends before they leave the country. But may we not hope that the period of future happiness to which Miss Bingley looks forward, may arrive earlier than she is aware, and that the delightful intercourse you have known as friends, will be renewed with yet greater satisfaction as sisters? – Mr Bingley will not be detained in London by them.'

'Caroline decidedly says that none of the party will return into Hertfordshire this winter. I will read it to you –

'When my brother left us yesterday, he imagined that the business which took him to London, might be concluded in three or four days, but as we are certain it cannot be so, and at the same time convinced that when Charles gets to town, he will be in no hurry to leave it again, we have determined on following him thither, that he may not be obliged to spend his vacant hours in a comfortless hotel. Many of my acquaintance are already there for the winter; I wish I could hear that you, my dearest friend, had any intention of making one in the croud, but of that I despair. I sincerely hope your Christmas in Hertfordshire may abound in the gaieties which that season generally brings, and that your beaux will be so numerous as to prevent your feeling the loss of the three, of whom, we shall deprive you.'

'It is evident by this,' added Jane, 'that he comes back no more this winter.'

'It is only evident that Miss Bingley does not mean he *should*.'

'Why will you think so? It must be his own doing. – He is his own master. But you do not know *all*. I *will* read you the passage which particularly hurts me. I will have no reserves from *you.*' 'Mr Darcy is impatient to see his sister, and to confess the truth, *we* are scarcely less eager to meet her again. I really do not think Georgiana Darcy has her equal for beauty, elegance, and accomplishments; and the affection she inspires in Louisa and myself, is heightened into something still more interesting, from the hope we dare to entertain of her being hereafter our sister. I do not know whether I ever before mentioned to you my feelings on this subject, but I will not leave the country without confiding them, and I trust you will not esteem them unreasonable. My brother admires her greatly already, he will have frequent opportunity now of seeing her on the most intimate footing, her relations all wish the connection as much as his own, and a sister's partiality is not misleading me, I think, when I call Charles most capable of engaging any woman's heart. With all these circumstances to favour an attachment and nothing to prevent it, am I wrong, my dearest Jane, in indulging the hope of an event which will secure the happiness of so many?'

'What think you of *this* sentence, my dear Lizzy?' – said Jane as she finished it. 'Is it not clear enough? – Does it not expressly declare that Caroline neither expects nor wishes me to be her sister; that she is perfectly convinced of her brother's indifference, and that if she suspects the nature of my feelings for him, she means (most kindly!) to put me on my guard? Can there be any other opinion on the subject?'

'Yes, there can; for mine is totally different. – Will you hear it?'

'Most willingly.'

'You shall have it in few words. Miss Bingley sees that her brother is in love with you, and wants him to marry Miss Darcy. She follows him to town in the hope of keeping him there, and tries to persuade you that he does not care about you.'

Jane shook her head.

'Indeed, Jane, you ought to believe me. – No one who has ever seen you together, can doubt his affection. Miss Bingley I am sure cannot. She is not such a simpleton. Could she have seen half as much love in Mr Darcy for herself, she would have ordered her wedding clothes. But the case is this. We are not rich enough, or grand enough for them; and she is the more anxious to get Miss Darcy for her brother, from the notion that when there has been *one* intermarriage, she may have less trouble in achieving a second; in which there is certainly some ingenuity, and I dare say it would succeed, if Miss de Bourgh were out of the way. But, my dearest Jane, you cannot seriously imagine that because Miss Bingley tells you her brother greatly admires Miss Darcy, he is in the smallest degree less sensible of *your* merit than when he took leave of you on Tuesday, or that it will be in her power to persuade him that instead of being in love with you, he is very much in love with her friend.'

'If we thought alike of Miss Bingley,' replied Jane, 'your representation of all this, might make me quite easy. But I know the foundation is unjust. Caroline is incapable of wilfully deceiving any one; and all that I can hope in this case, is that she is deceived herself.'

'That is right. – You could not have started a more happy idea, since you will not take comfort in mine. Believe her to be deceived by all means. You have now done your duty by her, and must fret no longer.'

'But, my dear sister, can I be happy, even supposing the best, in accepting a man whose sisters and friends are all wishing him to marry elsewhere?'

'You must decide for yourself,' said Elizabeth, 'and if upon mature deliberation, you find that the misery of disobliging his two sisters is more than equivalent to the happiness of being his wife, I advise you by all means to refuse him.'

'How can you talk so?' – said Jane faintly smiling, – 'You must know that though I should be exceedingly grieved at this disapprobation, I could not hesitate.'

'I did not think you would; – and that being the case, I cannot consider your situation with much compassion.'

'But if he returns no more this winter, my choice will never be required. A thousand things may arise in six months!'

The idea of his returning no more Elizabeth treated with the utmost contempt. It appeared to her merely the suggestion of Caroline's interested wishes, and she could not for a moment suppose that those wishes, however openly or artfully spoken, could influence a young man so totally independent of every one.

She represented to her sister as forcibly as possible what she felt on the subject, and had soon the pleasure of seeing its happy effect. Jane's temper was not desponding, and she was gradually led to hope, though the diffidence of affection sometimes overcame the hope, that Bingley would return to Netherfield and answer every wish of her heart.

They agreed that Mrs Bennet should only hear of the departure of the family, without being alarmed on the score of the gentleman's conduct; but even this partial communication gave her a good deal of concern, and she bewailed it as exceedingly unlucky that the ladies should happen to go away, just as they were all getting so intimate together. After lamenting it however at some length, she had the consolation of thinking that Mr Bingley would be soon down again and soon dining at Longbourn, and the conclusion of all was the comfortable declaration, that, though he had been invited only to a family dinner, she would take care to have two full courses.

CHAPTER TWENTY TWO

THE BENNETS WERE ENGAGED TO dine with the Lucases, and again during the chief of the day, was Miss Lucas so kind as to listen to Mr Collins. Elizabeth took an opportunity of thanking her. 'It keeps him in good humour,' said she, 'and I am more obliged to you than I can express.' Charlotte assured her friend of her satisfaction in being useful, and that it amply repaid her for the little sacrifice of her time. This was very amiable, but Charlotte's kindness extended farther than Elizabeth had any conception of; – its object was nothing less, than to secure her from any return of Mr Collins's addresses, by engaging them towards herself. Such was Miss Lucas's scheme; and appearances were so favourable that when they parted at night, she would have felt almost sure of success if he had not been to leave Hertfordshire so very soon. But here, she did injustice to the fire and independence of his character, for it led him to escape out of Longbourn House the next morning with admirable slyness, and hasten to Lucas Lodge to throw himself at her feet. He was anxious to avoid the notice of his cousins, from a conviction that if they saw him depart, they could not fail to conjecture his design, and he was not willing to have the attempt known till its success could be known likewise; for though feeling almost secure, and with reason, for Charlotte had been tolerably encouraging, he was comparatively diffident since the adventure of Wednesday. His reception however was of the most flattering kind. Miss Lucas perceived him from an upper window as he walked towards the house, and instantly set out to meet him accidentally in the lane. But little had she dared to hope that so much love and eloquence awaited her there.

In as short a time as Mr Collins's long speeches would allow, every thing was settled between them to the satisfaction of both; and as they entered the house, he earnestly entreated her to name the day that was to make him the happiest of men; and though such a solicitation must be waved for the present, the lady felt no inclination to trifle with his happiness. The stupidity with which he was favoured by nature, must guard his courtship from any charm that could make a woman wish for its continuance; and Miss Lucas, who accepted him solely from the pure and disinterested desire of an establishment, cared not how soon that establishment were gained.

Sir William and Lady Lucas were speedily applied to for their consent; and it was bestowed with a most joyful alacrity. Mr Collins's present circumstances made it a most eligible match for their daughter, to whom

So much love and eloquence

they could give little fortune; and his prospects of future wealth were exceedingly fair. Lady Lucas began directly to calculate with more interest than the matter had ever excited before, how many years longer Mr Bennet was likely to live; and Sir William gave it as his decided opinion, that whenever Mr Collins should be in possession of the Longbourn estate, it would be highly expedient that both he and his wife should make their appearance at St James's. The whole family in short were properly overjoyed on the occasion. The younger girls formed hopes of *coming out* a year or two sooner than they might otherwise have done; and the boys were relieved from their apprehension of Charlotte's dying an old maid. Charlotte herself was tolerably composed. She had gained her point, and had time to consider of it. Her reflections were in general satisfactory. Mr Collins to be sure was neither sensible nor agreeable; his society was irksome, and his attachment to her must be imaginary. But still he would be her husband. – Without thinking highly either of men or of matrimony, marriage had always been her object; it was the only honourable provision for well-educated young women of small fortune, and however uncertain of giving happiness, must be their pleasantest preservative from want. This preservative she had now obtained; and at the age of twenty-seven, without having ever been handsome, she felt all the good luck of it. The least agreeable circumstance in the business, was the surprise it must occasion to Elizabeth Bennet, whose friendship she valued beyond that of any other person. Elizabeth would wonder, and probably would blame her; and though her resolution was not to be shaken, her feelings must be hurt by such disapprobation. She resolved to give her the information herself, and therefore charged Mr Collins when he returned to Longbourn to dinner, to drop no hint of what had passed before any of the family. A promise of secrecy was of course very dutifully given, but it could not be kept without difficulty; for the curiosity excited by his long absence, burst forth in such very direct questions on his return, as required some ingenuity to evade, and he was at the same time exercising great self-denial, for he was longing to publish his prosperous love.

As he was to begin his journey too early on the morrow to see any of the family, the ceremony of leave-taking was performed when the ladies moved for the night; and Mrs Bennet with great politeness and cordiality said how happy they should be to see him at Longbourn again, whenever his other engagements might allow him to visit them.

'My dear Madam,' he replied, 'this invitation is particularly gratifying, because it is what I have been hoping to receive; and you may be very certain that I shall avail myself of it as soon as possible.'

They were all astonished; and Mr Bennet, who could by no means wish for so speedy a return, immediately said,

'But is there not danger of Lady Catherine's disapprobation here, my good sir? – You had better neglect your relations, than run the risk of offending your patroness.'

'My dear sir,' replied Mr Collins, 'I am particularly obliged to you for this friendly caution, and you may depend upon my not taking so material a step without her ladyship's concurrence.'

'You cannot be too much on your guard. Risk any thing rather than her displeasure; and if you find it likely to be raised by your coming to us again, which I should think exceedingly probable, stay quietly at home, and be satisfied that *we* shall take no offence.'

'Believe me, my dear sir, my gratitude is warmly excited by such affectionate attention; and depend upon it, you will speedily receive from me a letter of thanks for this, as well as for every other mark of your regard during my stay in Hertfordshire. As for my fair cousins, though my absence may not be long enough to render it necessary, I shall now take the liberty of wishing them health and happiness, not excepting my cousin Elizabeth.'

With proper civilities the ladies then withdrew; all of them equally surprised to find that he meditated a quick return. Mrs Bennet wished to understand by it that he thought of paying his addresses to one of her younger girls, and Mary might have been prevailed on to accept him. She rated his abilities much higher than any of the others; there was a solidity in his reflections which often struck her, and though by no means so clever as herself, she thought that if encouraged to read and improve himself by such an example as her's, he might become a very agreeable companion. But on the following morning, every hope of this kind was done away. Miss Lucas called soon after breakfast, and in a private conference with Elizabeth related the event of the day before.

The possibility of Mr Collins's fancying himself in love with her friend had once occurred to Elizabeth within the last day or two; but that Charlotte could encourage him, seemed almost as far from possibility as that she could encourage him herself, and her astonishment was consequently so great as to overcome at first the bounds of decorum, and she could not help crying out,

'Engaged to Mr Collins! my dear Charlotte, – impossible!'

The steady countenance which Miss Lucas had commanded in telling her story, gave way to a momentary confusion here on receiving so direct a reproach; though, as it was no more than she expected, she soon regained her composure, and calmly replied,

'Why should you be surprised, my dear Eliza? – Do you think it incredible that Mr Collins should be able to procure any woman's good opinion, because he was not so happy as to succeed with you?'

But Elizabeth had now recollected herself, and making a strong effort for it, was able to assure her with tolerable firmness that the prospect of their relationship was highly grateful to her, and that she wished her all imaginable happiness.

'I see what you are feeling,' replied Charlotte, – 'you must be surprised, very much surprised, – so lately as Mr Collins was wishing to marry you. But when you have had time to think it all over, I hope you will be satisfied with what I have done. I am not romantic you know. I never was. I ask only a comfortable home; and considering Mr Collins's character, connections, and situation in life, I am convinced that my chance of happiness with him is as fair, as most people can boast on entering the marriage state.'

Elizabeth quietly answered, 'Undoubtedly;' – and after an awkward pause, they returned to the rest of the family. Charlotte did not stay much longer, and Elizabeth was then left to reflect on what she had heard. It was a long time before she became at all reconciled to the idea of so unsuitable a match. The strangeness of Mr Collins's making two offers of marriage within three days, was nothing in comparison of his being now accepted. She had always felt that Charlotte's opinion of matrimony was not exactly like her own, but she could not have supposed it possible that when called into action, she would have sacrificed every better feeling to worldly advantage. Charlotte the wife of Mr Collins, was a most humiliating picture! – And to the pang of a friend disgracing herself and sunk in her esteem, was added the distressing conviction that it was impossible for that friend to be tolerably happy in the lot she had chosen.

Protested he must be entirely mistaken

CHAPTER TWENTY THREE

ELIZABETH WAS SITTING WITH HER mother and sisters, reflecting on what she had heard, and doubting whether she were authorised to mention it, when Sir William Lucas himself appeared, sent by his daughter to announce her engagement to the family. With many compliments to them, and much self-gratulation on the prospect of a connection between the houses, he unfolded the matter, – to an audience not merely wondering, but incredulous; for Mrs Bennet, with more perseverance than politeness, protested he must be entirely mistaken, and Lydia, always unguarded and often uncivil, boisterously exclaimed,

'Good Lord! Sir William, how can you tell such a story? – Do not you know that Mr Collins wants to marry Lizzy?'

Nothing less than the complaisance of a courtier could have borne without anger such treatment; but Sir William's good breeding carried him through it all; and though he begged leave to be positive as to the truth of his information, he listened to all their impertinence with the most forbearing courtesy.

Elizabeth, feeling it incumbent on her to relieve him from so unpleasant a situation, now put herself forward to confirm his account, by mentioning her prior knowledge of it from Charlotte herself; and endeavoured to put a stop to the exclamations of her mother and sisters, by the earnestness of her congratulations to Sir William, in which she was readily joined by Jane, and by making a variety of remarks on the happiness that might be expected from the match, the excellent character of Mr Collins, and the convenient distance of Hunsford from London.

Mrs Bennet was in fact too much overpowered to say a great deal while Sir William remained; but no sooner had he left them her feelings found a rapid vent. In the first place, she persisted in disbelieving the whole of the matter; secondly, she was very sure that Mr Collins had been taken in; thirdly, she trusted that they would never be happy together; and fourthly, that the match might be broken off. Two inferences, however, were plainly deduced from the whole; one, that Elizabeth was the real cause of all the mischief; and the other, that she herself had been barbarously used by them all; and on these two points she principally dwelt during the rest of the day. Nothing could console and nothing appease her. – Nor did that day wear out her resentment. A week elapsed before she could see Elizabeth without scolding her, a month passed away before she could speak to Sir William or Lady Lucas without being rude, and many months were gone before she could at all forgive their daughter.

Mr Bennet's emotions were much more tranquil on the occasion, and such as he did experience he pronounced to be of a most agreeable sort; for it gratified him, he said, to discover that Charlotte Lucas, whom he had been used to think tolerably sensible, was as foolish as his wife, and more foolish than his daughter!

Jane confessed herself a little surprised at the match; but she said less of her astonishment than of her earnest desire for their happiness; nor could Elizabeth persuade her to consider it as improbable. Kitty and Lydia were far from envying Miss Lucas, for Mr Collins was only a clergyman; and it affected them in no other way than as a piece of news to spread at Meryton.

Lady Lucas could not be insensible of triumph on being able to retort on Mrs Bennet the comfort of having a daughter well married; and she called at Longbourn rather oftener than usual to say how happy she was, though Mrs

Bennet's sour looks and ill-natured remarks might have been enough to drive happiness away.

Between Elizabeth and Charlotte there was a restraint which kept them mutually silent on the subject; and Elizabeth felt persuaded that no real confidence could ever subsist between them again. Her disappointment in Charlotte made her turn with fonder regard to her sister, of whose rectitude and delicacy she was sure her opinion could never be shaken, and for whose happiness she grew daily more anxious, as Bingley had now been gone a week, and nothing was heard of his return.

Jane had sent Caroline an early answer to her letter, and was counting the days till she might reasonably hope to hear again. The promised letter of thanks from Mr Collins arrived on Tuesday, addressed to their father, and written with all the solemnity of gratitude which a twelvemonth's abode in the family might have prompted. After discharging his conscience on that head, he proceeded to inform them, with many rapturous expressions, of his happiness in having obtained the affection of their amiable neighbour, Miss Lucas, and then explained that it was merely with the view of enjoying her society that he had been so ready to close with their kind wish of seeing him again at Longbourn, whither he hoped to be able to return on Monday fortnight; for Lady Catherine, he added, so heartily approved his marriage, that she wished it to take place as soon as possible, which he trusted would be an unanswerable argument with his amiable Charlotte to name an early day for making him the happiest of men.

Mr Collins's return into Hertfordshire was no longer a matter of pleasure to Mrs Bennet. On the contrary she was as much disposed to complain of it as her husband. – It was very strange that he should come to Longbourn instead of to Lucas Lodge; it was also very inconvenient and exceedingly troublesome. – She hated having visitors in the house while her health was so indifferent, and lovers were of all people the most disagreeable. Such were the gentle murmurs of Mrs Bennet, and they gave way only to the greater distress of Mr Bingley's continued absence.

Neither Jane nor Elizabeth were comfortable on this subject. Day after day passed away without bringing any other tidings of him than the report which shortly prevailed in Meryton of his coming no more to Netherfield the whole winter; a report which highly incensed Mrs Bennet, and which she never failed to contradict as a most scandalous falsehood.

Even Elizabeth began to fear – not that Bingley was indifferent – but that his sisters would be successful in keeping him away. Unwilling as she was to admit an idea so destructive of Jane's happiness, and so dishonourable to the stability of her lover, she could not prevent its frequently recurring. The united efforts of his two unfeeling sisters and of his overpowering friend, assisted by the attractions of Miss Darcy and the amusements of London,

Whenever she spoke in a low voice

might be too much, she feared, for the strength of his attachment.

As for Jane, *her* anxiety under this suspense was, of course, more painful than Elizabeth's; but whatever she felt she was desirous of concealing, and between herself and Elizabeth, therefore, the subject was never alluded to. But as no such delicacy restrained her mother, an hour seldom passed in which she did not talk of Bingley, express her impatience for his arrival, or even require Jane to confess that if he did not come back, she should think herself very ill used. It needed all Jane's steady mildness to bear these attacks with tolerable tranquillity.

Mr Collins returned most punctually on the Monday fortnight, but his reception at Longbourn was not quite so gracious as it had been on his first introduction. He was too happy, however, to need much attention; and luckily for the others, the business of love-making relieved them from a great deal of his company. The chief of every day was spent by him at Lucas Lodge, and he sometimes returned to Longbourn only in time to make an apology for his absence before the family went to bed.

Mrs Bennet was really in a most pitiable state. The very mention of any thing concerning the match threw her into an agony of ill humour, and wherever she went she was sure of hearing it talked of. The sight of Miss Lucas was odious to her. As her successor in that house, she regarded her with jealous abhorrence. Whenever Charlotte came to see them she concluded her to be anticipating the hour of possession; and whenever she spoke in a low voice to Mr Collins, was convinced that they were talking of the Longbourn estate, and resolving to turn herself and her daughters out of the house, as soon as Mr Bennet were dead. She complained bitterly of all this to her husband.

'Indeed, Mr Bennet,' said she, 'it is very hard to think that Charlotte Lucas should ever be mistress of this house, that *I* should be forced to make way for *her*, and live to see her take my place in it!'

'My dear, do not give way to such gloomy thoughts. Let us hope for better things. Let us flatter ourselves that I may be the survivor.'

This was not very consoling to Mrs Bennet, and, therefore, instead of making any answer, she went on as before,

'I cannot bear to think that they should have all this estate. If it was not for the entail I should not mind it.'

'What should not you mind?'

'I should not mind any thing at all.'

'Let us be thankful that you are preserved from a state of such insensibility.'

'I never can be thankful, Mr Bennet, for any thing about the entail. How any one could have the conscience to entail away an estate from one's own daughters I cannot understand; and all for the sake of Mr Collins too! – Why should *he* have it more than anybody else?'

'I leave it to yourself to determine,' said Mr Bennet.

CHAPTER TWENTY FOUR

MISS BINGLEY'S LETTER ARRIVED, AND put an end to doubt. The very first sentence conveyed the assurance of their being all settled in London for the winter, and concluded with her brother's regret at not having had time to pay his respects to his friends in Hertfordshire before he left the country.

Hope was over, entirely over; and when Jane could attend to the rest of the letter, she found little, except the professed affection of the writer, that could give her any comfort. Miss Darcy's praise occupied the chief of it. Her many attractions were again dwelt on, and Caroline boasted joyfully of their increasing intimacy, and ventured to predict the accomplishment of the wishes which had been unfolded in her former letter. She wrote also with great pleasure of her brother's being an inmate of Mr Darcy's house, and mentioned with raptures, some plans of the latter with regard to new furniture.

Elizabeth, to whom Jane very soon communicated the chief of all this, heard it in silent indignation. Her heart was divided between concern for her sister, and resentment against all the others. To Caroline's assertion of her brother's being partial to Miss Darcy she paid no credit. That he was really fond of Jane, she doubted no more than she had ever done; and much as she had always been disposed to like him, she could not think without anger, hardly without contempt, on that easiness of temper, that want of proper resolution which now made him the slave of his designing friends, and led him to sacrifice his own happiness to the caprice of their inclinations. Had his own happiness, however, been the only sacrifice, he might have been allowed to sport with it in what ever manner he thought best; but her sister's was involved in it, as she thought he must be sensible himself. It was a subject, in short, on which reflection would be long indulged, and must be unavailing. She could think of nothing else, and yet whether Bingley's regard had really died away, or were suppressed by his friends' interference; whether he had been aware of Jane's attachment, or whether it had escaped his observation; whichever were the case, though her opinion of him must be materially affected by the difference, her sister's situation remained the same, her peace equally wounded.

A day or two passed before Jane had courage to speak of her feelings to Elizabeth; but at last on Mrs Bennet's leaving them together, after a longer irritation than usual about Netherfield and its master, she could not help saying,

'Oh! that my dear mother had more command over herself; she can have no idea of the pain she gives me by her continual reflections on him. But I will not repine. It cannot last long. He will be forgot, and we shall all be as we are before.'

Elizabeth looked at her sister with incredulous solicitude, but said nothing.

'You doubt me,' cried Jane, slightly colouring; 'indeed you have no reason. He may live in my memory as the most amiable man of my acquaintance, but that is all. I have nothing either to hope or fear, and nothing to reproach him with. Thank God! I have not *that* pain. A little time therefore. – I shall certainly try to get the better.'

With a stronger voice she soon added, 'I have this comfort immediately, that it has not been more than an error of fancy on my side, and that it has done no harm to any one but myself.'

'My dear Jane!' exclaimed Elizabeth, 'you are too good. Your sweetness and disinterestedness are really angelic; I do not know what to say to you. I feel as if I had never done you justice, or loved you as you deserve.'

Miss Bennet eagerly disclaimed all extraordinary merit, and threw back the praise on her sister's warm affection.

'Nay,' said Elizabeth, 'this is not fair. *You* wish to think all the world respectable, and are hurt if I speak ill of any body. *I* only want to think *you* perfect, and you set yourself against it. Do not be afraid of my running into any excess, of my encroaching on your privilege of universal good will. You need not. There are few people whom I really love, and still fewer of whom I think well. The more I see of the world, the more am I dissatisfied with it; and every day confirms my belief of the inconsistency of all human characters, and of the little dependence that can be placed on the appearance of either merit or sense. I have met with two instances lately; one I will not mention; the other is Charlotte's marriage. It is unaccountable! in every view it is unaccountable!'

'My dear Lizzy, do not give way to such feelings as these. They will ruin your happiness. You do not make allowance enough for difference of situation and temper. Consider Mr Collins's respectability, and Charlotte's prudent, steady character. Remember that she is one of a large family; that as to fortune, it is a most eligible match; and be ready to believe, for every body's sake, that she may feel something like regard and esteem for our cousin.'

'To oblige you, I would try to believe almost any thing, but no one else could be benefited by such a belief as this; for were I persuaded that Charlotte had any regard for him, I should only think worse of her understanding, than I now do of her heart. My dear Jane, Mr Collins is a conceited, pompous, narrow-minded, silly man; you know he is, as well as I do; and you must feel, as well as I do, that the woman who marries him, cannot have a proper way of thinking. You shall not defend her, though it is Charlotte Lucas. You shall not, for the sake of one individual, change the meaning of principle and integrity, nor endeavour to persuade yourself or me, that selfishness is prudence, and insensibility of danger, security for happiness.'

'I must think your language too strong in speaking of both,' replied Jane, 'and I hope you will be convinced of it, by seeing them happy together. But enough of this. You alluded to something else. You mentioned *two* instances. I cannot misunderstand you, but I intreat you, dear Lizzy, not to pain me by thinking *that person* to blame, and saying your opinion of him is sunk. We must not be so ready to fancy ourselves intentionally injured. We must not expect a lively young man to be always so guarded and circumspect. It is very often nothing but our own vanity that deceives us. Women fancy admiration means more than it does.'

'And men take care that they should.'

'If it is designedly done, they cannot be justified; but I have no idea of there being so much design in the world as some persons imagine.'

'I am far from attributing any part of Mr Bingley's conduct to design,' said Elizabeth; 'but without scheming to do wrong, or to make others unhappy, there may be error, and there may be misery. Thoughtlessness, want of attention to other people's feelings, and want of resolution, will do the business.'

'And do you impute it to either of those?'

'Yes; to the last. But if I go on, I shall displease you by saying what I think of persons you esteem. Stop me whilst you can.'

'You persist, then, in supposing his sisters influence him.'

'Yes, in conjunction with his friend.'

'I cannot believe it. Why should they try to influence him? They can only wish his happiness, and if he is attached to me, no other woman can secure it.'

'Your first position is false. They may wish many things besides his happiness; they may wish his increase of wealth and consequence; they may wish him to marry a girl who has all the importance of money, great connections, and pride.'

'Beyond a doubt, they *do* wish him to chuse Miss Darcy,' replied Jane; 'but this may be from better feelings than you are supposing. They have known her much longer than they have known me; no wonder if they love her better. But, whatever may be their own wishes, it is very unlikely they should have opposed their brother's. What sister would think herself at liberty to do it, unless there were something very objectionable? If they believed him attached to me, they would not try to part us; if he were so, they could not succeed. By supposing such an affection, you make every body acting unnaturally and wrong, and me most unhappy. Do not distress me by the idea. I am not ashamed of having been mistaken – or, at least, it is slight, it is nothing in comparison of what I should feel in thinking ill of him or his sisters. Let me take it in the best light, in the light in which it may be understood.'

Elizabeth could not oppose such a wish; and from this time Mr Bingley's name was scarcely ever mentioned between them.

Mrs Bennet still continued to wonder and repine at his returning no more, and though a day seldom passed in which Elizabeth did not account for it clearly, there seemed little chance of her ever considering it with less perplexity. Her daughter endeavoured to convince her of what she did not believe herself, that his attentions to Jane had been merely the effect of a common and transient liking, which ceased when he saw her no more; but though the probability of the statement was admitted at the time, she had the same story to repeat every day. Mrs Bennet's best comfort was, that Mr Bingley must be down again in the summer.

Mr Bennet treated the matter differently. 'So, Lizzy,' said he one day, 'your sister is crossed in love I find. I congratulate her. Next to being married, a girl likes to be crossed in love a little now and then. It is something to think of, and gives her a sort of distinction among her companions. When is your turn to come? You will hardly bear to be long outdone by Jane. Now is your time. Here are officers enough at Meryton to disappoint all the young ladies in the country. Let Wickham be *your* man. He is a pleasant fellow, and would jilt you creditably.'

'Thank you, Sir, but a less agreeable man would satisfy me. We must not all expect Jane's good fortune.'

'True,' said Mr Bennet, 'but it is a comfort to think that, whatever of that kind may befall you, you have an affectionate mother who will always make the most of it.'

Mr Wickham's society was of material service in dispelling the gloom, which the late perverse occurrences had thrown on many of the Longbourn family. They saw him often, and to his other recommendations was now added that of general unreserve. The whole of what Elizabeth had already heard, his claims on Mr Darcy, and all that he had suffered from him, was now openly acknowledged and publicly canvassed; and every body was pleased to think how much they had always disliked Mr Darcy before they had known any thing of the matter.

Miss Bennet was the only creature who could suppose there might be any extenuating circumstances in the case, unknown to the society of Hertfordshire; her mild and steady candour always pleaded for allowances, and urged the possibility of mistakes – but by everybody else Mr Darcy was condemned as the worst of men.

CHAPTER TWENTY FIVE

AFTER A WEEK SPENT IN PROFESSIONS OF love and schemes of felicity, Mr Collins was called from his amiable Charlotte by the arrival of Saturday. The pain of separation, however, might be alleviated on his side, by preparations for the reception of his bride, as he had reason to hope, that shortly after his next return into Hertfordshire, the day would be fixed that was to make him the happiest of men. He took leave of his relations at Longbourn with as much solemnity as before; wished his fair cousins health and happiness again, and promised their father another letter of thanks.

On the following Monday, Mrs Bennet had the pleasure of receiving her brother and his wife, who came as usual to spend the Christmas at Longbourn. Mr Gardiner was a sensible, gentlemanlike man, greatly superior to his sister as well by nature as education. The Netherfield ladies would have had difficulty in believing that a man who lived by trade, and within view of his own warehouses, could have been so well bred and agreeable. Mrs Gardiner, who was several years younger than Mrs Bennet and Mrs Philips, was an amiable, intelligent, elegant woman, and a great favourite with all her Longbourn nieces. Between the two eldest and herself especially, there subsisted a very particular regard. They had frequently been staying with her in town.

The first part of Mrs Gardiner's business on her arrival, was to distribute her presents and describe the newest fashions. When this was done, she had a less active part to play. It became her turn to listen. Mrs Bennet had many grievances to relate, and much to complain of. They had all been ill-used since she last saw her sister. Two of her girls had been on the point of marriage, and after all there was nothing in it.

'I do not blame Jane,' she continued, 'for Jane would have got Mr Bingley, if she could. But Lizzy! Oh, sister! it is very hard to think that she might have been Mr Collins' wife by this time, had not it been for her own perverseness. He made her an offer in this very room, and she refused him. The consequence of it is that Lady Lucas will have a daughter married before I have, and that Longbourn estate is just as much entailed as ever. The Lucases are very artful people indeed, sister. They are all for what they can get. I am sorry to say it of them, but so it is. It makes me very nervous and poorly, to be thwarted so in my own family, and to have neighbours who think of themselves before anybody else. However, your coming just at this time is the greatest of comforts, and I am very glad to hear what you tell us, of long sleeves.'

Mrs Gardiner, to whom the chief of this news had been given before, in the course of Jane and Elizabeth's correspondence with her, made her sister a slight answer, and in compassion to her nieces turned the conversation.

When alone with Elizabeth afterwards, she spoke more on the subject. 'It seems likely to have been a desirable match for Jane,' said she, 'I am sorry it went off. But these things happen so often! A young man, such as you describe Mr Bingley, so easily falls in love with a pretty girl for a few weeks, and when accident separates them, so easily forgets her, that these sort of inconstancies are very frequent.'

'An excellent consolation in its way,' said Elizabeth, 'but it will not do for *us*. We do not suffer by *accident*. It does not often happen that the interference of friends will persuade a young man of independent fortune to think no more of a girl, whom he was violently in love with only a few days before.'

'But that expression of "violently in love" is so hackneyed, so doubtful, so indefinite, that it gives me very little idea. It is as often applied to feelings which arise from an half-hour's acquaintance, as to a real, strong attachment. Pray, how *violent was* Mr Bingley's love?'

'I never saw a more promising inclination. He was growing quite inattentive to other people, and wholly engrossed by her. Every time they met, it was more decided and remarkable. At his own ball he offended two or three young ladies, by not asking them to dance, and I spoke to him twice myself, without receiving an answer. Could there be finer symptoms? Is not general incivility the very essence of love?'

'Oh, yes! – of that kind of love which I suppose him to have felt. Poor Jane! I am sorry for her, because, with her disposition, she may not get over it immediately. It had better have happened to *you*, Lizzy; you would have laughed yourself out of it sooner. But do you think she would be prevailed on to go back with us? Change of scene might be of service – and perhaps a little relief from home, may be as useful as anything.'

Elizabeth was exceedingly pleased with this proposal, and felt persuaded of her sister's ready acquiescence.

'I hope,' added Mrs Gardiner, 'that no consideration with regard to this young man will influence her. We live in so different a part of town, all our connections are so different, and, as you well know, we go out so little, that

Offended two or three young ladies

it is very improbable they should meet at all, unless he really comes to see her.'

'And *that* is quite impossible; for he is now in the custody of his friend, and Mr Darcy would no more suffer him to call on Jane in such a part of London! My dear aunt, how could you think of it? Mr Darcy may perhaps have *heard* of such a place as Gracechurch Street, but he would hardly think a month's ablution enough to cleanse him from its impurities, were he once to enter it; and depend upon it, Mr Bingley never stirs without him.'

'So much the better. I hope they will not meet at all. But does not Jane correspond with the sister? *She* will not be able to help calling.'

'She will drop the acquaintance entirely.'

But in spite of the certainty in which Elizabeth affected to place this point, as well as the still more interesting one of Bingley's being withheld from seeing Jane, she felt a solicitude on the subject which convinced her, on examination, that she did not consider it entirely hopeless. It was possible, and sometimes she thought it profitable, that his affection might be re-animated, and the influence of his friends successfully combated by the more natural influence of Jane's attractions.

Miss Bennet accepted her aunt's invitation with pleasure; and the Bingley's were no otherwise in her thoughts at the time, than as she hoped that, by Caroline's not living in the same house with her brother, she might occasionally spend a morning with her, without any danger of seeing him.

The Gardiners staid a week at Longbourn; and what with the Philipses, the Lucases, and the officers, there was not a day without its engagement. Mrs Bennet had so carefully provided for the entertainment of her brother and sister, that they did not once sit down to a family dinner. When the engagement was for home, some of the officers always made part of it, of which officers Mr Wickham was sure to be one; and on these occasions, Mrs Gardiner, rendered suspicious by Elizabeth's warm commendation of him, narrowly observed them both. Without supposing them, from what she saw, to be very seriously in love, their preference of each other was plain enough to make her a little uneasy; and she resolved to speak to Elizabeth on the subject before she left Hertfordshire, and represented to her the imprudence of encouraging such an attachment.

To Mrs Gardiner, Wickham had one means of affording pleasure, unconnected with his general powers. About ten or a dozen years ago, before her marriage, she had spent a considerable time in that very part of Derbyshire, to which he belonged. They had, therefore, many acquaintances in common; and, though Wickham had been little there since the death of Darcy's father, five years before, it was yet in his power to give her fresher intelligence of her former friends, than she had been in the way of procuring.

Mrs Gardiner had seen Pemberley, and known the late Mr Darcy by character perfectly well. Here consequently was an inexhaustible subject of discourse. In comparing her recollection of Pemberley, with the minute description which Wickham could give, and in bestowing her tribute of praise on the character of its late possessor, she was delighting both him and herself. On being made acquainted with the present Mr Darcy's treatment of him, she tried to remember something of that gentleman's reputed disposition when quite a lad, which might agree with it, and was confident at last, that she recollected having heard Mr Fitzwilliam Darcy formerly spoken of as a very proud, ill-natured boy.

CHAPTER TWENTY SIX

MRS GARDINER'S CAUTION TO ELIZABETH was punctually and kindly given on the first favourable opportunity of speaking to her alone; after honestly telling her what she thought, she thus went on:

'You are too sensible a girl, Lizzy, to fall in love merely because you are warned against it; and, therefore, I am not afraid of speaking openly. Seriously, I would have you be on your guard. Do not involve yourself, or endeavour to involve him in an affection which the want of fortune would make so very imprudent. I have nothing to say against *him*; he is a most interesting young man; and if he had the fortune he ought to have, I should think you could not do better. But as it is – you must not let your fancy run away with you. You have sense, and we all expect you to use it. Your father would depend on *your* resolution and good conduct, I am sure. You must not disappoint your father.'

'My dear aunt, this is being serious indeed.'

'Yes, and I hope to engage you to be serious likewise.'

'Well, then, you need not be under any alarm. I will take care of myself, and of Mr Wickham to. He shall not be in love with me, if I can prevent it.'

'Elizabeth, you are not serious now.'

'I beg your pardon. I will try again. At present I am not in love with Mr Wickham; no, I certainly am not. But he is, beyond all comparison, the most agreeable man I ever saw – and if he becomes really attached to me – I believe it will be better that he should not. I see the imprudence of it. – Oh! *that* abominable Mr Darcy! – My father's opinion of me does me the greatest honour; and I should be miserable to forfeit it. My father, however, is partial to Mr Wickham. In short, my dear aunt, I should be very sorry to be the means of making any of you unhappy; but since we see every day that where there is affection, young people are seldom withheld by immediate want of fortune, from entering into engagements with each other, how can I promise to be wiser than so many of my fellow creatures if I am tempted, or how am I even to know that it would be wisdom to resist? All that I can promise you, therefore, is not to be in a hurry. I will not be in a hurry to believe myself his first object. When I am in company with him, I will not be wishing. In short, I will do my best.'

'Perhaps it will be as well, if you discourage his coming here so very often. At least, you should not *remind* your Mother of inviting him.'

'As I did the other day,' said Elizabeth, with a conscious smile; 'very true, it will be wise in me to refrain from *that*. But do not imagine that he is always here so often. It is on your account that he has been so frequently invited this week. You know my mother's ideas as to the necessity of constant company for her friends. But really, and upon my honour, I will try to do what I think to be wisest; and now, I hope you are satisfied.'

Her aunt assured her that she was; and Elizabeth having thanked her for the kindness of her hints, they parted; a wonderful instance of advice being given on such a point, without being resented.

Mr Collins returned into Hertfordshire soon after it had been quitted by the Gardiners and Jane; but as he took up his abode with the Lucases, his arrival was no great inconvenience to Mrs Bennet. His marriage was now fast approaching, and she was at length so far resigned as to think it inevitable and even repeatedly to say in an ill-natured tone that she '*wished* they might be happy.' Thursday was to be the wedding day, and on Wednesday Miss Lucas paid her farewell visit; and when she rose to take leave, Elizabeth, ashamed of her mother's ungracious and reluctant good wishes, and sincerely affected herself, accompanied her out of the room. As they went down stairs together, Charlotte said,

'I shall depend on hearing from you very often, Eliza.'

'*That* you certainly shall.'

'And I have another favour to ask. Will you come and see me?'

'We shall often meet, I hope, in Hertfordshire.'

'I am not likely to leave Kent for some time. Promise me, therefore, to come to Hunsford.'

Elizabeth could not refuse, though she foresaw little pleasure in the visit.

'My father and Maria are to come to me in March,' added Charlotte, 'and I hope you will consent to be of the party. Indeed, Eliza, you will be as welcome to me as either of them.'

The wedding took place; the bride and bridegroom set off for Kent from the church door, and every body had as much to say or to hear on the subject as usual. Elizabeth soon heard from her friend; and their correspondence was as regular and frequent as it had ever been; that it should be equally unreserved was impossible. Elizabeth could never address her without feeling that all the comfort of intimacy was over, and, though determined not to slacken as a correspondent, it was for the sake of what had been, rather than what was. Charlotte's first letters were received with a good deal of eagerness; there could not but be curiosity to know how she would speak of her new home, how she would like Lady Catherine, and how happy she would dare pronounce herself to be; though, when the letters were read, Elizabeth felt that Charlotte expressed herself on every point exactly as she might have foreseen. She wrote cheerfully, seemed surrounded with comforts, and mentioned nothing which she could not praise. The house, furniture, neighbourhood, and roads, were all to her taste, and Lady Catherine's behaviour was most friendly and obliging. It was Mr Collins's picture of Hunsford and Rosings rationally softened; and Elizabeth perceived that she must wait for her own visit there, to know the rest.

Jane had already written a few lines to her sister to announce their safe arrival in London; and when she wrote again, Elizabeth hoped it would be in her power to say something of the Bingleys.

Her impatience for this second letter was as well rewarded as impatience generally is. Jane had been a week in town, without either seeing or hearing from Caroline. She accounted for it, however, by supposing that her last letter to her friend from Longbourn, had by some accident been lost.

'My aunt,' she continued, 'is going to-morrow into that part of the town, and I shall take the opportunity of calling in Grosvenor-street.'

She wrote again when the visit was paid, and she had seen Miss Bingley. 'I did not think Caroline in spirits,' were her words, 'but she was very glad to see me, and reproached me for giving her no notice of my coming to London. I was right, therefore; my last letter had never reached her. I enquired after their brother, of course. He was well, but so much engaged with Mr Darcy, that they scarcely ever saw him. I found that Miss Darcy was expected to dinner. I wish I could see her. My visit was not long, as Caroline and Mrs Hurst were going out. I dare say I shall soon see them here.'

Elizabeth shook her head over this letter. It convinced her, that accident only could discover to Mr Bingley her sister's being in town.

Four weeks passed away, and Jane saw nothing of him. She endeavoured to persuade herself that she did not regret it; but she could no longer be blind to Miss Bingley's inattention. After waiting at home every morning for a fortnight, and inventing every evening a fresh excuse for her, the visitor did at last appear; but the shortness of her stay, and yet more, the alteration of her manner, would allow Jane to deceive herself no longer. The letter which she wrote on this occasion to her sister, will prove what she felt.

My dearest Lizzy, will, I am sure, be incapable of triumphing in her better judgement, at my expence, when I confess myself to have been entirely deceived in Miss Bingley's regard for me. But, my dear sister, though the event has proved you right, do not think me obstinate if I still assert, that, considering what her behaviour was, my confidence was as natural as your suspicion. I do not at all comprehend her reason for wishing to be intimate with me, but if the same circumstances were to happen again, I am sure I should be deceived again. Caroline did not return my visit till yesterday; and not a note, not a line, did I receive in the mean time. When she did come, it was evident that she had no pleasure in it; she made a slight, formal apology, for not calling before, said not a word of wishing to see me again, and was in every respect so altered a creature, that when she went away, I was perfectly resolved to continue the acquaintance no longer. I pity, though I cannot help blaming her. She was very wrong in singling me out as she did; I can safely say, that every advance to intimacy began on her side. But I pity her, because she must feel that she has been acting wrong, and because I am very sure that anxiety for her brother is the cause of it. I need not explain myself farther: and though we know this anxiety to be quite needless, yet if she feels it, it will easily account for her behaviour to me; and so deservedly dear as he is to his sister, whatever anxiety she may feel on his behalf, is natural and amiable. I cannot but wonder, however, at her having any such fears now, because, if he had at all cared about me, we must have met long, long ago. He knows of my being in town, I am certain, from something she said herself; and yet it should seem by her manner of talking, as if she wanted to persuade herself that he is really partial to Miss Darcy. I cannot understand it. If I were not afraid of judging harshly, I should be almost tempted to say, that there is a strong appearance of duplicity in all this. But I will endeavour to banish every painful thought, and think only of what will make me happy, your affection, and the invariable kindness of my dear uncle and aunt. Let me hear from you very soon. Miss Bingley said something of his never returning to Netherfield again, of giving up the house, but not with any certainty. We had better not mention it. I am extremely glad that you have such pleasant accounts from our friends at Hunsford. Pray go to see them, with Sir William and Maria. I am sure you will be very comfortable there.

Yours, &c.

This letter gave Elizabeth some pain; but her spirits returned as she considered that Jane would no longer be duped, by the sister at least. All expectation from the brother was not absolutely over. She would not even wish for any renewal of his attentions. His character sunk on every review of it; and as a punishment for him, as well as a possible advantage to Jane, she seriously hoped he might really soon marry Mr Darcy's sister, as, by Wickham's account, she would make him abundantly regret what he had thrown away.

Mrs Gardiner about this time reminded Elizabeth of her promise concerning that gentleman, and required information; and Elizabeth had such to send as might rather give contentment to her aunt than to herself. His apparent partiality had subsided, his attentions were over, he was the admirer of some one else. Elizabeth was watchful enough to see it all, but she could see it and write of it without material pain. Her heart had been but slightly touched, and her vanity was satisfied with believing that *she* would have been his only choice, had fortune permitted it. The sudden acquisition of ten thousand pounds was the most remarkable charm, of the young lady, to whom he was now rendering himself agreeable; but Elizabeth, less clear-sighted perhaps in his case than in Charlotte's, did not quarrel with him for his wish of independence. Nothing, on the contrary, could be more natural; and while able to suppose that it cost him a few struggles to relinquish her, she was ready to allow it a wise and desirable measure for both, and could very sincerely wish him happy.

All this was acknowledged to Mrs Gardiner; and after relating the circumstances, she thus went on: – 'I am now convinced, my dear aunt, that I have never been much in love; for had I really experienced that pure and elevating passion, I should at present detest his very name, and wish him all manner of evil. But my feelings are not only cordial towards *him*; they are even impartial towards Miss King. I cannot find out that I hate her at all, or that I am in the least unwilling to think her a very good sort of girl. There can be no love in all this. My watchfulness has been effectual; and though I should certainly be a more interesting object to all my acquaintance, were I distractedly in love with him, I cannot say that I regret my comparative insignificance. Importance may sometimes be purchased too dearly. Kitty and Lydia take his defection much more to heart than I do. They are young in the ways of the world, and not yet open to the mortifying conviction that handsome men must have something to live on, as well as the plain.'

On the stairs

CHAPTER TWENTY SEVEN

WITH NO GREATER EVENTS THAN THESE in the Longbourn family, and otherwise diversified by little beyond the walks to Meryton, sometimes dirty and sometimes cold, did January and February pass away. March was to take Elizabeth to Hunsford. She had not at first thought very seriously of going thither; but Charlotte, she soon found, was depending on the plan, and she gradually learned to consider it herself with greater pleasure as well as greater certainty. Absence had increased her desire of seeing Charlotte again, and weakened her disgust of Mr Collins. There was novelty in the scheme, and as, with such a mother and such uncompanionable sisters, home could not be faultless, a little change was not unwelcome for its own sake. The journey would moreover give her a peep at Jane; and, in short, as the time drew near, she would have been very sorry for any delay. Every thing, however, went on smoothly, and was finally settled according to Charlotte's first sketch. She was to accompany Sir William and his second daughter. The improvement of spending a night in London was added in time, and the plan became perfect as plan could be.

The only pain was in leaving her father, who would certainly miss her, and who, when it came to the point, so little liked her going, that he told her to write to him, and almost promised to answer her letter.

The farewell between herself and Mr Wickham was perfectly friendly; on his side even more. His present pursuit could not make him forget that Elizabeth had been the first to excite and to deserve his attention, the first to listen and to pity, the first to be admired; and in his manner of bidding her adieu, wishing her every enjoyment, reminding her of what she was to expect in Lady Catherine de Bourgh, and trusting their opinion of her – their opinion of every body – would always coincide, there was a solicitude, an interest which she felt must ever attach her to him with a most sincere regard; and she parted from him convinced, that whether married or single, he must always be her model of the amiable and pleasing.

Her fellow-travellers the next day, were not of a kind to make her think them less agreeable. Sir William Lucas, and his daughter Maria, a good humoured girl, but as empty-headed as himself, had nothing to say that could be worth hearing, and were listened to with about as much delight as the rattle of the chaise. Elizabeth loved absurdities, but she had known Sir William's too long. He could tell her nothing new of the wonders of his presentation and knighthood; and his civilities were worn out like his information.

It was a journey of only twenty-four miles, and they began it so early as to be in Gracechurch-street by noon. As they drove to Mr Gardiner's door, Jane was at a drawing-room window watching their arrival; when they entered the passage she was there to welcome them, and Elizabeth, looking earnestly in her face, was pleased to see it healthful and lovely as ever. On the stairs were a troop of little boys and girls, whose eagerness for their cousin's appearance would not allow them to wait in the drawing-room, and whose shyness, as they had not seen her for a twelvemonth, prevented their coming lower. All was joy and kindness. The day passed most pleasantly away; the morning in bustle and shopping, and the evening at one of the theatres.

Elizabeth then contrived to sit by her aunt. Their first subject was her sister; and she was more grieved than astonished to hear, in reply to her minute enquiries, that though Jane always struggled to support her spirits, there were periods of dejection. It was reasonable, however, to hope, that they would not continue long. Mrs Gardiner gave her the particulars also of Miss Bingley's visit to Gracechurch-street, and repeated conversations occurring at different times between Jane and herself, which proved that the former had, from her heart, given up the acquaintance.

Mrs Gardiner then rallied her niece on Wickham's desertion, and complimented her on bearing it so well.

'But, my dear Elizabeth,' she added, 'what sort of girl is Miss King? I should be sorry indeed to think our friend mercenary.'

'Pray, my dear aunt, what is the difference in matrimonial affairs, between the mercenary and the prudent motive? Where does discretion end, and avarice begin? Last Christmas you were afraid of his marrying me, because it would be imprudent; and now, because he is trying to get a girl with only ten thousand pounds, you want to find out that he is mercenary.'

'If you will only tell me what sort of girl Miss King is, I shall know what to think.'

'She is a very good kind of girl, I believe. I know no harm of her.'

'But he paid her not the smallest attention, till her grandfather's death made her mistress of this fortune.'

'No – why should he? If it was not allowable for him to gain *my* affections, because I had no money, what occasion could there be for making love to a girl whom he did not care about, and who was equally poor?'

'But there seems indelicacy in directing his attentions towards her, so soon after this event.'

'A man in distressed circumstances has not time for all those elegant decorums which other people may observe. If *she* does not object to it, why should *we*?'

'*Her* not objecting does not justify *him*. It only shews her being deficient in something herself – sense or feeling.'

'Well,' cried Elizabeth, 'have it as you choose. *He* shall be mercenary, and *she* shall be foolish.'

'No, Lizzy, that is what I do *not* choose. I should be sorry, you know, to think ill of a young man who has lived so long in Derbyshire.'

'Oh! if that is all, I have a very poor opinion of young men who live in Derbyshire; and their intimate friends who live in Hertfordshire are not much better. I am sick of them all. Thank Heaven! I am going to-morrow where I shall find a man who has not one agreeable quality, who has neither manner nor sense to recommend him. Stupid men are the only ones worth knowing, after all.'

'Take care, Lizzy; that speech savours strongly of disappointment.'

Before they were separated by the conclusion of the play, she had the unexpected happiness of an invitation to accompany her uncle and aunt in a tour of pleasure which they proposed taking in the summer.

'We have not quite determined how far it shall carry us,' said Mrs Gardiner, 'but perhaps to the Lakes.'

No scheme could have been more agreeable to Elizabeth, and her acceptance of the invitation was most ready and grateful. 'My dear, dear aunt,' she rapturously cried, 'what delight! what felicity! You give me fresh life and vigour. Adieu to disappointment and spleen. What are men to rocks and mountains? Oh! what hours of transport we shall spend! And when we *do* return, it shall not be like other travellers, without being able to give one accurate idea of any thing. We *will* know where we have gone – we *will* recollect what we have seen. Lakes, mountains, and rivers, shall not be jumbled together in our imaginations; nor, when we attempt to describe any particular scene, will we begin quarrelling about its relative situation. Let *our* first effusions be less insupportable than those of the generality of travellers.'

CHAPTER TWENTY EIGHT

EVERY OBJECT IN THE NEXT DAY'S journey was new and interesting to Elizabeth; and her spirits were in a state for enjoyment; for she had seen her sister looking so well as to banish all fear for her health, and the prospect of her northern tour was a constant source of delight.

When they left the high road for the lane to Hunsford, every eye was in search of the Parsonage, and every turning expected to bring it in view. The paling of Rosings Park was their boundary on one side. Elizabeth smiled at the recollection of all that she had heard of its inhabitants.

At length the Parsonage was discernible. The garden sloping to the road, the house standing in it, the green pales and the laurel hedge, every thing declared they were arriving. Mr Collins and Charlotte appeared at the door, and the carriage stopped at the small gate, which led by a short gravel walk to the house, amidst the nods and smiles of the whole party. In a moment they were all out of the chaise, rejoicing at the sight of each other. Mrs Collins welcomed her friend with the liveliest pleasure, and Elizabeth was more and more satisfied with coming, when she found herself so affectionately received. She saw instantly that her cousin's manners were not altered by his marriage; his formal civility was just what it had been, and he detained her some minutes at the gate to hear and satisfy his enquiries after all her family. They were then, with no other delay than his pointing out the neatness of the entrance, taken into the house; and as soon as they were in the parlour, he welcomed them a second time with ostentatious formality to his humble abode, and punctually repeated all his wife's offers of refreshment.

Elizabeth was prepared to see him in his glory; and she could not help fancying that in displaying the good proportion of the room, its aspect and its furniture, he addressed himself particularly to her, as if wishing to make her feel what she had lost in refusing him. But though every thing seemed neat and comfortable, she was not able to gratify him by any sigh of repentance; and rather looked with wonder at her friend that she could have so cheerful an air, with such a companion. When Mr Collins said any thing of which his wife might reasonably be ashamed, which certainly was not unseldom, she involuntarily turned her eye on Charlotte. Once or twice she could discern a faint blush; but in general Charlotte wisely did not hear. After sitting long enough to admire every article of furniture in the room, from the sideboard to the fender, to give an account of their journey and of all that had happened in London, Mr Collins invited them to take a stroll in the garden, which was large and well laid out, and to the cultivation of which he attended himself. The work in his garden was one of his most respectable pleasures; and Elizabeth admired the command of countenance with which Charlotte talked of the healthfulness of the exercise, and owned she encouraged it as much as possible. Here, leading the way through every walk and cross walk, and scarcely allowing them an interval to utter the praises he asked for, every view was pointed out with a minuteness which left beauty entirely behind. He could number the fields in every direction and could tell how many trees there were in the most distant clump. But of all the views which his garden, or which the country, or the kingdom could boast, none were to be compared with the prospect of Rosings, afforded by an opening in the trees that bordered the park nearly opposite the front of his house. It was a handsome modern building, well situated on rising ground.

From his garden, Mr Collins would have led them round his two meadows, but the ladies not having shoes to encounter the remains of a white frost, turned back; and while Sir William accompanied him, Charlotte took her sister and friend over the house, extremely well pleased, probably, to have the opportunity of shewing it without her husband's help. It was rather small, but well built and convenient; and every thing was fitted up and arranged with a neatness and consistency of which Elizabeth gave Charlotte all the credit. When Mr Collins could be forgotten, there was really a great air of comfort throughout, and by Charlotte's evident enjoyment of it, Elizabeth supposed he must be often forgotten.

She had already learnt that Lady Catherine was still in the country. It was spoken of again while they were at dinner, when Mr Collins, joining in, observed.

'Yes, Miss Elizabeth, you will have the honour of seeing Lady Catherine de Bourgh on the ensuing Sunday at church, and I need not say you will be delighted with her. She is all affability and condescension, and I doubt not but you will be honoured by some portion of her notice when service is over. I have scarcely any hesitation in saying that she will include you and my sister Maria in every invitation with which she honours us during your stay here. Her behaviour to my dear Charlotte is charming. We dine at Rosings twice every week, and are never allowed to walk home. Her ladyship's carriage is regularly ordered for us. I *should* say, one of her ladyship's carriages, for she has several.'

'Lady Catherine is a very respectable, sensible woman indeed,' added Charlotte, 'and a most attentive neighbour.'

'Very true, my dear, that is exactly what I say. She is the sort of woman whom one cannot regard with too much deference.'

The evening was spent chiefly in talking over Hertfordshire news, and telling again what had been already written; and when it closed, Elizabeth in the solitude of her chamber had to meditate upon Charlotte's degree of contentment, to understand her address in guiding, and composure in bearing with her husband, and to acknowledge that it was all done very well. She had also to anticipate how her visit would pass, the quiet tenor of their usual employments, the vexatious interruptions of Mr Collins, and the gaieties of their intercourse with Rosings. A lively imagination soon settled it all.

About the middle of the next day, as she was in her room getting ready for a walk, a sudden noise below seemed to speak the whole house in confusion; and after listening a moment, she heard somebody running up stairs in a violent hurry, and calling loudly after her. She opened the door,

In conversation with the ladies

and met Maria in the landing place, who, breathless with agitation, cried out,

'Oh, my dear Eliza! pray make haste and come into the dining-room, for there is such a sight to be seen! I will not tell you what it is. Make haste, and come down this moment.'

Elizabeth asked questions in vain; Maria would tell her nothing more, and down they ran into the dining-room, which fronted the lane, in quest of this wonder; it was two ladies stopping in a low phaeton at the garden gate.

'And is that all?' cried Elizabeth, 'I expected at least that the pigs were got into the garden, and here is nothing but Lady Catherine and her daughter!'

'La! my dear,' said Maria quite shocked at the mistake, 'it is not Lady Catherine. The old lady is Mrs Jenkinson, who lives with them. The other is Miss de Bourgh. Only look at her. She is quite a little creature. Who would have thought she could be so thin and small!'

'She is abominably rude to keep Charlotte out of doors in all this wind. Why does she not come in?'

'Oh! Charlotte says, she hardly ever does. It is the greatest of favours when Miss de Bourgh comes in.'

'I like her appearance,' said Elizabeth, struck with other ideas. 'She looks sickly and cross. – Yes, she will do for him very well. She will make him a very proper wife.'

Mr Collins and Charlotte were both standing at the gate in conversation with the ladies; and Sir William to Elizabeth's high diversion, was stationed in the doorway, in earnest contemplation of the greatness before him, and constantly bowing whenever Miss de Bourgh looked that way.

At length there was nothing more to be said; the ladies drove on, and the others returned into the house. Mr Collins no sooner saw the two girls than he began to congratulate them on their good fortune, which Charlotte explained by letting them know that the whole party was asked to dine at Rosings the next day.

'Lady Catherine,' said she, 'you have given me a treasure'

CHAPTER TWENTY NINE

MR COLLINS'S TRIUMPH IN CONSEQUENCE of this invitation was complete. The power of displaying the grandeur of his patroness to his wondering visitors, and of letting them see her civility towards himself and his wife, was exactly what he had wished for; and that an opportunity of doing it should be given so soon, was such an instance of Lady Catherine's condescension as he knew not how to admire enough.

'I confess,' said he, 'that I should not have been at all surprised by her Ladyship's asking us on Sunday to drink tea and spend the evening at Rosings. I rather expected, from my knowledge of her affability, that it would happen. But who could have foreseen such an attention as this? Who could have imagined that we should receive an invitation to dine there (an invitation moreover including the whole party) so immediately after your arrival!'

'I am the less surprised at what has happened,' replied Sir William, 'from that knowledge of what the manners of the great really are, which my situation in life has allowed me to acquire. About the Court, such instances of elegant breeding are not uncommon.'

Scarcely any thing was talked of the whole day or next morning, but their visit to Rosings. Mr Collins was carefully instructing them in what they were to expect, that the sight of such rooms, so many servants, and so splendid a dinner might not wholly overpower them.

When the ladies were separating for the toilette, he said to Elizabeth, 'Do not make yourself uneasy, my dear cousin, about your apparel. Lady Catherine is far from requiring that elegance of dress in us, which becomes herself and daughter. I would advise you merely to put on whatever of your clothes is superior to the rest, there is no occasion for any thing more. Lady Catherine will not think the worse of you for being simply dressed. She likes to have the distinction of rank preserved.'

While they were dressing, he came two or three times to their different doors, to recommend their being quick, as Lady Catherine very much objected to be kept waiting for her dinner. – Such formidable accounts of her Ladyship, and her manner of living, quite frightened Maria Lucas, who had been little used to company, and she looked forward to her introduction at Rosings, with as much apprehension, as her father had done to his presentation at St James's.

As the weather was fine, they had a pleasant walk of about half a mile across the park. – Every park has its beauty and its prospects; and Elizabeth saw much to be pleased with, though she could not be in such raptures as Mr Collins expected the scene to inspire, and was but slightly affected by his enumeration of the windows in front of the house, and his relation of what the glazing altogether had originally cost Sir Lewis de Bourgh.

When they ascended the steps to the hall, Maria's alarm was every moment increasing, and even Sir William did not look perfectly calm. – Elizabeth's courage did not fail her. She had heard nothing of Lady Catherine that spoke her awful from any extraordinary talents or miraculous virtue, and the mere stateliness of money and rank, she thought she could witness without trepidation.

From the entrance hall, of which Mr Collins pointed out, with a rapturous air, the fine proportion and finished ornaments, they followed the servants through an antichamber, to the room where Lady Catherine, her daughter, and Mrs Jenkinson were sitting. – Her ladyship, with great condescension, arose to receive them; and as Mrs Collins had settled it with her husband that the office of introduction should be her's, it was performed in a proper manner, without any of those apologies and thanks which he would have thought necessary.

In spite of having been at St James's, Sir William was so completely awed, by the grandeur surrounding him, that he had but just courage enough to make a very low bow, and take his seat without saying a word; and his daughter, frightened almost out of her senses, sat on the edge of her chair, not knowing which way to look. Elizabeth found herself quite equal to the scene, and could observe the three ladies before her composedly. – Lady

Catherine was a tall, large woman, with strongly-marked features, which might once have been handsome. Her air was not conciliating, nor was her manner of receiving them, such as to make her visitors forget their inferior rank. She was not rendered formidable by silence; but whatever she said, was spoken in so authoritative a tone, as marked her self-importance, and brought Mr Wickham immediately to Elizabeth's mind; and from the observation of the day altogether, she believed Lady Catherine to be exactly what he had represented.

When, after examining the mother, in whose countenance and deportment she soon found some resemblance to Mr Darcy, she turned her eyes on the daughter, she could almost have joined in Maria's astonishment, at her being so thin, and so small. There was neither in figure nor face, any likeness between the ladies. Miss de Bourgh was pale and sickly; her features, though not plain, were insignificant; and she spoke very little, except in a low voice, to Mrs Jenkinson, in whose appearance there was nothing remarkable, and who was entirely engaged in listening to what she said, and placing a screen in the proper direction before her eyes.

After sitting a few minutes, they were all sent to one of the windows, to admire the view, Mr Collins attending them to point out its beauties, and Lady Catherine kindly informing them that it was much better worth looking at in the summer.

The dinner was exceedingly handsome, and there were all the servants, and all the articles of plate which Mr Collins had promised; and, as he had likewise foretold, he took his seat at the bottom of the table, by her ladyship's desire, and looked as if he felt that life could furnish nothing greater. – He carved, and ate, and praised with delighted alacrity; and every dish was commended, first by him, and then by Sir William, who was now enough recovered to echo whatever his son in law said, in a manner which Elizabeth wondered Lady Catherine could bear. But Lady Catherine seemed gratified by their excessive admiration, and gave most gracious smiles, especially when any dish on the table proved a novelty to them. The party did not supply much conversation. Elizabeth was ready to speak whenever there was an opening, but she was seated between Charlotte and Miss de Bourgh – the former of whom was engaged in listening to Lady Catherine, and the latter said not a word to her all dinner time. Mrs Jenkinson was chiefly employed in watching how little Miss de Bourgh ate, pressing her to try some other dish, and fearing she were indisposed. Maria thought speaking out of the question, and the gentlemen did nothing but eat and admire.

When the ladies returned to the drawing room, there was little to be done but to hear Lady Catherine talk, which she did without any intermission till coffee came in, delivering her opinion on every subject in so decisive a manner as proved that she was not used to have her judgment controverted. She enquired into Charlotte's domestic concerns familiarly and minutely, and gave her a great deal of advice, as to the management of them all; told her how every thing ought to be regulated in so small a family as her's, and instructed her as to the care of her cows and her poultry. Elizabeth found that nothing was beneath this great Lady's attention, which could furnish her with an occasion of dictating to others. In the intervals of her discourse with Mrs Collins, she addressed a variety of questions to Maria and Elizabeth, but especially to the latter, of whose connections she knew the least, and who she observed to Mrs Collins, was a very genteel, pretty kind of girl. She asked her at different times, how many sisters she had, whether they were older or younger than herself, whether any of them were likely to be married, whether they were handsome, where they had been educated, what carriage her father kept, and what had been her mother's maiden name? – Elizabeth felt all the impertinence of her questions, but answered them very composedly. – Lady Catherine then observed,

'Your father's estate is entailed on Mr Collins, I think. For your sake,' turning to Charlotte, 'I am glad of it; but otherwise I see no occasion for entailing estates from the female line. – It was not thought necessary in Sir Lewis de Bourgh's family. – Do you play and sing, Miss Bennet?'

'A little.'

'Oh! then – some time or other we shall be happy to hear you. Our instrument is a capable one, probably superior to – You shall try it some day. – Do your sisters play and sing?'

'One of them does.'

'Why did not you all learn? – You ought all to have learned. The Miss Webbs all play, and their father has not so good an income as your's. – Do you draw?'

'No, not at all.'

'What, none of you?'

'Not one.'

'That is very strange. But I suppose you had no opportunity. Your mother should have taken you to town every spring for the benefit of masters.'

'My mother would have had no objection, but my father hates London.'

'Has your governess left you?'

'We never had any governess.'

'No governess! How was that possible? Five daughters brought up at home without a governess! – I never heard of such a thing. Your mother must have been quite a slave to your education.'

Elizabeth could hardly help smiling, as she assured her that had not been the case.

'Then, who taught you? who attended to you? Without a governess you must have been neglected.'

'Compared with some families, I believe we were; but such of us as wished to learn, never wanted the means. We were always encouraged to read, and had all the masters that were necessary. Those who chose to be idle, certainly might.'

'Aye, no doubt; but that is what a governess will prevent, and if I had known your mother, I should have advised her most strenuously to engage one. I always say that nothing is to be done in education without steady and regular instruction, and nobody but a governess can give it. It is wonderful how many families I have been the means of supplying in that way. I am always glad to get a young person well placed out. Four nieces of Mrs Jenkinson are most delightfully situated through my means; and it was but the other day, that I recommended another young person, who was merely acidentally mentioned to me, and the family are quite delighted with her. Mrs Collins, did I tell you of Lady Metcalfe's calling yesterday to thank me? She finds Miss Pope a treasure. "Lady Catherine," said she, "you have given me a treasure." Are any of your younger sisters out, Miss Bennet?'

"Yes, Ma'am, all.'

'All! – What, all five out at once? Very odd! – And you only the second. – The younger ones out before the elder are married! – Your younger sisters must be very young?'

'Yes, my youngest is not sixteen. Perhaps *she* is full young to be much in company. But really, Ma'am, I think it would be very hard upon younger sisters, that they should not have their share of society and amusement because the elder may not have the means or inclination to marry early. – The last born has as good a right to the pleasures of youth, as the first. And to be kept back on *such* a motive! – I think it would not be very likely to promote sisterly affection or delicacy of mind.'

'Upon my word,' said her Ladyship, 'you give your opinion very decidedly for so young a person. – Pray, what is your age?'

'With three younger sisters grown up,' replied Elizabeth smiling, 'your Ladyship can hardly expect me to own it.'

Lady Catherine seemed quite astonished at not receiving a direct answer; and Elizabeth suspected herself to be the first creature who had ever dared to trifle with so much dignified impertinence.

'You cannot be more than twenty, I am sure, – therefore you need not conceal your age.'

'I am not one and twenty.'

When the gentlemen had joined them, and tea was over, the card tables were placed. Lady Catherine, Sir William, and Mr and Mrs Collins sat down to quadrille; and as Miss de Bourgh chose to play at cassino, the two girls had the honour of assisting Mrs Jenkinson to make up her party. Their table was superlatively stupid. Scarcely a syllable was uttered that did not relate to the game, except when Mrs Jenkinson expressed her fears of Miss de Bourgh's being too hot or too cold, or having too much or too little light. A great deal more passed at the other table. Lady Catherine was generally speaking – stating the mistakes of the three others, or relating some anecdote of herself. Mr Collins was employed in agreeing to every thing her Ladyship said, thanking her for every fish he won, and apologising if he thought he won too many. Sir William did not say much. He was storing his memory with anecdotes and noble names.

When Lady Catherine and her daughter had played as long as they chose, the tables were broke up, the carriage was offered to Mrs Collins, gratefully accepted, and immediately ordered. The party then gathered round the fire to hear Lady Catherine determine what weather they were to have on the morrow. From these instructions they were summoned by the arrival of the coach, and with many speeches of thankfulness on Mr Collins's side, and as many bows on Sir William's, they departed. As soon as they had driven from the door, Elizabeth was called on by her cousin, to give her opinion of all that she had seen at Rosings, which, for Charlotte's sake, she made more favourable than it really was. But her commendation, though costing her some trouble, could by no means satisfy Mr Collins, and he was very soon obliged to take her Ladyship's praise into his own hands.

CHAPTER THIRTY

SIR WILLIAM STAID ONLY A WEEK at Hunsford; but his visit was long enough to convince him of his daughter's being most comfortably settled, and of her possessing such a husband and such a neighbour as were not often met with. While Sir William was with them, Mr Collins devoted his mornings to driving him out in his gig, and shewing him the country; but when he went away, the whole family returned to their usual employments, and Elizabeth was thankful to find that they did not see more of her cousin by the alteration, for the chief of the time between breakfast and dinner was now passed by him either at work in the garden, or in reading and writing, and looking out of window in his own book room, which fronted the road. The room in which the ladies sat was backwards. Elizabeth at first had rather wondered that Charlotte should not prefer the dining parlour for common use; it was a better sized room, and had a pleasanter aspect; but she soon saw that her friend had an excellent reason for what she did, for Mr Collins would undoubtedly have been much less in his own apartment, had they sat in one equally lively; and she gave Charlotte credit for the arrangement.

From the drawing room they could distinguish nothing in the lane, and were indebted to Mr Collins for the knowledge of what carriages went along, and how often especially Miss De Bourgh drove by in her phaeton, which he never failed coming to inform them of, though it happened almost every day. She not unfrequently stopped at the Parsonage, and had a few minutes' conversation with Charlotte, but was scarcely ever prevailed on to get out.

Very few days passed in which Mr Collins did not walk to Rosings, and not many in which his wife did not think it necessary to go likewise; and till Elizabeth recollected that there might be other family livings to be disposed of, she could not understand the sacrifice of so many hours. Now and then, they were honoured with a call from her Ladyship, and nothing escaped her observation that was passing in the room during these visits. She examined into their employments, looked at their work, and advised them to do it differently; found fault with the arrangement of the furniture, or detected the housemaid in negligence; and if she accepted any refreshment, seemed to do it only for the sake of finding out that Mrs Collins's joints of meat were too large for her family.

Elizabeth soon perceived that though this great lady was not in the commission of the peace for the county, she was a most active magistrate in her own parish, the minutest concerns of which were carried to her by Mr Collins; and whenever any of the cottagers were disposed to be quarrelsome, discontented or too poor, she sallied forth into the village to settle their differences, silence their complaints, and scold them into harmony and plenty.

The entertainment of dining at Rosings was repeated about twice a week; and, allowing for the loss of Sir William, and there being only one card table in the evening, every such entertainment was the counterpart of

He never failed to inform them

the first. Their other engagements were few; as the style of living of the neighbourhood in general, was beyond the Collinses' reach. This however was no evil to Elizabeth, and upon the whole she spent her time comfortably enough; there were half hours of pleasant conversation with Charlotte, and the weather was so fine for the time of year, that she had often great enjoyment out of doors. Her favourite walk, and where she frequently went while the others were calling on Lady Catherine, was along the open grove which edged that side of the park, where there was a nice sheltered path, which no one seemed to value but herself, and where she felt beyond the reach of Lady Catherine's curiosity.

In this quiet way, the first fortnight of her visit soon passed away. Easter was approaching, and the week preceding it, was to bring an addition to the family at Rosings, which in so small a circle must be important. Elizabeth had heard soon after her arrival, that Mr Darcy was expected there in the course of a few weeks, and though there were not many of her acquaintance whom she did not prefer, his coming would furnish one comparatively new to look at in their Rosings parties, and she might be amused in seeing how hopeless Miss Bingley's designs on him were, by his behaviour to his cousin, for whom he was evidently destined by Lady Catherine; who talked of his coming with the greatest satisfaction, spoke of him in terms of the highest admiration, and seemed almost angry to find that he had already been frequently seen by Miss Lucas and herself.

His arrival was soon known at the Parsonage, for Mr Collins was walking the whole morning within view of the lodges opening into Hunsford Lane, in order to have the earliest assurance of it; and after making his bow as the carriage turned into the Park, hurried home with the great intelligence. On the following morning he hastened to Rosings to pay his respects. There were two nephews of Lady Catherine to require them, for Mr Darcy had brought with him a Colonel Fitzwilliam, the younger son of his uncle, Lord – and to the great surprise of all the party, when Mr Collins returned the gentlemen accompanied him. Charlotte had seen them from her husband's room, crossing the road, and immediately running into the other, told the girls what an honour they might expect, adding,

'I may thank you, Eliza, for this piece of civility. Mr Darcy would never have come so soon to wait upon me.'

Elizabeth had scarcely time to disclaim all right to the compliment, before their approach was announced by the door-bell, and shortly afterwards the three gentlemen entered the room. Colonel Fitzwilliam, who led the way, was about thirty, not handsome, but in person and address most truly the gentleman. Mr Darcy looked just as he had been used to look in Hertfordshire, paid his compliments, with his usual reserve, to Mrs Collins; and whatever might be his feelings towards her friend, met her

The gentlemen accompanied him

with every appearance of composure. Elizabeth merely curtseyed to him, without saying a word.

Colonel Fitzwilliam entered into conversation directly with the readiness and ease of a well-bred man, and talked very pleasantly; but his cousin, after having addressed a slight observation on the house and garden to Mrs Collins, sat for some time without speaking to any body. At length, however, his civility was so far awakened as to enquire of Elizabeth after the health of her family. She answered him in the usual way, and after a moment's pause, added,

'My eldest sister has been in town these three months. Have you never happened to see her there?'

She was perfectly sensible that he never had; but she wished to see whether he would betray any consciousness of what had passed between the Bingleys and Jane; and she thought he looked a little confused as he answered that he had never been so fortunate as to meet Miss Bennet. The subject was pursued no farther, and the gentlemen soon afterwards went away.

CHAPTER THIRTY ONE

COLONEL FITZWILLIAM'S MANNERS WERE very much admired at the parsonage, and the ladies all felt that he must add considerably to the pleasure of their engagements at Rosings. It was some days, however, before they received any invitation thither, for while there were visitors in the house, they could not be necessary; and it was not till Easter-day, almost a week after the gentlemen's arrival, that they were honoured by such an attention, and then they were merely asked on leaving church to come there in the evening. For the last week they had seen very little of either Lady Catherine or her daughter. Colonel Fitzwilliam had called at the parsonage more than once during the time, but Mr Darcy they had only seen at church.

The invitation was accepted of course, and at a proper hour they joined the party in Lady Catherine's drawing room. Her ladyship received them civilly, but it was plain that their company was by no means so acceptable as when she could get nobody else; and she was, in fact, almost engrossed by her nephews, speaking to them, especially to Darcy, much more than to any other person in the room.

Colonel Fitzwilliam seemed really glad to see them; any thing was a welcome relief to him at Rosings; and Mrs Collins's pretty friend had moreover caught his fancy very much. He now seated himself by her, and talked so agreeably of Kent and Hertfordshire, of travelling and staying at home, of new books and music, that Elizabeth had never been half so well entertained in that room before; and they conversed with so much spirit and flow, as to draw the attention of Lady Catherine herself, as well as of Mr Darcy. *His* eyes had been soon and repeatedly turned towards them with a look of curiosity; and that her ladyship after a while shared the feeling, was more openly acknowledged, for she did not scruple to call out,

'What is that you are saying, Fitzwilliam? What is it you are talking of? What are you telling Miss Bennet? Let me hear what it is.'

'We are speaking of music, Madam,' said he, when no longer able to avoid a reply.

'Of music! Then pray speak aloud. It is of all subjects my delight. I must have my share in the conversation, if you are speaking of music. There are few people in England, I suppose, who have more true enjoyment of music than myself, or a better natural taste. If I had ever learnt, I should have been a great proficient. And so would Anne, if her health had allowed her to apply. I am confident that she would have performed delightfully. How does Georgiana get on, Darcy?'

Mr Darcy spoke with affectionate praise of his sister's proficiency.

'I am very glad to hear such a good account of her,' said Lady Catherine; 'and pray tell her from me, that she cannot expect to excel, if she does not practise a great deal.'

'I assure you, Madam,' he replied, 'that she does not need such advice. She practises very constantly.'

'So much the better. It cannot be done too much; and when I next write to her, I shall charge her not to neglect it on any account. I often tell young ladies, that no excellence in music is to be acquired, without constant practice. I have told Miss Bennet several times, that she will never play really well, unless she practises more; and though Mrs Collins has no instrument, she is very welcome, as I have often told her, to come to Rosings every day, and play on the piano-forte in Mrs Jenkinson's room. She would be in nobody's way, you know, in that part of the house.'

Mr Darcy looked a little ashamed of his aunt's ill breeding, and made no answer.

When coffee was over, Colonel Fitzwilliam reminded Elizabeth of having promised to play for him; and she sat down directly to the instrument. He drew a chair near her. Lady Catherine listened to half a song, and then talked, as before, to her other nephew; till the latter walked away from her, and moving with his usual deliberation towards the piano-forte, stationed himself so as to command a full view of the fair performer's countenance. Elizabeth saw what he was doing, and at the first convenient pause, turned to him with arch smile, and said,

'You mean to frighten me, Mr Darcy, by coming in all this state to hear me? But I will not be alarmed though your sister *does* play so well. There is a stubbornness about me that never can bear to be frightened at the will of others. My courage always rises with every attempt to intimidate me.'

'I shall not say that you are mistaken,' he replied, 'because you could not really believe me to entertain any design of alarming you; and I have had the pleasure of your acquaintance long enough to know, that you find great enjoyment in occasionally professing opinions which in fact are not your own.'

Elizabeth laughed heartily at this picture of herself, and said to Colonel Fitzwilliam, 'Your cousin will give you a very pretty notion of me, and teach you not to believe a word I say. I am particularly unlucky in meeting with a person so well able to expose my real character, in a part of the world, where I had hoped to pass myself off with some degree of credit. Indeed, Mr Darcy, it is very ungenerous in you to mention all that you knew to my disadvantage in Hertfordshire – and, give me leave to say, very impolitic too – for it is provoking me to retaliate, and such things may come out, as will shock your relations to hear.'

'I am not afraid of you,' said he, smilingly.

'Pray let me hear what you have to accuse him of,' cried Colonel Fitzwilliam. 'I should like to know how he behaves among strangers.'

'You shall hear then – but prepare yourself for something very dreadful. The first time of my ever seeing him in Hertfordshire, you must know, was at a ball – and at this ball, what do you think he did? He danced only four dances! I am sorry to pain you – but so it was. He danced only four dances, though gentlemen were scarce; and, to my certain knowledge, more than one young lady was sitting down in want of a partner. Mr Darcy, you cannot deny the fact.'

'I had not at that time the honour of knowing any lady in the assembly beyond my own party.'

'True; and nobody can ever be introduced in a ball room. Well, Colonel Fitzwilliam, what do I play next? My fingers wait your orders.'

'Perhaps,' said Darcy, 'I should have judged better, had I sought an introduction, but I am ill qualified to recommend myself to strangers.'

'Shall we ask your cousin the reason of this?' said Elizabeth, still addressing Colonel Fitzwilliam. 'Shall we ask him why a man of sense and education, and who has lived in the world, is ill qualified to recommend himself to strangers?'

'I can answer your question,' said Fitzwilliam, 'without applying to him. It is because he will not give himself the trouble.'

'I certainly have not the talent which some people possess,' said Darcy, 'of conversing easily with those I have never seen before. I cannot catch their tone of conversation, or appear interested in their concerns, as I often see done.'

'My fingers,' said Elizabeth, 'do not move over this instrument in the masterly manner which I see so many women's do. They have not the same force or rapidity, and do not produce the same expression. But then I have always supposed it to be my own fault – because I would not take the trouble of practising. It is not that I do not believe *my* fingers as capable as any other woman's of superior execution.'

Darcy smiled and said, 'You are perfectly right. You have employed your time much better. No one admitted to the privilege of hearing you, can think any thing wanting. We neither of us perform to strangers.'

Here they were interrupted by Lady Catherine, who called out to know what they were talking of. Elizabeth immediately began playing again. Lady Catherine approached, and, after listening for a few minutes, said to Darcy,

'Miss Bennet would not play at all amiss, if she practised more, and could have the advantage of a London master. She has a very good notion of fingering, though her taste is not equal to Anne's. Anne would have been a delightful performer, had her health allowed her to learn.'

Elizabeth looked at Darcy to see how cordially he assented to his cousin's praise; but neither at that moment nor at any other could she discern any symptom of love; and from the whole of his behaviour to Miss de Bourgh she derived this comfort for Miss Bingley, that he might have been just as likely to marry *her*, had she been his relation.

Lady Catherine continued her remarks on Elizabeth's performance, mixing with them many instructions on execution and taste. Elizabeth received them with all the forbearance of civility; and at the request of the gentlemen remained at the instrument till her Ladyship's carriage was ready to take them all home.

CHAPTER THIRTY TWO

ELIZABETH WAS SITTING BY HERSELF the next morning, and writing to Jane, while Mrs Collins and Maria were gone on business into the village, when she was startled by a ring at the door, the certain signal of a visitor. As she had heard no carriage, she thought it not unlikely to be Lady Catherine, and under that apprehension was putting away her half-finished letter that she might escape all impertinent questions, when the door opened, and to her very great surprise, Mr Darcy, and Mr Darcy only, entered the room.

He seemed astonished too on finding her alone, and apologised for his intrusion, by letting her know that he had understood all the ladies to be within.

They then sat down, and when her enquiries after Rosings were made, seemed in danger of sinking into total silence. It was absolutely necessary, therefore, to think of something, and in this emergence recollecting *when* she had seen him last in Hertfordshire, and feeling curious to know what he would say on the subject of their hasty departure, she observed,

'How very suddenly you all quitted Netherfield last November, Mr Darcy! It must have been a most agreeable surprise to Mr Bingley to see you all after him so soon; for, if I recollect right, he went but the day before. He and his sisters were well, I hope, when you left London.'

'Perfectly so – I thank you.'

She found that she was to receive no other answer – and, after a short pause, added,

'I think I have understood that Mr Bingley has not much idea of ever returning to Netherfield again?'

'I have never heard him say so; but it is probable that he may spend very little of his time there in future. He has many friends, and he is at a time of life when friends and engagements are continually increasing.'

'If he means to be but little at Netherfield, it would be better for the neighbourhood that he should give up the place entirely, for then we might possibly get a settled family there. But perhaps Mr Bingley did not take the house so much for the convenience of the neighbourhood as for his own, and we must expect him to keep or quit it on the same principle.'

'I should not be surprised,' said Darcy, 'if he were to give it up, as soon as any eligible purchase offers.'

Elizabeth made no answer. She was afraid of talking longer of his friend; and, having nothing else to say, was now determined to leave the trouble of finding a subject to him.

He took the hint, and soon began with, 'This seems a very comfortable house. Lady Catherine, I believe, did a great deal to it when Mr Collins first came to Hunsford.'

'I believe she did – and I am sure she could not have bestowed her kindness on a more grateful object.'

'Mr Collins appears very fortunate in his choice of a wife.'

'Yes, indeed; his friends may well rejoice in his having met with one of the very few sensible women who would have accepted him, or have made him happy if they had. My friend has an excellent understanding – though I am not certain that I consider her marrying Mr Collins as the wisest thing she ever did. She seems perfectly happy, however, and in a prudential light, it is certainly a very good match for her.'

'It must be very agreeable to her to be settled within so easy a distance of her own family and friends.'

'An easy distance do you call it? It is nearly fifty miles.'

'And what is fifty miles of good road? Little more than half a day's journey. Yes, I call it a *very* easy distance.'

'I should never have considered the distance as one of the *advantages* of the match,' cried Elizabeth. 'I should never have said Mrs Collins was settled *near* her family.'

'It is a proof of your own attachment to Hertfordshire. Any thing beyond the very neighbourhood of Longbourn, I suppose, would appear far.'

As he spoke there was a sort of smile, which Elizabeth fancied she understood; he must be supposing her to be thinking of Jane and Netherfield, and she blushed as she answered,

'I do not mean to say that a woman may not be settled too near her family. The far and the near must be relative, and depend on many varying circumstances. Where there is fortune to make the expence of travelling unimportant, distance becomes no evil. But that is not the case *here*. Mr and Mrs Collins have a comfortable income, but not such a one as will allow of frequent journeys – and I am persuaded my friend would not call herself *near* her family under less than *half* the present distance.'

Mr Darcy drew his chair a little towards her, and said, '*You* cannot have a right to such very strong local attachment. *You* cannot have been always at Longbourn.'

Elizabeth looked surprised. The gentleman experienced some change of feeling; he drew back his chair, took a newspaper from the table, and, glancing over it, said, in a colder voice,

'Are you pleased with Kent?'

A short dialogue on the subject of the country ensued, on either side calm and concise – and soon put an end to by the entrance of Charlotte and her sister, just returned from their walk. The tête-à-tête surprised them. Mr Darcy related the mistake which had occasioned his intruding on Miss Bennet, and after sitting a few minutes longer without saying much to any body, went away.

'What can be the meaning of this!' said Charlotte, as soon as he was gone. 'My dear Eliza he must be in love with you, or he would never have called on us in this familiar way.'

But when Elizabeth told of his silence, it did not seem very likely, even to Charlotte's wishes, to be the case; and after various conjectures, they could at last only suppose his visit to proceed from the difficulty of finding any

Accompanied by their aunt

thing to do, which was the more probable from the time of year. All field sports were over. Within doors there was Lady Catherine, books, and a billiard table, but gentlemen cannot be always within doors; and in the nearness of the Parsonage, or the pleasantness of the walk to it, or of the people who lived in it, the two cousins found a temptation from this period of walking thither almost every day. They called at various times of the morning, sometimes separately, sometimes together, and now and then accompanied by their aunt. It was plain to them all that Colonel Fitzwilliam came because he had pleasure in their society, a persuasion which of course recommended him still more; and Elizabeth was reminded by her own satisfaction in being with him, as well as by his evident admiration of her, of her former favourite George Wickham; and though, in comparing them, she saw there was less captivating softness in Colonel Fitzwilliam's manners, she believed he might have the best informed mind.

But why Mr Darcy came so often to the Parsonage, it was more difficult to understand. It could not be for society, as he frequently sat there ten minutes together without opening his lips; and when he did speak, it seemed the effect of necessity rather than of choice – a sacrifice to propriety, not a pleasure to himself. He seldom appeared really animated. Mrs Collins knew not what to make of him. Colonel Fitzwilliam's occasionally laughing at his stupidity, proved that he was generally different, which her own knowledge of him could not have told her; and as she would have liked to believe this change the effect of love, and the object of that love, her friend Eliza, she sat herself seriously to work to find it out. – She watched him whenever they were at Rosings, and whenever he came to Hunsford; but without much success. He certainly looked at her friend a great deal, but the expression of that look was disputable. It was an earnest, steadfast gaze, but she often doubted whether there were much admiration in it, and sometimes it seemed nothing but absence of mind.

She had once or twice suggested to Elizabeth the possibility of his being partial to her, but Elizabeth always laughed at the idea; and Mrs Collins did not think it right to press the subject, from the danger of raising expectations which might only end in disappointment; for in her opinion it admitted not of a doubt, that all her friend's dislike would vanish, if she could suppose him to be in her power.

In her kind schemes for Elizabeth, she sometimes planned her marrying Colonel Fitzwilliam. He was beyond comparison the pleasantest man; he certainly admired her, and his situation in life was most eligible; but, to counterbalance these advantages, Mr Darcy had considerable patronage in the church, and his cousin could have none at all.

CHAPTER THIRTY THREE

MORE THAN ONCE DID ELIZABETH IN her ramble within the Park, unexpectedly meet Mr Darcy. – She felt all the perverseness of the mischance that should bring him where no one else was brought; and to prevent its ever happening again, took care to inform him at first, that it was a favourite haunt of hers. – How it could occur a second time therefore was very odd! – Yet it did, and even a third. It seemed like wilful ill-nature, or a voluntary penance, for on these occasions it was not merely a few formal enquiries and an awkward pause and then away, but he actually thought it necessary to turn back and walk with her. He never said a great deal, nor did she give herself the trouble of talking or of listening much; but it struck her in the course of their third rencontre that he was asking some odd unconnected questions – about her pleasure in being at Hunsford, her love of solitary walks, and her opinion of Mr and Mrs Collins's happiness; and that in speaking of Rosings and her not perfectly understanding the house, he seemed to expect that whenever she came into Kent again she would be staying *there* too. His words seemed to imply it. Could he have Colonel Fitzwilliam in his thoughts? She supposed, if he meant any thing, he must mean an allusion to what might arise in that quarter. It distressed her a little, and she was quite glad to find herself at the gate in the pales opposite the Parsonage.

She was engaged one day as she walked, in re-perusing Jane's last letter, and dwelling on some passages which proved that Jane had not written in spirits, when, instead of being again surprised by Mr Darcy, she saw on looking up that Colonel Fitzwilliam was meeting her. Putting away the letter immediately and forcing a smile, she said,

'I did not know before that you ever walked this way.'

'I have been making the tour of the Park,' he replied, 'as I generally do every year, and intend to close it with a call at the Parsonage. Are you going much farther?'

'No, I should have turned in a moment.'

And accordingly she did turn, and they walked towards the Parsonage together.

'Do you certainly leave Kent on Saturday?' said she.

'Yes – if Darcy does not put it off again. But I am at his disposal. He arranges the business just as he pleases.'

'And if not able to please himself in the arrangement, he has at least great pleasure in the power of choice. I do not know any body who seems more to enjoy the power of doing what he likes than Mr Darcy.'

'He likes to have his own way very well,' replied Colonel Fitzwilliam. 'But so we all do. It is only that he has better means of having it than many others, because he is rich, and many others are poor. I speak feelingly. A younger son, you know, must be inured to self-denial and dependence.'

'In my opinion, the younger son of an Earl can know very little of either. Now, seriously, what have you ever known of self-denial and dependence? When have you been prevented by want of money from going wherever you chose, or procuring any thing you had a fancy for?'

'These are home questions – and perhaps I cannot say that I have experienced many hardships of that nature. But in matters of greater weight, I may suffer from the want of money. Younger sons cannot marry where they like.'

'Unless where they like women of fortune, which I think they very often do.'

'Our habits of expence make us too dependant, and there are not many in my rank of life who can afford to marry without some attention to money.'

'Is this,' thought Elizabeth, 'meant for me?' and she coloured at the idea; but, recovering herself, said in a lively tone, 'And pray, what is the usual price of an Earl's younger son? Unless the elder brother is very sickly, I suppose you would not ask above fifty thousand pounds.'

He answered her in the same style, and the subject dropped. To interrupt a silence which might make him fancy her affected with what had passed, she soon afterwards said,

'I imagine your cousin brought you down with him chiefly for the sake of having somebody at his disposal. I wonder he does not marry, to secure a lasting convenience of that kind. But, perhaps his sister does as well for the present, and, as she is under his sole care, he may do what he likes with her.'

'No,' said Colonel Fitzwilliam, 'that is an advantage which he must divide with me. I am joined with him in the guardianship of Miss Darcy.'

'Are you, indeed? And pray what sort of guardians do you make? Does your charge give you much trouble? Young ladies of her age, are sometimes a little difficult to manage, and if she has the true Darcy spirit, she may like to have her own way.'

As she spoke, she observed him looking at her earnestly, and the manner in which he immediately asked her why she supposed Miss Darcy likely to give them any uneasiness, convinced her that she had somehow or other got pretty near the truth. She directly replied,

'You need not be frightened. I never heard any harm of her; and I dare say she is one of the most tractable creatures in the world. She is a very great favourite with some ladies of my acquaintance, Mrs Hurst and Miss Bingley. I think I have heard you say that you know them.'

'I know them a little. Their brother is a pleasant gentleman-like man – he is a great friend of Darcy's.'

'Oh! yes,' said Elizabeth drily – 'Mr Darcy is uncommonly kind to Mr Bingley, and takes a prodigious deal of care of him.'

'Care of him! – Yes, I really believe Darcy *does* take care of him in those points where he most wants care. From something that he told me in our journey hither, I have reason to think Bingley very much indebted to him. But I ought to beg his pardon, for I have no right to suppose that Bingley was the person meant. It was all conjecture.'

'What is it you mean?'

'It is a circumstance which Darcy of course would not wish to be generally known, because if it were to get round to the lady's family, it would be an unpleasant thing.'

'You may depend upon my not mentioning it.'

'And remember that I have not much reason for supposing it to be Bingley. What he told me was merely this; that he congratulated himself on having lately saved a friend from the inconveniences of a most imprudent marriage, but without mentioning names or any other particulars, and I only suspected it to be Bingley from believing him the kind of young man to get into a scrape of that sort, and from knowing them to have been together the whole of last summer.'

'Did Mr Darcy give you his reasons for this interference?'

'I understood that there were some very strong objections against the lady.'

'And what arts did he use to separate them?'

'He did not talk to me of his own arts,' said Fitzwilliam smiling. 'He only told me, what I have now told you.'

Elizabeth made no answer, and walked on, her heart swelling with indignation. After watching her a little, Fitzwilliam asked her why she was so thoughtful.

'I am thinking of what you have been telling me,' said she. 'Your cousin's conduct does not suit my feelings. Why was he to be the judge?'

'You are rather disposed to call his interference officious?'

'I do not see what right Mr Darcy had to decide on the propriety of his friend's inclination, or why, upon his own judgment alone, he was to determine and direct in what manner that friend was to be happy.' 'But,' she continued, recollecting herself, 'as we know none of the particulars, it is not fair to condemn him. It is not to be supposed that there was much affection in the case.'

'That is not an unnatural surmise,' said Fitzwilliam, 'but it is lessening the honour of my cousin's triumph very sadly.'

This was spoken jestingly, but it appeared to her so just a picture of Mr Darcy, that she would not trust herself with an answer; and, therefore, abruptly changing the conversation, talked on indifferent matters till they reached the parsonage. There, shut into her own room, as soon as their visitor left them, she could think without interruption of all that she had heard. It was not to be supposed that any other people could be meant than those with whom she was connected. There could not exist in the world *two* men, over whom Mr Darcy could have such boundless influence. That he had been concerned in the measures taken to separate Mr Bingley and Jane, she had never doubted; but she had always attributed to Miss Bingley the principal design and arrangement of them. If his own vanity, however, did not mislead him, *he* was the cause, his pride and caprice were the cause of all that Jane had suffered, and still continued to suffer. He had ruined for a while every hope of happiness for the most affectionate, generous heart in the world; and no one could say how lasting an evil he might have inflicted.

'There were some very strong objections against the lady,' were Colonel Fitzwilliams's words, and these strong objections probably were, her having one uncle who was a country attorney, and another who was in business in London.

'To Jane herself,' she exclaimed, 'there could be possibility of objection. All loveliness and goodness as she is! Her understanding excellent, her mind improved, and her manners captivating. Neither could any thing be urged against my father, who, though with some peculiarities, has abilities which Mr Darcy himself need not disdain, and respectability which he will probably never reach.' When she thought of her mother indeed, her confidence gave way a little, but she would not allow that any objections *there* had material weight with Mr Darcy, whose pride, she was convinced, would receive a deeper wound from the want of importance in his friend's connections, than from their want of sense; and she was quite decided at last, that he had been partly governed by this worst kind of pride, and partly by the wish of retaining Mr Bingley for his sister.

The agitation and tears which the subject occasioned, brought on a headache; and it grew so much worse towards the evening that, added to her unwillingness to see Mr Darcy, it determined her not to attend her counsins to Rosings, where they were engaged to drink tea. Mrs Collins, seeing that she was really unwell, did not press her to go, and as much as possible prevented her husband from pressing her, but Mr Collins could not conceal his apprehension of Lady Catherine's being rather displeased by her staying at home.

CHAPTER THIRTY FOUR

WHEN THEY WERE GONE, ELIZABETH, as if intending to exasperate herself as much as possible against Mr Darcy, chose for her employment the examination of all the letters which Jane had written to her since her being in Kent. They contained no actual complaint, nor was there any revival of past occurrences, or any communication of present suffering. But in all, and in almost every line of each, there was a want of that cheerfulness which had been used to characterize her style, and which, proceeding from the serenity of a mind at ease with itself, and kindly disposed towards every one, had been scarcely ever clouded. Elizabeth noticed every sentence conveying the idea of uneasiness, with an attention which it had hardly received on the first perusal. Mr Darcy's shameful boast of what misery he had been able to inflict, gave her a keener sense of her sister's sufferings. It was some consolation to think that his visit to Rosings was to end on the day after the next, and a still greater, that in less than a fortnight she should herself be with Jane again, and enabled to contribute to the recovery of her spirits, by all that affection could do.

She could not think of Darcy's leaving Kent, without remembering that his cousin was to go with him; but Colonel Fitzwilliam had made it clear that he had no intentions at all, and agreeable as he was, she did not mean to be unhappy about him.

While settling this point, she was suddenly roused by the sound of the door bell, and her spirits were a little fluttered by the idea of its being Colonel Fitzwilliam himself, who had once before called late in the evening, and might now come to enquire particularly after her. But this idea was soon banished, and her spirits were very differently affected, when, to her utter amazement, she saw Mr Darcy walk into the room. In an hurried manner he immediately began an enquiry after her health, imputing his visit to a wish of hearing that she were better. She answered him with cold civility. He sat down a for a few moments, and then getting up walked about the room. Elizabeth was surprised, but said not a word. After a silence of several minutes he came towards her in an agitated manner, and thus began.

'In vain have I struggled. It will not do. My feelings will not be repressed. You must allow me to tell you how ardently I admire and love you.'

Elizabeth's astonishment was beyond expression. She stared, coloured, doubted, and was silent. This he considered sufficient encouragement, and the avowal of all that he felt and had long felt for her, immediately followed. He spoke well, but there were feelings besides those of the heart to be detailed, and he was not more eloquent on the subject of tenderness than of pride. His sense of her inferiority – of its being a degradation – of the family obstacles which judgment had always opposed to inclination, were dwelt on with a warmth which seemed due to the consequence he was wounding, but was very unlikely to recommend his suit.

In spite of her deeply-rooted dislike, she could not be insensible to the compliment of such a man's affection, and though her intentions did not vary for an instant, she was at first sorry for the pain he was to receive; till, roused to resentment by his subsequent language, she lost all compassion in anger. She tried, however, to compose herself to answer him with patience, when he should have done. He concluded with representing to her the strength of that attachment which, in spite of all his endeavours, he had found impossible to conquer; and with expressing his hope that it would now be rewarded by her acceptance of his hand. As he said this, she could easily see that he had no doubt of a favourable answer. He *spoke* of apprehension and anxiety, but his countenance expressed real security. Such a circumstance could only exasperate farther, and when he ceased, the colour rose into her cheeks, and she said.

'In such cases as this, it is, I believe, the established mode to express a sense of obligation for the sentiments avowed, however unequally they may be returned. It is natural that obligation should be felt, and if I could *feel* gratitude, I would now thank you. But I cannot – I have never desired your good opinion, and you have certainly bestowed it most unwillingly. I am sorry to have occasioned pain to any one. It has been most unconsciously done, however, and I hope will be of short duration. The feelings which, you tell me, have long prevented the acknowledgment of your regard, can have little difficulty in overcoming it after this explanation.'

Mr Darcy, who was leaning against the mantel-piece with his eyes fixed on her face, seemed to catch her words with no less resentment than surprise. His complexion became pale with anger, and the disturbance of his mind was visible in every feature. He was struggling for the appearance of composure, and would not open his lips, till he believed himself to have attained it. The pause was to Elizabeth's feelings dreadful. At length, in a voice of forced calmness, he said,

'And this is all the reply which I am to have the honour of expecting! I might, perhaps, wish to be informed why, with so little *endeavour* at civility, I am thus rejected. But it is of small importance.'

'I might as well enquire,' replied she, 'why with so evident a design of offending and insulting me, you chose to tell me that you liked me against your will, against your reason, and even against your character? Was not this some excuse for incivility, if I *was* uncivil? But I have other provocations. You know I have. Had not my own feelings decided against you, had they been indifferent, or had they even been favourable, do you think that any consideration would tempt me to accept the man, who has been the means of ruining, perhaps for ever, the happiness of a most beloved sister?'

As she pronounced these words, Mr Darcy changed colour; but the emotion was short, and he listened without attempting to interrupt her while she continued.

'I have every reason in the world to think ill of you. No motive can excuse the unjust and ungenerous part you acted *there*. You dare not, you cannot deny that you have been the principal, if not the only means of dividing them from each other, of exposing one to the censure of the world for caprice and instability, the other to its derision for disappointed hopes, and involving them both in misery of the acutest kind.'

She paused, and saw with no slight indignation that he was listening with an air which proved him wholly unmoved by any feeling of remorse. He even looked at her with a smile of affected incredulity.

'Can you deny that you have done it?' she repeated.

With assumed tranquillity he then replied, 'I have no wish of denying that I did every thing in my power to separate my friend from your sister, or that I rejoice in my success. Towards *him* I have been kinder than towards myself.'

Elizabeth disdained the appearance of noticing this civil reflection, but its meaning did not escape, nor was it likely to conciliate her.

'But it is not merely this affair,' she continued, 'on which my dislike is founded. Long before it had taken place, my opinion of you was decided. Your character was unfolded in the recital which I received many months ago from Mr Wickham. On this subject, what can you have to say? In what imaginary act of friendship can you here defend yourself? or under what misrepresentation, can you here impose upon others?'

'You take an eager interest in that gentleman's concerns,' said Darcy in a less tranquil tone, and with a heightened colour.

'Who that knows what his misfortunes have been, can help feeling an interest in him?'

'His misfortunes!' repeated Darcy contemptuously; 'yes, his misfortunes have been great indeed.'

'And of your infliction,' cried Elizabeth with energy. 'You have reduced him to his present state of poverty, comparative poverty. You have withheld the advantages, which you must know to have been designed for him. You have deprived the best years of his life, of that independence which was no less his due than his desert. You have done all this! and yet you can treat the mention of his misfortunes with contempt and ridicule.'

'And this,' cried Darcy, as he walked with quick steps across the room, 'is your opinion of me! This is the estimation in which you hold me! I thank you for explaining it so fully. My faults, according to this calculation, are heavy indeed! But perhaps,' added he, stopping in his walk, and turning towards her, 'these offences might have been overlooked, had not your pride been hurt by my honest confession of the scruples that had long prevented my forming any serious design. These bitter accusations might have been suppressed, had I with greater policy concealed my struggles, and flattered you into the belief of my being impelled by unqualified, unalloyed inclination; by reason, by reflection, by every thing. But disguise of every sort is my abhorrence. Nor am I ashamed of the feelings I related. They were natural and just. Could you expect me to rejoice in the inferiority of your connections? To congratulate myself on the hope of relations, whose condition in life is so decidedly beneath my own?'

Elizabeth felt herself growing more angry every moment; yet she tried to the utmost to speak with composure when she said,

'You are mistaken, Mr Darcy, if you suppose that the mode of your declaration affected me in any other way, than as it spared me the concern which I might have felt in refusing you, had you behaved in a more gentleman-like manner.'

She saw him start at this, but he said nothing, and she continued,

'You could not have made me the offer of your hand in any possible way that would have tempted me to accept it.'

Again his astonishment was obvious; and he looked at her with an expression of mingled incredulity and mortification. She went on.

'From the very beginning, from the first moment I may almost say, of my acquaintance with you, your manners impressing me with the fullest belief of your arrogance, your conceit, and your selfish disdain of the feelings of others, were such as to form that ground-work of disapprobation, on which succeeding events have built so immovable a dislike; and I had not known you a month before I felt that you were the last man in the world whom I could ever be prevailed on to marry.'

'You have said quite enough, madam. I perfectly comprehend your feelings, and have now only to be ashamed of what my own have been. Forgive me for having taken up so much of your time, and accept my best wishes for your health and happiness.' And with these words he hastily left the room, and Elizabeth heard him the next moment open the front door and quit the house.

The tumult of her mind was now painfully great. She knew not how to support herself, and from actual weakness sat down and cried for half an hour. Her astonishment, as she reflected on what had passed, was increased by every review of it. That she should receive an offer of marriage from Mr Darcy! that he should have been in love with her for so many months! so much in love as to wish to marry her in spite of all the objections which had made him prevent his friend's marrying her sister, and which must appear at least with equal force in his own case, was almost incredible! it was gratifying to have inspired unconsciously so strong an affection. But his pride, his abominable pride, his shameless avowal of what he had done with respect to Jane, his unpardonable assurance in acknowledging, though he could not justify it, and the unfeeling manner in which he had mentioned Mr Wickham, his cruelty towards whom he had not attempted to deny, soon overcame the pity which the consideration of his attachment had for a moment excited.

She continued in very agitating reflections till the sound of Lady Catherine's carriage made her feel how unequal she was to encounter Charlotte's observation, and hurried her away to her room.

CHAPTER THIRTY FIVE

ELIZABETH AWOKE THE NEXT MORNING to the same thoughts and meditations which had at length closed her eyes. She could not yet recover from the surprise of what had happened; it was impossible to think of any thing else, and totally indisposed for employment, she resolved soon after breakfast to indulge herself in air and exercise. She was proceeding directly to her favourite walk, when the recollection of Mr Darcy's sometimes coming there stopped her, and instead of entering the park, she turned up the lane, which led her farther from the turnpike road. The park paling was still the boundary on one side, and she soon passed one of the gates into the ground.

After walking two or three times along that part of the lane, she was tempted, by the pleasantness of the morning, to stop at the gates and look into the park. The five weeks which she had now passed in Kent, had made a great difference in the country, and every day was adding to the verdure of the early trees. She was on the point of continuing her walk, when she caught a glimpse of a gentleman within the sort of grove which edged the park; he was moving that way; and fearful of its being Mr Darcy, she was directly retreating. But the person who advanced, was now near enough to see her, and stepping forward with eagerness, pronounced her name. She had turned away, but on hearing herself called, though in a voice which proved it to be Mr Darcy, she moved again towards the gate. He had by that time reached it also, and holding out a letter, which she instinctively took, said with a look of haughty composure, 'I have been walking in the grove some time in the hope of meeting you. Will you do me the honour of reading that letter? – And then, with a slight bow, turned again into the plantation, and was soon out of sight.

With no expectation of pleasure, but with the strongest curiosity, Elizabeth opened the letter, and to her still increasing wonder, perceived an envelope containing two sheets of letter paper, written quite through, in a very close hand. – The envelope itself was likewise full. – Pursuing her way along the lane, she then began it. It was dated from Rosings, at eight o'clock in the morning, and was as follows: –

Be not alarmed, Madam, on receiving this letter, by the apprehension of its containing any repetition of those sentiments, or renewal of those offers, which were last night so disgusting to you. I write without any intention of paining you, or humbling myself, by dwelling on wishes, which, for the happiness of both, cannot be too soon forgotten; and the effort which the formation, and the perusal of this letter must occasion, should have been spared, had not my character required it to be written and read. You must, therefore, pardon the freedom with which I demand your attention; your feelings, I know, will bestow it unwillingly, but I demand it of your justice.

Two offences of a very different nature, and by no means of equal magnitude, you last night laid to my charge. The first mentioned was that, regardless of the sentiments of either, I had detached Mr Bingley from your sister, – and the other, that I had, in defiance of various claims, in defiance of honour and humanity, ruined the immediate prosperity, and blasted the prospects of Mr Wickham. – Wilfully and wantonly to have thrown off the companion of my youth, the acknowledged favourite of my father, a young man who had scarcely any other dependence than on our patronage, and who had been brought up to expect its exertion, would be a depravity, to which the separation of two young persons, whose affection could be the growth of only a few weeks, could bear no comparison. – But from the severity of that blame which was last night so liberally bestowed, respecting each circumstance, I shall hope to be in future secured, when the following account of my actions and their motives has been read. – If, in the explanation of them which is due to myself, I am under the necessity of relating feelings which may be offensive to your's, I can only say that I am sorry. – The necessity must be obeyed – and farther apology would be absurd. – I had not been long in Hertfordshire, before I saw, in common with others, that Bingley preferred your eldest sister, to any other young woman in the country. – But it was not till the evening of the dance at Netherfield that I had any apprehension of his feeling a serious attachment. – I had often seen him in love before. – At that ball, while I had the honour of dancing with you, I was first made acquainted, by Sir William Lucas's accidental information, that Bingley's attentions to your sister had given rise to a general expectation of their marriage. He spoke of it as a certain event, of which the time alone could be undecided. From that moment I observed my friend's behaviour attentively; and I could then perceive that his partiality for Miss Bennet was beyond what I had ever witnessed in him. Your sister I also watched. – Her look and manners were open, cheerful and engaging as ever, but without any symptom of peculiar regard, and I remained convinced from the evening's scrutiny, that though she received his attentions with pleasure, she did not invite them by any participation of sentiment. – If you have not been mistaken here, I must have been in an error. Your superior knowledge of your sister must make the latter probable. – If it be so, if I have been misled by such error, to inflict pain on her, your resentment has not been unreasonable. But I shall not scruple to assert, that the serenity of your sister's countenance and air was such, as might have given the most acute observer, a conviction that, however amiable her temper, her heart was not likely to be easily touched. – That I was desirous of believing her indifferent is certain, – but I will venture to say that my investigations and decisions are not usually influenced by my hopes or fears. – I did not believe her to be indifferent because I wished it; – I believed it on impartial conviction, as truly as I wished it in reason. – My objections to the marriage were not merely those, which I last night acknowledged to have required the utmost force of passion to put aside, in my own case; the want of connection could not be so great an evil to my friend as to me. – But there were other causes of repugnance; – causes which, though still existing, and existing to an equal degree in both instances, I had myself endeavoured to forget, because they were not immediately before me. – These causes must be stated, though briefly. – The situation of your mother's family, though objectionable, was nothing in comparison of that total want of propriety so frequently, so almost uniformly betrayed by herself, by your three younger sisters, and occasionally even by your father. – Pardon me. – It pains me to offend you. But amidst your concern for the defects of your nearest relations, and your displeasure at this representation of them, let it give you consolation to consider that, to have conducted yourselves so as to avoid any share of the like censure, is praise no less generally bestowed on you and your eldest sister, than it is honourable to the sense and disposition of both. – I will only say farther, that from what passed that evening, my opinion of all parties was confirmed, and every inducement heightened, which could have led me before, to preserve my friend from what I esteemed a most unhappy connection. – He left Netherfield for London, on the day following, as you, I am certain, remember, with the design of soon returning. – The part which I acted, is now to be explained. – His sisters' uneasiness had been equally excited with my own; our coincidence of feeling was soon discovered; and, alike sensible that no time was to be lost in detaching their brother, we shortly resolved on joining him directly in London. – We accordingly went – and there I readily engaged in the office of pointing out to my friend, the certain evils of such a choice. – I described, and enforced them earnestly. – But, however, this remonstrance might have staggered or delayed his determination, I do not suppose that it would ultimately have prevented the marriage, had it not been seconded by the assurance which I hesitated not in giving, of your sister's indifference. He had before believed her to return his affection with sincere, if not with equal regard. – But Bingley has great natural modesty, with a stronger dependence on my judgment than on his own. – To convince him, therefore, that he had deceived himself, was no very difficult point. To persuade him against returning into Hertfordshire, when that conviction had been given, was scarcely the work of a moment. – I cannot blame myself for having done thus much. There is but one part of my conduct in the whole affair, on which I do not reflect with satisfaction; it is that I condescended to adopt the measures of art so far as to conceal from him your sister's being in town. I knew it myself, as it was known to Miss Bingley, but her brother is even yet ignorant of it. – That they might have met without ill consequence, is perhaps probable; – but his regard did not appear to me enough extinguished for him to see her without some danger. – Perhaps this concealment, this disguise, was beneath me. – It is done, however, and it was done for the best. – On this subject I have nothing more to say, no other apology to offer. If I have wounded your sister's feelings, it was unknowingly done; and though the motives which governed me may to you very naturally appear insufficient, I have not yet learnt to condemn them. – With respect to that other, more weighty accusation, of having injured Mr Wickham, I can only refute it by laying before you the whole of his connection with my family.

Of what he has particularly *accused me I am ignorant; but of the truth of what I shall relate, I can summon more than one witness of undoubted veracity. Mr Wickham is the son of a very respectable man, who had for many years the management of all the Pemberley estates; and whose good conduct in the discharge of his trust, naturally inclined my father to be of service to him, and on George Wickham, who was his god-son, his kindness was therefore liberally bestowed. My father supported him at school, and afterwards at Cambridge; – most important assistance, as his own father, always poor from the extravagance of his wife, would have been unable to give him a gentleman's education. My father was not only fond of this young man's society, whose manners were always engaging; he had also the highest opinion of him, and hoping the church would be his profession, intended to provide for him in it. As for myself, it is many, many years since I first began to think of him in a very different manner. The vicious propensities – the want of principle which he was careful to guard from the knowledge of his best friend, could not escape the observation of a young man of nearly the same age with himself, and who had opportunities of seeing him in unguarded moments, which Mr Darcy could not have. Here again I shall give you pain – to what degree you only can tell. But whatever may be the sentiments which Mr Wickham has created, a suspicion of their nature shall not prevent me from unfolding his real character. It adds even another motive. My excellent father died about five years ago; and his attachment to Mr Wickham was to the last so steady, that in his will he particularly recommended it to me, to promote his advancement in the best manner that his profession might allow, and if he took orders, desired that a valuable family living might be his as soon as it became vacant. There was also a legacy of one thousand pounds. His own father did not long survive mine, and within half a year from these events, Mr Wickham wrote to inform me that, having finally resolved against taking orders, he hoped I should not think it unreasonable for him to expect some more immediate pecuniary advantage, in lieu of the preferment, by which he could not be benefited. He had some intention, he added, of studying the law, and I must be aware that the interest of one thousand pounds would be a very insufficient support therein. I rather wished, than believed him to be sincere; but at any rate, was perfectly ready to accede to his proposal. I knew that Mr Wickham ought not to be a clergyman. The business was therefore soon settled. He resigned all claim to assistance in the church, were it possible that he could ever be in a situation to receive it, and accepted in return three thousand pounds. All connection between us seemed now dissolved. I thought too ill of him, to invite him to Pemberley, or admit his society in town. In town I believe he chiefly lived, but his studying the law was a mere pretence, and being now free from all restraint, his life was a life of idleness and dissipation. For about three years I heard little of him; but on the decease of the incumbent of the living which had been designed for him, he applied to me again by letter for the presentation. His circumstances, he assured me, and I had no difficulty in believing it, were exceedingly bad. He had found the law a most unprofitable study, and was now absolutely resolved on being ordained, if I would present him to the living in question – of which he trusted there could be little doubt, as he was well assured that I had no other person to provide for, and I could not have forgotten my revered father's intentions. You will hardly blame me for refusing to comply with this entreaty, or for resisting every repetition of it. His resentment was in proportion to the distress of his circumstances – and he was doubtless as violent in his abuse of me to others, as in his reproaches to myself. After this period, every appearance of acquaintance was dropt. How he lived I know not. But last summer he was again most painfully obtruded on my notice. I must now mention a circumstance which I would wish to forget myself, and which no obligation less than the present should induce me to unfold to any human being. Having said thus much, I feel no doubt of your secrecy. My sister, who is more than ten years my junior, was left to the guardianship of my mother's nephew, Colonel Fitzwilliam, and myself. About a year ago, she was taken from school, and an establishment formed for her in London; and last summer she went with the lady who presided over it, to Ramsgate; and thither also went Mr Wickham, undoubtedly by design; for there proved to have been a prior acquaintance between him and Mrs Younge, in whose character we were most unhappily deceived; and by her connivance and aid, he so far recommended himself to Georgiana, whose affectionate heart retained a strong impression of his kindness to her as a child, that she was persuaded to believe herself in love, and to consent to an elopement. She was then but fifteen, which must be her excuse and after stating her imprudence, I am happy to add, that I owed the knowledge of it to herself. I joined them unexpectedly a day or two before the intended elopement, and then Georgiana, unable to support the idea of grieving and offending a brother whom she almost looked up to as a father, acknowledged the whole to me. You may imagine what I felt and how I acted. Regard for my sister's credit and feelings prevented any public exposure, but I wrote to Mr Wickham, who left the place immediately, and Mrs Younge was of course removed from her charge. Mr Wickham's chief object was unquestionably my sister's fortune, which is thirty thousand pounds; but I cannot help supposing that the hope of revenging himself on me, was a strong inducement. His revenge would have been complete indeed. This, madam, is a faithful narrative of every event in which we have been concerned together; and if you do not absolutely reject it as false, you will, I hope, acquit me henceforth of cruelty towards Mr Wickham. I know not in what manner, under what form of falsehood he has imposed on you; but his success is not perhaps to be wondered at, ignorant as you previously were of every thing concerning either. Detection could not be in your power, and suspicion certainly not in your inclination. You may possibly wonder why all this was not told you last night. But I was not then master enough of myself to know what could or ought to be revealed. For the truth of every thing here related, I can appeal more particularly to the testimony of Colonel Fitzwilliam, who from our near relationship and constant intimacy, and still more as one of the executors of my father's will, has been unavoidably acquainted with every particular of these transactions. If your abhorrence of* me *should make* my *assertions valueless, you cannot be prevented by the same cause from confiding in my cousin; and that there may be the possibility of consulting him, I shall endeavour to find some opportunity of putting this letter in your hands in the course of the morning. I will only add, God bless you.*

FITZWILLIAM DARCY.

CHAPTER THIRTY SIX

IF ELIZABETH, WHEN MR DARCY GAVE her the letter, did not expect it to contain a renewal of his offers, she had formed no expectation at all of its contents. But such as they were, it may be well supposed how eagerly she went through them, and what a contrariety of emotion they excited. Her feelings as she read were scarcely to be defined. With amazement did she first understand that he believed any apology to be in his power; and steadfastly was she persuaded that he could have no explanation to give, which a just sense of shame would not conceal. With a strong prejudice against every thing he might say, she began his account of what had happened at Netherfield. She read, with an eagerness which hardly left her power of comprehension, and from impatience of knowing what the next sentence might bring, was incapable of attending to the sense of the one before her eyes. His belief of her sister's insensibility, she instantly resolved to be false, and his account of the real, the worst objections to the match, made her too angry to have any wish of doing him justice. He expressed no regret for what he had done which satisfied her; his style was not penitent, but haughty. It was all pride and insolence.

But when this subject was succeeded by his account of Mr Wickham, when she read with somewhat clearer attention, a relation of events, which, if true, must overthrow every cherished opinion of his worth, and which bore so alarming an affinity to his own history of himself, her feelings were yet more acutely painful and more difficult of definition. Astonishment, apprehension, and even horror, oppressed her. She wished to discredit it entirely, repeatedly exclaiming, 'This must be false! This cannot be! This must be the grossest falsehood!' – and when she had gone through the whole letter, though scarcely knowing any thing of the last page or two, put it hastily away, protesting that she would not regard it, that she would never look in it again.

In this perturbed state of mind, with thoughts that could rest on nothing, she walked on; but it would not do; in half a minute the letter was unfolded again, and collecting herself as well as she could, she again began the mortifying perusal of all that related to Wickham, and commanded herself so far as to examine the meaning of every sentence. The account of his connection with the Pemberley family, was exactly what he had related himself; and the kindness of the late Mr Darcy, though she had not before known its extent, agreed equally well with his own words. So far each recital confirmed the other: but when she came to the will, the difference was great. What Wickham had said of the living was fresh in her memory, and as she recalled his very words, it was impossible not to feel that there was gross duplicity on one side or the other; and, for a few moments, she flattered herself that her wishes did not err. But when she read, and re-read with the closest attention, the particulars immediately following of Wickham's resigning all pretensions to the living, of his receiving in lieu, so considerable a sum as three thousand pounds, again was she forced to hesitate. She put down the letter, weighed every circumstance with what she meant to be impartiality – deliberated on the probability of each statement – but with little success. On both sides it was only assertion. Again she read on. But every line proved more clearly that the affair, which she had believed it impossible that any contrivance could so represent, as to render Mr Darcy's conduct in it less than infamous, was capable of a turn which must make him entirely blameless throughout the whole.

The extravagance and general profligacy which he scrupled not to lay to Mr Wickham's charge, exceedingly shocked her; the more so, as she could bring no proof of its injustice. She had never heard of him before his entrance into the –shire Militia, in which he had engaged at the persuasion of the young man, who, on meeting him accidentally in town, had there renewed a slight acquaintance. Of his former way of life, nothing had been known in Hertfordshire but what he told himself. As to his real character, had information been in her power, she had never felt a wish of enquiring. His countenance, voice, and manner, had established him at once in the possession of every virtue. She tried to recollect some instance of goodness, some distinguished trait of integrity or benevolence, that might rescue him from the attacks of Mr Darcy; or at least, by the predominance of virtue, atone for those casual errors, under which she would endeavour to class, what Mr Darcy had described as the idleness and vice of many years continuance. But no such recollection befriended her. She could see him instantly before her, in every charm of air and address; but she could remember no more substantial good than the general approbation of the neighbourhood, and the regard which his social powers had gained him in the mess. After pausing on this point a considerable while, she once more continued to read. But, alas! the story which followed of his designs on Miss Darcy, received some confirmation from what had passed between Colonel Fitzwilliam and herself only the morning before; and at last she was referred for the truth of every particular to Colonel Fitzwilliam himself – from whom she had previously received the information of his near concern in all his cousin's affairs, and whose character she had no reason to question. At one time she had almost resolved on applying to him, but the idea was checked by the awkwardness of the application, and at length wholly banished by the conviction that Mr Darcy would never have hazarded such a proposal, if he had not been well assured of his cousin's corroboration.

She perfectly remembered every thing that had passed in conversation between Wickham and herself, in their first evening at Mr Philip's. Many of his expressions were still fresh in her memory. She was *now* struck with the impropriety of such communications to a stranger, and wondered it had escaped her before. She saw the indelicacy of putting himself forward as he had done, and the inconsistency of his professions with his conduct. She remembered that he had boasted of having no fear of seeing Mr Darcy – that Mr Darcy might leave the country, but that *he* should stand his ground; yet he had avoided the Netherfield ball the very next week. She remembered

Meeting accidentally in town

also, that till the Netherfield family had quitted the country, he had told his story to no one but herself; but that after their removal, it had been every where discussed; that he had then no reserves, no scruples in sinking Mr Darcy's character, though he had assured her that respect for the father, would always prevent his exposing the son.

How differently did every thing now appear in which he was concerned! His attentions to Miss King were now the consequence of views solely and hatefully mercenary; and the mediocrity of her fortune proved no longer the moderation of his wishes, but his eagerness to grasp at any thing. His behaviour to herself could now have had no tolerable motive; he had either been deceived with regard to her fortune, or had been gratifying his vanity by encouraging the preference which she believed she had most incautiously shewn. Every lingering struggle in his favour grew fainter and fainter; and in farther justification of Mr Darcy, she could not but allow that Mr Bingley, when questioned by Jane, had long ago asserted his blamelessness in the affair; that proud and repulsive as were his manners, she had never, in the whole course of their acquaintance, an acquaintance which had latterly brought them much together, and given her a sort of intimacy with his ways, seen any thing that betrayed him to be unprincipled or unjust – any thing that spoke him of irreligious or immoral habits. That among his own connections he was esteemed and valued – that even Wickham had allowed him merit as a brother, and that she had often heard him speak so affectionately of his sister as to prove him capable of *some* amiable feeling. That had his actions been what Wickham represented them, so gross a violation of every thing right could hardly have been concealed from the world; and that friendship between a person capable of it, and such an amiable man as Mr Bingley, was incomprehensible.

She grew absolutely ashamed of herself. – Of neither Darcy nor Wickham could she think, without feeling that she had been blind, partial, prejudiced, absurd.

'How despicably have I acted!' she cried. – 'I, who have prided myself on my discernment! – I, who have valued myself on my abilities! who have often disdained the generous candour of my sister, and gratified my vanity, in useless or blameable distrust. – How humiliating is this discovery! – Yet, how just a humiliation! – Had I been in love, I could not have been more wretchedly blind. But vanity, not love, has been my folly. – Pleased with the preference of one, and offended by the neglect of the other, on the very beginning of our acquaintance, I have courted prepossession and ignorance, and driven reason away, where either were concerned. Till this moment, I never knew myself.'

From herself to Jane – from Jane to Bingley, her thoughts were in a line which soon brought to her recollection that Mr Darcy's explanation *there*, had appeared very insufficient; and she read it again. Widely different was the effect of a second perusal. – How could she deny that credit to his assertions, in one instance, which she had been obliged to give in the other? – He declared himself to have been totally unsuspicious of her sister's attachment; – and she could not help remembering what Charlotte's opinion had always been. – Neither could she deny the justice of his description of Jane. – She felt that Jane's feelings, though fervent, were little displayed, and that there was a constant complacency in her air and manner, not often united with great sensibility.

When she came to that part of the letter in which her family were mentioned, in terms of such mortifying, yet merited reproach, her sense of shame was severe. The justice of the charge struck her too forcibly for denial, and the circumstances to which he particularly alluded, as having passed at the Netherfield ball, and as confirming all his first disapprobation, could not have made a stronger impression on his mind than on hers.

The compliment to herself and her sister, was not unfelt. It soothed, but it could not console her for the contempt which had been thus self-attracted by the rest of her family; – and as she considered that Jane's disappointment had in fact been the work of her nearest relations, and reflected how materially the credit of both must be hurt by such impropriety of conduct, she felt depressed beyond any thing she had ever known before.

After wandering along the lane for two hours, giving way to every variety of thought; re-considering events, determining probabilities, and reconciling herself as well as she could, to a change so sudden and so important, fatigue, and a recollection of her long absence, made her at length return home; and she entered the house with the wish of appearing cheerful as usual, and the resolution of repressing such reflections as must make her unfit for conversation.

She was immediately told, that the two gentlemen from Rosings had each called during her absence; Mr Darcy, only for a few minutes to take leave, but that Colonel Fitzwilliam had been sitting with them at least an hour, hoping for her return, and almost resolving to walk after her till she could be found. – Elizabeth could but just *affect* concern in missing him; she really rejoiced at it. Colonel Fitzwilliam was no longer an object. She could think only of her letter.

His parting obeisance

CHAPTER THIRTY SEVEN

THE TWO GENTLEMEN LEFT ROSINGS the next morning; and Mr Collins having been in waiting near the lodges, to make them his parting obeisance, was able to bring home the pleasing intelligence, of their appearing in very good health, and in as tolerable spirits as could be expected, after the melancholy scene so lately gone through at Rosings. To Rosings he then hastened to console Lady Catherine, and her daughter; and on his return, brought back, with great satisfaction, a message from her Ladyship, importing that she felt herself so dull as to make her very desirous of having them all to dine with her.

Elizabeth could not see Lady Catherine without recollecting, that had she chosen it, she might by this time have been presented to her, as her future niece; nor could she think, without a smile, of what her ladyship's indignation would have been. 'What would she have said? – how would she have behaved?' were questions with which she amused herself.

Their first subject was the diminution of the Rosings party. – 'I assure you, I feel it exceedingly,' said Lady Catherine; 'I believe nobody feels the loss of friends so much as I do. But I am particularly attached to these young men; and know them to be so much attached to me! – They were excessively sorry to go! But so they always are. The dear colonel rallied his spirits tolerably till just at last; but Darcy seemed to feel it most acutely, more I think than last year. His attachment to Rosings, certainly increases.'

Mr Collins had a compliment, and an allusion to throw in here, which were kindly smiled on by the mother and daughter.

Lady Catherine observed, after dinner, that Miss Bennet seemed out of spirits, and immediately accounting for it herself, by supposing that she did not like to go home again so soon, she added,

'But if that is the case, you must write to your mother to beg that you may stay a little longer. Mrs Collins will be very glad of your company, I am sure.'

'I am much obliged to your ladyship for your kind invitation,' replied Elizabeth, 'but it is not in my power to accept it. – I must be in town next Saturday.'

'Why, at that rate, you will have been here only six weeks. I expected you to stay two months. I told Mrs Collins so before you came. There can be no occasion for your going so soon. Mrs Bennet could certainly spare you for another fortnight.'

Dawson

'But my father cannot. – He wrote last week to hurry my return.'

'Oh! your father of course may spare you, if your mother can. – Daughters are never of so much consequence to a father. And if you will stay another *month* complete, it will be in my power to take one of you as far as London, for I am going there early in June, for a week; and as Dawson does not object to the Barouche box, there will be very good room for one of you – and indeed, if the weather should happen to be cool, I should not object to taking you both, as you are neither of you large.'

'You are all kindness, Madam; but I believe we must abide by our original plan.'

Lady Catherine seemed resigned.

'Mrs Collins, you must send a servant with them. You know I always speak my mind, and I cannot bear the idea of two young women travelling post by themselves. It is highly improper. You must contrive to send somebody. I have the greatest dislike in the world to that sort of thing. – Young women should always be properly guarded and attended, according to their situation in life. When my niece Georgiana went to Ramsgate last summer, I made a point of her having two men servants go with her. – Miss Darcy, the daughter of Mr Darcy, of Pemberley, and Lady Anne, could not have appeared with propriety in a different manner. – I am excessively attentive to all those things. You must send John with the young ladies, Mrs Collins. I am glad it occurred to me to mention it; for it would really be discreditable to *you* to let them go alone.'

'My uncle is to send a servant for us.'

'Oh! – Your uncle! – He keeps a man-servant, does he? – I am very glad you have somebody who thinks of those things. Where shall you change horses? – Oh! Bromley, of course.– If you mention my name at the Bell, you will be attended to.'

Lady Catherine had many other questions to ask respecting their journey, and as she did not answer them all herself, attention was necessary, which Elizabeth believed to be lucky for her; or, with a mind so occupied, she might have forgotten where she was. Reflection must be reserved for solitary hours; whenever she was alone, she gave way to it as the greatest relief; and not a day went by without a solitary walk, in which she might indulge in all the delight of unpleasant recollections.

Mr Darcy's letter, she was in a fair way of soon knowing by heart. She studied every sentence: and her feelings towards its writer were at times widely different. When she remembered the style of his address, she was still full of indignation; but when she considered how unjustly she had condemned and upbraided him, her anger was turned against herself; and his disappointed feelings became the object of compassion. His attachment excited gratitude, his general character respect; but she could not approve him; nor could she for a moment repent her refusal, or feel the slightest inclination ever to see him again. In her own past behaviour, there was a constant source of vexation and regret; and in the unhappy defects of her family a subject of yet heavier chagrin. They were hopeless of remedy. Her father, contented with laughing at them, would never exert himself to restrain the wild giddiness of his youngest daughters; and her mother, with manners so far from right herself, was entirely insensible of the evil. Elizabeth had frequently united with Jane in an endeavour to check the imprudence of Catherine and Lydia; but while they were supported by their mother's indulgence, what chance could there be of improvement? Catherine, weak-spirited, irritable, and completely under Lydia's guidance, had been always affronted by their advice; and Lydia, self-willed and careless, would scarcely give them a hearing. They were ignorant, idle, and vain. While there was an officer in Meryton, they would flirt with him; and while Meryton was within a walk of Longbourn, they would be going there for ever.

Anxiety on Jane's behalf, was another prevailing concern, and Mr Darcy's explanation, by restoring Bingley to all her former good opinion, heightened the sense of what Jane had lost. His affection was proved to have been sincere, and his conduct cleared of all blame, unless any could attach to the implicitness of his confidence in his friend. How grievous then was the thought that, of a situation so desirable in every respect, so replete with advantage, so promising for happiness, Jane had been deprived, by the folly and indecorum of her own family!

When to these recollections was added the development of Wickham's character, it may be easily believed that the happy spirits which had seldom been depressed before, were now so much affected as to make it almost impossible for her to appear tolerably cheerful.

Their engagements at Rosings were as frequent during the last week of her stay, as they had been at first. The very last evening was spent there; and her Ladyship again enquired minutely into the particulars of their journey, gave them directions as to the best methods of packing, and was so urgent on the necessity of placing gowns in the only right way, that Maria thought herself obliged, on her return, to undo all the work of the morning, and pack her trunk afresh.

When they parted, Lady Catherine, with great condescension, wished them a good journey, and invited them to come to Hunsford again next year; and Miss de Bourgh exerted herself so far as to curtsey and hold out her hand to both.

The elevation of his feelings

CHAPTER THIRTY EIGHT

ON SATURDAY MORNING ELIZABETH and Mr Collins met for breakfast a few minutes before the others appeared; and he took the opportunity of paying the parting civilities which he deemed indispensably necessary.

'I know not, Miss Elizabeth,' said he, 'whether Mrs Collins has yet expressed her sense of your kindness in coming to us, but I am very certain you will not leave the house without receiving her thanks for it. The favour of your company has been much felt, I assure you. We know how little there is to tempt any one to our humble abode. Out plain manner of living, our small rooms, and few domestics, and the little we see of the world, must make Hunsford extremely dull to a young lady like yourself; but I hope you will believe us grateful for the condescension, and that we have done every thing in our power to prevent your spending your time unpleasantly.'

Elizabeth was eager with her thanks and assurances of happiness. She had spent six weeks with great enjoyment; and the pleasure of being with Charlotte, and the kind attentions she had received, must make *her* feel the obliged. Mr Collins was gratified; and with a more smiling solemnity replied,

'It gives me the greatest pleasure to hear that you have passed your time not disagreeably. We have certainly done our best; and most fortunately having it in our power to introduce you to very superior society, and from our connection with Rosings, the frequent means of varying the humble home scene, I think we may flatter ourselves that your Hunsford visit cannot have been entirely irksome. Our situation with regard to Lady Catherine's family is indeed the sort of extraordinary advantage and blessing which few can boast. You see on what a footing we are. You see how continually we are engaged there. In truth I must acknowledge that, with all the disadvantages of this humble parsonage, I should not think any one abiding in it an object of compassion, while they are sharers of our intimacy at Rosings.'

Words were insufficient for the elevation of his feelings; and he was obliged to walk about the room, while Elizabeth tried to unite civility and truth in a few short sentences.

'You may, in fact, carry a very favourable report of us into Hertfordshire, my dear cousin. I flatter myself at least that you will be able to do so. Lady Catherine's great attentions to Mrs Collins you have been a daily witness of; and altogether I trust it does not appear that your friend has drawn an unfortunate – but on this point it will be as well to be silent. Only let me

They had forgotten to leave any message

assure you, my dear Miss Elizabeth, that I can from my heart most cordially wish you equal felicity in marriage. My dear Charlotte and I have but one mind and one way of thinking. There is in every thing a most remarkable resemblance of character and ideas between us. We seem to have been designed for each other.'

Elizabeth could safely say that it was a great happiness where that was the case, and with equal sincerity could add that she firmly believed and rejoiced in his domestic comforts. She was not sorry, however, to have the recital of them interrupted by the entrance of the lady from whom they sprung. Poor Charlotte! – it was melancholy to leave her to such society! – But she had chosen it with her eyes open; and though evidently regretting that her visitors were to go, she did not seem to ask for compassion. Her home and her housekeeping, her parish and her poultry, and all their dependent concerns, had not yet lost their charms.

At length the chaise arrived, the trunks were fastened on, the parcels placed within, and it was pronounced to be ready. After an affectionate parting between the friends, Elizabeth was attended to the carriage by Mr Collins, and as they walked down the garden, he was commissioning her with his best respects to all her family, not forgetting his thanks for the kindness he had received at Longbourn in the winter, and his compliments to Mr and Mrs Gardiner, though unknown. He then handed her in, Maria followed, and the door was on the point of being closed, when he suddenly reminded them, with some consternation, that they had hitherto forgotten to leave any message for the ladies of Rosings.

'But,' he added, 'you will of course wish to have your humble respects delivered to them, with your grateful thanks for their kindness to you while you have been here.'

Elizabeth made no objection; – the door was then allowed to be shut, and the carriage drove off.

'Good gracious!' cried Maria, after a few minutes silence, 'it seems but a day or two since we first came! – and yet how many things have happened!'

'A great many indeed,' said her companion with a sigh.

'We have dined nine times at Rosings, besides drinking tea there twice! – How much I shall have to tell!'

Elizabeth privately added, 'And how much I shall have to conceal.'

Their journey was performed without much conversation, or any alarm; and within four hours of their leaving Hunsford, they reached Mr Gardiner's house, where they were to remain a few days.

Jane looked well, and Elizabeth had little opportunity of studying her spirits, amidst the various engagements which the kindness of her aunt had reserved for them. But Jane was to go home with her, and at Longbourn there would be leisure enough for observation.

It was not without an effort meanwhile that she could wait even for Longbourn, before she told her sister of Mr Darcy's proposals. To know that she had the power of revealing what would so exceedingly astonish Jane, and must, at the same time, so highly gratify whatever of her own vanity she had not yet been able to reason away, was such a temptation to openness as nothing could have conquered, but the state of indecision in which she remained, as to the extent of what she should communicate; and her fear, if she once entered on the subject, of being hurried into repeating something of Bingley, which might only grieve her sister farther.

'How nicely we are crammed in!'

CHAPTER THIRTY NINE

IT WAS THE SECOND WEEK IN MAY, in which the three young ladies set out together from Gracechurch-street, for the town of — in Hertfordshire; and, as they drew near the appointed inn where Mr Bennet's carriage was to meet them, they quickly perceived, in token of the coachman's punctuality, both Kitty and Lydia looking out of a dining room up stairs. These two girls had been above an hour in the place, happily employed in visiting an opposite milliner, watching the sentinel on guard, and dressing a salad and cucumber.

After welcoming their sisters, they triumphantly displayed a table set out with such cold meat as an inn larder usually affords, exclaiming, 'Is not this nice? is not this an agreeable surprise?'

'And we mean to treat you all,' added Lydia; 'but you must lend us the money, for we have just spent ours at the shop out there.' Then shewing her purchases: 'Look here, I have bought this bonnet. I do not think it is very pretty; but I thought I might as well buy it as not. I shall pull it to pieces as soon as I get home, and see if I can make it up any better.'

And when her sisters abused it as ugly, she added, with perfect unconcern, 'Oh! but there were two or three much uglier in the shop; and when I have bought some prettier-coloured satin to trim it with fresh, I think it will be very tolerable. Besides, it will not much signify what one wears this summer, after the –shire have left Meryton, and they are going in a fortnight.'

'Are they indeed?' cried Elizabeth, with the greatest satisfaction.

'They are going to be encamped near Brighton; and I do so want papa to take us all there for the summer! It would be such a delicious scheme, and I dare say would hardly cost any thing at all. Mamma would like to go too of all things! Only think what a miserable summer else we shall have!'

'Yes,' thought Elizabeth, '*that* would be a delightful scheme, indeed, and completely do for us at once. Good Heaven! Brighton, and a whole campful of soldiers, to us, who have been overset already by one poor regiment of militia, and the monthly balls of Meryton.'

'Now I have got some news for you,' said Lydia, as they sat down to table. 'What do you think? It is excellent news, capital news, and about a certain person that we all like.'

Jane and Elizabeth looked at each other, and the waiter was told that he need not stay. Lydia laughed, and said,

'Aye, that is just like your formality and discretion. You thought the waiter must not hear, as if he cared! I dare say he often hears worse things said than I am going to say. But he is an ugly fellow! I am glad he is gone. I never saw such a long chin in my life. Well, but now for my news: it is about dear Wickham; too good for the waiter, is not it? There is no danger of Wickham's marrying Mary King. There's for you! She is gone down to her uncle at Liverpool; gone to stay. Wickham is safe.'

'And Mary King is safe!' added Elizabeth; 'safe from a connection imprudent as to fortune.'

'She is a great fool for going away, if she liked him.'

'But I hope there is no strong attachment on either side,' said Jane.

'I am sure there is not on *his*. I will answer for it he never cared three straws about her. Who *could* about such a nasty little freckled thing?'

Elizabeth was shocked to think that, however incapable of such coarseness of *expression* herself, the coarseness of the *sentiment* was little other than her own breast had formerly harboured and fancied liberal!

As soon as all had ate, and the elder ones paid, the carriage was ordered; and after some contrivance, the whole party, with all their boxes, workbags, and parcels, and the unwelcome addition of Kitty's and Lydia's purchases, were seated in it.

'How nicely we are crammed in!' cried Lydia. 'I am glad I bought my bonnet, if it is only for the fun of having another bandbox! Well, now let us be quite comfortable and snug, and talk and laugh all the way home. And in the first place, let us hear what has happened to you all, since you went away. Have you seen any pleasant men? Have you had any flirting? I was in great hopes that one of you would have got a husband before you came back. Jane will be quite an old maid soon, I declare. She is almost three and twenty! Lord, how ashamed I should be of not being married before three and twenty! My aunt Philips wants you so to get husbands, you can't think. She says Lizzy had better have taken Mr Collins; but I do not think there would have been any fun in it. Lord! how I should like to be married before any of you; and then I would chaperon you about to all the balls. Dear me! we had such a good piece of fun the other day at Colonel Forster's. Kitty and me were to spend the day there, and Mrs Forster promised to have a little dance in the evening; (by the bye, Mrs Forster and me are *such* friends!) and so she asked the two Harringtons to come, but Harriet was ill, and so Pen was forced to come by herself; and then, what do you think we did? We dressed up Chamberlayne in woman's clothes, on purpose to pass for a lady, – only think what fun! Not a soul knew of it, but Col and Mrs Forster, and Kitty and me, except my aunt, for we were forced to borrow one of her gowns; and you cannot imagine how well he looked! When Denny, and Wickham, and Pratt, and two or three more of the men came in, they did not know him in the least. Lord! how I laughed! and so did Mrs Forster. I thought I should have died. And *that* made the men suspect something, and then they soon found out what was the matter.'

With such kind of histories of their parties and good jokes, did Lydia, assisted by Kitty's hints and additions, endeavour to amuse her companions all the way to Longbourn. Elizabeth listened as little as she could, but there was no escaping the frequent mention of Wickham's name.

Their reception at home was most kind. Mrs Bennet rejoiced to see Jane in undiminished beauty; and more than once during dinner did Mr Bennet say voluntarily to Elizabeth,

'I am glad you are come back, Lizzy.'

Their party in the dining-room was large, for almost all the Lucases came to meet Maria and hear the news: and various were the subjects which occupied them; Lady Lucas was enquiring of Maria across the table, after the welfare and poultry of her eldest daughter; Mrs Bennet was doubly engaged, on one hand collecting an account of the present fashions from Jane, who sat some way below her, and on the other, retailing them all to the younger Miss Lucases; and Lydia, in a voice rather louder than any other person's was enumerating the various pleasures of the morning to any body who would hear her.

'Oh! Mary,' said she, 'I wish you had gone with us, for we had such fun! as we went along, Kitty and me drew up all the blinds, and pretended there was nobody in the coach; and I should have gone so all the way, if Kitty had not been sick; and when we got to the George, I do think we behaved very handsomely, for we treated the other three with the nicest cold luncheon in the world, and if you would have gone, we would have treated you too. And then when we came away it was such fun! I thought we never should have got into the coach. I was ready to die of laughter. And then we were so merry all the way home! we talked and laughed so loud, that any body might have heard us ten miles off!'

To this, Mary very gravely replied, 'Far be it from me, my dear sister, to depreciate such pleasures. They would doubtless be congenial with the generality of female minds. But I confess they would have no charms for *me*. I should infinitely prefer a book.'

But of this answer Lydia heard not a word. She seldom listened to any body for more than half a minute, and never attended to Mary at all.

In the afternoon Lydia was urgent with the rest of the girls to walk to Meryton and see how every body went on; but Elizabeth steadily opposed the scheme. It should not be said, that the Miss Bennets could not be at home half a day before they were in pursuit of the officers. There was another reason too for her opposition. She dreaded seeing Wickham again, and was resolved to avoid it as long as possible. The comfort to *her*, of the regiment's approaching removal, was indeed beyond expression. In a fortnight they were to go, and once gone, she hoped there could be nothing more to plague her on his account.

She had not been many hours at home, before she found that the Brighton scheme, of which Lydia had given them a hint at the inn, was under frequent discussion between her parents. Elizabeth saw directly that her father had not the smallest intention of yielding; but his answers were at the same time so vague and equivocal, that her mother, though often disheartened, had never yet despaired of succeeding at last.

CHAPTER FORTY

ELIZABETH'S IMPATIENCE TO ACQUAINT Jane with what had happened could no longer be overcome; and at length resolving to suppress every particular in which her sister was concerned, and preparing her to be surprised, she related to her the next morning the chief of the scene between Mr Darcy and herself.

Miss Bennet's astonishment was soon lessened by the strong sisterly partiality which made any admiration of Elizabeth appear perfectly natural; and all surprise was shortly lost in other feelings. She was sorry that Mr Darcy should have delivered his sentiments in a manner so little suited to recommend them; but still more was she grieved for the unhappiness which her sister's refusal must have given him.

'His being so sure of succeeding, was wrong,' said she; 'and certainly ought not to have appeared; but consider how much it must increase his disappointment.'

'Indeed,' replied Elizabeth, 'I am heartily sorry for him; but he has other feelings which will probably soon drive away his regard for me. You do not blame me, however, for refusing him?'

'Blame you! Oh, no.'

'But you blame me for having spoken so warmly of Wickham.'

'No – I do not know that you were wrong in saying what you did.'

'But you *will* know it, when I have told you what happened the very next day.'

She then spoke of the letter, repeating the whole of its contents as far as they concerned George Wickham. What a stroke was this for poor Jane! who would willingly have gone through the world without believing that so much wickedness existed in the whole race of mankind, as was here collected in one individual. Nor was Darcy's vindication, though grateful to her feelings, capable of consoling her for such discovery. Most earnestly did she labour to prove the probability of error, and seek to clear one, without involving the other.

'This will not do,' said Elizabeth. 'You never will be able to make both of them good for any thing. Take your choice, but you must be satisfied with only one. There is but such a quantity of merit between them; just enough to make one good sort of man; and of late it has been shifting about pretty much. For my part, I am inclined to believe it all Mr Darcy's, but you shall do as you chuse.'

It was some time, however, before a smile could be extorted from Jane.

'I do not know when I have been more shocked,' said she. 'Wickham so very bad! It is almost past belief. And poor Mr Darcy! dear Lizzy, only consider what he must have suffered. Such a disappointment! and with the knowledge of your ill opinion too! and having to relate such a thing of his sister! It is really too distressing. I am sure you must feel it so.'

'Oh! no, my regret and compassion are all done away by seeing you so full of both. I know you will do him such ample justice, that I am growing every moment more unconcerned and indifferent. Your profusion makes me saving; and if you lament over him much longer, my heart will be as light as a feather.'

'Poor Wickham; there is such an expression of goodness in his countenance! such an openness and gentleness in his manner.'

'There certainly was some great mismanagement in the education of those two young men. One has got all the goodness, and the other all the appearance of it.'

'I never thought Mr Darcy so deficient in the *appearance* of it as you used to do.'

'And yet I meant to be uncommonly clever in taking so decided a dislike to him, without any reason. It is such a spur to one's genius, such an opening for wit to have a dislike of that kind. One may be continually abusive without saying any thing just; but one cannot be always laughing at a man without now and then stumbling on something witty.'

'Lizzy, when you first read that letter, I am sure you could not treat the matter as you do now.'

'Indeed I could not. I was uncomfortable enough. I was very uncomfortable, I may say unhappy. And with no one to speak to, of what I felt, no Jane to comfort me and say that I had not been so very weak and vain and nonsensical as I knew I had! Oh! how I wanted you!'

'How unfortunate that you should have used such very strong expressions in speaking of Wickham to Mr Darcy, for now they *do* appear wholly undeserved.'

'Certainly. But the misfortune of speaking with bitterness, is a most natural consequence of the prejudices I had been encouraging. There is one point, on which I want your advice. I want to be told whether I ought, or ought not to make our acquaintance in general understand Wickham's character.'

Miss Bennet paused a little and then replied, 'Surely there can be no occasion for exposing him so dreadfully. What is your own opinion?'

'That it ought not to be attempted. Mr Darcy has not authorised me to make his communication public. On the contrary every particular relative to his sister, was meant to be kept as much as possible to myself; and if I endeavour to undeceive people as to the rest of his conduct, who will believe me? The general prejudice against Mr Darcy is so violent, that it would be the death of half the good people in Meryton, to attempt to place him in an amiable light. I am not equal to it. Wickham will soon be gone; and therefore it will not signify to anybody here, what he really is. Sometime hence it will be all found out, and then we may laugh at their stupidity in not knowing it before. At present I will say nothing about it.'

'You are quite right. To have his errors made public might ruin him for ever. He is now perhaps sorry for what he has done, and anxious to re-establish a character. We must not make him desperate.'

The tumult of Elizabeth's mind was allayed by this conversation. She had got rid of two of the secrets which had weighed on her for a fortnight, and was certain of a willing listener in Jane, whenever she might wish to talk again of either. But there was still something lurking behind, of which prudence forbad the disclosure. She dared not relate the other half of Mr Darcy's letter, nor explain to her sister how sincerely she had been valued by his friend. Here was knowledge in which no one could partake; and she was sensible that nothing less than a perfect understanding between the parties could justify her in throwing off this last incumbrance of mystery. 'And then,' said she, 'if that very improbable event should ever take place, I shall merely be able to tell what Bingley may tell in a much more agreeable manner himself. The liberty of communication cannot be mine till it has lost all its value!'

She was now, on being settled at home, at leisure to observe the real state of her sister's spirits. Jane was not happy. She still cherished a very tender affection for Bingley. Having never even fancied herself in love before, her regard had all the warmth of first attachment, and from her age and disposition, greater steadiness than first attachments often boast; and so fervently did she value his remembrance, and prefer him to every other man, that all her good sense, and all her attention to the feelings of her friends, were requisite to check the indulgence of those regrets, which must have been injurious to her own health and their tranquillity.

'Well Lizzy,' said Mrs Bennet one day, 'what is your opinion *now* of this sad business of Jane's? For my part, I am determined never to speak of it again to anybody. I told my sister Philips so the other day. But I cannot find out that Jane saw any thing of him in London. Well, he is a very undeserving young man – and I do not suppose there is the least chance in the world of her ever getting him now. There is no talk of his coming to Netherfield again in the summer; and I have enquired of every body too, who is likely to know.'

'I do not believe that he will ever live at Netherfield any more.'

'Oh, well! it is just as he chooses. Nobody wants him to come. Though I

'I am determined never to speak of it again'

shall always say that he used my daughter extremely ill; and if I was her, I would not have put up with it. Well, my comfort is, I am sure Jane will die of a broken heart, and then he will be sorry for what he has done.'

But as Elizabeth could not receive comfort from any such expectation, she made no answer.

'Well, Lizzy,' continued her mother soon afterwards, 'and so the Collinses live very comfortable, do they? Well, well, I only hope it will last. And what sort of table do they keep? Charlotte is an excellent manager, I dare say. If she is half as sharp as her mother, she is saving enough. There is nothing extravagant in *their* housekeeping, I dare say.'

'No, nothing at all.'

'A great deal of good management, depend upon it. Yes, yes. *They* will take care not to outrun their income. *They* will never be distressed for money. Well, much good may it do them! And so, I suppose, they often talk of having Longbourn when your father is dead. They look upon it quite as their own, I dare say, whenever that happens.'

'It was a subject which they could not mention before me.'

'No. It would have been strange if they had. But I make no doubt, they often talk of it between themselves. Well, if they can be easy with an estate that is not lawfully their own, so much the better. I should be ashamed of having one that was only entailed on me.'

'When Colonel Miller's regiment went away'

CHAPTER FORTY ONE

THE FIRST WEEK OF THEIR RETURN was soon gone. The second began. It was the last of the regiment's stay in Meryton, and all the young ladies in the neighbourhood were drooping apace. The dejection was almost universal. The elder Miss Bennets alone were still able to eat, drink, and sleep, and pursue the usual course of their employments. Very frequently were they reproached for this insensibility by Kitty and Lydia, whose own misery was extreme, and who could not comprehend such hard-heartedness in any of the family.

'Good Heaven! What is to become of us! What are we to do!' would they often exclaim in the bitterness of woe. 'How can you be smiling so, Lizzy?'

Their affectionate mother shared all their grief; she remembered what she had herself endured on a similar occasion, five and twenty years ago.

'I am sure,' said she, 'I cried for two days together when Colonel Miller's regiment went away. I thought I should have broke my heart.'

'I am sure I shall break *mine*,' said Lydia.

'If one could but go to Brighton!' observed Mrs Bennet.

'Oh, yes! – if one could but go to Brighton! But papa is so disagreeable.'

'A little sea-bathing would set me up for ever.'

'And my aunt Philips is sure it would do *me* a great deal of good,' added Kitty.

Such were the kind of lamentations resounding perpetually through Longbourn-house. Elizabeth tried to be diverted by them; but all sense of pleasure was lost in shame. She felt anew the justice of Mr Darcy's objections; and never had she before been so much disposed to pardon his interference in the views of his friend.

But the gloom of Lydia's prospect was shortly cleared away; for she received an invitation from Mrs Forster, the wife of the Colonel of the regiment, to accompany her to Brighton. This invaluable friend was a very young woman, and very lately married. A resemblance in good humour and good spirits had recommended her and Lydia to each other, and out of their *three* months' acquaintance they had been intimate *two*.

The rapture of Lydia on this occasion, her adoration of Mrs Forster, the delight of Mrs Bennet, and the mortification of Kitty, are scarcely to be described. Wholly inattentive to her sister's feelings, Lydia flew about the house in restless ecstasy, calling for every one's congratulations, and laughing and talking with more violence than ever; whilst the luckless Kitty continued in the parlour repining at her fate in terms as unreasonable as her accent was peevish.

'I cannot see why Mrs Forster should not ask *me* as well as Lydia,' said she, 'though I am *not* her particular friend. I have just as much right to be asked as she has, and more too, for I am two years older.'

In vain did Elizabeth attempt to make her reasonable, and Jane to make her resigned. As for Elizabeth herself, this invitation was so far from exciting in her the same feelings as in her mother and Lydia, that she considered it as the death-warrant of all possibility of common sense for the latter; and detestable as such a step must make her were it known, she could not help secretly advising her father not to let her go. She represented to him all the improprieties of Lydia's general behaviour, the little advantage she could derive from the friendship of such a woman as Mrs Forster, and the probability of her being yet more imprudent with such a companion at Brighton, where the temptations must be greater than at home. He heard her attentively, and then said,

'Lydia will never be easy till she has exposed herself in some public place or other, and we can never expect her to do it with so little expense or inconvenience to her family as under the present circumstances.'

'If you were aware,' said Elizabeth, 'of the very great disadvantage to us all, which must arise from the public notice of Lydia's unguarded and imprudent manner; nay, which has already arisen from it, I am sure you would judge differently in the affair.'

'Already arisen!' repeated Mr Bennet. 'What, has she frightened away some of your lovers? Poor little Lizzy! But do not be cast down. Such squeamish youths as cannot bear to be connected with a little absurdity, are not worth a regret. Come, let me see the list of the pitiful fellows who have been kept aloof by Lydia's folly.'

'Indeed you are mistaken. I have no such injuries to resent. It is not of peculiar, but of general evils, which I am now complaining. Our importance, our respectability in the world, must be affected by the wild volatility, the assurance and disdain of all restraint which mark Lydia's character. Excuse me – for I must speak plainly. If you, my dear father, will not take the trouble of checking her exuberant spirits, and of teaching her that her present pursuits are not to be the business of her life, she will soon be beyond the reach of amendment. Her character will be fixed, and she will, at sixteen, be the most determined flirt that ever made herself and her family ridiculous. A flirt too, in the worst and meanest degree of flirtation; without any attraction beyond youth and a tolerable person; and from the ignorance and emptiness of her mind, wholly unable to ward off any portion of that universal contempt which her rage for admiration will excite. In this danger Kitty is also comprehended. She will follow wherever Lydia leads. Vain, ignorant, idle, and absolutely uncontrolled! Oh! my dear father, can you suppose it possible that they will not be censured and despised wherever they are known, and that their sister will not be often involved in the disgrace?'

Mr Bennet saw that her whole heart was in the subject; and affectionately taking her hand, said in reply,

'Do not make yourself uneasy, my love. Wherever you and Jane are known, you must be respected and valued; and you will not appear to less advantage for having a couple of – or I may say, three very silly sisters. We shall have no peace at Longbourn if Lydia does not go to Brighton. Let her go then. Colonel Forster is a sensible man, and will keep her out of any real mischief; and she is luckily too poor to be an object of prey to any body. At Brighton she will be of less importance even as a common flirt than she has been here. The officers will find women better worth their notice. Let us hope, therefore, that her being there may teach her her own insignificance. At any rate, she cannot grow many degrees worse, without authorizing us to lock her up for the rest of her life.'

With this answer Elizabeth was forced to be content; but her own opinion continued the same, and she left him disappointed and sorry. It was not in her nature, however, to increase her vexations, by dwelling on them. She was confident of having performed her duty, and to fret over unavoidable evils, or augment them by anxiety, was no part of her disposition.

Had Lydia and her mother known the substance of her conference with her father, their indignation would hardly have found expression in their united volubility. In Lydia's imagination, a visit to Brighton comprised every possibility of earthly happiness. She saw with the creative eye of fancy, the streets of that gay bathing place covered with officers. She saw herself the object of attention, to tens and to scores of them at present unknown. She saw all the glories of the camp; its tents stretched forth in beauteous uniformity of lines, crowded with the young and the gay, and dazzling with scarlet; and to complete the view, she saw herself seated beneath a tent, tenderly flirting with at least six officers at once.

Had she known that her sister sought to tear her from such prospects and such realities as these, what would have been her sensations? They could have been understood only by her mother, who might have felt nearly the

Tenderly flirting

same. Lydia's going to Brighton was all that consoled her from the melancholy conviction of her husband's never intending to go there himself.

But they were entirely ignorant of what had passed; and their raptures continued with little intermission to the very day of Lydia's leaving home.

Elizabeth was now to see Mr Wickham for the last time. Having been frequently in company with him since her return, agitation was pretty well over; the agitations of former partiality entirely so. She had even learnt to detect, in the very gentleness which had first delighted her, an affectation and a sameness to disgust and weary. In his present behaviour to herself, moreover, she had a fresh source of displeasure, for the inclination he soon testified of renewing those attentions which had marked the early part of their acquaintance, could only serve, after what had since passed, to provoke her. She lost all concern for him in finding herself thus selected as the object of such idle and frivolous gallantry; and while she steadily repressed it, could not but feel the reproof contained in his believing, that however long, and for whatever cause, his attentions had been withdrawn, her vanity would be gratified and her preference secured at any time by their renewal.

On the very last day of the regiment's remaining in Meryton, he dined with others of the officers at Longbourn; and so little was Elizabeth disposed to part from him in good humour, that on his making some enquiry as to the manner in which her time had passed at Hunsford, she mentioned Colonel Fitzwilliam's and Mr Darcy's having both spent three weeks at Rosings, and asked him if he were acquainted with the former.

He looked surprised, displeased, alarmed; but with a moment's recollection and a returning smile, replied, that he had formerly seen him often; and after observing that he was a very gentleman-like man, asked her how she had liked him. Her answer was warmly in his favour. With an air of indifference he soon afterwards added, 'How long did you say that he was at Rosings?'

'Nearly three weeks.'

'And you saw him frequently?'

'Yes, almost every day.'

'His manners are very different from his cousin's.'

'Yes, very different. But I think Mr Darcy improves on acquaintance.'

'Indeed!' cried Wickham with a look which did not escape her. 'And pray may I ask?' but checking himself, he added in a gayer tone, 'Is it in address that he improves? Has he deigned to add ought of civility to his ordinary style? for I dare not hope,' he continued in a lower and more serious tone, 'that he is improved in essentials.'

'Oh, no!' said Elizabeth. 'In essentials, I believe, he is very much what he ever was.'

While she spoke, Wickham looked as if scarcely knowing whether to rejoice over her words, or to distrust their meaning. There was a something in her countenance which made him listen with an apprehensive and anxious attention, while she added,

'When I said that he improved on acquaintance, I did not mean that either his mind or manners were in a state of improvement, but that from knowing him better, his disposition was better understood.'

Wickham's alarm now appeared in a heightened complexion and agitated look; for a few minutes he was silent; till, shaking off his embarrassment, he turned to her again, and said in the gentlest of accents,

'You, who so well know my feelings towards Mr Darcy, will readily comprehend how sincerely I must rejoice that he is wise enough to assume even the *appearance* of what is right. His pride, in that direction, may be of service, if not to himself, to many others, for it must deter him from such foul misconduct as I have suffered by. I only fear that the sort of cautiousness, to which you, I imagine, have been alluding, is merely adopted on his visits to his aunt, of whose good opinion and judgment he stands much in awe. His fear of her, has always operated, I know, when they were together; and a good deal is to be imputed to his wish of forwarding the match with Miss de Bourgh, which I am certain he has very much at heart.'

Elizabeth could not repress a smile at this, but she answered only by a slight inclination of the head. She saw that he wanted to engage her on the old subject of his grievances, and she was in no humour to indulge him. The rest of the evening passed with the *appearance*, on his side, of usual cheerfulness, but with no farther attempt to distinguish Elizabeth; and they parted at last with mutual civility, and possibly a mutual desire of never meeting again.

When the party broke up, Lydia returned with Mrs Forster to Meryton, from whence they were to set out early the next morning. The separation between her and her family was rather noisy than pathetic. Kitty was the only one who shed tears; but she did weep from vexation and envy. Mrs Bennet was diffuse in her good wishes for the felicity of her daughter, and impressive in her injunctions that she would not miss the opportunity of enjoying herself as much as possible; advice, which there was every reason to believe would be attended to; and in the clamorous happiness of Lydia herself in bidding farewell, the more gentle adieus of her sisters were uttered without being heard.

The arrival of the Gardiners

CHAPTER FORTY TWO

HAD ELIZABETH'S OPINION BEEN ALL drawn from her own family, she could not have formed a very pleasing picture of conjugal felicity or domestic comfort. Her father captivated by youth and beauty, and that appearance of good humour, which youth and beauty generally give, had married a woman whose weak understanding and illiberal mind, had very early in their marriage put an end to all real affection for her. Respect, esteem, and confidence, had vanished for ever; and all his views of domestic happiness were overthrown. But Mr Bennet was not of a disposition to seek comfort for the disappointment which his own imprudence had brought on, in any of those pleasures which too often console the unfortunate for their folly or their vice. He was fond of the country and of books; and from these tastes had arisen his principal enjoyments. To his wife he was very little otherwise indebted, than as her ignorance and folly had contributed to his amusement. This is not the sort of happiness which a man would in general wish to owe to his wife; but where other powers of entertainment are wanting, the true philosopher will derive benefit from such as are given.

Elizabeth, however, had never been blind to the impropriety of her father's behaviour as a husband. She had always seen it with pain; but respecting his abilities, and grateful for his affectionate treatment of herself, she endeavoured to forget what she could not overlook, and to banish from her thoughts that continual breach of conjugal obligation and decorum which, in exposing his wife to the contempt of her own children, was so highly reprehensible. But she had never felt so strongly as now, the disadvantages which must attend the children of so unsuitable a marriage, nor ever been so fully aware of the evils arising from so ill-judged a direction of talents; talents which rightly used, might at least have preserved the respectability of his daughters, even if incapable of enlarging the mind of his wife.

When Elizabeth had rejoiced over Wickham's departure, she found little other cause for satisfaction in the loss of the regiment. Their parties abroad were less varied than before; and at home she had a mother and sister whose constant repinings at the dullness of every thing around them, threw a real gloom over their domestic circle; and, though Kitty might in time regain her natural degree of sense, since the disturbers of her brain were removed, her other sister, from whose disposition greater evil might be apprehended, was likely to be hardened in all her folly and assurance, by a situation of such double danger as a watering place and a camp. Upon the whole, therefore, she found, what has been sometimes found before, that an event to which she had looked forward with impatient desire, did not in taking place, bring all the satisfaction she had promised herself. It was consequently necessary to name some other period for the commencement of actual felicity; to have some other point on which her wishes and hopes might be fixed, and by again enjoying the pleasure of anticipation, console herself for the present, and prepare for another disappointment. Her tour to the Lakes was now the object of her happiest thoughts; it was her best consolation for all the uncomfortable hours, which the discontentedness of her mother and Kitty made inevitable; and could she have included Jane in the scheme, every part of it would have been perfect.

'But it is fortunate,' thought she, 'that I have something to wish for. Were the whole arrangement complete, my disappointment would be certain. But here, by carrying with me one ceaseless source of regret in my sister's absence, I may reasonably hope to have all my expectations of pleasure realized. A scheme of which every part promises delight, can never be successful; and general disappointment is only warded off by the defence of some little peculiar vexation.'

When Lydia went away, she promised to write very often and very minutely to her mother and Kitty; but her letters were always long expected, and always very short. Those to her mother, contained little else, than that they were just returned from the library, where such and such officers had attended them, and where she had seen such beautiful ornaments as made her quite wild; that she had a new gown, or a new parasol, which she would have described more fully, but was obliged to leave off in a violent hurry, as Mrs Forster called her, and they were going to the camp; – and from her correspondence with her sister, there was still less to be learnt – for her letters to Kitty, though rather longer, were much too full of lines under the words to be made public.

After the first fortnight or three weeks of her absence, health, good humour and cheerfulness began to re-appear at Longbourn. Everything wore a happier aspect. The families who had been in town for the winter came back again and summer finery and summer engagements arose. Mrs Bennet was restored to her usual querulous serenity, and by the middle of June Kitty was so much recovered as to be able to enter Meryton without tears; an event of such happy promise as to make Elizabeth hope, that by the following Christmas, she might be so tolerably reasonable as not to mention an officer above once a day, unless by some cruel and malicious arrangement at the war-office, another regiment should be quartered in Meryton.

The time fixed for the beginning of their Northern tour was now fast approaching; and a fortnight only was wanting of it, when a letter arrived from Mrs Gardiner, which at once delayed its commencement and curtailed its extent. Mr Gardiner would be prevented by business from setting out till a fortnight later in July, and must be in London again within a month; and as that left too short a period for them to go so far, and see so much as they had proposed, or at least to see it with the leisure and comfort they had built on, they were obliged to give up the Lakes, and substitute a more contracted tour; and according to the present plan, were to go no farther northward than Derbyshire. In that country, there was enough to be seen, to occupy the chief of their three weeks; and to Mrs Gardiner it had a peculiarly strong attraction. The town where she had formerly passed some years of her life, and where they were now to spend a few days, was probably as great an object of her curiosity, as all the celebrated beauties of Matlock, Chatsworth, Dovedale, or the Peak.

Elizabeth was excessively disappointed; she had set her heart on seeing the Lakes; and still thought there might have been time enough. But it was her business to be satisfied – and certainly her temper to be happy; and all was soon right again.

With the mention of Derbyshire, there were many ideas connected. It was impossible for her to see the word without thinking of Pemberley and its owner. 'But surely,' said she, 'I may enter his county with impunity, and rob it of a few petrified spars without his perceiving me.'

The period of expectation was now doubled. Four weeks were to pass away before her uncle and aunt's arrival. But they did pass away, and Mr and Mrs Gardiner, with their four children, did at length appear at Longbourn. The children, two girls of six and eight years old, and two younger boys, were to be left under the particular care of their cousin Jane, who was the general favourite, and whose steady sense and sweetness of temper exactly adapted her for attending to them in every way – teaching them, playing with them, and loving them.

The Gardiners staid only one night at Longbourn, and set off the next morning with Elizabeth in pursuit of novelty and amusement. One enjoyment was certain – that of suitableness as companions; a suitableness which comprehended health and temper to bear inconveniences – cheerfulness to enhance every pleasure – and affection and intelligence, which might supply it among themselves if there were disappointments abroad.

It is not the object of this work to give a description of Derbyshire, nor of any of the remarkable places through which their route thither lay; Oxford, Blenheim, Warwick, Kenelworth, Birmingham, &c. are sufficiently known. A small part of Derbyshire is all the present concern. To the little town of Lambton, the scene of Mrs Gardiner's former residence, and where she had lately learned that some acquaintance still remained, they bent their steps, after having seen all the principal wonders of the country; and within five miles of Lambton, Elizabeth found from her aunt, that Pemberley was situated. It was not in their direct road, nor more than a mile or two out of it. In talking over their route the evening before, Mrs Gardiner expressed an inclination to see the place again. Mr Gardiner declared his willingness, and Elizabeth was applied to for her approbation.

'My love, should not you like to see a place of which you have heard so much?' said her aunt. 'A place too, with which so many of your acquaintance are connected. Wickham passed all his youth there, you know.'

Elizabeth was distressed. She felt that she had no business at Pemberley, and was obliged to assume a disinclination for seeing it. She must own that she was tired of great houses; after going over so many, she really had no pleasure in fine carpets or satin curtains.

Mrs Gardiner abused her stupidity. 'If it were merely a fine house richly furnished,' said she, 'I should not care about it myself; but the grounds are delightful. They have some of the finest woods in the country.'

Elizabeth said no more – but her mind could not acquiesce. The possibility of meeting Mr Darcy, while viewing the place, instantly occurred. It would be dreadful! She blushed at the very idea; and thought it would be better to speak openly to her aunt, than to run such a risk. But against this, there were objections; and she finally resolved that it could be the last resource, if her private enquiries as to the absence of the family, were unfavourably answered.

Accordingly, when she retired at night, she asked the chambermaid whether Pemberley were not a very fine place, what was the name of its proprietor, and with no little alarm, whether the family were down for the summer. A most welcome negative followed the last question – and her alarms being now removed, she was at leisure to feel a great deal of curiosity to see the house herself; and when the subject was revived the next morning, and she was again applied to, could readily answer, and with a proper air of indifference, that she had not really any dislike to the scheme.

To Pemberley, therefore, they were to go.

CHAPTER FORTY THREE

ELIZABETH, AS THEY DROVE ALONG, watched for the first appearance of Pemberley Woods with some perturbation; and when at length they turned in at the lodge, her spirits were in a high flutter.

The park was very large, and contained great variety of ground. They entered it in one of its lowest points, and drove for some time through a beautiful wood, stretching over a wide extent.

Elizabeth's mind was too full for conversation, but she saw and admired every remarkable spot and point of view. They gradually ascended for half a mile, and then found themselves at the top of a considerable eminence, where the wood ceased, and the eye was instantly caught by Pemberley House, situated on the opposite side of a valley, into which the road with some abruptness wound. It was a large, handsome, stone building, standing well on rising ground, and backed by a ridge of high woody hills; – and in front, a stream of some natural importance was swelled into greater, but without any artificial appearance. Its banks were neither formal, nor falsely adorned. Elizabeth was delighted. She had never seen a place for which nature had done more, or where natural beauty had been so little counteracted by an awkward taste. They were all of them warm in their admiration; and at that moment she felt, that to be mistress of Pemberley might be something!

They descended the hill, crossed the bridge, and drove to the door; and, while examining the nearer aspect of the house, all her apprehensions of meeting its owner returned. She dreaded lest the chambermaid had been mistaken. On aplying to see the place, they were admitted into the hall; and Elizabeth, as they waited for the housekeeper, had leisure to wonder at her being where she was.

The housekeeper came; a respectable-looking, elderly woman, much less fine, and more civil, than she had any notion of finding her. They followed her into the dining-parlour. It was a large, well-proportioned room, handsomely fitted up. Elizabeth, after slightly surveying it, went to a window to enjoy its prospect. The hill, crowned with wood, from which they had descended, receiving increased abruptness from the distance, was a beautiful object. Every disposition of the ground was good; and she looked on the whole scene, the river, the trees scattered on its banks, and the winding of the valley, as far as she could trace it, with delight. As they passed into other rooms, these objects were taking different positions; but from every window there were beauties to be seen. The rooms were lofty and handsome, and their furniture suitable for the fortune of their proprietor; but Elizabeth saw, with admiration of his taste, that it was neither gaudy nor uselessly fine; with less of splendor, and more real elegance, than the furniture of Rosings.

'And of this place,' thought she, 'I might have been mistress! With these rooms I might now have been familiarly acquainted! Instead of viewing them as a stranger, I might have rejoiced in them as my own, and welcomed to them as visitors my uncle and aunt. – But no,' – recollecting herself, – 'that could never be: my uncle and aunt would have been lost to me: I should not have been allowed to invite them.'

This was a lucky recollection – it saved her from something like regret.

She longed to enquire of the housekeeper, whether her master were really absent, but had not courage for it. At length, however, the question was asked by her uncle; and she turned away with alarm, while Mrs Reynolds replied, that he was, adding, 'but we expect him to-morrow, with a large party of friends.' How rejoiced was Elizabeth that their own journey had not by any circumstance been delayed a day!

Her aunt now called her to look at a picture. She approached, and saw the likeness of Mr Wickham suspended, amongst several other miniatures, over the mantlepiece. Her aunt asked her, smilingly, how she liked it. The housekeeper came forward, and told them it was the picture of a young gentleman, the son of her late master's steward, who had been brought up by him at his own expence. – 'He is now gone into the army,' she added, 'but I am afraid he has turned out very wild.'

Mrs Gardiner looked at her niece with a smile, but Elizabeth could not return it.

'And that,' said Mrs Reynolds, pointing to another of the miniatures, 'is my master – and very like him. It was drawn at the same time as the other – about eight years ago.'

'I have heard much of your master's fine person,' said Mrs Gardiner, looking at the picture; 'it is a handsome face. But, Lizzy, you can tell us whether it is like or not.'

Mrs Reynolds's respect for Elizabeth seemed to increase on this intimation of her knowing her master.

'Does that young lady know Mr Darcy?'

Elizabeth coloured, and said – 'A little.'

'And do not you think him a very handsome gentleman, Ma'am?'

'Yes, very handsome.'

'I am sure *I* know none so handsome; but in the gallery up stairs you will see a finer, larger picture of him than this. This room was my late master's favourite room, and these miniatures are just as they used to be then. He was very fond of them.'

This accounted to Elizabeth for Mr Wickham's being among them.

Mrs Reynolds then directed their attention to one of Miss Darcy, drawn when she was only eight years old.

'And is Miss Darcy as handsome as her brother?' said Mr Gardiner.

'Oh! yes – the handsomest young lady that ever was seen; and so accomplished! – She plays and sings all day long. In the next room is a new instrument just come down for her – a present from my master; she comes here to-morrow with him.'

Mr Gardiner, whose manners were easy and pleasant, encouraged her communicativeness by his questions and remarks; Mrs Reynolds, either from pride or attachment, had evidently great pleasure in talking of her master and his sister.

'Is your master much at Pemberley in the course of the year?'

'Not so much as I could wish, Sir; but I dare say he may spend half his time here; and Miss Darcy is always down for the summer months.'

'Except,' thought Elizabeth, 'when she goes to Ramsgate.'

'If your master would marry, you might see more of him.'

'Yes, Sir; but I do not know when *that* will be. I do not know who is good enough for him.'

Mr and Mrs Gardiner smiled. Elizabeth could not help saying, 'It is very much to his credit, I am sure, that you should think so.'

'I say no more than the truth, and what every body will say that knows him,' replied the other. Elizabeth thought this was going pretty far; and she listened with increasing astonishment as the housekeeper added, 'I have never had a cross word from him in my life, and I have known him ever since he was four years old.'

This was praise, of all others most extraordinary, most opposite to her ideas. That he was not a good-tempered man, had been her firmest opinion. Her keenest attention was awakened; she longed to hear more, and was grateful to her uncle for saying,

'There are very few people of whom so much can be said. You are lucky in having such a master.'

'Yes, Sir, I know I am. If I was to go through the world, I could not meet with a better. But I have always observed, that they who are good-natured when children, are good-natured when they grow up; and he was always the sweetest-tempered, most generous-hearted, boy in the world.'

Elizabeth almost stared at her. – 'Can this be Mr Darcy!' thought she.

'His father was an excellent man,' said Mrs Gardiner.

'Yes, Ma'am, that he was indeed; and his son will be just like him – just as affable to the poor.'

Elizabeth listened, wondered, doubted, and was impatient for more. Mrs Reynolds could interest her on no other point. She related the subject of the pictures, the dimensions of the rooms, and the price of the furniture, in vain. Mr Gardiner, highly amused by the kind of family prejudice, to which he attributed her excessive commendation of her master, soon led again to the subject; and she dwelt with energy on his many merits, as they proceeded together up the great staircase.

'He is the best landlord, and the best master,' said she, 'that ever lived. Not like the wild young men now-a-days, who think of nothing but themselves. There is not one of his tenants or servants but what will give him a good name. Some people call him proud; but I am sure I never saw any thing of it. To my fancy, it is only because he does not rattle away like other young men.'

'In what an amiable light does this place him!' thought Elizabeth.

'This fine account of him,' whispered her aunt, as they walked, 'is not quite consistent with his behaviour to our poor friend.'

'Perhaps we might be deceived.'

'That is not very likely; our authority was too good.'

On reaching the spacious lobby above, they were shewn into a very pretty sitting-room, lately fitted up with greater elegance and lightness than the apartments below; and were informed that it was but just done, to give pleasure to Miss Darcy, who had taken a liking to the room, when last at Pemberley.

'He is certainly a good brother,' said Elizabeth, as she walked towards one of the windows.

Mrs Reynolds anticipated Miss Darcy's delight, when she should enter the room. 'And this is always the way with him,' she added. – 'Whatever can give his sister any pleasure, is sure to be done in a moment. There is nothing he would not do for her.'

The picture gallery, and two or three of the principal bedrooms, were all that remained to be shewn. In the former were many good paintings; but Elizabeth knew nothing of the art; and from such as had been already visible below, she had willingly turned to look at some drawings of Miss Darcy's, in crayons, whose subjects were usually more interesting, and also more intelligible.

In the gallery there were many family portraits, but they could have little to fix the attention of a stranger. Elizabeth walked on in quest of the only face whose features would be known to her. At last it arrested her – and she beheld a striking resemblance of Mr Darcy, with such a smile over the face, as she remembered to have sometimes seen, when he looked at her. She stood several minutes before the picture in earnest contemplation, and returned to it again before they quitted the gallery. Mrs Reynolds informed them, that it had been taken in his father's life time.

There was certainly at this moment, in Elizabeth's mind, a more gentle sensation towards the original, than she had ever felt in the height of their acquaintance. The commendation bestowed on him by Mrs Reynolds was of no trifling nature. What praise is more valuable than the praise of an intelligent servant? As a brother, a landlord, a master, she considered how many people's happiness were in his guardianship! – How much of pleasure or pain it was in his power to bestow! – How much of good or evil must be done by him! Every idea that had been brought forward by the housekeeper was favourable to his character, and as she stood before the canvas, on which he was represented, and fixed his eyes upon herself, she thought of his regard with a deeper sentiment of gratitude than it had ever raised before; she remembered its warmth, and softened its impropriety of expression.

When all of the house that was open to general inspection had been seen, they returned down stairs, and taking leave of the housekeeper, were consigned over to the gardener, who met them at the hall door.

As they walked across the lawn towards the river, Elizabeth turned back to look again; her uncle and aunt stopped also, and while the former was conjecturing as to the date of the building, the owner of it himself suddenly came forward from the road, which led behind it to the stables.

They were within twenty yards of each other, and so abrupt was his appearance, that it was impossible to avoid his sight. Their eyes instantly met, and the cheeks of each were overspread with the deepest blush. He absolutely started, and for a moment seemed immoveable from surprise; but shortly recovering himself, advanced towards the party, and spoke to Elizabeth, if not in terms of perfect composure, at least of perfect civility.

She had instinctively turned away; but, stopping on his approach, received his compliments with an embarrassment impossible to be overcome. Had his first appearance, or his resemblance to the picture they had just been examining, been insufficient to assure the other two that they now saw Mr Darcy, the gardener's expression of surprise, on beholding his master, must immediately have told it. They stood a little aloof while he was talking to their niece, who, astonished and confused, scarcely dared lift her eyes to his face, and knew not what answer she returned to his civil enquiries after her family. Amazed at the alteration in his manner since they last parted, every sentence that he uttered was increasing her embarrassment;

and every idea of the impropriety of her being found there, recurring to her mind, the few minutes in which they continued together, were some of the most uncomfortable of her life. Nor did he seem much more at ease; when he spoke, his accent had none of its usual sedateness; and he repeated his enquiries as to the time of her having left Longbourn, and of her stay in Derbyshire, so often, and in so hurried a way, as plainly spoke the distraction of his thoughts.

At length, every idea seemed to fail him; and, after standing a few moments without saying a word, he suddenly recollected himself, and took leave.

The others then joined her, and expressed their admiration of his figure; but Elizabeth heard not a word, and, wholly engrossed by her own feelings, followed them in silence. She was overpowered by shame and vexation. Her coming there was the most unfortunate, the most ill-judged thing in the world! How strange must it appear to him! In what a disgraceful light might it not strike so vain a man! It might seem as if she had purposely thrown herself in his way again! Oh! why did she come? or, why did he thus come a day before he was expected? Had they been only ten minutes sooner, they should have been beyond the reach of his discrimination, for it was plain that he was that moment arrived, that moment alighted from his horse or his carriage. She blushed again and again over the perverseness of the meeting. And his behaviour, so strikingly altered, – what could it mean? That he should even speak to her was amazing! – but to speak with such civility, to enquire after her family! Never in her life had she seen his manners so little dignified, never had he spoken with such gentleness as on this unexpected meeting. What a contrast did it offer to his last address in Rosing's Park, when he put his letter into her hand! She knew not what to think, nor how to account for it.

They had now entered a beautiful walk by the side of the water, and every step was bringing forward a nobler fall of ground, or a finer reach of the woods to which they were approaching; but it was some time before Elizabeth was sensible of any of it; and, though she answered mechanically to the repeated appeals of her uncle and aunt, and seemed to direct her eyes to such objects as they pointed out, she distinguished no part of the scene. Her thoughts were all fixed on that one spot of Pemberley House, whichever it might be, where Mr Darcy then was. She longed to know what at that moment was passing in his mind; in what manner he thought of her, and whether, in defiance of every thing, she was still dear to him. Perhaps he had been civil, only because he felt himself at ease; yet there had been *that* in his voice, which was not like ease. Whether he had felt more of pain or of pleasure in seeing her, she could not tell, but he certainly had not seen her with composure.

At length, however, the remarks of her companions on her absence of mind roused her, and she felt the necessity of appearing more like herself.

They entered the woods, and bidding adieu to the river for a while, ascended some of the higher grounds; whence, in spots where the opening of the trees gave the eye power to wander, were many charming views of the valley, the opposite hills, with the long range of woods overspreading many, and occasionally part of the stream. Mr Gardiner expressed a wish of going round the whole Park, but feared it might be beyond a walk. With a triumphant smile, they were told, that it was ten miles round. It settled the matter; and they pursued the accustomed circuit; which brought them again, after some time, in a descent among hanging woods, to the edge of the water, in one of its narrowest parts. They crossed it by a simple bridge, in character with the general air of the scene; it was a spot less adorned than any they had yet visited; and the valley, here contracted into a glen, allowed room only for the stream, and a narrow walk amidst the rough coppice-wood which bordered it. Elizabeth longed to explore its windings; but when they had crossed the bridge, and perceived their distance from the house, Mrs Gardiner, who was not a great walker, could go no farther, and thought only of returning to the carriage as quickly as possible. Her niece was, therefore, obliged to submit, and they took their way towards the house on the opposite side of the river, in the nearest direction; but their progress was slow, for Mr Gardiner, though seldom able to indulge the taste, was very fond of fishing, and was so much engaged in watching the occasional appearance of some trout in the water, and talking to the man about them, that he advanced but little. Whilst wandering on in this slow manner, they were again surprised, and Elizabeth's astonishment was quite equal to what it had been at first, by the sight of Mr Darcy approaching them, and at no great distance. The walk being here less sheltered than on the other side, allowed them to see him before they met. Elizabeth, however astonished, was at least more prepared for an interview than before, and resolved to appear and to speak with calmness, if he really intended to meet them. For a few moments, indeed, she felt that he would probably strike into some other path. This idea lasted while a turning in the walk concealed him from their view; the turning past, he was immediately before them. With a glance she saw, that he had lost none of his recent civility; and, to imitate his politeness, she began, as they met, to admire the beauty of the place; but she had not got beyond the words 'delightful,' and 'charming,' when some unlucky recollections obtruded, and she fancied that praise of Pemberley from her, might be mischievously construed. Her colour changed, and she said no more.

Mrs Gardiner was standing a little behind; and on her pausing, he asked her, if she would do him the honour of introducing him to her friends. This was a stroke of civility for which she was quite unprepared; and she could hardly suppress a smile, at his being now seeking the acquaintance of some of those very people, against whom his pride had revolted, in his offer to herself. 'What will be his surprise,' thought she, 'when he knows who they are! He takes them now for people of fashion.'

The introduction, however, was immediately made; and as she named their relationship to herself, she stole a sly look at him, to see how he bore it; and was not without the expectation of his decamping as fast as he could from such disgraceful companions. That he was *surprised* by the connexion was evident; he sustained it however with fortitude, and so far from going away, turned back with them, and entered into conversation with Mr Gardiner. Elizabeth could not but be pleased, could not but triumph. It was consoling, that he should know she had some relations for whom there was no need to blush. She listened most attentively to all that passed between them, and gloried in every expression, every sentence of her uncle, which marked his intelligence, his taste, or his good manners.

The conversation soon turned upon fishing, and she heard Mr Darcy invite him, with the greatest civility, to fish there as often as he chose, while he continued in the neighbourhood, offering at the same time to supply him with fishing tackle, and pointing out those parts of the stream where there was usually most sport. Mrs Gardiner, who was walking arm in arm with Elizabeth, gave her a look expressive of her wonder. Elizabeth said nothing, but it gratified her exceedingly; the compliment must be all for herself. Her astonishment, however, was extreme; and continually was she repeating, 'Why is he so altered? From what can it proceed? It cannot be for *me*, it cannot be for *my* sake that his manners are thus softened. My reproofs at Hunsford could not work such a change as this. It is impossible that he should still love me.'

After walking some time in this way, the two ladies in front, the two gentlemen behind, on resuming their places, after descending to the brink of the river for the better inspection of some curious water-plant, there chanced to be a little alteration. It originated in Mrs Gardiner, who, fatigued by the exercise of the morning, found Elizabeth's arm inadequate to her support, and consequently preferred her husband's. Mr Darcy took her place by her niece, and they walked on together. After a short silence, the lady first spoke. She wished him to know that she had been assured of his absence before she came to the place, and accordingly began by observing, that his arrival had been very unexpected – 'for your housekeeper,' she added, 'informed us that you would certainly not be here till to-morrow; and indeed, before we left Bakewell, we understood that you were not immediately expected in the country.' He acknowledged the truth of it all; and said that business with his steward had occasioned his coming forward a few hours before the rest of the party with whom he had been travelling. 'They will join me early to-morrow,' he continued, 'and among them are some who will claim an acquaintance with you, – Mr Bingley and his sisters.'

Elizabeth answered only by a slight bow. Her thoughts were instantly driven back to the time when Mr Bingley's name had been last mentioned between them; and if she might judge from his complexion, *his* mind was not very differently engaged.

'There is also one other person in the party,' he continued after a pause, 'who more particularly wishes to be known to you, – Will you allow me, or do I ask too much, to introduce my sister to your acquaintance during your stay at Lambton?'

The surprise of such an application was great indeed; it was too great for her to know in what manner she acceded to it. She immediately felt that whatever desire Miss Darcy might have of being acquainted with her, must be the work of her brother, and without looking farther, it was satisfactory; it was gratifying to know that his resentment had not made him think really ill of her.

They now walked on in silence; each of them deep in thought. Elizabeth was not comfortable; that was impossible; but she was flattered and pleased. His wish of introducing his sister to her, was a compliment of the highest kind. They soon outstripped the others, and when they had reached the carriage, Mr and Mrs Gardiner were half a quarter of a mile behind.

He then asked her to walk into the house – but she declared herself not tired, and they stood together on the lawn. At such a time, much might have been said, and silence was very awkward. She wanted to talk, but there seemed an embargo on every subject. At last she recollected that she had been travelling, and they talked of Matlock and Dove Dale with great perseverance. Yet time and her aunt moved slowly – and her patience and her ideas were nearly worn out before the tête-à-tête was over. On Mr and Mrs Gardiner's coming up, they were all pressed to go into the house and take some refreshment; but this was declined, and they parted on each side with the utmost politeness. Mr Darcy handed the ladies into the carriage, and when it drove off Elizabeth saw him walking slowly towards the house.

The observations of her uncle and aunt now began; and each of them pronounced him to be infinitely superior to any thing they had expected. 'He is perfectly well behaved, polite, and unassuming,' said her uncle.

'There *is* something a little stately in him to be sure,' replied her aunt, 'but it is confined to his air, and is not unbecoming. I can now say with the housekeeper, that though some people may call him proud, *I* have seen nothing of it.'

'I was never more surprised than by his behaviour to us. It was more than civil; it was really attentive; and there was no necessity for such attention. His acquaintance with Elizabeth was very trifling.'

'To be sure, Lizzy,' said her aunt, 'he is not so handsome as Wickham; or rather he has not Wickham's countenance, for his features are perfectly good. But how came you to tell us that he was so disagreeable?'

Elizabeth excused herself as well as she could; said that she had liked him better when they met in Kent than before, and that she had never seen him so pleasant as this morning.

'But perhaps he may be a little whimsical in his civilities,' replied her uncle. 'Your great men often are; and therefore I shall not take him at his word about fishing, as he might change his mind another day, and warn me off his grounds.'

Elizabeth felt that they had entirely mistaken his character, but said nothing.

'From what we have seen of him,' continued Mrs Gardiner, 'I really should not have thought that he could have behaved in so cruel a way by any body, as he has done by poor Wickham. He has not an ill-natured look. On the contrary, there is something of dignity in his countenance, that would not give one an unfavourable idea of his heart. But to be sure, the good lady who shewed us the house, did give him a most flaming character! I could hardly help laughing aloud sometimes. But he is a liberal master, I suppose, and *that* in the eye of a servant comprehends every virtue.'

Elizabeth here felt herself called on to say something in vindication of his behaviour to Wickham; and therefore gave them to understand, in as guarded a manner as she could, that by what she had heard from his relations in Kent, his actions were capable of a very different construction; and that his character was by no means so faulty, nor Wickham's so amiable, as they had been considered in Hertfordshire. In confirmation of this, she related the particulars of all the pecuniary transactions in which they had been connected, without actually naming her authority, but stating it to be such as might be relied on.

Mrs Gardiner was surprised and concerned; but as they were now approaching the scene of her former pleasures, every idea gave way to the charm of recollection; and she was too much engaged in pointing out to her husband all the interesting spots in its environs, to think of any thing else. Fatigued as she had been by the morning's walk, they had no sooner dined than she set off again in quest of her former acquaintance, and the evening was spent in the satisfactions of an intercourse renewed after many years discontinuance.

The occurrences of the day were too full of interest to leave Elizabeth much attention for any of these new friends; and she could do nothing but think, and think with wonder, of Mr Darcy's civility, and above all, of his wishing her to be acquainted with his sister.

CHAPTER FORTY FOUR

ELIZABETH HAD SETTLED IT THAT Mr Darcy would bring his sister to visit her, the very day after her reaching Pemberley; and was consequently resolved not to be out of sight of the inn the whole of that morning. But her conclusion was false; for on the very morning after their own arrival at Lambton, these visitors came. They had been walking about the place with some of their new friends, and were just returned to the inn to dress themselves for dining with the same family, when the sound of a carriage drew them to a window, and they saw a gentleman and lady in a curricle, driving up the street. Elizabeth immediately recognizing the livery, guessed what it meant, and imparted no small degree of surprise to her relations, by acquainting them with the honour which she expected. Her uncle and aunt were all amazement; and the embarrassment of her manner as she spoke, joined to the circumstance itself, and many of the circumstances of the preceding day, opened to them a new idea on the business. Nothing had ever suggested it before, but they now felt that there was no other way of accounting for such attentions from such a quarter, than by supposing a partiality for their niece. While these newlyborn notions were passing in their heads, the perturbation of Elizabeth's feelings was every moment increasing. She was quite amazed at her own discomposure; but amongst other causes of disquiet, she dreaded lest the partiality of the brother should have said too much in her favour; and more than commonly anxious to please, she naturally suspected that every power of pleasing would fail her.

She retreated from the window, fearful of being seen; and as she walked up and down the room, endeavouring to compose herself, saw such looks of enquiring surprise in her uncle and aunt, as made every thing worse.

Miss Darcy and her brother appeared, and this formidable introduction took place. With astonishment did Elizabeth see, that her new acquaintance was at least as much embarrassed as herself. Since her being at Lambton, she had heard that Miss Darcy was exceedingly proud; but the observations of a very few minutes convinced her, that she was only exceedingly shy. She found it difficult to obtain even a word from her beyond a monosyllable.

Miss Darcy was tall, and on a larger scale than Elizabeth; and, though little more than sixteen, her figure was formed, and her appearance womanly and graceful. She was less handsome than her brother, but there was sense and good humour in her face, and her manners were perfectly unassuming and gentle. Elizabeth, who had expected to find in her as acute and unembarrassed an observer as ever Mr Darcy had been, was much relieved by discerning such different feelings.

They had not been long together, before Darcy told her that Bingley was also coming to wait on her; and she had barely time to express her satisfaction, and prepare for such a visitor, when Bingley's quick step was heard on the stairs, and in a moment he entered the room. All Elizabeth's anger against him had been long done away; but, had she still felt any, it could hardly have stood its ground against the unaffected cordiality with which he expressed himself, on seeing her again. He enquired in a friendly, though general way, after her family, and looked and spoke with the same good-humoured ease that he had ever done.

To Mr and Mrs Gardiner he was scarcely a less interesting personage than to herself. They had long wished to see him. The whole party before them, indeed, excited a lively attention. The suspicions which had just arisen of Mr Darcy and their niece, directed their observation towards each with an earnest, though guarded, enquiry; and they soon drew from those enquiries the full conviction that one of them at least knew what it was to love. Of the lady's sensations they remained a little in doubt; but that the gentleman was overflowing with admiration was evident enough.

Elizabeth, on her side, had much to do. She wanted to ascertain the feelings of each of her visitors, she wanted to compose her own, and to make herself agreeable to all; and in the latter object, where she feared most to fail, she was most sure of success, for those to whom she endeavoured to give pleasure were prepossessed in her favour. Bingley was ready, Georgiana was eager, and Darcy determined, to be pleased.

In seeing Bingley, her thoughts naturally flew to her sister; and oh! how ardently did she long to know, whether any of his were directed in a like manner. Sometimes she could fancy, that he talked less than on former occasions, and once or twice pleased herself with the notion that as he looked at her, he was trying to trace a resemblance. But, though this might be imaginary, she could not be deceived as to his behaviour to Miss Darcy, who had been set up as a rival of Jane. No look appeared on either side that spoke particular regard. Nothing occurred between them that could justify the hopes of his sister. On this point she was soon satisfied; and two or three little circumstances occurred ere they parted, which, in her anxious interpretation, denoted a recollection of Jane, not untinctured by tenderness, and a wish of saying more that might lead to the mention of her, had he dared. He observed to her, at a moment when the others were talking together, and in a tone which had something of real regret, that it 'was a

To make herself agreeable to all

very long time since he had had the pleasure of seeing her'; and, before she could reply, he added, 'It is above eight months. We have not met since the 26th of November, when we were all dancing together at Netherfield.'

Elizabeth was pleased to find his memory so exact; and he afterwards took occasion to ask her, when unattended to by any of the rest, whether *all* her sisters were at Longbourn. There was not much in the question, nor in the preceding remark, but there was a look and a manner which gave them meaning.

It was not often that she could turn her eyes on Mr Darcy himself; but, whenever she did catch a glimpse, she saw an expression of general complaisance, and in all that he said, she heard an accent so far removed from hauteur or disdain of his companions, as convinced her that the improvement of manners which she had yesterday witnessed, however temporary its existence might prove, had at least outlived one day. When she saw him thus seeking the acquaintance, and courting the good opinion of people, with whom any intercourse a few months ago would have been a disgrace; when she saw him thus civil, not only to herself, but to the very relations whom he had openly disdained, and recollected their last lively scene in Hunsford Parsonage, the difference, the change was so great, and struck so forcibly on her mind, that she could hardly restrain her astonishment from being visible. Never, even in the company of his dear friends at Netherfield, or his dignified relations at Rosings, had she seen him so desirous to please, so free from self-consequence, or unbending reserve as now, when no importance could result from the success of his endeavours, and when even the acquaintance of those to whom his attentions were addressed, would draw down the ridicule and censure of the ladies both of Netherfield and Rosings.

Their visitors staid with them above half an hour, and when they arose to depart, Mr Darcy called on his sister to join him in expressing their wish of seeing Mr and Mrs Gardiner, and Miss Bennet, to dinner at Pemberley, before they left the country. Miss Darcy, though with a diffidence which marked her little in the habit of giving invitations, readily obeyed. Mrs Gardiner looked at her niece, desirous of knowing how *she*, whom the invitation most concerned, felt disposed as to its acceptance, but Elizabeth had turned away her head. Presuming, however, that this studied avoidance spoke rather a momentary embarrassment, than any dislike of the proposal, and seeing in her husband, who was fond of society, a perfect willingness to accept it, she ventured to engage for her attendance, and the day after the next was fixed on.

Bingley expressed great pleasure in the certainty of seeing Elizabeth again, having still a great deal to say to her, and many enquiries to make after all their Hertfordshire friends. Elizabeth, construing all this into a wish of hearing her speak of her sister, was pleased; and on this account, as well as some others, found herself, when her visitors left them, capable of considering the last half hour with some satisfaction, though while it was passing, the enjoyment of it had been little. Eager to be alone, and fearful of enquiries or hints from her uncle and aunt, she staid with them only long enough to hear their favourable opinion of Bingley, and then hurried away to dress.

But she had no reason to fear Mr and Mrs Gardiner's curiosity; it was not their wish to force her communication. It was evident that she was much better acquainted with Mr Darcy than they had before any idea of; it was evident that he was very much in love with her. They saw much to interest, but nothing to justify enquiry.

Of Mr Darcy it was now a matter of anxiety to think well; and, as far as their acquaintance reached, there was no fault to find. They could not be untouched by his politeness, and had they drawn his character from their own feelings, and his servant's report, without any reference to any other account, the circle in Hertfordshire to which he was known, would not have recognised it for Mr Darcy. There was now an interest, however, in believing the housekeeper; and they soon became sensible, that the authority of a servant who had known him since he was four years old, and whose own manners indicated respectability, was not to be hastily rejected. Neither had any thing occurred in the intelligence of their Lambton friends, that could materially lessen its weight. They had nothing to accuse him of but pride; pride he probably had, and if not, it would certainly be imputed by the inhabitants of a small market-town, where the family did not visit. It was acknowledged, however, that he was a liberal man, and did much good among the poor.

With respect to Wickham, the travellers soon found that he was not held there in much estimation; for though the chief of his concerns, with the son of his patron, were imperfectly understood, it was yet a well known fact that, on his quitting Derbyshire, he had left many debts behind him, which Mr Darcy afterwards discharged.

As for Elizabeth, her thoughts were at Pemberley this evening more than the last; and the evening, though as it passed it seemed long, was not long enough to determine her feelings towards *one* in that mansion; and she lay awake two whole hours, endeavouring to make them out. She certainly did not hate him. No; hatred had vanished long ago, and she had almost as long been ashamed of ever feeling a dislike against him, that could be so called. The respect created by the conviction of his valuable qualities, though at first unwillingly admitted, had for some time ceased to be repugnant to her feelings; and it was now heightened into somewhat of a friendlier nature, by the testimony so highly in his favour, and bringing forward his disposition in so amiable a light, which yesterday had produced. But above all, above respect and esteem, there was a motive within her of good will which could not be overloked. It was gratitude. – Gratitude, not merely for having once loved her, but for loving her still well enough, to forgive all the petulance and acrimony of her manner in rejecting him, and all the unjust accusations accompanying her rejection. He who, she had been persuaded, would avoid her as his greatest enemy, seemed, on this accidental meeting, most eager to preserve the acquaintance, and without any indelicate display of regard, or any peculiarity of manner, where their two selves only were concerned, was soliciting the good opinion of her friends, and bent on making her known to his sister. Such a change in a man of so much pride, excited not only astonishment but gratitude – for to love, ardent love, it must be attributed; and as such its impression on her was of a sort to be encouraged, as by no means unpleasing, though it could not be exactly defined. She respected, she esteemed, she was grateful to him, she felt a real interest in his welfare; and she only wanted to know how far she wished that welfare to depend upon herself, and how far it would be for the happiness of both that she should employ the power, which her fancy told her she still possessed, of bringing on the renewal of his addresses.

It had been settled in the evening, between the aunt and niece, that such a striking civility as Miss Darcy's, in coming to them on the very day of her arrival at Pemberley, for she had reached it only to a late breakfast, ought to be imitated, though it could not be equalled, by some exertion of politeness on their side; and, consequently, that it would be highly expedient to wait on her at Pemberley the following morning. They were, therefore, to go. – Elizabeth was pleased, though, when she asked herself the reason, she had very little to say in reply.

Mr Gardiner left them soon after breakfast. The fishing scheme had been renewed the day before, and a positive engagement made of his meeting some of the gentlemen at Pemberley by noon.

Engaged by the river

CHAPTER FORTY FIVE

CONVINCED AS ELIZABETH NOW WAS that Miss Bingley's dislike of her had originated in jealousy, she could not help feeling how very unwelcome her appearance at Pemberley must be to her, and was curious to know with how much civility on that lady's side, the acquaintance would now be renewed.

On reaching the house, they were shewn through the hall into the saloon, whose northern aspect rendered it delightful for summer. Its windows opening to the ground, admitted a most refreshing view of the high woody hills behind the house, and of the beautiful oaks and Spanish chestnuts which were scattered over the intermediate lawn.

In this room they were received by Miss Darcy, who was sitting there with Mrs Hurst and Miss Bingley, and the lady with whom she lived in London. Georgiana's reception of them was very civil; but attended with all that embarrassment which, though proceeding from shyness and the fear of doing wrong, would easily give to those who felt themselves inferior, the belief of her being proud and reserved. Mrs Gardiner and her niece, however, did her justice, and pitied her.

By Mrs Hurst and Miss Bingley, they were noticed only by a curtsey; and on their being seated, a pause, awkward as such pauses must always be, succeeded for a few moments. It was first broken by Mrs Annesley, a genteel, agreeable-looking woman, whose endeavour to introduce some kind of discourse, proved her to be more truly well bred than either of the others; and between her and Mrs Gardiner, with occasional help from Elizabeth, the conversation was carried on. Miss Darcy looked as if she wished for courage enough to join in it; and sometimes did venture a short sentence, when there was least danger of its being heard.

Elizabeth soon saw that she was herself closely watched by Miss Bingley, and that she could not speak a word, especially to Miss Darcy, without calling her attention. This observation would not have prevented her from trying to talk to the latter, had they not been seated at an inconvenient distance; but she was not sorry to be spared the necessity of saying much. Her own thoughts were employing her. She expected every moment that some of the gentlemen would enter the room. She wished, she feared that the master of the house might be amongst them; and whether she wished or feared it most, she could scarcely determine. After sitting in this manner a quarter of an hour, without hearing Miss Bingley's voice, Elizabeth was roused by receiving from her a cold enquiry after the health of her family. She answered with equal indifference and brevity, and the other said no more.

The next variation which their visit afforded was produced by the entrance of servants with cold meat, cake, and a variety of all the finest fruits in season; but this did not take place till after many a significant look and smile from Mrs Annesley to Miss Darcy had been given, to remind her of her post. There was now employment for the whole party; for though they could not all talk, they could all eat; and the beautiful pyramids of grapes, nectarines, and peaches, soon collected them round the table.

While thus engaged, Elizabeth had a fair opportunity of deciding whether she most feared or wished for the appearance of Mr Darcy, by the feelings which prevailed on his entering the room; and then, though but a moment before she had believed her wishes to predominate, she began to regret that he came.

He had been some time with Mr Gardiner, who, with two or three other gentlemen from the house, was engaged by the river, and had left him only on learning that the ladies of the family intended a visit to Georgiana that morning. No sooner did he appear, than Elizabeth wisely resolved to be perfectly easy and unembarrassed; – a resolution the more necessary to be made, but perhaps not the more easily kept, because she saw that the suspicions of the whole party were awakened against them, and that there was scarcely an eye which did not watch his behaviour when he first came into the room. In no countenance was attentive curiosity so strongly marked as in Miss Bingley's, in spite of the smiles which overspread her face whenever she spoke to one of its objects; for jealousy had not yet made her desperate, and her attentions to Mr Darcy were by no means over. Miss Darcy, on her brother's entrance, exerted herself much more to talk; and Elizabeth saw that he was anxious for his sister and herself to get acquainted, and forwarded, as much as possible, every attempt at conversation on either side. Miss Bingley saw all this likewise; and, in the imprudence of anger, took the first opportunity of saying, with sneering civility,

'Pray, Miss Eliza, are not the –shire militia removed from Meryton? They must be a great loss to *your* family.'

In Darcy's presence she dared not mention Wickham's name; but Elizabeth instantly comprehended that he was uppermost in her thoughts; and the various recollections connected with him gave her a moment's distress; but, exerting herself vigorously to repel the ill-natured attack, she presently answered the question in a tolerably disengaged tone. While she spoke, an involuntary glance shewed her Darcy with an heightened complexion, earnestly looking at her, and his sister overcome with confusion, and unable to lift up her eyes. Had Miss Bingley known what pain she was then giving her beloved friend, she undoubtedly would have refrained from the hint; but she had merely intended to discompose Elizabeth, by bringing forward the idea of a man to whom she believed her partial, to make her betray a sensibility which might injure her in Darcy's opinion, and perhaps to remind the latter of all the follies and absurdities, by which some part of her family were connected with that corps. Not a syllable had ever reached her of Miss Darcy's meditated elopement. To no creature had it been revealed, where sccrecy was possible, except to Elizabeth; and from all Bingley's connections her brother was particularly anxious to conceal it, from that very wish which Elizabeth had long ago attributed to him, of their becoming hereafter her own. He had certainly formed such a plan, and without meaning that it should affect his endeavour to separate him from Miss Bennet, it is probable that it might add something to his lively concern for the welfare of his friend.

Elizabeth's collected behaviour, however, soon quieted his emotion; and as Miss Bingley, vexed and disappointed, dared not approach nearer to Wickham, Georgiana also recovered in time, though not enough to be able to speak any more. Her brother, whose eye she feared to meet, scarcely recollected her interest in the affair, and the very circumstance which had been designed to turn his thoughts from Elizabeth, seemed to have fixed them on her more, and more cheerfully.

Their visit did not continue long after the question and answer above-mentioned; and while Mr Darcy was attending them to their carriage, Miss Bingley was venting her feelings in criticisms on Elizabeth's person, behaviour, and dress. But Georgiana would not join her. Her brother's recommendation was enough to ensure her favour; his judgment could not err, and he had spoken in such terms of Elizabeth, as to leave Georgiana without the power of finding her otherwise than lovely and amiable. When Darcy returned to the saloon, Miss Bingley could not help repeating to him some part of what she had been saying to his sister.

'How very ill Eliza Bennet looks this morning, Mr Darcy,' she cried; 'I never in my life saw any one so much altered as she is since the winter. She is grown so brown and coarse! Louisa and I were agreeing that we should not have known her again.'

However little Mr Darcy might have liked such an address, he contented himself with coolly replying, that he perceived no other alteration than her being rather tanned, – no miraculous consequence of travelling in the summer.

'For my own part,' she rejoined, 'I must confess that I never could see any beauty in her. Her face is too thin; her complexion has no brilliancy; and her features are not at all handsome. Her nose wants character; there is nothing marked in its lines. Her teeth are tolerable, but not out of the common way; and as for her eyes, which have sometimes been called so fine, I never could perceive any thing extraordinary in them. They have a sharp, shrewish look, which I do not like at all; and in her air altogether, there is a self-sufficiency without fashion, which is intolerable.'

Persuaded as Miss Bingley was that Darcy admired Elizabeth, this was not the best method of recommending herself; but angry people are not always wise; and in seeing him at last look somewhat nettled, she had all the success she expected. He was resolutely silent however; and, from a determination of making him speak, she continued,

'I remember, when we first knew her in Hertfordshire, how amazed we all were to find that she was a reputed beauty; and I particularly recollect your saying one night, after they had been dining at Netherfield, "*She* a beauty! – I should as soon call her mother a wit." But afterwards she seemed to improve on you, and I believe you thought her rather pretty at one time.'

'Yes,' replied Darcy, who could contain himself no longer, 'but *that* was only when I first knew her, for it is many months since I have considered her as one of the handsomest women of my acquaintance.'

He then went away, and Miss Bingley was left to all the satisfaction of having forced him to say what gave no one any pain but herself.

Mrs Gardiner and Elizabeth talked of all that had occurred, during their visit, as they returned, except what had particularly interested them both. The looks and behaviour of every body they had seen were discussed, except of the person who had mostly engaged their attention. They talked of his sister, his friends, his house, his fruit, of every thing but himself; yet Elizabeth was longing to know what Mrs Gardiner thought of him, and Mrs Gardiner would have been highly gratified by her niece's beginning the subject.

CHAPTER FORTY SIX

ELIZABETH HAD BEEN A GOOD DEAL DISAPPOINTED in not finding a letter from Jane, on their first arrival at Lambton; and this disappointment had been renewed on each of the mornings that had now been spent there; but on the third, her repining was over, and her sister justified by the receipt of two letters from her at once, on one of which was marked that it had been missent elsewhere. Elizabeth was not surprised at it, as Jane had written the direction remarkably ill.

They had just been preparing to walk as the letters came in; and her uncle and aunt, leaving her to enjoy them in quiet, set off by themselves. The one missent must be first attended to; it had been written five days ago. The beginning contained an account of all their little parties and engagements, with such news as the country afforded; but the latter half, which was dated a day later, and written in evident agitation, gave more important intelligence. It was to this effect:

'Since writing the above, dearest Lizzy, something has occurred of a most unexpected and serious nature; but I am afraid of alarming you – be assured that we are all well. What I have to say relates to poor Lydia. An express came at twelve last night, just as we were all gone to bed, from Colonel Forster, to inform us that she was gone off the Scotland with one of his officers; to own the truth, with Wickham! – Imagine our surprise. To Kitty, however, it does not seem so wholly unexpected. I am very, very sorry. So imprudent a match on both sides! – But I am willing to hope the best, and that his character has been misunderstood. Thoughtless and indiscreet I can easily believe him, but this step (and let us rejoice over it) marks nothing bad at heart. His choice is disinterested at least, for he must know my father can give her nothing. Our poor mother is sadly grieved. My father bears it better. How thankful am I, that we never let them know what has been said against him; we must forget it ourselves. They were off Saturday night about twelve, as is conjectured, but were not missed till yesterday morning at eight. The express was sent off directly. My dear Lizzy, they must have passed within ten miles of us. Colonel Forster gives us reason to expect him here soon. Lydia left a few lines for his wife, informing her of their intention. I must conclude, for I cannot be long from my poor mother. I am afraid you will not be able to make it out, but I hardly know what I have written.'

Without allowing herself time for consideration, and scarcely knowing what she felt, Elizabeth on finishing this letter, instantly seized the other, and opening it with the utmost impatience, read as follows: it had been written a day later than the conclusion of the first.

'By this time, my dearest sister, you have received my hurried letter; I wish this may be more intelligible, but though not confined for time, my head is so bewildered that I cannot answer for being coherent. Dearest Lizzy, I hardly know what I would write, but I have bad news for you, and it cannot be delayed. Imprudent as a marriage between Mr Wickham and our poor Lydia would be, we are now anxious to be assured it has taken place, for there is but too much reason to fear they are not gone to Scotland. Colonel Forster came yesterday, having left Brighton the day before, not many hours after the express. Though Lydia's short letter to Mrs F. gave them to understand that they were going to Gretna Green, something was dropped by Denny expressing his belief that W. never intended to go there, or to marry Lydia at all, which was repeated to Colonel F. who instantly taking the alarm, set off from B. intending to trace their route. He did trace them easily to Clapham, but no farther; for on entering that place they removed into a hackney-coach and dismissed the chaise that brought them from Epsom. All that is known after this is, that they were seen to continue the London road. I know not what to think. After making every possible enquiry on that side London, Colonel F. came on into Hertfordshire, anxiously renewing them at all the turnpikes, and at the inns in Barnet and Hatfield, but without any success, no such people had been seen to pass through. With the kindest concern he came on to Longbourn, and broke his apprehensions to us in a manner most creditable to his heart. I am sincerely grieved for him and Mrs F. but no one can throw any blame on them. Our distress, my dear Lizzy, is very great. My father and mother believe the worst, but I cannot think so ill of him. Many circumstances might make it more eligible for them to be married privately in town than to pursue their first plan; and even if *he* could form such a design against a young woman of Lydia's connections, which is not likely, can I suppose her so lost to every thing? – Impossible. I grieve to find, however, that Colonel F. is not disposed to depend upon their marriage; he shook his head when I expressed my hopes, and said he feared W. was not a man to be trusted. My poor mother is really ill and keeps her room. Could she exert herself it would be better, but this is not to be expected; and as to my father, I never in my life saw him so affected. Poor Kitty has anger for having concealed their attachment; but as it was a matter of confidence one cannot wonder. I am truly glad, dearest Lizzy, that you have been spared something of these distressing scenes; but now as the first shock is over, shall I own that I long for your return? I am not so selfish, however, as to press for it, if inconvenient. Adieu. I take up my pen again to do, what I have just told you I would not, but circumstances are such, that I cannot help earnestly begging you all to come here, as soon as possible. I know my dear uncle and aunt so well, that I am not afraid of requesting it, though I have still something more to ask of the former. My father is going to London with Colonel Forster instantly, to try to discover her. What he means to do, I am sure I know not; but his excessive distress will not allow him to pursue any measure in the best and safest way, and Colonel Forster is obliged to be at Brighton again to-morrow evening. In such an exigence my uncle's advice and assistance would be every thing in the world; he will immediately comprehend what I must feel, and I rely upon his goodness.'

'Oh! where, where is my uncle?' cried Elizabeth, darting from her seat as she finished the letter, in eagerness to follow him, without losing a moment of the time so precious; but as she reached the door, it was opened by a servant, and Mr Darcy appeared. Her pale face and impetuous manner made him start, and before he could recover himself enough to speak, she, in whose mind every idea was superseded by Lydia's situation, hastily exclaimed, 'I beg your pardon, but I must leave you. I must find Mr Gardiner this moment, on business that cannot be delayed; I have not an instant to lose.'

'Good God! what is the matter?' cried he, with more feeling than politeness; then recollecting himself, 'I will not detain you a minute, but let me, or let the servant, go after Mr and Mrs Gardiner. You are not well enough; – you cannot go yourself.

Elizabeth hesitated, but her knees trembled under her, and she felt how little would be gained by her attempting to pursue them. Calling back the servant, therefore, she commissioned him, though in so breathless an accent

'I have not an instant to lose'

as made her almost unintelligible, to fetch his master and mistress home, instantly.

On his quitting the room, she sat down, unable to support herself, and looking so miserably ill, that it was impossible for Darcy to leave her, or to refrain from saying, in a tone of gentleness and commiseration, 'Let me call your maid. Is there nothing you could take, to give you present relief? – A glass of wine; – shall I get you one? – You are very ill.'

'No, I thank you;' she replied, endeavouring to recover herself. 'There is nothing the matter with me. I am quite well. I am only distressed by some dreadful news which I have just received from Longbourn.'

She burst into tears as she alluded to it, and for a few minutes could not speak another word. Darcy, in wretched suspense, could only say something indistinctly of his concern, and observe her in compassionate silence. At length, she spoke again. 'I have just had a letter from Jane, with such dreadful news. It cannot be concealed from any one. My youngest sister has left all her friends – has eloped; – has thrown herself into the power of – of Mr Wickham. They are gone off together from Brighton. *You* know him too well to doubt the rest. She has no money, no connections, nothing that can tempt him to – she is lost for ever.'

Darcy was fixed in astonishment. 'When I consider,' she added, in a yet more agitated voice, 'that *I* might have prevented it! – *I* who knew what he was. Had I but explained some part of it only – some part of what I learnt, to my own family! Had his character been known, this could not have happened. But it is all, all too late now.'

'I am grieved, indeed,' cried Darcy; 'grieved – shocked. But is it certain, absolutely certain?'

'Oh yes! – They left Brighton together on Sunday night, and were traced almost to London, but not beyond; they are certainly not gone to Scotland.'

'And what has been done, what has been attempted, to recover her?'

'My father is gone to London, and Jane has written to beg my uncle's immediate assistance, and we shall be off, I hope, in half an hour. But nothing can be done; I know very well that nothing can be done. How is such a man to be worked on? How are they even to be discovered? I have not the smallest hope. It is every way horrible!'

Darcy shook his head in silent acquiescence.

'When *my* eyes were opened to his real character. – Oh! had I known what I ought, what I dared, to do! But I knew not – I was afraid of doing too much. Wretched, wretched, mistake!'

Darcy made no answer. He seemed scarcely to hear her, and was walking up and down the room in earnest meditation; his brow contracted, his air gloomy. Elizabeth soon observed, and instantly understood it. Her power was sinking; every thing *must* sink under such a proof of family weakness, such an assurance of the deepest disgrace. She could neither wonder nor condemn, but the belief of his self-conquest brought nothing consolatory to her bosom, afforded no palliation of her distress. It was, on the contrary, exactly calculated to make her understand her own wishes; and never had she so honestly felt that she could have loved him, as now, when all love must be vain.

But self, though it would intrude, could not engross her, Lydia – the humiliation, the misery, she was bringing on them all, soon swallowed up every private care; and covering her face with her handkerchief, Elizabeth was soon lost to every thing else; and, after a pause of several minutes, was only recalled to a sense of her situation by the voice of her companion, who, in a manner, which though it spoke compassion, spoke likewise restraint, said, 'I am afraid you have been long desiring my absence, nor have I any thing to plead in excuse of my stay, but real, though unavailing, concern. Would to heaven that any thing could be either said or done on my part, that might offer consolation to such distress. – But I will not torment you with vain wishes, which may seem purposely to ask for your thanks. This unfortunate affair will, I fear, prevent my sister's having the pleasure of seeing you at Pemberley to day.'

'Oh, yes. Be so kind as to apologize for us to Miss Darcy. Say that urgent business calls us home immediately. Conceal the unhappy truth as long as it is possible. – I know it cannot be long.'

He readily assured her of his secrecy – again expressed his sorrow for her distress, wished it a happier conclusion than there was at present reason to hope, and leaving his compliments for her relations, with only one serious, parting, look, went away.

As he quitted the room, Elizabeth felt how improbable it was that they should ever see each other again on such terms of cordiality as had marked their several meetings in Derbyshire; and as she threw a retrospective glance over the whole of their acquaintance, so full of contradictions and varieties, sighed at the perverseness of those feelings which would now have promoted its continuance, and would formerly have rejoiced in its termination.

If gratitude and esteem are good foundations of affection, Elizabeth's change of sentiment will be neither improbable nor faulty. But if otherwise, if the regard springing from such sources is unreasonable or unnatural, in comparison of what is so often described as arising on a first interview with its object, and even before two words have been exchanged, nothing can be said in her defence, except that she had given somewhat of a trial to the latter method, in her partiality for Wickham, and that its ill-success might perhaps authorize her to seek the other less interesting mode of attachment. Be that as it may, she saw him go with regret; and in this early example of what Lydia's infamy must produce, found additional anguish as she reflected on that wretched business. Never, since reading Jane's second letter, had she entertained a hope of Wickham's meaning to marry her. No one but Jane, she thought, could flatter herself with such an expectation. Surprise was the least of her feelings on this development. While the contents of the first letter remained on her mind, she was all surprise – all astonishment that Wickham should marry a girl, whom it was impossible he could marry for money; and how Lydia could ever have attached him, had appeared incomprehensible. But now it was all too natural. For such an attachment as this, she might have sufficient charms; and though she did not suppose Lydia to be deliberately engaging in an elopement, without the intention of marriage, she had no difficulty in believing that neither her virtue nor her understanding would preserve her from falling an easy prey.

She had never perceived, while the regiment was in Hertfordshire, that Lydia had any partiality for him, but she was convinced that Lydia had wanted only encouragement to attach herself to any body. Sometimes one officer, sometimes another had been her favourite, as their attentions raised them in her opinion. Her affections had been continually fluctuating, but never without an object. The mischief of neglect and mistaken indulgence towards such a girl. – Oh! how acutely did she now feel it.

She was wild to be at home – to hear, to see, to be upon the spot, to share with Jane in the cares that must now fall wholly upon her, in a family so deranged; a father absent, a mother incapable of exertion, and requiring constant attendance; and though almost persuaded that nothing could be done for Lydia, her uncle's interference seemed of the utmost importance, and till he entered the room, the misery of her impatience was severe. Mr and Mrs Gardiner had hurried back in alarm, supposing, by the servant's account, that their niece was taken suddenly ill; – but satisfying them instantly on that head, she eagerly communicated the cause of their summons, reading the two letters aloud, and dwelling on the postscript of the last, with trembling energy. – Though Lydia had never been a favourite with them, Mr and Mrs Gardiner could not but be deeply affected. Not Lydia only, but all were concerned in it; and after the first exclamations of surprise and horror, Mr Gardiner readily promised every assistance in his power. – Elizabeth, though expecting no less, thanked him with tears of gratitude; and all three being actuated by one spirit, every thing relating to their journey was speedily settled. They were to be off as soon as possible. 'But what is to be done about Pemberley?' cried Mrs Gardiner, 'John told us Mr Darcy was here when you sent for us; – was it so?'

'Yes; and I told him we should not be able to keep our engagement. *That* is all settled.'

'That is all settled;' repeated the other, as she ran into her room to prepare. 'And are they upon such terms as for her to disclose the real truth! Oh, that I knew how it was!'

But wishes were vain; or at best could serve only to amuse her in the hurry and confusion of the following hour. Had Elizabeth been at leisure to be idle, she would have remained certain that all employment was impossible to one so wretched as herself; but she had her share of business as well as her aunt, and amongst the rest there were notes to be written to all their friends in Lambton, with false excuses for their sudden departure. An hour, however, saw the whole completed; and Mr Gardiner meanwhile having settled his account at the inn, nothing remained to be done but to go; and Elizabeth, after all the misery of the morning, found herself, in a shorter space of time than she could have supposed, seated in the carriage, and on the road to Longbourn.

The first pleasing earnest of their welcome

CHAPTER FORTY SEVEN

'I HAVE BEEN THINKING IT OVER AGAIN, Elizabeth,' said her uncle, as they drove from the town; 'and really, upon serious consideration, I am much more inclined than I was to judge as your eldest sister does of the matter. It appears to me so very unlikely, that any young man should form such a design against a girl who is by no means unprotected or friendless and who was actually staying in his colonel's family, that I am strongly inclined to hope the best. Could he expect that her friends would not step forward? Could he expect to be noticed again by the regiment, after such an affront to Colonel Forster? His temptation is not adequate to the risk.'

'Do you really think so?' cried Elizabeth, brightening up for a moment.

'Upon my word,' said Mrs Gardiner, 'I begin to be of your uncle's opinion. It is really too great a violation of decency, honour, and interest, for him to be guilty of it. I cannot think so very ill of Wickham. Can you, yourself, Lizzy, so wholly give him up, as to believe him capable of it?'

'Not perhaps of neglecting his own interest. But of every other neglect I can believe him capable. If, indeed, it should be so! But I dare not hope it. Why should they not go on to Scotland, if that had been the case?'

'In the first place,' replied Mr Gardiner, 'there is no absolute proof that they are not gone to Scotland.'

'Oh! but their removing from the chaise into an hackney coach is such a presumption! And, besides, no traces of them were to be found on the Barnet road.'

'Well, then – supposing them to be in London. They may be there, though for the purpose of concealment, for no more exceptionable purpose. It is not likely that money should be very abundant on either side; and it might strike them that they could be more economically, though less expeditiously, married in London, than in Scotland.'

'But why all this secrecy? Why any fear of detection? Why must their marriage be private? Oh! no, no, this it not likely. His most particular friend, you see by Jane's account, was persuaded of his never intending to marry her. Wickham will never marry a woman without some money. He cannot afford it. And what claims has Lydia, what attractions has she beyond youth, health, and good humour, that could make him for her sake, forego every chance of benefiting himself by marrying well? As to what restraint the apprehension of disgrace in the corps might throw on a dishonourable elopement with her, I am not able to judge; for I know nothing of the effects that such a step might produce. But as to your other objection, I am afraid it will hardly hold good. Lydia has no brothers to step forward; and he might imagine, from my father's behaviour, from his indolence and the little attention he has ever seemed to give to what was going forward in his family, that *he* would do as little, and think as little about it, as any father could do, in such a matter.'

'But can you think that Lydia is so lost to every thing but love of him, as to consent to live with him on any other terms than marriage?'

'It does seem, and it is most shocking indeed,' replied Elizabeth, with tears in her eyes, 'that a sister's sense of decency and virtue in such a point should admit of doubt. But, really, I know not what to say. Perhaps I am not doing her justice. But she is very young; she has never been taught to think on serious subjects; and for the last half year, nay, for a twelvemonth, she has been given up to nothing but amusement and vanity. She has been allowed to dispose of her time in the most idle and frivolous manner, and to adopt any opinions that came in her way. Since the –shire were first quartered in Meryton, nothing but love, flirtation, and officers, have been in her head. She has been doing every thing in her power by thinking and talking on the subject, to give greater – what shall I call it? susceptibility to her feelings; which are naturally lively enough. And we all know that Wickham has every charm of person and address than can captivate a woman.'

'But you see that Jane,' said her aunt, 'does not think so ill of Wickham, as to believe him capable of the attempt.'

'Of whom does Jane ever think ill? And who is there, whatever might be their former conduct, that she would believe capable of such an attempt, till it were proved against them? But Jane knows, as well as I do, what Wickham really is. We both know that he has been profligate in every sense of the word. That he has neither integrity nor honour. That he is as false and deceitful, as he is insinuating.'

'And do you really know all this?' cried Mrs Gardiner, whose curiosity as to the mode of her intelligence was all alive.

'I do, indeed,' replied Elizabeth, colouring. 'I told you the other day, of his infamous behaviour to Mr Darcy; and you, yourself, when last at Longbourn, heard in what manner he spoke of the man, who had behaved with such forbearance and liberality towards him. And there are other circumstances which I am not at liberty – which it is not worth while to relate; but his lies about the whole Pemberley family are endless. From what he said of Miss Darcy, I was thoroughly prepared to see a proud, reserved, disagreeable girl. Yet he knew to the contrary himself. He must know that she was as amiable and unpretending as we have found her.'

'But does Lydia know nothing of this? Can she be ignorant of what you and Jane seem so well to understand?'

'Oh, yes! – that, that is the worst of all. Till I was in Kent, and saw so much both of Mr Darcy and his relation, Colonel Fitzwilliam, I was ignorant of the truth myself. And when I returned home, the –shire was to leave Meryton in a week or fortnight's time. As that was the case, neither Jane, to whom I related the whole, nor I, thought it necessary to make our knowledge public; for of what use could it apparently be to any one, that the good opinion which all the neighbourhood had of him, should be overthrown? And even when it was settled that Lydia should go with Mrs Forster, the necessity of opening her eyes to his character never occurred to me. That *she* could be in any danger from the deception never entered my head. That such a consequence as *this* should ensue, you may easily believe was far enough from my thoughts.'

'When they all removed to Brighton, therefore, you had no reason, I suppose, to believe them fond of each other.'

'Not the slightest. I can remember no symptom of affection on either side; and had any thing of the kind been perceptible, you must be aware that ours is not a family, on which it could be thrown away. When first he entered the corps, she was ready enough to admire him; but so we all were. Every girl in, or near Meryton, was out of her senses about him for the first two months; but he never distinguished *her* by any particular attention, and, consequently, after a moderate period of extravagant and wild admiration, her fancy for him gave way, and others of the regiment, who treated her with more distinction, again became her favourites.'

It may be easily believed, that however little of novelty could be added to their fears, hopes, and conjectures, on this interesting subject, by its repeated discussion, no other could detain them from it long, during the whole of the journey. From Elizabeth's thoughts it was never absent. Fixed there by the keenest of all anguish, self reproach, she could find no interval of ease or forgetfulness.

They travelled as expeditiously as possible; and sleeping one night on the road, reached Longbourn by dinner-time the next day. It was a comfort to Elizabeth to consider that Jane could not have been wearied by long expectations.

The little Gardiners, attracted by the sight of a chaise, were standing on the steps of the house, as they entered the paddock; and when the carriage drove up to the door, the joyful surprise that lighted up their faces, and displayed itself over their whole bodies, in a variety of capers and frisks, was the first pleasing earnest of their welcome.

Elizabeth jumped out; and, after giving each of them an hasty kiss, hurried into the vestibule, where Jane, who came running down stairs from her mother's apartment, immediately met her.

Elizabeth, as she affectionately embraced her, whilst tears filled the eyes of both, lost not a moment in asking whether any thing had been heard of the fugitives.

'Not yet,' replied Jane. 'But now that my dear uncle is come, I hope everything will be well.'

'Is my father in town?'

'Yes, he went on Tuesday as I wrote you word.'

'And have you heard from him often?'

'We have heard only once. He wrote me a few lines on Wednesday, to say that he arrived in safety, and to give me his directions, which I particularly begged him to do. He merely added, that he should not write again, till he had something of importance to mention.'

'And my mother – How is she? How are you all?'

'My mother is tolerably well, I trust; though her spirits are greatly shaken. She is up stairs, and will have great satisfaction in seeing you all. She does not yet leave her dressing-room. Mary and Kitty, thank Heaven! are quite well.'

'But you – How are you?' cried Elizabeth, 'You look pale. How much you must have gone through!'

Her sister, however, assured her, of her being perfectly well; and their conversation, which had been passing while Mr and Mrs Gardiner were engaged with their children, was now put an end to, by the approach of the whole party. Jane ran to her uncle and aunt, and welcomed and thanked them both, with alternate smiles and tears.

When they were all in the drawing room, the questions which Elizabeth had already asked, were of course repeated by the others, and they soon found that Jane had no intelligence to give. The sanguine hope of good, however, which the benevolence of her heart suggested, had not yet deserted her; she still expected that it would all end well, and that every morning would bring some letter, either from Lydia or her father, to explain their proceedings, and perhaps announce the marriage.

Mrs Bennet, to whose apartment they all repaired, after a few minutes conversation together, received them exactly as might be expected; with tears and lamentations of regret, invectives against the villainous conduct of Wickham, and complaints of her own sufferings and ill usage; blaming every body but the person to whose ill judging indulgence the errors of her daughter must be principally owing.

'If I had been able,' said she, 'to carry my point of going to Brighton, with all my family, *this* would not have happened; but poor dear Lydia had nobody to take care of her. Why did the Forsters ever let her go out of their sight? I am sure there was some great neglect or other on their side, for she is not the kind of girl to do such a thing, if she had been well looked after. I always thought they were very unfit to have the charge of her; but I was over-ruled, as I always am. Poor dear child! And now here's Mr Bennet gone away, and I know he will fight Wickham, wherever he meets him, and then he will be killed, and what is to become of us all? The Collinses will turn us out, before he is cold in his grave; and if you are not kind to us, brother, I do not know what we shall do.'

They all exclaimed against such terrific ideas; and Mr Gardiner, after general assurances of his affection for her and all her family, told her that he meant to be in London the very next day, and would assist Mr Bennet in every endeavour for recovering Lydia.

'Do not give way to useless alarm,' added he, 'though it is right to be prepared for the worst, there is no occasion to look on it as certain. It is not quite a week since they left Brighton. In a few days more, we may gain some news of them, and till we know that they are not married, and have no design of marrying, do not let us give the matter over as lost. As soon as I get to town, I shall go to my brother, and make him come home with me to Gracechurch Street, and then we may consult together as to what is to be done.'

'Oh my dear brother,' replied Mrs Bennet, 'that is exactly what I could most wish for. And now do, when you get to town, find them out, wherever they may be; and if they are not married already, *make* them marry. And as for wedding clothes, do not let them wait for that, but tell Lydia she shall have as much money as she chuses, to buy them, after they are married. And, above all things, keep Mr Bennet from fighting. Tell him what a dreadful state I am in, – that I am frightened out of my wits; and have such tremblings, such flutterings all over me, such spasms in my side, and pains in my head, and such beatings at heart, that I can get no rest by night nor by day. And tell my dear Lydia, not to give any directions about her clothes, till she has seen me, for she does not know which are the best warehouses. Oh, brother, how kind you are! I know you will contrive it all.'

But Mr Gardiner, though he assured her again of his earnest endeavours in the cause, could not avoid recommending moderation to her, as well as in her hopes as her fears; and, after talking with her in this manner till dinner was on table, they left her to vent all her feelings on the housekeeper, who attended, in the absence of her daughters.

Though her brother and sister were persuaded that there was no real occasion for such a seclusion from the family, they did not attempt to oppose it, for they knew that she had not prudence enough to hold her tongue before the servants, while they waited at table, and judged it better that *one* only of the household, and the one whom they could most trust, should comprehend all her fears and solicitude on the subject.

In the dining-room they were soon joined by Mary and Kitty, who had been too busily engaged in their separate apartments, to make their appearance before. One came from her books, and the other from her toilette. The faces of both, however, were tolerably calm; and no change was visible in either except that the loss of her favourite sister, or the anger which she had herself incurred in the business, had given something more of fretfulness than usual, to the accents of Kitty. As for Mary, she was mistress enough of herself to whisper to Elizabeth with a countenance of grave reflection, soon after they were seated at table,

'This is a most unfortunate affair; and will probably be much talked of. But we must stem the tide of malice, and pour into the wounded bosoms of each other, the balm of sisterly consolation.'

Then, perceiving in Elizabeth no inclination of replying, she added, 'Unhappy as the event must be for Lydia, we may draw from it this useful lesson; that loss of virtue in a female is irretrievable – that one false step involves her in endless ruin – that her reputation is no less brittle than it is beautiful, – and that she cannot be too much guarded in her behaviour towards the undeserving of the other sex.'

Elizabeth lifted up her eyes in amazement, but was too much oppressed to make any reply. Mary, however, continued to console herself with such kind of moral extractions from the evil before them.

In the afternoon, the two elder Miss Bennets were able to be for half an hour by themselves; and Elizabeth instantly availed herself of the opportunity of making many enquiries, which Jane was equally eager to satisfy. After joining in general lamentations over the dreadful sequel of this event, which Elizabeth considered as all but certain, and Miss Bennet could not assert to be wholly impossible; the former continued the subject, by saying, 'But tell me all and every thing about it, which I have not already heard. Give me farther particulars. What did Colonel Forster say? Had they no apprehension of any thing before the elopement took place? They must have seen them together for ever.'

'Colonel Forster did own that he had often suspected some partiality, especially on Lydia's side, but nothing to give him any alarm. I am so grieved for him. His behaviour was attentive and kind to the utmost. He *was* coming to us, in order to assure us of his concern, before he had any idea of their now being gone to Scotland: when that apprehension first got abroad, it hastened his journey.'

'And was Denny convinced that Wickham would not marry? Did he know of their intending to go off? Had Colonel Forster seen Denny himself?'

'Yes; but when questioned by *him* Denny denied knowing any thing of their plan, and would not give his real opinion about it. He did not repeat his persuasion of their not marrying – and from *that*, I am inclined to hope, he might have been misunderstood before.'

'And till Colonel Forster came himself, not one of you entertained a doubt, I suppose, of their being really married?'

'How was it possible that such an idea should enter our brains! I felt a little uneasy – a little fearful of my sister's happiness with him in marriage, because I knew that his conduct had not been always quite right. My father and mother knew nothing of that, they only felt how imprudent a match it must be. Kitty then owned, with a very natural triumph on knowing more than the rest of us, that in Lydia's last letter, she had prepared her for such a step. She had known, it seems, of their being in love with each other, many weeks.'

'But not before they went to Brighton?'

'No, I believe not.'

'And did Colonel Forster appear to think ill of Wickham himself? Does he know his real character?'

'I must confess that he did not speak so well of Wickham as he formerly did. He believed him to be imprudent and extravagant. And since this sad affair has taken place, it is said, that he left Meryton greatly in debt; but I hope this may be false.'

'Oh, Jane, had we been less secret, had we told what we knew of him, this could not have happened!'

'Perhaps it would have been better,' replied her sister. 'But to expose the former faults of any person, without knowing what their present feelings were, seemed unjustifiable. We acted with the best intentions.'

'Could Colonel Forster repeat the particulars of Lydia's note to his wife?'

'He brought it with him for us to see.'

Jane then took it from her pocket-book, and gave it to Elizabeth. There were the contents:

My Dear Harriet,

You will laugh when you know where I am gone, and I cannot help laughing myself at your surprise tomorrow morning, as soon as I am missed. I am going to Gretna Green, and if you cannot guess with who, I shall think you a simpleton, for there is but one man in the world I love, so think it no harm to be off. You need not send them word at Longbourn of my going, if you do not like it, for it will make the surprise the greater, when I write to them, and sign my name Lydia Wickham. What a good joke it will be! I can hardly write for laughing. Pray make my excuses to Pratt, for not keeping my engagement, and dancing with him to night. Tell him I hope he will excuse me when he knows all, and tell him I will dance with him at the next ball we meet, with great pleasure. I shall send for my clothes when I get to Longbourn; but I wish you would tell Sally to mend a great slit in my working muslin gown, before they are packed up. Good bye. Give my love to Colonel Forster, I hope you will drink to our good journey.

Your affectionate friend,

LYDIA BENNET.

'Oh! thoughtless, thoughtless Lydia!' cried Elizabeth when she had finished it. 'What a letter is this, to be written at such a moment. But at least it shews, that *she* was serious in the object of her journey. Whatever he might afterwards persuade her to, it was not on her side a *scheme* of infamy. My poor father! how he must have felt it!'

'I never saw any one so shocked. He could not speak a word for full ten minutes. My mother was taken ill immediately, and the whole house in such confusion!'

'Oh! Jane,' cried Elizabeth, 'was there a servant belonging to it, who did not know the whole story before the end of the day?'

'I do not know. – I hope there was. – But to be guarded at such a time, is very difficult. My mother was in hysterics, and though I endeavoured to give her every assistance in my power, I am afraid I did not do so much as I might have done! But the horror of what might possibly happen, almost took from me my faculties.'

'Your attendance upon her, has been too much for you. You do not look well. Oh! that I had been with you, you have had every care and anxiety upon yourself alone.'

'Mary and Kitty have been very kind, and would have shared in every fatigue, I am sure, but I did not think it right for either of them. Kitty is slight and delicate, and Mary studies so much, that her hours of repose should not be broken in on. My aunt Philips came to Longbourn on Tuesday, after my father went away; and was so good as to stay until Thursday with me. She was of great use and comfort to us all, and Lady Lucas has been very kind; she walked here on Wednesday morning to condole with us, and offered her services, or any of her daughters, if they could be of use to us.'

'She had better have stayed at home,' cried Elizabeth; 'perhaps she *meant* well, but, under such a misfortune as this, one cannot see too little of one's neighbours. Assistance is impossible; condolence, insufferable. Let them triumph over us at a distance, and be satisfied.'

She then proceeded to enquire into the measures which her father had intended to pursue, while in town, for the recovery of his daughter.

'He meant, I believe,' replied Jane, 'to go to Epsom, the place where they last changed horses, see the postilions, and try if any thing could be made out from them. His principal object must be, to discover the number of the hackney coach which took them from Clapham. It had come with a fare from London; and as he thought the circumstance of a gentleman and lady's removing from one carriage into another, might be remarked, he meant to make enquiries at Clapham. If he could any how discover at what house the coachman had before set down his fare, he determined to make enquiries there, and hoped it might not be impossible to find out the stand and number of the coach. I do not know of any other designs that he had formed; but he was in such a hurry to be gone, and his spirits so greatly discomposed, that I had difficulty in finding out even so much as this.'

The Post

CHAPTER FORTY EIGHT

THE WHOLE PARTY WERE IN HOPES OF a letter from Mr Bennet the next morning, but the post came in without bringing a single line from him. His family knew him to be on all common occasions, a most negligent and dilatory correspondent, but at such a time, they had hoped for exertion. They were forced to conclude, that he had no pleasing intelligence to send, but even of *that* they would have been glad to be certain. Mr Gardiner had waited only for the letters before he set off.

When he was gone, they were certain at least of receiving constant information of what was going on, and their uncle promised, at parting, to prevail on Mr Bennet to return to Longbourn, as soon as he could, to the great consolation of his sister, who considered it as the only security for her husband's not being killed in a duel.

Mrs Gardiner and the children were to remain in Hertfordshire a few days longer, as the former thought her presence might be serviceable to her nieces. She shared in their attendance on Mrs Bennet, and was a great comfort to them, in their hours of freedom. Their other aunt also visited them frequently, and always, as she said, with the design of cheering and heartening them up, though as she never came without reporting some fresh instance of Wickham's extravagance or irregularity, she seldom went away without leaving them more dispirited than she found them.

All Meryton seemed striving to blacken the man, who, but three months before, had been almost an angel of light. He was declared to be in debt to every tradesman in the place, and his intrigues, all honoured with the title of seduction, had been extended into every tradesman's family. Every body declared that he was the wickedest young man in the world; and every body began to find out, that they had always distrusted the appearance of his goodness. Elizabeth, though she did not credit above half of what was said, believed enough to make her former assurance of her sister's ruin still more certain; and even Jane, who believed still less of it, became almost hopeless, more especially as the time was now come, when if they had gone to Scotland, which she had never before entirely despaired of, they must in all probability have gained some news of them.

Mr Gardiner left Longbourn on Sunday; on Tuesday, his wife received a letter from him; it told them, that on his arrival, he had immediately found out his brother, and persuaded him to come to Gracechurch street. That Mr Bennet had been to Epsom and Clapham, before his arrival, but without gaining any satisfactory information; and that he was now determined to enquire at all the principal hotels in town, as Mr Bennet thought it possible they might have gone to one of them, on their first coming to London, before they procured lodgings. Mr Gardiner himself did not expect any success from this measure, but as his brother was eager in it, he meant to assist him in pursuing it. He added, that Mr Bennet seemed wholly disinclined at present, to leave London, and promised to write again very soon. There was also a postscript to this effect.

'I have written to Colonel Forster to desire him to find out, if possible, from some of the young man's intimates in the regiment, whether Wickham has any relations or connections, who would be likely to know in what part of the town he has now concealed himself. If there were any one, that one could apply to, with a probability of gaining such a clue as that, it might be of essential consequence. At present we have nothing to guide us. Colonel Forster will, I dare say, do every thing in his power to satisfy us on this head. But, on second thoughts, perhaps Lizzy could tell us, what relations he has now living, better than any other person.'

Elizabeth was at no loss to understand from whence this deference for her authority proceeded; but it was not in her power to give any information of so satisfactory a nature, as the compliment deserved.

She had never heard of his having had any relations, except a father and mother, both of whom had been dead many years. It was possible, however, that some of his companions in the –shire, might be able to give more information; and, though she was not very sanguine in expecting it, the application was a something to look forward to.

Every day at Longbourn was now a day of anxiety; but the most anxious part of each was when the post was expected. The arrival of letters was the first grand object of every morning's impatience. Through letters, whatever of good or bad was to be told, would be communicated, and every succeeding day was expected to bring some news of importance.

But before they heard again from Mr Gardiner, a letter arrived for their father, from a different quarter, from Mr Collins; which, as Jane had received directions to open all that came for him in his absence, she accordingly read; and Elizabeth, who knew what curiosities his letters always were, looked over her, and read it likewise. It was as follows:

MY DEAR SIR,

I feel myself called upon by our relationship, and my situation in life, to condole with you on the grievous affliction you are now suffering under, of which we were yesterday informed by a letter from Hertfordshire. Be assured, my dear Sir, that Mrs Collins and myself sincerely sympathise with you, and all your respectable family, in your present distress, which must be of the bitterest kind, because proceeding from a cause which no time can remove. No arguments shall be wanting on my part, that can alleviate so severe a

'To whom I have related the affair'

misfortune; or that may comfort you, under a circumstance that must be of all others most afflicting to a parent's mind. The death of your daughter would have been a blessing in comparison of this. And it is the more to be lamented, because there is reason to suppose, as my dear Charlotte informs me, that this licentiousness of behaviour in your daughter, has proceeded from a faulty degree of indulgence, though, at the same time, for the consolation of yourself and Mrs Bennet, I am inclined to think that her own disposition must be naturally bad, or she could not be guilty of such an enormity, at so early an age. Howsoever that may be, you are grievously to be pitied, in which opinion I am not only joined by Mrs Collins, but likewise by lady Catherine and her daughter, to whom I have related the affair. They agree with me in apprehending that this false step in one daughter, will be injurious to the fortunes of all the others, for who, as lady Catherine herself condescendingly says, will connect themselves with such a family. And this consideration leads me moreover to reflect with augmented satisfaction on a certain event of last November, for had it been otherwise, I must have been involved in all your sorrow and disgrace. Let me advise you then, my dear Sir, to console yourself as much as possible, to throw off your unworthy child from your affection for ever, and leave her to reap the fruits of her own heinous offence.

I am, dear Sir, &c. &c.

Mr Gardiner did not write again, till he had received an answer from Colonel Forster; and then he had nothing of a pleasant nature to send. It was not known that Wickham had a single relation, with whom he kept up any connection, and it was certain that he had no near one living. His former acquaintances had been numerous; but since he had been in the militia, it did not appear that he was on terms of particular friendship with any of them. There was no one therefore who could be pointed out, as likely to give any news of him. And in the wretched state of his own finances, there was a very powerful motive for secrecy, in addition to his fear of discovery by Lydia's relations, for it had just transpired that he had left gaming debts behind him, to a very considerable amount. Colonel Forster believed that more than a thousand pounds would be necessary to clear his expences at Brighton. He owed a good deal in the town, but his debts of honour were still more formidable. Mr Gardiner did not attempt to conceal these particulars from the Longbourn family; Jane heard them with horror. 'A gamester!' she cried. 'This is wholly unexpected. I had not an idea of it.'

Mr Gardiner added in his letter, that they might expect to see their father at home on the following day, which was Saturday. Rendered spiritless by the ill-success of all their endeavours, he had yielded to his brother-in-law's intreaty that he would return to his family, and leave it to him to do, whatever occasion might suggest to be advisable for continuing their pursuit. When Mrs Bennet was told of this, she did not express so much satisfaction as her children expected, considering what her anxiety for his life had been before.

'What, is he coming home, and without poor Lydia!' she cried. 'Sure he will not leave London before he has found them. Who is to fight Wickham, and make him marry her, if he comes away?'

As Mrs Gardiner began to wish to be at home, it was settled that she and her children should go to London, at the same time that Mr Bennet came from it. The coach, therefore, took them the first stage of their journey, and brought its master back to Longbourn.

Mrs Gardiner went away in all the perplexity about Elizabeth and her Derbyshire friend, that had attended her from that part of the world. His name had never been voluntarily mentioned before them by her niece; and the kind of half-expectation which Mrs Gardiner had formed, of their being followed by a letter from him, had ended in nothing. Elizabeth had received none since her return, that could come from Pemberley.

The present unhappy state of the family, rendered any other excuse for the lowness of her spirits unnecessary; nothing, therefore, could be fairly conjectured from *that*, though Elizabeth, who was by this time tolerably well acquainted with her own feelings, was perfectly aware, that, had she known nothing of Darcy, she could have borne the dread of Lydia's infamy somewhat better. It would have spared her, she thought, one sleepless night out of two.

When Mr Bennet arrived, he had all the appearance of his usual philosophic composure. He said as little as he had ever been in the habit of saying; made no mention of the business that had taken him away, and it was some time before his daughters had courage to speak of it.

It was not till the afternoon, when he joined them at tea, that Elizabeth ventured to introduce the subject; and then, on her briefly expressing her sorrow for what he must have endured, he replied, 'Say nothing of that. Who should suffer but myself? It has been my own doing, and I ought to feel it.'

'You must not be too severe upon yourself,' replied Elizabeth.

'You may well warn me against such an evil. Human nature is so prone to fall into it! No, Lizzy, let me once in my life feel how much I have been to blame. I am not afraid of being overpowered by the impression. It will pass away soon enough.'

'Do you suppose them to be in London?'

'Yes; where else can they be so well concealed?'

'And Lydia used to want to go to London,' added Kitty.

'She is happy, then,' said her father, drily; 'and her residence there will probably be of some duration.'

Then, after a short silence, he continued, 'Lizzy, I bear you no ill-will for being justified in your advice to me last May, which, considering the event, shews some greatness of mind.'

They were interrupted by Miss Bennet, who came to fetch her mother's tea.

'This is a parade,' cried he, 'which does one good; it gives such an elegance to misfortune! Another day I will do the same; I will sit in my library, in my night cap and powdering gown, and give as much trouble as I can, – or, perhaps, I may defer it, till Kitty runs away.'

'I am not going to run away, Papa,' said Kitty, fretfully; 'if *I* should ever go to Brighton, I would behave better than Lydia.'

'*You* go to Brighton! – I would not trust you so near it as East Bourne, for fifty pounds! No, Kitty, I have at last learnt to be cautious, and you will feel the effects of it. No officer is ever to enter my house again, nor even to pass through the village. Balls will be absolutely prohibited, unless you stand up with one of your sisters. And you are never to stir out of doors, till you can prove, that you have spent ten minutes of every day in a rational manner.'

Kitty, who took all these threats in a serious light, began to cry.

'Well, well, said he, 'do not make yourself unhappy. If you are a good girl for the next ten years, I will take you to a review at the end of them.'

CHAPTER FORTY NINE

TWO DAYS AFTER MR BENNET'S RETURN, as Jane and Elizabeth were walking together in the shrubbery behind the house, they saw the housekeeper coming towards them, and, concluding that she came to call them to their mother, went forward to meet her; but, instead of the expected summons, when they approached her, she said to Miss Bennet, 'I beg your pardon, madam, for interrupting you, but I was in hopes you might have got some good news from town, so I took the liberty of coming to ask.'

'What do you mean, Hill? We have heard nothing from town.'

'Dear madam,' cried Mrs Hill, in great astonishment, 'don't you know there is an express come for master from Mr Gardiner? He has been here this half hour, and master has had a letter.'

Away ran the girls, too eager to get in to have time for speech. They ran through the vestibule into the breakfast room; from thence to the library; – their father was in neither; and they were on the point of seeking him up stairs with their mother, when they were met by the butler, who said,

'If you are looking for my master, ma'am, he is walking towards the little copse.'

Upon this information, they instantly passed through the hall once more, and ran across the lawn after their father, who was deliberately pursuing his way towards a small wood on one side of the paddock.

Jane, who was not so light, nor so much in the habit of running as Elizabeth, soon lagged behind, while her sister, panting for breath, came up with him, and eagerly cried out,

'Oh, Papa, what news? what news? have you heard from my uncle?'

'Yes, I have had a letter from him by express.'

'Well, and what news does it bring? good or bad?'

'What is there of good to be expected?' said he, taking the letter from his pocket; 'but perhaps you would like to read it.'

Elizabeth impatiently caught it from his hand. Jane now came up.

'Read it aloud,' said their father, 'for I hardly know myself what it is about.'

Gracechurch-street, Monday,

MY DEAR BROTHER, *August 2.*

At last I am able to send you some tidings of my niece, and such as, upon the whole, I hope will give you satisfaction. Soon after you left me on Saturday, I was fortunate enough to find out in what part of London they were. The particulars, I reserve till we meet. It is enough to know they are discovered. I have seen them both –

'Then it is, as I always hoped,' cried Jane: 'they are married!'

Elizabeth read on:

I have seen them both. They are not married, nor can I find there was any intention of being so; but if you are willing to perform the engagements which I have ventured to make on your side, I hope it will not be long before they are. All that is required of you is, to assure to your daughter, by settlement, her

'But perhaps you would like to read it'

equal share of the five thousand pounds, secured among your children after the decease of yourself and my sister; and, moreover, to enter into an engagement of allowing her, during your life, one hundred pounds per annum. These are conditions, which, considering every thing, I had no hesitation in complying with, as far as I thought myself privileged, for you. I shall send this by express, that no time may be lost in bringing me your answer. You will easily comprehend, from these particulars, that Mr Wickham's circumstances are not so hopeless as they are generally believed to be. The world has been deceived in that respect; and I am happy to say, there will be some little money, even when all his debts are discharged, to settle on my niece, in addition to her own fortune. If, as I conclude will be the case, you send me full powers to act in your name, throughout the whole of this business, I will immediately give directions to Haggerston for preparing a proper settlement. There will not be the smallest occasion for your coming to town again; therefore, stay quietly at Longbourn, and depend on my diligence and care. Send back your answer as soon as you can, and be careful to write explicitly. We have judged it best, that my niece should be married from this house, of which I hope you will approve. She comes to us to-day. I shall write again as soon as any thing more is determined on. Your's, &c. EDW. GARDINER.

'Is it possible!' cried Elizabeth, when she had finished. 'Can it be possible that he will marry her?'

'Wickham is not so undeserving, then, as we have thought him;' said her sister. 'My dear father, I congratulate you.'

'And have you answered the letter?' said Elizabeth.

'No; but it must be done soon.'

Most earnestly did she then intreat him to lose no more time before he wrote.

'Oh! my dear father,' she cried, 'come back, and write immediately. Consider how important every moment is, in such a case.'

'Let me write for you,' said Jane, 'if you dislike the trouble yourself.'

'I dislike it very much,' he replied; 'but it must be done.'

And so saying, he turned back with them, and walked towards the house.

'And may I ask?' said Elizabeth, 'but the terms, I suppose, must be complied with.'

'Complied with! I am only ashamed of his asking so little.'

'And they *must* marry! Yet he is *such* a man!'

'Yes, yes, they must marry. There is nothing else to be done. But there are two things that I want very much to know: – one is, how much money your uncle has laid down, to bring it about; and the other, how I am ever to pay him.'

'Money! my uncle!' cried Jane, 'what do you mean, Sir?'

'I mean, that no man in his senses, would marry Lydia on so slight a temptation as one hundred a-year during my life, and fifty after I am gone.'

'That is very true,' said Elizabeth; 'though it had not occurred to me before. His debts to be discharged, and something still to remain! Oh! it must be my uncle's doings! Generous, good man, I am afraid he has distressed himself. A small sum would not do all this.'

'No,' said her father, 'Wickham's a fool, if he takes her with a farthing less than ten thousand pounds. I should be sorry to think so ill of him, in the very beginning of our relationship.'

'Ten thousand pounds! Heaven forbid! How is half such a sum to be repaid?'

Mr Bennet made no answer, and each of them, deep in thought, continued silent till they reached the house. Their father then went to the library to write, and the girls walked into the breakfast-room.

'And they are really to be married!' cried Elizabeth, as soon as they were by themselves. 'How strange this is! And for *this* we are to be thankful. That they should marry, small as is their chance of happiness, and wretched as is his character, we are forced to rejoice! Oh, Lydia!'

'I comfort myself with thinking,' replied Jane, 'that he certainly would not marry Lydia, if he had not a real regard for her. Though our kind uncle has done something towards clearing him, I cannot believe that ten thousand pounds, or any thing like it, has been advanced. He has children of his own, and may have more. How could he spare half ten thousand pounds?'

'If we are ever able to learn what Wickham's debts have been,' said Elizabeth, 'and how much is settled on his side on our sister, we shall exactly know what Mr Gardiner has done for them, because Wickham has not sixpence of his own. The kindness of my uncle and aunt can never be requited. Their taking her home, and affording her their personal protection and countenance, is such a sacrifice to her advantage, as years of gratitude cannot enough acknowledge. By this time she is actually with them! If such goodness does not make her miserable now, she will never deserve to be happy! What a meeting for her, when she first sees my aunt!'

'We must endeavour to forget all that has passed on either side,' said Jane: 'I hope and trust they will yet be happy. His consenting to marry her is a proof, I will believe, that he is come to a right way of thinking. Their mutual affection will steady them; and I flatter myself they will settle so quietly, and live in so rational a manner, as may in time make their past imprudence forgotten.'

'Their conduct has been such,' replied Elizabeth, 'as neither you, nor I, nor any body, can ever forget. It is useless to talk of it.'

It now occurred to the girls that their mother was in all likelihood perfectly ignorant of what had happened. They went to the library, therefore, and asked their father, whether he would not wish them to make it known to her. He was writing, and, without raising his head, coolly replied,

'Just as you please.'

'May we take my uncle's letter to read to her?'

'Take whatever you like, and get away.'

Elizabeth took the letter from his writing table, and they went up stairs together. Mary and Kitty were both with Mrs Bennet: one communication would, therefore, do for all. After a slight preparation for good news, the letter was read aloud. Mrs Bennet could hardly contain herself. As soon as Jane had read Mr Gardiner's hope of Lydia's being soon married, her joy burst forth, and every following sentence added to its exuberance. She was now in an irritation as violent from delight, as she had ever been fidgetty from alarm and vexation. To know that her daughter would be married was enough. She was disturbed by no fear for her felicity, nor humbled by any remembrance of her misconduct.

'My dear, dear Lydia!' she cried: 'This is delightful indeed! – She will be married – I shall see her again! – She will be married at sixteen! – My good, kind brother! – I knew how it would be – I knew he would manage every thing. How I long to see her! and to see dear Wickham too! but the clothes, the wedding clothes! I will write to my sister Gardiner about them directly. Lizzy, my dear, run down to your father, and ask him how much he will give her. Stay, stay, I will go myself. Ring the bell, Kitty, for Hill. I will put on my things in a moment. My dear, dear Lydia! – How merry we shall be together when we meet!'

Her eldest daughter endeavoured to give some relief to the violence of these transports, by leading her thoughts to the obligations which Mr Gardiner's behaviour laid them all under.

'For we must attribute this happy conclusion,' she added, 'in a great measure, to his kindness. We are persuaded that he has pledged himself to assist Mr Wickham with money.'

'Well,' cried her mother, 'it is all very right; who should do it but her own uncle? If he had not had a family of his own, I and my children must have had all his money you know, and it is the first time we have ever had any thing from him, except a few presents. Well! I am so happy. In a short time, I shall have a daughter married. Mrs Wickham! How well it sounds. And she was only sixteen last June. My dear Jane, I am in such a flutter, that I am sure I can't write; so I will dictate, and you write for me. We will settle with your father about the money afterwards; but the things should be ordered immediately.'

She was then proceeding to all the particulars of calico, muslin, and cambric, and would shortly have dictated some very plentiful orders, had not Jane, though with some difficulty, persuaded her to wait, till her father was at leisure to be consulted. One day's delay she observed, would be of small importance; and her mother was too happy, to be quite so obstinate as usual. Other schemes too came into her head.

'I will go to Meryton,' said she, 'as soon as I am dressed, and tell the good, good news to my sister Philips. And as I come back, I can call on Lady Lucas and Mrs Long. Kitty, run down and order the carriage. An airing would do me a great deal of good, I am sure. Girls, can I do any thing for you in Meryton? Oh! here comes Hill. My dear Hill, have you heard the good news? Miss Lydia is going to be married; and you shall all have a bowl of punch, to make merry at her wedding.'

Mrs Hill began instantly to express her joy. Elizabeth received her congratulations amongst the rest, and then, sick of this folly, took refuge in her own room, that she might think with freedom.

Poor Lydia's situation must, at best, be bad enough; but that it was no worse, she had need to be thankful. She felt it so; and though, in looking forward, neither rational happiness nor worldly prosperity, could be justly expected for her sister; in looking back to what they had feared, only two hours ago, she felt all the advantages of what they had gained.

The spiteful old ladies

CHAPTER FIFTY

MR BENNET HAD VERY OFTEN WISHED, before this period of his life, that, instead of spending his whole income, he had laid by an annual sum, for the better provision of his children, and of his wife, if she survived him. He now wished it more than ever. Had he done his duty in that respect, Lydia need not have been indebted to her uncle, for whatever of honour or credit could now be purchased for her. The satisfaction of prevailing on one of the most worthless young men in Great Britain to be her husband, might then have rested in its proper place.

He was seriously concerned, that a cause of so little advantage to any one, should be forwarded at the sole expence of his brother-in-law, and he was determined, if possible, to find out the extent of his assistance, and to discharge the obligation as soon as he could.

When first Mr Bennet had married, economy was held to be perfectly useless; for, of course, they were to have a son. This son was to join in cutting off the entail, as soon as he should be of age, and the widow and younger children would by that means be provided for. Five daughters successively entered the world, but yet the son was to come; and Mrs Bennet, for many years after Lydia's birth, had been certain that he would. This event had at last been despaired of, but it was then too late to be saving. Mrs Bennet had no turn for economy, and her husband's love of independence had alone prevented their exceeding their income.

Five thousand pounds was settled by marriage articles on Mrs Bennet and the children. But in what proportions it should be divided amongst the latter, depended on the will of the parents. This was one point, with regard to Lydia at least, which was now to be settled, and Mr Bennet could have no hesitation in acceding to the proposal before him. In terms of grateful acknowledgment for the kindness of his brother, though expressed most concisely, he then delivered on paper his perfect approbation of all that was done, and his willingness to fulfil the engagements that had been made for him. He had never before supposed that, could Wickham be prevailed on to marry his daughter, it would be done with so little inconvenience to himself, as by the present arrangement. He would scarcely be ten pounds a-year the loser, by the hundred that was to be paid them; for what with her board and pocket allowance, and the continual presents in money, which passed to her, through her mother's hands, Lydia's expences had been very little within that sum.

That it should be done with such trifling exertion on his side, to, was another very welcome surprise; for his chief wish at present, was to have as little trouble in the business as possible. When the first transports of rage which had produced his activity in seeking her were over, he naturally returned to all his former indolence. His letter was soon dispatched; for though dilatory in undertaking business, he was quick in its execution. He begged to know farther particulars of what he was indebted to his brother; but was too angry with Lydia, to send any message to her.

The good news quickly spread through the house; and with proportionate speed through the neighbourhood. It was borne in the latter with decent philosophy. To be sure it would have been more for the advantage of conversation, had Miss Lydia Bennet come upon the town; or, as the happiest alternative, been secluded from the world, in some distant farm house. But there was much to be talked of, in marrying her; and the good-natured wishes for her well-doing, which had proceeded before, from all the spiteful old ladies in Meryton, lost but little of their spirit in this change of circumstances, because with such an husband, her misery was considered certain.

It was a fortnight since Mrs Bennet had been down stairs, but on this happy day, she again took her seat at the head of her table, and in spirits oppressively high. No sentiment of shame gave a damp to her triumph. The marriage of a daughter, which had been the first object of her wishes, since

Jane was sixteen, was now on the point of accomplishment, and her thoughts and her words ran wholly on those attendants of elegant nuptials, fine muslins, new carriages, and servants. She was busily searching through the neighbourhood for a proper situation for her daughter, and, without knowing or considering what their income might be, rejected many as deficient in size and importance.

'Haye-Park might do,' said she, 'if the Gouldings would quit it, or the great house at Stoke, if the drawing-room were larger; but Ashworth is too far off! I could not bear to have her ten miles from me; and as for Purvis Lodge, the attics are dreadful.'

Her husband allowed her to talk on without interruption, while the servants remained. But when they had withdrawn, he said to her, 'Mrs Bennet, before you take any, or all of these houses, for your son and daughter, let us come to a right understanding. Into *one* house in this neighbourhood, they shall never have admittance. I will not encourage the impudence of either, by receiving them at Longbourn.'

A long dispute followed this declaration; but Mr Bennet was firm: it soon led to another; and Mrs Bennet found, with amazement and horror, that her husband would not advance a guinea to buy clothes for his daughter. He protested that she should receive from him no mark of affection whatever, on the occasion. Mrs Bennet could hardly comprehend it. That his anger could be carried to such a point of inconceivable resentment, as to refuse his daughter a privilege, without which her marriage would scarcely seem valid, exceeded all that she could believe possible. She was more alive to the disgrace, which the want of new clothes must reflect on her daughter's nuptials, than to any sense of shame at her eloping and living with Wickham, a fortnight before they took place.

Elizabeth was now most heartily sorry that she had, from the distress of the moment, been led to make Mr Darcy acquainted with their fears for her sister; for since her marriage would so shortly give the proper termination to the elopement, they might hope to conceal its unfavourable beginning, from all those who were not immediately on the spot.

She had no fear of its spreading farther, through his means. There were few people on whose secrecy she would have more confidently depended; but at the same time, there was no one, whose knowledge of a sister's frailty would have mortified her so much. Not, however, from any fear of disadvantage from it, individually to herself; for at any rate, there seemed a gulf impassable between them. Had Lydia's marriage been concluded on the most honourable terms, it was not to be supposed that Mr Darcy would connect himself with a family, where to every other objection would now be added, an alliance and relationship of the nearest kind with the man whom he so justly scorned.

From such a connection she could not wonder that he should shrink. The wish of procuring her regard, which she had assured herself of his feeling in Derbyshire, could not in rational expectation survive such a blow as this. She was humbled, she was grieved; she repented, though she hardly knew of what. She became jealous of his esteem, when she could no longer hope to be benefited by it. She wanted to hear of him, when there seemed the least chance of gaining intelligence. She was convinced that she could have been happy with him; when it was no longer likely they should meet.

What a triumph for him, as she often thought, could he know that the proposals which she had proudly spurned only four months ago, would now have been gladly and gratefully received! He was as generous, she doubted not, as the most generous of his sex. But while he was mortal, there must be a triumph.

She began now to comprehend that he was exactly the man, who, in disposition and talents, would most suit her. His understanding and temper, though unlike her own, would have answered all her wishes. It was an union that must have been to the advantage of both; by her ease and liveliness, his mind might have been softened, his manners improved, and from his judgment, information, and knowledge of the world, she must have received benefit of greater importance.

But no such happy marriage could now teach the admiring multitude what connubial felicity really was. An union of a different tendency, and precluding the possibility of the other, was soon to be formed in their family.

How Wickham and Lydia were to be supported in tolerable independence, she could not imagine. But how little of permanent happiness could belong to a couple who were only brought together because their passions were stronger than their virtue, she could easily conjecture.

Mr Gardiner soon wrote again to his brother. To Mr Bennet's acknowledgments he briefly replied, with assurances of his eagerness to promote the welfare of any of his family; and concluded with intreaties that the subject might never be mentioned to him again. The principal purport of his letter was to inform them, that Mr Wickham had resolved on quitting the Militia.

'It was greatly my wish that he should do so,' he added,

as soon as his marriage was fixed on. And I think you will agree with me, in considering a removal from the corps as highly desirable, both on his account and my niece's. It is Mr Wickham's intention to go into the regulars; and, among his former friends, there are still some who are able and willing to assist him in the army. He has the promise of an ensigncy in General —'s regiment, now quartered in the North. It is an advantage to have it so far from this part of the kingdom. He promises fairly, and I hope among different people, where they may each have a character to preserve, they will both be more prudent. I have written to Colonel Forster, to inform him of our present arrangements, and to request that he will satisfy the various creditors of Mr Wickham in and near Brighton, with assurances of speedy payment, for which I have pledged myself. And will you give yourself the trouble of carrying similar assurances to his creditors in Meryton, of whom I shall subjoin a list. according to his information. He has given in all his debts; I hope at least he has not deceived us. Haggerston has our directions, and all will be completed in a week. They will then join his regiment, unless they are first invited to Longbourn; and I understand from Mrs Gardiner, that my niece is very desirous of seeing you all, before she leaves the South. She is well, and begs to be dutifully remembered to you and her mother. – Your's, &c.

E. Gardiner.

Mr Bennet and his daughters saw all the advantages of Wickham's removal from the –shire, as clearly as Mr Gardiner could do. But Mrs Bennet, was not so well pleased with it. Lydia's being settled in the North, just when she had expected most pleasure and pride in her company, for she had by no means given up her plan of their residing in Hertfordshire, was a severe disappointment; and besides, it was such a pity that Lydia should be taken from a regiment where she was acquainted with every body, and had so many favourites.

'She is so fond of Mrs Forster,' said she, 'it will be quite shocking to send her away! And there are several of the young men, too, that she likes very much. The officers may not be so pleasant in General —'s regiment.'

His daughter's request, for such it might be considered, of being admitted into her family again, before she set off for the North, received at first an absolute negative. But Jane and Elizabeth, who agreed in wishing, for the sake of their sister's feelings and consequence, that she should be noticed on her marriage by her parents, urged him so earnestly, yet so rationally and so mildly, to receive her and her husband at Longbourn, as soon as they were married, that he was prevailed on to think as they thought, and act as they wished. And their mother had the satisfaction of knowing, that she should be able to shew her married daughter in the neighbourhood, before she was banished to the North. When Mr Bennet wrote again to his brother, therefore, he sent his permission for them to come; and it was settled, that as soon as the ceremony was over, they should proceed to Longbourn. Elizabeth was surprised, however, that Wickham should consent to such a scheme, and, had she consulted only her own inclination, any meeting with him would have been the last object of her wishes.

With an affectionate smile

CHAPTER FIFTY ONE

THEIR SISTER'S WEDDING DAY ARRIVED; and Jane and Elizabeth felt for her probably more than she felt for herself. The carriage was sent to meet them at –, and they were to return in it, by dinner-time. Their arrival was dreaded by the elder Miss Bennets; and Jane more especially, who gave Lydia the feelings which would have attended herself, had *she* been the culprit, was wretched in the thought of what her sister must endure.

They came. The family were assembled in the breakfast room, to receive them. Smiles decked the face of Mrs Bennet, as the carriage drove up to the door; her husband looked impenetrably grave; her daughters, alarmed, anxious, uneasy.

Lydia's voice was heard in the vestibule; the door was thrown open, and she ran into the room. Her mother stepped forwards, embraced her, and welcomed her with rapture; gave her hand with an affectionate smile to Wickham, who followed his lady, and wished them both joy, with an alacrity which shewed no doubt of their happiness.

Their reception from Mr Bennet, to whom they then turned, was not quite so cordial. His countenance rather gained in austerity; and he scarcely opened his lips. The easy assurance of the young couple, indeed, was enough to provoke him. Elizabeth was disgusted, and even Miss Bennet was shocked. Lydia was Lydia still; untamed, unabashed, wild, noisy, and fearless. She turned from sister to sister, demanding their congratulations, and when at length they all sat down, looked eagerly round the room, took notice of some little alteration in it, and observed, with a laugh, that it was a great while since she had been there.

Wickham was not at all more distressed than herself, but his manners were always so pleasing, that had his character and his marriage been exactly what they ought, his smiles and his easy address, while he claimed their relationship, would have delighted them all. Elizabeth had not before believed him quite equal to such assurance; but she sat down, resolving within herself, to draw no limits in future to the impudence of an impudent man. *She* blushed, and Jane blushed; but the cheeks of the two who caused their confusion, suffered no variation of colour.

There was no want of discourse. The bride and her mother could neither of them talk fast enough; and Wickham, who happened to sit near Elizabeth, began enquiring after his acquaintance in that neighbourhood, with a good humoured ease, which she felt very unable to equal in her replies. They seemed each of them to have the happiest memories in the world. Nothing of the past was recollected with pain; and Lydia led voluntarily to subjects, which her sisters would not have alluded to for the world.

'Only think of its being three months,' she cried, 'since I went away; it seems but a fortnight I declare; and yet there have been things enough happened in the time. Good gracious! when I went away, I am sure I had no more idea of being married till I came back again! though I thought it would be very good fun if I was.'

Her father lifted up his eyes. Jane was distressed. Elizabeth looked expressively at Lydia; but she, who never heard nor saw any thing of which she chose to be insensible, gaily continued, 'Oh! mamma, do the people here abouts know I am married to-day? I was afraid they might not; and we overtook William Goulding in his curricle, so I was determined he should know it, and so I let down the side glass next to him, and took off my glove, and let my hand just rest upon the window frame, so that he might see the ring, and then I bowed and smiled like any thing.'

Elizabeth could bear it no longer. She got up, and ran out of the room;

and returned no more, till she heard them passing through the hall to the dining parlour. She then joined them soon enough to see Lydia, with anxious parade, walk up to her mother's right hand, and hear her say to her eldest sister, 'Ah! Jane, I take your place now, and you must go lower, because I am a married woman.'

It was not to be supposed that time would give Lydia that embarrassment, from which she had been so wholly free at first. Her ease and good spirits increased. She longed to see Mrs Philips, the Lucasses, and all their other neighbours, and to hear herself called 'Mrs Wickham,' by each of them; and in the mean time, she went after dinner to shew her ring and boast of being married, to Mrs Hill and the two housemaids.

'Well, mamma,' said she, when they were all returned to the breakfast room, 'and what do you think of my husband? Is not he a charming man? I am sure my sisters must all envy me. I only hope they may have half my good luck. They must all go to Brighton. That is the place to get husbands. What a pity it is, mamma, we did not all go.'

'Very true; and if I had my will, we should. But my dear Lydia, I don't at all like your going such a way off. Must it be so?'

'Oh, lord! yes; – there is nothing in that. I shall like it of all things. You and papa, and my sisters, must come down and see us. We shall be at Newcastle all the winter, and I dare say there will be some balls, and I will take care to get good partners for them all.'

'I should like it beyond any thing!' said her mother.

'And then when you go away, you may leave one or two of my sisters behind you; and I dare say I shall get husbands for them before the winter is over.'

'I thank you for my share of the favour,' said Elizabeth; 'but I do not particularly like your way of getting husbands.'

Their visitors were not to remain above ten days with them. Mr Wickham had received his commission before he left London, and he was to join his regiment at the end of a fortnight.

No one but Mrs Bennet, regretted that their stay would be so short; and she made the most of the time, by visiting about with her daughter, and having very frequent parties at home. These parties were acceptable to all; to avoid a family circle was even more desirable to such as did think, than such as did not.

Wickham's affection for Lydia, was just what Elizabeth had expected to find it; not equal to Lydia's for him. She had scarcely needed her present observation to be satisfied, from the reason of things, that their elopement had been brought on by the strength of her love, rather than by his; and she would have wondered why, without violently caring for her, he chose to elope with her at all, had she not felt certain that his flight was rendered necessary by distress of circumstances; and if that were the case, he was not the young man to resist an opportunity of having a companion.

Lydia was exceedingly fond of him. He was her dear Wickham on every occasion; no one was to be put in competition with him. He did every thing best in the world; and she was sure he would kill more birds on the first of September, than any body else in the country.

One morning, soon after their arrival, as she was sitting with her two elder sisters, she said to Elizabeth,

'Lizzy, I never gave *you* an account of my wedding, I believe. You were not by, when I told mamma, and the others, all about it. Are not you curious to hear how it was managed?'

'No really,' replied Elizabeth; 'I think there cannot be too little said on the subject.'

'La! You are so strange! But I must tell you how it went off. We were married, you know, at St Clement's, because Wickham's lodgings were in that parish. And it was settled that we should all be there by eleven o'clock. My uncle and aunt and I were to go together; and the others were to meet us at the church. Well, Monday morning came, and I was in such a fuss! I was so afraid you know that something would happen to put it off, and then I should have gone quite distracted. And there was my aunt, all the time I was dressing, preaching and talking away just as if she was reading a sermon. However, I did not hear above one word in ten, for I was thinking, you may suppose, of my dear Wickham. I longed to know whether he would be married in his blue coat.

'Well, and so we breakfasted at ten as usual; I thought it would never be over; for, by the bye, you are to understand, that my uncle and aunt were horrid unpleasant all the time I was with them. If you'll believe me, I did not once put my foot out of doors, though I was there a fortnight. Not one party, or scheme, or any thing. To be sure London was rather thin, but however the little Theatre was open. Well, and so just as the carriage came to the door, my uncle was called away upon business to that horrid man Mr Stone. And then, you know, when once they get together, there is no end of it. Well, I was so frightened I did not know what to do, for my uncle was to give me away; and if we were beyond the hour, we could not be married all day. But, luckily, he came back again in ten minutes time, and then we all set out. However, I recollected afterwards, that if he *had* been prevented going, the wedding need not be put off, for Mr Darcy might have done as well.'

'Mr Darcy!' repeated Elizabeth, in utter amazement.

'Oh, yes! – he was to come there with Wickham, you know. But gracious me! I quite forgot! I ought not to have said a word about it. I promised them so faithfully! What will Wickham say? It was to be such a secret!'

'If it was to be secret,' said Jane, 'say not another word on the subject. You may depend upon my seeking no further.'

'Oh! certainly,' said Elizabeth, though burning with curiosity; 'we will ask you no questions.'

'Thank you,' said Lydia, 'for if you did, I should certainly tell you all, and then Wickham would be angry.'

On such encouragement to ask, Elizabeth was forced to put it out of her power, by running away.

But to live in ignorance on such a point was impossible; or at least it was impossible not to try for information. Mr Darcy had been at her sister's wedding. It was exactly a scene, and exactly among people, where he had apparently least to do, and least temptation to go. Conjectures as to the meaning of it, rapid and wild, hurried into her brain; but she was satisfied with none. Those that best pleased her, as placing his conduct in the noblest light, seemed most improbable. She could not bear such suspense; and hastily seizing a sheet of paper, wrote a short letter to her aunt, to request an explanation of what Lydia had dropt, if it were compatible with the secrecy which had been intended.

'You may readily comprehend,' she added, 'what my curiosity must be to know how a person unconnected with any of us, and (comparatively speaking) a stranger to our family, should have been amongst you at such a time. Pray write instantly, and let me understand it – unless it is, for very cogent reasons, to remain in the secrecy which Lydia seems to think necessary; and then I must endeavour to be satisfied with ignorance.'

'Not that I *shall* though,' she added to herself, as she finished the letter; 'and my dear aunt, if you do not tell me in an honourable manner, I shall certainly be reduced to tricks and stratagems to find it out.'

Jane's delicate sense of honour would not allow her to speak to Elizabeth privately of what Lydia had let fall; Elizabeth was glad of it; – till it appeared whether her enquiries would receive any satisfaction, she had rather be without a confidante.

'I am sure she did not listen'

CHAPTER FIFTY TWO

ELIZABETH HAD THE SATISFACTION OF receiving an answer to her letter, as soon as she possibly could. She was no sooner in possession of it, than hurrying into the little copse, where she was least likely to be interrupted, she sat down on one of the benches, and prepared to be happy; for the length of the letter convinced her that it did not contain a denial.

Gracechurch-street, Sept. 6.

MY DEAR NIECE,

I have just received your letter, and shall devote this whole morning to answering it, as I foresee that a little *writing will not comprise what I have to tell you. I must confess myself surprised by your application; I did not expect it from* you. *Don't think me angry, however, for I only mean to let you know, that I had not imagined such enquiries to be necessary on* your *side. If you do not choose to understand me, forgive my impertinence. Your uncle is as much surprised as I am – and nothing but the belief of your being a party concerned, would have allowed him to act as he has done. But if you are really innocent and ignorant, I must be more explicit. On the very day of my coming home from Longbourn, your uncle had a most unexpected visitor. Mr Darcy called, and was shut up with him several hours. It was all over before I arrived; so my curiosity was not so dreadfully racked as* your's *seems to have been. He came to tell Mr Gardiner that he had found out where your sister and Mr Wickham were, and that he had seen and talked with them both. Wickham repeatedly, Lydia once. From what I can collect, he left Derbyshire only one day after ourselves, and came to town with the resolution of hunting for them. The motive professed, was his conviction of its being owing to himself that Wickham's worthlessness had not been so well known, as to make it impossible for any young woman of character, to love or confide in him. He generously imputed the whole to his mistaken pride, and confessed that he had before thought it beneath him, to lay his private actions open to the world. His character was to speak for itself. He called it, therefore, his duty to step forward, and endeavour to remedy an evil, which had been brought on by himself. If he* had another *motive, I am sure it would never disgrace him. He had been some days in town, before he was able to discover them; but he had something to direct his search, which was more than* we *had; and the consciousness of this, was another reason for his resolving to follow us. There is a lady, it seems, a Mrs Younge, who was some time ago governess to Miss Darcy, and was dismissed from her charge on some cause of disapprobation, though he did not say what. She then took a large house in Edward-street, and has since maintained herself by letting lodgings. This Mrs Younge was, he knew, intimately acquainted with Wickham; and he went to her for intelligence of him, as soon as he got to town. But it was two or three days before he could get from her what he wanted. She would not betray her trust, I suppose, without bribery and corruption, for she really did know where her friend was to be found. Wickham indeed had gone to her, on their first arrival in London, and had she been able to receive them into her house, they would have taken up their abode with her. At length, however, our kind friend procured the wished-for direction. They were in —street. He saw Wickham, and afterwards insisted on seeing Lydia. His first object with her, he acknowledged, had been to persuade her to quit her present disgraceful situation, and return to her friends as soon as they could be prevailed on to receive her, offering his assistance, as far as it would go. But he found Lydia absolutely resolved on remaining where she was. She cared for none of her friends, she wanted no help of his, she would not hear of leaving Wickham. She was sure they should be married some time or other, and it did not much signify when. Since such were her feelings, it only remained, he thought, to* secure and expedite a marriage, which, in his very first conversation with Wickham, he easily learnt, had never been his design. He confessed himself obliged to leave the regiment, on account of some debts of honour, which were very pressing; and scrupled not to lay all the ill-consequence of Lydia's flight, on her own folly alone. He meant to resign his commission immediately; and as to his future situation, he could conjure very little about it. He must go somewhere, but he did not know where, and he knew he should have nothing to live on. Mr Darcy asked him why he had not married your sister at once. Though Mr Bennet was not imagined to be very rich, he would have been able to do something for him, and his situation must have been benefited by marriage. But he found, in reply to this question, that Wickham still cherished the hope of more effectually making his fortune by marriage, in some other country. Under such circumstances, however, he was not likely to be proof against the temptation of immediate relief. They met several times, for there was much to be discussed. Wickham of course wanted more than he could get; but at length was reduced to be reasonable. Every thing being settled between them, Mr Darcy's next step was to make your uncle acquainted with it, and he first called in Gracechurch-street the evening before I came home. But Mr Gardiner could not be seen, and Mr Darcy found, on further enquiry, that your father was still with him, but would quit town the next morning. He did not judge your father to be a person whom he could so properly consult as your uncle, and therefore readily postponed seeing him, till after the departure of the former. He did not leave his name, and till the next day, it was only known that a gentleman had called on business. On Saturday he came again. Your father was gone, your uncle at home, and, as I said before, they had a great deal of talk together. They met again on Sunday, and then I saw him too. It was not all settled before Monday: as soon as it was, the express was sent off to Longbourn. But our visitor was very obstinate. I fancy, Lizzy, that obstinancy is the real defect of his character after all. He has been accused of many faults at different times; but this is the true one. Nothing was to be done that he did not do himself; though I am sure (and I do not speak it to be thanked, therefore say nothing about it,) your uncle would most readily have settled the whole. They battled it together for a long time, which was more than either the gentleman or lady concerned in it deserved. But at last your uncle was forced to yield, and instead of being allowed to be of use to his niece, was forced to put up with only having the probable credit of it, which went sorely against the grain; and I really believe your letter this morning gave him great pleasure, because it required an explanation that would rob him of his borrowed feathers, and give the praise where it was due. But, Lizzy, this must go no farther than yourself, or Jane at most. You know pretty well, I suppose, what has been done for the young people. His debts are to be paid, amounting, I believe, to considerably more than a thousand pounds, another thousand in *addition to her own settled upon* her, *and his commission purchased. The reason why all this was to be done by him alone, was such as I have given above. It was owing to him, to his reserve, and want of proper consideration, that Wickham's character had been so misunderstood, and consequently that he had been received and noticed as he was. Perhaps there was some truth in* this; *though I doubt whether* his *reserve, or* anybody's *reserve, can be answerable for the event. But in spite of all this fine talking, my dear Lizzy, you may rest perfectly assured, that your uncle would never have yielded, if we had not given him credit for* another interest *in the affair. When all this was resolved on, he returned again to his friends, who were still staying at Pemberley; but it was agreed that he should be in London once more when the wedding took place, and all money matters were then to receive the last finish. I believe I have now told you every thing. It is a relation which you tell me is to give you great surprise; I hope at least it will not afford you any displeasure. Lydia came to us; and Wickham had constant admission to the house.* He *was exactly what he had been, when I knew him in Hertfordshire; but I would not tell you how little I was satisfied with* her *behaviour while she staid with us, if I had not perceived, by Jane's letter last Wednesday, that her conduct on coming home was exactly of a piece with it, and therefore what I now tell you, can give you no fresh pain. I talked to her repeatedly in the most serious manner, representing to her all the wickedness of what she had done, and all the unhappiness she had brought on her family. If she heard me, it was by good luck, for I am sure she did not listen. I was sometimes quite provoked, but then I recollected my dear Elizabeth and Jane, and for their sakes had patience with her. Mr Darcy was punctual in his return, and as Lydia informed you, attended the wedding. He dined with us the next day, and was to leave town again on Wednesday or Thursday. Will you be very angry with me, my dear Lizzy, if I take this opportunity of saying (what I was never bold enough to say before) how much I like him. His behaviour to us has, in every respect, been as pleasing as when we were in Derbyshire. His understanding and opinions all please me; he wants nothing but a little more liveliness, and* that, *if he marry* prudently, *his wife may teach him. I thought him very sly; – he hardly ever mentioned your name. But slyness seems the fashion. Pray forgive me, if I have been very presuming, or at least do not punish me so far, as to exclude me from P. I shall never be quite happy till I have been all round the park. A low phaeton, with a nice little pair of ponies, would be the very thing. But I must write no more. The children have been wanting me this half hour.*

Your's, very sincerely,

M. GARDINER.

The contents of this letter threw Elizabeth into a flutter of spirits, in which it was difficult to determine whether pleasure or pain bore the greatest share. The vague and unsettled suspicions which uncertainty had produced of what Mr Darcy might have been doing to forward her sister's match, which she had feared to encourage, as an exertion of goodness too great to be probable, and at the same time dreaded to be just, from the pain of obligation, were proved beyond their greatest extent to be true! He had followed them purposely to town, he had taken on himself all the trouble and mortification attendant on such a research; in which supplication had been necessary to a woman whom he must abominate and despise, and where he was reduced to meet, frequently meet, reason with, persuade, and finally bribe, the man whom he always most wished to avoid, and whose very name it was punishment to him to pronounce. He had done all this for a girl whom he could neither regard nor esteem. Her heart did whisper, that he had done it for her. But it was a hope shortly checked by other considerations, and she soon felt that even her vanity was insufficient, when required to depend on his affection for her, for a woman who had already refused him, as able to overcome a sentiment so natural as abhorrence against relationship with Wickham. Brother-in-law of Wickham! Every kind of pride must revolt from the connection. He had to be sure done much. She was ashamed to think how much. But he had given a reason for his interference, which asked no extraordinary stretch of belief. It was reasonable that he should feel he had been wrong; he had liberality, and he had the means of exercising it; and though she would not place herself as his principal inducement, she could, perhaps, believe, that remaining partiality to her, might assist his endeavours in a cause where her peace of mind must be materially concerned. It was painful, exceedingly painful, to know that they were under obligations to a person who could never receive a return. They owed the restoration of Lydia, her character, every thing to him. Oh! how heartily did she grieve over every ungracious sensation she had ever encouraged, every saucy speech she had ever directed towards him. For herself she was humbled; but she was proud of him. Proud that in a cause of compassion and honour, he had been able to get the better of himself. She read over her aunt's commendation of him again and again. It was hardly enough; but it pleased her. She was even sensible of some pleasure, though mixed with regret, on finding how steadfastly both she and her uncle had been persuaded that affection and confidence subsisted between Mr Darcy and herself.

She was roused from her seat, and her reflections, by someone's approach; and before she could strike into another path, she was overtaken by Wickham.

'I am afraid I interrupt your solitary ramble, my dear sister?' said he, as he joined her.

'You certainly do,' she replied with a smile; 'but it does not follow that the interruption must be unwelcome.'

'I should be sorry indeed, if it were. *We* were always good friends; and now we are better.'

'True. Are the others coming out?'

'I do not know. Mrs Bennet and Lydia are going in the carriage to Meryton. And so, my dear sister, I find from our uncle and aunt, that you have actually seen Pemberley.'

She replied in the affirmative.

'I almost envy you the pleasure, and yet I believe it would be too much for me, or else I could take it in my way to Newcastle. And you saw the old housekeeper, I suppose? Poor Reynolds, she was always very fond of me. But of course she did not mention my name to you.'

'Yes, she did.'

'And what did she say?'

'That you were gone into the army, and she was afraid had – not turned out well. At such a distance as *that*, you know, things are strangely misrepresented.'

'Certainly,' he replied, biting his lips. Elizabeth hoped she had silenced him; but he soon afterwards said,

'I was surprised to see Darcy in town last month. We passed each other several times. I wonder what he can be doing there.'

'Perhaps preparing for his marriage with Miss de Bourgh,' said Elizabeth. 'It must be something particular, to take him there at this time of year.'

'Undoubtedly. Did you see him while you were at Lambton? I thought I understood from the Gardiners that you had.'

'Yes; he introduced us to his sister.'

'And do you like her?'

'Very much.'

'I have heard, indeed, that she is uncommonly improved within this year or two. When I last saw her, she was not very promising. I am very glad you liked her. I hope she will turn out well.'

'I dare say she will; she has got over the most trying age.'

'Did you go by the village of Kympton?'

'I do not recollect that we did.'

'I mention it, because it is the living which I ought to have had. A most delightful place! – Excellent Parsonage House! It would have suited me in every respect.'

'How should you have liked making sermons?'

'Exceedingly well. I should have considered it as part of my duty, and the exertion would soon have been nothing. One ought not to repine; – but, to be sure, it would have been such a thing for me! The quiet, the retirement of such a life, would have answered all my ideas of happiness! But it was not to be. Did you ever hear Darcy mention the circumstance, when you were in Kent?'

'I *have* heard from authority, which I thought *as good*, that it was left you conditionally only, and at the will of the present patron.'

'You have. Yes, there was something in *that*; I told you so from the first, you may remember.'

'I *did* hear, too, that there was a time, when sermon-making was not so palatable to you as it seems to be at present; that you actually declared your resolution of never taking orders, and that the business had been compromised accordingly.'

'You did! and it was not wholly without foundation. You may remember what I told you on that point, when first we talked of it.'

They were now almost at the door of the house, for she had walked fast to get rid of him; and unwilling for her sister's sake, to provoke him, she only said in reply, with a good-humoured smile.

'Come, Mr Wickham, we are brother and sister, you know. Do not let us quarrel about the past. In future, I hope we shall be always of one mind.'

She held out her hand; he kissed it with affectionate gallantry, though he hardly knew how to look, and they entered the house.

Mr Darcy with him

CHAPTER FIFTY THREE

MR WICKHAM WAS SO PERFECTLY SATISFIED with this conversation, that he never again distressed himself, or provoked his dear sister Elizabeth, by introducing the subject of it; and she was pleased to find that she had said enough to keep him quiet.

The day of his and Lydia's departure soon came, and Mrs Bennet was forced to submit to a separation, which, as her husband by no means entered into her scheme of their all going to Newcastle, was likely to continue at least a twelvemonth.

'Oh! my dear Lydia,' she cried, 'when shall we meet again?'

'Oh, lord! I don't know. Not these two or three years perhaps.'

'Write to me very often, my dear.'

'As often as I can. But you know married women have never much time for writing. My sisters may write to *me*. They will have nothing else to do.'

Mr Wickham's adieus were much more affectionate than his wife's. He smiled, looked handsome, and said many pretty things.

'He is as fine a fellow,' said Mr Bennet, as soon as they were out of the house, 'as ever I saw. He simpers, and smirks, and makes love to us all. I am prodigiously proud of him. I defy even Sir William Lucas himself, to produce a more valuable son-in-law.'

The loss of her daughter made Mrs Bennet very dull for several days.

'I often think,' said she, 'that there is nothing so bad as parting with one's friends. One seems so forlorn without them.'

This is the consequence you see, Madam, of marrying a daughter,' said Elizabeth. 'It must make you better satisfied that your other four are single.'

'It is no such thing. Lydia does not leave me because she is married; but only because her husband's regiment happens to be so far off. If that had been nearer, she would not have gone so soon.'

But the spiritless condition which this event threw her into, was shortly relieved, and her mind opened again to the agitation of hope, by an article of news, which then began to be in circulation. The housekeeper at Netherfield had received orders to prepare for the arrival of her master, who was coming down in a day or two, to shoot there for several weeks. Mrs Bennet was quite in the fidgets. She looked at Jane, and smiled, and shook her head by turns.

'Well, well, and so Mr Bingley is coming down, sister,' (for Mrs Philips first brought her the news.) 'Well, so much the better. Not that I care about it, though. He is nothing to us, you know, and I am sure *I* never want to see him again. But, however, he is very welcome to come to Netherfield, if he likes it. And who knows what *may* happen? But that is nothing to us. You know, sister, we agreed long ago never to mention a word about it. And so, it is quite certain he is coming?'

'You may depend on it,' replied the other, 'for Mrs Nicholls was in Meryton last night; I saw her passing by, and went out myself on purpose to know the truth of it; and she told me that it was certain true. He comes down on Thursday at the latest, very likely on Wednesday. She was going to the butcher's, she told me, on purpose to order in some meat on Wednesday, and she has got three couple of ducks, just fit to be killed.'

Miss Bennet had not been able to hear of his coming, without changing colour. It was many months since she had mentioned his name to Elizabeth; but now, as soon as they were alone together, she said,

'I saw you look at me to day, Lizzy, when my aunt told us of the present report; and I know I appeared distressed. But don't imagine it was from any silly cause. I was only confused for the moment, because I felt that I *should* be looked at. I do assure you, that the news does not affect me either with pleasure or pain. I am glad of one thing, that he comes alone; because we shall see the less of him. Not that I am afraid of *myself*, but I dread other people's remarks.'

Elizabeth did not know what to make of it. Had she not seen him in

Derbyshire, she might have supposed him capable of coming there, with no other view than what was acknowledged; but she still thought him partial to Jane, and she wavered as to the greater probability of his coming there *with* his friend's permission, or being bold enough to come without it.

'Yet it is hard,' she sometimes thought, 'that this poor man cannot come to a house, which he has legally hired, without raising all this speculation! I *will* leave him to himself.'

In spite of what her sister declared, and really believed to be her feelings, in the expectation of his arrival, Elizabeth could easily perceive that her spirits were affected by it. They were more disturbed, more unequal, than she had often seen them.

The subject which had been so warmly canvassed between their parents, about a twelvemonth ago, was now brought forward again.

'As soon as ever Mr Bingley comes, my dear,' said Mrs Bennet, 'you will wait on him of course.'

'No, no. You forced me into visiting him last year, and promised if I went to see him, he should marry one of my daughters. But it ended in nothing, and I will not be sent on a fool's errand again.'

His wife represented to him how absolutely necessary such an attention would be from all the neighbouring gentlemen, on his returning to Netherfield.

''Tis an etiquette I despise,' said he. 'If he wants our society, let him seek it. He knows where we live. I will not spend *my* hours in running after my neighbours every time they go away, and come back again.'

'Well, all I know is, that it will be abominably rude if you do not wait on him. But, however, that shan't prevent my asking him to dine here, I am determined. We must have Mrs Long and the Gouldings soon. That will make thirteen with ourselves, so there will be just room at table for him.'

Consoled by this resolution, she was the better able to bear her husband's incivility; though it was very mortifying to know that her neighbours might all see Mr Bingley in consequence of it, before *they* did. As the day of his arrival drew near,

'I begin to be sorry that he comes at all,' said Jane to her sister. 'It would be nothing; I could see him with perfect indifference, but I can hardly bear to hear it thus perpetually talked of. My mother means well; but she does not know, no one can know how much I suffer from what she says. Happy shall I be, when his stay at Netherfield is over!'

'I wish I could say any thing to comfort you,' replied Elizabeth; 'but it is wholly out of my power. You must feel it; and the usual satisfaction of preaching patience to a sufferer is denied me, because you have always so much.'

Mr Bingley arrived. Mrs Bennet, through the assistance of servants, contrived to have the earliest tidings of it, that the period of anxiety and fretfulness on her side, might be as long as it could. She counted the days that must intervene before their invitation could be sent; hopeless of seeing him before. But on the third morning after his arrival in Hertfordshire, she saw him from her dressing-room window, enter the paddock, and ride towards the house.

Her daughters were eagerly called to partake of her joy. Jane resolutely kept her place at the table; but Elizabeth, to satisfy her mother, went to the window – she looked, – she saw Mr Darcy with him, and sat down again by her sister.

'There is a gentleman with him, mamma,' said Kitty; 'who can it be?'

'Some acquaintance or other, my dear, I suppose; I am sure I do not know.'

'La!' replied Kitty, 'it looks just like that man that used to be with him before. Mr what's his name. That tall, proud man.'

'Good gracious! Mr Darcy! – and so it does I vow. Well, any friend of Mr Bingley's will always be welcome here to be sure; but else I must say that I hate the very sight of him.'

Jane looked at Elizabeth with surprise and concern. She knew but little of their meeting in Derbyshire, and therefore felt for the awkwardness which must attend her sister, in seeing him almost for the first time after receiving his explanatory letter. Both sisters were uncomfortable enough. Each felt for the other, and of course for themselves; and their mother talked on, of her dislike of Mr Darcy, and her resolution to be civil to him only as Mr Bingley's friend, without being heard by either of them. But Elizabeth had sources of uneasiness which could not be suspected by Jane, to whom she had never yet had courage to shew Mrs Gardiner's letter, or to relate her own change of sentiment towards him. To Jane, he could be only a man whose proposals she had refused, and whose merit she had undervalued; but to her own more extensive information, he was the person, to whom the whole family were indebted for the first of benefits, and whom she regarded herself with an interest, if not quite so tender, at least as reasonable and just, as what Jane felt for Bingley. Her astonishment at his coming – at his coming to Netherfield, to Longbourn, and voluntarily seeking her again, was almost equal to what she had known on first witnessing his altered behaviour in Derbyshire.

The colour which had been driven from her face, returned for half a minute with an additional glow, and a smile of delight added lustre to her eyes, as she thought for that space of time, that his affection and wishes must still be unshaken. But she would not be secure.

'Let me first see how he behaves,' said she; 'it will then be early enough for expectation.'

She sat intently at work, striving to be composed, and without daring to lift up her eyes, till anxious curiosity carried them to the face of her sister, as the servant was approaching the door. Jane looked a little paler than usual but more sedate than Elizabeth had expected. On the gentlemen's appearing, her colour increased; yet she received them with tolerable ease, and with a propriety of behaviour equally free from any symptom of resentment, or any unnecessary complaisance.

Elizabeth said as little either as civility would allow, and sat down again to her work, with an eagerness which it did not often command. She had ventured only one glance at Darcy. He looked serious as usual; and she thought, more as he had been used to look in Hertfordshire, than as she had seen him at Pemberley. But, perhaps he could not in her mother's presence be what he was before her uncle and aunt. It was a painful, but not an improbable, conjecture.

Bingley, she had likewise seen for an instant, and in that short period saw him looking both pleased and embarrassed. He was received by Mrs Bennet with a degree of civility, which made her two daughters ashamed, especially when contrasted with the cold and ceremonious politeness of her curtsey and address to his friend.

Elizabeth particularly, who knew that her mother owed to the latter the preservation of her favourite daughter from irremediable infamy, was hurt and distressed to a most painful degree by a distinction, so ill applied.

Darcy, after enquiring of her how Mr and Mrs Gardiner did, a question which she could not answer without confusion, said scarcely any thing. He was not seated by her; perhaps that was the reason of his silence; but it had not been so in Derbyshire. There he had talked to her friends, when he could not to herself. But now several minutes elapsed, without bringing the sound of his voice; and when occasionally, unable to resist the impulse of curiosity, she raised her eyes to his face, she as often found him looking at Jane, as at herself, and frequently on no object but the ground. More thoughtfulness, and less anxiety to please than when they last met, were plainly expressed. She was disappointed, and angry with herself for being so.

'Could I expect it to be otherwise!' said she. 'Yet why did he come?'

She was in no humour for conversation with anyone but himself; and to him she had hardly courage to speak.

She enquired after his sister, but could do no more.

'It is a long time, Mr Bingley, since you went away,' said Mrs Bennet.

He readily agreed to it.

'I began to be afraid you would never come back again. People *did* say, you meant to quit the place entirely at Michaelmas; but, however, I hope it is not true. A great many changes have happened in the neighbourhood, since you went away. Miss Lucas is married and settled. And one of my own daughters. I suppose you have heard of it; indeed, you must have seen it in the papers. It was in the Times and the Courier, I know; though it was not put in as it ought to be. It was only said, "Lately, George Wickham, Esq. to Miss Lydia Bennet," without there being a syllable said of her father, or the place where she lived, or any thing. It was my brother Gardiner's drawing up too, and I wonder how he came to make such an awkward business of it. Did you see it?'

Bingley replied that he did, and made his congratulations. Elizabeth dared not lift up her eyes. How Mr Darcy looked, therefore, she could not tell.

'It is a delightful thing, to be sure, to have a daughter well married,' continued her mother, 'but at the same time, Mr Bingley, it is very hard to have her taken such a way from me. They are gone down to Newcastle, a place quite northward, it seems, and there they are to stay. I do not know how long. His regiment is there; for I suppose you have heard of his leaving the –shire, and of his being gone into the regulars. Thank Heaven! he has *some* friends, though perhaps not so many as he deserves.'

Elizabeth, who knew this to be levelled at Mr Darcy, was in such misery of shame, that she could hardly keep her seat. It drew from her, however, the exertion of speaking, which nothing else had so effectually done before; and she asked Bingley, whether he meant to make any stay in the country at present. A few weeks, he believed.

'When you have killed all your own birds, Mr Bingley,' said her mother, 'I beg you will come here, and shoot as many as you please, on Mr Bennet's manor. I am sure he will be vastly happy to oblige you, and will save all the best of the covies for you.'

Elizabeth's misery increased, at such unnecessary, such officious attention! Were the same fair prospect to arise at present, as had flattered them a year ago, every thing, she was persuaded, would be hastening to the same vexatious conclusion. At that instant she felt, that years of happiness could not make Jane or herself amends, for moments of such painful confusion.

'The first wish of my heart,' said she to herself, 'is never more to be in company with either of them. Their society can afford no pleasure, that will atone for such wretchedness as this! Let me never see either one or the other again!'

Yet the misery, for which years of happiness were to offer no compensation, received soon afterwards material relief, from observing how much the beauty of her sister re-kindled the admiration of her former lover. When first he came in, he had spoken to her but little; but every five minutes seemed to be giving her more of his attention. He found her as handsome as she had been last year; as good natured, and as unaffected, though not quite so chatty. Jane was anxious that no difference should be perceived in her at all, and was really persuaded that she talked as much as ever. But her mind was so busily engaged, that she did not always know when she was silent.

When the gentlemen rose to go away, Mrs Bennet was mindful of her intended civility, and they were invited and engaged to dine at Longbourn in a few days time.

'You are quite a visit in my debt, Mr Bingley,' she added, 'for when you went to town last winter, you promised to take a family dinner with us, as soon as you returned. I have not forgot, you see; and I assure you, I was very much disappointed that you did not come back and keep your engagement.'

Bingley looked a little silly at this reflection, and said something of his concern, at having been prevented by business. They then went away.

Mrs Bennet had been strongly inclined to ask them to stay and dine there, that day; but, though she always kept a very good table, she did not think any thing less than two courses, could be good enough for a man, on whom she had such anxious designs, or satisfy the appetite and pride of one who had ten thousand a year.

Jane happened to look round

CHAPTER FIFTY FOUR

AS SOON AS THEY WERE GONE, ELIZABETH walked out to recover her spirits; or in other words, to dwell without interruption on those subjects that must deaden them more. Mr Darcy's behaviour astonished and vexed her.

'Why, if he came only to be silent, grave, and indifferent,' said she, 'did he come at all?'

She could settle it in no way that gave her pleasure.

'He could be still amiable, still pleasing, to my uncle and aunt, when he was in town; and why not to me? If he fears me, why come hither? If he no longer cares for me, why silent? Teazing, teazing, man! I will think no more about him.'

Her resolution was for a short time involuntarily kept by the approach of her sister, who joined her with a cheerful look, which shewed her better satisfied with their visitors, than Elizabeth.

'Now,' said she, 'that this first meeting is over, I feel perfectly easy. I know my own strength, and I shall never be embarrassed again by his coming. I am glad he dines here on Tuesday. It will then be publicly seen, that on both sides, we meet only as common and indifferent acquaintance.'

'Yes, very indifferent indeed,' said Elizabeth, laughingly. 'Oh, Jane, take care.'

'My dear Lizzy, you cannot think me so weak, as to be in danger now.'

'I think you are in very great danger of making him as much in love with you as ever.'

They did not see the gentlemen again till Tuesday; and Mrs Bennet, in the meanwhile, was giving way to all the happy schemes, which the good humour, and common politeness of Bingley, in half an hour's visit, had revived.

On Tuesday there was a large party assembled at Longbourn; and the two, who were most anxiously expected, to the credit of their punctuality as sportsmen, were in very good time. When they repaired to the dining-room, Elizabeth eagerly watched to see whether Bingley would take the place, which, in all their former parties, had belonged to him, by her sister. Her prudent mother, occupied by the same ideas, forbore to invite him to sit by herself. On entering the room, he seemed to hesitate; but Jane happened to look around, and happened to smile: it was decided. He placed himself by her.

Elizabeth, with a triumphant sensation, looked towards his friend. He bore it with noble indifference, and she would have imagined that Bingley had received his sanction to be happy, had she not seen his eyes likewise turned towards Mr Darcy, with an expression of half-laughing alarm.

His behaviour to her sister was such, during dinner time, as shewed an admiration of her, which, though more guarded than formerly, persuaded Elizabeth, that if left wholly to himself, Jane's happiness, and his own, would be speedily secured. Though she dared not depend upon the consequence, she yet received pleasure from observing his behaviour. It gave her all the animation that her spirits could boast; for she was in no cheerful humour. Mr Darcy was almost as far from her, as the table could divide them. He was on one side of her mother. She knew how little such a situation would give pleasure to either, or make either appear to advantage. She was not near enough to hear any of their discourse, but she could see how seldom they spoke to each other, and how formal and cold was their manner, whenever they did. Her mother's ungraciousness, made the sense of what they owed him more painful to Elizabeth's mind; and she would, at times, have given any thing to be privileged to tell him, that his kindness was neither unknown nor unfelt by the whole of the family.

She was in hopes that the evening would afford some opportunity of bringing them together; that the whole of the visit would not pass away without enabling them to enter into something more of conversation, than the mere ceremonious salutation attending his entrance. Anxious and uneasy, the period which passed in the drawing-room, before the gentlemen came, was wearisome and dull to a degree, that almost made her uncivil. She looked forward to their entrance, as the point on which all her chance of pleasure for the evening must depend.

'If he does not come to me, *then*,' said she, 'I shall give him up for ever.'

The gentlemen came; and she thought he looked as if he would have answered her hopes; but, alas! the ladies had crowded round the table, where Miss Bennet was making tea, and Elizabeth pouring out the coffee, in so close a confederacy, that there was not a single vacancy near her, which would admit of a chair. And on the gentlemen's approaching, one of the girls moved closer to her than ever, and said, in a whisper,

'The men shan't come and part us, I am determined. We want none of them, do we?'

Darcy had walked away to another part of the room. She followed him with her eyes, envied every one to whom he spoke, had scarcely patience enough to help anybody to coffee; and then was enraged against herself for being so silly!

'A man who has once been refused! How could I ever be foolish enough to expect a renewal of his love? Is there one among the sex, who would not protest against such a weakness as a second proposal to the same woman? There is no indignity so abhorrent to their feelings!'

She was a little revived, however, by his bringing back his coffee cup himself; and she seized the opportunity of saying,

'Is your sister at Pemberley still?'

'Yes, she will remain there till Christmas.'

'And quite alone? Have all her friends left her?'

'Mrs Annesley is with her. The others have been gone on to Scarborough, these three weeks.'

She could think of nothing more to say; but if he wished to converse with her, he might have better success. He stood by her, however, for some minutes, in silence; and, at last, on the young lady's whispering to Elizabeth again, he walked away.

When the tea-things were removed, and the card tables placed, the ladies all rose, and Elizabeth was then hoping to be soon joined by him, when all her views were overthrown, by seeing him fall a victim to her mother's rapacity for whist players, and in a few moments after seated with the rest of the party. She now lost every expectation of pleasure. They were confined for the evening at different tables, and she had nothing to hope, but that his eyes were so often turned towards her side of the room, as to make him play as unsuccessfully as herself.

Mrs Bennet had designed to keep the two Netherfield gentlemen to supper; but their carriage was unluckily ordered before any of the others, and she had no opportunity of detaining them.

'Well girls,' said she, as soon as they were left to themselves, 'What say you to the day? I think every thing has passed off uncommonly well, I assure you. The dinner was as well dressed as any I ever saw. The venison was roasted to a turn – and everybody said, they never saw so fat a haunch. The soup was fifty times better than what we had at the Lucas's last week; and even Mr Darcy acknowledged, that the partridges were remarkably well done; and I suppose he has two or three French cooks at least. And, my dear Jane, I never saw you look in greater beauty. Mrs Long said so too, for I asked her whether you did not. And what do you think she said besides? "Ah! Mrs Bennet, we shall have her at Netherfield at last." She did indeed. I do think Mrs Long is as good a creature as ever lived – and her nieces are very pretty behaved girls, and not at all handsome: I like them prodigiously.'

Mrs Bennet, in short, was in very great spirits; she had seen enough of Bingley's behaviour to Jane, to be convinced that she would get him at last; and her expectations of advantage to her family, when in a happy humour, were so far beyond reason, that she was quite disappointed at not seeing him there again the next day, to make his proposals.

'It has been a very agreeable day,' said Miss Bennet to Elizabeth. 'The

Mrs Long and her nieces

party seemed so well selected, so suitable one with the other. I hope we may often meet again.'

Elizabeth smiled.

'Lizzy, you must not do so. You must not suspect me. It mortifies me. I assure you that I have now learnt to enjoy his conversation as an agreeable and sensible young man, without having a wish beyond it. I am perfectly satisfied from what his manners now are, that he never had any design of engaging my affection. It is only that he is blessed with greater sweetness of address, and a stronger desire of generally pleasing than any other man.'

'You are very cruel,' said her sister, 'you will not let me smile, and are provoking me to it every moment.'

'How hard it is in some cases to be believed!'

'And how impossible in others!'

'But why should you wish to persuade me that I feel more than I acknowledge?'

'That is a question which I hardly know how to answer. We all love to instruct, though we can teach only what is not worth knowing. Forgive me; and if you persist in indifference, do not make *me* your confidante.'

'Lizzy, my dear, I want to speak to you'

CHAPTER FIFTY FIVE

A FEW DAYS AFTER THIS VISIT, Mr Bingley called again, and alone. His friend had left him that morning for London, but was to return home in ten days time. He sat with them above an hour, and was in remarkably good spirits. Mrs Bennet invited him to dine with them; but, with many expressions of concern, he confessed himself engaged elsewhere.

'Next time you call,' said she, 'I hope we shall be more lucky.'

He should be particularly happy at any time, &c. &c.; and if she would give him leave, would take an early opportunity of waiting on them.

'Can you come to-morrow?'

Yes, he had no engagement at all for to-morrow; and her invitation was accepted with alacrity.

He came, and in such very good time, that the ladies were none of them dressed. In ran Mrs Bennet to her daughter's room, in her dressing gown, and with her hair half finished, crying out,

'My dear Jane, make haste and hurry down. He is come – Mr Bingley is come. – He is, indeed. Make haste, make haste. Here, Sarah, come to Miss Bennet this moment, and help her on with her gown. Never mind Miss Lizzy's hair.'

'We will be down as soon as we can,' said Jane; 'but I dare say Kitty is forwarder than either of us, for she went up stairs half an hour ago.'

'Oh! hang Kitty! what has she to do with it? Come be quick, be quick! where is your sash my dear?'

But when her mother was gone, Jane would not be prevailed on to go down without one of her sisters.

The same anxiety to get them by themselves, was visible again in the evening. After tea, Mr Bennet retired to the library, as was his custom, and Mary went up stairs to her instrument. Two obstacles of the five being thus removed, Mrs Bennet sat looking and winking at Elizabeth and Catherine for a considerable time, without making any impression on them. Elizabeth would not observe her; and when at last Kitty did, she very innocently said 'What is the matter mamma? What do you keep winking at me for? What am I to do?'

'Nothing child, nothing. I did not wink at you.' She then sat still five minutes longer; but unable to waste such a precious occasion, she suddenly got up, and saying to Kitty,

'Come here, my love, I want to speak to you,' took her out of the room. Jane instantly gave a look at Elizabeth, which spoke her distress at such premeditation, and her intreaty that *she* would not give into it. In a few minutes, Mrs Bennet half opened the door and called out,

'Lizzy, my dear, I want to speak with you.'

Elizabeth was forced to go.

'We may as well leave them by themselves you know;' said her mother as soon as she was in the hall. 'Kitty and I are going up stairs to sit in my dressing room.'

Elizabeth made no attempt to reason with her mother, but remained quietly in the hall, till she and Kitty were out of sight, then returned into the drawing room.

Mrs Bennet's schemes for this day were ineffectual. Bingley was every thing that was charming, except the professed lover of her daughter. His ease and cheerfulness rendered him a most agreeable addition to their evening party; and he bore with the ill-judged officiousness of the mother, and heard all her silly remarks with a forbearance and command of countenance, particularly grateful to the daughter.

He scarcely needed an invitation to stay to supper; and before he went away, an engagement was formed, chiefly through his own and Mrs Bennet's means, for his coming to shoot with her husband.

After this day, Jane said no more of her indifference. Not a word passed between the sisters concerning Bingley; but Elizabeth went to bed in the happy belief that all must speedily be concluded, unless Mr Darcy returned within the stated time. Seriously, however, she felt tolerably persuaded that all this must have taken place with that gentleman's concurrence.

Bingley was punctual to his appointment; and he and Mr Bennet spent the morning together, as had been agreed on. The latter was much more agreeable than his companion expected. There was nothing of presumption or folly in Bingley, that could provoke his ridicule, or disgust him into silence; and he was more communicative, and less eccentric than the other had ever seen him. Bingley of course returned with him to dinner; and in the evening Mrs Bennet's invitation was again at work to get every body away from him and her daughter. Elizabeth, who had a letter to write, went into the breakfast room for that purpose soon after tea; for as the others were all going to sit down to cards, she could not be wanted to counteract her mother's schemes.

But on returning to the drawing room, when her letter was finished, she saw, to her infinite surprise, there was reason to fear that her mother had been too ingenious for her. On opening the door, she perceived her sister and Bingley standing together over the hearth, as if engaged in earnest conversation; and had this led to no suspicion, the faces of both as they hastily turned round, and moved away from each other, would have told it all. *Their* situation was awkward enough; but *her's* she thought was still worse. Not a syllable was uttered by either; and Elizabeth was on the point of going away again, when Bingley, who as well as the other had sat down, suddenly rose, and whispering a few words to her sister, ran out of the room.

Jane could have no reserves from Elizabeth, where confidence would give pleasure; and instantly embracing her, acknowledged, with the liveliest emotion, that she was the happiest creature in the world.

''Tis too much!' she added, 'by far too much. I do not deserve it. Oh! why is not every body as happy?'

Elizabeth's congratulations were given with a sincerity, a warmth, a delight, which words could but poorly express. Every sentence of kindness was a fresh source of happiness to Jane. But she would not allow herself to stay with her sister, or say half that remained to be said, for the present. 'I must go instantly to my mother;' she cried. 'I would not on any account trifle with her affectionate solicitude; or allow her to hear it from any one but myself. He is gone to my father already. Oh! Lizzy, to know that what I have to relate will give such pleasure to all my dear family! how shall I bear so much happiness!'

She then hastened away to her mother, who had purposely broken up the card party, and was sitting up stairs with Kitty.

Elizabeth, who was left by herself, now smiled at the rapidity and ease with which an affair was finally settled, that had given them so many previous months of suspense and vexation.

'And this,' said she, 'is the end of all his friend's anxious circumspection! of all his sister's falsehood and contrivance! the happiest, wisest, most reasonable end!'

In a few minutes she was joined by Bingley, whose conference with her father had been short and to the purpose.

'Where is your sister?' said he hastily, as he opened the door.

'With my mother up stairs. She will be down in a moment I dare say.'

He then shut the door, and coming up to her, claimed the good wishes and affection of a sister. Elizabeth honestly and heartily expressed her delight in the prospect of their relationship. They shook hands with great cordiality; and then till her sister came down, she had to listen to all he had to say, of his own happiness, and of Jane's perfections; and in spite of his being a lover, Elizabeth really believed all his expectations of felicity, to be rationally founded, because they had for basis the excellent understanding, and super-excellent disposition of Jane, and a general similarity of feeling and taste between her and himself.

It was an evening of no common delight to them all; the satisfaction of Miss Bennet's mind gave a glow of such sweet animation to her face, as made her look handsomer than ever. Kitty simpered and smiled, and hoped her turn was coming soon. Mrs Bennet could not give her consent, or speak her approbation in terms warm enough to satisfy her feelings, though she talked to Bingley of nothing else, for half an hour; and when Mr Bennet joined them at supper, his voice and manner plainly shewed how really happy he was.

Not a word, however, passed his lips in allusion to it, till their visitor took his leave for the night; but as soon as he was gone, he turned to his daughter and said,

'Jane, I congratulate you. You will be a very happy woman.'

Jane went to him instantly, kissed him, and thanked him for his goodness.

'You are a good girl;' he replied, 'and I have great pleasure in thinking you will be so happily settled. I have not a doubt of your doing very well together. Your tempers are by no means unlike. You are each of you so complying, that nothing will ever be resolved on; so easy, that every servant will cheat you; and so generous, that you will always exceed your income.'

'I hope not so. Imprudence or thoughtlessness in money matters, would be unpardonable in *me*.'

'Exceed their income! My dear Mr Bennet,' cried his wife, 'what are you talking of? Why, he has four or five thousand a-year, and very likely more.' Then addressing her daughter, 'Oh, my dear, dear Jane, I am so happy! I am sure I sha'nt get a wink of sleep all night. I knew how it would be. I always said it must be so, at last. I was sure you could not be so beautiful for nothing! I remember, as soon as ever I saw him, when he first came into Hertfordshire last year, I thought how likely it was that you should come together. Oh! he is the handsomest young man that ever was seen!'

Wickham, Lydia, were all forgotten. Jane was beyond competition her favourite child. At that moment, she cared for no other. Her younger sisters soon began to make interest with her for objects of happiness which she might in future be able to dispense.

Mary petitioned for the use of the library at Netherfield; and Kitty begged very hard for a few balls there every winter.

Bingley, from this time, was of course a daily visitor at Longbourn; coming frequently before breakfast, and always remaining till after supper; unless when some barbarous neighbour, who could not be enough detested, had given him an invitation to dinner, which he thought himself obliged to accept.

Elizabeth had now but little time for conversation with her sister; for while he was present, Jane had no attention to bestow on anyone else; but she found herself considerably useful to both of them, in those hours of separation that must sometimes occur. In the absence of Jane, he always attached himself to Elizabeth, for the pleasure of talking of her; and when Bingley was gone, Jane constantly sought the same means of relief.

'He has made me so happy,' said she, one evening, 'by telling me, that he was totally ignorant of my being in town last spring! I had not believed it possible.'

'I suspected as much,' replied Elizabeth. 'But how did he account for it?'

'It must have been his sister's doing. They were certainly no friends to his acquaintance with me, which I cannot wonder at, since he might have chosen so much more advantageously in many respects. But when they see, as I trust they will, that their brother is happy with me, they will learn to be contented, and we shall be on good terms again; though we can never be what we once were to each other.'

'That is the most unforgiving speech,' said Elizabeth, 'that I ever heard you utter. Good girl! It would vex me, indeed, to see you again the dupe of Miss Bingley's pretended regard.'

'Would you believe it, Lizzy, that when he went to town last November, he really loved me, and nothing but a persuasion of *my* being indifferent, would have prevented his coming down again!'

'He made a little mistake to be sure; but it is to the credit of his modesty.'

This naturally introduced a panegyric from Jane on his diffidence, and the little value he put on his own good qualities.

Elizabeth was pleased to find, that he had not betrayed the interference of his friend, for, though Jane had the most generous and forgiving heart in the world, she knew it was a circumstance which must prejudice her against him.

'I am certainly the most fortunate creature that ever existed!' cried Jane. 'Oh! Lizzy, why am I thus singled from my family, and blessed above them all! If I could see *you* as happy! If there *were* but such another man for you!'

'If you were to give me forty such men, I never could be so happy as you. Till I have your disposition, your goodness, I never can have your happiness. No, no, let me shift for myself; and, perhaps, if I have very good luck, I may meet with another Mr Collins in time.'

The situation of affairs in the Longbourn family could not be long a secret. Mrs Bennet was privileged to whisper it to Mrs Philips, and *she* ventured, without any permission, to do the same by all her neighbours in Meryton.

The Bennets were speedily pronounced to be the luckiest family in the world, though only a few weeks before, when Lydia had first run away, they had been generally proved to be marked out for misfortune.

CHAPTER FIFTY SIX

ONE MORNING, ABOUT A WEEK AFTER Bingley's engagement with Jane had been formed, as he and the females of the family were sitting together in the dining room, their attention was suddenly drawn to the window, by the sound of a carriage; and they perceived a chaise and four driving up the lawn. It was too early in the morning for visitors, and besides, the equipage did not answer to that of any of their neighbours. The horses were post; and neither the carriage, nor the livery of the servant who preceded it, were familiar to them. As it was certain, however, that somebody was coming, Bingley instantly prevailed on Miss Bennet to avoid the confinement of such an intrusion, and walk away with him into the shrubbery. They both set off, and the conjectures of the remaining three continued, though with little satisfaction, till the door was thrown open, and their visitor entered. It was Lady Catherine de Bourgh.

They were of course all intending to be surprised; but their astonishment was beyond their expectation; and on the part of Mrs Bennet and Kitty, though she was perfectly unknown to them, even inferior to what Elizabeth felt.

She entered the room with an air more than usually ungracious, made no other reply to Elizabeth's salutation, than a slight inclination of the head, and sat down without saying a word. Elizabeth had mentioned her name to her mother, on her ladyship's entrance, though no request of introduction had been made.

Mrs Bennet all amazement, though flattered by having a guest of such high importance, received her with the utmost politeness. After sitting for a moment in silence, she said very stiffly to Elizabeth,

'I hope you are well, Miss Bennet. That lady I suppose is your mother.'

Elizabeth replied very concisely that she was.

'And *that* I suppose is one of your sisters.'

'Yes, madam,' said Mrs Bennet, delighted to speak to lady Catherine. 'She is my youngest girl but one. My youngest of all, is lately married, and my eldest is some-where about the grounds, walking with a young man, who I believe will soon become a part of the family.'

'You have a very small park here,' returned lady Catherine after a short silence.

'It is nothing in comparison of Rosings, my lady, I dare say; but I assure you it is much larger than Sir William Lucas's.'

'This must be a most inconvenient sitting room for the evening, in summer; the windows are full west.'

Mrs Bennet assured her that they never sat there after dinner; and then added,

'May I take the liberty of asking your ladyship whether you left Mr and Mrs Collins well.'

'Yes, very well. I saw them the night before last.'

Elizabeth now expected that she would produce a letter for her from Charlotte, as it seemed the only probable motive for her calling. But no letter appeared, and she was completely puzzled.

Mrs Bennet, with great civility, begged her ladyship to take some refreshment; but Lady Catherine very resolutely, and not very politely, declined eating any thing; and then rising up, said to Elizabeth,

'Miss Bennet, there seemed to be a prettyish kind of a little wilderness on one side of your lawn. I should be glad to take a turn in it, if you will favour me with your company.'

'Go, my dear,' cried her mother, 'and shew her ladyship about the different walks. I think she will be pleased with the hermitage.'

Elizabeth obeyed, and running into her own room for her parasol, attended her noble guest down stairs. As they passed through the hall, Lady Catherine opened the doors into the dining-parlour and drawing-room, and pronouncing them, after a short survey, to be decent loking rooms, walked on.

Her carriage remained at the door, and Elizabeth saw that her waiting-woman was in it. They proceeded in silence along the gravel walk that led to the copse; Elizabeth was determined to make no effort for conversation with a woman, who was now more than usually insolent and disagreeable.

'How could I ever think her like her nephew?' said she, as she looked in her face.

As soon as they entered the copse, Lady Catherine began in the following manner: –

'You can be at no loss, Miss Bennet, to understand the reason of my journey hither. Your own heart, your own conscience, must tell you why I come.'

Elizabeth looked with unaffected astonishment.

'Indeed, you are mistaken, Madam. I have not been at all able to account for the honour of seeing you here.'

'Miss Bennet,' replied her ladyship, in an angry tone, 'you ought to know, that I am not to be trifled with. But however insincere you may choose to be, you shall not find *me* so. My character has ever been celebrated

After a short survey

for its sincerity and frankness, and in a cause of such moment as this, I shall certainly not depart from it. A report of a most alarming nature, reached me two days ago. I was told, that not only your sister was on the point of being most advantageously married, but that *you*, that Miss Elizabeth Bennet, would, in all likelihood, be soon aferwards united to my nephew, my own nephew, Mr Darcy. Though I *know* it must be a scandalous falsehood; though I would not injure him so much as to suppose the truth of it possible, I instantly resolved on setting off for this place, that I might make my sentiments known to you.'

'If you believed it impossible to be true,' said Elizabeth, colouring with astonishment and disdain, 'I wonder you took the trouble of coming so far. What would your ladyship propose by it?'

'At once to insist upon having such a report universally contradicted.'

'Your coming to Longbourn, to see me and my family,' said Elizabeth, coolly, 'will be rather a confirmation of it; if, indeed, such a report is in existence.'

'If! do you then pretend to be ignorant of it? Has it not been industriously circulated by yourselves? Do you not know that such a report is spread abroad?'

'I never heard that it was.'

'And can you likewise declare, that there is no *foundation* for it?'

'I do not pretend to possess equal frankness with your ladyship. *You* may ask questions which *I* shall not choose to answer.'

'This is not to be borne. Miss Bennet, I insist on being satisfied. Has he, has my nephew, made you an offer of marriage?'

'Your ladyship has declared it to be impossible.'

'It ought to be so; it must be so, while he retains the use of his reason. But *your* arts and allurements may, in a moment of infatuation, have made him forget what he owes to himself and to all his family. You may have drawn him in.'

'If I had, I shall be the last person to confess it.'

'Miss Bennet, do you know who I am? I have not been accustomed to such language as this. I am almost the nearest relation he has in the world, and am entitled to know all his dearest concerns.'

'But you are not entitled to know *mine*; nor will such behaviour as this, ever induce me to be explicit.'

'Let me be rightly understood. This match, to which you have the presumption to aspire, can never take place. No, never. Mr Darcy is engaged to *my daughter*. Now what have you to say?'

'Only this; that if he is so, you can have no reason to suppose he will make an offer to me.'

Lady Catherine hesitated for a moment, and then replied,

'The engagement between them is of a peculiar kind. From their infancy, they have been intended for each other. It was the favourite wish of *his* mother, as well as of her's. While in their cradles, we planned the union: and now, at the moment when the wishes of both sisters would be accomplished, in their marriage, to be prevented by a young woman of inferior birth, of no importance in the world, and wholly unallied to the family! Do you pay no regard to the wishes of his friends? To his tacit engagement with Miss de Bourgh? Are you lost to every feeling of propriety and delicacy? Have you not heard me say, that from his earliest hours he was destined for his cousin?'

'Yes, and I had heard it before. But what is that to me? If there is no other objection to my marrying your nephew, I shall certainly not be kept from it, by knowing that his mother and aunt wished him to marry Miss de Bourgh. You both did as much as you could, in planning the marriage. Its completion depended on others. If Mr Darcy is neither by honour nor inclination confined to his cousin, why is not he to make another choice? And if I am that choice, why may not I accept him?'

'Because honour, decorum, prudence, nay, interest, forbid it. Yes, Miss Bennet, interest; for do not expect to be noticed by his family or friends, if you wilfully act against the inclinations of all. You will be censured, slighted, and despised, by every one connected with him. Your alliance will be a disgrace; your name will never even be mentioned by any of us.'

'These are heavy misfortunes,' replied Elizabeth. 'But the wife of Mr Darcy must have such extraordinary sources of happiness necessarily attached to her situation, that she could, upon the whole, have no cause to repine.'

'Obstinate, headstrong girl! I am ashamed of you! Is this your gratitude for my attentions to you last spring? Is nothing due to me on that score?

'Let us sit down. You are to understand, Miss Bennet, that I came here with the determined resolution of carrying my purpose; nor will I be dissuaded from it. I have not been used to submit to any person's whims. I have not been in the habit of brooking disappointment.'

'*That* will make your ladyship's situation at present more pitiable; but it will have no effect on *me*.'

'I will not be interrupted. Hear me in silence. My daughter and my nephew are formed for each other. They are descended on the maternal side, from the same noble line; and, on the father's, from respectable, honourable, and ancient, though untitled families. Their fortune on both sides is splendid. They are destined for each other by the voice of every member of their respective houses; and what is to divide them? The upstart pretensions of a young woman without family, connections, or fortune. Is this to be endured! But it must not, shall not be. If you were sensible of your own good, you would not wish to quit the sphere, in which you have been brought up.'

'In marrying your nephew, I should not consider myself as quitting that sphere. He is a gentleman; I am a gentleman's daughter; so far we are equal.'

'True. You *are* a gentleman's daughter. But who was your mother? Who are your uncles and aunts? Do not imagine me ignorant of their condition.'

'Whatever my connections may be,' said Elizabeth, 'if your nephew does not object to them, they can be nothing to *you*.'

'Tell me once for all, are you engaged to him?'

Though Elizabeth would not, for the mere purpose of obliging Lady Catherine, have answered this question; she could not but say, after a moment's deliberation,

'I am not.'

Lady Catherine seemed pleased.

'And will you promise me, never to enter into such an engagement?'

'I will make no promise of the kind.'

'Miss Bennet I am shocked and astonished. I expected to find a more reasonable young woman. But do not deceive yourself into a belief that I will ever recede. I shall not go away, till you have given me the assurance I require.'

'And I certainly *never* shall give it. I am not to be intimidated into anything so wholly unreasonable. Your ladyship wants Mr Darcy to marry your daughter; but would my giving you the wished-for promise, make *their* marriage at all more probable? Supposing him to be attached to me, would *my* refusing to accept his hand, make him wish to bestow it on his cousin? Allow me to say, Lady Catherine, that the arguments with which you have supported this extraordinary application, have been as frivolous as the application was ill-judged. You have widely mistaken my character, if you think I can be worked on by such persuasions as these. How far your nephew might approve of your interference in *his* affairs, I cannot tell; but you have certainly no right to concern yourself in mine. I must beg, therefore, to be importuned no farther on the subject.'

'Not so hasty, if you please. I have by no means done. To all the objections I have already urged, I have still another to add. I am no stranger to the particulars of your youngest sister's infamous elopement. I know it all; that the young man's marrying her, was a patched-up business, at the expence of your father and uncles. And is *such* a girl to be my nephew's sister? Is *her* husband, is the son of his late father's steward, to be his brother? Heaven and earth! – of what are you thinking? Are the shades of Pemberley to be thus polluted?'

'You can *now* have nothing farther to say,' she resentfully answered. 'You have insulted me, in every possible method. I must beg to return to the house.'

And she rose as she spoke. Lady Catherine rose also, and they turned back. Her ladyship was highly incensed.

'You have no regard, then, for the honour and credit of my nephew! Unfeeling, selfish girl! Do you not consider that a connection with you, must disgrace him in the eyes of everybody?'

'Lady Catherine, I have nothing farther to say. You know my sentiments.'

'You are then resolved to have him?'

'I have said no such thing. I am only resolved to act in that manner, which will, in my own opinion, constitute my happiness, without reference to *you*, or to any person so wholly unconnected with me.'

'It is well. You refuse, then, to oblige me. You refuse to obey the claims of duty, honour, and gratitude. You are determined to ruin him in the opinion of all his friends, and make him the contempt of the world.'

'Neither duty, nor honour, nor gratitude,' replied Elizabeth, 'have any possible claim on me, in the present instance. No principle of either, would be violated by my marriage with Mr Darcy. And with regard to the resentment of his family, or the indignation of the world, if the former *were* excited by his marrying me, it would not give me one moment's concern – and the world in general would have too much sense to join in the scorn.'

'And this is your real opinion! This is your final resolve! Very well. I shall now know how to act. Do not imagine, Miss Bennet, that your ambition will ever be gratified. I came to try you. I hoped to find you reasonable; but depend upon it I will carry my point.'

In this manner Lady Catherine talked on, till they were at the door of the carriage, when turning hastily round, she added,

'I take no leave of you, Miss Bennet: I send no compliments to your mother. You deserve no such attention. I am most seriously displeased.'

Elizabeth made no answer; and without attempting to persuade her ladyship to return into the house, walked quietly into it herself. She heard the carriage drive away as she proceeded up stairs. Her mother impatiently met her at the door of the dressing-room, to ask why Lady Catherine would not come in again and rest herself.

'She did not choose it,' said her daughter, 'she would go.'

'She is a very fine-looking woman! and her calling here was prodigiously civil! for she only came, I suppose, to tell us the Collinses were well. She is on her road somewhere, I dare say, and so passing through Meryton, thought she might as well call on you. I suppose she had nothing particular to say to you, Lizzy?'

Elizabeth was forced to give into a little falsehood here; for to acknowledge the substance of their conversation was impossible.

CHAPTER FIFTY SEVEN

THE DISCOMPOSURE OF SPIRITS, WHICH this extraordinary visit threw Elizabeth into, could not be easily overcome; nor could she for many hours, learn to think of it less than incessantly. Lady Catherine it appeared, had actually taken the trouble of this journey from Rosings, for the sole purpose of breaking off her supposed engagement with Mr Darcy. It was a rational scheme to be sure! but from what the report of their engagement could originate, Elizabeth was at a loss to imagine; till she recollected that *his* being the intimate friend of Bingley, and *her* being the sister of Jane, was enough, at a time when the expectation of one wedding, made every body eager for another, to supply the idea. She had not herself forgotten to feel that the marriage of her sister must bring them more frequently together. And her neighbours at Lucas lodge, therefore, (for through their communication with the Collinses, the report she concluded had reached Lady Catherine) had only set *that* down, as almost certain and immediate, which *she* had looked forward to as possible, at some future time.

In revolving Lady Catherine's expressions, however, she could not help feeling some uneasiness as to the possible consequence of her persisting in this interference. From what she had said of her resolution to prevent their marriage, it occurred to Elizabeth that she must meditate an application to her nephew; and how *he* might take a similar representation of the evils attached to a connection with her, she dared not pronounce. She knew not the exact degree of his affection for his aunt, or his dependence on her judgment, but it was natural to suppose that he thought much higher of her ladyship than *she* could do; and it was certain, that in enumerating the miseries of a marriage with *one*, whose immediate connections were so unequal to his own, his aunt would address him on his weakest side. With his notions of dignity, he would probably feel that the arguments, which to Elizabeth had appeared weak and ridiculous, contained much good sense and solid reasoning.

If he had been wavering before, as to what he should do, which had often seemed likely, the advice and intreaty of so near a relation might settle every doubt, and determine him at once to be as happy, as dignity unblemished could make him. In that case he would return no more. Lady Catherine might see him in her way through town; and his engagement to Bingley of coming again to Netherfield must give way.

'If, therefore, an excuse for not keeping his promise, should come to his friend within a few days,' she added, 'I shall know how to understand it. I shall then give over every expectation, every wish of his constancy. If he is satisfied with only regretting me, when he might have obtained my affections and hand, I shall soon cease to regret him at all.'

The surprise of the rest of the family, on hearing who their visitor had been, was very great; but they obligingly satisfied it, with the same kind of supposition, which had appeased Mrs Bennet's curiosity; and Elizabeth was spared from much teazing on the subject.

The next morning, as she was going down stairs, she was met by her father, who came out of his library with a letter in his hand.

'Lizzy,' said he, 'I was going to look for you; come into my room.'

She followed him thither; and her curiosity to know what he had to tell her, was heightened by the supposition of its being in some manner connected with the letter he held. It suddenly struck her that it might be from Lady Catherine; and she anticipated with dismay all the consequent explanations.

She followed her father to the fire place, and they both sat down. He then said,

'I have received a letter this morning that has astonished me exceedingly. As it principally concerns yourself, you ought to know its contents. I did not know before, that I had *two* daughters on the brink of matrimony. Let me congratulate you, on a very important conquest.'

The colour now rushed into Elizabeth's cheeks in the instantaneous conviction of its being a letter from the nephew, instead of the aunt; and she was undetermined whether most to be pleased that he explained himself at all, or offended that this letter was not rather addressed to herself; when her father continued,

'You look conscious. Young ladies have great penetration in such matters as these; but I think I may defy even *your* sagacity, to discover the name of your admirer. This letter is from Mr Collins.'

'From Mr Collins! and what can *he* have to say?'

'Something very much to the purpose of course. He begins with congratulations on the approaching nuptials of my eldest daughter, of which it seems he has been told, by some of the good-natured, gossiping Lucases. I shall not sport with your impatience, by reading what he says on that point. What relates to yourself, is as follows.' 'Having thus offered you the sincere congratulations of Mrs Collins and myself on this happy event, let me now add a short hint on the subject of another of which we have been advertised by the same authority. Your daughter Elizabeth, it is presumed, will not long bear the name of Bennet, after her elder sister has resigned it, and the chosen partner of her fate, may be reasonably looked up to, as one of the most illustrious personages in this land.'

'Can you possibly guess Lizzy, who is meant by this?' 'This young gentleman is blessed in a peculiar way, with every thing the heart of mortal can most desire, – splendid property, noble kindred, and extensive patronage. Yet in spite of all these temptations, let me warn my cousin Elizabeth, and yourself, of what evils you may incur, by a precipitate closure with this gentleman's proposals, which, of course, you will be inclined to take immediate advantage of.'

'Have you any idea, Lizzy, who this gentleman is? But now it comes out.'

'My motive for cautioning you, is as follows. We have reason to imagine that his aunt, Lady Catherine de Bourgh, does not look on the match with a friendly eye.'

'*Mr Darcy*, you see, is the man! Now, Lizzy, I think I *have* surprised you. Could he, or the Lucases, have pitched on any man, within the circle of our acquaintance, whose name would have given the lie more effectually to what they related? Mr Darcy, who never looks at any woman but to see a blemish, and who probably never looked at *you* in his life! It is admirable!'

Elizabeth tried to join in her father's pleasantry, but could only force one most reluctant smile. Never had his wit been directed in a manner so little agreeable to her.

'Are you not diverted?'

'Oh! yes. Pray read on.'

'After mentioning the likelihood of this marriage to her ladyship last night, she immediately, with her usual condescension, expressed what she felt on the occasion; when it became apparent, that on the score of some family objections on the part of my cousin, she would never give her consent to what she termed so disgraceful a match. I thought it my duty to give the speediest intelligence of this to my cousin, that she and her noble admirer may be aware of what they are about, and not run hastily into a marriage which has not been properly sanctioned.' 'Mr Collins moreover adds,' 'I am truly rejoiced that my cousin Lydia's sad business has been so well hushed up, and am only concerned that their living together before the marriage took place, should be so generally known. I must not, however, neglect the duties of my station, or refrain from declaring my amazement, at hearing that you received the young couple into your house as soon as they were married. It was an encouragement of vice; and had I been the rector of Longbourn, I should very strenuously have opposed it. You ought certainly to forgive them as christians, but never to admit them in your sight, or allow their names to be mentioned in your hearing.' '*That* is his notion of christian forgiveness! The rest of his letter is only about his dear

Charlotte's situation, and his expectation of a young olive-branch. But, Lizzy, you look as if you did not enjoy it. You are not going to be *Missish*, I hope, and pretend to be affronted at an idle report. For what do we live, but to make sport for our neighbours, and laugh at them in our turn?'

'Oh!' cried Elizabeth, 'I am excessively diverted. But it is so strange!'

'Yes – *that* is what makes it amusing. Had they fixed on any other man it would have been nothing; but *his* perfect indifference, and *your* pointed dislike, make it so delightfully absurd! Much as I abominate writing, I would not give up Mr Collins's correspondence for any consideration. Nay, when I read a letter of his, I cannot help giving him the preference even over Wickham, much as I value the impudence and hypocrisy of my son-in-law. And pray, Lizzie, what said Lady Catherine about this report? Did she call to refuse her consent?'

To this question his daughter replied only with a laugh; and as it had been asked without the least suspicion, she was not distressed by his repeating it. Elizabeth had never been more at a loss to make her feelings appear what they were not. It was necessary to laugh, when she would rather have cried. Her father had most cruelly mortified her, by what he said of Mr Darcy's indifference, and she could do nothing but wonder at such a want of penetration, or fear that perhaps, instead of his seeing too *little*, she might have fanciced too *much*.

The efforts of his aunt

CHAPTER FIFTY EIGHT

INSTEAD OF RECEIVING ANY SUCH letter of excuse from his friend, as Elizabeth half expected Mr Bingley to do, he was able to bring Darcy with him to Longbourn before many days had passed after Lady Catherine's visit. The gentlemen arrived early; and, before Mrs Bennet had time to tell him of their having seen his aunt, of which her daughter sat in momentary dread, Bingley, who wanted to be alone with Jane, proposed their all walking out. It was agreed to. Mrs Bennet was not in the habit of walking, Mary could never spare time, but the remaining five set off together. Bingley and Jane, however, soon allowed the others to outstrip them. They lagged behind, while Elizabeth, Kitty, and Darcy, were to entertain each other. Very little was said by either; Kitty was too much afraid of him to talk; Elizabeth was secretly forming a desperate resolution; and perhaps he might be doing the same.

They walked towards the Lucases, because Kitty wished to call upon Maria; and as Elizabeth saw no occasion for making it a general concern, when Kitty left them, she went boldly on with him alone. Now was the moment for her resolution to be executed, and, while her courage was high, she immediately said,

'Mr Darcy, I am a very selfish creature; and, for the sake of giving relief to my own feelings, care not how much I may be wounding your's. I can no longer help thanking you for your unexampled kindness to my poor sister. Ever since I have known it, I have been most anxious to acknowledge to you how gratefully I feel it. Were it known to the rest of my family, I should not have merely my own gratitude to express.'

'I am sorry, exceedingly sorry,' replied Darcy, in a tone of surprise and emotion, 'that you have ever been informed of what may, in a mistaken light, have given you uneasiness. I did not think Mrs Gardiner was so little to be trusted.'

'You must not blame my aunt. Lydia's thoughtlessness first betrayed to me that you had been concerned in the matter; and, of course, I could not rest till I knew the particulars. Let me thank you again and again, in the name of all my family, for that generous compassion which induced you to take so much trouble, and bear so many mortifications, for the sake of discovering them.'

'If you *will* thank me,' he replied, 'let it be for yourself alone. That the wish of giving happiness to you, might add force to the other inducements which led me on, I shall not attempt to deny. But your *family* owe me nothing. Much as I respect them, I believe, I thought only of *you*.'

Elizabeth was too much embarrassed to say a word. After a short pause, her companion added, 'You are too generous to trifle with me. If your feelings are still what they were last April, tell me so at once. *My* affections and wishes are unchanged, but one word from you will silence me on this subject for ever.'

Elizabeth feeling all the more than common awkwardness and anxiety of his situation, now forced herself to speak; and immediately, though not very fluently, gave him to understand, that her sentiments had undergone so material a change, since the period to which he alluded, as to make her receive with gratitude and pleasure, his present assurances. The happiness which this reply produced, was such as he had probably never felt before; and he expressed himself on the occasion as sensibly and as warmly as a man violently in love can be supposed to do. Had Elizabeth been able to encounter his eye, she might have seen how well the expression of heart-felt delight, diffused over his face, became him; but, though she could not look, she could listen, and he told her of feelings, which, in proving of what importance she was to him, made his affection every moment more valuable.

They walked on, without knowing in what direction. There was too much to be thought, and felt, and said, for attention to any other objects.

She soon learnt that they were indebted for their present good understanding to the efforts of his aunt, who *did* call on him in her return through London, and there relate her journey to Longbourn, its motive, and the substance of her conversation with Elizabeth; dwelling emphatically on every expression of the latter, which, in her ladyship's apprehension, peculiarly denoted her perverseness and assurance, in the belief that such a relation must assist her endeavours to obtain that promise from her nephew, which *she* had refused to give. But, unluckily for her ladyship, its effect had been exactly contrariwise.

'It taught me to hope,' said he, 'as I had scarcely ever allowed myself to hope before. I knew enough of your disposition to be certain, that, had you been absolutely, irrevocably decided against me, you would have acknowledged it to Lady Catherine, frankly and openly.'

Elizabeth coloured and laughed as she replied. 'Yes, you know enough of my *frankness* to believe me capable of *that*. After abusing you so abominably to your face, I could have no scruple in abusing you to all your relations.'

'What did you say of me, that I did not deserve? For, though your accusations were ill-founded, formed on mistaken premises, my behaviour to you at the time, had merited the severest reproof. It was unpardonable. I cannot think of it without abhorrence.'

'We will not quarrel for the greater share of blame annexed to that evening,' said Elizabeth. 'The conduct of neither, if strictly examined, will be irreproachable; but since then, we have both, I hope, improved in civility.'

'I cannot be so easily reconciled to myself. The recollection of what I then said, of my conduct, my manners, my expressions during the whole of it, is now, and has been many months, inexpressibly painful to me. Your reproof, so well applied, I shall never forget: "had you behaved in a more gentleman-like manner." Those were your words. You know not, you can scarcely conceive, how they have tortured me; – though it was some time, I confess, before I was reasonable enough to allow their justice.'

'I was certainly very far from expecting them to make so strong an impression. I had not the smallest idea of their being ever felt in such a way.'

'I can easily believe it. You thought me then devoid of every proper feeling, I am sure you did. The turn of your countenance I shall never forget, as you said that I could not have addressed you in any possible way, that would induce you to accept me.'

'Oh! do not repeat what I then said. These recollections will not do at all. I assure you, that I have long been most heartily ashamed of it.'

Darcy mentioned his letter. 'Did it,' said he, 'did it *soon* make you think better of me? Did you, on reading it, give any credit to its contents?'

She explained what its effect on her had been, and how gradually all her former prejudices had been removed.

'I knew,' said he, 'that what I wrote must give you pain, but it was necessary. I hope you have destroyed the letter. There was one part especially, the opening of it, which I should dread your having the power of reading again. I can remember some expressions which might justly make you hate me.'

'The letter shall certainly be burnt, if you believe it essential to the preservation of my regard; but, though we have both reason to think my opinions not entirely unalterable, they are not, I hope, quite so easily changed as that implies.'

'When I wrote that letter,' replied Darcy, 'I believed myself perfectly calm and cool, but I am since convinced that it was written in a dreadful bitterness of spirit.'

'The letter, perhaps, began in bitterness, but it did not end so. The adieu is charity itself. But think no more of the letter. The feelings of the person who wrote, and the person who received it, are now so widely different from what they were then, that every unpleasant circumstance attending it, ought to be forgotten. You must learn some of my philosophy. Think only of the past as its remembrance gives you pleasure.'

'I cannot give you credit for any philosophy of the kind. *Your* retrospections must be so totally void of reproach, that the contentment arising from them, is not of philosophy, but what is much better, of ignorance. But with *me*, it is not so. Painful recollections will intrude, which cannot, which ought not to be repelled. I have been a selfish being all my life, in practice, though not in principle. As a child I was taught what was *right*, but I was not taught to correct my temper. I was given good principles, but left to follow them in pride and conceit. Unfortunately an only son, (for many years an only *child*) I was spoilt by my parents, who though good themselves, (my father particularly, all that was benevolent and amiable,) allowed, encouraged, almost taught me to be selfish and overbearing, to care for none beyond my own family circle, to think meanly of all the rest of the world, to *wish* at least to think meanly of their sense and worth compared with my own. Such I was, from eight to eight and twenty; and such I might still have been but for you, dearest, loveliest Elizabeth! What do I not owe you! You taught me a lesson, hard indeed at first, but most advantageous. By you, I was properly humbled. I came to you without a doubt of my reception. You shewed me how insufficient were all my pretensions to please a woman worthy of being pleased.'

'Had you then persuaded yourself that I should?'

'Indeed I had. What will you think of my vanity? I believed you to be wishing, expecting my addresses.'

'My manners must have been in fault, but not intentionally I assure you. I never meant to deceive you, but my spirits might often lead me wrong. How you must have hated me after *that* evening?'

'Hate you! I was angry perhaps at first, but my anger soon began to take a proper direction.'

'I am almost afraid of asking what you thought of me; when we met at Pemberley. You blamed me for coming?'

'No indeed; I felt nothing but surprise.'

'Your surprise could not be greater than *mine* in being noticed by you. My conscience told me that I deserved no extraordinary politeness, and I confess that I did not expect to receive *more* than my due.'

'My object *then*,' replied Darcy, 'was to shew you, by every civility in my power, that I was not so mean as to resent the past; and I hoped to obtain your forgiveness, to lessen your ill opinion, by letting you see that your reproofs had been attended to. How soon any other wishes introduced themselves I can hardly tell, but I believe in about half an hour after I had seen you.'

He then told her of Georgiana's delight in her acquaintance, and of her disappointment at its sudden interruption; which naturally leading to the cause of that interruption, she soon learnt that his resolution of following her from Derbyshire in quest of her sister, had been formed before he quitted the inn, and that his gravity and thoughtfulness there, had arisen from no other struggles than what such a purpose must comprehend.

She expressed her gratitude again, but it was too painful a subject to each, to be dwelt on farther.

After walking several miles in a leisurely manner, and too busy to know any thing about it, they found at last, on examining their watches, that it was time to be at home.

'What could become of Mr Bingley and Jane!' was a wonder which introduced the discussion of *their* affairs. Darcy was delighted with their engagement; his friend had given him the earliest information of it.

'I must ask whether you were surprised?' said Elizabeth.

'Not at all. When I went away, I felt that it would soon happen.'

'That is to say, you had given your permission. I guessed as much.' And though he exclaimed at the term, she found that it had been pretty much the case.

'On the evening before my going to London,' said he, 'I made a confession to him, which I believe I ought to have made long ago. I told him of all that had occurred to make my former interference in his affairs, absurd and impertinent. His surprise was great. He had never had the slightest suspicion. I told him, moreover, that I believed myself mistaken in supposing, as I had done, that your sister was indifferent to him; and as I could easily perceive that his attachment to her was unabated, I felt no doubt of their happiness together.'

Elizabeth could not help smiling at his easy manner of directing his friend.

'Did you speak from your own observation,' said she, 'when you told him that my sister loved him, or merely from my information last spring?'

'From the former. I had narrowly observed her during the two visits which I had lately made her here; and I was convinced of her affection.'

'And your assurance of it, I suppose, carried immediate conviction to him.'

'It did. Bingley is most unaffectedly modest. His diffidence had prevented his depending on his own judgment in so anxious a case, but his reliance on mine, made every thing easy. I was obliged to confess one thing, which for a time, and not unjustly, offended him. I could not allow myself to conceal that your sister had been in town three months last winter, that I had known it, and purposely kept it from him. He was angry. But his anger, I am persuaded, lasted no longer than he remained in any doubt of your sister's sentiments. He has heartily forgiven me now.'

Elizabeth longed to observe that Mr Bingley had been a most delightful friend; so easily guided that his worth was invaluable; but she checked herself. She remembered that he had yet to learn to be laughed at, and it was rather too early to begin. In anticipating the happiness of Bingley, which of course was to be inferior only to his own, he continued the conversation till they reached the house. In the hall they parted.

Unable to utter a syllable

CHAPTER FIFTY NINE

'MY DEAR LIZZY, WHERE CAN YOU have been walking to?' was a question which Elizabeth received from Jane as soon as she entered the room, and from all the others when they sat down to table. She had only to say in reply, that they had wandered about, till she was beyond her own knowledge. She coloured as she spoke; but neither that, nor any thing else, awakened a suspicion of the truth.

The evening passed quietly, unmarked by any thing extraordinary. The acknowledged lovers talked and laughed, the unacknowledged were silent. Darcy was not of a disposition in which happiness overflows in mirth; and Elizabeth, agitated and confused, rather *knew* that she was happy, than *felt* herself to be so; for, besides the immediate embarrassment, there were other evils before her. She anticipated what would be felt in the family when her situation became known; she was aware that no one liked him but Jane; and even feared that with the others it was a *dislike* which not all his fortune and consequence might do away.

At night she opened her heart to Jane. Though suspicion was very far from Miss Bennet's general habits, she was absolutely incredulous here.

'You are joking, Lizzy. This cannot be! – engaged to Mr Darcy! No, no, you shall not deceive me. I know it to be impossible.'

'This is a wretched beginning indeed! My sole dependence was on you; and I am sure nobody else will believe me, if you do not. Yet, indeed, I am in earnest. I speak nothing but the truth. He still loves me, and we are engaged.'

Jane looked at her doubtingly. 'Oh, Lizzy! it cannot be. I know how much you dislike him.'

'You know nothing of the matter. *That* is all to be forgot. Perhaps I did not always love him so well as I do now. But in such cases as these, a good memory is unpardonable. This is the last time I shall ever remember it myself.'

Miss Bennet still looked all amazement. Elizabeth again, and more seriously assured her of its truth.

'Good Heaven! can it be really so! Yet now I must believe you,' cried Jane. 'My dear, dear Lizzy, I would – I do congratulate you – but are you certain? forgive the question – are you quite certain that you can be happy with him?'

'There can be no doubt of that. It is settled between us already, that we are to be the happiest couple in the world. But are you pleased, Jane? Shall you like to have such a brother?'

'Very, very much. Nothing could give either Bingley or myself more delight. But we considered it, we talked of it as impossible. And do you really love him quite well enough? Oh, Lizzy! do any thing rather than marry without affection. Are you quite sure that you feel what you ought to do?'

'Oh, yes! You will only think I feel *more* than I ought to do, when I tell you all.'

'What do you mean?'

'Why, I must confess, that I love him better than I do Bingley. I am afraid you will be angry.'

'My dearest sister, now *be* serious. I want to talk very seriously. Let me know every thing that I am to know, without delay. Will you tell me how long you have loved him?'

'It has been coming on so gradually, that I hardly know when it began. But I believe I must date it from my first seeing his beautiful grounds at Pemberley.'

Another intreaty that she would be serious, however, produced the desired effect; and she soon satisfied Jane by her solemn assurances of attachment. When convinced on that article, Miss Bennet had nothing farther to wish.

'Now I am quite happy,' she said, 'for you will be as happy as myself. I always had a value for him. Were it for nothing but his love of you, I must always have esteemed him; but now, as Bingley's friend and your husband, there can be only Bingley and yourself more dear to me. But Lizzy, you have been very sly, very reserved with me. How little did you tell me of what passed at Pemberley and Lambton! I owe all that I know of it, to another, not to you.'

Elizabeth told her the motives of her secrecy. She had been unwilling to mention Bingley; and the unsettled state of her own feelings had made her equally avoid the name of his friend. But now she would no longer conceal from her, his share in Lydia's marriage. All was acknowledged, and half the night spent in conversation.

'Good gracious!' cried Mrs Bennet, as she stood at a window the next morning, 'if that disagreeable Mr Darcy is not coming here again with our dear Bingley! What can he mean by being so tiresome as to be always coming here? I had no notion but he would go a shooting, or something or other, and not disturb us with his company. What shall we do with him? Lizzy, you must walk out with him again, that he may not be in Bingley's way.'

Elizabeth could hardly help laughing at so convenient a proposal; yet was really vexed that her mother should be always giving him such an epithet.

As soon as they entered, Bingley looked at her so expressively, and shook hands with such warmth, as left no doubt of his good information; and he soon afterwards said aloud, 'Mr Bennet, have you no more lanes hereabouts in which Lizzy may lose her way again to-day?'

'I advise Mr Darcy, and Lizzy, and Kitty,' said Mrs Bennet, 'to walk to Oakham Mount this morning. It is a nice long walk, and Mr Darcy has never seen the view.'

'It may do very well for the others,' replied Mr Bingley; 'but I am sure it will be too much for Kitty. Won't it, Kitty?'

Kitty owned that she had rather stay at home. Darcy professed a great curiosity to see the view from the Mount, and Elizabeth silently consented. As she went up stairs to get ready, Mrs Bennet followed her, saying,

'I am quite sorry, Lizzy, that you should be forced to have that disagreeable man all to yourself. But I hope you will not mind it: it is all for Jane's sake, you know; and there is no occasion for talking to him, except just now and then. So, do not put yourself to inconvenience.'

During their walk, it was resolved that Mr Bennet's consent should be asked in the course of the evening. Elizabeth reserved to herself the application for her mother's. She could not determine how her mother would take it; sometimes doubting whether all his wealth and grandeur would be enough to overcome her abhorrence of the man. But whether she were violently set against the match, or violently delighted with it, it was certain that her manner would be equally ill adapted to do credit to her sense; and she could no more bear that Mr Darcy should hear the first raptures of her joy, than the first vehemence of her disapprobation.

In the evening, soon after Mr Bennet withdrew to the library, she saw Mr Darcy rise also and follow him, and her agitation on seeing it was extreme. She did not fear her father's opposition, but he was going to be made unhappy, and that it should be through her means, that *she*, his favourite child, should be distressing him by her choice, should be filling him with fears and regrets in disposing of her, was a wretched reflection, and she sat in misery till Mr Darcy appeared again, when, looking at him, she was a little relieved by his smile. In a few minutes he approached the table where she was sitting with Kitty; and, while pretending to admire her work, said in a whisper, 'Go to your father, he wants you in the library.' She was gone directly.

Her father was walking about the room, looking grave and anxious. 'Lizzy,' said he, 'what are you doing? Are you out of your senses, to be accepting this man? Have not you always hated him?'

How earnestly did she then wish that her former opinions had been more reasonable, her expressions more moderate! It would have spared her from explanations and professions which it was exceedingly awkward to give; but they were now necessary, and she assured him with some confusion, of her attachment to Mr Darcy.

'Or in other words, you are determined to have him. He is rich, to be sure, and you may have more fine clothes and fine carriages than Jane. But will they make you happy?'

'Have you any other objection,' said Elizabeth, 'than your belief of my indifference?'

'None at all. We all know him to be a proud, unpleasant sort of man; but this would be nothing if you really liked him.'

'I do, I do like him,' she replied, with tears in her eyes, 'I love him. Indeed he has no improper pride. He is perfectly amiable. You do not know what he really is; then pray do not pain me by speaking of him in such terms.'

'Lizzy,' said her father, 'I have given him my consent. He is the kind of man, indeed, to whom I should never dare refuse any thing, which he condescended to ask. I now give it to *you*, if you are resolved on having him. But let me advise you to think better of it. I know your disposition, Lizzy. I know that you could be neither happy nor respectable, unless you truly esteemed your husband; unless you looked up to him as a superior. Your lively talents would place you in the greatest danger in an unequal marriage. You could scarcely escape discredit and misery. My child, let me not have the grief of seeing *you* unable to respect your partner in life. You know not what you are about.'

Elizabeth, still more affected, was earnest and solemn in her reply; and at length, by repeated assurances that Mr Darcy was really the object of her choice, by explaining the gradual change which her estimation of him had undergone, relating her absolute certainty that his affection was not the work of a day, but had stood the test of many months suspense, and enumerating with energy all his good qualities, she did conquer her father's incredulity, and reconcile him to the match.

'Well, my dear,' said he, when she ceased speaking, 'I have no more to say. If this be the case, he deserves you. I could not have parted with you, my Lizzy, to any one less worthy.'

To complete the favourable impression, she then told him what Mr Darcy had voluntarily done for Lydia. He heard her with astonishment.

'This is an evening of wonders, indeed! And so, Darcy did every thing; made up the match, gave the money, paid the fellow's debts, and got him his commission! So much the better. It will save me a world of trouble and economy. Had it been your uncle's doing, I must and *would* have paid him; but these violent young lovers carry every thing their own way. I shall offer to pay him to-morrow; he will rant and storm about his love for you, and there will be an end of the matter.'

He then recollected her embarrassment a few days before, on his reading Mr Collins's letter; and after laughing at her some time, allowed her at last to go – saying, as she quitted the room, 'If any young men come for Mary or Kitty, send them in, for I am quite at leisure.'

Elizabeth's mind was now relieved from a very heavy weight; and, after half an hour's quiet reflection in her own room, she was able to join the others with tolerable composure. Every thing was too recent for gaiety, but the evening passed tranquilly away; there was no longer any thing material to be dreaded, and the comfort of ease and familiarity would come in time.

When her mother went up to her dressing-room at night, she followed her, and made the important communication. Its effect was most extraordinary; for on first hearing it, Mrs Bennet sat quite still, and unable to utter a syllable. Nor was it under many, many minutes, that she could comprehend what she heard; though not in general backward to credit what was for the advantage of her family, or that came in the shape of a lover to any of them. She began at length to recover, to fidget about in her chair, get up, sit down again, wonder, and bless herself.

'Good gracious! Lord bless me! only think! dear me! Mr Darcy! Who would have thought it! And is it really true? Oh! my sweetest Lizzy! how rich and how great you will be! What pin-money, what jewels, what carriages you will have! Jane's is nothing to it – nothing at all. I am so pleased

– so happy. Such a charming man! – so handsome! so tall! – Oh, my dear Lizzy! pray apologise for my having disliked him so much before. I hope he will overlook it. Dear, dear Lizzy. A house in town! Every thing that is charming! Three daughters married! Ten thousand a year! Oh, Lord! What will become of me. I shall go distracted.'

This was enough to prove that her approbation need not be doubted: and Elizabeth, rejoicing that such an effusion was heard only by herself, soon went away. But before she had been three minutes in her own room, her mother followed her.

'My dearest child,' she cried, 'I can think of nothing else! Ten thousand a year, and very likely more! 'Tis as good as a Lord! And a special licence. You must and shall be married by a special licence. But my dearest love, tell me what dish Mr Darcy is particularly fond of, that I may have it to-morrow.'

This was a sad omen of what her mother's behaviour to the gentleman himself might be; and Elizabeth found, that though in the certain possession of his warmest affection, and secure of her relations' consent, there was still something to be wished for. But the morrow passed off much better than she expected; for Mrs Bennet luckily stood in such awe of her intended son-in-law, that she ventured not to speak to him, unless it was in her power to offer him any attention, or mark her deference for his opinion.

Elizabeth had the satisfaction of seeing her father taking pains to get acquainted with him; and Mr Bennet soon assured her that he was rising every hour in his esteem.

'I admire all my three sons-in-law highly,' said he. 'Wickham, perhaps, is my favourite; but I think I shall like *your* husband quite as well as Jane's.'

The obsequious civility

CHAPTER SIXTY

ELIZABETH'S SPIRITS SOON RISING to playfulness again, she wanted Mr Darcy to account for his having ever fallen in love with her. 'How could you begin?' said she. 'I can comprehend your going on charmingly, when you had once made a beginning; but what could set you off in the first place?'

'I cannot fix on the hour, or the spot, or the look, or the words, which laid the foundation. It is too long ago. I was in the middle before I knew that I *had* begun.'

'My beauty you had early withstood, and as for my manners – my behaviour to *you* was at least always bordering on the uncivil, and I never spoke to you without rather wishing to give you pain than not. Now be sincere; did you admire me for my impertinence?'

'For the liveliness of your mind, I did.'

'You may as well call it impertinence at once. It was very little less. The fact is, that you were sick of civility, of deference, of officious attention. You were disgusted with the women who were always speaking and looking, and thinking for *your* approbation alone. I roused, and interested you, because I was so unlike *them*. Had you not been really amiable you would have hated me for it; but in spite of the pains you took to disguise yourself, your feelings were always noble and just; and in your heart, you thoroughly despised the persons who so assiduously courted you. There – I have saved you the trouble of accounting for it; and really, all things considered, I begin to think it perfectly reasonable. To be sure, you knew no actual good of me – but nobody thinks of *that* when they fall in love.'

'Was there no good in your affectionate behaviour to Jane, while she was ill at Netherfield?'

'Dearest Jane! who could have done less for her? But make a virtue of it by all means. My good qualities are under your protection, and you are to exaggerate them as much as possible; and, in return, it belongs to me to find occasions for teazing and quarrelling with you as often as may be; and I shall begin directly by asking you what made you so unwilling to come to the point at last. What made you so shy of me, when you first called, and afterwards dined here? Why, especially, when you called, did you look as if you did not care about me?'

'Because you were grave and silent, and gave me no encouragement.'

'But I was embarrassed.'

'And so was I.'

'You might have talked to me more when you came to dinner.'

'A man who had felt less, might.'

'How unlucky that you should have a reasonable answer to give, and that I should be so reasonable as to admit it! But I wonder how long you *would* have gone on, if you had been left to yourself. I wonder when you *would* have spoken, if I had not asked you! My resolution of thanking you for your kindness to Lydia had certainly great effect. *Too much*, I am afraid; for what becomes of the moral, if our comfort springs from a breach of promise, for I ought not to have mentioned the subject? This will never do.'

'You need not distress yourself. The moral will be perfectly fair. Lady Catherine's unjustifiable endeavours to separate us, were the means of removing all my doubts. I am not indebted for my present happiness to your eager desire of expressing your gratitude. I was not in a humour to wait for any opening of your's. My aunt's intelligence had given me hope, and I was determined at once to know every thing.'

'Lady Catherine has been of infinite use, which ought to make her happy, for she loves to be of use. But tell me, what did you come down to Netherfield for? Was it merely to ride to Longbourn and be embarrassed? or had you intended any more serious consequence?'

'My real purpose was to see *you*, and to judge, if I could, whether I might ever hope to make you love me. My avowed one, or what I avowed to myself, was to see whether your sister were still partial to Bingley, and if she were, to make the confession to him which I have since made.'

'Shall you ever have courage to announce to Lady Catherine, what is to befall her?'

'I am more likely to want time than courage, Elizabeth. But it ought to be done, and if you will give me a sheet of paper, it shall be done directly.'

'And if I had not a letter to write myself, I might sit by you, and admire the evenness of your writing, as another young lady once did. But I have an aunt, too, who must not be longer neglected.'

From an unwillingness to confess how much her intimacy with Mr Darcy had been over-rated, Elizabeth had never yet answered Mrs Gardiner's long letter, but now, having *that* to communicate which she knew would be most welcome, she was almost ashamed to find, that her uncle and aunt had already lost three days of happiness, and immediately wrote as follows:

I would have thanked you before, my dear aunt, as I ought to have done, for your long, kind, satisfactory, detail of particulars; but to say the truth, I was too cross to write. You supposed more than really existed. But now *suppose as much as you chuse; give a loose to your fancy, indulge your imagination in every possible flight which the subject will afford, and unless you believe me actually married, you cannot greatly err. You must write again very soon, and praise him a great deal more than you did in your last. I thank you, again and again, for not going to the Lakes. How could I be so silly as to wish it! Your idea of the ponies is delightful. We will go round the Park every day. I am the happiest creature in the world. Perhaps other people have said so before, but not one with such justice. I am happier even than Jane; she only smiles, I laugh. Mr Darcy sends you all the love in the world, that he can spare from me. You are all to come to Pemberley at Christmas. Your's &c.*

Mr Darcy's letter to Lady Catherine, was in a different style; and still different from either, was what Mr Bennet sent to Mr Collins, in reply to his last.

DEAR SIR,

I must trouble you once more for congratulations. Elizabeth will soon be the wife of Mr Darcy. Console Lady Catherine as well as you can. But, if I were you, I would stand by the nephew. He has more to give.

Your's sincerely, &c.

Miss Bingley's congratulations to her brother, on his approaching marriage, were all that was affectionate and insincere. She wrote even to Jane on the occasion, to express her delight, and repeat all her former professions of regard. Jane was not deceived, but she was affected; and though feeling no reliance on her, could not help writing her a much kinder answer than she knew was deserved.

The joy which Miss Darcy expressed on receiving similar information, was as sincere as her brother's in sending it. Four sides of paper were insufficient to contain all her delight, and all her earnest desire of being loved by her sister.

Before any answer could arrive from Mr Collins, or any congratulations to Elizabeth, from his wife, the Longbourn family heard that the Collinses were come themselves to Lucas lodge. The reason of this sudden removal was soon evident. Lady Catherine had been rendered so exceedingly angry by the contents of her nephew's letter, that Charlotte, really rejoicing in the match, was anxious to get away till the storm was blown over. At such a moment, the arrival of her friend was a sincere pleasure to Elizabeth, though in the course of their meeting she must sometimes think the pleasure dearly bought, when she saw Mr Darcy exposed to all the parading and obsequious civility of her husband. He bore it however with admirable calmness. He could even listen to Sir William Lucas, when he complimented him on carrying away the brightest jewel of the country, and expressed his hopes of their all meeting frequently at St James's, with very decent composure. If he did shrug his shoulders, it was not till Sir William was out of sight.

Mrs Philips's vulgarity was another, and perhaps a greater tax on his forbearance; and though Mrs Philips, as well as her sister, stood in too much awe of him to speak with the familiarity which Bingley's good humour encouraged, yet, whenever she *did* speak, she must be vulgar. Nor was her respect for him, though it made her more quiet, at all likely to make her more elegant. Elizabeth did all she could, to shield him from the frequent notice of either, and was ever anxious to keep him to herself, and to those of her family with whom he might converse without mortification; and though the uncomfortable feelings arising from all this took from the season of courtship much of its pleasure, it added to the hope of the future; and she looked forward with delight to the time when they should be removed from society so little pleasing to either, to all the comfort and elegance of their family party at Pemberley.

CHAPTER SIXTY ONE

HAPPY FOR ALL HER MATERNAL FEELINGS was the day on which Mrs Bennet got rid of her two most deserving daughters. With what delighted pride she afterwards visited Mrs Bingley and talked of Mrs Darcy may be guessed. I wish I could say, for the sake of her family, that the accomplishment of her earnest desire in the establishment of so many of her children, produced so happy an effect as to make her a sensible, amiable, well-informed woman for the rest of her life; though perhaps it was lucky for her husband, who might not have relished domestic felicity in so unusual a form, that she still was occasionally nervous and invariably silly.

Mr Bennet missed his second daughter exceedingly; his affection for her drew him oftener from home than any thing else could do. He delighted in going to Pemberley, especially when he was least expected.

Mr Bingley and Jane remained at Netherfield only a twelve-month. So near a vicinity to her mother and Meryton relations was not desirable even to *his* easy temper, or *her* affectionate heart. The darling wish of his sisters was then gratified; he bought an estate in a neighbouring county to Derbyshire, and Jane and Elizabeth, in addition to every other source of happiness, were within thirty miles of each other.

Kitty, to her very material advantage, spent the chief of her time with her two elder sisters. In society so superior to what she had generally known, her improvement was great. She was not of so ungovernable a temper as Lydia, and, removed from the influence of Lydia's example, she became, by proper attention and management, less irritable, less ignorant, and less insipid. From the farther disadvantage of Lydia's society she was of course carefully kept, and though Mrs Wickham frequently invited her to come and stay with her, with the promise of balls and young men, her father would never consent to her going.

Mary was the only daughter who remained at home; and she was necessarily drawn from the pursuit of accomplishments by Mrs Bennet's being quite unable to sit alone. Mary was obliged to mix more with the world, but she could still moralize over every morning visit; and as she was no longer mortified by comparisons between her sisters' beauty and her own, it was suspected by her father that she submitted to the change without much reluctance.

As for Wickham and Lydia, their characters suffered no revolution from the marriage of her sisters. He bore with philosophy the conviction that Elizabeth must now become acquainted with whatever of his ingratitude and falsehood had before been unknown to her; and in spite of every thing, was not wholly without hope that Darcy might yet be prevailed on to make his fortune. The congratulatory letter which Elizabeth received from Lydia on her marriage, explained to her that, by his wife at least, if not by himself, such a hope was cherished. The letter was to this effect:

My Dear Lizzy,

I wish you joy. If you love Mr Darcy half as well as I do my dear Wickham, you must be very happy. It is a great comfort to have you so rich, and when you have nothing else to do, I hope you will think of us. I am sure Wickham would like a place at court very much, and I do not think we shall have quite money enough to live upon without some help. Any place would do, of about three or four hundred a year; but, however, do not speak to Mr Darcy about it, if you had rather not.

Your's, &c.

As it happened that Elizabeth had *much* rather not, she endeavoured in her answer to put an end to every intreaty and expectation of the kind. Such relief, however, as it was in her power to afford, by the practice of what might be called economy in her own private expences, she frequently sent them. It had always been evident to her that such an income as theirs, under the direction of two persons so extravagant in their wants, and heedless of the future, must be very insufficient to their support; and whenever they changed their quarters, either Jane or herself were sure of being applied to, for some little assistance towards discharging their bills. Their manner of living, even when the restoration of peace dismissed them to a home, was unsettled in the extreme. They were always moving from place to place in quest of a cheap situation, and always spending more than they ought. His affection for her soon sunk into indifference; her's lasted a little longer; and in spite of her youth and her manners, she retained all the claims to reputation which her marriage had given her.

Though Darcy could never receive *him* at Pemberley, yet, for Elizabeth's sake, he assisted him farther in his profession. Lydia was occasionally a visitor there, when her husband was gone to enjoy himself in London or Bath; and with the Bingleys they both of them frequently staid so long, that even Bingley's good humour was overcome, and he proceeded so far as to *talk* of giving them a hint to be gone.

Miss Bingley was very deeply mortified by Darcy's marriage; but as she thought it advisable to retain the right of visiting at Pemberley, she dropt all her resentment; was fonder than ever of Georgiana, almost as attentive to Darcy as heretofore, and paid off every arrear of civility to Elizabeth.

Pemberley was now Georgiana's home; and the attachment of the sisters was exactly what Darcy had hoped to see. They were able to love each other, even as well as they intended. Georgiana had the highest opinion in the world of Elizabeth; though at first she often listened with an astonishment bordering on alarm, at her lively, sportive, manner of talking to her brother. He, who had always inspired in herself a respect which almost overcame her affection, she now saw the object of open pleasantry. Her mind received knowledge which had never before fallen in her way. By Elizabeth's instructions she began to comprehend that a woman may take liberties with her husband, which a brother will not always allow in a sister more than ten years younger than himself.

Lady Catherine was extremely indignant on the marriage of her nephew; and as she gave way to all the genuine frankness of her character, in her reply to the letter which announced its arrangement, she sent him language so very abusive, especially of Elizabeth, that for some time all intercourse was at an end. But at length, by Elizabeth's persuasion, he was prevailed on to overlook the offence, and seek a reconciliation; and, after a little farther resistance on the part of his aunt, her resentment gave way, either to her affection for him, or her curiosity to see how his wife conducted herself; and she condescended to wait on them at Pemberley, in spite of that pollution which its woods had received, not merely from the presence of such a mistress, but the visits of her uncle and aunt from the city.

With the Gardiners, they were always on the most intimate terms. Darcy, as well as Elizabeth, really loved them; and they were both ever sensible of the warmest gratitude towards the persons who, by bringing her into Derbyshire, had been the means of uniting them.

Mansfield Park

CHAPTER ONE

ABOUT THIRTY YEARS AGO, Miss Maria Ward, of Huntingdon, with only seven thousand pounds, had the good luck to captivate Sir Thomas Bertram, of Mansfield Park, in the county of Northampton, and to be thereby raised to the rank of a baronet's lady, with all the comforts and consequences of an handsome house and large income. All Huntingdon exclaimed on the greatness of the match, and her uncle, the lawyer, himself allowed her to be at least three thousand pounds short of any equitable claim to it. She had two sisters to be benefited by her elevation; and such of their acquaintances as thought Miss Ward and Miss Frances quite as handsome as Miss Maria, did not scruple to predict their marrying with almost equal advantage. But there certainly are not so many men of large fortune in the world as there are pretty women to deserve them. Miss Ward, at the end of half-a-dozen years, found herself obliged to be attached to the Rev. Mr Norris, a friend of her brother-in-law, with scarcely any private fortune, and Miss Frances fared yet worse. Miss Ward's match, indeed, when it came to the point, was not contemptible; Sir Thomas being happily able to give his friend an income in the living of Mansfield; and Mr and Mrs Norris began their career of conjugal felicity with very little less than a thousand a year. But Miss Frances married, in the common phrase, to disoblige her family, and by fixing on a lieutenant of marines, without education, fortune, or connections, did it very thoroughly. She could hardly have made a more untoward choice. Sir Thomas Bertram had interest which, from principle as well as pride – from a general wish of doing right, and a desire of seeing all that were connected with him in situations of respectability, he would have been glad to exert for the advantage of Lady Bertram's sister; but her husband's profession was such as no interest could reach; and before he had time to devise any other method of assisting them, an absolute breach between the sisters had taken place. It was the natural result of the conduct of each party, and such as a very imprudent marriage almost always produces. To save herself from useless remonstrance, Mrs Price never wrote to her family on the subject till actually married. Lady Bertram, who was a woman of very tranquil feelings, and a temper remarkably easy and indolent, would have contented herself with merely giving up her sister, and thinking no more of the matter; but Mrs Norris had a spirit of activity, which could not be satisfied till she had written a long and angry letter to Fanny, to point out the folly of her conduct, and threaten her with all its possible ill consequences. Mrs Price, in her turn, was injured and angry; and an answer, which comprehended each sister in its bitterness, and bestowed such very disrespectful reflections on the pride of Sir Thomas, as Mrs Norris could not possibly keep to herself, put an end to all intercourse between them for a considerable period.

Their homes were so distant, and the circles in which they moved so distinct, as almost to preclude the means of ever hearing of each other's existence during the eleven following years, or, at least, to make it very wonderful to Sir Thomas, that Mrs Norris should ever have it in her power to tell them, as she now and then did, in an angry voice, that Fanny had got another child. By the end of eleven years, however, Mrs Price could no longer afford to cherish pride or resentment, or to lose one connection that might possibly assist her. A large and still increasing family, an husband disabled for active service, but not the less equal to company and good liquor, and a very small income to supply their wants, made her eager to regain the friends she had so carelessly sacrificed; and she addressed Lady Bertram in a letter which spoke so much contrition and despondence, such a superfluity of children, and such a want of almost every thing else, as could not but dispose them all to a reconciliation. She was preparing for her ninth lying-in; and after bewailing the circumstance, and imploring their countenance as sponsors to the expected child, she could not conceal how important she felt they might be to the future maintenance of the eight already in being. Her eldest was a boy of ten years old, a fine spirited fellow, who longed to be out in the world; but what could she do? Was there any chance of his being hereafter useful to Sir Thomas in the concerns of his West Indian property? No situation would be beneath him; or what did Sir Thomas think of Woolwich? or how could a boy be sent out to the East?

The letter was not unproductive. It re-established peace and kindness, Sir Thomas sent friendly advice and professions, Lady Bertram dispatched money and baby-linen, and Mrs Norris wrote the letters.

Such were its immediate effects, and within a twelvemonth a more important advantage to Mrs Price resulted from it. Mrs Norris was often observing to the others that she could not get her poor sister and her family out of her head, and that, much as they had all done for her, she seemed to be wanting to do more; and at length she could not but own it to be her wish that poor Mrs Price should be relieved from the charge and expense of one child entirely out of her great number.

'What if they were among them to undertake the care of her eldest daughter, a girl now nine years old, of an age to require more attention than her poor mother could possibly give? The trouble and expense of it to them would be nothing, compared with the benevolence of the action.' Lady Bertram agreed with her instantly. 'I think we cannot do better,' said she; 'let us send for the child.'

Sir Thomas could not give so instantaneous and unqualified a consent. He debated and hesitated: it was a serious charge; a girl so brought up must be adequately provided for, or there would be cruelty instead of kindness in taking her from her family. He thought of his own four children, of his two sons, of cousins in love, etc.; but no sooner had he deliberately begun to state his objections, then Mrs Norris interrupted him with a reply to them all, whether stated or not.

'My dear Sir Thomas, I perfectly comprehend you, and do justice to the generosity and delicacy of your notions, which, indeed, are quite of a piece with your general conduct; and I entirely agree with you in the main as to the propriety of doing every thing one could by way of providing for a child one had in a manner taken into one's own hands; and I am sure I should be the last person in the world to withhold my mite upon such an occasion. Having no children of my own, who should I look to in any little matter I may ever have to bestow, but the children of my sisters? And I am sure Mr Norris is too just – but you know I am a woman of few words and professions. Do not let us be frightened from a good deed by a trifle. Give a girl an education, and introduce her properly into the world, and ten to one but she has the means of settling well, without further expense to any body. A niece of ours, Sir Thomas, I may say, or, at least, of *yours*, would not grow up in this neighbourhood without many advantages. I don't say she would be so handsome as her cousins. I dare say she would not; but she would be introduced into the society of this country under such very favourable circumstances as, in all human probability, would get her a creditable establishment. You are thinking of your sons; but do not you know that of all things upon earth *that* is the least likely to happen, brought up as they would be, always together like brothers and sisters? It is morally impossible. I never knew an instance of it. It is, in fact, the only sure way of providing against the connection. Suppose her a pretty girl, and seen by Tom or Edmund for the first time seven years hence, and I dare say there would be mischief. The very idea of her having been suffered to grow up at a distance from us all in poverty and neglect, would be enough to make either of the dear, sweet-tempered boys in love with her. But breed her up with them from this time, and suppose her even to have the beauty of an angel, and she will never be more to either than a sister.'

'There is a great deal of truth in what you say,' replied Sir Thomas, 'and far be it from me to throw any fanciful impediment in the way of a plan which would be so consistent with the relative situations of each. I only meant to observe, that it ought not to be lightly engaged in, and that to make it really serviceable to Mrs Price, and creditable to ourselves, we must secure to the child, or consider ourselves engaged to secure to her hereafter, as circumstances may arise, the provision of a gentle-woman, if no such establishment should offer as you are so sanguine in expecting.'

'I thoroughly understand you,' cried Mrs Norris; 'You are everything that is generous and considerate, and I am sure we shall never disagree on this point. Whatever I can do, as you well know, I am always ready enough to do for the good of those I love; and, though I could never feel for this little girl the hundredth part of the regard I bear your own dear children, nor consider her, in any respect, so much my own, I should hate myself if I were capable of neglecting her. Is not she a sister's child? And could I bear to see her want while I had a bit of bread to give her? My dear Sir Thomas, with all my faults I have a warm heart; and, poor as I am, would rather deny myself the necessaries of life than do an ungenerous thing. So, if you are not against it, I will write to my poor sister to-morrow, and make the proposal; and, as soon as matters are settled, *I* will engage to get the child to Mansfield; *you* shall have no trouble about it. My own trouble, you know, I never regard. I will send Nanny to London on purpose, and she may have a bed at her cousin the saddler's, and the child be appointed to meet her there. They may easily get her from Portsmouth to town by the coach, under the care of any creditable person that may chance to be going. I dare say there is always some reputable tradesman's wife or other going up.'

Except to the attack on Nanny's cousin, Sir Thomas no longer made any objection, and a more respectable, though less economical rendezvous being accordingly substituted, every thing was considered as settled, and the pleasures of so benevolent a scheme were already enjoyed. The division of gratifying sensations ought not, in strict justice, to have been equal; for Sir Thomas was fully resolved to be the real and consistent patron of the selected child, and Mrs Norris had not the least intention of being at any expense whatever in her maintenance. As far as walking, talking, and contriving reached, she was thoroughly benevolent, and nobody knew better how to dictate liberality to others; but her love of money was equal to her love of directing, and she knew quite as well how to save her own as to spend that of her friends. Having married on a narrower income than she had been used to look forward to, she had, from the first, fancied a very strict line of economy necessary; and what was begun as a matter of prudence, soon grew into a matter of choice, as an object of that needful solicitude which there were no children to supply. Had there been a family to provide for, Mrs Norris might never have saved her money; but having no care of that kind, there was nothing to impede her frugality, or lessen the comfort of making a yearly addition to an income which they had never lived up to. Under this infatuating principle, counteracted by no real affection for her sister, it was impossible for her to aim at more than the credit of projecting and arranging so expensive a charity; though perhaps she might so little know herself, as to walk home to the Parsonage, after this conversation, in the happy belief of being the most liberal-minded sister and aunt in the world.

When the subject was brought forward again, her views were more fully explained; and, in reply to Lady Bertram's calm inquiry of 'Where shall the child come to first, sister, to you or to us?' Sir Thomas heard with some surprise that it would be totally out of Mrs Norris's power to take any share in the personal charge of her. He had been considering her as a particularly welcome addition at the Parsonage, as a desirable companion to an aunt who had no children of her own; but he found himself wholly mistaken. Mrs Norris was sorry to say, that the little girl's staying with them, at least as things were then, was quite out of the question. Poor Mr Norris's indifferent state of health made it an impossibility; he could no more bear the noise of a child than he could fly; if, indeed, he should ever get well of his gouty complaints, it would be a different matter; she should then be glad to take her turn, and think nothing of the inconvenience; but just now poor Mr Norris took up every moment of her time, and the very mention of such a thing she was sure would distract him.

'Then she had better come to us,' said Lady Bertram, with the utmost composure. After a short pause, Sir Thomas added with dignity: 'Yes; let her home be in this house. We will endeavour to do our duty by her, and she will, at least, have the advantage of companions of her own age, and of a regular instructress.'

'Very true,' cried Mrs Norris, 'which are both very important considerations; and it will be just the same to Miss Lee, whether she has three girls to teach or only two – there can be no difference. I only wish I could be more useful; but you see I do all in my power. I am not one of those that spare their own trouble; and Nanny shall fetch her, however it may put me to inconvenience to have my chief counsellor away for three days. I suppose, sister, you will put the child in the little white attic, near the old nurseries. It will be much the best place for her, so near Miss Lee, and not far from the girls, and close by the housemaids, who could either of them help to dress her, you know, and take care of her clothes, for I suppose you would not think it fair to expect Ellis to wait on her as well as the others. Indeed, I do not see that you could possibly place her any where else.'

Lady Bertram made no opposition.

'I hope she will prove a well-disposed girl,' continued Mrs Norris, 'and be sensible of her uncommon good fortune in having such friends.'

'Should her disposition be really bad,' said Sir Thomas, 'we must not, for our own children's sake, continue her in the family; but there is no reason to expect so great an evil. We shall probably see much to wish altered in her, and must prepare ourselves for gross ignorance, some meanness of opinions, and very distressing vulgarity of manner; but these are not incurable faults; nor, I trust, can they be dangerous for her associates. Had my daughters been *younger* than herself, I should have considered the introduction of such a companion as a matter of very serious moment; but, as it is, I hope there can be nothing to fear for *them*, and every thing to hope for *her*, from the association.'

'That is exactly what I think,' cried Mrs Norris, 'and what I was saying to my husband this morning. It will be an education for the child, said I, only being with her cousins; if Miss Lee taught her nothing, she would learn to be good and clever from *them*.'

'I hope she will not tease my poor pug,' said Lady Bertram: 'I have but just got Julia to leave it alone.'

'There will be some difficulty in our way, Mrs Norris,' observed Sir Thomas, 'as to the distinction proper to be made between the girls as they grow up: how to preserve in the minds of my *daughters* the consciousness of what they are, without making them think too lowly of their cousin; and how, without depressing her spirits too far, to make her remember that she is not a *Miss Bertram*. I should wish to see them very good friends, and would, on no account, authorise in my girls the smallest degree of arrogance towards their relation; but still they cannot be equals. Their rank, fortune, rights, and expectations will always be different. It is a point of great delicacy, and you must assist us in our endeavours to choose exactly the right line of conduct.'

Mrs Norris was quite at his service; and though she perfectly agreed with him as to its being a most difficult thing, encouraged him to hope that between them it would be easily managed.

It will be readily believed that Mrs Norris did not write to her sister in vain. Mrs Price seemed rather surprised that a girl should be fixed on, when she had so many fine boys, but accepted the offer most thankfully, assuring them of her daughter's being a very well-disposed, good-humoured girl, and trusting they would never have cause to throw her off. She spoke of her further as somewhat delicate and puny, but was sanguine in the hope of her being materially better for change of air. Poor woman! She probably thought change of air might agree with many of her children.

CHAPTER TWO

THE LITTLE GIRL PERFORMED her long journey in safety; and at Northampton was met by Mrs Norris, who thus regaled in the credit of being foremost to welcome her, and in the importance of leading her into the others, and recommending her to their kindness.

Fanny Price was at this time just ten years old, and though there might not be much in her first appearance to captivate, there was at least nothing to disgust her relations. She was small for her age, with no glow of complexion, nor any other striking beauty; exceedingly timid and shy, and shrinking from notice; but her air, though awkward, was not vulgar, her voice was sweet, and when she spoke her countenance was pretty. Sir Thomas and Lady Bertram received her very kindly; and Sir Thomas, seeing how much she needed encouragement, tried to be all that was conciliating; but he had to work against a most untoward gravity of deportment; and Lady Bertram, without taking half so much trouble, or speaking one word where he spoke ten, by the mere aid of a good-humoured smile, became immediately the less awful character of the two.

The young people were all at home, and sustained their share in the introduction very well, with much good humour, and no embarrassment, at least on the part of the sons, who, at seventeen and sixteen, and tall for their age, had all the grandeur of men in the eyes of their little cousin. The two girls were more at a loss from being younger and in greater awe of their father, who addressed them on the occasion with rather an injudicious particularity. But they were too much used to company and praise to have anything like natural shyness; and their confidence increasing from their cousin's total want of it, they were soon able to take a full survey of her face and her frock in easy indifference.

They were a remarkably fine family, the sons very well-looking, the daughters decidedly handsome, and all of them well grown and forward for their age, which produced as striking a difference between the cousins in person, as education had given to their address; and no one would have supposed the girls so nearly of an age as they really were. There was in fact but two years between the youngest and Fanny. Julia Bertram was only twelve, and Maria but a year older. The little visitor meanwhile was as unhappy as possible. Afraid of every body, ashamed of herself, and longing for the home she had left, she knew not how to look up, and could scarcely speak to be heard, or without crying. Mrs Norris had been talking to her the whole way from Northampton of her wonderful good fortune, and the extraordinary degree of gratitude and good behaviour which it ought to produce, and her consciousness of misery was therefore increased by the idea of its being a wicked thing for her not to be happy. The fatigue, too, of so long a journey, became soon no trifling evil. In vain were the well-meant condescensions of Sir Thomas, and all the officious prognostications of Mrs Norris that she would be a good girl; in vain did Lady Bertram smile and make her sit on the sofa with herself and pug, and vain was even the sight of a gooseberry tart towards giving her comfort; she could scarcely swallow two mouthfuls before tears interrupted her, and sleep seeming to be her likeliest friend, she was taken to finish her sorrows in bed.

'This is not a very promising beginning,' said Mrs Norris, when Fanny had left the room. 'After all that I said to her as we came along, I though she would have behaved better; I told her how much might depend upon her acquitting herself well at first. I wish there may not be a sulkiness of temper – her poor mother had a good deal; but we must make allowances for such a child – and I do not know that her being sorry to leave her home is really against her, for, with all its faults, it *was* her home, and she cannot as yet understand how much she has changed for the better; but then there is moderation in all things.'

It required a longer time, however, than Mrs Norris was inclined to allow, to reconcile Fanny to the novelty of Mansfield Park, and the

In vain did Lady Bertram smile and make her sit on the sofa with herself and Pug

separation from every body she had been used to. Her feelings were very acute, and too little understood to be properly attended to. Nobody meant to be unkind, but nobody put themselves out of their way to secure her comfort.

The holiday allowed to the Miss Bertrams the next day, on purpose to afford leisure for getting acquainted with, and entertaining their young cousin, produced little union. They could not but hold her cheap on finding that she had but two sashes, and had never learned French; and when they perceived her to be little struck with the duet they were so good as to play, they could do no more than make her a generous present of some of their least valued toys, and leave her to herself, while they adjourned to whatever might be the favourite holiday sport of the moment, making artificial flowers or wasting gold paper.

Fanny, whether near or from her cousins, whether in the schoolroom, the drawing-room, or the shrubbery, was equally forlorn, finding something to fear in every person and place. She ws disheartened by Lady Bertram's silence, awed by Sir Thomas's grave looks, and quite overcome by Mrs Norris's admonitions. Her elder cousins mortified her by reflections on her size, and abashed her by noticing her shyness; Miss Lee wondered at her ignorance, and the maid servants sneered at her clothes; and when to these sorrows was added the idea of the brothers and sisters among whom she had always been important as playfellow, instructress, and nurse, the despondence that sunk her little heart was severe.

The grandeur of the house astonished, but could not console her. The rooms were too large for her to move in with ease; whatever she touched she expected to injure, and she crept about in constant terror of some thing or other; often retreating towards her own chamber to cry; and the little girl who was spoken of in the drawing-room when she left it at night, as seeming so desirably sensible of her peculiar good fortune, ended every day's sorrows by sobbing herself to sleep. A week had passed in this way, and no suspicion of it conveyed by her quiet passive manner, when she was found one morning by her cousin Edmund, the youngest of the sons, sitting crying on the attic stairs.

'My dear little cousin,' said he, with all the gentleness of an excellent nature, 'what can be the matter?' And sitting down by her, was at great pains to overcome her shame in being so surprised, and persuade her to speak openly. 'Was she ill? Or was anybody angry with her? Or had she quarrelled with Maria and Julia? Or was she puzzled about any thing in her lesson that he could explain? Did she, in short, want any thing he could possibly get her, or do for her?' For a long while no answer could be obtained beyond a 'No, no – not at all – no, thank you'; but he still persevered; and no sooner had he begun to revert to her own home, than her increased sobs explained to him where the grievance lay. He tried to console her.

'You are sorry to leave mamma, my dear little Fanny,' said he, 'which shows you to be a very good girl; but you must remember that you are with relations and friends, who all love you, and wish to make you happy. Let us walk out in the park, and you shall tell me all about your brothers and sisters.'

On pursuing the subject, he found that, dear as all these brothers and sisters generally were, there was one among them who ran more in her thoughts than the rest. It was William whom she talked of most, and wanted most to see. William, the eldest, a year older than herself, her constant companion and friend; her advocate with her mother (of whom he was the darling) in every distress. 'William did not like she should come away; he had told her he should miss her very much indeed.' 'But William will write to you, I dare say.' 'Yes, he had promised he would, but he had told *her* to write first.' 'And when shall you do it?' She hung her head and answered, hesitatingly, 'She did not know; she had not any paper.'

'If that will be all your difficulty, I will furnish you with paper and every other material, and you may write your letter whenever you choose. Would it make you happy to write to William?'

'Yes, very.'

'Then let it be done now. Come with me into the breakfast-room, we shall find every thing there, and be sure of having the room to ourselves.'

'But, cousin, will it go to the post?'

'Yes, depend upon me it shall; it shall go with the other letters; and, as your uncle will frank it, it will cost William nothing.'

'My uncle!' repeated Fanny, with a frightened look.

'Yes, when you have written the letter, I will take it to my father to frank.'

Fanny thought it a bold measure, but offered no further resistance; and they went together into the breakfast-room, where Edmund prepared her paper and ruled her lines with all the good-will that her brother could himself have felt, and probably with somewhat more exactness. He continued with her the whole time of her writing, to assist her with his penknife or his orthography, as either were wanted; and added to these attentions, which she felt very much, a kindness to her brother which delighted her beyond all the rest. He wrote with his own hand his love to his cousin William, and sent him half a guinea under the seal. Fanny's feelings on the occasion were such as she believed herself incapable of expressing; but her countenance and a few artless words fully conveyed all their gratitude and delight, and her cousin began to find her an interesting object. He talked to her more, and, from all that she said, was convinced of her having an affectionate heart, and a strong desire of doing right; and he could perceive her to be further entitled to attention, by great sensibility of her situation, and great timidity. He had never knowingly given her pain, but he now felt that she required more positive kindness and with that view endeavoured, in the first place, to lessen her fears of them all, and gave her especially a great deal of good advice as to playing with Maria and Julia, and being as merry as possible.

From this day Fanny grew more comfortable. She felt that she had a friend, and the kindness of her cousin Edmund gave her better spirits with every body else. The place became less strange, and the people less formidable; and if there were some amongst them whom she could not cease to fear, she began at least to know their ways, and to catch the best manner of conforming to them. The little rusticities and awkwardnesses which had at first made grievous inroads on the tranquillity of all, and not least of herself, necessarily wore away, and she was no longer materially afraid to appear before her uncle, not did her Aunt Norris's voice make her start very much. To her cousins she became occasionally an acceptable companion. Though unworthy, from inferiority of age and strength, to be their constant associate, their pleasures and schemes were sometimes of a nature to make a third very useful, especially when that third was of an obliging, yielding temper; and they could not but own, when their aunt inquired into her faults, or their brother Edmund urged her claims to their kindness, that 'Fanny was good natured enough.'

Edmund was uniformly kind himself; and she had nothing worse to endure on the part of Tom than that sort of merriment which a young man of seventeen will always think fair with a child of ten. He was just entering into life, full of spirits, and with all the liberal dispositions of an eldest son, who feels born only for expense and enjoyment. His kindness to his little cousin was consistent with his situation and rights: he made her some very pretty presents, and laughed at her.

As her appearance and spirits improved, Sir Thomas and Mrs Norris thought with greater satisfaction of their benevolent plan; and it was pretty soon decided between them that, though far from clever, she showed a tractable disposition, and seemed likely to give them little trouble. A mean opinion of her abilities was not confined to *them*. Fanny could read, work, or write, but she had been taught nothing more; and as her cousins found her ignorant of many things with which they had been long familiar, they thought her prodigiously stupid, and for the first two or three weeks were continually bringing some fresh report of it into the drawing-room. 'Dear mamma, only think, my cousin cannot put the map of Europe together – or my cousin cannot tell the principal rivers in Russia – or she never heard of Asia Minor – or she does not know the difference between water-colours and crayons! How strange! Did you ever hear anything so stupid?'

'My dear,' their considerate aunt would reply, 'it is very bad, but you must not expect everybody to be as forward and quick at learning as yourself.'

'But, aunt, she is really so very ignorant! Do you know, we asked her last night which way she would go to get to Ireland; and she said she should cross to the Isle of Wight. She thinks of nothing but the Isle of Wight, and she calls it *the Island*, as if there were no other island in the world. I am sure I should have been ashamed of myself, if I had not known better long before I was so old as she is. I cannot remember the time when I did not know a great deal that she has not the least notion of yet. How long ago it is, aunt, since we used to repeat the chronological order of the kings of England, with the dates of their accession, and most of the principal events of their reigns!'

'Yes,' added the other; 'and of the Roman emperors as low as Severus; besides a great deal of the heathen mythology, and all the metals, semi-metals, planets, and distinguished philosophers.'

'Very true, indeed, my dears, but you are blessed with wonderful memories, and your poor cousin has probably none at all. There is a vast deal of difference in memories, as well as in everything else, and therefore you must make allowance for your cousin, and pity her deficiency. And remember that, if you are ever so forward and clever yourselves, you should always be modest; for, much as you know already, there is a great deal more for you to learn.'

'Yes, I know there is, till I am seventeen. But I must tell you another thing of Fanny, so odd and so stupid. Do you know, she says she does not want to learn either music or drawing.'

'To be sure, my dear, that is very stupid indeed, and shows a great want of genius and emulation. But, all things considered, I do not know whether it is not as well that it should be so, for, though you know (owing to me) your papa and mamma are so good as to bring her up with you, it is not at all necessary that she should be as accomplished as you are; on the contrary, it is much more desirable that there should be a difference.'

Such were the counsels by which Mrs Norris assisted to form her nieces' minds; and it is not very wonderful that, with all their promising talents and early information, they should be entirely deficient in the less common acquirements of self-knowledge, generosity and humility. In every thing but disposition, they were admirably taught. Sir Thomas did not know what was wanting, because, though a truly anxious father, he was not outwardly affectionate, and the reserve of his manner repressed all the flow of their spirits before him.

To the education of her daughters Lady Bertram paid not the smallest attention. She had not time for such cares. She was a woman who spent her days in sitting, nicely dressed, on a sofa, doing some long piece of needlework, of little use and no beauty, thinking more of her pug than her children, but very indulgent to the latter, when it did not put herself to inconvenience, guided in everything important by Sir Thomas and in smaller concerns by her sister. Had she possessed greater leisure for the service of her girls, she would probably have supposed it unnecessary, for they were under the care of a governess, with proper masters, and could want nothing more. As for Fanny's being stupid at learning, 'she could only say it was very unlucky, but some people *were* stupid, and Fanny must take more pains: she did not know what else was to be done; and, except her being so dull, she must add she saw no harm in the poor little thing, and always found her very handy, and quick in carrying messages, and fetching what she wanted?

Fanny, with all her faults of ignorance and timidity, was fixed at Mansfield Park, and learning to transfer in its favour much of her attachment to her former home, grew up there not unhappily among her cousins. There was no positive ill-nature in Maria or Julia; and though Fanny was often mortified by their treatment of her, she thought too lowly of her own claims to feel injured by it.

From about the time of her entering the family, Lady Bertram, in consequence of a little ill-health, and a greater deal of indolence, gave up the house in town, which she had been used to occupy every spring, and remained wholly in the country, leaving Sir Thomas to attend to his duty in Parliament with whatever increase or diminution of comfort might arise from her absence. In the country, therefore, the Miss Bertrams continued to exercise their memories, practise their duets, and grow tall and womanly; and their father saw them becoming in person, manner and accomplishments every thing that could satisfy his anxiety. His eldest son was careless and extravagant, and had already given him much uneasiness; but his other children promised him nothing but good. His daughters, he felt, while they retained the name of Bertram, must be giving it new grace, and in quitting it, he trusted, would extend its respectable alliances; and the character of Edmund, his strong good sense and uprightness of mind, bid most fairly for utility, honour and happiness to himself and all his connections. He was to be a clergyman.

Amid the cares and the complacency which his own children suggested, Sir Thomas did not forget to do what he could for the children of Mrs Price: he assisted her liberally in the education and disposal of her sons as they became old enough for a determinate pursuit; and Fanny, though almost totally separated from her family, was sensible of the truest satisfaction in hearing of any kindness towards them, or of anything at all promising in their situation or conduct. Once, and once only in the course of many years, had she the happiness of being with William. Of the rest she saw nothing; nobody at home seemed to want her; but William determining, soon after her removal, to be a sailor, was invited to spend a week with his sister in Northamptonshire, before he went to sea. Their eager affection and meeting, their exquisite delight in being together, their hours of happy mirth, and moments of serious conference, may be imagined; as well as the sanguine views and spirits of the boy even to the last, and the misery of the girl when he left her. Luckily the visit happened in the Christmas holidays, when she could directly look for comfort to her cousin Edmund; and he told her such charming things of what William was to do and be hereafter, in consequence of his profession, as made her gradually admit that the separation might have some use. Edmund's friendship never failed her: his leaving Eton for Oxford made no change in his kind disposition, and only afforded more frequent opportunities of proving them. Without any display of doing more than the rest, or any fear of doing too much, he was always true to her interests, and considerate of her feelings, trying to make her good qualities understood, and to conquer the diffidence which prevented their being more apparent; giving her advice, consolation and encouragement.

Kept back as she was by every body else, his single support could not bring her forward; but his attentions were otherwise of the highest importance in assisting the improvement of her mind, and extending its pleasures. He knew her to be clever, to have a quick apprehension as well as good sense, and a fondness for reading, which, properly directed, must be an education in itself. Miss Lee taught her French, and heard her read the daily portion of history; but he recommended the books which charmed her leisure hours, he encouraged her taste, and corrected her judgment; he made reading useful by talking to her of what she read and heightened its attraction by judicious praise. In return for such services, she loved him better than any body in the world except William; her heart was divided between the two.

CHAPTER THREE

THE FIRST EVENT OF ANY importance in the family was the death of Mr Norris, which happened when Fanny was about fifteen, and necessarily introduced alterations and novelties. Mrs Norris, on quitting the Parsonage, removed first to the Park, and afterwards to a small house of Sir Thomas's in the village, and consoled herself for the loss of her husband by considering that she could do very well without him; and for her reduction of income by the evident necessity of stricter economy.

The living was hereafter for Edmund; and, had his uncle died a few years sooner, it would have been duly given to some friend to hold till he were old enough for orders. But Tom's extravagance had, previous to that event, been so great as to render a different disposal of the next presentation necessary, and the younger brother must help to pay for the pleasures of the elder. There was another family living actually held for Edmund; but though circumstance had made the arrangement somewhat easier to Sir Thomas's conscience, he could not but feel it to be an act of injustice and he earnestly tried to impress his eldest son with the same conviction in the hope of its producing a better effect than any thing he had yet been able to say or do.

'I blush for you, Tom,' said he, in his most dignified manner; 'I blush for the expedient which I am driven on, and I trust I may pity your feelings as a brother on the occasion. You have robbed Edmund for ten, twenty, thirty years, perhaps for life, of more than half the income which ought to be his. It may hereafter be in my power, or in yours (I hope it will) to procure him better preferment; but it must not be forgotten, that no benefit of that sort would have been beyond his natural claims on us, and that nothing can, in fact, be an equivalent for the certain advantage which he is now obliged to forego through the urgency of your debts.'

Tom listened with some shame and some sorrow; but escaping as quickly as possible, could soon with cheerful selfishness reflect, firstly, that he had not been half so much in debt as some of his friends; secondly, that his father had made a most tiresome piece of work of it; and thirdly, that the future incumbent, whoever he might be, would, in all probability, die very soon.

On Mr Norris's death, the presentation became the right of a Dr Grant, who came consequently to reside at Mansfield; and on proving to be a hearty man of forty-five, seemed likely to disappoint Mr Bertram's calculations. But 'no, he was a short-necked, apoplectic sort of fellow, and, plied well with good things, would soon pop off.'

He had a wife about fifteen years his junior, but no children; and they entered the neighbourhood with the usual fair report of being very respectable, agreeable people.

The time was now come when Sir Thomas expected his sister-in-law to claim her share in their niece, the change in Mrs Norris's situation, and the improvement in Fanny's age, seeming not merely to do away any former objection to their living together, but even to give it the most decided eligibility; and as his own circumstances were rendered less fair than heretofore, by some recent losses on his West India estate, in addition to his eldest son's extravagance, it became not undesirable to himself to be relieved from the expense of her support, and the obligation of her future provision. In the fullness of his belief that such a thing must be, he mentioned its probability to his wife; and the first time of the subject's occurring to her again happening to be when Fanny was present, she calmly observed to her: 'So, Fanny, you are going to leave us, and live with my sister. How shall you like it?'

Fanny was too much surprised to do more than repeat her aunt's words, 'Going to leave you?'

'Yes, my dear; why should you be astonished? You have been years with us, and my sister always meant to take you when Mr Norris died. But you must come up and tack on my patterns all the same.'

The news was as disagreeable to Fanny as it had been unexpected. She had never received kindness from her Aunt Norris, and could not love her.

'I shall be very sorry to go away,' said she, with a faltering voice.

'Yes, I dare say you will; *that's* natural enough. I suppose you have had as little to vex you since you came into this house as any creature in the world.'

'I hope I am not ungrateful, aunt,' said Fanny, modestly.

'No, my dear; I hope not. I have always found you a very good girl.'

'And I am never to live here again?'

'Never, my dear; but you are sure of a comfortable home. It can make very little difference to you, whether you are in one house or the other.'

Fanny left the room with a very sorrowful heart: she could not feel the difference to be so small, she could not think of living with her aunt with any thing like satisfaction. As soon as she met with Edmund, she told him her distress.

'Cousin,' said she, 'some thing is going to happen which I do not like at all; and though you have often persuaded me into being reconciled to things that I disliked at first, you will not be able to do it now. I am going to live entirely with my Aunt Norris.'

'Indeed!'

'Yes: my Aunt Bertram has just told me so. It is quite settled. I am to leave Mansfield Park, and go to the White House, I suppose, as soon as she is removed there.'

'Well, Fanny, and if the plan were not unpleasant to you, I should call it an excellent one.'

'Oh, cousin!'

'It has every thing else in its favour. My aunt is acting like a sensible woman in wishing for you. She is choosing a friend and companion exactly where she ought, and I am glad her love of money does not interfere. You will be what you ought to be to her. I hope it does not distress you very much, Fanny.'

'Indeed it does; I cannot like it. I love this house and every thing in it: I shall love nothing there. You know how uncomfortable I feel with her.'

'I can say nothing for her manner to you as a child; but it was the same with us all, or nearly so. She never knew how to be pleasant to children. But you are now of an age to be treated better; I think she *is* behaving better already; and when you are her only companion, you *must* be important to her.'

'I can never be important to anyone.'

'What is to prevent you?'

'Every thing. My situation, my foolishness, and awkwardness.'

'As to your foolishness and awkwardness, my dear Fanny, believe me, you never have a shadow of either, but in using the words so improperly. There is no reason in the world why you should not be important where you are known. You have good sense, and a sweet temper, and I am sure you have a grateful heart, that could never receive kindness without wishing to return it. I do not know any better qualification for a friend and companion.'

'You are too kind,' said Fanny, colouring at such praise; 'how shall I ever thank you as I ought, for thinking so well of me? Oh! cousin, if I am to go away, I shall remember your goodness to the last moment of my life.'

'Why, indeed, Fanny, I should hope to be remembered at such a distance as the White House. You speak as if you were going two hundred miles off instead of only across the park; but you will belong to us almost as much as ever. The two families will be meeting every day in the year. The only difference will be that living with your aunt, you will necessarily be brought forward as you ought to be. *Here*, there are too many whom you can hide behind; but with *her* you will be forced to speak for yourself.'

'Oh! do not say so.'

'I must say it, and say it with pleasure. Mrs Norris is much better fitted than my mother for having the charge of you now. She is of a temper to do a great deal for any body she really interests herself about, and she will force you to do justice to your natural powers.'

Fanny sighed, and said, 'I cannot see things as you do; but I ought to believe you to be right rather than myself, and I am very much obliged to you for trying to reconcile me to what must be. If I could suppose my aunt really to care for me, it would be delightful to feel myself of consequence to any body. *Here*, I know, I am of none, and yet I love the place so well.'

'The place, Fanny, is what you will not quit, though you quit the house. You will have as free a command of the park and gardens as ever. Even *your* constant little heart need not take fright at such a nominal change. You will have the same walks to frequent, the same library to choose from, the same people to look at, the same horse to ride.'

'Very true. Yes, dear old grey pony! Ah! cousin, when I remember how

'How much I used to dread riding'

much I used to dread riding, what terrors it gave me to hear it talked of as likely to do me good (oh! how I have trembled at my uncle's opening his lips if horses were talked of), and then think of the kind pains you took to reason and persuade me out of my fears, and convince me that I should like it after a little while, and feel how right you proved to be, I am inclined to hope you may always prophesy as well.'

'And I am quite convinced that your being with Mrs Norris will be as good for your mind as riding has been for your health, and as much for your ultimate happiness, too.'

So ended their discourse, which for any very appropriate service it could render Fanny, might as well have been spared, for Mrs Norris had not the smallest intention of taking her. It had never occurred to her, on the present occasion, but as a thing to be carefully avoided. To prevent its being expected, she had fixed on the smallest habitation which could rank as genteel among the buildings of Mansfield parish, the White House being only just large enough to receive herself and her servants, and allow a spare room for a friend, of which she made a very particular point. The spare rooms at the Parsonage had never been wanted, but the absolute necessity of a spare room for a friend was now never forgotten. Not all her precautions, however, could save her from being suspected of some thing better; or, perhaps, her very display of the importance of a spare room might have misled Sir Thomas to suppose it really intended for Fanny. Lady Bertram soon brought the matter to a certainty, by carelessly observing to Mrs Norris:

'I think, sister, we need not keep Miss Lee any longer, when Fanny goes to live with you.'

Mrs Norris almost started. 'Live with me, dear Lady Bertram! What do you mean?'

'Is she not to live with you? I thought you had settled it with Sir Thomas.'

'Me! never. I spoke a syllable about it to Sir Thomas, nor he to me. Fanny live with me! The last thing in the world for me to think of, or for any body to wish that really knows us both. Good heaven! What could I do with Fanny? Me? A poor, helpless, forlorn widow, unfit for any thing, my spirits quite broken down; what could I do with a girl at her time of life? A girl of fifteen! The very age of all others to need most attention and care, and put the cheerfullest spirits to the test! Sure Sir Thomas could not seriously expect such a thing! Sir Thomas is too much my friend. Nobody that wishes me well, I am sure, would propose it. How came Sir Thomas to speak to you about it?'

'Indeed, I do not know. I suppose he thought it best.'

'But what did he say? He could not say he *wished* me to take Fanny. I am sure in his heart he could not wish me to do it.'

'No; he only said he thought it very likely; and I thought so too. We both thought it would be a comfort to you. But if you do not like it, there is no more to be said. She is no incumbrance here.'

'Dear sister, if you consider my unhappy state, how can she be any comfort to me? Here am I, a poor desolate widow, deprived of the best of husbands, my health gone in attending and nursing him, my spirits still worse, all my peace in this world destroyed, with hardly enough to support me in the rank of a gentlewoman, and enable me to live so as not to disgrace the memory of the dear departed – what possible comfort could I have in taking such a charge upon me as Fanny? If I could wish it for my own sake, I would not do so unjust a thing by the poor girl. She is in good hands, and sure of doing well. I must struggle through my sorrows and difficulties as I can.'

'Then you will not mind living by yourself quite alone?'

'Dear Lady Bertram, what am I fit for but solitude? Now and then I shall hope to have a friend in my little cottage (I shall always have a bed for a friend); but the most part of my future days will be spent in utter seclusion. If I can but make both ends meet, that's all I ask for.'

'I hope, sister, things are not so very bad with you neither, considering Sir Thomas says you will have six hundred a year.'

'Lady Bertram, I do not complain. I know I cannot live as I have done, but I must retrench where I can, and learn to be a better manager. I *have been* a liberal housekeeper enough, but I shall not be ashamed to practise economy now. My situation is as much altered as my income. A great many things were due from poor Mr Norris, as clergyman of the parish, that cannot be expected from me. It is unknown how much was consumed in our kitchen by odd comers and goers. At the White House, matters must be better looked after. I *must* live within my income, or I shall be miserable; and I own it would give me great satisfaction to be able to do rather more, to lay by a little at the end of the year.'

'I dare say you will. You always do, don't you?'

'My object, Lady Bertram, is to be of use to those that come after me. It is for your children's good that I wish to be richer. I have nobody else to care for; but I should be very glad to think I could leave a little trifle among them worth their having.'

'You are very good, but do not trouble yourself about them. They are sure of being well provided for. Sir Thomas will take care of that.'

'Why, you know, Sir Thomas's means will be rather straitened if the Antigua estate is to make such poor returns.'

'Oh! *that* will soon be settled. Sir Thomas has been writing about it, I know.'

'Well, Lady Bertram,' said Mrs Norris, moving to go, 'I can only say that my sole desire is to be of use to your family; and so, if Sir Thomas should ever speak again about my taking Fanny, you will be able to say that my health and spirits put it quite out of the question; besides that, I really should not have a bed to give her, for I must keep a spare room for a friend.'

Lady Bertram repeated enough of this conversation to her husband to convince him how much he had mistaken his sister-in-law's views; and she was from that moment perfectly safe from all expectation, or the slightest allusion to it from him. He could not but wonder at her refusing to do any thing for a niece whom she had been so forward to adopt; but, as she took early care to make him, as well as Lady Bertram, understand, that whatever she possessed was designed for their family, he soon grew reconciled to a distinction which, at the same time that it was advantageous and complimentary to them, would enable him better to provide for Fanny himself.

Fanny soon learnt how unnecessary had been her fears of a removal: and her spontaneous, untaught felicity on the discovery, conveyed some consolation to Edmund for his disappointment in what he had expected to be so essentially serviceable to her. Mrs Norris took possession of the White House, the Grants arrived at the Parsonage, and these events over, everything at Mansfield went on for some time as usual.

The Grants, showing a disposition to be friendly and sociable, gave great satisfaction in the main among their new acquaintances. They had their faults, and Mrs Norris soon found them out. The Doctor was very fond of eating, and would have a good dinner every day; and Mrs Grant, instead of contriving to gratify him at little expense, gave her cook as high wages as they did at Mansfield Park, and was scarcely ever seen in her offices. Mrs Norris could not speak with any temper of such grievances, nor of the quantity of butter and eggs that were regularly consumed in the house. 'Nobody loved plenty and hospitality more than herself; nobody more hated pitiful doings; the Parsonage, she believed, had never been wanting in comforts of any sort, had never borne a bad character in *her time*, but this was a way of going on that she could not understand. A fine lady in a country parsonage was quite out of place. *Her* store-room, she thought, might have been good enough for Mrs Grant to go into. Enquire where she would, she could not find out that Mrs Grant had ever had more than five thousand pounds.'

Lady Bertram listened without much interest to this sort of invective. She could not enter into the wrongs of an economist, but she felt all the injuries of beauty in Mrs Grant's being so well settled in life without being handsome, and expressed her astonishment on that point almost as often, though not so diffusely, as Mrs Norris discussed the other.

These opinions had been hardly canvassed a year before another event arose of such importance in the family, as might fairly claim some place in the thoughts and conversation of the ladies. Sir Thomas found it expedient to go to Antigua himself, for the better arrangement of his affairs, and he took his eldest son with him, in the hope of detaching him from some bad connections at home. They left England with the probability of being nearly a twelvemonth absent.

The necessity of the measure in a pecuniary light, and the hope of its utility to his son, reconciled Sir Thomas to the effort of quitting the rest of his family, and of leaving his daughters to the direction of others at their present most interesting time of life. He could not think Lady Bertram quite equal to supply his place with them, or rather, to perform what should have been her own; but, in Mrs Norris's watchful attention, and in Edmund's judgment, he had sufficient confidence to make him go without fears for their conduct.

Lady Bertram did not at all like to have her husband leave her; but she was not disturbed by any alarm for his safety, or solicitude for his comfort, being one of those persons who think nothing can be dangerous or difficult, or fatiguing, to any body but themselves.

The Miss Bertrams were much to be pitied on the occasion; not for their sorrow, but for their want of it. Their father was no object of love to them; he had never seemed the friend of their pleasures, and his absence was unhappily most welcome. They were relieved by it from all restraint; and without aiming at one gratification that would probably have been forbidden by Sir Thomas, they felt themselves immediately at their own disposal, and to have every indulgence within their reach. Fanny's relief, and her consciousness of it, was quite equal to her cousins'; but a more tender nature suggested that her feelings were ungrateful, and she really grieved because she could not grieve. 'Sir Thomas, who had done so much for her and her brothers, and who was gone perhaps never to return! That she should see him go without a tear! It was a shameful insensibility.' He had said to her, moreover, on the very last morning, that he hoped she might see William again in the course of the ensuing winter, and had charged her to write and invite him to Mansfield, as soon as the squadron to which he belonged should be known to be in England. 'This was so thoughtful and kind!' and would he only have smiled upon her, and called her 'my dear Fanny' while he said it, every former frown or cold address might have been forgotten. But he had ended his speech in a way to sink her in sad mortification, by adding, 'If William does come to Mansfield, I hope you may be able to convince him that the many years which have passed since you parted have not been spent on your side entirely without improvement; though, I fear, he must find his sister at sixteen in some respects too much like his sister at ten.' She cried bitterly over this reflection when her uncle was gone; and her cousins, on seeing her with red eyes, set her down as a hypocrite.

CHAPTER FOUR

TOM BERTRAM HAD OF LATE SPENT so little of his time at home, that he could be only nominally missed; and Lady Bertram was soon astonished to find how very well they did even without his father, how well Edmund could supply his place in carving, talking to the steward, writing to the attorney, settling with the servants, and equally saving her from all possible fatigue or exertion in every particular, but that of directing her letters.

The earliest intelligence of the travellers' safe arrival at Antigua, after a favourable voyage, was received; though not before Mrs Norris had been indulging in very dreadful fears, and trying to make Edmund participate them whenever she could get him alone; and as she depended on being the first person made acquainted with any fatal catastrophe, she had already arranged the manner of breaking it to all the others, when Sir Thomas's assurances of their both being alive and well, made it necessary to lay by her agitation and affectionate preparatory speeches for a while.

The winter came and passed without their being called for; the accounts continued perfectly good; and Mrs Norris, in promoting gaieties for her nieces, assisting their toilets, displaying their accomplishments, and looking about for their future husbands, had so much to do as, in addition to all her own household cares, some interference in those of her sister, and Mrs Grant's wasteful doings to overlook, left her very little occasion to be occupied in fears for the absent.

The Miss Bertrams were now fully established among the belles of the neighbourhood; and as they joined to beauty and brilliant acquirements a manner naturally easy, and carefully formed to general civility and obligingness, they possessed its favour as well as its admiration. Their vanity was in such good order, that they seemed to be quite free from it, and gave themselves no airs; while the praise attending such behaviour, secured and brought round by their aunt, served to strengthen them in believing they had no faults.

Lady Bertram did not go into public with her daughters. She was too indolent even to accept a mother's gratification in witnessing their success and enjoyment at the expense of any personal trouble, and the charge was made over to her sister, who desired nothing better than a post of such honourable representation, and very thoroughly relished the means it afforded her of mixing in society without having horses to hire.

Fanny had no share in the festivities of the season; but she enjoyed being avowedly useful as her aunt's companion, when they called away the rest of the family; and, as Miss Lee had left Mansfield, she naturally became everything to Lady Bertram during the night of a ball or a party. She talked to her, listened to her, read to her; and the tranquillity of such evenings, her perfect security in such a *tête-à-tête* from any sound of unkindness, was unspeakably welcome to a mind which had seldom known a pause in its alarms or embarrassments. As to her cousins' gaieties, she loved to hear an account of them, especially of the balls, and whom Edmund had danced with; but thought too lowly of her own situation to imagine she should ever be admitted to the same, and listened, therefore, without an idea of any nearer concern in them. Upon the whole, it was a comfortable winter to her; for though it brought no William to England, the never-failing hope of his arrival was worth much.

The ensuing spring deprived her of her valued friend the old grey pony; and for some time she was in danger of feeling the loss in her health as well as in her affections; for in spite of the acknowledged importance of her riding on horseback, no measures were taken for mounting her again, 'because,' as it was observed by her aunts, 'she might ride one of her cousins' horses at any time when they did not want them,' and as the Miss Bertrams regularly wanted their horses every fine day, and had no idea of carrying their obliging manners to the sacrifice of any real pleasure, that time, of course, never came. They took their cheerful rides in the fine mornings of April and May; and Fanny either sat at home the whole day with one aunt, or walked beyond her strength at the instigation of the other; Lady Bertram holding exercise to be as unnecessary for every body as it was unpleasant to herself; and Mrs Norris, who was walking all day, thinking every body ought to walk as much. Edmund was absent at this time, or the evil would have been earlier remedied. When he returned, to understand how Fanny was situated, and perceived its ill effects, there seemed with him but one thing to be done; and that 'Fanny must have a horse,' was the resolute declaration with which he opposed whatever could be urged by the supineness of his mother, or the economy of his aunt, to make it appear unimportant. Mrs Norris could not help thinking that some steady old thing might be found among the numbers belonging to the Park, that would do vastly well; or, that one might be borrowed of the steward; or that perhaps Dr Grant might now and then lend them the pony he sent to the post. She could not but consider it as absolutely unnecessary, and even improper, that Fanny should have a regular lady's horse of her own, in the style of her cousins. She was sure Sir Thomas never intended it: and she must say, that to be making such a purchase in his absence, and adding to the great expenses of his stable, at a time when a large part of his income was unsettled, seemed to her very unjustifiable. 'Fanny must have a horse,' was Edmund's only reply. Mrs

Norris could not see it in the same light. Lady Bertram did: she entirely agreed with her son as to the necessity of it, and as to its being considered necessary by his father; she only pleaded against there being any hurry; she only wanted him to wait till Sir Thomas's return, and then Sir Thomas might settle it all himself. He would be at home in September, and where would be the harm of only waiting till September?

Though Edmund was much more displeased with his aunt than with his mother, as evincing least regard for her niece, he could not help paying more attention to what she said, and at length determined on a method of proceeding which would obviate the risk of his father's thinking he had done too much, and at the same time procure for Fanny the immediate means of exercise, which he could not bear she should be without. He had three horses of his own, but not one that would carry a woman. Two of them were hunters; the third, a useful road-horse. This third he resolved to exchange for for one that his cousin might ride; he knew where such a one was to be met with; and having once made up his mind, the whole business was soon completed. The new mare proved a treasure; with a very little trouble she became exactly calculated for the purpose, and Fanny was then put in almost full possession of her. She had not supposed before, that anything could ever suit her like the old grey pony; but her delight in Edmund's mare was far beyond any former pleasure of the sort; and the addition it was ever receiving in the consideration of that kindness from which her pleasure sprung, was beyond all her words to express. She regarded her cousin as an example of every thing good and great, as possessing worth, which no one but herself could ever appreciate, and as entitled to such gratitude from her, as no feelings could be strong enough to pay. Her sentiments towards him were compounded of all that was respectful, grateful, confiding and tender.

As the horse continued in name, as well as fact, the property of Edmund, Mrs Norris could tolerate its being for Fanny's use; and had Lady Bertram ever thought about her own objection again, he might have been excused in her eyes for not waiting till Sir Thomas' return in September, for when September came, Sir Thomas was still abroad, and without any near prospect of finishing his business. Unfavourable circumstances had suddenly arisen at a moment when he was beginning to turn all his thoughts towards England; and the very great uncertainty in which everything was then involved determined him on sending home his son, and waiting the final arrangement by himself. Tom arrived safely, bringing an excellent account of his father's health; but to very little purpose, as far as Mrs Norris was concerned. Sir Thomas's sending away his son seemed to her so like a parent's care, under the influence of a foreboding of evil to himself, that she could not help feeling dreadful presentiments; and as the long evenings of autumn came on, was so terribly haunted by these ideas, in the sad solitariness of her cottage, as to be obliged to take daily refuge in the dining-room of the Park. The return of winter engagements, however, was not without its effects; and in the course of their progress, her mind became so pleasantly occupied in superintending the fortunes of her eldest niece, as tolerably to quiet her nerves. 'If poor Sir Thomas were fated never to return, it would be peculiarly consoling to see their dear Maria well married,' she very often thought; always when they were in the company of men of fortune, and particularly on the introduction of a young man who had recently succeeded to one of the largest estates and finest places in the country.

Mr Rushworth was from the first struck with the beauty of Miss Bertram, and, being inclined to marry, soon fancied himself in love. He was a heavy young man, with not more than common sense; but as there was nothing disagreeable in his figure or address, the young lady was well pleased with her conquest. Being now in her twenty-first year, Maria Bertram was beginning to think matrimony a duty, and as a marriage with Mr Rushworth would give her the enjoyment of a larger income than her father's, as well as ensure her the house in town, which was now a prime object, it became, by the same rule of moral obligation, her evident duty to marry Mr Rushworth if she could. Mrs Norris was most zealous in promoting the match, by every suggestion and contrivance likely to enhance its desirableness to either party; and, among other means, by seeking an intimacy with the gentleman's mother, who at present lived with him, and to whom she even forced Lady Bertram to go through ten miles of indifferent road to pay a morning visit. It was not long before a good understanding took place between this lady and herself. Mrs Rushworth acknowledged herself very desirous that her son should marry, and declared that of all the young ladies she had ever seen, Miss Bertram seemed, by her amiable qualities and accomplishments, the best adapted to make him happy. Mrs Norris accepted the compliment, and admired the nice discernment of character which could so well distinguish merit. Maria was indeed the pride and delight of them all – perfectly faultless – an angel; and, of course, so surrounded by admirers, must be difficult in her choice: but yet, as far as Mrs Norris could allow herself to decide on so short an acquaintance, Mr Rushworth appeared precisely the young man to deserve and attach her.

After dancing with each other at a proper number of balls, the young people justified these opinions, and an engagement, with a due reference to the absent Sir Thomas, was entered into, much to the satisfaction of their respective families, and of the general lookers-on of the neighbourhood, who had, for many weeks past, felt the expediency of Mr Rushworth's marrying Miss Bertram.

It was some months before Sir Thomas's consent could be received; but, in the meanwhile, as no one felt a doubt of his most cordial pleasure in the connection, the intercourse of the two families was carried on without restraint, and no other attempt made at secrecy, than Mrs Norris's talking of it everywhere as a matter of not to be talked of at present.

Edmund was the only one of the family who could see a fault in the business; but no representation of his aunt's could induce him to find Mr Rushworth a desirable companion. He could allow his sister to be the best judge of her own happiness, but he was not pleased that her happiness should centre in a large income; nor could he refrain from often saying to himself, in Mr Rushworth's company, 'If this man had not twelve thousand a year, he would be a very stupid fellow.'

Sir Thomas, however, was truly happy in the prospect of an alliance so unquestionably advantageous, and of which he heard nothing but the perfectly good and agreeable. It was a connection exactly of the right sort – in the same county, and the same interest – and his most hearty concurrence was conveyed as soon as possible. He only conditioned that the marriage should not take place before his return, which he was again looking eagerly forward to. He wrote in April, and had strong hopes of settling every thing to his entire satisfaction, leaving Antigua before the end of the summer.

Such was the state of affairs in the month of July; and Fanny had just reached her eighteenth year, when the society of the village received an addition in the brother and sister of Mrs Grant, a Mr and Miss Crawford, the children of her mother by a second marriage. They were young people of fortune. The son had a good estate in Norfolk, the daughter twenty thousand pounds. As children, their sister had been always very fond of them; but, as her own marriage had been soon followed by the death of their common parent, which left them to the care of a brother of their father, of whom Mrs Grant knew nothing, she had scarcely seen them since. In their uncle's house they had found a kind home. Admiral and Mrs Crawford, though agreeing in nothing else, were united in affection for these children, or, at least, were not further adverse in their feelings than that each had their favourite, to whom they showed the greatest fondness of the two. The Admiral delighted in the boy, Mrs Crawford doted on the girl; and it was the lady's death which now obliged her *protégée*, after some months' further trial at her uncle's house, to find another home. Admiral Crawford was a man of vicious conduct, who chose, instead of retaining his niece, to bring his mistress under his own roof; and to this Mrs Grant was indebted for her sister's proposal of coming to her, a measure quite as welcome on one side as it could be expedient on the other; for Mrs Grant, having by this time run through the usual resources of ladies residing in the country without a family of children – having more than filled her favourite sitting-room with pretty furniture, and made a choice collection of plants and poultry – was very much in want of some variety at home. The arrival, therefore, of a sister whom she had always loved, and now hoped to retain with her as long as she remained single, was highly agreeable; and her chief anxiety was, lest Mansfield should not satisfy the habits of a young woman who had been mostly used to London.

Miss Crawford was not entirely free from similar apprehensions, though they arose principally from doubts of her sister's style of living and tone of society; and it was not till after she had tried in vain to persuade her brother to settle with her at his own country house, that she could resolve to hazard herself among her other relations. To anything like a permanence of abode, or limitation of society, Henry Crawford had, unluckily, a great dislike; he could not accommodate his sister in an article of such importance; but he escorted her, with the utmost kindness, into Northamptonshire and as readily engaged to fetch her away again, at half an hour's notice, whenever she were weary of the place.

The meeting was very satisfactory on each side. Miss Crawford found a sister without preciseness or rusticity – a sister's husband who looked the gentleman, and a house commodious and well fitted up; and Mrs Grant received in those whom she hoped to love better than ever, a young man and woman of very prepossessing appearance. Mary Crawford was remarkably pretty; Henry, though not handsome, had air and countenance; the manners of both were lively and pleasant, and Mrs Grant immediately gave them credit for everything else. She was delighted with each, but Mary was her dearest object; and having never been able to glory in beauty of her own, she thoroughly enjoyed the power of being proud of her sister's. She had not waited for her arrival to look out for a suitable match for her; she had fixed on Tom Bertram; the eldest son of a baronet was not too good for a girl of twenty thousand pounds, with all the elegance and accomplishments which Mrs Grant foresaw in her; and being a warmhearted, unreserved woman, Mary had not been there three hours in the house before she told her what she had planned.

Miss Crawford was glad to find a family of such consequence so very near them, and not at all displeased either at her sister's early care, or the choice it had fallen on. Matrimony was her object, provided she could marry well: and having seen Mr Bertram in town, she knew that objection could no more be made to his person than to his situation in life. While she treated it as a joke, therefore, she did not forget to think of it seriously. The scheme was soon repeated to Henry.

'And now,' added Mrs Grant, 'I have thought of something to make it complete. I should dearly love to settle you both in this country; and therefore, Henry, you shall marry the youngest Miss Bertram, a nice, handsome, good-humored, accomplished girl, who will make you very happy.'

Henry bowed and thanked her.

'My dear sister,' said Mary, 'if you can persuade him into any thing of the sort, it will be a fresh matter of delight to me to find myself allied to any body so clever, and I shall only regret that you have not half-a-dozen daughters to dispose of. If you can persuade Henry to marry, you must have the address of a Frenchwoman. All that English abilities can do has been tried already. I have three very particular friends who have been all dying for him in their turn; and the pains which they, their mothers (very clever women), as well as my dear aunt and myself, have taken to reason, coax, or trick him into marrying, is inconceivable! He is the most horrible flirt that can be imagined. If your Miss Bertrams do not like to have their hearts broke let them avoid Henry.'

'My dear brother, I will not believe this of you.'

'No, I am sure you are too good. You will be kinder than Mary. You will allow for the doubts of youth and inexperience. I am of a cautious temper, and unwilling to risk my happiness in a hurry. Nobody can think more highly of the matrimonial state than myself. I consider the blessing of a wife as most justly described in those discreet lines of the poet '"Heavens's *last* best gift."'

'There, Mrs Grant, you see how he dwells on one word, and only look at his smile. I assure you he is very detestable; the Admiral's lessons have quite spoiled him.'

'I pay very little regard,' said Mrs Grant, 'to what any young person says on the subject of marriage. If they profess a disinclination for it, I only set it down that they have not yet seen the right person.'

Dr Grant laughingly congratulated Miss Crawford on feeling no disinclination to the state herself.

'Oh yes! I am not at all ashamed of it. I would have every body marry if they can do it properly: I do not like to have people throw themselves away: but every body should marry as soon as they can do it to advantage.'

CHAPTER FIVE

THE YOUNG PEOPLE WERE PLEASED with each other from the first. On each side there was much to attract, and their acquaintance soon promised as early an intimacy as good manners would warrant. Miss Crawford's beauty did her no disservice with the Miss Bertrams. They were too handsome themselves to dislike any woman for being so too, and were almost as much charmed as their brothers with her lively dark eyes, clear-brown complexion, and general prettiness. Had she been tall, full formed, and fair, it might have been more of a trial: but as it was, there could be no comparison; and she was most allowably a sweet, pretty girl, while they were the finest young women in the country.

Her brother was not handsome; no, when they first saw him he was absolutely plain, black and plain; but still he was the gentleman, with a pleasing address. The second meeting proved him not so very plain; he was plain, to be sure, but then he had so much countenance, and his teeth were so good, and he was so well made, that one soon forgot he was plain; and after a third interview, after dining in company with him at the Parsonage, he was no longer allowed to be called so by any body. He was, in fact, the most agreeable young man the sisters had ever known, and they were equally delighted with him. Miss Bertram's engagement made him in equity the property of Julia, of which Julia was fully aware; and before he had been at Mansfield a week, she was quite ready to be fallen in love with.

Maria's notions on the subject were more confused and indistinct. She did not want to see or understand. 'There could be no harm in her liking an agreeable man – every body knew her situation – Mr Crawford must take care of himself.' Mr Crawford did not mean to be in any danger! the Miss Bertrams were worth pleasing, and were ready to be pleased; and he began with no object of making them like him. He did not want them to die of love; but with sense and temper which ought to have made him judge and feel better, he allowed himself great latitude on such points.

'I like your Miss Bertrams exceedingly, sister,' said he, as he returned from attending them to their carriage after the said dinner visit; 'they are very elegant, agreeable girls.'

'So they are, indeed, and I am delighted to hear you say it. But you like Julia best.'

'Oh yes! I like Julia best.'

'But do you really? for Miss Bertram is in general thought the handsomest.'

'So I should suppose. She has the advantage in every feature, and I prefer her countenance; but I like Julia best; Miss Bertram is certainly the handsomest, and I have found her the most agreeable, but I shall always like Julia best, because you order me.'

'I shall not talk to you, Henry, but I know you *will* like her best at last.'

'Do not I tell you that I like her best at *first*?'

'And besides, Miss Bertram is engaged. Remember that, my dear brother. Her choice is made.'

'Yes, and I like her the better for it. An engaged woman is always more agreeable than a disengaged. She is satisfied with herself. Her cares are over, and she feels that she may exert all her powers of pleasing without suspicion. All is safe with a lady engaged; no harm can be done.'

'Why, as to that, Mr Rushworth is a very good sort of young man, and it is a great match for her.'

'But Miss Bertram does not care three straws for him; *that* is your opinion of your intimate friend. *I* do not subscribe to it. I am sure Miss Bertram is very much attached to Mr Rushworth. I could see it in her eyes, when he was mentioned. I think too well of Miss Bertram to suppose she would ever give her hand without her heart.'

'Mary, how shall we manage him?'

'We must leave him to himself, I believe. Talking does no good. He will be taken in at last.'

'But I would not have him *taken in*; I would not have him duped; I would have it all fair and honourable.'

Attending them to their carriage

'Oh dear! let him stand his chance and be taken in. It will do just as well. Every body is taken in at some period or other.'

'Not always in marriage, dear Mary.'

'In marriage especially. With all due respect to such of the present company as chance to be married, my dear Mrs Grant, there is not one in a hundred of either sex who is not taken in when they marry. Look where I will, I see that it *is* so; and I feel that it *must* be so, when I consider that it is, of all transactions, the one in which people expect most from others, and are least honest themselves.'

'Ah! You have been in a bad school for matrimony, in Hill Street.'

'My poor aunt had certainly little cause to love the state; but, however, speaking from my own observation, it is a manœuvring business. I know so many who have married in the full expectation and confidence of some one particular advantage in the connection, or accomplishment, or good quality in the person, who have found themselves entirely deceived, and been obliged to put up with exactly the reverse. What is this but a take in?'

'My dear child, there must be a little imagination here. I beg your pardon, but I cannot quite believe you. Depend upon it, you see but half. You see the evil, but you do not see the consolation. There will be little rubs and disappointments everywhere, and we are all apt to expect too much; but then, if one scheme of happiness fails, human nature turns to another; if the first calculation is wrong we make a second better; we find comfort somewhere – and those evil-minded observers, dearest Mary, who make much of a little, are more taken in and deceived than the parties themselves.'

'Well done, sister! I honour your *esprit de corps*. When I am a wife, I mean to be just as staunch myself; and I wish my friends in general would be so too. It would save me many a heart-ache.'

'You are as bad as your brother, Mary; but we will cure you both. Mansfield shall cure you both, and without any taking in. Stay with us, and we will cure you.'

The Crawfords, without wanting to be cured, were very willing to stay. Mary was satisfied with the Parsonage as a present home and Henry equally ready to lengthen his visit. He had come, intending to spend only a few days with them; but Mansfield promised well, and there was nothing to call him elsewhere. It delighted Mrs Grant to keep them both with her, and Dr Grant was exceedingly well contented to have it so: a talking pretty young woman like Miss Crawford is always pleasant society to an indolent, stay-at-home man; and Mr Crawford's being his guest was an excuse for drinking claret every day.

The Miss Bertrams' admiration of Mr Crawford was more rapturous than anything which Miss Crawford's habits made her likely to feel. She acknowledged, however, that the Mr Bertrams were very fine young men, that two such young men were not often seen together even in London, and that their manners, particularly those of the eldest, were very good. *He* had been much in London, and had more liveliness and gallantry than Edmund, and must, therefore, be preferred; and indeed, his being the eldest was another strong claim. She had felt an early presentiment that she *should* like the eldest best. She knew it was her way.

Tom Bertram must have been thought pleasant, indeed, at any rate; he was the sort of young man to be generally liked, his agreeableness was of the kind to be oftener found agreeable than some endowments of a higher stamp, for he had easy manners, excellent spirits, a large acquaintance, and a great deal to say: and the reversion of Mansfield Park, and a baronetcy, did no harm to all this. Miss Crawford soon felt that he and his situation might do. She looked about her with due consideration, and found almost every thing in his favour, a park, a real park, five miles round, a spacious modern-built house, so well placed and well screened as to deserve to be in any collection of engravings of gentlemen's seats in the kingdom, and wanting only to be completely new furnished – pleasant sisters, a quiet mother, and an agreeable man himself – with the advantage of being tied up from much gaming at present by a promise to his father, and of being Sir Thomas hereafter. It might do very well; she believed she should accept him; and she began accordingly to interest herself a little about the horse which he had to run at the B—— races.

These races were to call him away not long after their acquaintance began; and as it appeared that the family did not, from his usual goings on, expect him back again for many weeks, it would bring his passion to an early proof. Much was said on his side to induce her to attend the races, and schemes were made for a large party to them, with all the eagerness of inclination, but it would only do to be talked of.

And Fanny, what was *she* doing and thinking all this while? and what was *her* opinion of the new-comers? Few young ladies of eighteen could be less called on to speak their opinion than Fanny. In a quiet way, very little attended to, she paid her tribute of admiration to Miss Crawford's beauty; but as she still continued to think Mr Crawford very plain, in spite of her two cousins having repeatedly proved the contrary she never mentioned *him*. The notice which she excited herself, was to this effect. 'I begin now to understand you all, except Miss Price,' said Miss Crawford, as she was walking with the Mr Bertrams. 'Pray, is she out, or is she not? I am puzzled. She dined at the Parsonage, with the rest of you, which seemed like being *out*; and yet she says so little, that I can hardly suppose she is.'

Edmund, to whom this was chiefly addressed, replied, 'I believe I know what you mean, but I will not undertake to answer the question. My cousin is grown up. She has the age and sense of a woman, but the outs and not outs are beyond me.'

'And yet, in general, nothing can be more easily ascertained. The distinction is so broad. Manners as well as appearance are, generally speaking, so totally different. Till now, I could not have supposed it possible to be mistaken as to a girl's being out or not. A girl not out, has always the same sort of dress: a close bonnet, for instance; looks very demure, and never says a word. You may smile, but it is so, I assure you; and except that it is some times carried a little too far, it is all very proper. Girls should be quiet and modest. The most objectionable part is, that the alteration of manners on being introduced into company is frequently too sudden. They sometimes pass in such very little time from reserve to quite the opposite – to confidence! *That* is the faulty part of the present system. One does not like to see a girl of eighteen or nineteen so immediately up to every thing – and perhaps when one has seen her hardly able to speak the year before. Mr Bertram, I dare say *you* have sometimes met with such changes.'

'I believe I have, but this is hardly fair; I see what you are at. You are quizzing me and Miss Anderson.'

'No, indeed. Miss Anderson! I do not know who or what you mean. I am quite in the dark. But I *will* quiz you with a great deal of pleasure, if you will tell me what about.'

'Ah! you carry it off very well, but I cannot be quite so far imposed on. You must have had Miss Anderson in your eye, in describing an altered young lady. You paint too accurately for mistake. It was exactly so. The Andersons of Baker Street. We were speaking of them the other day, you know. Edmund, you have heard me mention Charles Anderson. The circumstance was precisely as this lady has represented it. When Anderson first introduced me to his family, about two years ago, his sister was not *out*, and I could not get her to speak to me. I sat there an hour one morning waiting for Anderson, with only her and a little girl or two in the room, the governess being sick or run away, and the mother in and out every moment with letters of business, and I could hardly get a word or a look from the young lady – nothing like a civil answer – she screwed up her mouth, and turned from me with such an air! I did not see her again for a twelvemonth. She was then *out*. I met her at Mrs Holford's, and did not recollect her. She came up to me, claimed me as an acquaintance, stared me out of countenance, and talked and laughed till I did not know which way to look. I felt that I must be the jest of the room at the time, and Miss Crawford, it is plain, has heard the story.'

'And a very pretty story it is, and with more truth in it, I dare say, than does credit to Miss Anderson. It is too common a fault. Mothers certainly

'I did not know which way to look'

have not yet got quite the right way of managing their daughters. I do not know where the error lies. I do not pretend to set people right, but I do see that they are often wrong.'

'Those who are showing the world what female manners *should* be,' said Mr Bertram gallantly, 'are doing a great deal to set them right.'

'The error is plain enough,' said the less courteous Edmund; 'such girls are ill brought up. They are given wrong notions from the beginning. They are always acting upon motives of vanity, and there is no more real modesty in their behaviour *before* they appear in public than afterwards.'

'I do not know,' replied Miss Crawford, hesitatingly. 'Yes, I cannot agree with you there. It is certainly the modestest part of the business. It is much worse to have girls *not out*, give themselves the same airs and take the same liberties as if they were, which I *have* seen done. *That* is worse than anything – quite disgusting!'

'Yes, *that* is very inconvenient, indeed,' said Mr Bertram. 'It leads one astray; one does not know what to do. The close bonnet and demure air you described so well (and nothing was ever juster), tell one what is expected; but I got into a dreadful scrape last year from the want of them. I went down to Ramsgate for a week with a friend last September, just after my return from the West Indies. My friend Sneyd – you have heard me speak of Sneyd, Edmund – his father, and mother, and sisters, were all new to me. When we reached Albion Place, they were out; we went after them, and found them on the pier; Mrs and the two Miss Sneyds, with others of their acquaintances. I made my bow in form; and as Mrs Sneyd was surrounded by men, attached myself to one of her daughters, walked by her side all the way home, and made myself as agreeable as I could; the young lady, perfectly easy in her manners, and as ready to talk as to listen. I had not a suspicion that I could be doing anything wrong. They looked just the same: both well dressed, with veils and parasols like other girls; but I afterwards found that I had been giving all my attention to the youngest, who was not *out*, and had most excessively offended the eldest. Miss Augusta ought not to have been noticed for the next six months; and Miss Sneyd, I believe, has never forgiven me.'

'That was bad, indeed. Poor Miss Sneyd! Though I have no younger sister, I feel for her. To be neglected before one's time must be very vexatious; but it was entirely her mother's fault. Miss Augusta should have been with her governess. Such half and half doings never prosper. But now I must be satisfied about Miss Price. Does she go to balls? Does she dine out everywhere, as well as at my sister's?'

'No,' replied Edmund; 'I do not think she has ever been to a ball. My mother seldom goes into company herself, and dines nowhere but with Mrs Grant, and Fanny stays at home with *her*.'

'Oh, then the point is clear. Miss Price is *not* out.'

CHAPTER SIX

MR. BERTRAM SET OFF FOR B—, and Miss Crawford was prepared to find a great chasm in their society, and to miss him decidedly in the meetings which were now becoming almost daily between the families; and on their all dining together at the Park soon after his going, she re-took her chosen place near the bottom of the table, fully expecting to feel a most melancholy difference in the change of masters. It would be a very flat business, she was sure. In comparison with his brother, Edmund would have nothing to say. The soup would be sent round in a most spiritless manner, wine drank without any smiles or agreeable trifling, and the venison cut up without supplying one pleasant anecdote of any former haunch, or a single entertaining story, about 'my friend such a one.' She must try to find amusement in what was passing at the upper end of the table, and in observing Mr Rushworth, who was now making his appearance at Mansfield for the first time since the Crawfords' arrival. He had been visiting a friend in the neighbouring county, and that friend having recently had his grounds laid out by an improver, Mr Rushworth was returned with his head full of the subject, and very eager to be improving his own place in the same way; and though not saying much to the purpose, could talk of nothing else. The subject had been already handled in the drawing-room; it was revived in the dining-parlour. Miss Bertram's attention and opinion was evidently his chief aim; and though her deportment showed rather conscious superiority than any solicitude to oblige him, the mention of Sotherton Court, and the ideas attached to it, gave her a feeling of complacency, which prevented her from being very ungracious.

'I wish you could see Compton,' said he, 'it is the most complete thing! I never saw a place so altered in my life. I told Smith I did not know where I was. The approach, *now*, is one of the finest things in the country; you see the house in the most surprising manner. I declare, when I got back to Sotherton yesterday, it looked like a prison – quite a dismal old prison.'

'Oh, for shame!' cried Mrs Norris. 'A prison, indeed! Sotherton Court is the noblest old place in the world.'

'It wants improvement, ma'am, beyond any thing. I never saw a place that wanted so much improvement in my life: and it is so forlorn, that I do not know what can be done with it.'

'No wonder that Mr Rushworth should think so at present,' said Mrs

Grant to Mrs Norris, with a smile; 'but depend upon it, Sotherton will have *every* improvement in time which his heart can desire.'

'I must try to do some thing with it,' said Mr Rushworth, 'but I do not know what. I hope I shall have some good friend to help me.'

'Your best friend upon such an occasion,' said Miss Bertram calmly, 'would be Mr Repton, I imagine.'

'That is what I was thinking of. As he has done so well by Smith, I think I had better have him at once. His terms are five guineas a day.'

'Well, and if they were *ten*,' cried Mrs Norris, 'I am sure *you* need not regard it. The expense need not be any impediment. If I were you, I should not think of the expense. I would have everything done in the best style, and made as nice as possible. Such a place as Sotherton Court deserves everything that taste and money can do. You have space to work upon there, and grounds that will well reward you. For my own part, if I had anything within the fiftieth part of the size of Sotherton, I should be always planting and improving, for, naturally, I am excessively fond of it. It would be too ridiculous for me to attempt anything where I am now with my little half acre. It would be quite a burlesque. But if I had more room, I should take a prodigious delight in improving and planting. We did a vast deal in that way at the Parsonage: we made it quite a place from what it was when we first had it. You young ones do not remember much about it, perhaps; but if dear Sir Thomas were here, he could tell you what improvements we made: and a great deal more would have been done, but for poor Mr Norris's sad state of health. He could hardly ever get out, poor man, to enjoy any thing, and *that* disheartened me from doing several things that Sir Thomas and I used to talk of. If it had not been for *that*, we should have carried on the garden wall, and made the plantation to shut out the churchyard, just as Dr Grant has done. We were always doing something as it was. It was only the spring twelvemonth before Mr Norris's death, that we put in the apricot against the stable wall, which is now grown such a noble tree, and getting to such perfection, sir,' addressing herself then to Dr Grant.

'The tree thrives well, beyond a doubt, madam,' replied Dr Grant. 'The soil is good; and I never pass it without regretting that the fruit should be so little worth the trouble of gathering.'

'Sir, it is a Moor Park, we bought it as a Moor Park, and it cost us – that is, it was a present from Sir Thomas, but I saw the bill – and I know it cost seven shillings, and was charged as a Moor Park.'

'You were imposed on, ma'am,' replied Dr Grant: 'these potatoes have as much the flavour of a Moor Park apricot as the fruit from that tree. It is an insipid fruit at the best; but a good apricot is eatable, which none from my garden are.'

'The truth is, ma'am,' said Mrs Grant, pretending to whisper across the table to Mrs Norris, 'that Dr Grant hardly knows what the natural taste of our apricot is: he is scarcely ever indulged with one, for it is so valuable a fruit, with a little assistance, and ours is such a remarkably large, fair sort, that what with early tarts and preserves, my cook contrives to get them all.'

Mrs Norris, who had begun to redden, was appeased; and, for a little while, other subjects took place of the improvements of Sotherton. Dr Grant and Mrs Norris were seldom good friends; their acquaintance had begun in dilapidations, and their habits were totally dissimilar.

After a short interruption, Mr Rushworth began again. 'Smith's place is the admiration of all the country; and it was a mere nothing before Repton took it in hand. I think I shall have Repton.'

'Mr Rushworth,' said Lady Bertram, 'if I were you, I would have a very pretty shrubbery. One likes to get out into a shrubbery in fine weather.'

Mr Rushworth was eager to assure her ladyship of his acquiescence, and tried to make out something complimentary; but, between his submission to *her* taste, and his having always intended the same himself, with superadded objects of professing attention to the comfort of ladies in general, and of insinuating that there was one only whom he was anxious to please, he grew puzzled, and Edmund was glad to put an end to his speech by a proposal of wine. Mr Rushworth, however, though not usually a great talker, had still more to say on the subject next his heart; 'Smith has not much above a hundred acres altogether, in his grounds, which is little enough, and makes it more surprising that the place can have been so improved. Now, at Sotherton, we have a good seven hundred, without reckoning the water meadows; so that I think, if so much could be done at Compton, we need not despair. There have been two or three fine old trees cut down, that grew too near the house, and it opens the prospect amazingly, which makes me think that Repton, or any body of that sort, would certainly have the avenue at Sotherton down; the avenue that leads from the front to the top of the hill, you know,' turning to Miss Bertram particularly as he spoke. But Miss Bertram thought it most becoming to reply:

'The avenue! Oh! I do not recollect it. I really know very little of Sotherton.'

Fanny, who was sitting on the other side of Edmund, exactly opposite Miss Crawford, and who had been attentively listening, now looked at him, and said, in a low voice:

'Cut down an avenue! What a pity! Does it not make you think of Cowper? "Ye fallen avenues, once more I mourn your fate unmerited."'

He smiled as he answered, 'I am afraid the avenue stands a bad chance, Fanny.'

'I should like to see Sotherton before it is cut down, to see the place as it is now, in its old state; but I do not suppose I shall.'

'Have you never been there? No, you never can; and, unluckily, it is out of distance for a ride. I wish we could contrive it.'

'Oh! it does not signify. Whenever I do see it, you will tell me how it has been altered.'

'I collect,' said Miss Crawford, 'that Sotherton is an old place, and a place of some grandeur. In any particular style of building?'

'The house was built in Elizabeth's time, and is a large, regular, brick building; heavy, but respectable looking, and has many good rooms. It is ill placed. It stands in one of the lowest spots of the park; in that respect, unfavourable for improvement. But the woods are fine, and there is a stream, which, I dare say, might be made a good deal of. Mr Rushworth is quite right, I think, in meaning to give it a modern dress, and I have no doubt that it will be all done extremely well.'

Miss Crawford listened with submission, and said to herself, 'He is a well-bred man; he makes the best of it.'

'I do not wish to influence Mr Rushworth,' he continued; 'but, had I a place to new-fashion, I should not put myself into the hands of an improver. I would rather have an inferior degree of beauty, of my own choice, and acquired progressively. I would rather abide by my own blunders than by his.'

'*You* would know what you were about, of course; but that would not suit *me*. I have no eye of ingenuity for such matters, but as they are before me; and had I a place of my own in the country, I should be most thankful to any Mr Repton who would undertake it, and give me as much beauty as he could for my money; and I should never look at it till it was complete.'

'It would be delightful to *me* to see the progress of it all,' said Fanny.

'Ay, you have been brought up to it. It was no part of my education; and the only dose I ever had, being administered by not the first favourite in the world, has made me consider improvements *in hand* as the greatest of nuisances. Three years ago, the Admiral, my honoured uncle, bought a cottage at Twickenham for us all to spend our summers in; and my aunt and I went down to it quite in raptures; but it being excessively pretty, it was soon found necessary to be improved, and for three months we were all dirt and confusion, without a gravel walk to step on, or a bench fit for use. I would have every thing as complete as possible in the country, shrubberies and flower-gardens, and rustic seats innumerable: but it must all be done without my care. Henry is different, he loves to be doing.'

Edmund was sorry to hear Miss Crawford, whom he was disposed to admire, speak so freely of her uncle. It did not suit his sense of propriety, and he was silenced, till induced by further smiles and liveliness, to put the matter by for the present.

'Mr Bertram,' said she, 'I have tidings of my harp at last. I am assured that it is safe at Northampton; and there it has probably been these ten days, in spite of the solemn assurances we have so often received to the contrary.' Edmund expressed his pleasure and surprise. 'The truth is, that our inquiries were too direct; we sent a servant, we went ourselves: this will not do seventy miles from London; but this morning we heard of it in the right way. It was seen by some farmer, and he told the miller, and the miller told the butcher, and the butcher's son-in-law left word at the shop.'

'I am very glad that you have heard of it, by whatever means, and hope there will be no further delay.'

'I am to have it to-morrow; but, how do you think it is to be conveyed? Not by a wagon or cart: oh no! nothing of that kind could be hired in the village. I might as well have asked for porters and a hand-barrow.'

'You would find it difficult, I dare say, just now, in the middle of a very late hay harvest, to hire a horse and cart?'

'I was astonished to find what a piece of work was made of it! To want a horse and cart in the country seemed impossible, so I told my maid to speak for one directly; and as I cannot look out of my dressing-closet without seeing one farm-yard, not walk in the shrubbery without passing another, I thought it would be only ask and have, and was rather grieved that I could not give the advantage to all. Guess my surprise when I found that I had been asking the most unreasonable, most impossible thing in the world; had offended all the farmers, all the labourers, all the hay in the parish! As for Dr Grant's bailiff, I believe I had better keep out of *his* way; and my brother-in-law himself, who is all kindness in general, looked rather black upon me, when he found what I had been at.'

'You could not be expected to have thought on the subject before; but when you *do* think of it, you must see the importance of getting in the grass. The hire of a cart at any time might not be so easy as you suppose; our farmers are not in the habit of letting them out: but, in harvest, it must be quite out of their power to spare a horse.'

'I shall understand all your ways in time; but, coming down with the true London maxim, that every thing is to be got with money, I was a little embarrassed at first by the sturdy independence of your country customs. However, I am to have my harp fetched to-morrow. Henry, who is good nature itself, has offered to fetch it in his barouche. Will it not be honourably conveyed?'

Edmund spoke of the harp as his favourite instrument, and hoped to be soon allowed to hear her. Fanny had never heard the harp at all, and wished for it very much.

'I shall be most happy to play to you both,' said Miss Crawford; 'at least as long as you can like to listen: probably much longer, for I dearly love music myself, and where the natural taste is equal the player must always be best off, for she is gratified in more ways than one. Now, Mr Bertram, if you write to your brother, I entreat you to tell him that my harp *is* come; he heard so much of my misery about it. And you may say, if you please, that I shall prepare my most plaintive airs against his return, in compassion to his feelings, as I know his horse will lose.'

'If I write, I will say whatever you wish me; but I do not, at present, foresee any occasion for writing.'

'No, I dare say, not if he were to be gone a twelvemonth would you ever write to him, nor he to you, if it could be helped. The occasion would never be foreseen. What strange creatures brothers are! You would not write to each other but upon the most urgent necessity in the world; and when obliged to take up a pen to say that such a horse is ill, or such a relation dead, it is done in the fewest possible words. You have but one style among you. I know it perfectly. Henry, who is in every other respect exactly what a brother should be, who loves me, consults me, confides in me, and will talk to me by the hour together, has never yet turned the page in a letter; and very often it is nothing more than – "Dear Mary, I am just arrived. Bath seems full and everything as usual. Yours sincerely." That is the true manly style; that is a complete brother's letter.'

'When they are at a distance from all their family,' said Fanny, colouring for William's sake, 'they can write long letters.'

'Miss Price has a brother at sea,' said Edmund, 'whose excellence as a correspondent makes her think you too severe upon us.'

'At sea, has she? In the king's service, of course?'

Fanny would rather have had Edmund tell the story, but his determined silence obliged her to relate her brother's situation; her voice was animated in speaking of his profession, and the foreign stations he had been on; but she could not mention the number of years that he had been absent without tears in her eyes. Miss Crawford civilly wished him an early promotion.

'Do you know any thing of my cousin's captain?' said Edmund; 'Captain Marshall? You have a large acquaintance in the navy, I conclude?'

'Among admirals, large enough; but,' with an air of grandeur, 'we know very little of the inferior ranks. Post-captains may be very good sort of men, but they do not belong to *us*. Of various admirals I could tell you a great deal; of them and their flags, and the gradation of their pay, and their bickerings and jealousies. But, in general, I can assure you that they are all passed over, and all very ill used. Certainly, my home at my uncle's brought me acquainted with a circle of admirals. Of *Rears* and *Vices*, I saw enough. Now do not be suspecting me of a pun, I entreat.'

Edmund again felt grave, and only replied, 'It is a noble profession.'

'Yes, the profession is well enough under two circumstances; if it make the fortune, and there be discretion in spending it; but, in short, it is not a favourite profession of mine. It has never worn an amiable form to *me*.'

Edmund reverted to the harp, and was again very happy in the prospect of hearing her play.

The subject of improving grounds, meanwhile, was still under consideration among the others; and Mrs Grant could not help addressing her brother, though it was calling his attention from Miss Julia Bertram.

'My dear Henry, have *you* nothing to say? You have been an improver yourself, and from what I hear of Everingham, it may vie with any place in England. Its natural beauties, I am sure, are great. Everingham, as it *used* to be, was perfect in my estimation; such a happy fall of ground, and such timber! What would I not give to see it again.'

'Nothing could be so gratifying to me as to hear your opinion of it,' was his answer; 'but I fear there would be some disappointment: you would not

A circle of admirals

find it equal to your present ideas. In extent, it is a mere nothing; you would be surprised at its insignificance; and, as for improvement, there was very little for me to do – too little; I should like to have been busy much longer.'

'You are fond of the sort of thing?' said Julia.

'Excessively; but what with the natural advantages of the ground, which pointed out, even to a very young eye, what little remained to be done, and my own consequent resolutions, I had not been of age three months before Everingham was all that it is now. My plan was laid at Westminster, a little altered, perhaps, at Cambridge, and at one-and-twenty executed. I am inclined to envy Mr Rushworth for having so much happiness yet before him. I have been a devourer of my own.'

'Those who see quickly, will resolve quickly, and act quickly,' said Julia. '*You* can never want employment. Instead of envying Mr Rushworth, you should assist him with your opinion.'

Mrs Grant, hearing the latter part of this speech, enforced it warmly; persuaded that no judgment could be equal to her brother's; and as Miss Bertram caught at the idea likewise, and gave it her full support, declaring that, in her opinion, it was infinitely better to consult with friends and disinterested advisers, than immediately to throw the business into the hands of a professional man, Mr Rushworth was very ready to request the favour of Mr Crawford's assistance; and Mr Crawford, after properly depreciating his own abilities, was quite at his service in any way that could be useful. Mr Rushworth then began to propose Mr Crawford's doing him the honour of coming over to Sotherton, and taking a bed there; when Mrs Norris, as if reading in her two nieces' minds their little approbation of a plan which was to take Mr Crawford away, interposed with an amendment.

'There can be no doubt of Mr Crawford's willingness; but why should not more of us go? Why should not we make a little party? Here are many that would be interested in your improvements, my dear Mr Rushworth, and that would like to hear Mr Crawford's opinion on the spot, and that might be of some small use to you with *their* opinions; and for my own part, I have been long wishing to wait upon your good mother again; nothing but having no horses of my own could have made me so remiss; but now I could go and sit a few hours with Mrs Rushworth, while the rest of you walked about and settled things, and then we could all return to a late dinner here, or dine at Sotherton, just as might be most agreeable to your mother, and have a pleasant drive home by moonlight. I dare say Mr Crawford would take my two nieces and me in his barouche, and Edmund can go on horseback, you know, sister, and Fanny will stay at home with you.'

Lady Bertram made no objection; and every one concerned in the going was forward in expressing their ready concurrence, excepting Edmund, who heard it all and said nothing.

CHAPTER SEVEN

'WELL, FANNY, AND HOW DO YOU like Miss Crawford *now*?' said Edmund the next day, after thinking some time on the subject himself. 'How did you like her yesterday?'

'Very well – very much. I like to hear her talk. She entertains me; and she is so extremely pretty, that I have great pleasure in looking at her.'

'It is her countenance that it is so attractive. She has a wonderful play of feature! But was there nothing in her conversation that struck you, Fanny, as not quite right?'

'Oh, yes! she ought not to have spoken of her uncle as she did. I was quite astonished. An uncle with whom she has been living so many years, and who, whatever his faults may be, is so very fond of her brother, treating him, they say, quite like a son. I could not have believed it!'

'I thought you would be struck. It was very wrong; very indecorous.'

'And very ungrateful, I think.'

'Ungrateful is a strong word. I do not know that her uncle has any claim to her *gratitude*; his wife certainly had; and it is the warmth of her respect for her aunt's memory which misleads her here. She is awkwardly circumstanced. With such warm feelings and lively spirits it must be difficult to do justice to her affection for Mrs Crawford, without throwing a shade on the Admiral. I do not pretend to know which was most to blame in their disagreements, though the Admiral's present conduct might incline one to the side of his wife; but it is natural and amiable that Miss Crawford should acquit her aunt entirely. I do not censure her *opinions*: but there certainly *is* impropriety in making them public.'

'Do not you think,' said Fanny, after a little consideration, 'that this impropriety is a reflection itself upon Mrs Crawford, as her niece has been entirely brought up by her? She cannot have given her right notions of what was due to the Admiral.'

'That is a fair remark. Yes, we must suppose the faults of the niece to have been those of the aunt; and it makes one more sensible of the disadvantages she has been under. But I think her present home must do her good. Mrs Grant's manners are just what they ought to be. She speaks of her brother with a very pleasing affection.'

'Yes, except as to his writing her such short letters. She made me almost laugh; but I cannot rate so very highly the love or good nature of a brother, who will not give himself the trouble of writing any thing worth reading to his sisters, when they are separated. I am sure William would never have used *me* so, under any circumstances. And what right had she to suppose that *you* would not write long letters when you were absent?'

'The right of a lively mind, Fanny, seizing whatever may contribute to its own amusement or that of others; perfectly allowable, when untinctured by ill humour or roughness; and there is not a shadow of either in the countenance or manner of Miss Crawford: nothing sharp, or loud, or coarse. She is perfectly feminine, except in the instances we have been speaking of. *There* she cannot be justified. I am glad you saw it all as I did.'

Having formed her mind and gained her affections, he had a good chance of her thinking like him; though at this period, and on this subject, there began now to be some danger of dissimilarity, for he was in a line of admiration of Miss Crawford, which might lead him where Fanny could not follow. Miss Crawford's attractions did not lessen. The harp arrived, and rather added to her beauty, wit, and good humour; for she played with the greatest obligingness, with an expression and taste which were peculiarly becoming, and there was something clever to be said at the close of every air. Edmund was at the Parsonage every day, to be indulged with his favourite instrument: one morning secured an invitation for the next; for the lady could not be unwilling to have a listener, and every thing was soon in a fair train.

A young woman, pretty, lively, with a harp as elegant as herself, and both placed near a window cut down to the ground and opening on a little lawn, surrounded by shrubs in the rich foliage of summer, was enough to catch any man's heart. The season, the scene, the air, were all favourable to tenderness and sentiment. Mrs Grant and her tambour frame were not without their use: it was all in harmony; and as every thing will turn to account when love is once set going, even the sandwich tray, and Dr Grant doing the honours of it, were worth looking at. Without studying the business, however, or knowing what he was about, Edmund was beginning, at the end of a week of such intercourse, to be a good deal in love; and to the credit of the lady it may be added, that, without his being a man of the world or an elder brother, without any of the arts of flattery or the gaieties of small talk, he began to be agreeable to her. She felt it to be so, though she had not foreseen, and could hardly understand it; for he was not pleasant by any common rule; he talked no nonsense; he paid no compliments; his opinions were unbending, his attentions tranquil and simple. There was a charm, perhaps in his sincerity, his steadiness, his integrity, which Miss Crawford might be equal to feel, though not equal to discuss with herself. She did not think very much about it, however: he pleased her for the present; she liked to have him near her; it was enough.

Fanny could not wonder that Edmund was at the Parsonage every morning; she would gladly have been there too, might she have gone in uninvited and unnoticed, to hear the harp; neither could she wonder that, when the evening stroll was over, and the two families parted again, he should think it right to attend Mrs Grant and her sister to their home, while Mr Crawford was devoted to the ladies of the Park; but she thought it a very bad exchange; and if Edmund were not there to mix the wine and water for her, would rather go without it than not. She was a little surprised that he could spend so many hours with Miss Crawford, and not see more of the sort of fault which he had already observed, and of which *she* was almost always reminded by a something of the same nature whenever she was in her company; but so it was. Edmund was fond of speaking to her of Miss Crawford, but he seemed to think it enough that the Admiral had since been spared; and she scrupled to point out her own remarks to him, lest it should appear like ill nature. The first actual pain which Miss Crawford occasioned her was the consequence of an inclination to learn to ride, which the former caught soon after her being settled at Mansfield, from the example of the young ladies at the Park, and which, when Edmund's acquaintance with her increased, led to his encouraging the wish, and the offer of his own quiet mare for the purpose of her first attempts, as the best fitted for a beginner, that either stable could furnish. No pain, no injury, however, was designed by him to his cousin in this offer: *she* was not to lose a day's exercise by it. The mare was only to be taken down to the Parsonage half an hour before her rides were to begin; and Fanny on its being first proposed, so far from feeling slighted, was almost overpowered with gratitude that he should be asking her leave for it.

Miss Crawford made her first essay with great credit to herself, and no inconvenience to Fanny. Edmund, who had taken down the mare and presided at the whole, returned with it in excellent time, before either Fanny or the steady old coachman, who always attended her when she rode without her cousins, were ready to set forward. The second day's trial was not so guiltless. Miss Crawford's enjoyment of riding was such, that she did not know how to leave off. Active and fearless, and, though rather small, strongly made, she seemed formed for a horsewoman; and to the pure genuine pleasure of the exercise, something was probably added in Edmund's attendance and instructions, and something more in the conviction of very much surpassing her sex in general by her early progress, to make her unwilling to dismount. Fanny was ready and waiting and Mrs Norris was beginning to scold her for not being gone, and still no horse was announced, no Edmund appeared. To avoid her aunt, and look for him, she went out.

The houses, though scarcely half a mile apart, were not within sight of each other; but, by walking fifty yards from the hall door, she could look down the park, and command a view of the Parsonage and all its demesnes, gently rising beyond the village road; and in Dr Grant's meadow she immediately saw the group: Edmund and Miss Crawford both on horseback, riding side by side, Dr and Mrs Grant, and Mr Crawford, with two or three grooms, standing about and looking on. A happy party it appeared to her, all interested in one object: cheerful beyond a doubt, for the sound of merriment ascended even to her. It was a sound which did not make *her* cheerful; she wondered that Edmund should forget her, and felt a pang. She could not turn her eyes from the meadow; she could not help watching all that passed. At first Miss Crawford and her companion made the circuit of the field, which was not small, at a foot's pace; then, at *her* apparent suggestion, they rose into a canter; and to Fanny's timid nature it was most astonishing to see how well she sat. After a few minutes, they stopped entirely. Edmund was close to her; he was speaking to her; he was evidently directing her management of the bridle; he had hold of her hand; she saw it, or the imagination supplied what the eye could not reach. She must not wonder at all this; what could be more natural than that Edmund should be making himself useful, and proving his good nature by any one? She could not but think, indeed, that Mr Crawford might as well have saved him the trouble; that it would have been particularly proper and becoming in a brother to have done it himself; but Mr Crawford, with all his boasted good-nature, and all his coachmanship, probably knew nothing of the matter, and had no active kindness in comparison of Edmund. She began to think it rather hard upon the mare to have such double duty; if she were forgotten, the poor mare should be remembered.

Her feelings for one and the other were soon a little tranquillised, by seeing the party in the meadow disperse, and Miss Crawford still on horseback, but attended by Edmund on foot, pass through a gate into the lane, and so into the park, and make towards the spot where she stood. She began then to be afraid of appearing rude and impatient; and walked to meet them with a great anxiety to avoid the suspicion.

'My dear Miss Price,' said Miss Crawford, as soon as she was at all within hearing. 'I am come to make my own apologies for keeping you waiting; but I have nothing in the world to say for myself. I knew it was very late, and that I was behaving extremely ill; and therefore, if you please, you must forgive me. Selfishness must always be forgiven, you know, because there is no hope of a cure.'

Fanny's answer was extremely civil, and Edmund added his conviction that she could be in no hurry. 'For there is more than time enough for my cousin to ride twice as far as she ever goes,' said he, 'and you have been promoting her comfort by preventing her from setting off half-an-hour sooner; clouds are now coming up, and she will not suffer from the heat as she would have done then. I wish *you* may not be fatigued by so much exercise. I wish you had saved yourself this walk home.'

'No part of it fatigues me but getting off this horse, I assure you,' said she, as she sprang down with his help; 'I am very strong. Nothing ever fatigues me, but doing what I do not like. Miss Price, I give way to you with a very bad grace; but I sincerely hope you will have a pleasant ride, and that I may have nothing but good to hear of this dear, delightful, beautiful animal.'

The old coachman, who had been waiting about with his own horse, now joining them, Fanny was lifted on hers, and they set off across another part of the park; her feelings of discomfort not lightened by seeing, as she looked back, that the others were walking down the hill together to the village; nor did her attendant do her much good by his comments on Miss Crawford's great cleverness as a horsewoman, which he had been watching with an interest almost equal to her own.

'It is a pleasure to see a lady with such a good heart for riding!' said he. 'I never see one sit a horse better. She did not seem to have thought of fear. Very different from you, miss, when you first began, six years ago come next Easter. Lord bless you! how you did tremble when Sir Thomas first had you put on!'

In the drawing-room Miss Crawford was also celebrated. Her merit in being gifted by Nature with strength and courage, was fully appreciated by the Miss Bertrams; her delight in riding was like their own; her early excellence in it was like their own, and they had great pleasure in praising it.

'I was sure she would ride well,' said Julia; 'she has the make for it. Her figure is as neat as her brother's.'

'Yes,' added Maria, 'and her spirits are as good, and she has the same energy of character. I cannot but think that good horsemanship has a great deal to do with the mind.'

When they parted at night, Edmund asked Fanny whether she meant to ride the next day.

'No, I do not know – not if you want the mare,' was her answer. 'I do not want her at all for myself,' said he; 'but whenever you are next inclined to stay at home, I think Miss Crawford would be glad to have her a longer time – for a whole morning, in short. She has a great desire to get as far as Mansfield Common; Mrs Grant has been telling her of its fine views, and I have no doubt of her being perfectly equal to it. But any morning will do for this. She would be extremely sorry to interfere with you. It would be very wrong if she did. *She* rides only for pleasure; *you* for health.'

'I shall not ride to-morrow, certainly,' said Fanny; 'I have been out very often lately, and would rather stay at home. You know I am strong enough now to walk very well.'

Edmund looked pleased, which must be Fanny's comfort, and the ride to Mansfield Common took place the next morning: the party included all the young people but herself, and was much enjoyed at the time, and doubly enjoyed again in the evening discussion. A successful scheme of this sort

There were many other views to be shown

generally brings on another; and the having been to Mansfield Common disposed them all for going somewhere else the day after. There were many other views to be shown; and though the weather was hot, there were shady lanes wherever they wanted to go. A young party is always provided with a shady lane. Four fine mornings successively were spent in this manner, in showing the Crawfords the country, and doing the honours of its finest spots. Everything answered; it was all gaiety and good humour, the heat only supplying inconvenience enough to be talked of with pleasure – till the fourth day, when the happiness of one of the party was exceedingly clouded. Miss Bertram was the one. Edmund and Julia were invited to dine at the Parsonage, and *she* was excluded. It was meant and done by Mrs Grant, with perfect good humour, on Mr Rushworth's account, who was partly expected at the Park that day; but it was felt as a very grievous injury, and her good manners were severely taxed to conceal her vexation and anger till she reached home. As Mr Rushworth did *not* come, the injury was increased, and she had not even the relief of showing her power over him; she could only be sullen to her mother, aunt, and cousin, and throw as great a gloom as possible over their dinner and dessert.

Between ten and eleven, Edmund and Julia walked into the drawing-room, fresh with the evening air, glowing and cheerful, the very reverse of what they found in the three ladies sitting there, for Maria would scarcely raise her eyes from her book, and Lady Bertram was half asleep; and even Mrs Norris discomposed by her niece's ill humour, and having asked one or two questions about the dinner, which were not immediately attended to, seemed almost determined to say no more. For a few minutes, the brother and sister were too eager in their praise of the night and their remarks on the stars, to think beyond themselves; but when the first pause came, Edmund, looking around, said, 'But where is Fanny? Is she gone to bed?'

'No, not that I know of,' replied Mrs Norris; 'she was here a moment ago.'

Her own gentle voice speaking from the other end of the room, which was a very long one, told them that she was on the sofa. Mrs Norris began scolding.

'That is a very foolish trick, Fanny, to be idling away all the evening upon a sofa. Why cannot you come and sit here, and emply yourself as *we* do? If you have no work of your own, I can supply you from the poor basket. There is all the new calico, that was bought last week, not touched yet. I am sure I almost broke my back by cutting it out. You should learn to think of other people; and take my word for it, it is a shocking trick for a young person to be always lolling upon a sofa.'

Before half this was said, Fanny was returned to her seat at the table, and had taken up her work again; and Julia, who was in high good humour, from the pleasures of the day, did her the justice of exclaiming, 'I must say, ma'am, that Fanny is as little upon the sofa as any body in the house.'

'Fanny,' said Edmund, after looking at her attentively, 'I am sure you have the headache.'

She could not deny it, but said it was not very bad.

'I can hardly believe you,' he replied; 'I know your looks too well. How long have you had it?'

'Since a little before dinner. It is nothing but the heat.'

'Did you go out in the heat?'

'Go out! to be sure she did,' said Mrs Norris: 'would you have her stay within such a fine day as this? Were not we *all* out? Even your mother was out to-day for above an hour.'

'Yes, indeed, Edmund,' added her ladyship, who had been thoroughly awakened by Mrs Norris's sharp reprimand to Fanny; 'I was out above an hour. I sat three-quarters of an hour in the flower-garden, while Fanny cut the roses, and very pleasant it was, I assure you, but very hot. It was shady enough in the alcove, but I declare I quite dreaded the coming home again.'

'Fanny has been cutting roses, has she?'

'Yes, and I am afraid they will be the last this year. Poor thing! *She* found it hot enough; but they were so full blown that one could not wait.'

'There was no help for it, certainly,' rejoined Mrs Norris, in a rather softened voice; 'but I question whether her headache might not be caught *then*, sister. There is nothing so likely to give it as standing and stooping in a hot sun; but I dare say it will be well to-morrow. Suppose you let her have your aromatic vinegar; I always forget to have mine filled.'

'She has got it,' said Lady Bertram; 'she has had it ever since she came back from your house the second time.'

'What!' cried Edmund; 'has she been walking as well as cutting roses, walking across the hot park to your house, and doing it twice, ma'am! No wonder her head aches.'

Mrs Norris was talking to Julia, and did not hear.

'I was afraid it would be too much for her,' said Lady Bertram; 'but when the roses were gathered, your aunt wished to have them, and then you know they must be taken home.'

'But were there roses enough to oblige her to go twice?'

'No, but they were to be put into the spare room to dry; and, unluckily, Fanny forgot to lock the door of the room and bring away the key, so she was obliged to go again.'

Edmund got up and walked about the room, saying, 'And could nobody be employed on such an errand but Fanny? Upon my word, ma'am, it has been a very ill-managed business.'

'I am sure I do not know how it was to have been done better,' cried Mrs Norris, unable to be longer deaf; 'unless I had gone myself, indeed, but I cannot be in two places at once; and I was talking to Mr Green at that very time about your mother's dairymaid, by *her* desire, and had promised John Groom to write to Mrs Jefferies about his son, and the poor fellow was waiting for me half an hour. I think nobody can justly accuse me of sparing myself upon any occasion, but really I cannot do every thing at once. And as for Fanny's just stepping down to my house for me – it is not much above a quarter of a mile – I cannot think I was unreasonable to ask it. How often do I pace it three times a day, early and late, aye, and in all weathers too, and say nothing about it?'

'I wish Fanny had half your strength, ma'am.'

'If Fanny would be more regular in her exercise, she would not be knocked up so soon. She has not been out on horseback now this long while, and I am persuaded, that when she does not ride, she ought to walk. If she had been riding before, I should not have asked it of her. But I thought it would rather do her good after being stooping among the roses; for there is nothing so refreshing as a walk after a fatigue of that kind; and though the sun was strong, it was not so very hot. Between ourselves, Edmund,' nodding significantly at his mother, 'it was cutting the roses, and dawdling about in the flower-garden, that did the mischief.'

'I am afraid it was, indeed,' said the more candid Lady Bertram, who had overheard her; 'I am very much afraid she caught the headache there, for the heat was enough to kill anybody. It was as much as I could bear myself. Sitting and calling to pug, and trying to keep him from the flowerbeds, was almost too much for me.'

Edmund said no more to either lady; but going quietly to another table, on which the supper tray yet remained, brought a glass of Madeira to Fanny, and obliged her to drink the greater part. She wished to be able to decline it; but the tears, which a variety of feelings created, made it easier to swallow than to speak.

Vexed as Edmund was with his mother and aunt, he was still more angry with himself. His own forgetfulness of her was worse than any thing which they had done. Nothing of this would have happened had she been properly considered; but she had been left four days together without any choice of companions or exercise, and without any excuse for avoiding whatever her unreasonable aunts might require. He was ashamed to think that for four days together she had not had the power of riding, and very seriously resolved, however unwilling he must be to check a pleasure of Miss Crawford's, that it should never happen again.

Fanny went to bed with her heart as full as on the first evening of her arrival at the Park. The state of her spirits had probably had its share in her indisposition; for she had been feeling neglected and been struggling against discontent and envy for some days past. As she leant on the sofa, to which she had retreated that she might not be seen, the pain of her mind had been much beyond that in her head; and the sudden change which Edmund's kindness had then occasioned, made her hardly know how to support herself.

CHAPTER EIGHT

FANNY'S RIDES RECOMMENCED THE very next day; and as it was a pleasant fresh-feeling morning, less hot than the weather had lately been, Edmund trusted that her losses both of health and pleasure would be soon made good. While she was gone, Mr Rushworth arrived, escorting his mother, who came to be civil and to show her civility especially, in urging the execution of the plan for visiting Sotherton, which had been started a fortnight before, and which, in consequence of her subsequent absence from home, had since lain dormant. Mrs Norris and her nieces were all well pleased with its revival, and an early day was named, and agreed to, provided Mr Crawford should be disengaged; the young ladies did not forget that stipulation, and though Mrs Norris would willingly have answered for his being so, they would neither authorise the liberty, nor run the risk; and at last, on a hint from Miss Bertram, Mr Rushworth discovered that the most proper thing to be done was for him to walk down to the Parsonage directly, and call on Mr Crawford, and inquire whether Wednesday would suit him or not.

Before his return, Mrs Grant and Miss Crawford came in. Having been out some time, and taken a different route to the house, they had not met him. Comfortable hopes, however, were given that he would find Mr Crawford at home. The Sotherton scheme was mentioned of course. It was hardly possible, indeed, that anything else should be talked of, for Mrs Norris was in high spirits about it; and Mrs Rushworth, a well-meaning, civil, prosing, pompous woman, who thought nothing of consequence but as it related to her own and her son's concerns, had not yet given over pressing Lady Bertram to be of the party. Lady Bertram constantly declined it; but her placid manner of refusal made Mrs Rushworth still think she wished to come, till Mrs Norris's more numerous words and louder tone convinced her of the truth.

'The fatigue would be too much for my sister, a great deal too much, I assure you, my dear Mrs Rushworth. Ten miles there, and ten back, you know. You must excuse my sister on this occasion, and accept of our two dear girls and myself without her. Sotherton is the only place that could give her a *wish* to go so far, but it cannot be, indeed. She will have a companion in Fanny Price, you know, so it will all do very well; and as for Edmund, as he is not here to speak for himself, I will answer for his being most happy to join the party. He can go on horseback, you know.'

Mrs Rushworth being obliged to yield to Lady Bertram's staying at home, could only be sorry. 'The loss of her ladyship's company would be a great drawback, and she should have been extremely happy to have seen the young lady too, Miss Price, who had never been at Sotherton yet, and it was a pity she should not see the place.'

'You are very kind, you are all kindness, my dear madam,' cried Mrs Norris; 'but as to Fanny, she will have opportunities in plenty of seeing Sotherton. She has time enough before her; and her going now is quite out of the question. Lady Bertram could not possibly spare her.'

'Oh no! I cannot do without Fanny.'

Mrs Rushworth proceeded next, under the conviction that everybody must be wanting to see Sotherton, to include Miss Crawford in the invitation; and though Mrs Grant, who had not been at the trouble of visiting Mrs Rushworth on her coming into the neighbourhood, civilly declined it on her own account, she was glad to secure any pleasure for her sister; and Mary, properly pressed and persuaded, was not long in accepting her share of the civility. Mr Rushworth came back from the Parsonage successful; and Edmund made his appearance just in time to learn what had been settled for Wednesday, to attend Mrs Rushworth to her carriage, and walk half-way down the park with the two other ladies.

On his return to the breakfast-room, he found Mrs Norris trying to make up her mind as to whether Miss Crawford's being of the party were desirable or not, or whether her brother's barouche would not be full without her. The Miss Bertrams laughed at the idea, assuring her that the barouche would hold four perfectly well, independent of the box, on which *one* might go with him.

'But why is it necessary,' said Edmund, 'that Crawford's carriage, or his *only*, should be employed? Why is no use to be made of my mother's chaise? I could not, when the scheme was first mentioned the other day, understand why a visit from the family were not to be made in the carriage of the family.'

'What!' cried Julia; 'go, boxed up three in a postchaise in this weather, when we may have seats in a barouche! No, my dear Edmund, that will not quite do.'

'Besides,' said Maria, 'I know that Mr Crawford depends upon taking us. After what passed at first, he would claim it as a promise.'

'And, my dear Edmund,' added Mrs Norris, 'taking out *two* carriages when *one* will do, would be trouble for nothing; and, between ourselves, coachman is not very fond of the roads between this and Sotherton; he always complains bitterly of the narrow lanes scratching his carriage, and you know one should not like to have dear Sir Thomas, when he comes home, find all the varnish scratched off.'

'That would not be a very handsome reason for using Mr Crawford's,' said Maria; 'but the truth is, that Wilcox is a stupid old fellow, and does not know how to drive. I will answer for it, that we shall find no inconvenience from narrow roads on Wednesday.'

'There is no hardship, I suppose, nothing unpleasant,' said Edmund, 'in going on the barouche box.'

'Unpleasant!' cried Maria; 'oh dear! I believe it would be generally thought the favourite seat. There can be no comparison as to one's view of the country. Probably Miss Crawford will choose the barouche box herself.'

'There can be no objection, then, to Fanny's going with you; there can be no doubt of your having room for her.'

'Fanny!' repeated Mrs Norris; 'my dear Edmund, there is no idea of her going with us. She stays with her aunt. I told her Mrs Rushworth so. She is not expected.'

'You can have no reason, I imagine, madam,' said he, addressing his mother, 'for wishing Fanny *not* to be of the party, but as it relates to yourself, to your own comfort. If you could do without her, you would not wish to keep her at home?'

'To be sure not, but I *cannot* do without her.'

'You can, if I stay at home with you, as I mean to do.'

There was a general cry out at this. 'Yes,' he continued, 'there is no necessity for my going, and I mean to stay at home. Fanny has a great desire to see Sotherton. I know she wishes it very much. She has not often a gratification of the kind, and I am sure, ma'am, you would be glad to give her the pleasure now?'

'Oh yes! very glad, if your aunt sees no objection.'

Mrs Norris was very ready with the only objection which could remain – their having positively assured Mrs Rushworth that Fanny could not go, and the very strange appearance there would consequently be in taking her, which seemed to her a difficulty quite impossible to be got over. It must have the strangest appearance! It would be something so very unceremonious, so bordering on disrespect for Mrs Rushworth, whose own manners were such a pattern of good breeding and attention, that she really did not feel equal to it. Mrs Norris had no affection for Fanny, and no wish of procuring her pleasure at any time; but her opposition to Edmund *now*, arose more from partiality for her own scheme, because it *was* her own, than from anything else. She felt that she had arranged everything extremely well, and that any alteration must be for the worse. When Edmund, therefore, told her in reply, as he did when she would give him the hearing, that she need not distress herself on Mrs Rushworth's account, because he had taken the opportunity as he walked with her through the hall of mentioning Miss Price as one who would probably be of the party, and had directly received a very sufficient invitation for his cousin, Mrs Norris was too much vexed to submit with a very good grace, and would only say, 'Very well, very well, just as you choose, settle it your own way, I am sure I do not care about it.'

'It seems very odd,' said Maria, 'that you should be staying at home instead of Fanny.'

'I am sure she ought to be very much obliged to you,' added Julia, hastily leaving the room as she spoke, from a consciousness that she ought to offer to stay at home herself.

'Fanny will feel quite as grateful as the occasion requires,' was Edmund's reply only, and the subject dropped.

Fanny's gratitude, when she heard the plan, was in fact much greater than her pleasure. She felt Edmund's kindness with all, and more than all, the sensibility which he, unsuspicious of her fond attachment, could be aware of; but that he should forego any enjoyment on her account gave her pain, and her own satisfaction in seeing Sotherton would be nothing without him.

The next meeting of the two Mansfield families produced another alteration in the plan, and one that was admitted with general approbation. Mrs Grant offered herself as companion for the day to Lady Bertram in lieu of her son, and Dr Grant was to join them at dinner. Lady Bertram was very well pleased to have it so, and the young ladies were in spirits again. Even Edmund was very thankful for an arrangement which restored him to his share of the party; and Mrs Norris thought it an excellent plan, and had it at her tongue's end, and was on the point of proposing it, when Mrs Grant spoke.

Wednesday was fine, and soon after breakfast the barouche arrived, Mr Crawford driving his sisters; and as everybody was ready, there was nothing to be done but for Mrs Grant to alight, and the others to take their places. The place of all places, the envied seat, the post of honour, was unappropriated. To whose happy lot was it to fall? While each of the Miss Bertrams were meditating how best, and with the most appearance of obliging the others, to secure it, the matter was settled by Mrs Grant's saying, as she stepped from the carriage, 'As there are five of you, it will be better that one should sit with Henry; and as you were saying lately that you wished you could drive, Julia, I think this will be a good opportunity for you to take a lesson.'

Happy Julia! Unhappy Maria! The former was on the barouche-box in a moment, the latter took her seat within, in gloom and mortification; and the carriage drove off amid the good wishes of the two remaining ladies, and the barking of pug in his mistress's arms.

Their road was through a pleasant country; and Fanny, whose rides had never been extensive, was soon beyond her knowledge, and was very happy in observing all that was new, and admiring all that was pretty. She was not often invited to join in the conversation of the others, nor did she desire it. Her own thoughts and reflections were habitually her best companions; and, in observing the appearance of the country, the bearings of the roads, the difference of soil, the state of the harvest, the cottages, the cattle, the children, she found entertainment that could only have been heightened by having Edmund to speak of what she felt. That was the only point of resemblance between her and the lady who sat by her; in everything but a value for Edmund, Miss Crawford was very unlike her. She had none of Fanny's delicacy of taste, of mind, of feeling; she saw Nature, inanimate Nature, with little observation; her attention was all for men and women, her talents for the light and lively. In looking back after Edmund, however, when there was any stretch of road behind them, or when he gained on them in ascending a considerable hill, they were united, and a 'there he is' broke at the same moment from them both, more than once.

For the first seven miles Miss Bertram had very little real comfort; her prospect always ended in Mr Crawford and her sister sitting side by side, full

Their road was through a pleasant country

of conversation and merriment; and to see only his expressive profile as he turned with a smile to Julia, or to catch the laugh of the other, was a perpetual source of irritation, which her own sense of propriety could but just smooth over. When Julia looked back, it was with a countenance of delight, and whenever she spoke to them, it was in the highest spirits: 'her view of the country was charming, she wished they could all see it,' etc.; but her only offer of exchange was addressed to Miss Crawford, as they gained the summit of a long hill, and was not more inviting than this: 'Here is a fine burst of country. I wish you had my seat, but I dare say you will not take it, let me press you ever so much'; and Miss Crawford could hardly answer, before they were moving again at a good pace.

When they came within the influence of Sotherton associations, it was better for Miss Bertram, who might be said to have two strings to her bow. She had Rushworth-feelings, and Crawford-feelings, and in the vicinity of Sotherton, the former had considerable effect. Mr Rushworth's consequence was hers. She could not tell Miss Crawford that 'those woods belonged to Sotherton'; she could not carelessly observe that 'she believed that it was now all Mr Rushworth's property on each side of the road,' without elation of heart; and it was a pleasure to increase with their approach to the capital freehold mansion, and ancient manorial residence of the family, with all its rights of court-leet and court-baron.

'Now, we shall have no more rough road, Miss Crawford; our difficulties are over. The rest of the way is such as it ought to be. Mr Rushworth has made it since he succeeded to the estate. Here begins the village. Those cottages are really a disgrace. The church spire is reckoned remarkably handsome. I am glad the church is not so close to the great house as often happens in old places. The annoyance of the bells must be terrible. There is the Parsonage; a tidy-looking house, and I understand the clergyman and his wife are very decent people. Those are almshouses, built by some of the family. To the right is the steward's house; he is a very respectable man. Now we are coming to the lodge-gates; but we have nearly a mile through the park still. It is not ugly, you see, at this end; there is some fine timber, but the situation of the house is dreadful. We go down hill to it for half a mile, and it is a pity, for it would not be an ill-looking place if it had a better approach.'

Miss Crawford was not slow to admire; she pretty well guessed Miss Bertram's feelings, and made it a point of honour to promote her enjoyment to the utmost. Mrs Norris was all delight and volubility; and even Fanny had something to say in admiration, and might be heard with complacency. Her eye was eagerly taking in every thing within her reach; and after being at some pains to get a view of the house, and observing that 'it was a sort of building which she could not look at but with respect,' she added: 'Now, where is the avenue? The house fronts the east, I perceive. The avenue, therefore, must be at the back of it. Mr Rushworth talked of the west front.'

'Yes, it is exactly behind the house; begins at a little distance, and ascends for half a mile to the extremity of the grounds. You may see something of it here – something of the more distant trees. It is oak entirely.'

Miss Bertram could now speak with decided information of what she had known nothing about when Mr Rushworth had asked her opinion; and her spirits were in as happy a flutter as vanity and pride could furnish, when they drove up to the spacious stone steps before the principal entrance.

CHAPTER NINE

MR RUSHWORTH WAS AT THE DOOR to receive his fair lady; and the whole party were welcomed by him with due attention. In the drawing-room they were met with equal cordiality by the mother, and Miss Bertram had all the distinction with each that she could wish. After the business of arriving was over, it was first necessary to eat, and the doors were thrown open to admit them through one or two intermediate rooms into the appointed dining-parlour, where a collation was prepared with abundance and elegance. Much was said, and much was ate, and all went well. The particular object of the day was then considered. How would Mr Crawford like, in what manner would he choose, to take a survey of the grounds? Mr Rushworth mentioned his curricle, Mr Crawford suggested the greater desirableness of some carriage which might convey more than two. 'To be depriving themselves of the advantage of other eyes and other judgments, might be an evil even beyond the loss of present pleasure.'

Mrs Rushworth proposed that the chaise should be taken also; but this was scarcely received as an amendment: the young ladies neither smiled nor spoke. Her next proposition, of showing the house to such of them as had not been before, was more acceptable, for Miss Bertram was pleased to have its size displayed, and all were glad to be doing something.

The whole party rose accordingly, and under Mrs Rushworth's guidance were shown through a number of rooms, all lofty, and many large, and amply furnished in the taste of fifty years back, with shining floors, solid mahogany, rich damask, marble, gilding and carving, each handsome in its way. Of pictures there were abundance, and some few good, but the larger part were family portraits, no longer anything to anybody except Mrs Rushworth, who had been at great pains to learn all that the housekeeper could teach, and was now almost equally well qualified to show the house. On the present occasion, she addressed herself chiefly to Miss Crawford and Fanny, but there was no comparison in the willingness of their attention; for Miss Crawford, who had seen scores of great houses, and cared for none of them, had only the appearance of civilly listening, while Fanny, to whom everything was almost as interesting as it was new, attended with unaffected earnestness to all that Mrs Rushworth could relate of the family in former times, its rise and grandeur, regal visits and loyal efforts, delighted to connect anything with history already known, or warm her imagination with scenes of the past.

The situation of the house excluded the possibility of much prospect from any of the rooms; and while Fanny and some of the others were attending Mrs Rushworth, Henry Crawford was looking grave and shaking his head at the windows. Every room on the west front looked across a lawn to the beginning of the avenue immediately beyond tall iron palisades and gates.

Having visited many more rooms than could be supposed to be of any other use than to contribute to the window tax, and find employment for housemaids, 'Now,' said Mrs Rushworth, 'we are coming to the chapel, which properly we ought to enter from above, and look down upon; but as we are quite among friends, I will take you in this way, if you will excuse me.'

They entered. Fanny's imagination had prepared her for something grander than a mere spacious, oblong room, fitted up for the purpose of devotion; with nothing more striking or more solemn than the profusion of mahogany, and the crimson velvet cushions appearing over the ledge of the family gallery above. 'I am disappointed,' said she, in a low voice to Edmund. 'This is not my idea of a chapel. There is nothing awful here, nothing melancholy, nothing grand. Here are no aisles, no arches, no inscriptions, no banners. No banners, cousin, to be "blown by the night wind of heaven." No signs that a "Scottish monarch sleeps below."'

'You forget, Fanny, how lately all this has been built, and for how confined a purpose, compared with the old chapels of castles and monasteries. It was only for the private use of the family. They have been buried, I suppose, in the parish church. *There* you must look for the banners and the achievements.'

'It was foolish of me not to think of all that; but I am disappointed.'

Mrs Rushworth began her relation. 'This chapel was fitted up as you see it, in James the Second's time. Before that period, as I understand, the pews were only wainscot; and there is some reason to think that the linings and cushions of the pulpit and family seat were only purple cloth; but this is not quite certain. It is a handsome chapel, and was formerly in constant use both morning and evening. Prayers were always read in it by the domestic chaplain, within the memory of many; but the late Mr Rushworth left it off.'

'Every generation has its improvements,' said Miss Crawford, with a smile, to Edmund.

Mrs Rushworth was gone to repeat her lesson to Mr Crawford; and Edmund, Fanny and Miss Crawford remained in a cluster together.

'It is a pity,' cried Fanny, 'that the custom should have been discontinued. It was a valuable part of former times. There is something in a chapel and chaplain so much in character with a great house, with one's ideas of what such a household should be! A whole family assembling regularly for the purpose of prayer is fine!'

'Very fine, indeed,' said Miss Crawford, laughing. 'It must do the heads of the family a great deal of good to force all the poor housemaids and footmen to leave business and pleasure, and say their prayers here twice a day, while they are inventing excuses themselves for staying away.'

'*That* is hardly Fanny's idea of a family assembling,' said Edmund. 'If the master and mistress do *not* attend themselves, there must be more harm than good in the custom.'

'At any rate, it is safer to leave people to their own devices on such subjects. Everybody likes to go their own way – to choose their own time and manner of devotion. The obligation of attendance, the formality, the restraint, the length of time – altogether it is a formidable thing, and what nobody likes; and if the good people who used to kneel and gape in that gallery could have foreseen that the time would ever come when men and women might lie another ten minutes in bed when they woke with a headache, without danger of reprobation because chapel was missed, they would have jumped with joy and envy. Cannot you imagine with what unwilling feelings the former belles of the house of Rushworth did many a time repair to this chapel? The young Mrs Eleanors and Mrs Bridgets – starched up into seeming piety, but with heads full of something very different – especially if the poor chaplain were not worth looking at – and, in those days, I fancy parsons were very inferior even to what they are now.'

For a few moments she was unanswered. Fanny coloured and looked at Edmund, but felt too angry for speech; and *he* needed a little recollection before he could say, 'Your lively mind can hardly be serious even on serious subjects. You have given us an amusing sketch, and human nature cannot say it was not so. We must all feel *at times* the difficulty of fixing our thoughts as we could wish; but if you are supposing it a frequent thing, that is to say, a weakness grown into a habit from neglect, what could be expected from the *private* devotions of such persons? Do you think the minds which are suffered, which are indulged in wanderings in a chapel, would be more collected in a closet?'

'Yes, very likely. They would have two chances at least in their favour. There would be less to distract the attention from without, and it would not be tried so long.'

'The mind which does not struggle against itself under *one* circumstance, would find objects to distract it in the *other*, I believe; and the influence of the place and of example may often rouse better feelings than are begun with. The greater length of the service, however, I admit to be sometimes too hard a stretch upon the mind. One wishes it were not so; but I have not yet left Oxford long enough to forget what chapel prayers are.'

While this was passing, the rest of the party being scattered about the chapel, Julia called Mr Crawford's attention to her sister, by saying, 'Do look at Mr Rushworth and Maria, standing side by side, exactly as if the ceremony were going to be performed. Have not they completely the air of it?'

Mr Crawford smiled his acquiescence, and stepping forward to Maria, said, in a voice which she only could hear, 'I do not like to see Miss Bertram so near the altar.'

Starting, the lady instinctively moved a step or two, but recovering herself in a moment, affected to laugh, and asked him in a tone not much louder, 'If he would give her away?'

'I am afraid I should do it very awkwardly,' was his reply, with a look of meaning.

Julia, joining them at the moment, carried on the joke. 'Upon my word, it is really a pity that it should not take place directly, if we had but a proper licence, for here we are all together, and nothing in the world could be more snug and pleasant.' And she talked and laughed about it with so little caution, as to catch the comprehension of Mr Rushworth and his mother, and expose her sister to the whispered gallantries of her lover, while Mrs Rushworth spoke with proper smiles and dignity of its being a most happy event to her whenever it took place.

'If Edmund were but in orders!' cried Julia, and running to where he stood with Miss Crawford and Fanny: 'My dear Edmund, if you were but in orders now, you might perform the ceremony directly. How unlucky that you are not ordained; Mr Rushworth and Maria are quite ready.'

Miss Crawford's countenance, as Julia spoke, might have amused a disinterested observer. She looked almost aghast under the new idea she was receiving. Fanny pitied her. 'How distressed she will be at what she said just now,' passed across her mind.

'Ordained!' said Miss Crawford; 'what, are you to be a clergyman?'

'Yes; I shall take orders soon after my father's return; probably at Christmas.'

Miss Crawford rallying her spirits, and recovering her complexion, replied only, 'If I known this before, I would have spoken of the cloth with more respect,' and turned the subject.

The chapel was soon afterwards left to the silence and stillness which reigned in it, with few interruptions, throughout the year. Miss Bertram, displeased with her sister, led the way, and all seemed to feel that they had been there long enough.

The lower part of the house had been now entirely shown, and Mrs Rushworth, never weary in the cause, would have proceeded towards the principal staircase, and taken them through all the rooms above, if her son had not interposed with a doubt of there being time enough. 'For if,' said he, with a sort of self-evident proposition which many a clearer head does not always avoid, 'we are *too long* going over the house, we shall not have time for what is to be done out of doors. It is past two, and we are to dine at five.'

Mrs Rushworth submitted; and the question of surveying the grounds with the who and the how was likely to be more fully agitated, and Mrs Norris was beginning to arrange by what junction of carriages and horses most could be done, when the young people, meeting with an outward door, temptingly open on a flight of steps which led immediately to turf and shrubs, and all the sweets of pleasure-grounds, as by one impulse, one wish for air and liberty, all walked out.

'Suppose we turn down here for the present,' said Mrs Rushworth, civilly taking the hint and following them. 'Here are the greatest number of our plants, and here are the curious pheasants.'

'Query,' said Mr Crawford, looking round him, 'whether we may not find something to employ us here, before we go further? I see walls of great promise. Mr Rushworth, shall we summon a council on this lawn?'

'James,' said Mrs Rushworth to her son, 'I believe the wilderness will be new to all the party. The Miss Bertrams have never seen the wilderness yet.'

No objection was made, but for some time there seemed no inclination to move in any plan, or to any distance. All were attracted at first by the plants or the pheasants, and all dispersed about in happy independence. Mr Crawford was the first to move forward, to examine the capabilities of that end of the house. The lawn, bounded on each side by a high wall, contained beyond the first planted area a bowling-green, and beyond the bowling-green a long terrace walk, backed by iron palisades, and commanding a view over them into the tops of the trees of the wilderness immediately adjoining. It was a good spot for fault-finding. Mr Crawford was soon followed by Miss Bertram and Mr Rushworth; and when, after a little time, the others began to form into parties, these three were found in busy consultation on the terrace by Edmund, Miss Crawford, and Fanny, who seemed as naturally to unite, and who, after a short participation of their regrets and difficulties, left them and walked on. The remaining three, Mrs Rushworth, Mrs Norris, and Julia, were still far behind; for Julia, whose happy star no longer prevailed, was obliged to keep by the side of Mrs Rushworth, and restrain her impatient feet to that lady's slow pace, while her aunt, having fallen in with the housekeeper, who was come out to feed the pheasants, was lingering behind in gossip with her. Poor Julia, the only one out of the nine not tolerably satisfied with their lot, was now in a state of complete penance, and as different from the Julia of the barouche-box as could well be imagined. The politeness which she had been brought up to practise as a duty made it impossible for her to escape; while the want of that higher species of self-command, that just consideration of others, that knowledge of her own heart, that principle of right, which had not formed any essential part of her education, made her miserable under it.

'This is insufferably hot,' said Miss Crawford, when they had taken one turn on the terrace, and were drawing a second time to the door in the middle which opened to the wilderness. 'Shall any of us object to being comfortable? Here is a nice little wood, if one can but get into it. What happiness if the door should not be locked! But of course it is; for in these great places the gardeners are the only people who can go where they like.'

The door, however, proved not to be locked, and they were all agreed in turning joyfully through it, and leaving the unmitigated glare of day behind. A considerable flight of steps landed them in the wilderness, which was a planted wood of about two acres, and though chiefly of larch and laurel, and beech cut down, and though laid out with too much regularity, was darkness and shade, and natural beauty, compared with the bowling-green and the terrace. They all felt the refreshment of it, and for some time could only walk and admire. At length, after a short pause, Miss Crawford began with: 'So you are to be a clergyman, Mr Bertram. This is rather a surprise to me.'

'Why should it surprise you? You must suppose me designed for some profession, and might perceive that I am neither a lawyer, nor a soldier, nor a sailor.'

'Very true; but, in short, it had not occurred to me. And you know there is generally an uncle or a grandfather to leave a fortune to the second son.'

'A very praiseworthy practice,' said Edmund, 'but not quite universal. I am one of the exceptions, and *being* one, must do something for myself.'

'But why are you to be a clergyman? I thought *that* was always the lot of the youngest, where there were many to choose before him.'

'Do you think the church itself never chosen, then?'

'*Never* is a black word. But yes, in the *never* of conversation, which means *not very often*, I do think it. For what is to be done in the church? Men love to distinguish themselves, and in either of the other lines distinction may be gained, but not in the church. A clergyman is nothing.'

'The *nothing* of conversation has its gradations, I hope, as well as the *never*. A clergyman cannot be high in state or fashion. He must not head mobs, or set the tone in dress. But I cannot call that situation nothing which has the charge of all that is of the first importance to mankind individually or collectively considered, temporally and eternally, which has the guardianship of religion and morals, and consequently of the manners which result from their influence. No one here can call the *office* nothing. If the man who holds it is so, it is by the neglect of his duty, by foregoing its just importance, and stepping out of his place to appear what he ought not to appear.'

'*You* assign greater consequence to the clergyman than one has been used to hear given, or than I can quite comprehend. One does not see much of this influence and importance in society, and how can it be acquired where they are so seldom seen themselves? How can two sermons a week, even supposing them worth hearing, supposing the preacher to have the sense to prefer Blair's to his own, do all that you speak of – govern the conduct and fashion the manners of a large congregation for the rest of the week? One scarcely sees a clergyman out of his pulpit.'

'*You* are speaking of London, *I* am speaking of the nation at large.'

'The metropolis, I imagine, is a pretty fair sample of the rest.'

'Not, I should hope, of the proportion of virtue to vice throughout the kingdom. We do not look in great cities for our best morality. It is not there that respectable people of any denomination can do most good; and it certainly is not there that the influence of the clergy can be most felt. A fine preacher is followed and admired; but it is not in fine preaching only that a good clergyman will be useful in his parish and his neighbourhood, where the parish and neighbourhood are of a size capable of knowing his private character, and observing his general conduct, which in London can rarely be the case. The clergy are lost there in the crowds of their parishioners. They are known to the largest part only as preachers. And with regard to their influencing public matters, Miss Crawford must not misunderstand me, or suppose I mean to call them the arbiters of good breeding, the regulators of refinement and courtesy, the masters of the ceremonies of life. The *manners* I speak of might rather be called *conduct*, perhaps, the result of good principles; the effect, in short, of those doctrines which it is their duty to teach and recommend; and it will, I believe, be everywhere found, that as the clergy are, or are not what they ought to be, so are the rest of the nation.'

'Certainly,' said Fanny, with gentle earnestness.

'There,' cried Miss Crawford, 'you have quite convinced Miss Price already.'

'I wish I could convince Miss Crawford too.'

'I do not think you ever will,' said she, with an arch smile; 'I am just as much surprised now as I was at first that you should intend to take orders. You really are fit for something better. Come, do change your mind. It is not too late. Go into the law.'

'Go into the law! With as much ease as I was told to go into this wilderness.'

'Now you are going to say something about law being the worst wilderness of the two, but I forestall you; remember. I have forestalled you.'

'You need not hurry when the object is only to prevent my saying a bon-mot, for there is not the least wit in my nature. I am a very matter-of-fact, plain-spoken being, and may blunder on the borders of a repartee for half-an-hour together without striking it out.'

A general silence succeeded. Each was thoughtful. Fanny made the first interruption by saying: 'I wonder that I should be tired with only walking in this sweet wood; but the next time we come to a seat, if it is not disagreeable to you, I should be glad to sit down for a little while.'

'My dear Fanny,' cried Edmund, immediately drawing her arm within his, 'how thoughtless I have been! I hope you are not very tired. Perhaps,' turning to Miss Crawford, 'my other companion may do me the honour of taking an arm.'

'Thank you, but I am not at all tired.' She took it, however, as she spoke, and the gratification of having her do so, of feeling such a connection for the first time, made him a little forgetful of Fanny. 'You scarcely touch me,' said he. 'You do not make me of any use. What a difference in the weight of a woman's arm from that of a man! At Oxford I have been a good deal used to have a man lean on me for the length of a street, and you are only a fly in comparison.'

'I am really not tired, which I almost wonder at; for we must have walked at least a mile in this wood. Do not you think we have?'

'Not half a mile,' was his sturdy answer; for he was not yet so much in love as to measure distance, or reckon time, with feminine lawlessness.

'Oh! you do not consider how much we have wound about. We have taken such a very serpentine course, and the wood itself must be half a mile long in a straight line, for we have never seen the end of it yet since we left the first great path.'

'But if you remember, before we left that first great path, we saw directly to the end of it. We looked down the whole vista, and saw it closed by iron gates, and it could not have been more than a furlong in length.'

'Oh! I know nothing of your furlongs, but I am sure it is a very long wood, and that we have been winding in and out ever since we came into it; and therefore, when I say that we have walked a mile in it, I must speak within compass.'

'We have been exactly a quarter of an hour here,' said Edmund, taking out his watch. 'Do you think we are walking four miles an hour?'

'Oh! do not attack me with your watch. A watch is always too fast or too slow. I cannot be dictated to by a watch.'

A few steps further brought them out at the bottom of the very walk they had been talking of; and standing back, well shaded and sheltered, and looking over a ha-ha into the park, was a comfortable-sized bench on which they all sat down.

'I am afraid you are very tired, Fanny,' said Edmund, observing her; 'why would you not speak sooner? This will be a bad day's amusement for you if you are to be knocked up. Every sort of exercise fatigues her so soon, Miss Crawford, except riding.'

'How abominable in you, then, to let me engross her horse as I did all last week! I am ashamed of you and of myself, but it shall never happen again.'

'*Your* attentiveness and consideration make me more sensible of my own neglect. Fanny's interest seems in safer hands with you than with me.'

'That she should be tired now, however, gives me no surprise; for there is nothing in the course of one's duties so fatiguing as what we have been doing this morning: seeing a great house, dawdling from one room to another, straining one's eyes and one's attention, hearing what one does not understand, admiring what one does not care for. It is generally allowed to be the greatest bore in the world, and Miss Price has found it so, though she did not know it.'

'I shall soon be rested,' said Fanny; 'to sit in the shade on a fine day, and look upon verdure, is the most perfect refreshment.'

After sitting a little while, Miss Crawford was up again. 'I must move,' said she, 'resting fatigues me. I have looked across the ha-ha till I am weary. I must go and look through that iron gate at the same view, without being able to see it so well.'

Edmund left the seat likewise. 'Now, Miss Crawford, if you will look up the walk, you will convince yourself that it cannot be half a mile long, or or half half a mile.'

'It is an immense distance,' said she; 'I see *that* with a glance.'

He still reasoned with her, but in vain. She would not calculate, she would not compare. She would only smile and assert. The greatest degree of rational consistency could not have been more engaging, and they talked with mutual satisfaction. At last it was agreed that they should endeavour to determine the dimensions of the wood by walking a little more about it. They would go to the end of it, in the line they were then in (for there was a straight green walk along the bottom by the side of the ha-ha), and perhaps turn a little way in some other direction, if it seemed likely to assist them, and be back in a few minutes. Fanny said she was rested, and would have moved too, but this was not suffered. Edmund urged her remaining where she was with an earnestness which she could not resist, and she was left on the bench to think with pleasure of her cousin's care, but with great regret that she was not stronger. She watched them till they had turned the corner, and listened till all sound of them had ceased.

CHAPTER TEN

A QUARTER OF AN HOUR, TWENTY MINUTES, passed away, and Fanny was still thinking of Edmund, Miss Crawford, and herself, without interruption from anyone. She began to be surprised at being left so long, and to listen with an anxious desire of hearing their steps and their voices again. She listened, and at length she heard; she heard voices and feet approaching; but she had just satisfied herself that it was not those she wanted, when Miss Bertram, Mr Rushworth, and Mr Crawford, issued from the same path which she had trod herself, and were before her.

'Miss Price all alone!' and 'My dear Fanny, how comes this?' were the first salutations. She told her story. 'Poor dear Fanny,' cried her cousin, 'how ill you have been used by them! You had better have stayed with us.'

Then seating herself with a gentleman on each side, she resumed the conversation which had engaged them before, and discussed the possibility of improvements with much animation. Nothing was fixed on; but Henry Crawford was full of ideas and projects, and, generally speaking, whatever he proposed was immediately approved, first by her, and then by Mr Rushworth, whose principal business seemed to be to hear the others, and who scarcely risked an original thought of his own beyond a wish that they had seen his friend Smith's place.

After some minutes spent in this way, Miss Bertram, observing the iron gate, expressed a wish of passing through it into the park, that their views and their plans might be more comprehensive. It was the very thing of all others to be wished, it was the best, it was the only way of proceeding with any advantage, in Henry Crawford's opinion, and he directly saw a knoll not half a mile off, which would give them exactly the requisite command of the house. Go therefore they must to that knoll, and through that gate; but the gate was locked. Mr Rushworth wished he had brought the key; he had been very near thinking whether he should not bring the key; he was determined he would never come without the key again; but still this did not remove the present evil. They could not get through; and as Miss Bertram's inclination for so doing did by no means lessen, it ended in Mr

Rushworth's declaring outright that he would go and fetch the key. He set off accordingly.

'It is undoubtedly the best thing we can do now, as we are so far from the house already,' said Mr Crawford, when he was gone.

'Yes, there is nothing else to be done. But now, sincerely, do not you find the place altogether worse than you expected?'

'No, indeed, far otherwise. I find it better, grander, more complete in its style, though that style may not be the best. And to tell you the truth,' speaking rather lower, 'I do not think that *I* shall ever see Sotherton again with so much pleasure as I do now. Another summer will hardly improve it to me.'

After a moment's embarrassment the lady replied: 'You are too much a man of the world not to see with the eyes of the world. If other people think Sotherton improved, I have no doubt that you will.'

'I am afraid I am not quite so much the man of the world as might be good for me in some points. My feelings are not quite so evanescent, nor my memory of the past under such easy dominion as one finds to be the case with men of the world.'

This was followed by a short silence. Miss Bertram began again. 'You seemed to enjoy your drive here very much this morning. I was glad to see you so well entertained. You and Julia were laughing the whole way.'

'Were we? Yes, I believe we were; but I have not the least recollection at what. Oh! I believe I was relating to her some ridiculous stories of an old Irish groom of my uncle's. Your sister loves to laugh.'

'You think her more lighthearted than I am.'

'More easily amused,' he replied, 'consequently, you know,' smiling, 'better company. I could not have hoped to entertain *you* with Irish anecdotes during a ten miles' drive.'

'Naturally, I believe, I am as lively as Julia, but I have more to think of now.'

'You have, undoubtedly; and there are situations in which very high spirits would denote insensibility. Your prospects, however, are too fair to justify want of spirits. You have a very smiling scene before you.'

'Do you mean literally or figuratively? Literally, I conclude. Yes, certainly the sun shines, and the park looks very cheerful. But unluckily that iron gate, that ha-ha, give me a feeling of restraint and hardship. "I cannot get out," as the starling said.' As she spoke, and it was with expression, she walked to the gate: he followed her. 'Mr Rushworth is so long fetching this key!'

'And for the world you would not get out without the key and without Mr Rushworth's authority and protection, or I think you might with little difficulty pass round the edge of the gate, here, with my assistance; I think it might be done, if you really wished to be more at large, and could allow yourself to think it not prohibited.'

'Prohibited! Nonsense! I certainly can get out that way, and I will. Mr Rushworth will be here in a moment, you know; we shall not be out of sight.'

'Or if we are, Miss Price will be so good as to tell him he will find us near that knoll: the grove of oak on the knoll.'

Fanny, feeling all this to be wrong, could not help making an effort to prevent it. 'You will hurt yourself against those spikes; you will tear your gown; you will be in danger of slipping into the ha-ha. You had better not go.'

Her cousin was safe on the other side while these words were spoken, and, smiling with all the good humour of success, she said: 'Thank you, my dear Fanny, but I and my gown are alive and well, and so good-bye.'

Fanny was again left to her solitude, and with no increase of pleasant feelings, for she was sorry for almost all that she had seen and heard, astonished at Miss Bertram, and angry with Mr Crawford. By taking a circuitous route, and, as it appeared to her, very unreasonable direction to the knoll, they were soon beyond her eye; and for some minutes longer she remained without sight or sound of any companion. She seemed to have the little wood all to herself. She could almost have thought that Edmund and Miss Crawford had left it, but that it was impossible for Edmund to forget her so entirely.

She was again roused from disagreeable musings by sudden footsteps: somebody was coming at a quick pace down the principal walk. She expected Mr Rushworth, but it was Julia, who, hot and out of breath, and with a look of disappointment, cried out on seeing her: 'Heyday! Where are the others? I thought Maria and Mr Crawford were with you.'

Fanny explained.

'A pretty trick, upon my word! I cannot see them anywhere,' looking eagerly into the park. 'But they cannot be very far off, and I think I am equal to as much as Maria, even without help.'

'But, Julia, Mr Rushworth will be here in a moment with the key. Do wait for Mr Rushworth.'

'Not I, indeed. I have had enough of the family for one morning. Why, child, I have but this moment escaped from his horrible mother. Such a penance as I have been enduring, while you were sitting here so composed and so happy! It might have been as well, perhaps, if you had been in my place, but you always contrive to keep out of these scrapes.'

This was a most unjust reflection, but Fanny could allow for it, and let it pass: Julia was vexed, and her temper was hasty; but she felt that it would not last, and therefore taking no notice, only asked her if she had not seen Mr Rushworth.

'Yes, yes, we saw him. He was posting away as if upon life and death, and could but just spare time to tell us his errand, and where you all were.'

'It is a pity he should have so much trouble for nothing.'

'*That* is Miss Maria's concern. I am not obliged to punish myself for *her* sins. The mother I could not avoid, as long as my tiresome aunt was dancing about with the housekeeper, but the son I *can* get away from.'

And she immediately scrambled across the fence, and walked away, not attending to Fanny's last question of whether she had seen any thing of Miss Crawford and Edmund. The sort of dread in which Fanny now sat of seeing Mr Rushworth, prevented her thinking so much of their continued absence, however, as she might have done. She felt that he had been very ill used, and was quite unhappy in having to communicate what had passed. He joined her within five minutes after Julia's exit; though she made the best of the story, he was evidently mortified and displeased in no common degree. At first he scarcely said any thing; his looks only expressed his extreme surprise and vexation, and he walked to the gate and stood there, without seeming to know what to do.

'They desired me to stay; my cousin Maria charged me to say that you would find them at that knoll, or thereabouts.'

'I do not believe I shall go any further,' said he, sullenly; 'I see nothing of them. By the time I get to the knoll, they may be gone some where else. I have had walking enough.'

And he sat down with a most gloomy countenance by Fanny.

'I am very sorry,' said she; 'it is very unlucky.' And she longed to be able to say some thing more to the purpose.

After an interval of silence, 'I think they might as well have stayed for me,' said he.

'Miss Bertram thought you would follow her.'

'I should not have had to follow her if she had stayed.'

This could not be denied, and Fanny was silenced. After another pause, he went on: 'Pray, Miss Price, are you such a great admirer of this Mr Crawford as some people are? For my part, I can see nothing in him.'

'I do not think him at all handsome.'

'Handsome! Nobody can call such an undersized man handsome. He is not five foot nine. I should not wonder if he was not more than five foot eight. I think he is an ill-looking fellow. In my opinion, these Crawfords are no addition at all. We did very well without them.'

A small sigh escaped Fanny here, and she did not know how to contradict him.

'If I had made any difficulty about fetching the key, there might have been some excuse, but I went the very moment she said she wanted it.'

'Nothing could be more obliging than your manner, I am sure, and I dare say you walked as fast as you could; but still it is some distance, you know, from this spot, to the house, quite into the house; and when people are waiting they are bad judges of time, and every half minute seems like five.'

He got up and walked to the gate again, and 'wished he had had the key about him at the time.' Fanny thought she discerned in his standing there an indication of relenting, which encouraged her to another attempt, and she said, therefore: 'It is a pity you should not join them. They expected to have a better view of the house from that part of the park, and will be thinking how it may be improved; and nothing of that sort, you know, can be settled without you.'

She found herself more successful in sending away, than in retaining a companion. Mr Rushworth was worked on. 'Well,' said he, 'if you really think I had better go: it would be foolish to bring the key for nothing.' And letting himself out, he walked off without further ceremony.

Fanny's thoughts were now all engrossed by the two who had left her so long ago, and getting quite impatient, she resolved to go in search of them. She followed their steps along the bottom walk, and had just turned up into another, when the voice and the laugh of Miss Crawford once more caught her ear; the sound approached, and a few more windings brought them before her. They were just returned into the wilderness from the park, to which a side gate, not fastened, had tempted them very soon after their leaving her, and they had been across a portion of the park into the very avenue which Fanny had been hoping the whole morning to reach at last, and had been sitting down under one of the trees. This was their history. It was evident that they had been spending their time pleasantly, and were not aware of the length of their absence. Fanny's best consolation was in being assured that Edmund had wished for her very much, and that he should certainly have come back for her, had she not been tired already; but this was not quite sufficient to do away with the pain of having been left a whole hour, when he had talked of only a few minutes, nor to banish the sort of curiosity she felt, to know what they had been conversing about all that time; and the result of the whole was to her disappointment and depression, as they prepared by general agreement to return to the house.

On reaching the bottom of the steps to the terrace, Mrs Rushworth and Mrs Norris presented themselves at the top, just ready for the wilderness, at the end of an hour and a half from their leaving the house. Mrs Norris had been too well employed to move faster. Whatever cross accidents had occurred to intercept the pleasures of her nieces, she had found a morning of complete enjoyment; for the housekeeper, after a great many courtesies on

Convinced him it was an ague, and promised him a charm for it

the subject of pheasants, had taken her to the dairy, told her all about their cows, and given her the receipt for a famous cream cheese; and since Julia's leaving them, they had been met by the gardener, with whom she had made a most satisfactory acquaintance, for she had set him right as to his grandson's illness, convinced him that it was an ague, and promised him a charm for it; and he, in return, had shown her all his choicest nursery of plants, and actually presented her with a very curious specimen of heath.

On this rencontre they all returned to the house together, there to lounge away the time as they could with sofas, and chit-chat, and *Quarterly Reviews*, till the return of the others, and the arrival of dinner. It was late before the Miss Bertrams and the two gentlemen came in, and their ramble did not appear to have been more than partially agreeable, or at all productive of anything useful with regard to the object of the day. By their own accounts they had been all walking after each other, and the junction which had taken place at last seemed, to Fanny's observation, to have been as much too late for re-establishing harmony, as it confessedly had been for determining on any alteration. She felt, as she looked at Julia and Mr Rushworth, that hers was not the only dissatisfied bosom amongst them; there was gloom on the face of each. Mr Crawford and Miss Bertram were much more gay, and she thought that he was taking particular pains, during dinner, to do away any little resentment of the other two, and restore general good humour.

Dinner was soon followed by tea and coffee, a ten miles' drive home allowed no waste of hours; and from the time of their sitting down to table, it was a quick succession of busy nothings till the carriage came to the door, and Mrs Norris, having fidgeted about, and obtained a few pheasants' eggs and a cream cheese from the housekeeper, and made abundance of civil speeches to Mrs Rushworth, was ready to lead the way. At the same moment, Mr Crawford, approaching Julia, said: 'I hope I am not to lose my companion, unless she is afraid of the evening air in so exposed a seat.' The request had not been foreseen, but was very graciously received, and Julia's day was likely to end almost as well as it began. Miss Bertram had made up her mind to something different, and was a little disappointed; but her conviction of being really the one preferred comforted her under it, and enabled her to receive Mr Rushworth's parting attentions as she ought. He was certainly better pleased to hand her into the barouche than to assist her in ascending the box, and his complacency seemed confirmed by the arrangement.

'Well, Fanny, this has been a fine day for you, upon my word,' said Mrs Norris, as they drove through the park. 'Nothing but pleasure from beginning to end! I am sure you ought to be very much obliged to your Aunt Bertram and me, for contriving to let you go. A pretty good day's amusement you have had!'

Maria was just discontented enough to say directly: 'I think *you* have done pretty well yourself, ma'am. Your lap seems full of good things, and here is a basket of something between us, which has been knocking my elbow unmercifully.'

'My dear, it is only a beautiful little heath, which that nice old gardener would make me take; but if it is in your way, I will have it in my lap directly. There, Fanny, you shall carry that parcel for me; take great care of it; do not let it fall; it is a cream cheese, just like the excellent one we had at dinner. Nothing would satisfy that good old Mrs Whitaker, but my taking one of the cheeses. I stood out as long as I could, till the tears almost came into her eyes, and I knew it was just the sort that my sister would be delighted with.

That Mrs Whitaker is a treasure! She was quite shocked when I asked her whether wine was allowed at the second table, and she has turned away two housemaids for wearing white gowns. Take care of the cheese, Fanny. Now I can manage the other parcel and the basket very well.'

'What else have you been spunging?' said Maria, half pleased that Sotherton should be so complimented.

'Spunging, my dear! It is nothing but four of those beautiful pheasants' eggs, which Mrs Whitaker would quite force upon me; she would not take a denial. She said it must be such an amusement to me, as she understood I lived quite alone, to have a few living creatures of that sort; and so to be sure it will. I shall get the dairymaid to set them under the first spare hen, and if they come to good I can have them moved to my own house and borrow a coop; and it will be a great delight to me in my lonely hours to attend to them. And if I have good luck your mother shall have some.'

It was a beautiful evening, mild and still, and the drive was as pleasant as the serenity of Nature could make it; but when Mrs Norris ceased speaking, it was altogether a silent drive to those within. Their spirits were in general exhausted; and to determine whether the day had afforded most pleasure or pain, might occupy the meditations of almost all.

CHAPTER ELEVEN

THE DAY AT SOTHERTON, with all its imperfections, afforded the Miss Bertrams much more agreeable feelings than were derived from the letters from Antigua, which soon afterwards reached Mansfield. It was much pleasanter to think of Henry Crawford than of their father; and to think of their father in England again within a certain period, which these letters obliged them to do, was a most unwelcome exercise.

November was the black month fixed for his return. Sir Thomas wrote of it with as much decision as experience and anxiety could authorise. His business was so nearly concluded as to justify him in proposing to take his passage in the September packet, and he consequently looked forward with the hope of being with his beloved family again early in November.

Maria was more to be pitied than Julia; for to her the father brought a husband, and the return of the friend most solicitous for her happiness would unite her to the lover, on whom she had chosen that happiness should depend. It was a gloomy prospect, and all she could do was to throw a mist over it, and hope when the mist cleared away she should see some thing else. It would hardly be *early* in November, there were generally delays, a bad passage or *some thing*; that favouring *some thing* which everybody who shuts their eyes while they look, or their understandings while they reason, feels the comfort of. It would probably be the middle of November at least; the middle of November was three months off. Three months comprised thirteen weeks. Much might happen in thirteen weeks.

Sir Thomas would have been deeply mortified by a suspicion of half that his daughters felt on the subject of his return, and would hardly have found consolation in a knowledge of the interest it excited in the breast of another young lady. Miss Crawford, on walking up with her brother to spend the evening at Mansfield Park, heard the good news; and though seeming to have no concern in the affair beyond politeness, and to have vented all her feelings in a quiet congratulation, heard it with an attention not so easily satisfied. Mrs Norris gave the particulars of the letters, and the subject was dropped; but after tea, as Miss Crawford was standing at an open window with Edmund and Fanny looking out on a twilight scene, while the Miss Bertrams, Mr Rushworth, and Henry Crawford were all busy with candles at the pianoforte, she suddenly revived it by turning round towards the group, and saying, 'How happy Mr Rushworth looks! He is thinking of November.'

Edmund looked round at Mr Rushworth too, but had nothing to say. 'Your father's return will be a very interesting event.'

'It will, indeed, after such an absence; an absence not only long, but including so many dangers.'

'It will be the forerunner also of other interesting events; your sister's marriage, and your taking orders.'

'Yes.'

'Don't be affronted,' said she, laughing, 'but it does put me in mind of some of the old heathen heroes, who, after performing great exploits in a foreign land, offered sacrifices to the gods on their safe return.'

'There is no sacrifice in the case,' replied Edmund, with a serious smile, and glancing at the pianoforte again, 'it is entirely her own doing.'

'Oh yes! I know it is. I was merely joking. She has done no more than what every young woman would do; and I have no doubt of her being extremely happy. My other sacrifice of course you do not understand.'

'My taking orders, I assure you, is quite as voluntary as Maria's marrying.'

'It is fortunate that your inclination and your father's convenience should accord so well. There is a very good living kept for you, I understand, hereabouts.'

'Which you suppose has biassed me?'

'But *that* I am sure it has not,' cried Fanny.

'Thank you for your good word, Fanny, but it is more than I would affirm myself. On the contrary, the knowing that there was such provision for me probably did bias me. Nor can I think it wrong that it should. There was no natural disinclination to be overcome, and I see no reason why a man should make a worse clergyman for knowing that he will have a competence early in life. I was in safe hands. I hope I should not have been influenced myself in a wrong way, and I am sure my father was too conscientious to have allowed it. I have no doubt that I was biassed, but I think it was blamelessly.'

'It is the same sort of thing,' said Fanny, after short pause, 'as for the son of an admiral to go into the navy or the son of a general to be in the army, and nobody sees any thing wrong in that. Nobody wonders that they should

Busy at the pianoforte

prefer the line where their friends can serve them best, or suspects them to be less in earnest in it than they appear.'

'No, my dear Miss Price, and for reasons good. The profession, either navy or army, is its own justification. It has everything in its favour; heroism, danger, bustle, fashion. Soldiers and sailors are always acceptable in society. Nobody can wonder that men are soldiers and sailors.'

'But the motives of a man who takes orders with the certainty of preferment may be fairly suspected, you think?' said Edmund. 'To be justified in your eyes, he must do it in the most complete uncertainty of any provision.'

'What! take orders without a living! No; that is madness indeed; absolute madness.'

'Shall I ask you how the church is to be filled, if a man is neither to take orders with a living, nor without? No; for you certainly would not know what to say. but I must beg some advantage to the clergyman from your own argument. As he cannot be influenced by those feelings which you rank highly as temptation and reward to the soldier and sailor, in their choice of a profession, as heroism, and noise, and fashion, are all against him, he ought to be less liable to the suspicion of wanting sincerity or good intentions in the choice of his.'

'Oh! no doubt he is very sincere in preferring an income ready made, to the trouble of working for one: and has the best intentions of doing nothing all the rest of his days but eat, drink, and grow fat. It is indolence, Mr Bertram, indeed. Indolence and love of ease; a want of all laudable ambition, of taste for good company, or of inclination to take the trouble of being agreeable, which makes men clergymen. A clergyman has nothing to do but be slovenly and selfish; read the newspaper, watch the weather, and quarrel with his wife. His curate does all the work, and the business of his own life is to dine.'

'There are such clergymen, no doubt, but I think they are not so common as to justify Miss Crawford in esteeming it their general character. I suspect that in this comprehensive and (may I say) commonplace censure, you are not judging from yourself, but from prejudiced persons, whose opinions you have been in the habit of hearing. It is impossible that your own observation can have given you much knowledge of the clergy. You can have been personally acquainted with very few of a set of men you condemn so conclusively. You are speaking what you have been told at your uncle's table.'

'I speak what appears to me the general opinion; and where an opinion is general, it is usually correct. Though *I* have not seen much of the domestic lives of clergymen, it is seen by too many to leave any deficiency of information.'

'Where any one body of educated men, of whatever denomination, are condemned indiscriminately, there must be a deficiency of information, or (smiling) of some thing else. Your uncle, and his brother admirals, perhaps knew little of clergymen beyond the chaplains whom, good or bad, they were always wishing away.'

'Poor William! He has met with great kindness from the chaplain of the Antwerp,' was a tender apostrophe of Fanny's, very much to the purpose of her own feelings if not of the conversation.

'I have been so little addicted to take my opinions from my uncle,' said Miss Crawford, 'that I can hardly suppose – and since you push me so hard, I must observe, that I am not entirely without the means of seeing what clergymen are, being at this present time the guest of my own brother, Dr Grant. And though Dr Grant is most kind and obliging to me, and though he is really a gentlemen, and, I dare say, a good scholar and clever, and often preaches good sermons, and is very respectable, *I* see him to be an indolent, selfish bon vivant, who must have his palate consulted in every thing; who will not stir a finger for the convenience of any one; and who, moreover, if the cook makes a blunder, is out of humour with his excellent wife. To own the truth, Henry and I were partly driven out this very evening by a disappointment about a green goose, which he could not get the better of. My poor sister was forced to stay and bear it.'

'I do not wonder at your disapprobation, upon my word. It is a great defect of temper, made worse by a very faulty habit of self-indulgence; and to see your sister suffering from it must be exceedingly painful to such feelings as yours. Fanny, it goes against us. We cannot attempt to defend Dr Grant.'

'No,' replied Fanny, 'but we need not give up his profession for all that; because, whatever profession Dr Grant had chosen, he would have taken a – not a good temper into it; and as he must, either in the navy or army, have had a great many more people under his command than he has now, I think more would have been made unhappy by him as a sailor or soldier than as a clergyman. Besides, I cannot but suppose that whatever there may be to wish otherwise in Dr Grant, would have been in a greater danger of becoming worse in a more active and worldly profession, where he would have had less time and obligation – where he might have escaped that knowledge of himself, the *frequency*, at least, of that knowledge which it is impossible he should escape as he is now. A man – a sensible man like Dr Grant, cannot be in the habit of teaching others, their duty every week, cannot go to church twice every Sunday, and preach such very good sermons in so good a manner as he does, without being the better for it himself. It must make him think; and I have no doubt that he oftener endeavours to restrain himself than he would if he had been any thing but a clergyman.'

'We cannot prove to the contrary, to be sure; but I wish you a better fate, Miss Price, than to be the wife of a man whose amiableness depends upon his own sermons; for, though he may preach himself into a good humour every Sunday, it will be bad enough to have him quarrelling about green geese from Monday morning till Saturday night.'

'I think the man who could often quarrel with Fanny,' said Edmund, affectionately, 'must be beyond the reach of any sermons.'

Fanny turned further into the window; and Miss Crawford had only time to say, in a pleasant manner, 'I fancy Miss Price has been more used to deserve praise than to hear it;' when being earnestly invited by the Miss Bertrams to join in a glee, she tripped off to the instrument, leaving Edmund looking after her in an ecstasy of admiration of all her many virtues, from her obliging manners down to her light and graceful tread.

'There goes good humour, I am sure,' said he presently. 'There goes a temper which would never give pain! How well she walks! and how readily she falls in with the inclination of others! joining them the moment she is asked. What a pity,' he added, after an instant's reflection, 'that she should have been in such hands!'

Fanny agreed to it, and had the pleasure of seeing him continue at the window with her, in spite of the expected glee; and of having his eyes soon turned, like hers, towards the scene without, where all that was solemn, and soothing, and lovely, appeared in the brilliancy of an unclouded night, and the contrast of the deep shade of the woods. Fanny spoke her feelings. 'Here's harmony!' said she; 'here's repose! Here's what may leave all painting and all music behind, and what poetry can only attempt to describe! Here's what may tranquillise every care, and lift the heart to rapture! When I look out on such a night as this, I feel as if there could be neither wickedness nor sorrow in the world; and there certainly would be less of both if the sublimity of Nature were more attended to, and people were carried more out of themselves by contemplating such a scene.'

'I like to hear your enthusiasm, Fanny. It is a lovely night, and they are much to be pitied who have not been taught to feel, in some degree, as you do; who have not, at least, been given a taste for Nature in early life. They lose a great deal.'

'*You* taught me to think and feel on the subject, cousin.'

'I had a very apt scholar. There's Arcturus looking very bright.'

'Yes, and the Bear. I wish I could see Cassiopeia.'

'We must go out on the lawn for that. Should you be afraid?'

'Not in the least. It is a great while since we have had any star-gazing.'

'Yes, I do not know how it has happened.' The glee began. 'We will stay till this is finished, Fanny,' said he, turning his back on the window; and as it advanced, she had the mortification of seeing him advance too, moving forward by gentle degrees towards the instrument, and when it ceased, he was close by the singers, among the most urgent in requesting to hear the glee again.

Fanny sighed alone at the window till scolded away by Mrs Norris's threats of catching cold.

CHAPTER TWELVE

SIR THOMAS WAS TO RETURN IN November, and his eldest son had duties to call him earlier home. The approach of September brought tidings of Mr Bertram, first in a letter to the gamekeeper and then in a letter to Edmund; and by the end of August he arrived himself, to be gay, agreeable, and gallant again as occasion served, or Miss Crawford demanded; to tell of races and Weymouth, and parties and friends, to which she might have listened six weeks before with some interest, and altogether to give her the fullest conviction, by the power of actual comparison, of her preferring his younger brother.

It was very vexatious, and she was heartily sorry for it; but so it was; and so far from now meaning to marry the elder, she did not even want to attract him beyond what the simplest claims of conscious beauty required; his lengthened absence from Mansfield, without any thing but pleasure in view, and his own will to consult, made it perfectly clear that he did not care about her; and his indifference was so much more than equalled by her own, that, were he now to step forth the owner of Mansfield Park, the Sir Thomas complete, which he was to be in time, she did not believe she could accept him.

The season and duties which brought Mr Bertram back to Mansfield took Mr Crawford into Norfolk. Everingham could not do without him in the beginning of September. He went for a fortnight – a fortnight of such dullness to the Miss Bertrams as ought to have put them both on their guard, and made even Julia admit, in her jealousy of her sister, the absolute necessity of distrusting his attentions, and wishing him not to return; and a fortnight of sufficient leisure, in the intervals of shooting and sleeping, to have convinced the gentleman that he ought to keep longer away, had he been more in the habit of examining his own motives, and of reflecting to what the indulgence of his idle vanity was tending; but, thoughtless and selfish from prosperity and bad example, he would not look beyond the present moment. The sisters, handsome, clever, and encouraging, were an amusement to his sated mind; and finding nothing in Norfolk to equal the social pleasures of Mansfield, he gladly returned to it at the time appointed, and was welcomed thither quite as gladly by those whom he came to trifle with further.

Maria, with only Mr Rushworth to attend to her, and doomed to the repeated details of his day's sport, good or bad, his boast of his dogs, his jealousy of his neighbours, his doubts of their qualifications, and his zeal after poachers, subjects which will not find their way to female feelings without some talent on one side or some attachment on the other, had missed Mr Crawford grievously; and Julia, unengaged and unemployed, felt all the right of missing him much more. Each sister believed herself the favourite. Julia might be justified in so doing by the hints of Mrs Grant, inclined to credit what she wished, and Maria by the hints of Mr Crawford himself. Every thing returned into the same channel as before his absence; his manners being to each so animated and agreeable as to lose no ground with either, and just stopping short of the consistence, the steadiness, the solicitude, and the warmth which might excite general notice.

Fanny was the only one of the party who found anything to dislike; but since the day at Sotherton, she could never see Mr Crawford with either sister without observation, and seldom without wonder or censure; and had her confidence in her own judgment been equal to her exercise of it in every other respect, had she been sure that she was seeing clearly, and judging candidly, she would probably have made some important communications to her usual confidant. As it was, however, she only hazarded a hint, and the hint was lost. 'I am rather surprised,' said she, 'that Mr Crawford should come back again so soon, after being here so long before, full seven weeks; for I had understood he was so very fond of change and moving about, that I thought something would certainly occur when he was once gone, to take him elsewhere. He is used to much gayer places than Mansfield.'

'It is to his credit,' was Edmund's answer; 'and I dare say it gives his sister pleasure. She does not like his unsettled habits.'

'What a favourite he is with my cousins!'

'Yes, his manners to women are such as must please. Mrs Grant, I believe, suspects him of a preference for Julia; I have never seen much symptom of it, but I wish it may be so. He has no faults but what a serious attachment would remove.'

'If Miss Bertram were not engaged,' said Fanny, cautiously, 'I could sometimes almost think that he admired her more than Julia.'

'Which is, perhaps, more in favour of his liking Julia best, than you, Fanny, may be aware; for I believe it often happens, that a man, before he has quite made up his own mind, will distinguish the sister or intimate friend of the woman he is really thinking of, more than the woman herself. Crawford has too much sense to stay here if he found himself in any danger from Maria; and I am not at all afraid for her, after such a proof as she has given, that her feelings are not strong.'

Fanny supposed she must have been mistaken, and meant to think differently in future; but with all that submission to Edmund could do, and all the help of the coinciding looks and hints which she occasionally noticed in some of the others, and which seemed to say that Julia was Mr Crawford's choice, she knew not always what to think. She was privy, one evening, to the hopes of her Aunt Norris on the subject, as well as to her feelings, and the feelings of Mrs Rushworth, on a point of some similarity, and could not help wondering as she listened; and glad would she have been not to be obliged to listen, for it was while all the other young people were dancing, and she sitting, most unwillingly, among the chaperons at the fire, longing for the re-entrance of her elder cousin, on whom all her own hopes of a partner then depended. It was Fanny's first ball, though without the preparation or splendour of many a young lady's first ball, being the thought only of the afternoon, built on the late acquisition of a violin player in the servant's hall, and the possibility of raising five couples with the help of Mrs Grant and a new intimate friend of Mr Bertram's just arrived on a visit. It had, however, been a very happy one to Fanny through four dances, and she was quite grieved to be losing even a quarter of an hour. While waiting and wishing, looking now at the dancers and now at the door, this dialogue between the two above-mentioned ladies was forced on her:

'I think, ma'am,' said Mrs Norris – her eyes directed towards Mr Rushworth and Maria, who were partners for the second time, 'we shall see some happy faces again now.'

'Yes, ma'am, indeed,' replied the other with a stately simper, 'there will be some satisfaction in looking on *now*, and I think it was rather a pity they should have been obliged to part. Young folks in their situation should be excused complying with the common forms. I wonder my son did not propose it.'

'I dare say he did, ma'am. Mr Rushworth is never remiss. But dear Maria has such a strict sense of propriety, so much of that true delicacy which one seldom meets with now-a-days, Mrs Rushworth – that wish of avoiding particularity! Dear ma'am, only look at her face at this moment; how different from what it was the two last dances!'

Miss Bertram did indeed look happy, her eyes were sparkling with pleasure, and she was speaking with great animation, for Julia and her partner, Mr Crawford, were close to her; they were all in a cluster together. How she had looked before, Fanny could not recollect, for she had been dancing with Edmund herself, and had not thought about her.

Mrs Norris continued, 'It is quite delightful, ma'am, to see young people so properly happy, so well suited, and so much the thing! I cannot but think of dear Sir Thomas's delight. And what do you say, ma'am, to the chance of another match? Mr Rushworth has set a good example and such things are very catching.'

Mrs Rushworth, who saw nothing but her son, was quite at a loss. 'The couple above, ma'am. Do you see no symptoms there?'

'Oh dear! Miss Julia and Mr Crawford. Yes, indeed, a very pretty match. What is his property?'

'Four thousand a year.'

'Very well. Those who have not more, must be satisfied with what they have. Four thousand a year is a pretty estate, and he seems a very genteel, steady young man, so I hope Miss Julia will be very happy.'

'It is not a settled thing, ma'am, yet. We only speak of it among friends. But I have very little doubt it *will be*. He is growing extremely particular in his attentions.'

Fanny could listen no further. Listening and wondering were all suspended for a time, for Mr Bertram was in the room again; and though feeling it would be a great honour to be asked by him, she thought it must happen. He came towards their little circle; but instead of asking her to dance, drew a chair near her, and gave her an account of the present state of a sick horse, and the opinion of the groom, from whom he had just parted. Fanny found that it was not to be, and in the modesty of her nature immediately felt that she had been unreasonable in expecting it.

When he had told of his horse, he took a newspaper from the table, and looking over it, said in a languid way, 'If you want to dance, Fanny, I will stand up with you.' With more than equal civility the offer was declined; she did not wish to dance. 'I am glad of it,' said he, in a much brisker tone, and throwing down the newspaper again, 'for I am tired to death. I only wonder how the good people can keep it up so long. They had need be *all* in love, to find any amusement in such folly; and so they are, I fancy. If you look at them you may see they are so many couple of lovers – all but Yates and Mrs Grant – and, between ourselves, she, poor woman, must want a lover as much as any one of them. A desperate dull life hers must be with the doctor,' making a sly face as he spoke towards the chair of the latter, who proving, however, to be close at his elbow, made so instantaneous a change of expression and subject necessary, as Fanny, in spite of every thing, could hardly help laughing at. 'A strange business this in America, Dr Grant! What is your opinion? I always come to you to know what I am to think of public matters.'

'My dear Tom,' cried his aunt soon afterwards, 'as you are not dancing, I dare say you will have no objection to join us in a rubber; shall you?' Then leaving her seat, and coming to him to enforce the proposal, added in a whisper, 'We want to make a table for Mrs Rushworth, you know. Your mother is quite anxious about it, but cannot very well spare time to sit down herself, because of her fringe. Now, you, and I, and Dr Grant, will just do; and though *we* play but half-crowns, you know, you may bet half-guineas with *him*.'

'I should be most happy,' replied he aloud, and jumping up with alacrity, 'it would give me the greatest pleasure; but that I am this moment going to dance. Come, Fanny,' taking her hand, 'do not be dawdling any longer, or the dance will be over.'

Fanny was led off very willingly, though it was impossible for her to feel much gratitude towards her cousin, or distinguish, as he certainly did, between the selfishness of another person and his own.

'A pretty modest request upon my word,' he indignantly exclaimed as they walked away. 'To want to nail me to a card table for the next two hours with herself and Dr Grant, who are always quarrelling, and that poking old woman, who knows no more of whist than of algebra. I wish my good aunt would be a little less busy! And to ask me in such a way too! without ceremony, before them all, so as to leave me no possibility of refusing. *That* is what I dislike most particularly. It raises my spleen more than any thing to have the pretence of being asked, of being given a choice, and at the same time addressed in such a way as to oblige one to do the very thing, whatever it be! If I had not luckily thought of standing up with you I could not have got out of it. It is a great deal too bad. But when my aunt has got a fancy in her head, nothing can stop her.'

CHAPTER THIRTEEN

THE HONOURABLE JOHN YATES, this new friend, had not much to recommend him beyond habits of fashion and expense, and being the younger son of a lord with a tolerable independence; and Sir Thomas would probably have thought his introduction at Mansfield by no means desirable. Mr Bertram's acquaintance with him had begun at Weymouth, where they had spent ten days together in the same society, and the friendship, if friendship it might be called, had been proved and perfected by Mr Yates's being invited to take Mansfield in his way, whenever he could, and by his promising to come; and he did come rather earlier than had been expected, in consequence of the sudden breaking-up of a large party assembled for gaiety at the house of another friend, which he had left Weymouth to join. He came on the wings of disappointment, and with his head full of acting, for it had been a theatrical party; and the play in which he had borne a part was within two days of representation, when the sudden death of one of the nearest connections of the family had destroyed the scheme and dispersed the performers. To be so near happiness, so near fame, so near the long paragraph in praise of the private theatricals at Ecclesford, the seat of the

Right Hon Lord Ravenshaw, in Cornwall, which would of course have immortalised the whole party for at least a twelvemonth! and being so near, to lose it all, was an injury to be keenly felt, and Mr Yates could talk of nothing else. Ecclesford and its theatre, with its arrangements and dresses, rehearsals, and jokes, was his never-failing subject, and to boast of the past his only consolation.

Happily for him, a love of the theatre is so general, an itch for acting so strong among young people, that he could hardly out-talk the interest of his hearers. From the first casting of the parts, to the epilogue, it was all bewitching, and there were few who did not wish to have been a party concerned, or would have hesitated to try their skill. The play had been *Lovers' Vows*, and Mr Yates was to have been Count Cassel. 'A trifling part,' said he, 'and not at all to my taste, and such a one as I certainly would not accept again; but I was determined to make no difficulties. Lord Ravenshaw and the duke had appropriated the only two characters worth playing before I reached Ecclesford; and though Lord Ravenshaw offered to resign his to me, it was impossible to take it, you know. I was sorry for *him* that he should have so mistaken his powers, for he was no more equal to the Baron – a little man with a weak voice, always hoarse after the first ten minutes. It must have injured the piece materially; but *I* was resolved to make no difficulties. Sir Henry thought the duke not equal to Frederick, but that was because Sir Henry wanted the part himself; whereas it was certainly in the best hands of the two. I was surprised to see Sir Henry such a stick. Luckily the strength of the piece did not depend upon him. Our Agatha was inimitable, and the duke was thought very great by many. And upon the whole it would certainly have gone off wonderfully.'

'It was a hard case, upon my word;' and, 'I do think you were very much to be pitied,' were the kind responses of listening sympathy.

'It is not worth complaining about; but to be sure the poor old dowager could not have died at a worse time; and it is impossible to help wishing that the news could have been suppressed for just the three days we wanted. It was but three days; and being only a grandmother, and all happening two hundred miles off, I think there would have been no great harm, and it *was* suggested, I know; but Lord Ravenshaw, who I suppose is one of the most correct men in England, would not hear of it.'

'An afterpiece instead of a comedy,' said Mr Bertram. 'Lovers' vows were at an end, and Lord and Lady Ravenshaw left to act My Grandmother by themselves. Well, the jointure may comfort *him*; and perhaps, between friends, he began to tremble for his credit and his lungs in the Baron, and was not sorry to withdraw; and to make *you* amends. Yates, I think we must raise a little theatre at Mansfield, and ask you to be our manager.'

This, though the thought of the moment, did not end with the moment;

for the inclination to act was awakened, and in no one more strongly than in him who was now master of the house; and who having so much leisure as to make almost any novelty a certain good, had likewise such a degree of lively talents and comic taste, as were exactly adapted to the novelty of acting. The thought returned again and again. 'Oh, for the Ecclesford theatre and scenery to try something with!' Each sister could echo the wish; and Henry Crawford, to whom, in all the riot of his gratifications it was yet an untasted pleasure, was quite alive at the idea. 'I really believe,' said he, 'I could be fool enough at this moment to undertake any character that ever was written, from Shylock or Richard III down to the singing hero of a farce in his scarlet coat and cocked hat. I feel as if I could be any thing or every thing; as if I could rant and storm, or sigh, or cut capers in any tragedy or comedy in the English language. Let us be doing some thing. Be it only half a play, an act, a scene; what should prevent us? Not these countenances, I am sure,' looking towards the Miss Bertrams, 'and for a theatre, what signifies a theatre? We shall be only amusing ourselves. Any room in this house might suffice.'

'We must have a curtain,' said Tom Bertram; 'a few yards of green baize for a curtain, and perhaps that may be enough.'

'Oh, quite enough!' cried Mr Yates, 'with only just a side wing or two run up, doors in flat, and three or four scenes to be let down; nothing more would be necessary on such a plan as this. For mere amusement among ourselves, we should want nothing more.'

'I believe we must be satisfied with *less*,' said Maria. 'There would not be time, and other difficulties would arise. We must rather adopt Mr Crawford's views, and make the *performance*, not the *theatre*, our object. Many parts of our best plays are independent of scenery.'

'Nay,' said Edmund, who began to listen with alarm. 'Let us do nothing by halves. If we are to act, let it be in a theatre completely fitted up with pit, boxes, and gallery, and let us have a play entire from beginning to end; so as it be a German play, no matter what, with a good tricking, shifting afterpiece, and a figure-dance, and a hornpipe, and a song between the acts. If we do not outdo Ecclesford, we do nothing.'

'Now, Edmund, do not be disagreeable,' said Julia. 'Nobody loves a play better than you do, or can have gone much further to see one.'

'True, to see real acting, good hardened real acting; but I would hardly walk from this room to the next to look at the raw efforts of those who have not been bred to the trade: a set of gentlemen and ladies, who have all the disadvantages of education and decorum to struggle through.'

After a short pause, however, the subject still continued, and was discussed with unabated eagerness, every one's inclination increasing by the discussion, and a knowledge of the inclination of the rest; and though nothing was settled but that Tom Bertram would prefer a comedy, and his sisters and Henry Crawford a tragedy, and that nothing in the world could be easier than to find a piece which would please them all, the resolution to act something or other seemed so decided, as to make Edmund quite uncomfortable. He was determined to prevent it, if possible, though his mother, who equally heard the conversation, which passed at table, did not evince the least disapprobation.

The same evening afforded him an opportunity of trying his strength. Maria, Julia, Henry Crawford, and Mr Yates were in the billiard-room. Tom returning from them into the drawing-room, where Edmund was standing thoughtfully by the fire, while Lady Bertram was on the sofa at a little distance, and Fanny close beside her, arranging her work, thus began as he entered:

'Such a horribly vile billiard-table as ours is not to be met with, I believe, above ground. I can stand it no longer, and I think, I may say, that nothing shall ever tempt me to it again; but one good thing I have just ascertained; it is the very room for a theatre, precisely the shape and length for it; and the doors at the further end, communicating with each other, as they may be made to do in five minutes, by merely moving the bookcase in my father's room, is the very thing we could have desired, if we had set down to wish for it; and my father's room will be an excellent green room. It seems to join the billiard-room on purpose.'

'You are not serious, Tom, in meaning to act?' said Edmund, in a low voice, as his brother approached the fire.

'Not serious! never more so, I assure you. What is there to surprise you in it?'

'I think it would be very wrong. In a *general* light, private theatricals are open to some objections, but as *we* are circumstanced, I must think it would be highly injudicious, and more than injudicious, to attempt any thing of the kind. It would show great want of feeling on my father's account, absent as he is, and in some degree of constant danger; and it would be imprudent, I think, with regard to Maria, whose situation is a very delicate one, considering everything, extremely delicate.'

'You take up a thing so seriously! as if we were going to act three times a week till my father's return, and invite all the country. But it is not to be a display of that sort. We mean nothing but a little amusement among ourselves, just to vary the scene, and exercise our powers in some thing new. We want no audience, no publicity. We may be trusted, I think, in choosing some play most perfectly unexceptionable; and I can conceive no greater harm or danger to any of us in conversing in the elegant written language of some respectable author than in chattering in words of our own. I have no fears, and no scruples. And as to my father's being absent, it is so far from an

Just falling into a gentle doze

objection, that I consider it rather as a motive; for the expectation of his return must be a very anxious period to my mother; and if we can be the means of amusing that anxiety, and keeping up her spirits for the next few weeks, I shall think our time very well spent, and so, I am sure, will he. It is a *very* anxious period for her.'

As he said this, each looked towards their mother. Lady Bertram, sunk back in one corner of the sofa, the picture of health, wealth, ease, and tranquillity, was just falling into a gentle doze, while Fanny was getting through the few difficulties of her work for her.

Edmund smiled and shook his head.

'By jove! this won't do,' cried Tom, throwing himself into a chair with a hearty laugh. 'To be sure, my dear mother, your anxiety – I was unlucky there.'

'What is the matter?' asked her ladyship, in the heavy tone of one half roused, 'I was not asleep.'

'Oh, dear no, ma'am, nobody suspected you! Well, Edmund,' he continued, returning to the former subject, posture, and voice, as soon as Lady Bertram began to nod again, 'but *this* I *will* maintain, that we shall be doing no harm.'

'I cannot agree with you; I am convinced that my father would totally disapprove it.'

'And I am convinced to the contrary. Nobody is fonder of the exercise of talent in young people, or promotes it more than my father, and for any thing of the acting, spouting, reciting kind, I think he has always a decided taste. I am sure he encouraged it in us as boys. How many a time have we mourned over the dead body of Julius Cæsar, and *to be'd* and not *to be'd*, in this very room, for his amusement? And I am sure, *my name was Norval*, every evening of my life through one Christmas holidays.'

'It was a very different thing. You must see the difference yourself. My father wished us, as schoolboys, to speak well, but he would never wish his grown-up daughters to be acting plays. His sense of decorum is strict.'

'I know all that,' said Tom, displeased. 'I know my father as well as you do; and I'll take care that his daughters do nothing to distress him. Manage your own concerns, Edmund, and I'll take care of the rest of the family.'

'If you are resolved on acting,' replied the persevering Edmund, 'I must hope it will be in a very small and quiet way; and I think a theatre ought not to be attempted. It would be taking liberties with my father's house in his absence which could not be justified.'

'For everything of that nature, I will be answerable,' said Tom, in a decided tone. 'His house shall not be hurt. I have quite as great an interest in being careful of his house as you can have; and as to such alterations as I was suggesting just now, such as moving a bookcase, or unlocking a door; or even as using the billiard-room for the space of a week without playing at billiards in it, you might just as well suppose he would object to our sitting more in this room, and less in the breakfast-room, than we did before he went away, or to my sister's pianoforte being moved from one side of the room to the other. Absolute nonsense!'

'The innovation, if not wrong as an innovation, will be wrong as an expense.'

'Yes, the expense of such an undertaking would be prodigious! Perhaps it might cost a whole twenty pounds. Something of a theatre we must have undoubtedly, but it will be on the simplest plan; a green curtain and a little carpenter's work, and that's all; and as the carpenter's work may be all done at home by Christopher Jackson himself, it will be too absurd to talk of expense; and as long as Jackson is employed, everything will be right with Sir Thomas. Don't imagine that nobody in this house can see or judge but yourself. Don't act yourself, if you do not like it, but don't expect to govern every body else.'

'No, as to acting myself,' said Edmund, '*that* I absolutely protest against.'

Tom walked out of the room as he said it, and Edmund was left to sit down and stir the fire in thoughtful vexation.

Fanny, who had heard it all, and borne Edmund company in every feeling throughout the whole, now ventured to say, in her anxiety to suggest some comfort, 'Perhaps they may not be able to find any play to suit them. Your brother's taste, and your sisters', seem very different.'

'I have no hope there, Fanny. If they persist in the scheme, they will find some thing. I shall speak to my sisters and try to dissuade *them*, and that is all I can do.'

'I should think my Aunt Norris would be on your side.'

'I dare say she would, but she has no influence with either Tom or my sisters that could be of any use; and if I cannot convince them myself, I shall let things take their course, without attempting it through her. Family squabbling is the greatest evil of all, and we had better do any thing than be altogether by the ears.'

His sisters, to whom he had an opportunity of speaking the next morning, were quite as impatient of his advice, quite as unyielding to his representation, quite as determined in the cause of pleasure, as Tom. Their mother had no objection to the plan, and they were not in the least afraid of their father's disapprobation. There could be no harm in what had been done in so many respectable families, and by so many women of the first consideration; and it must be scrupulousness run mad, that could see anything to censure in a plan like theirs, comprehending only brothers and sisters, and intimate friends, and which would never be heard of beyond themselves. Julia *did* seem inclined to admit that Maria's situation might require particular caution and delicacy – but that could not extend to *her* – *she* was at liberty; and Maria evidently considered her engagement as only raising her so much more above restraint, and leaving her less occasion than Julia, to consult either father or mother. Edmund had little to hope, but he was still urging the subject, when Henry Crawford entered the room, fresh from the Parsonage, calling out, 'No want of hands in our theatre, Miss

Bertram. No want of understrappers; my sister desires her love, and hopes to be admitted into the company, and will be happy to take the part of any old duenna, or tame confidante, that you may not like to do yourselves.'

Maria gave Edmund a glance, which meant, 'What say you now? Can we be wrong if Mary Crawford feels the same?' And Edmund, silenced, was obliged to acknowledge that the charm of acting might well carry fascination to the mind of genius; and with the ingenuity of love, to dwell more on the obliging, accommodating purport of the message than on anything else.

The scheme advanced. Opposition was vain; and as to Mrs Norris, he was mistaken in supposing she would wish to make any. She started no difficulties that were not talked down in five minutes by her eldest nephew and niece, who were all-powerful with her; and, as the whole arrangement was to bring very little expense to anybody, and none at all to herself, as she foresaw in it all the comfort of hurry, bustle, and importance, and derived the immediate advantage of fancying herself obliged to leave her own house, where she had been living a month at her own cost, and take up her abode in theirs, that every hour might be spent in their service, she was, in fact, exceedingly delighted with the project.

CHAPTER FOURTEEN

FANNY SEEMED NEARER BEING RIGHT than Edmund had supposed. The business of finding a play that would suit every body proved to be no trifle; and the carpenter had received his orders and taken his measurements, had suggested and removed at least two sets of difficulties, and having made the necessity of an enlargement of plan and expense fully evident, was already at work, while a play was still to seek. Other preparations were also in hand. An enormous roll of green baize had arrived from Northampton, and been cut out by Mrs Norris (with a saving by her good management, of full three quarters of a yard), and was actually forming into a curtain by the housemaids, and still the play was wanting; and as two or three days passed away in this manner, Edmund began almost to hope that none might ever be found.

There were, in fact, so many things to be attended to, so many people to be pleased, so many best characters required, and above all, such a need that the play should be at once both tragedy and comedy, that there did seem as little chance of a decision as anything pursued by youth and zeal could hold out.

On the tragic side were the Miss Bertrams, Henry Crawford and Mr

Yates; on the comic, Tom Bertram, not *quite* alone, because it was evident that Mary Crawford's wishes, though politely kept back, inclined the same way: but his determinateness and his power seemed to make allies unnecessary; and, independent of this great irreconcilable difference, they wanted a piece containing very few characters in the whole, but every character first-rate, and three principal women. All the best plays were run over in vain. Neither *Hamlet*, nor *Macbeth*, nor *Othello*, nor *Douglas*, nor *The Gamester*, presented anything that could satisfy even the tragedians; and *The Rivals*, *The School for Scandal*, *Wheel of Fortune*, *Heir at Law*, and a long et cetera, were successively dismissed with yet warmer objections. No piece could be proposed that did not supply some body with a difficulty, and on one side or the other it was a continual repetition of, 'Oh no, *that* will never do! Let us have no ranting tragedies. Too many characters. Not a tolerable woman's part in the play. Anything but *that*, my dear Tom. It would be impossible to fill it up. One could not expect anybody to take such a part. Nothing but buffoonery from beginning to end. *That* might do, perhaps, but for the low parts. If I *must* give my opinion, I have always thought it the most insipid play in the English language, *I* do not wish to make objections; I shall be happy to be of any use, but I think we could not choose worse.'

Fanny looked on and listened, not unamused to observe the selfishness which, more or less disguised, seemed to govern them all, and wondering how it would end. For her own gratification she could have wished that some thing might be acted, for she had never seen even half a play, but every thing of higher consequence was against it.

'This will never do,' said Tom Bertram at last. 'We are wasting time most abominably. Some thing must be fixed on. No matter what, so that some thing is chosen. We must not be so nice. A few characters too many must not frighten us. We must *double* them. We must descend a little. If a part is insignificant, the greater our credit in making any thing of it. From this moment, *I* make no difficulties. I take any part you choose to give me, so as it be comic. Let it but be comic, I condition for nothing more.'

For about the fifth time he then proposed *The Heir at Law*, doubting only whether to prefer Lord Duberley or Dr Pangloss for himself; and very earnestly, but very unsuccessfully, trying to persuade the others that there were some fine tragic parts in the rest of the dramatis personaæ.

The pause which followed this fruitless effort was ended by the same speaker, who taking up one of the many volumes of plays that lay on the table, and turning it over, suddenly exclaimed – '*Lovers' Vows*! And why should not *Lovers' Vows* do for *us* as well as for the Ravenshaws? How came it never to be thought of before? It strikes me as if it would do exactly. What say you all? Here are two capital tragic parts for Yates and Crawford, and here is the rhyming Butler for me, if nobody else wants it; a trifling part, but the sort of thing I should not dislike, and, as I said before, I am determined to take any thing and do my best. And as for the rest, they may be filled up by any body. It is only Count Cassel and Anhalt.'

The suggestion was generally welcome. Everybody was growing weary of indecision, and the first idea with everybody was, that nothing had been proposed before so likely to suit them all. Mr Yates was particularly pleased: he had been sighing and longing to do the Baron at Ecclesford, had grudged every rant of Lord Ravenshaw's and been forced to re-rant it all in his own room. To storm through Baron Wildenheim was the height of his theatrical ambition; and with the advantage of knowing half the scenes by heart already, he did now with the greatest alacrity, offer his services for the part. To do him justice, however, he did not resolve to appropriate it; for remembering that there was some very good ranting ground in Frederick, he professed an equal willingness for that. Henry Crawford was ready to take either. Whichever Mr Yates did not choose would perfectly satisfy him, and a short parley of compliment ensued. Miss Bertram, feeling all the interest of an Agatha in the question, took on her to decide it, by observing to Mr Yates, that this was a point in which height and figure ought to be considered, and that *his* being the tallest, seemed to fit him peculiarly for the Baron. She was acknowledged to be quite right, and the two parts being accepted accordingly, she was certain of the proper Frederick. Three of the characters were now cast, besides Mr Rushworth, who was always answered for by Maria as willing to do anything, when Julia, meaning, like her sister, to be Agatha, began to be scrupulous on Miss Crawford's account.

'This is not behaving well by the absent,' said she. 'Here are not women enough. Amelia and Agatha may do for Maria and me, but here is nothing for your sister, Mr Crawford.'

Mr Crawford desired *that* might not be thought of: he was very sure his sister had no wish of acting but as she might be useful, and that she would not allow herself to be considered in the present case. But this was immediately opposed by Tom Bertram, who asserted the part of Amelia to be in every respect the property of Miss Crawford, if she would accept it. 'It falls as naturally, as necessarily, to her,' said he, 'as Agatha does to one or other of my sisters. It can be no sacrifice on their side, for it is highly comic.'

A short silence followed. Each sister looked anxious; for each felt the best claim to Agatha, and was hoping to have it pressed on her by the rest. Henry Crawford, who meanwhile had taken up the play, and with seeming carelessness was turning over the first act, soon settled the business.

'I must entreat Miss *Julia* Bertram,' said he, 'not to engage in the part of Agatha, or it will be the ruin of all my solemnity. You must not, indeed you must not (turning to her). I could not stand your countenance dressed up in woe and paleness. The many laughs we have had together would infallibly come across me, and Frederick and his knapsack would be obliged to run away.'

Pleasantly, courteously, it was spoken; but the manner was lost in the matter to Julia's feelings. She saw a glance at Maria, which confirmed the injury to herself: it was a scheme, a trick; she was slighted, Maria was preferred; the smile of triumph which Maria was trying to suppress showed how well it was understood; and before Julia could command herself enough to speak, her brother gave his weight against her too, by saying, 'Oh yes! Maria must be Agatha. Maria will be the best Agatha. Though Julia fancies she prefers tragedy, I would not trust her in it. There is nothing of tragedy about her. She has not the look of it. Her features are not tragic features, and she walks too quick, and speaks too quick, and would not keep her countenance. She had better do the old country-woman: the Cottager's Wife; you had, indeed, Julia. Cottager's Wife is a very pretty part, I assure you. The old lady relieves the high-flown benevolence of her husband with a good deal of spirit. You shall be Cottager's Wife.'

'Cottager's Wife!' cried Mr Yates. 'What are you talking of? The most trivial, paltry, insignificant part; the merest commonplace; not a tolerable speech in the whole. Your sister do that! It is an insult to propose it. At Ecclesford the governess was to have done it. We all agreed that it could not be offered to any body else. A little more justice, Mr Manager, if you please. You do not deserve the office, if you cannot appreciate the talents of your company a little better.'

'Why, as to *that*, my good friend, till I and my company have really acted there must be some guess work; but I mean no disparagement to Julia. We cannot have two Agatha's, and we must have one Cottager's Wife; and I am sure I set her the example of moderation myself in being satisfied with the old Butler. If the part is trifling she will have more credit in making something of it; and if she is so desperately bent against every thing humorous, let her take Cottager's speeches instead of Cottager's Wife's and so change the parts all through; *he* is solemn and pathetic enough, I am sure. It could make no difference in the play, and as for Cottager himself, when he has got his wife's speeches, *I* would undertake him with all my heart.'

'With all your partiality for Cottager's Wife,' said Henry Crawford, 'it will be impossible to make anything of it fit for your sister, and we must not suffer her good nature to be imposed on. We must not *allow* her to accept the part. She must not be left to her own complaisance. Her talents will be wanted in Amelia. Amelia is a character more difficult to be well represented than even Agatha. I consider Amelia is the most difficult character in the whole piece. It requires great powers, great nicety, to give her playfulness and simplicity without extravagance. I have seen good actresses fail in the part. Simplicity, indeed, is beyond the reach of almost every actress by profession. It requires a delicacy of feeling which they have not. It requires a gentlewoman – a Julia Bertram. You *will* undertake it, I hope?' turning to her with a look of anxious entreaty, which softened her a little; but while she hesitated what to say, her brother again interposed with Miss Crawford's better claim.

'No, no, Julia must not be Amelia. It is not at all the part for her. She would not like it. She would not do well. She is too tall and robust. Amelia should be a small, light, girlish, skipping figure. It is fit for Miss Crawford, and Miss Crawford only. She looks the part, and I am persuaded will do it admirably.'

Without attending to this, Henry Crawford continued his supplication. 'You must oblige us,' said he, 'indeed you must. When you have studied the character, I am sure you will feel it suit you. Tragedy may be your choice, but it will certainly appear that comedy chooses *you*. You will be to visit me in prison with a basket of provisions; you will not refuse to visit me in prison? I think I see you coming in with your basket?'

The influence of his voice was felt. Julia wavered; but was he only trying to soothe and pacify her, and make her overlook the previous affront? She distrusted him. The slight had been most determined. He was, perhaps, but at treacherous play with her. She looked suspiciously at her sister; Maria's countenance was to decide it; if she were vexed and alarmed – but Maria looked all serenity and satisfaction, and Julia well knew that on this ground Maria could not be happy but at her expense. With hasty indignation, therefore, and a tremulous voice, she said to him, 'You do not seem afraid of not keeping your countenance when I come in with a basket of provisions – though one might have supposed – but it is only as Agatha that I was to be so overpowering!' She stopped, Henry Crawford looked rather foolish, and as if he did not know what to say. Tom Bertram began again:

'Miss Crawford must be Amelia. She will be an excellent Amelia.'

'Do not be afraid of *my* wanting the character,' cried Julia, with angry quickness: 'I am *not* to be Agatha, and I am sure I will do nothing else; and as to Amelia, it is of all parts in the world most disgusting to me. I quite detest her. An odious, little, pert, unnatural, impudent girl. I have always protested against comedy, and this is comedy in its worst form.' And so saying, she walked hastily out of the room, leaving awkward feelings to more than one, but exciting small compassion in any except Fanny, who had been a quiet auditor of the whole, and who could not think of her as under the agitations of *jealousy* without great pity.

A short silence succeeded her leaving them; but her brother soon returned to business and *Lovers' Vows*, and was eagerly looking over the play, with Mr Yates' help, to ascertain what scenery would be necessary, while Maria and Henry Crawford conversed together in an under voice, and the declaration with which she began of, 'I am sure I would give up the part of Julia most willingly, but that though I shall probably do it very ill, I feel persuaded *she* would do it worse,' was doubtless receiving all the compliments it called for.

When this had lasted some time, the division of the party was completed by Tom Bertram and Mr Yates walking off together to consult further in the room now beginning to be called *the Theatre*, and Miss Bertram's resolving to go down to the Parsonage herself with the offer of Amelia to Miss Crawford; and Fanny remained alone.

The first use she made of her solitude was to take up the volume which had been left on the table, and begin to acquaint herself with the play of which she had heard so much. Her curiosity was all awake, and she ran through it with an eagerness which was suspended only by intervals of astonishment, that it could be chosen in the present instance, that it could be proposed and accepted in a private theatre! Agatha and Amelia appeared to her in their different ways so totally improper for home representation; the situation of one, and the language of the other, so unfit to be expressed by any woman of modesty, that she could hardly suppose her cousins could be aware of what they were engaging in; and longed to have them roused as soon as possible by the remonstrance which Edmund would certainly make.

CHAPTER FIFTEEN

MISS CRAWFORD ACCEPTED THE PART very readily; and soon after Miss Bertram's return from the Parsonage, Mr Rushworth arrived, and another character was consequently cast. He had the offer of Count Cassel and Anhalt, and at first did not know which to choose, and wanted Miss Bertram to direct him; but upon being made to understand the different style of the characters, and which was which, and recollecting that he had once seen the play in London, and had thought Anhalt a very stupid fellow, he soon decided for the Count. Miss Bertram approved the decision, for the less he had to learn the better; and though she could not sympathise in his wish that the Count and Agatha might be to act together, nor wait very patiently while he was slowly turning over the leaves with the hope of still discovering such a scene, she very kindly took his part in hand, and curtailed every speech that admitted being shortened; besides pointing out the necessity of his being very much dressed, and choosing his colours. Mr

Rushworth liked the idea of his finery very well, though affecting to despise it; and was too much engaged with what his own appearance would be to think of the others, or draw any of those conclusions, or feel any of that displeasure which Maria had been half prepared for.

Thus much was settled before Edmund, who had been out all the morning, knew any thing of the matter; but when he entered the drawing-room before dinner, the buzz of discussion was high between Tom, Maria, and Mr Yates; and Mr Rushworth stepped forward with great alacrity to tell him the agreeable news.

'I am to have another fine fancy suit'

'We have got a play,' said he. 'It is to be *Lovers' Vows*; and I am to be Count Cassel, and am come in first with a blue dress, and a pink satin cloak, and afterwards am to have another fine fancy suit, by way of a shooting-dress. I do not know how I shall like it.'

Fanny's eyes followed Edmund, and her heart beat for him as she heard this speech, and saw his look and felt what his sensations must be.

'*Lovers' Vows*!' in a tone of the greatest amazement, was his only reply to Mr Rushworth, and he turned towards his brother and sisters as if hardly doubting a contradiction.

'Yes,' cried Mr Yates. 'After all our debatings and difficulties, we find there is nothing that will suit us altogether so well, nothing so unexceptionable as *Lovers' Vows*. The wonder is that it should not have been thought of before. My stupidity was abominable, for here we have all the advantage of what I saw at Ecclesford; and it is so useful to have anything of a model! We have cast almost every part.'

'But what do you do for women?' said Edmund gravely, and looking at Maria.

Maria blushed in spite of herself as she answered, 'I take the part which Lady Ravenshaw was to have done, and (with a bolder eye) Miss Crawford is to be Amelia.'

'I should not have thought it the sort of play to be so easily filled up, with *us*,' replied Edmund, turning away to the fire, where sat his mother, aunt, and Fanny, and seating himself with a look of great vexation.

Mr Rushworth followed him to say, 'I come in three times, and have two-and-forty speeches. That's something, is not it? But I do not much like the idea of being so fine. I shall hardly know myself in a blue dress, and a pink satin cloak.'

Edmund could not answer him. In a few minutes Mr Bertram was called out of the room to satisfy some doubts of the carpenter; and being accompanied by Mr Yates, and followed soon afterwards by Mr Rushworth, Edmund almost immediately took the opportunity of saying, 'I cannot before Mr Yates speak what I feel as to this play, without reflecting on his friends at Ecclesford; but I must now, my dear Maria, tell *you*, that I think it exceedingly unfit for private representation, and that I hope you will give it up. I cannot but suppose you *will* when you have read it carefully over. Read only the first act aloud to either mother or aunt, and see how you can approve it. It will not be necessary to send you to your *father*'s judgment, I am convinced.'

'We see things very differently,' cried Maria. 'I am perfectly acquainted with the play, I assure you; and with a very few omissions, and so forth, which will be made, of course, I can see nothing objectionable in it; and *I* am not the *only* young woman you find, who thinks it very fit for private representation.'

'I am sorry for it,' was his answer; 'but in this matter it is *you* who are to lead. *You* must set the example. If others have blundered, it is your place to put them right, and show them what true delicacy is. In all points of decorum, *your* conduct must be law to the rest of the party.'

This picture of her consequence had some effect, for no one loved better to lead than Maria; and with far more good humour she answered, 'I am much obliged to you, Edmund; you mean very well, I am sure; but I still think you see things too strongly; and I really cannot undertake to harangue all the rest upon a subject of this kind. *There* would be the greatest indecorum, I think.'

'Do you imagine that I could have such an idea in my head? No: let your conduct be the only harangue. Say that, on examining the part, you feel yourself unequal to it; that you find it requiring more exertion and confidence than you can be supposed to have. Say this with firmness, and it will be quite enough. All who can distinguish will understand your motive. The play will be given up, and your delicacy honoured as it ought.'

'Do not act anything improper, my dear,' said Lady Bertram. 'Sir Thomas would not like it. Fanny, ring the bell; I must have my dinner. To be sure Julia is dressed by this time.'

'I am convinced, madam,' said Edmund, preventing Fanny, 'that Sir Thomas would not like it.'

'There, my dear, do you hear what Edmund says?'

'If I were to decline the part,' said Maria, with renewed zeal, 'Julia would certainly take it.'

'What!' cried Edmund, 'if she knew your reasons!'

'Oh! she might think the difference between us – the difference in our situations – that *she* need not be so scrupulous as *I* might feel necessary. I am sure she would argue so. No: you must excuse me; I cannot retract my consent; it is too far settled, every body would be so disappointed, Tom would be quite angry; and if we are so very nice, we shall never act any thing.'

'I was just going to say the very same thing,' said Mrs Norris. 'If every play is to be objected to, you will act nothing, and the preparations will be all so much money thrown away, and I am sure *that* would be a discredit to us all. I do not know the play; but, as Maria says, if there is anything a little too warm (and it is so with most of them) it can be easily left out. We must not be over precise, Edmund. As Mr Rushworth is to act too, there can be no harm. I only wish Tom had known his own mind when the carpenters began, for there was the loss of half a day's work about the side-doors. The curtain will be a good job, however. The maids do their work very well, and I think we shall be able to send back some dozens of the rings. There is no occasion to put them so very close together. I *am* of some use, I hope, in preventing waste and making the most of things. There should always be one steady head to superintend so many young ones. I forgot to tell Tom of some thing that happened to me this very day. I had been looking about me in the poultry yard, and was just coming out, when who should I see but Dick Jackson, making up to the servants' hall-door with two bits of deal board in his hand, bringing them to father you may be sure; mother had chanced to send him on a message to father, and then father had bid him bring up them two bits of board, for he could not know how do without them. I knew what all this meant, for the servants' dinner-bell was ringing at the very moment over our heads; and as I hate such encroaching people (the Jacksons are very encroaching, I have always said so: just the sort of people to get all they can), I said to the boy directly (a great lubberly fellow of ten years old, you know, who ought to be ashamed of himself); '*I'll* take the boards to your father, Dick, so get you home again as fast as you can.' The boy looked very silly, and turned away without offering a word, for I believe I might speak pretty sharp; and I dare say it will cure him of coming marauding about the house for one while. I hate such greediness; so good as your father is to the family, employing the man all the year round!'

Nobody was at the trouble of an answer; the others soon returned; and Edmund found that to have endeavoured to set them right must be his only satisfaction.

Dinner passed heavily. Mrs Norris related again her triumph over Dick Jackson, but neither play nor preparation were otherwise much talked of, for Edmund's disapprobation was felt even by his brother, though he would not have owned it. Maria, wanting Henry Crawford's animating support, thought the subject better avoided. Mr Yates, who was trying to make himself agreeable to Julia, found her gloom less impenetrable on any topic than that of his regret at her secession from their company; and Mr Rushworth, having only his own part and his own dress in his head, had soon talked away all that could be said of either.

But the concerns of the theatre were suspended only for an hour or two: there was still a great deal to be settled; and the spirits of evening giving fresh courage, Tom, Maria, and Mr Yates, soon after their being reassembled in the drawing-room, seated themselves in committee at a separate table, with the play open before them, and were just getting deep in the subject, when a most welcome interruption was given by the entrance of Mr and Miss Crawford, who, late and dark and dirty as it was, could not help coming, and were received with the most grateful joy.

'Well, how do you go on?' and 'What have you settled?' and 'Oh! we can do nothing without you,' followed the first salutations; and Henry Crawford was soon seated with the other three at the table, while his sister made her way to Lady Bertram, and with pleasant attention was complimenting *her*. 'I must really contratulate your ladyship,' said she, 'on

A most welcome interruption

the play being chosen; for though you have borne it with exemplary patience, I am sure you must be sick of all our noise and difficulties. The actors may be glad, but the by-standers must be infinitely more thankful for a decision; and I do sincerely give you joy, madam, as well as Mrs Norris, and everybody else who is in the same predicament,' glancing half fearfully, half slyly, beyond Fanny to Edmund.

She was very civilly answered by Lady Bertram, but Edmund said nothing. His being only a by-stander was not disclaimed. After continuing in chat with the party round the fire a few minutes, Miss Crawford returned to the party round the table; and standing by them, seemed to interest herself in their arrangements till, as if struck by a sudden recollection, she exclaimed, 'My good friends, you are most composedly at work upon these cottages and ale-houses, inside and out; but pray, let me know my fate in the meanwhile. Who is to be Anhalt? What gentleman among you am I to have the pleasure of making love to?'

For a moment no one spoke; and then many spoke together to tell the same melancholy truth, that they had not yet got any Anhalt. 'Mr Rushworth was to be Count Cassel, but no one had yet undertaken Anhalt.'

'I had my choice of the parts,' said Mr Rushworth; 'but I thought I should like the Count best, though I do not much relish the finery I am to have.'

'You choose very wisely, I am sure,' replied Miss Crawford, with a brightened look; 'Anhalt is a heavy part.'

'*The Count* has two-and-forty speeches,' returned Mr Rushworth, 'which is no trifle.'

'I am not at all surprised,' said Miss Crawford, after a short pause, 'at this want of an Anhalt. Amelia deserves no better. Such a forward young lady might well frighten the men.'

'I should be but too happy in taking the part, if it were possible,' cried Tom; 'but, unluckily, the Butler and Anhalt are in together. I will not entirely give it up, however; I will try what can be done – I will look it over again.'

'Your *brother* should take the part,' said Mr Yates, in a low voice. 'Do you not think he would?'

'*I* shall not ask him,' replied Tom, in a cold determined manner.

Miss Crawford talked of some thing else, and soon afterwards rejoined the party at the fire.

'They do not want me at all,' said she, seating herself. 'I only puzzle them, and oblige them to make civil speeches. Mr Edmund Bertram, as you do not act yourself, you will be a disinterested adviser; and, therefore, I apply to *you*. What shall we do for an Anhalt? Is it practicable for any of the others to double it? What is your advice?'

'My advice,' said he calmly, 'is that you change the play.'

'*I* should have no objection,' she replied; 'for though I should not particularly dislike the part of Amelia, if well supported, that is, if every thing went well, I shall be sorry to be an inconvenience; but as they do not choose to hear your advice at *that table* (looking round), it certainly will not be taken.'

Edmund said no more.

'If *any* part could tempt *you* to act, I suppose it would be Anhalt,' observed the lady archly, after a short pause; 'for he is a clergyman, you know.'

'*That* circumstance would by no means tempt me,' he replied, 'for I should be sorry to make the character ridiculous by bad acting. It must be very difficult to keep Anhalt from appearing a formal solemn lecturer; and the man who chooses the profession itself, is, perhaps, one of the last who would wish to represent it on the stage.'

Miss Crawford was silenced, and with some feelings of resentment and mortification, moved her chair considerably nearer the tea-table, and gave all her attention to Mrs Norris, who was presiding there.

'Fanny,' cried Tom Bertram, from the other table, where the conference was eagerly carrying on, and the conversation incessant, 'we want your services.'

Fanny was up in a moment, expecting some errand; for the habit of employing her in that way was not yet overcome, in spite of all that Edmund could do.

'Oh! we do not want to disturb you from your seat. We do not want your *present* services. We shall only want you in our play. You must be Cottager's Wife.'

'Me!' cried Fanny, sitting down again with a most frightened look. 'Indeed, you must excuse me. I could not act any thing if you were to give me the world. No, indeed, I cannot act.'

'Indeed, but you must, for we cannot excuse you. It need not frighten you; it is a nothing of a part, a mere nothing, not above half-a-dozen speeches altogether, and it will not much signify if nobody hears a word you say, so you may be as creep-mouse as you like, but we must have you to look at.'

'If you are afraid of half-a-dozen speeches,' cried Mr Rushworth, 'what would you do with such a part as mine? I have forty-two to learn.'

'It is not that I am afraid of learning by heart,' said Fanny, shocked to find herself at that moment the only speaker in the room, and to feel that almost every eye was upon her; 'but I really cannot act.'

'Yes, yes, you can act well enough for *us*. Learn your part, and we will teach you all the rest. You have only two scenes, and as I shall be Cottager, I'll put you in and push you about, and you will do it very well, I'll answer for it.'

'No, indeed, Mr Bertram, you must excuse me. You cannot have an idea. It would be absolutely impossible for me. If I were to undertake it, I should only disappoint you.'

'Phoo! Phoo! Do not be so shamefaced. You'll do it very well. Every allowance will be made for you. We do not expect perfection. You must get a brown gown, and a white apron, and a mob cap, and we must make you a few wrinkles, and a little of the crowsfoot at the corner of your eyes, and you will be a very proper, little old woman.'

'You must excuse me, indeed you must excuse me,' cried Fanny, growing more and more red from excessive agitation, and looking distressfully at Edmund, who was kindly observing her; but unwilling to exasperate his brother by interference, gave her only an encouraging smile. Her entreaty had no effect on Tom; he only said again what he had said before, and it was not merely Tom, for the requisition was now backed by Maria, and Mr Crawford, and Mr Yates, with an urgency which differed from his but in being more gentle or more ceremonious, and which altogether was quite overpowering to Fanny; and before she could breathe after it, Mrs Norris completed the whole by thus addressing her in a whisper at once angry and audible: 'What a piece of work here is about nothing; I am quite ashamed of you, Fanny, to make such a difficulty of obliging your cousins in a trifle of this sort – so kind as they are to you! Take the part with a good grace, and let us hear no more of the matter, I entreat.'

'Do not urge her, madam,' said Edmund. 'It is not fair to urge her in this manner. You see she does not like to act. Let her choose for herself, as well as the rest of us. Her judgment may be quite as safely trusted. Do not urge her any more.'

'I am not going to urge her,' replied Mrs Norris sharply; 'but I shall think her a very obstinate, ungrateful girl, if she does not do what her aunt and cousins wish her; very ungrateful, indeed, considering who and what she is.'

Edmund was too angry to speak; but Miss Crawford looking for a moment with astonished eyes at Mrs Norris, and then at Fanny, whose tears were beginning to show themselves, immediately said, with some keenness, 'I do not like my situation; this *place* is too hot for me,' and moved away her chair to the opposite side of the table, close to Fanny, saying to her, in a kind, low whisper, as she placed herself, 'Never mind, my dear Miss Price, this is a cross evening; everybody is cross and teasing, but do not let us mind them'; and with pointed attention continued to talk to her and endeavour to raise her spirits, in spite of being out of spirits herself. By a look at her brother, she prevented any further entreaty from the theatrical board, and the really good feelings by which she was almost purely governed, were rapidly restoring her to all the little she had lost in Edmund's favour.

Fanny did not love Miss Crawford; but she felt very much obliged to her for her present kindness; and when, from taking notice of her work, and wishing *she* could work as well, and begging for the pattern, and supposing Fanny was now preparing for her *appearance*, as of course she would come out when her cousin was married, Miss Crawford proceeded to inquire if she had heard lately from her brother at sea, and said that she had quite a curiosity to see him, and imagined him a very fine young man, and advised Fanny to get his picture drawn before he went to sea again, she could not help admitting it to be very agreeable flattery, or help listening and answering with more animation than she had intended.

The consultation upon the play still went on, and Miss Crawford's attention was first called from Fanny, by Tom Bertram's telling her, with infinite regret, that he found it absolutely impossible for him to undertake the part of Anhalt in addition to the Butler: he had been most anxiously trying to make it out to be feasible, but it would not do; he must give it up. 'But there will not be the smallest difficulty in filling it,' he added. 'We have but to speak the word; we may pick and choose. I could name, at this moment, at least six young men within six miles of us, who are wild to be admitted into our company, and there are one or two that would not disgrace us; I should not be afraid to trust either of the Olivers or Charles Maddox. Tom Oliver is a very clever fellow, and Charles Maddox is as gentlemanlike a man as you will see anywhere, so I will take my horse early to-morrow morning and ride over to Stoke, and settle with one of them.'

While he spoke, Maria was looking apprehensively round at Edmund in full expectation that he must oppose such an enlargement of the plan as this: so contrary to all their first protestations; but Edmund said nothing. After a moment's thought, Miss Crawford calmly replied, 'As far as I am concerned, I can have no objection to anything that you all think eligible. Have I ever seen either of the gentlemen? Yes, Mr Charles Maddox dined at my sister's one day, did not he, Henry? A quiet looking young man. I remember him. Let *him* be applied to, if you please, for it will be less unpleasant for me than to have a perfect stranger.'

Charles Maddox was to be the man. Tom repeated his resolution of going to him early on the morrow; and though Julia, who had scarcely opened her lips before, observed in a sarcastic manner, and with a glance first at Maria, and then at Edmund, that 'the Mansfield theatricals would enliven the whole neighbourhood exceedingly,' Edmund still held his peace, and showed his feelings only by a determined gravity.

'I am not very sanguine as to our play,' said Miss Crawford, in an under voice to Fanny, after some consideration; 'and I can tell Mr Maddox that I shall shorten some of *his* speeches, and a great many of *my own* before we rehearse together. It will be very disagreeable, and by no means what I expected.'

CHAPTER SIXTEEN

IT WAS NOT IN MISS CRAWFORD'S power to talk Fanny into any real forgetfulness of what had passed. When the evening was over, she went to bed, full of it, her nerves still agitated by the shock of such an attack from her cousin Tom, so public and so persevered in, and her spirits sinking under her aunt's unkind reflection and reproach. To be called into notice in such a manner, to hear that it was but the prelude to something so infinitely worse, to be told that she must do what was so impossible as to act; and then to have the charge of obstinacy and ingratitude follow it, enforced with such a hint at the dependence of her situation, had been too distressing at the time to make the remembrance when she was alone much less so, especially with the superadded dread of what the morrow might produce in continuation of the subject. Miss Crawford had protected her only for the time; and if she were applied to again among themselves with all the authoritative urgency that Tom and Maria were capable of, and Edmund perhaps away, what should she do? She fell asleep before she could answer the question, and found it quite as puzzling when she awoke the next morning. The little white attic, which had continued her sleeping room ever since her first entering the family, proving incompetent to suggest any reply, she had recourse, as soon as she was dressed, to another apartment more spacious and more meet for walking about in and thinking, and of which she had now for some time been almost equally mistress. It had been their schoolroom; so called till the Miss Bertrams would not allow it to be called so any longer, and inhabited as such to a later period. There Miss Lee had lived, and there they had read and written, and talked and laughed, till within the last three years, when she had quitted them. The room had then become useless, and for some time was quite deserted, except by Fanny, when she visited her plants, or wanted one of the books, which she was still glad to keep there, from the deficiency of space and accommodation in her little chamber above; but gradually, as her value for the comforts of it increased, she had added to her possessions, and spent more of her time there; and having nothing to oppose her, had so naturally and so artlessly worked herself into it, that it was now generally admitted to be hers. The East Room, as it had been called ever since Maria Bertram was sixteen, was now considered Fanny's, almost as decidedly as the white attic: the smallness of the one making the use of the other so evidently reasonable, that the Miss Bertrams, with every superiority in their own apartments which their own sense of superiority could demand, were entirely approving it; and Mrs Norris, having stipulated for there never being a fire in it on Fanny's account, was tolerably resigned to her having the use of what nobody else wanted, though the terms in which she sometimes spoke of the indulgence seemed to imply that it was the best room in the house.

The aspect was so favourable, that even without a fire it was habitable in many an early spring and late autumn morning, to such a willing mind as Fanny's; and while there was a gleam of sunshine, she hoped not to be driven from it entirely, even when winter came. The comfort of it in her hours of leisure was extreme. She could go there after any thing unpleasant below, and find immediate consolation in some pursuit, or some train of thought at hand. Her plants, her books – of which she had been a collector from the first hour of her commanding a shilling – her writing-desk and her works of charity and ingenuity, were all within her reach; or if indisposed for employment, if nothing but musing would do, she could scarcely see an object in that room which had not an interesting remembrance connected with it. Every thing was a friend, or bore her thoughts to a friend; and though there had been sometimes much of suffering to her, though her motives had often been misunderstood, her feelings disregarded; and her comprehension undervalued; though she had known the pains of tyranny, or ridicule, and neglect; yet almost every recurrence of either had led to something consolatory; her Aunt Bertram had spoken for her, or Miss Lee had been encouraging, or, what was yet more frequent or more dear, Edmund had been her champion and her friend; he had supported her cause or explained her meaning; he had told her not to cry, or had given her some proof of affection which made her tears delightful, and the whole was now so blended together, so harmonised by distance, that every former affliction had its charm. The room was most dear to her, and she would not have changed its furniture for the handsomest in the house, though what had been originally plain, had suffered all the ill-usage of children; and its greatest elegancies and ornaments were a faded footstool of Julia's work, too ill done for the drawing-room, three transparencies, made in a rage for transparencies, for the three lower panes of one window, where Tintern Abbey held its station between a cave in Italy and a moonlight lake in Cumberland, a collection of family profiles, thought unworthy of being any where else, over the mantelpiece, and by their side, and pinned against the wall, a small sketch of a ship sent four years ago from the Mediterranean by William, with H.M.S. *Antwerp* at the bottom, in letters as tall as the mainmast.

To this nest of comforts Fanny now walked down to try its influence on an agitated, doubting spirit, to see if by looking at Edmund's profile she could catch any of his counsel, or by giving air to her geraniums she might inhale a breeze of mental strength herself. But she had more than fears of her own perseverance to remove: she had begun to feel undecided as to what she *ought to do*; and as she walked round the room her doubts were increasing. Was she *right* in refusing what was so warmly asked, so strongly wished for – what might be so essential to a scheme on which some of those to whom she owed the greatest complaisance had set their hearts? Was it not ill-nature, selfishness, and a fear of exposing herself? And would Edmund's judgment, would his persuasion of Sir Thomas's disapprobation of the whole, be enough to justify her in a determined denial in spite of all the rest? It would be so horrible to her to act, that she was inclined to suspect the truth and purity of her own scruples; and as she looked around her, the claims of her cousins to being obliged were strengthened by the sight of present upon present that she had received from them. The table between the windows was covered with work-boxes and netting-boxes which had been given her at different times, principally by Tom; and she grew bewildered as to the amount of the debt which all these kind remembrances produced. A tap at the door roused her in the midst of this attempt to find her way to her duty, and her gentle 'come in' was answered by the appearance of one, before whom all her doubts were wont to be laid. Her eyes brightened at the sight of Edmund.

'Can I speak with you, Fanny, for a few minutes?' said he.

'Yes, certainly.'

'I want to consult. I want your opinion.'

'My opinion!' she cried, shrinking from such a compliment, highly as it gratified her.

'Yes, your advice and opinion. I do not know what to do. This acting scheme gets worse and worse, you see. They have chosen almost as bad a play as they could, and now, to complete the business, are going to ask the help of a young man very slightly known to any of us. This is the end of all the privacy and propriety which was talked about at first. I know no harm of Charles Maddox; but the excessive intimacy which must spring from his being admitted among us in this manner is highly objectionable, the *more* than intimacy – the familiarity. I cannot think of it with any patience; and it does appear to me an evil of such magnitude as must, *if possible*, be prevented. Do not you see it in the same light?'

'Yes; but what can be done? Your brother is so determined.'

'There is but *one* thing to be done, Fanny. I must take Anhalt myself. I am well aware that nothing else will quiet Tom.'

Fanny could not answer him.

'It is not at all what I like,' he continued. 'No man can like being driven into the *appearance* of such inconsistency. After being known to oppose the scheme from the beginning, there is absurdity in the face of my joining them *now*, when they are exceeding their first plan in every respect; but I can think of no other alternative. Can you, Fanny?'

'No,' said Fanny slowly, 'not immediately, but—'

'But what? I see your judgment is not with me. Think it a little over. Perhaps you are not so much aware as I am of the mischief that *may*, of the unpleasantness that *must* arise from a young man's being received in this manner; domesticated among us; authorised to come at all hours, and placed suddenly on a footing which must do away all restraints. To think only of the licence which every rehearsal must tend to create. It is all very bad! Put yourself in Miss Crawford's place, Fanny. Consider what it would be to act Amelia with a stranger. She has a right to be felt for, because she evidently feels for herself. I heard enough of what she said to you last night to understand her unwillingness to be acting with a stranger; and as she probably engaged in the part with different expectations – perhaps without considering the subject enough to know what was likely to be – it would be ungenerous, it would be really wrong to expose her to it. Her feelings ought to be respected. Does it not strike you so, Fanny? You hesitate.'

'I am sorry for Miss Crawford; but I am more sorry to see you drawn in to do what you had resolved against, and what you are known to think will be disagreeable to my uncle. It will be such a triumph to the others!'

'They will not have much cause of triumph when they see how infamously I act. But, however, triumph there certainly will be, and I must brave it. But if I can be the means of restraining the publicity of the business, of limiting the exhibition, of concentrating our folly, I shall be well repaid. As I am now, I have no influence, I can do nothing: I have offended them, and they will not hear me; but when I have put them in good humour by this concession, I am not without hopes of persuading them to confine the representation within a much smaller circle than they are now in the high road for. This will be a material gain. My object is to confine it to Mrs Rushworth and the Grants. Will not this be worth gaining?'

'Yes, it will be a great point.'

'But still it has not your approbation. Can you mention any other measure by which I have a chance of doing equal good?'

'No, I cannot think of any thing else.'

'Give me your approbation, then, Fanny. I am not comfortable without it.'

'Oh cousin!'

'If you are against me, I ought to distrust myself, and yet— But it is absolutely impossible to let Tom go on in this way, riding about the country in quest of any body who can be persuaded to act – no matter whom: the look of a gentleman is to be enough. I thought *you* would have entered more into Miss Crawford's feelings.'

'No doubt she will be very glad. It must be a great relief to her,' said Fanny, trying for greater warmth of manner.

'She never appeared more amiable than in her behaviour to you last night. It gave her a very strong claim on my goodwill.'

'She *was* very kind, indeed, and I am glad to have her spared —'

She could not finish the generous effusion. Her conscience stopped her in the middle, but Edmund was satisfied.

'I shall walk down immediately after breakfast,' said he, 'and am sure of giving pleasure there. And, now, dear Fanny, I will not interrupt you any longer. You want to be reading. But I could not be easy till I had spoken to you, and come to a decision. Sleeping or waking, my head has been full of this matter all night. It is an evil, but I am certainly making it less than it might be. If Tom is up, I shall go to him directly and get it over, and when we meet at breakfast we shall be all in high good humour at the prospect of acting the fool together with such unanimity. *You* in the meanwhile will be taking a trip into China, I suppose. How does Lord Macartney go on? (opening a volume on the table and then taking up some others). And here are Crabbe's *Tales*, and *The Idler*, at hand to relieve you, if you tire of your great book. I admire your little establishment exceedingly; and as soon as I am gone, you will empty your head of all this nonsense of acting, and sit comfortably down to your table. But do not stay here to be cold.'

He went; but there was no reading, no China, no composure for Fanny. He had told her the most extraordinary, the most inconceivable, the most unwelcome news; and she could think of nothing else. To be acting! After all his objections – objections so just and so public! After all that she had heard him say, and seen him look, and known him to be feeling. Could it be possible? Edmund so inconsistent! Was he not deceiving himself? Was he not wrong? Alas! it was all Miss Crawford's doing. She had seen her influence in every speech, and was miserable. The doubts and alarms as to her own conduct, which had previously distressed her, and which had all slept while she listened to him, were become of little consequence now. This deeper anxiety swallowed them up. Things should take their course; she cared not how it ended. Her cousins might attack, but could hardly teaze her. She was beyond their reach; and if at last obliged to yield – no matter – it was all misery *now*.

CHAPTER SEVENTEEN

IT WAS, INDEED, A TRIUMPHANT day to Mr Bertram and Maria. Such a victory over Edmund's discretion had been beyond their hopes, and was most delightful. There was no longer any thing to disturb them in their darling project, and they congratulated each other in private on the jealous weakness to which they attributed the change, with all the glee of feelings gratified in every way. Edmund might still look grave, and say he did not like the scheme in general, and must disapprove the play in particular; their point was gained; he was to act, and he was driven to it by force of selfish inclinations only. Edmund had descended from that moral elevation which he had maintained before, and they were both as much the better as the happier for the descent.

They behaved very well, however, to *him* on the occasion, betraying no exultation beyond the lines about the corners of the mouth, and seemed to think it as great an escape to be quit of the intrusion of Charles Maddox, as if they had been forced into admitting him against their inclination. 'To have it quite in their own family circle was what they had particularly wished. A stranger among them would have been the destruction of all their comfort'; and when Edmund, pursuing that idea, gave a hint of his hope as to the limitation of the audience, they were ready, in the complaisance of the moment, to promise any thing. It was all good humour and encouragement. Mrs Norris offered to contrive his dress, Mr Yates assured him that Anhalt's last scene with the Baron admitted a good deal of action and emphasis, and Mr Rushworth undertook to count his speeches.

'Perhaps,' said Tom, '*Fanny* may be more disposed to oblige us now. Perhaps you may persuade *her*.'

'No, she is quite determined. She certainly will not act.'

'Oh! very well.' And not another word was said; but Fanny felt herself again in danger, and her indifference to the danger was beginning to fail her already.

There were not fewer smiles at the Parsonage than at the Park on this change in Edmund; Miss Crawford looked very lovely in hers, and entered with such an instantaneous renewal of cheerfulness into the whole affair, as could have but one effect on him. 'He was certainly right in respecting such feelings; he was glad he had determined on it.' And the morning wore away in satisfactions very sweet, if not very sound. One advantage resulted from it to Fanny; at the earnest request of Miss Crawford, Mrs Grant had, with her usual good humour, agreed to undertake the part for which Fanny had been wanted; and this was all that occurred to gladden *her* heart during the day; and even this, when imparted by Edmund, brought a pang with it, for it was Miss Crawford to whom she was obliged; it was Miss Crawford whose kind exertions were to excite her gratitude, and whose merit in making them was spoken of with a glow of admiration. She was safe; but peace and safety were unconnected here. Her mind had been never farther from peace. She could not feel that she had done wrong herself, but she was disquieted in every other way. Her heart and her judgment were equally against Edmund's decision: she could not acquit his unsteadiness, and his happiness under it made her wretched. She was full of jealousy and agitation. Miss Crawford came with looks of gaiety which seemed an insult, with friendly expressions towards herself which she could hardly answer calmly. Everybody around her was gay and busy, prosperous and important; each had their object of interest, their part, their dress, their favourite scene, their friends and confederates: all were finding employment in consultations and comparisons, or diversion in the playful conceits they suggested. She alone was sad and insignificant; she had no share in any thing; she might go or stay; she might be in the midst of their noise, or retreat from it to the solitude of the East Room, without being seen or missed. She could almost think any thing would have been preferable to this. Mrs Grant was of consequence: *her* good nature had honourable mention: her taste and her time were considered; her presence was wanted; she was sought for, and attended, and praised; and Fanny was at first in some danger of envying her the character she had accepted. But reflection brought better feelings, and showed her that Mrs Grant was entitled to respect, which could never have belonged to *her*; and that, had she received even the greatest, she could never have been easy in joining a scheme which, considering only her uncle, she must condemn altogether.

Fanny's heart was not absolutely the only saddened one amongst them, as she soon began to acknowledge to herself. Julia was a sufferer, too, though not quite so blamelessly.

Henry Crawford had trifled with her feelings; but she had very long allowed, and even sought his attentions with a jealousy of her sister so reasonable as ought to have been their cure; and now that the conviction of his preference for Maria had been forced on her, she submitted to it without any alarm for Maria's situation, or any endeavour at rational tranquillity for herself. She either sat in gloomy silence, wrapped in such gravity as nothing could subdue, no curiosity touch, no wit amuse; or allowing the attentions of Mr Yates, was talking with forced gaiety to him alone, and ridiculing the acting of the others.

For a day or two after the affront was given Henry Crawford had endeavoured to do it away by the usual attack of gallantry and compliment, but he had not cared enough about it to persevere against a few repulses; and becoming soon too busy with his play to have time for more than one flirtation, he grew indifferent to the quarrel, or rather thought it a lucky occurrence, as quietly putting an end to what might ere long have raised expectations in more than Mrs Grant. She was not pleased to see Julia excluded from the play, and sitting by disregarded; but as it was not a matter which really involved her happiness, as Henry must be the best judge of his own, and as he did assure her, with a most persuasive smile, that neither he nor Julia had ever had a serious thought of each other, she could only renew her former caution as to the elder sister, entreat him not to risk his tranquillity by too much admiration there, and then gladly take her share in any thing that brought cheerfulness to the young people in general, and that did so particularly promote the pleasure of the two so dear to her.

'I rather wonder Julia is not in love with Henry,' was her observation to Mary.

'I dare say she is,' replied Mary coldly. 'I imagine both sisters are.'

'Both! No, no, that must not be. Do not give him a hint of it. Think of Mr Rushworth!'

'You had better tell Miss Bertram to think of Mr Rushworth. It may do *her* some good. I often think of Mr Rushworth's property and independence and wish them in other hands; but I never think of *him*. A man might represent the county with such an estate; a man might escape a profession and represent the county.'

'I dare say he *will* be in parliament soon. When Sir Thomas comes I dare say he will be in for some borough, but there has been nobody to put him in the way of doing any thing yet.'

'Sir Thomas is to achieve many mighty things when he comes home,' said Mary, after a pause. 'Do you remember Hawkins Browne's "Address to Tobacco," in imitation of Pope?

> Blest leaf! whose aromatic gales dispense
> To Templars modesty, to Parsons sense.

I will parody them:

> Blest Knight! whose dictatorial looks dispense
> To Children affluence, to Rushworth sense.

Will not that do, Mrs Grant? Everything seems to depend upon Sir Thomas's return.'

'You will find his consequence very just and reasonable when you see him in his family, I assure you. I do not think we do so well without him. He has a fine dignified manner, which suits the head of such a house, and keeps every body in their place. Lady Bertram seems more of a cipher now than when he is at home; and nobody else can keep Mrs Norris in order. But, Mary, do not fancy that Maria Bertram cares for Henry. I am sure *Julia* does not, or she would not have flirted as she did last night with Mr Yates; and though he and Maria are very good friends, I think she likes Sotherton too well to be inconstant.'

'I would not give much for Mr Rushworth's chance, if Henry stepped in before the articles were signed.'

'If you have such a suspicion, some thing must be done; and as soon as the play is all over, we will talk to him seriously, and make him know his own mind; and if he means nothing, we will send him off, though he is Henry, for a time.'

Julia *did* suffer, however, though Mrs Grant discerned it not, and though it escaped the notice of many of her own family likewise. She had loved, she did love still, and she had all the suffering which a warm temper and a high spirit were likely to endure under the disappointment of a dear, though irrational hope, with a strong sense of ill-usage. Her heart was sore and angry, and she was capable only of angry consolations. The sister with whom she was used to be on easy terms was now become her greatest enemy: they were alienated from each other; and Julia was not superior to the hope of some distressing end to the attentions which were still carrying on there, some punishment to Maria for conduct so shameful towards herself as well as towards Mr Rushworth. With no material fault of temper, or difference of opinion, to prevent their being very good friends while their interests were the same, the sisters, under such a trial as this, had not affection or principle enough to make them merciful or just, to give them honour or compassion. Maria felt her triumph, and pursued her purpose, careless of Julia; and Julia could never see Maria distinguished by Henry Crawford without trusting that it would create jealousy, and bring a public disturbance at last.

Fanny saw and pitied much of this in Julia; but there was no outward fellowship between them. Julia made no communication, and Fanny took no liberties. They were two solitary sufferers, or connected only by Fanny's consciousness.

The inattention of the two brothers and the aunt to Julia's discomposure, and their blindness to its true cause, must be imputed to the fullness of their own minds. They were totally preoccupied. Tom was engrossed by the concerns of his theatre, and saw nothing that did not immediately relate to it. Edmund, between his theatrical and his real part – between Miss Crawford's claims and his own conduct – between love and consistency, was equally unobservant; and Mrs Norris was too busy in contriving and directing the general little matters of the company, superintending their various dresses with economical expedience, for which nobody thanked her, and saving, with delighted integrity, half-a-crown here and there to the absent Sir Thomas, to have leisure for watching the behaviour, or guarding the happiness of his daughters.

CHAPTER EIGHTEEN

EVERYTHING WAS NOW IN A regular train; theatre, actors, actresses and dresses were all getting forward; but though no other great impediments arose, Fanny found, before many days were past, that it was not all uninterrupted enjoyment to the party themselves, and that she had not to witness the continuance of such unanimity and delight, as had been almost too much for her at first. Everybody began to have their vexation. Edmund had many. Entirely against *his* judgment, a scene painter arrived from town, and was at work, much to the increase of the expenses, and, what was worse, of the éclat of their proceedings; and his brother, instead of being really guided by him as to the privacy of the representation, was giving an invitation to every family who came in his way. Tom himself began to fret over the scene painter's slow progress, and to feel the miseries of waiting. He had learned his part – all parts, for he took every trifling one that could be united with the Butler, and began to be impatient to be acting; and every day thus unemployed was tending to increase his sense of the insignificance of all his parts together, and make him more ready to regret that some other play had not been chosen.

Fanny, being always a very courteous listener, and often the only listener at hand, came in for the complaints and the distresses of most of them. *She* knew that Mr Yates was in general thought to rant dreadfully; that Mr Yates was disappointed in Henry Crawford; that Tom Bertram spoke so quick he would be unintelligible; that Mrs Grant spoiled everything by laughing; that Edmund was behind-hand with his part, and that it was a misery to have any thing to do with Mr Rushworth, who was wanting a prompter through every speech. She knew, also, that poor Mr Rushworth could seldom get any body to rehearse with him; *his* complaint came before her as well as the rest; and so decided to her eye was her cousin Maria's avoidance of him and so needlessly often the rehearsal of the first scene between her and Mr Crawford, that she had soon all the terror of other complaints from *him*. So far from being all satisfied and all enjoying, she found every body requiring some thing they had not, and giving occasion of discontent to the others. Every body had a part either too long or too short; nobody would attend as they ought; nobody would remember on which side they were to come in; nobody but the complainer would observe any directions.

Fanny believed herself to derive as much innocent enjoyment from the play as any of them; Henry Crawford acted well, and it was a pleasure to her to creep into the theatre, and attend the rehearsal of the first act, in spite of the feelings it excited in some speeches for Maria. Maria, she also thought, acted well, too well; and after the first rehearsal or two, Fanny began to be their only audience, and sometimes as prompter, sometimes as spectator, was often very useful. As far as she could judge, Mr Crawford was considerably the best actor of all; he had more confidence then Edmund, more judgment than Tom, more talent and taste than Mr Yates. She did not like him as a man, but she must admit him to be the best actor, and on this point there were not many who differed from her. Mr Yates, indeed, exclaimed against his tameness and insipidity; and the day came at last when Mr Rushworth turned to her with a black look and said: 'Do you think there is any thing so very fine in all this? For the life and soul of me, I cannot admire him; and between ourselves, to see such an undersized, little, mean-looking man, set up for a fine actor, is very ridiculous in my opinion.'

From this moment there was a return of his former jealousy, which Maria, from increasing hopes of Crawford, was at little pains to remove, and the chances of Mr Rushworth's ever attaining to the knowledge of his two-and-forty speeches became much less. As to his ever making any thing *tolerable* of them, nobody had the smallest idea of that except his mother; *she*, indeed, regretted that his part was not more considerable, and deferred coming over to Mansfield till they were forward enough in their rehearsal to comprehend all his scenes; but the others aspired at nothing beyond his remembering the catch-word, and the first line of his speech, and being able to follow the prompter through the rest. Fanny, in her pity and kindheartedness, was at great pains to teach him how to learn, giving him all the helps and directions in her power, trying to make an artificial memory for him, and learning every word of his part herself, but without being much the forwarder.

Many uncomfortable, anxious, apprehensive feelings she certainly had; but with all these, and other claims on her time and attention, she was as far from finding herself without employment or utility amongst them, as without a companion in uneasiness; quite as far from having no demand on her leisure as on her compassion. The gloom of her first anticipations was proved to have been unfounded. She was occasionally useful to all; she was perhaps as much at peace as any.

There was a great deal of needlework to be done, moreover, in which her help was wanted; and that Mrs Norris thought her quite as well off as the rest was evident by the manner in which she claimed it: 'Come, Fanny,' she cried, 'these are fine times for you, but you must not be always walking from one room to the other, and doing the lookings-on at your ease, in this way; I want you here. I have been slaving myself till I can hardly stand, to contrive Mr Rushworth's cloak without sending for any more satin; and now I think you may give me your help in putting it together. There are but three seams, you may do them in a trice. It would be lucky for me if I had nothing but the executive part to do. *You* are best off, I can tell you; but if nobody did more than *you*, we should not get on very fast.'

Fanny took the work very quietly, without attempting any defence; but her kinder Aunt Bertram observed on her behalf:

'One cannot wonder, sister, that Fanny *should* be delighted; it is all new to her, you know; you and I used to be very fond of a play ourselves, and so am I still; and as soon as I am a little more at leisure, *I* mean to look in at their rehearsals too. What is the play about, Fanny, you have never told me?'

'Oh! sister, pray do not ask her now; for Fanny is not one of those who can talk and work at the same time. It is about lovers' vows.'

'I believe,' said Fanny to her Aunt Bertram, 'there will be three acts rehearsed to-morrow evening, and that will give you an opportunity of seeing all the actors at once.'

'You had better stay till the curtain is hung,' interposed Mrs Norris; 'the curtain will be hung in a day or two – there is very little sense in a play without a curtain – and I am much mistaken if you do not find it drawn up into very handsome festoons.'

Lady Bertram seemed quite resigned to waiting. Fanny did not share her aunt's composure; she thought of the morrow a great deal, for if the three acts were rehearsed, Edmund and Miss Crawford would then be acting together for the first time; the third act would bring a scene between them which interested her most particularly, and which she was longing and dreading to see how they would perform. The whole subject of it was love – a marriage of love was to be described by the gentleman, and very little short of a declaration of love be made by the lady.

She had read, and read the scene again with many painful, many wondering emotions, and looked forward to their representation of it as a circumstance almost too interesting. She did not *believe* they had yet rehearsed it, even in private.

The morrow came, the plan for the evening continued, and Fanny's consideration of it did not become less agitated. She worked very diligently under her aunt's directions, but her diligence and her silence concealed a very absent, anxious mind; and about noon she made her escape with her work to the East Room, that she might have no concern in another, and, as she deemed it, most unnecessary rehearsal of the first act, which Henry Crawford was just proposing, desirous at once of having her time to herself, and of avoiding the sight of Mr Rushworth. A glimpse, as she passed through the hall, of the two ladies walking up from the Parsonage, made no change in her wish of retreat, and she worked and meditated in the East Room, undisturbed, for a quarter of an hour, when a gentle tap at the door was followed by the entrance of Miss Crawford.

'Am I right? yes; this is the East Room. My dear Miss Price, I beg your pardon, but I have made my way to you on purpose to entreat your help.'

Fanny, quite surprised, endeavoured to show herself mistress of the room by her civilities, and looked at the bright bars of her empty grate with concern.

'Thank you; I am quite warm, very warm. Allow me to stay here a little while, and do have the goodness to hear my third act. I have brought my book, and if you would but rehearse it with me, I should be so obliged! I came here to-day intending to rehearse it with Edmund – by ourselves – against the evening, but he is not in the way; and if he *were*, I do not think I could go through it with *him*, till I have hardened myself a little; for really there *is* a speech or two— You will be so good, won't you?'

Fanny was most civil in her assurances, though she could not give them in a very steady voice.

'Have you ever happened to look at the part I mean?' continued Miss Crawford, opening her book. 'Here it is. I did not think much of it at first – but, upon my word— There, look at *that* speech, and *that*, and *that*. How am I ever to look him in the face and say such things? Could you do it? But then he is your cousin, which makes all the difference. You must rehearse it with me, that I may fancy *you* him, and get on by degrees. You *have* a look of *his* sometimes.'

'Have I? I will do my best with the greatest readiness; but I must *read* the part, for I can *say* very little of it.'

'None of it, I suppose. You are to have the book, of course. Now for it. We must have two chairs at hand for you to bring forward to the front of the stage. There – very good schoolroom chairs, not made for a theatre, I dare say; much more fitted for little girls to sit and kick their feet against when they are learning a lesson. What would your governess and your uncle say to see them used for such a purpose? Could Sir Thomas look in upon us just now, he would bless himself, for we are rehearsing all over the house. Yates is storming away in the dining-room. I heard him as I came upstairs, and the theatre is engaged of course by those indefatigable rehearsers, Agatha and Frederick. If *they* are not perfect, I *shall* be surprised. By the bye, I looked in upon them five minutes ago, and it happened to be exactly at one of the times when they were trying *not* to embrace, and Mr Rushworth was with me. I thought he began to look a little queer, so I turned it off as well as I could, by whispering to him, "We shall have an excellent Agatha, there is something so *maternal* in her manner, so completely *maternal* in her voice and countenance." Was not that well done of me? He brightened up directly. Now for my soliloquy.'

She began, and Fanny joined in with all the modest feeling which the idea of representing Edmund was so strongly calculated to inspire; but with looks and voice so truly feminine, as to be no very good picture of a man. With such an Anhalt, however, Miss Crawford had courage enough; and they had got through half the scene, when a tap at the door brought a pause, and the entrance of Edmund, the next moment, suspended it all.

Surprise, consciousness, and pleasure appeared in each of the three on this unexpected meeting; and as Edmund was come on the very same business that had brought Miss Crawford, consciousness and pleasure were likely to be more than momentary in *them*. He, too, had his book, and was seeking Fanny, to ask her to rehearse with him, and help him to prepare for the evening, without knowing Miss Crawford to be in the house; and great was the joy and animation of being thus thrown together, of comparing schemes, and sympathising in praise of Fanny's kind offices.

She could not equal them in their warmth. *Her* spirits sank under the glow of theirs, and she felt herself becoming too nearly nothing to both, to have any comfort in having been sought by either. They must now rehearse together. Edmund proposed, urged, entreated it, till the lady, not very unwilling at first, could refuse no longer, and Fanny was wanted only to prompt and observe them. She was invested, indeed, with the office of judge and critic, and earnestly desired to exercise it and tell them all their faults; but from doing so every feeling within her shrank – she could not, would not, dared not, attempt it; had she been otherwise qualified for criticism, her conscience must have restrained her from venturing at disapprobation. She believed herself to feel too much of it in the aggregate for honesty or safety in particulars. To prompt them must be enough for her; and it was sometimes *more* than enough; for she could not always pay attention to the book. In watching them she forgot herself; and, agitated by the increasing spirit of Edmund's manner, had once closed the page and turned away exactly as he wanted help. It was imputed to very reasonable weariness, and she was thanked and pitied; but she deserved their pity more than she hoped they would ever surmise. At last the scene was over, and Fanny forced herself to add her praise to the compliments each was giving the other; and when again alone, and able to recall the whole, she was inclined to believe their performance would indeed, have such nature and feeling in it as must ensure their credit, and make it a very suffering exhibition to herself. Whatever might be its effect, however, she must stand the brunt of it again that very day.

The first regular rehearsal of the three first acts was certainly to take place in the evening: Mrs Grant and the Crawfords were engaged to return for that purpose as soon as they could after dinner; and every one concerned was looking forward with eagerness. There seemed a general diffusion of cheerfulness on the occasion. Tom was enjoying such an advance towards the end; Edmund was in spirits from the morning's rehearsal, and little vexations seemed everywhere smoothed away. All were alert and impatient; the ladies moved soon, the gentlemen soon followed them, and with the exception of Lady Bertram, Mrs Norris and Julia, everybody was in the theatre at an early hour; and, having lighted it up as well as its unfinished state admitted, were waiting only the arrival of Mrs Grant and the Crawfords to begin.

They did not wait long for the Crawfords, but there was no Mrs Grant. She could not come. Dr Grant, professing an indisposition, for which he had little credit with his fair sister-in-law, could not spare his wife.

'Dr Grant is ill,' said she, with mock solemnity. 'He has been ill ever since he did not eat any of the pheasant to-day. He fancied it tough, sent away his plate, and has been suffering ever since.'

Here was disappointment! Mrs Grant's non-attendance was sad indeed. Her pleasant manners and cheerful conformity made her always valuable amongst them; but *now* she was absolutely necessary. They could not act, they could not rehearse with any satisfaction without her. The comfort of the whole evening was destroyed. What was to be done? Tom, as Cottager,

'My father is come!'

was in despair. After a pause of perplexity, some eyes began to be turned towards Fanny, and a voice or two to say, 'If Miss Price would be so good as to *read* the part.' She was immediately surrounded by supplications, everybody asked it, even Edmund said, 'Do, Fanny, if it is not *very* disagreeable to you.'

But Fanny still hung back. She could not endure the idea of it. Why was not Miss Crawford to be applied to as well? Or why had not she rather gone to her own room, as she had felt to be safest, instead of attending the rehearsal at all? She had known it would irritate and distress her; she had known it her duty to keep away. She was properly punished.

'You have only to *read* the part,' said Henry Crawford, with renewed entreaty.

'And I do believe she can say every word of it,' added Maria, 'for she could put Mrs Grant right the other day in twenty places. Fanny, I am sure you know the part.'

Fanny could not say she did *not*; and as they all persevered, as Edmund repeated his wish, and with a look of even fond dependence on her good nature, she must yield. She would do her best. Everybody was satisfied; and she was left to the tremors of a most palpitating heart, while the others prepared to begin.

They *did* begin; and being too much engaged in their own noise to be struck by an unusual noise in the other part of the house, had proceeded some way, when the door of the room was thrown open, and Julia, appearing at it, with a face all aghast, exclaimed, 'My father is come! He is in the hall at this moment.'

CHAPTER NINETEEN

HOW IS THE CONSTERNATION OF the party to be described? To the greater number it was a moment of absolute horror. Sir Thomas in the house! All felt the instantaneous conviction. Not a hope of imposition or mistake was harboured anywhere. Julia's looks were an evidence of the fact that made it indisputable; and after the first starts and exclamations, not a word was spoken for half a minute; each with an altered countenance was looking at some other, and almost each was feeling it a stroke the most unwelcome, most ill-timed, most appalling! Mr Yates might consider it only as a vexatious interruption for the evening, and Mr Rushworth might imagine it a blessing; but every other heart was sinking under some degree of self-condemnation or undefined alarm, every other heart was suggesting,

'What will become of us? What is to be done now?' It was a terrible pause; and terrible to every ear were the corroborating sounds of opening doors and passing footsteps.

Julia was the first to move and speak again. Jealousy and bitterness had been suspended: selfishness was lost in the common cause; but at the moment of her appearance, Frederick was listening with looks of devotion to Agatha's narrative, and pressing her hand to his heart; and as soon as she could notice this, and see that, in spite of the shock of her words, he still kept his station and retained her sister's hand, her wounded heart swelled again with injury, and looking as red as she had been white before, she turned out of the room, saying, '*I* need not be afraid of appearing before him.'

Her going roused the rest; and at the same moment the two brothers stepped forward, feeling the necessity of doing some thing. A very few words between them were sufficient. The case admitted no difference of opinion; they must go to the drawing-room directly. Maria joined them with the same intent, just then the stoutest of the three; for the very circumstance which had driven Julia away was to her the sweetest support. Henry Crawford's retaining her hand at such a moment, a moment of such peculiar proof and importance, was worth ages of doubt and anxiety. She hailed it as an earnest of the most serious determination, and was equal even to encounter her father. They walked off, utterly heedless of Mr Rushworth's repeated question of, 'Shall I go too? Had not I better go too? Will not it be right for me to go too?' But they were no sooner through the door than Henry Crawford undertook to answer the anxious enquiry, and, encouraging him by all means to pay his respects to Sir Thomas without delay, sent him after the others with delighted haste.

Fanny was left with with only the Crawfords and Mr Yates. She had been quite overlooked by her cousins; and as her own opinion of her claims on Sir Thomas's affection was much too humble to give her any idea of classing herself with his children, she was glad to remain behind and gain a little breathing time. Her agitation and alarm exceeded all that was endured by the rest, by the right of a disposition which not even innocence could keep from suffering. She was nearly fainting: all her former habitual dread of her uncle was returning, and with it compassion for him and for almost every one of the party on the development before him, with solicitude on Edmund's account indescribable. She had found a seat, where in excessive trembling she was enduring all these fearful thoughts, while the other three, no longer under any restraint, were giving vent to their feelings of vexation, lamenting over such an unlooked-for premature arrival as a most untoward event, and without mercy wishing poor Sir Thomas had been twice as long on his passage, or were still in Antigua.

The Crawfords were more warm on the subject than Mr Yates, from better understanding the family, and judging more clearly of the mischief that must ensue. The ruin of the play was to them a certainty: they felt the total destruction of the scheme to be inevitably at hand; while Mr Yates considered it only as a temporary interruption, a disaster for the evening, and could even suggest the possibility of the rehearsal being renewed after tea, when the bustle of receiving Sir Thomas were over, and he might be at leisure to be amused by it. The Crawfords laughed at the idea; and having soon agreed on the propriety of their walking quietly home and leaving the family to themselves, proposed Mr Yates's accompanying them and spending the evening at the Parsonage. But Mr Yates, having never been with those who thought much of parental claims, or family confidence, could not perceive that any thing of the kind was necessary; and therefore, thanking them, said: 'He preferred remaining where he was, that he might pay his respects to the old gentleman handsomely, since he *was* come; and besides, he did not think it would be fair by the others to have every body run away.'

Fanny was just beginning to collect herself, and to feel that if she stayed longer behind it might seem disrespectful, when this point was settled, and being commissioned with the brother and sister's apology, saw them preparing to go as she quitted the room herself to perform the dreadful duty of appearing before her uncle.

Too soon did she find herself at the drawing-room door; and after pausing a moment for what she knew would not come, for a courage which the outside of no door had ever supplied to her, she turned the lock in desperation, and the lights of the drawing-room, and all the collected family, were before her. As she entered, her own name caught her ear. Sir Thomas was at that moment looking round him and saying, 'But where is Fanny? Why do not I see my little Fanny?' – and on perceiving her, came forward with a kindness which astonished and penetrated her, calling her his dear Fanny, kissing her affectionately, and observing with decided pleasure how much she was grown! Fanny knew not how to feel, nor where to look. She was quite oppressed. He had never been so kind, so *very* kind to her in his life. His manner seemed changed, his voice was quick from the agitation of joy; and all that had been awful in his dignity seemed lost in tenderness. He led her nearer the light and looked at her again – enquired particularly after her health, and then correcting himself, observed that he need *not* enquire, for her appearance spoke sufficiently on that point. A fine blush having succeeded the previous paleness of her face, he was justified in his belief of her equal improvement in health and beauty. He enquired next after her family, especially William; and his kindness altogether was such as made her reproach herself for loving him so little, and thinking his return a misfortune; and when, on having courage to lift her eyes to his face, she saw that he was grown thinner, and had the burnt, fagged, worn look of fatigue and a hot climate, every tender feeling was increased, and she was miserable in considering how much unsuspected vexation was probably ready to burst on him.

Sir Thomas was indeed the life of the party, who at his suggestion now seated themselves round the fire. He had the best right to be the talker; and the delight of his sensations in being again in his own house, in the centre of his family, after such a separation, made him communicative and chatty in a very unusual degree; and he was ready to give every information as to his voyage, and answer every question of his two sons almost before it was put. His business in Antigua had latterly been prosperously rapid, and he came directly from Liverpool, having had an opportunity of making his passage thither in a private vessel, instead of waiting for the packet; and all the little particulars of his proceedings and events, his arrivals and departures, were most promptly delivered, as he sat by Lady Bertram and looked with heartfelt satisfaction on the faces around him – interrupting himself more than once, however, to remark on his good fortune in finding them all at home – coming unexpectedly as he did – all collected together exactly as he could have wished, but dared not depend on. Mr Rushworth was not forgotten; a most friendly reception and warmth of hand-shaking had already met him, and with pointed attention he was now included in the objects most intimately connected with Mansfield. There was nothing disagreeable in Mr Rushworth's appearance, and Sir Thomas was liking him already.

By not one of the circle was he listened to with such unbroken, unalloyed enjoyment as by his wife, who was really extremely happy to see him, and whose feelings were so warmed by his sudden arrival as to place her nearer agitation than she had been for the last twenty years. She had been *almost* fluttered for a few minutes, and still remained so sensibly animated as to put away her work, move pug from her side, and give all her attention and all the rest of her sofa to her husband. She had no anxieties for any body to cloud *her* pleasure: her own time had been irreproachably spent during his absence: she had done a great deal of carpet work, and made many yards of fringe; and she would have answered as freely for the good conduct and useful pursuits of all the young people as for her own. It was so agreeable to her to see him again and hear him talk, to have her ear amused and her whole comprehensions filled by his narratives, that she began particularly to feel how dreadfully she must have missed him, and how impossible it would have been for her to bear a lengthened absence.

Mrs Norris was by no means to be compared in happiness to her sister. Not that *she* was incommoded by many fears of Sir Thomas's disapprobation when the present state of his house should be known, for her judgment had been so blinded that, except by the instinctive caution with which she had whisked away Mr Rushworth's pink satin cloak as her brother-in-law entered, she could hardly be said to show any sign of alarm; but she was vexed by the *manner* of his return. It had left her nothing to do. Instead of being sent for out of the room, and seeing him first, and having to spread the happy news through the house, Sir Thomas, with a very reasonable dependence, perhaps, on the nerves of his wife and children, had sought no confidant but the butler, and had been following him almost instantaneously into the drawing-room. Mrs Norris felt herself defrauded of an office on which she had always depended, whether his arrival or his death were to be the thing unfolded; and was now trying to be in a bustle without having anything to bustle about, and labouring to be important where nothing was wanted but tranquillity and silence. Would Sir Thomas have consented to eat, she might have gone to the housekeeper with troublesome directions, and insulted the footmen with injunctions of despatch; but Sir Thomas resolutely declined all dinner; he would take nothing, nothing till tea came – he would rather wait for tea. Still Mrs Norris was at intervals urging something different; and in the most interesting moment of his passage to England, when the alarm of a French privateer was at the height, she burst through his recital with the proposal of soup. 'Sure, my dear Sir Thomas, a basin of soup would be a much better thing for you than tea. Do have a basin of soup.'

Sir Thomas could not be provoked. 'Still the same anxiety for everybody's comfort, my dear Mrs Norris,' was his answer. 'But, indeed, I would rather have nothing but tea.'

'Well, then, Lady Bertram, suppose you speak for tea directly; suppose you hurry Baddeley a little; he seems behindhand to-night.' She carried this point, and Sir Thomas's narrative proceeded.

At length there was a pause. His immediate communications were exhausted, and it seemed enough to be looking joyfully around him, now at one, now at another of the beloved circle; but the pause was not long: in the elation of her spirits Lady Bertram became talkative, and what were the sensations of her children upon hearing her say: 'How do you think the young people have been amusing themselves lately, Sir Thomas? They have been acting. We have been all alive with acting.'

'Indeed! And what have you been acting?'

'Oh! They'll tell you all about it.'

'The *all* will soon be told,' cried Tom hastily, and with affected unconcern; 'but it is not worth while to bore my father with it now. You will hear enough of it to-morrow, sir. We have just been trying, by way of doing something, and amusing my mother, just within the last week, to get up a few scenes, a mere trifle. We have had such incessant rains almost since

October began, that we have been nearly confined to the house for days together. I have hardly taken out a gun since the third. Tolerable sport the first three days, but there has been no attempting anything since. The first day I went over Mansfield Wood, and Edmund took the copses beyond Easton, and we brought home six brace between us, and might each have killed six times as many; but we respect your pheasants, sir, I assure you, as much as you could desire. I do not think you will find your woods by any means worse stocked than they were. *I* never saw Mansfield Wood so full of pheasants in my life as this year. I hope you will take a day's sport there yourself, sir, soon.'

For the present the danger was over, and Fanny's sick feeling subsided; but when tea was soon afterwards brought in, and Sir Thomas, getting up, said that he found that he could not be any longer in the house without just looking into his own dear room, every agitation was returning. He was gone before any thing had been said to prepare him for the change he must find there; and a pause of alarm followed his disappearance. Edmund was the first to speak:

'Some thing must be done,' said he.

'It is time to think of our visitors,' said Maria, still feeling her hand pressed to Henry Crawford's heart, and caring little for any thing else. 'Where did you leave Miss Crawford, Fanny?'

Fanny told of their departure, and delivered their message.

'Then poor Yates is all alone,' cried Tom. 'I will go and fetch him. He will be no bad assistant when it all comes out.'

To the theatre he went, and reached it just in time to witness the first meeting of his father and his friend. Sir Thomas had been a good deal surprised to find candles burning in his room; and on casting his eye round it, to see other symptoms of recent habitation and a general air of confusion in the furniture. The removal of the bookcase from before the billiard-room door struck him especially, but he had scarcely more than time to feel astonished at all this, before there were sounds from the billiard-room to astonish him still further. Some one was talking there in a very loud accent; he did not know the voice – *more* than talking – almost hallooing. He stepped to the door, rejoicing at that moment in having the means of immediate communication, and, opening it, found himself on the stage of a theatre, and opposed to a ranting young man, who appeared likely to knock him down backwards. At the very moment of Yates perceiving Sir Thomas, and giving perhaps the very best start he had ever given in the whole course of his rehearsals, Tom Bertram entered at the other end of the room; and never had he found greater difficulty in keeping his countenance. His father's looks of solemnity and amazement on this, his first appearance on any stage, and the gradual metamorphosis of the impassioned Baron

A ranting young man

Wildenheim into the well-bred and easy Mr Yates, making his bow and apology to Sir Thomas Bertram, was such an exhibition, such a piece of true acting, as he would not have lost upon any account. It would be the last – in all probability the last scene on that stage; but he was sure there could not be a finer. The house would close with the greatest éclat.

There was little time, however, for the indulgence of any images of merriment. It was necessary for him to step forward, too, and assist the introduction, and with many awkward sensations he did his best. Sir

Thomas received Mr Yates with all the appearance of cordiality which was due to his own character, but was really as far from pleased with the necessity of the acquaintance as with the manner of its commencement. Mr Yates's family and connections were sufficiently known to him, to render his introduction as the 'particular friend,' another of the hundred particular friends of his son, exceedingly unwelcome; and it needed all the felicity of being again at home, and all the forbearance it could supply, to save Sir Thomas from anger on finding himself thus bewildered in his own house, making part of a ridiculous exhibition in the midst of theatrical nonsense, and forced in so untoward a moment to admit the acquaintance of a young man whom he felt sure of disapproving, and whose easy indifference and volubility in the course of the first five minutes seemed to mark him the most at home of the two.

Tom understood his father's thoughts, and heartily wishing he might be always as well disposed to give them but partial expression, began to see more clearly than he had ever done before, that there might be some ground of offence, that there might be some reason for the glance his father gave towards the ceiling and stucco of the room; and that when he enquired with mild gravity after the fate of the billiard-table, he was not proceeding beyond a very allowable curiosity. A few minutes were enough for such unsatisfactory sensations on each side; and Sir Thomas having exerted himself so far as to speak a few words of calm approbation in reply to an eager appeal of Mr Yates, as to the happiness of the arrangement, the three gentlemen returned to the drawing-room together, Sir Thomas with an increase of gravity which was not lost on all.

'I come from your theatre,' said he, composedly, as he sat down; 'I found myself in it rather unexpectedly. Its vicinity to my own room—but in every respect, indeed, it took me by surprise, as I had not the smallest suspicion of your acting having assumed so serious a character. It appears a neat job, however, as far as I could judge by candle-light, and does my friend Christopher Jackson credit.' And then he would have changed the subject, and sipped his coffee in peace over domestic matters of a calmer hue; but Mr Yates, without discernment to catch Sir Thomas's meaning, or diffidence, or delicacy, or discretion enough to allow him to lead the discourse while he mingled among the others with the least obtrusiveness himself, would keep him on the topic of the theatre, would torment him, with questions and remarks relative to it, and finally would make him hear the whole history of his disappointment at Ecclesford. Sir Thomas listened most politely, but found much to offend his ideas of decorum, and confirm his ill opinion of Mr Yates's habits of thinking, from the beginning to the end of the story; and when it was over, could give him no other assurance of sympathy than what a slight bow conveyed.

'This was, in fact, the origin of *our* acting,' said Tom, after a moment's thought. 'My friend Yates brought the infection from Ecclesford, and it spread – as those things always spread, you know, sir – the faster, probably, from *your* having so often encouraged the sort of thing in us formerly. It was like treading old ground again.'

Mr Yates took the subject from his friend as soon as possible, and immediately gave Sir Thomas an account of what they had done and were doing; told him of the gradual increase of their views, the happy conclusion of their first difficulties, and present promising state of affairs; relating everything with so blind an interest as made him not only totally unconscious of the uneasy movements of many of his friends as they sat, the change of countenance, the fidget, the hem! of unquietness, but prevented him even from seeing the expression of the face on which his own eyes were fixed – from seeing Sir Thomas's dark brows contract as he looked with enquiring earnestness at his daughters and Edmund, dwelling particularly on the latter, and speaking a language, a remonstrance, a reproof, which *he* felt at his heart. Not less acutely was it felt by Fanny, who had edged back her chair behind her aunt's end of the sofa, and, screened from notice herself, saw all that was passing before her. Such a look of reproach at Edmund from his father she could never have expected to witness; and to feel that it was in any degree deserved was an aggravation indeed. Sir Thomas's look implied, 'On your judgment, Edmund, I depended; what have you been about?' She knelt in spirit to her uncle, and her bosom swelled to utter, 'Oh, not to *him*! Look so to all the others, but not to *him*!'

Mr Yates was still talking. 'To own the truth, Sir Thomas, we were in the middle of a rehearsal when you arrived this evening. We were going through the three first acts, and not unsuccessfully upon the whole. Our company is now so dispersed, from the Crawfords being gone home, that nothing more can be done to-night; but if you will give us the honour of your company to-morrow evening, I should not be afraid of the result. We bespeak your indulgence, you understand, as young performers; we bespeak your indulgence.'

'My indulgence shall be given, sir,' replied Sir Thomas gravely, 'but without any other rehearsal.' And with a relenting smile he added, 'I come home to be happy and indulgent.' Then turning away towards any or all of the rest, he tranquilly said, 'Mr and Miss Crawford were mentioned in my last letters from Mansfield. Do you find them agreeable acquaintances?'

Tom was the only one at all ready with an answer, but he being entirely without particular regard for either, without jealousy either in love or acting, could speak very handsomely of both. 'Mr Crawford was a most pleasant gentlemanlike man; his sister a sweet, pretty, elegant, lively girl.'

Mr Rushworth could be silent no longer. 'I do not say he is not gentlemanlike, considering; but you should tell your father he is not above five feet eight, or he will be expecting a well-looking man.'

Sir Thomas did not quite understand this, and looked with some surprise at the speaker.

'If I must say what I think,' continued Mr Rushworth, 'in my opinion it is very disagreeable to be always rehearsing. It is having too much of a good thing. I am not so fond of acting as I was at first. I think we are a great deal better employed, sitting comfortably here among ourselves and doing nothing.'

Sir Thomas looked again, and then replied with an approving smile, 'I am happy to find our sentiments on this subject so much the same. It gives me sincere satisfaction. That I should be cautious and quick-sighted, and feel many scruples which my children do *not* feel, is perfectly natural; and equally so that *my* value for domestic tranquillity, for a home which shuts out noisy pleasures, should much exceed theirs. But at your time of life to feel all this, is a most favourable circumstance for yourself, and for every body connected with you; and I am sensible of the importance of having an ally of such weight.'

Sir Thomas meant to be giving Mr Rushworth's opinion in better words than he could find himself. He was aware that he must not expect a genius in Mr Rushworth; but as a well-judging, steady young man, with better notions than his elocution would do justice to, he intended to value him very highly. It was impossible for many of the others not to smile. Mr Rushworth hardly knew what to do with so much meaning; but by looking, as he really felt, most exceedingly pleased with Sir Thomas's good opinion, and saying scarcely any thing, he did his best towards preserving that good opinion a little longer.

CHAPTER TWENTY

EDMUND'S FIRST OBJECT the next morning was to see his father alone, and give him a fair statement of the whole acting scheme, defending his own share in it as far only as he could then, in a soberer moment, feel his motives to deserve, and acknowledging, with perfect ingenuousness, that his concession had been attended with such partial good as to make his judgment in it very doubtful. He was anxious, while vindicating himself, to say nothing unkind of the others; but there was only one amongst them whose conduct he could mention without some necessity of defence or palliation. 'We have all been more or less to blame,' said he, 'every one of us, excepting Fanny. Fanny is the only one who has been consistent. *Her* feelings have been steadily against it from first to last. She never ceased to think of what was due to you. You will find Fanny every thing you could wish.'

Sir Thomas saw all the impropriety of such a scheme among such a party, and at such a time, as strongly as his son had ever supposed he must; he felt it too much, indeed, for many words; and having shaken hands with Edmund, meant to try to lose the disagreeable impression, and forget how much he had been forgotten himself as soon as he could, after the house had been cleared of every object enforcing the remembrance, and restored to its proper state. He did not enter into any remonstrance with his other children: he was more willing to believe they felt their error, than to run the risk of investigation. The reproof of an immediate conclusion of everything, the sweep of every preparation, would be sufficient.

There was one person, however, in the house, whom he could not leave to learn his sentiments merely through his conduct. He could not help giving Mrs Norris a hint of his having hoped that her advice might have been interposed to prevent what her judgment must certainly have disapproved. The young people had been very inconsiderate in forming the plan; they ought to have been capable of a better decision themselves; but they were young, and, excepting Edmund, he believed, of unsteady characters; and with greater surprise, therefore, he must regard her acquiescence in their wrong measures, her countenance of their unsafe amusements, then that such measures and such amusements should have been suggested. Mrs Norris was a little confounded and as nearly being silenced as ever she had been in her life; for she was ashamed to confess having never seen any of the impropriety which was so glaring to Sir Thomas, and would not have admitted that her influence was insufficient – that she might have talked in vain. Her only resource was to get out of the subject as fast as possible, and turn the current of Sir Thomas's ideas into a happier channel. She had a great deal to insinuate in her own praise as to *general* attention to the interest and comfort of his family, much exertion and many sacrifices to glance at in the form of hurried walks and sudden removals from her own fireside, and many excellent hints of distrust and economy to Lady Bertram and Edmund to detail, whereby a most considerable saving had always arisen, and more than one bad servant been detected. But her chief strength lay in Sotherton. Her greatest support and glory was in having formed the connection with the Rushworths. *There* she was impregnable. She took to herself all the credit of bringing Mr Rushworth's admiration of Maria to any effect. 'If I had not been active,' said she, 'and made a point of being introduced to his mother, and then prevailed on my sister to pay the first visit, I am as certain as I sit here that nothing would have come of it; for Mr Rushworth is the sort of amiable modest young man who wants a great deal of encouragement, and there were girls enough on the catch for him if we had been idle. But I left no stone unturned. I was ready to move heaven and earth to persuade my sister, and at last I did persuade her. You know the distance to Sotherton; it was in the middle of winter, and the roads almost impassable, but I did persuade her.'

'I know how great, how justly great, your influence is with Lady Bertram and her children, and am the more concerned that it should not have been—'

'My dear Sir Thomas, if you had seen the state of the roads *that* day! I

'To advise him not to venture'

though we should never have got through them, though we had the four horses of course; and poor old coachman would attend us, out of his great love and kindness, though he was hardly able to sit the box on account of the rheumatism which I had been doctoring him for ever since Michaelmas. I cured him at last; but he was very bad all the winter – and this was such a day, I could not help going to him up in his room before we set off to advise him not to venture: he was putting on his wig; so I said, "Coachman, you had much better not go; your Lady and I shall be very safe; you know how steady Stephen is, and Charles has been upon the leaders so often now, that I am sure there is no fear." But, however, I soon found it would not do; he was bent upon going, and as I hate to be worrying and officious, I said no more; but my heart quite ached for him at every jolt, and when we got into the rough lanes about Stoke, where, what with frost and snow upon beds of stones, it was worse than anything you can imagine, I was quite in an agony about him. And then the poor horses too! To see them straining away! You know how I always feel for the horses. And when we got to the bottom of Sandcroft Hill, what do you think I did? You will laugh at me; but I got out and walked up. I did indeed. It might not be saving them much, but it was some thing, and I could not bear to sit at my ease, and be dragged up at the expense of those noble animals. I caught a dreadful cold, but *that* I did not regard. My object was accomplished in the visit.'

'I hope we shall always think the acquaintance worth any trouble that might be taken to establish it. There is nothing very striking in Mr Rushworth's manners, but I was pleased last night with what appeared to be his opinion on *one* subject; his decided preference of a quiet family party to the bustle and confusion of acting. He seemed to feel exactly as one could wish.'

'Yes, indeed, and the more you know of him the better you will like him. He is not a shining character, but he has a thousand good qualities; and is so disposed to look up to you, that I am quite laughed at about it, for everybody considers it as my doing. "Upon my word, Mrs Norris," said Mrs Grant, the other day, "if Mr Rushworth were a son of your own, he could not hold Sir Thomas in greater respect."'

Sir Thomas gave up the point, foiled by her evasions, disarmed by her flattery; and was obliged to rest satisfied with the conviction that where the present pleasure of those she loved was at stake, her kindness did sometimes overpower her judgment.

It was a busy morning with him. Conversation with any of them occupied but a small part of it. He had to reinstate himself in all the wonted concerns of his Mansfield life; to see his steward and his bailiff; to examine and compute, and, in the intervals of business, to walk into his stables and his gardens, and nearest plantations; but active and methodical, he had not only done all this before he resumed his seat as master of the house at dinner, he had also set the carpenter to work in pulling down what had been so lately put up in the billiard-room, and given the scene-painter his dismissal, long enough to justify the pleasing belief of his being then at least as far off as Northampton. The scene-painter was gone, having spoilt only the floor of one room, ruined all the coachman's sponges, and made five of the under-servants idle and dissatisfied; and Sir Thomas was in hopes that another day or two would suffice to wipe away every outward memento of what had been, even to the destruction of every unbound copy of *Lovers' Vows* in the house, for he was burning all that met his eye.

Mr Yates was beginning now to understand Sir Thomas's intentions, though as far as ever from understanding their source. He and his friend had been out with their guns the chief of the morning, and Tom had taken the opportunity of explaining, with proper apologies for his father's particularity, what was to be expected. Mr Yates felt it as acutely as might be supposed. To be a second time disappointed in the same way was an instance of very severe ill luck; and his indignation was such, that had it not been for delicacy towards his friend, and his friend's youngest sister, he believed he should certainly attack the baronet on the absurdity of his proceedings, and argue him into a little more rationality. He believed this very stoutly while he was in Mansfield Wood, and all the way home; but there was a something in Sir Thomas, when they sat round the same table, which made Mr Yates think it wiser to let him pursue his own way, and feel the folly of it without question. He had known many disagreeable fathers before, and often been struck with the inconveniences they occasioned, but never, in the whole course of his life, had he seen one of that class, so unintelligibly moral, so infamously tyrannical as Sir Thomas. He was not a man to be endured but for his children's sake, and he might be thankful to his fair daughter Julia that Mr Yates did yet mean to stay a few days longer under his roof.

The evening passed with external smoothness, though almost every mind was ruffled; and the music which Sir Thomas called for from his daughters helped to conceal the want of real harmony. Maria was in a good deal of agitation. It was of the utmost consequence to her that Crawford should now lose no time in declaring himself, and she was disturbed that even a day should be gone by without seeming to advance that point. She had been expecting to see him the whole morning, and all the evening, too, was still expecting him. Mr Rushworth had set off early with the great news for Sotherton; and she had fondly hoped for such an immediate éclaircissement as might save him the trouble of ever coming back again. But they had seen no one from the Parsonage, not a creature, and had heard no tidings beyond a friendly note of congratulation and enquiry from Mrs Grant to Lady Bertram. It was the first day for many, many weeks, in which the families had been wholly divided. Four-and-twenty hours had never passed before, since August last began, without bringing them together in some way or other. It was a sad, anxious day; and the morrow, though differing in the sort of evil, did by no means bring less. A few moments of feverish enjoyment were followed by hours of acute suffering. Henry Crawford was again in the house; he walked up with Dr Grant, who was anxious to pay his respects to Sir Thomas, and at rather an early hour they were ushered into the breakfast-room, where were most of the family. Sir Thomas soon appeared, and Maria saw with delight and agitation the introduction of the man she loved to her father. Her sensations were indefinable, and so were they a few minutes afterwards upon hearing Henry Crawford, who had a chair between herself and Tom, ask the latter in an under voice, whether there were any plans for resuming the play after the present happy interruption (with a courteous glance at Sir Thomas), because, in that case, he should make a point of returning to Mansfield at any time required by the party: he was going away immediately, being to meet his uncle at Bath without delay: but if there were any prospect of a renewal of *Lovers' Vows*, he should hold himself positively engaged, he should break through every other claim; he should absolutely condition with his uncle for attending them whenever he might be wanted. The play should not be lost by *his* absence.

'From Bath, Norfolk, London, York; wherever I may be,' said he: 'I will attend you from any place in England, at an hour's notice.'

It was well at that moment that Tom had to speak and not his sister. He could immediately say with easy fluency, 'I am sorry you are going; but as to our play, *that* is all over – entirely at an end – (looking significantly at his father). The painter was sent off yesterday, and very little will remain of the theatre to-morrow. I knew how *that* would be from the first. It is early for Bath. You will find nobody there.'

'It is about my uncle's usual time.'

'When do you think of going?'

'I may, perhaps, get as far as Banbury to-day.'

'Whose stables do you use at Bath?' was the next question; and while this branch of the subject was under discussion, Maria, who wanted neither pride nor resolution, was preparing to encounter her share of it with tolerable calmness.

To her he soon turned, repeating much of what he had already said with only a softened air and stronger expression of regret. But what availed his expressions or his air? He was going, and, if not voluntarily going, voluntarily intending to stay away; for, excepting what might be due to his uncle, his engagements were all self-imposed. He might talk of necessity, but she knew his independence. The hand which had so pressed hers to his

Good wishes for a pleasant journey

heart! the hand and the heart were alike motionless and passive now! Her spirit supported her, but the agony of her mind was severe. She had not long to endure what arose from listening to language which his actions contradicted, or to bury the tumult of her feelings under the restraint of society; for general civilities soon called his notice from her, and the farewell visit, as it then became openly acknowledged, was a very short one. He was gone – he had touched her hand for the last time, he had made his parting bow, and she might seek directly all that solitude could do for her. Henry Crawford was gone, gone from the house, and within two hours afterwards from the parish; and so ended all the hopes his selfish vanity had raised in Maria and Julia Bertram.

Julia could rejoice that he was gone. His presence was beginning to be odious to her; and if Maria gained him not, she was now cool enough to dispense with any other revenge. She did not want exposure to be added to desertion. Henry Crawford gone, she could even pity her sister.

With a purer spirit did Fanny rejoice in the intelligence. She heard it at dinner, and felt it a blessing. By all the others it was mentioned with regret; and his merits honoured with due gradation of feeling, from the sincerity of Edmund's too partial regard, to the unconcern of his mother speaking entirely by rote. Mrs Norris began to look about her, and wonder that his falling in love with Julia had come to nothing; and could almost fear that she had been remiss herself in forwarding it; but with so many to care for, how was it possible for even *her* activity to keep pace with her wishes?

Another day or two, and Mr Yates was gone likewise. In *his* departure Sir Thomas felt the chief interest; wanting to be alone with his family, the presence of a stranger superior to Mr Yates must have been irksome; but of him, trifling and confident, idle and expensive, it was every way vexatious. In himself he was wearisome, but as the friend of Tom and the admirer of Julia he became offensive. Sir Thomas had been quite indifferent to Mr Crawford's going or staying; but his good wishes for Mr Yates's having a pleasant journey, as he walked with him to the hall door, were given with genuine satisfaction. Mr Yates had stayed to see the destruction of every theatrical preparation at Mansfield, the removal of every thing appertaining to the play: he left the house in all the soberness of its general character; and Sir Thomas hoped, in seeing him out of it, to be rid of the worst object connected with the scheme, and the last that must be inevitably reminding him of its existence.

Mrs Norris contrived to remove one article from his sight that might have distressed him. The curtain over which she had presided with such talent and such success, went off with her to her cottage, where she happened to be particularly in want of green baize.

CHAPTER TWENTY ONE

SIR THOMAS'S RETURN MADE a striking change in the ways of the family, independent of *Lovers' Vows*. Under his government, Mansfield was an altered place. Some members of their society sent away, and the spirits of many others saddened – it was all sameness and gloom compared with the past – a sombre family party rarely enlivened. There was little intercourse with the Parsonage. Sir Thomas, drawing back from intimacies in general, was particularly disinclined, at this time, for any engagements but in one quarter. The Rushworths were the only addition to his own domestic circle which he could solicit.

Edmund did not wonder that such should be his father's feelings, nor could he regret anything but the exclusion of the Grants. 'But they,' he observed to Fanny, 'have a claim. They seem to belong to us; they seem to be part of ourselves. I could wish my father were more sensible of their very great attention to my mother and sisters while he was away. I am afraid they may feel themselves neglected. But the truth is, that my father hardly knows them. They had not been here a twelvemonth when he left England. If he knew them better, he would value their society as it deserves; for they are in fact exactly the sort of people he would like. We are sometimes a little in want of animation among ourselves: my sisters seem out of spirits, and Tom is certainly not at his ease. Dr and Mrs Grant would enliven us, and make our evenings pass away with more enjoyment even to my father.'

'Do you think so?' said Fanny: 'in my opinion, my uncle would not like *any* addition. I think he values the very quietness you speak of, and that the repose of his own family circle is all he wants. And it does not appear to me that we are more serious than we used to be – I mean before my uncle went abroad. As well as I can recollect it was always much the same. There was never much laughing in his presence; or, if there is any difference it is not more I think than such an absence has a tendency to produce at first. There must be a sort of shyness; but I cannot recollect that our evenings formerly were ever merry, except when my uncle was in town. No young people's are, I suppose, when those they look up to are at home.'

'I believe you are right, Fanny,' was his reply, after a short consideration. 'I believe our evenings are rather returned to what they were, than assuming a new character. The novelty was in their being lively. Yet, how strong the impression that only a few weeks will give! I have been feeling as if we had never lived so before.'

'I suppose I am graver than other people,' said Fanny. 'The evenings do not appear long to me. I love to hear my uncle talk of the West Indies. I could listen to him for an hour together. It entertains *me* more than many other things have done; but then I am unlike other people, I dare say.'

'Why should you dare say *that*?' (smiling). 'Do you want to be told that you are only unlike other people in being more wise and discreet? But when did you, or any body, ever get a compliment from me, Fanny? Go to my father if you want to be complimented. He will satisfy you. Ask your uncle what he thinks, and you will hear compliments enough: and though they may be chiefly on your person, you must put up with it, and trust to his seeing as much beauty of mind in time.'

Such language was so new to Fanny that it quite embarrassed her.

'Your uncle thinks you very pretty, dear Fanny – and that is the long and the short of the matter. Any body but myself would have made some thing more of it, and any body but you would resent that you had not been thought very pretty before; but the truth is, that your uncle never did admire you till now – and now he does. Your complexion is so improved! and you have gained so much countenance! and your figure – nay, Fanny, do not turn away about it – it is but an uncle. If you cannot bear an uncle's admiration, what is to become of you? You must really begin to harden yourself to the idea of being worth looking at. You must try not to mind growing up into a pretty woman.'

'Oh! don't talk so, don't talk so,' cried Fanny, distressed by more feelings than he was aware of; but seeing that she was distressed, he had done with the subject, and only added more seriously—

'Your uncle is disposed to be pleased with you in every respect; and I only wish you would talk to him more. You are one of those who are too silent in the evening circle.'

'But I do talk to him more than I used. I am sure I do. Did not you hear me ask him about the slave-trade last night?'

'I did – and was in hopes the question would be followed up by others. It would have pleased your uncle to be enquired of farther.'

'And I longed to do it – but there was such a dead silence! And while my cousins were sitting by without speaking a word, or seeming at all interested in the subject, I did not like – I thought it would appear as if I wanted to set myself off at their expense, by showing a curiosity and pleasure in his information which he must wish his own daughters to feel.'

'Miss Crawford was very right in what she said of you the other day: that you seemed almost as fearful of notice and praise as other women were of neglect. We were talking of you at the Parsonage, and those were her words. She has great discernment. I know nobody who distinguishes characters better. For so young a woman it is remarkable! She certainly understands *you* better than you are understood by the greater part of those who have known you so long; and with regard to some others, I can perceive, from occasional lively hints, the unguarded expressions of the moment, that she could define *many* as accurately did not delicacy forbid it. I wonder what she thinks of my father! She must admire him as a fine-looking man, with most gentlemanlike, dignified, consistent manners, but, perhaps, having seen him so seldom, his reserve may be a little repulsive. Could they be much together. I feel sure of their liking each other. He would enjoy her liveliness, and she has talents to value his powers. I wish they met more frequently! I hope she does not suppose there is any dislike on his side.'

'She must know herself too secure of the regard of all the rest of you,' said

Fanny, with half a sigh, 'to have any such apprehension. And Sir Thomas's wishing just at first to be only with his family is so very natural, that she can argue nothing from that. After a little while I dare say we shall be meeting again in the same sort of way, allowing for the difference of the time of year.'

'This is the first October that she has passed in the country since her infancy. I do not call Tunbridge or Cheltenham the country; and November is a still more serious month, and I can see that Mrs Grant is very anxious for her not finding Mansfield dull as winter comes on.'

Fanny could have said a great deal, but it was safer to say nothing, and leave untouched all Miss Crawford's resources, her accomplishments, her spirits, her importance, her friends, lest it should betray her into any observations seemingly unhandsome. Miss Crawford's kind opinion of herself deserved at least a grateful forbearance, and she began to talk of some thing else.

'To-morrow, I think, my uncle dines at Sotherton and you and Mr Bertram too. We shall be quite a small party at home. I hope my uncle may continue to like Mr Rushworth.'

'That is impossible, Fanny. He must like him less after to-morrow's visit, for we shall be five hours in his company. I should dread the stupidity of the day, if there were not a much greater evil to follow – the impression it must leave on Sir Thomas. He cannot much longer deceive himself. I am sorry for them all, and would give some thing that Rushworth and Maria had never met.'

In this quarter, indeed, disappointment was impending over Sir Thomas. Not all his good-will for Mr Rushworth, not all Mr Rushworth's deference for him, could prevent him from soon discerning some part of the truth – that Mr Rushworth was an inferior young man, as ignorant in business as in books, with opinions in general unfixed, and without seeming much aware of it himself.

He had expected a very different son-in-law; and beginning to feel grave on Maria's account, tried to understand *her* feelings. Little observation there was necessary to tell him that indifference was the most favourable state they could be in. Her behaviour to Mr Rushworth was careless and cold. She could not, did not like him. Sir Thomas resolved to speak seriously to her. Advantageous as would be the alliance, and long standing and public as was the engagement, her happiness must not be sacrificed to it. Mr Rushworth had, perhaps, been accepted on too short an acquaintance, and, on knowing him better, she was repenting.

With solemn kindness Sir Thomas addressed her; told her his fears, enquired into her wishes, entreated her to be open and sincere, and assured her that every inconvenience should be braved, and the connection entirely given up, if she felt herself unhappy in the prospect of it. He would act for her and release her. Maria had a moment's struggle as she listened, and only a moment's; when her father ceased, she was able to give her answer immediately, decidedly, and with no apparent agitation. She thanked him for his great attention, his paternal kindness, but he was quite mistaken in supposing she had the smallest desire of breaking through her engagement, or was sensible of any change of opinion or inclination since her forming it. She had the highest esteem for Mr Rushworth's character and disposition, and could not have a doubt of her happiness with him.

Sir Thomas was satisfied; too glad to be satisfied, perhaps, to urge the matter quite so far as his judgment might have dictated to others. It was an alliance which he could not have relinquished without pain; and thus he reasoned. Mr Rushworth was young enough to improve: Mr Rushworth must and would improve in good society; and if Maria could now speak so securely of her happiness with him, speaking certainly without the prejudice, the blindness of love, she ought to be believed. Her feelings, probably, were not acute; he had never supposed them to be so; but her comforts might not be less on that account; and if she could dispense with seeing her husband a leading, shining character, there would certainly be every thing else in her favour. A well-disposed young woman, who did not marry for love, was in general but the more attached to her own family; and the nearness of Sotherton to Mansfield must naturally hold out the greatest temptation, and would, in all probability, be a continual supply of the most amiable and innocent enjoyments. Such and such-like were the reasonings of Sir Thomas, happy to escape the embarrassing evils of a rupture, the wonder, the reflections, the reproach that must attend it; happy to secure a marriage which would being him such an addition of respectability and influence and very happy to think any thing of his daughter's disposition that was most favourable for the purpose.

To her the conference closed as satisfactorily as to him. She was in a state of mind to be glad that she had secured her fate beyond recall; that she had pledged herself anew to Sotherton; that she was safe from the possibility of giving Crawford the triumph of governing her actions, and destroying her prospects; and retired in proud resolve, determined only to behave more cautiously to Mr Rushworth in future, that her father might not be again suspecting her.

Had Sir Thomas applied to his daughter within the first three or four days after Henry Crawford's leaving Mansfield, before her feelings were at all tranquillised, before she had given up every hope of him, or absolutely resolved on enduring his rival, her answer might have been different; but after another three or four days, when there was no return, no letter, no message, no symptom of a softened heart, no hope of advantage from separation her mind became cool enough to seek all the comfort that pride and self-revenge could give.

Henry Crawford had destroyed her happiness, but he should not know that he had done it; he should not destroy her credit, her appearance, her prosperity too. He should not have to think of her as pining in the retirement of Mansfield for *him*, rejecting Sotherton and London, independence and splendour, for *his* sake. Independence was more needful than ever; the want of it at Mansfield more sensibly felt. She was less and less able to endure the restraint which her father imposed. The liberty which his absence had given was now become absolutely necessary. She must escape from him and Mansfield as soon as possible, and find consolation in fortune and consequence, bustle and the world, for a wounded spirit. Her mind was quite determined, and varied not.

To such feelings delay, even the delay of much preparation, would have been an evil, and Mr Rushworth could hardly be more impatient for the marriage than herself. In all the important preparations of the mind she was complete: being prepared for matrimony by an hatred of home, restraint, and tranquillity; by the misery of disappointed affection, and contempt of the man she was to marry. The rest might wait. The preparation of new carriages and furniture might wait for London and spring, when her own taste could have fairer play.

The principals being all agreed in this respect, it soon appeared that a very few weeks would be sufficient for such arrangements as must precede the wedding.

Mrs Rushworth was quite ready to retire, and make way for the fortunate young woman whom her dear son had selected; and very early in November removed herself, her maid, her footman, and her chariot, with true dowager propriety, to Bath, there to parade over the wonders of Sotherton in her evening parties; enjoying them as thoroughly, perhaps, in the animation of a card-table as she had ever done on the spot; and before the middle of the same month the ceremony had taken place which gave Sotherton another mistress.

It was a very proper wedding. The bride was elegantly dressed; the two bridesmaids were duly inferior; her father gave her away; her mother stood with salts in her hand, expecting to be agitated; her aunt tried to cry; and the service was impressively read by Dr Grant. Nothing could be objected to when it came under the discussion of the neighbourhood, except that the carriage which conveyed the bride and bridegroom and Julia from the church door to Sotherton was the same chaise which Mr Rushworth had used for a twelvemonth before. In every thing else the etiquette of the day might stand the strictest investigation.

It was done, and they were gone. Sir Thomas felt as an anxious father must feel, and was indeed experiencing much of the agitation which his wife had been apprehensive of for herself, but had fortunately escaped. Mrs Norris, most happy to assist in the duties of the day, by spending it at the

Park to support her sister's spirits, and drinking the health of Mr and Mrs Rushworth in a supernumerary glass or two, was all joyous delight; for she had made the match; she had done every thing and no one would have supposed, from her confident triumph, that she had ever heard of conjugal infelicity in her life or could have the smallest insight into the disposition of the niece who had been brought up under her eye.

The plan of the young couple was to proceed, after a few days, to Brighton, and take a house there for some weeks. Every public place was new to Maria, and Brighton is almost as gay in winter as in summer. When the novelty of amusement there was over, it would be time for the wider range of London.

Julia was to go with them to Brighton. Since rivalry between the sisters had ceased, they had been gradually recovering much of their former good understanding; and were at last sufficiently friends to make each of them exceedingly glad to be with the other at such a time. Some other companion than Mr Rushworth was of the first consequence to his lady; and Julia was quite as eager for novelty and pleasure as Maria, though she might not have struggled through so much to obtain them, and could better bear a subordinate situation.

Their departure made another material change at Mansfield, a chasm which required some time to fill up. The family circle became greatly contracted; and though the Miss Bertrams had latterly added little to its gaiety, they could not but be missed. Even their mother missed them; and how much more their tender-hearted cousin, who wandered about the house, and thought of them, and felt for them, with a degree of affectionate regret which they had never done much to deserve!

CHAPTER TWENTY TWO

FANNY'S CONSEQUENCE INCREASED on the departure of her cousins. Becoming, as she then did, the only young woman in the drawing-room, the only occupier of that interesting division of a family in which she had hitherto held so humble a third, it was impossible for her not to be more looked at, more thought of and attended to, than she had ever been before; and 'Where is Fanny?' became no uncommon question even without her being wanted for any one's convenience.

Not only at home did her value increase, but at the Parsonage too. In that house which she had hardly entered twice a year since Mr Norris's death, she became a welcome, an invited guest, and in the gloom and dirt of a

November day, most acceptable to Mary Crawford. Her visits there, beginning by chance, were continued by solicitation. Mrs Grant, really eager to get any change for her sister, could, by the easiest self-deceit, persuade herself that she was doing the kindest thing by Fanny, and giving her the most important opportunities of improvement in pressing her frequent calls.

Fanny having been sent into the village on some errand by her Aunt Norris, was overtaken by a heavy shower close to the Parsonage; and being descried from one of the windows endeavouring to find shelter under the branches and lingering leaves of an oak just beyond their premises, was forced, though not without some modest reluctance on her part, to come in. A civil servant she had withstood; but when Dr Grant himself went out with an umbrella, there was nothing to be done but to be very much ashamed, and to get into the house as fast as possible; and to poor Miss Crawford, who had just been contemplating the dismal rain in a very desponding state of mind, sighing over the ruin of all her plan of exercise for that morning, and of every chance of seeing a single creature beyond themselves for the next twenty-four hours, the sound of a little bustle at the front door, and the sight of Miss Price dripping with wet in the vestibule, was delightful. The value of an event on a wet day in the country was most forcibly brought before her. She was all alive again directly, and among the most active in being useful to Fanny, in detecting her to be wetter than she would at first allow, and providing her with dry clothes; and Fanny, after being obliged to submit to all this attention, and to being assisted and waited on by mistresses and maids, being also obliged, on returning downstairs, to be fixed in their drawing-room for an hour while the rain continued, the blessing of something fresh to see and think of was thus extended to Miss Crawford, and might carry on her spirits to the period of dressing and dinner.

The two sisters were so kind to her, and so pleasant, that Fanny might have enjoyed her visit could she have believed herself not in the way, and could she have foreseen that the weather would certainly clear at the end of the hour, and save her from the shame of having Dr Grant's carriage and horses out to take her home, with which she was threatened. As to anxiety for any alarm that her absence in such weather might occasion at home, she had nothing to suffer on that score; for as her being out was known only to her two aunts, she was perfectly aware that none would be felt, and that in whatever cottage Aunt Norris might choose to establish her during the rain, her being in such a cottage would be indubitable to Aunt Bertram.

It was beginning to look brighter, when Fanny, observing a harp in the room, asked some questions about it, which soon led to an acknowledgment of her wishing very much to hear it, and a confession, which could hardly be believed, of her having never yet heard it since its being in Mansfield. To Fanny herself it appeared a very simple and natural circumstance. She had scarcely ever been at the Parsonage since the instrument's arrival, there had been no reason that she should; but Miss Crawford, calling to mind an early expressed wish on the subject, was concerned at her own neglect; and 'Shall I play to you now?' and 'What will

Dr Grant himself came out with an umbrella

you have?' were questions immediately following with the readiest good humour.

She played accordingly; happy to have a new listener, and a listener who seemed so much obliged, so full of wonder at the performance, and who showed herself not wanting in taste. She played till Fanny's eyes, straying to the window on the weather's being evidently fair, spoke what she felt must be done.

'Another quarter of an hour,' said Miss Crawford, 'and we shall see how it will be. Do not run away the first moment of its holding up. Those clouds look alarming.'

'But they are passed over,' said Fanny. 'I have been watching them. This weather is all from the south.'

'South or north, I know a black cloud when I see it; and you must not set forward while it is so threatening. And besides I want to play something more to you – a very pretty piece – and your cousin Edmund's prime favourite. You must stay and hear your cousin's favourite.'

Fanny felt that she must; and though she had not waited for that sentence to be thinking of Edmund, such a memento made her particularly awake to his idea, and she fancied him sitting in that room again and again, perhaps in the very spot where she sat now, listening with constant delight to the favourite air, played, as it appeared to her, with superior tone and expression; and though pleased with it herself, and glad to like whatever was liked by him, she was more sincerely impatient to go away at the conclusion of it than she had been before; and on this being evident, she was so kindly asked to call again, to take them in her walk whenever she could, to come and hear more of the harp, that she felt it necessary to be done, if no objection arose at home.

Such was the origin of the sort of intimacy which took place between them within the first fortnight after the Miss Bertrams' going away – an intimacy resulting principally from Miss Crawford's desire of some thing new, and which had little reality in Fanny's feelings. Fanny went to her every two or three days: it seemed a kind of fascination: she could not be easy without going, and yet it was without loving her, without ever thinking like her, without any sense of obligation for being sought after now when nobody else was to be had; and deriving no higher pleasure from her conversation than occasional amusement, and *that* often at the expense of her judgment, when it was raised by pleasantry on people or subjects which she wished to be respected. She went, however, and they sauntered about together many an half-hour in Mrs Grant's shrubbery, the weather being unusually mild for the time of year; and venturing sometimes even to sit down on one of the benches now comparatively unsheltered, remaining there perhaps till, in the midst of some tender ejaculation of Fanny's on the sweets of so protracted an autumn, they were forced by the sudden swell of a cold gust shaking down the last few yellow leaves about them, to jump up and walk for warmth.

'This is pretty, very pretty,' said Fanny, looking around her as they were thus sitting together one day; 'every time I come into this shrubbery I am more struck with its growth and beauty. Three years ago this was nothing but a rough hedgerow along the upper side of the field, never thought of as any thing or capable of becoming any thing; and now it is converted into a walk, and it would be difficult to say whether most valuable as a convenience or an ornament; and perhaps, in another three years we may be forgetting – almost forgetting what it was before. How wonderful, how very wonderful the operations of time and the changes of the human mind!' And following the latter train of thought, she soon afterwards added: 'If any one faculty of our nature may be called *more* wonderful than the rest, I do think it is memory. There seems something more speakingly incomprehensible in the powers, the failures, the inequalities of memory, than in any other of our intelligences. The memory is sometimes so retentive, so serviceable, so obedient: at others, so bewildered and so weak; and at others again, so tyrannic, so beyond control! We are, to be sure, a miracle every way; but our powers of recollecting and of forgetting do seem peculiarly past finding out.'

Miss Crawford, untouched and inattentive, had nothing to say; and Fanny, perceiving it, brought back her own mind to what she thought must interest.

'It may seem impertinent in *me* to praise, but I must admire the taste Mrs Grant has shown in all this. There is such a quiet simplicity in the plan of the walk! Not too much attempted!'

'Yes,' replied Miss Crawford, carelessly, 'it does very well for a place of this sort. One does not think of extent *here*; and between ourselves, till I came to Mansfield, I had not imagined a country parson ever aspired to a shrubbery, or anything of the kind.'

'I am so glad to see the evergreens thrive!' said Fanny, in reply. 'My uncle's gardener always says the soil here is better than his own, and so it appears from the growth of the laurels and evergreens in general. The evergreen! How beautiful, how welcome, how wonderful the evergreen! When one thinks of it, how astonishing a variety of nature! In some countries we know the tree that sheds its leaf is the variety, but that does not make it less amazing, that the same soil and the same sun should nurture plants differing in the first rule and law of their existence. You will think me rhapsodising; but when I am out of doors, especially when I am sitting out of doors, I am very apt to get into this sort of wondering strain. One cannot fix one's eyes on the commonest natural production without finding food for a rambling fancy.'

'To say the truth,' replied Miss Crawford, 'I am some thing like the famous Doge at the court of Louis XIV; and may declare that I see no wonder in this shrubbery equal to seeing myself in it. If any body had told me a year ago that this place would be my home, that I should be spending month after month here, as I have done, I certainly should not have believed them. I have now been here nearly five months; and, moreover, the quietest five months I ever passed.'

'*Too* quiet for you, I believe.'

'I should have thought so *theoretically* myself, but,' and her eyes brightened as she spoke, 'take it all and all, I never spent so happy a summer. But then,' with a more thoughtful air and lowered voice, 'there is no saying what it may lead to.'

Fanny's heart beat quick, and she felt quiet unequal to surmising or soliciting anything more. Miss Crawford, however, with renewed animation, soon went on—

'I am conscious of being far better reconciled to a country residence than I had ever expected to be. I can even suppose it pleasant to spend *half* the year in the country, under certain circumstances, very pleasant. An elegant, moderate-sized house in the centre of family connections; continual engagements among them; commanding the first society in the neighbourhood; looked-up to, perhaps, as leading it even more than those of larger fortune, and turning from the cheerful round of such amusements to nothing worse than a *tête-à-tête* with the person one feels most agreeable in the world. There is nothing frightful in such a picture, is there, Miss Price? One need not envy the new Mrs Rushworth with such a home as *that*.' 'Envy Mrs Rushworth!' was all that Fanny attempted to say. 'Come, come, it would be very unhandsome in us to be severe on Mrs Rushworth, for I look forward to our owing her a great many gay, brilliant, happy hours. I expect we shall be all very much at Sotherton another year. Such a match as Miss Bertram has made is a public blessing; for the first pleasures of Mr Rushworth's wife must be to fill her house, and give the best balls in the country.'

Fanny was silent, and Miss Crawford relapsed into thoughtfulness, till suddenly looking up at the end of a few minutes, she exclaimed, 'Ah, here he is.' It was not Mr Rushworth, however, but Edmund, who then appeared walking towards them with Mrs Grant. 'My sister and Mr Bertram. I am so glad your eldest cousin is gone, that he *may* be Mr Bertram again. There is some thing in the sound of Mr *Edmund* Bertram so formal, so pitiful, so younger-brother-like, that I detest it.'

'How differently we feel!' cried Fanny. 'To me, the sound of *Mr* Bertram is so cold and nothing-meaning, so entirely without warmth or character! It just stands for a gentleman, and that's all. But there is nobleness in the name of Edmund. It is a name of heroism and renown; of kings, princes, and knights; and seems to breathe the spirit of chivalry and warm affections.'

'I grant you the name is good in itself, and *Lord* Edmund or *Sir* Edmund sound delightfully; but sink it under the chill, the annihilation of a Mr and Mr Edmund is not more than Mr John or Mr Thomas. Well, shall we join and disappoint them of half their lecture upon sitting down out of doors at this time of year, by being up before they can begin?'

Edmund met them with particular pleasure. It was the first time of his seeing them together since the beginning of that better acquaintance which he had been hearing of with great satisfaction. A friendship between two so very dear to him was exactly what he could have wished: and to the credit of the lover's understanding, be it stated, that he did not by any means consider Fanny as the only, or even as the greater gainer by such a friendship.

'Well,' said Miss Crawford, 'and do you not scold us for our imprudence? What do you think we have been sitting down for but to be talked to about it, and entreated and supplicated never to do so again?'

'Perhaps I might have scolded,' said Edmund, 'if either of you had been sitting down alone; but while you do wrong together, I can overlook a great deal.'

'They cannot have been sitting long,' cried Mrs Grant, 'for when I went up for my shawl I saw them from the staircase window, and then they were walking.'

'And really,' added Edmund, 'the day is so mild, that your sitting down for a few minutes can be hardly thought imprudent. Our weather must not always be judged by the calendar. We may sometimes take greater liberties in November than in May.'

'Upon my word,' cried Miss Crawford, 'you are two of the most disappointing and unfeeling kind friends I ever met with! There is no giving you a moment's uneasiness. You do not know how much we have been suffering, nor what chills we have felt! But I have long thought Mr Bertram one of the worst subjects to work on, in any little manœuvre against common sense, that a woman could be plagued with. I had very little hope of *him* from the first; but you, Mrs Grant, my sister, my own sister, I think I had a right to alarm you a little.'

'Do not flatter yourself, my dearest Mary. You have not the smallest chance of moving me. I have my alarms, but they are quite in a different quarter; and if I could have altered the weather, you would have had a good sharp east wind blowing on you the whole time – for here are some of my plants which Robert *will* leave out because the nights are so mild, and I know the end of it will be, that we shall have a sudden change of weather, a hard frost setting in all at once, taking everybody (at least Robert) by surprise, and I shall lose every one; and what is worse, cook has just been telling me that the turkey, which I particularly wished not to be dressed till Sunday, because I know how much more Dr Grant would enjoy it on

Sunday after the fatigues of the day, will not keep beyond to-morrow. These are some thing like grievances, and make me think the weather most unseasonably close.'

'The sweets of housekeeping in a country village!' said Miss Crawford, archly. 'Commend me to the nurseryman and the poulterer.'

'My dear child, commend Dr Grant to the deanery of Westminster or St Paul's, and I should be as glad of your nurseryman and poulterer as you could be. But we have no such people in Mansfield. What would you have me do?'

'Oh! you can do nothing but what you do already: be plagued very often, and never lose your temper.'

'Thank you; but there is no escaping these little vexations, Mary, live where we may; and when you are settled in town and I come to see you, I dare say I shall find you with yours, in spite of the nurseryman and the poulterer – or perhaps on their very account. Their remoteness and unpunctuality, or their exorbitant charges and frauds, will be drawing forth bitter lamentations.'

'I mean to be too rich to lament or to feel any thing of the sort. A large income is the best recipe for happiness I ever heard of. It certainly may secure all the myrtle and turkey part of it.'

'You intend to be very rich?' said Edmund, with a look which, to Fanny's eye, had a great deal of serious meaning.

'To be sure. Do not you? Do not we all?'

'I cannot intend any thing which it must be so completely beyond my power to command. Miss Crawford may choose her degree of wealth. She has only to fix on her number of thousands a year, and there can be no doubt of their coming. My intentions are only not to be poor.'

'By moderation and economy, and bringing down your wants to your income, and all that. I understand you – and a very proper plan it is for a person at your time of life, with such limited means and indifferent connections. What can *you* want but a decent maintenance? You have not much time before you; and your relations are in no situation to do any thing for you, or to mortify you by the contrast of their own wealth and consequence. Be honest and poor, by all means – but I shall not envy you; I do not think I shall even respect you. I have a much greater respect for those that are honest and rich.'

'Your degree of respect for honesty, rich or poor, is precisely what I have no manner of concern with. I do not mean to be poor. Poverty is exactly what I have determined against. Honesty, in the something between, in the middle state of worldly circumstances, is all that I am anxious for your not looking down on.'

'But I do look down upon it, if it might have been higher. I must look down upon any thing contented with obscurity when it might rise to distinction.'

'But how may it rise? How may my honesty at least rise to any distinction?'

This was not so very easy a question to answer, and occasioned an 'Oh!' of some length from the fair lady before she could add, 'You ought to be in parliament, or you should have gone into the army ten years ago.'

'*That* is not much to the purpose now; and as to my being in parliament, I believe I must wait till there is an especial assembly for the representation of younger sons who have little to live on. No, Miss Crawford,' he added, in a more serious tone, 'there *are* distinctions which I should be miserable if I thought myself without any chance – absolutely without chance or possibility of obtaining – but they are of a different character.'

A look of consciousness, as he spoke, and what seemed a consciousness of manner on Miss Crawford's side as she made some laughing answer, was sorrowful food for Fanny's observation; and finding herself quite unable to attend as she ought to Mrs Grant, by whose side she was now following the others, she had nearly resolved on going home immediately, and only waited for courage to say so, when the sound of the great clock at Mansfield Park, striking three, made her feel that she had really been much longer absent than usual, and brought the previous self-enquiry, of whether she should take leave or not just then, and how, to a very speedy issue. With undoubting decision she directly began her adieus; and Edmund began at the same time to recollect that his mother had been enquiring for her, and that he had walked down to the Parsonage on purpose to bring her back.

Fanny's hurry increased; and without in the least expecting Edmund's attendance, she would have hastened away alone; but the general pace was quickened, and they all accompanied her into the house through which it was necessary to pass. Dr Grant was in the vestibule, and as they stopped to speak to him she found from Edmund's manner that he *did* mean to go with her. He, too, was taking leave. She could not but be thankful. In the moment of parting, Edmund was invited by Dr Grant to eat his mutton with him the next day; and Fanny had barely time for an unpleasant feeling on the occasion, when Mrs Grant, with sudden recollection, turned to her and asked for the pleasure of her company too. This was so new an attention, so perfectly new a circumstance in the events of Fanny's life, that she was all surprise and embarrassment; and while stammering out her great obligation, and her – 'but she did not suppose it would be in her power,' was looking at Edmund for his opinion and help. But Edmund, delighted with her having such an happiness offered, and ascertaining with half a look and half a sentence, that she had no objection but on her aunt's account, could not imagine that his mother would make any difficulty of sparing her, and therefore gave his decided open advice that the invitation should be accepted; and though Fanny would not venture, even on his encouragement, to such a flight of audacious independence, it was soon settled, that if nothing was heard to the contrary, Mrs Grant might expect her.

'And you know what your dinner will be,' said Mrs Grant, smiling – 'the turkey, and I assure you a very fine one; for, my dear,' turning to her husband, 'cook insists upon the turkey's being dressed to-morrow.'

'Very well, very well,' cried Dr Grant, 'all the better; I am glad to hear you have anything so good in the house. But Miss Price and Mr Edmund Bertram, I dare say, would take their chance. We none of us want to hear the bill of fare. A friendly meeting, and not a fine dinner, is all we have in view. A turkey, or a goose, or a leg of mutton, or whatever you and your cook choose to give us.'

The two cousins walked home together; and, except in the immediate discussion of this engagement, which Edmund spoke of with the warmest satisfaction, as so particularly desirable for her in the intimacy which he saw with so much pleasure established, it was a silent walk; for having finished that subject, he grew thoughtful and indisposed for any other.

CHAPTER TWENTY THREE

'BUT WHY SHOULD MRS GRANT ask Fanny?' said Lady Bertram. 'How came she to think of asking Fanny? Fanny never dines there, you know, in this sort of way. I cannot spare her, and I am sure she does not want to go. Fanny, you do not want to go, do you?'

'If you put such a question to her,' cried Edmund, preventing his cousin's speaking, 'Fanny will immediately say No; but I am sure, my dear mother, she would like to go; and I can see no reason why she should not.'

'I cannot imagine why Mrs Grant should think of asking her? She never did before. She used to ask your sisters now and then, but she never asked Fanny.'

'If you cannot do without me, ma'am—' said Fanny, in a self-denying tone.

'But my mother will have my father with her all the evening.'

'To be sure, so I shall.'

'Suppose you take my father's opinion, ma'am.'

'That's well thought of. So I will, Edmund, I will ask Sir Thomas, as soon as he comes in, whether I can do without her.'

'As you please, ma'am on that head; but I meant my father's opinion as to the *propriety* of the invitation's being accepted or not; and I think he will consider it a right thing by Mrs Grant, as well as by Fanny, that being the *first* invitation it should be accepted.'

'I do not know. We will ask him. But he will be very much surprised that Mrs Grant should ask Fanny at all.'

'There was nothing more to be said, or that could be said, to any purpose, till Sir Thomas were present; but the subject involving, as it did, her own evening's comfort for the morrow, was so much uppermost in Lady Bertram's mind, that half an hour afterwards, on his looking in for a minute in his way from his plantation to his dressing-room, she called him back again, when he had almost closed the door, with 'Sir Thomas, stop a moment – I have something to say to you.'

Her tone of calm languor, for she never took the trouble of raising her voice, was always heard and attended to; and Sir Thomas came back. Her story began; and Fanny immediately slipped out of the room; for to hear herself the subject of any discussion with her uncle was more than her nerves could bear. She was anxious, she knew – more anxious perhaps than she ought to be – for what was it after all whether she went or stayed? but if her uncle were to be a great while considering and deciding, and with very grave looks, and those grave looks directed to her, and at last decide against her, she might not be able to appear properly submissive and indifferent. Her cause, meanwhile, went on well. It began, on Lady Bertram's part, with – 'I have something to tell you that will surprise you. Mrs Grant has asked Fanny to dinner.'

'Well,' said Sir Thomas, as if waiting more to accomplish the surprise.

'Edmund wants her to go. But how can I spare her?'

'She will be late,' said Sir Thomas, taking out his watch, 'but what is your difficulty?'

Edmund found himself obliged to speak and fill up the blanks in his mother's story. He told the whole; and she had only to add, 'So strange! for Mrs Grant never used to ask her.'

'But is it not very natural,' observed Edmund, 'that Mrs Grant should wish to procure so agreeable a visitor for her sister?'

'Nothing can be more natural,' said Sir Thomas, after a short deliberation; 'nor, were there no sister in the case, could any thing, in my opinion, be more natural. Mrs Grant's showing civility to Miss Price, to Lady Bertram's niece, could never want explanation. The only surprise I can feel is, that this should be the *first* time of its being paid. Fanny was perfectly right in giving only a conditional answer. She appears to feel as she ought. But as I conclude that she must wish to go, since all young people like to be together, I can see no reason why she should be denied the indulgence.'

'But can I do without her, Sir Thomas?'

'Indeed I think you may.'

'She always makes tea, you know, when my sister is not here.'

'Your sister, perhaps, may be prevailed on to spend the day with us, and I shall certainly be at home.'

'Very well, then, Fanny may go, Edmund.'

The good news soon followed her. Edmund knocked at her door in his way to his own.

'Well, Fanny, it is all happily settled, and without the smallest hesitation on your uncle's side. He had but one opinion. You are to go.'

'Thank you, I am *so* glad,' was Fanny's instinctive reply; though when she had turned from him and shut the door, she could not help feeling, 'And yet why should I be glad? for am I not certain of seeing or hearing some thing there to pain me?'

In spite of this conviction, however, she was glad. Simple as such an engagement might appear in other eyes, it had novelty and importance in hers, for excepting the day at Sotherton, she had scarcely ever dined out before; and though now going only half a mile, and only to three people, still it was dining out, and all the little interests of preparation were enjoyments in themselves. She had neither sympathy nor assistance from those who ought to have entered into her feelings and directed her taste; for Lady Bertram never thought of being useful to any body, and Mrs Norris, when she came on the morrow, in consequence of an early call and invitation from Sir Thomas, was in a very ill humour, and seemed intent only on lessening her niece's pleasure, both present and future, as much as possible.

'Upon my word, Fanny, you are in high luck to meet with such attention and indulgence! You ought to be very much obliged to Mrs Grant for thinking of you, and to your aunt for letting you go, and you ought to look upon it as something extraordinary; for I hope you are aware that there is no real occasion for your going into company in this sort of way, or ever dining out at all; and it is what you must not depend upon ever being repeated. Nor must you be fancying that the invitation is meant as any particular compliment to *you*; the compliment is intended to your uncle and aunt and me. Mrs Grant thinks it a civility due to *us* to take a little notice of you, or else it would never have come into her head, and you may be very certain, that if your cousin Julia had been at home, you would not have been asked at all.'

Mrs Norris had now so ingeniously done away all Mrs Grant's part of the favour, that Fanny, who found herself expected to speak, could only say that she was very much obliged to her Aunt Bertram for sparing her, and that she was endeavouring to put her aunt's evening work in such a state as to prevent her being missed.

'Oh! depend upon it, your aunt can do very well without you, or you would not be allowed to go. *I* shall be here, so you may be quite easy about your aunt. And I hope you will have a very *agreeable* day, and find it all mighty *delightful*. But I must observe that five is the very awkwardest of all possible numbers to sit down to table; and I cannot but be surprised that such an *elegant* lady as Mrs Grant should not contrive better! And round their enormous great wide table, too, which fills up the room so dreadfully! Had the Doctor been contented to take my dining table when I came away, as any body in their senses would have done, instead of having that absurd new one of his own, which is wider, literally wider than the dinner table here, how infinitely better it would have been! and how much more he would have been respected! for people are never respected when they step out of their proper sphere. Remember *that*, Fanny. Five – only five to be sitting round that table. However, you will have dinner enough on it for ten, I dare say.'

Mrs Norris fetched breath, and went on again.

'The nonsense and folly of people's stepping out of their rank and trying to appear above themselves, makes me think it right to give *you* a hint, Fanny, now that you are going into company without any of us; and I do beseech and entreat you not to be putting yourself forward, and talking and giving your opinion as if you were one of your cousins, as if you were dear Mrs Rushworth or Julia. *That* will never do, believe me. Remember, wherever you are, you must be the lowest and last; and though Miss Crawford is in a manner at home at the Parsonage, you are not to be taking place of her. And as to coming away at night, you are to stay just as long as Edmund chooses. Leave him to settle *that*.'

'Yes, ma'am, I should not think of any thing else.'

'And if it should rain, which I think exceedingly likely, for I never saw it more threatening for a wet evening in my life, you must manage as well as you can, and not be expecting the carriage to be sent for you. I certainly do not go home to-night, and, therefore, the carriage will not be out on my account; so you must make up your mind to what may happen, and take your things accordingly.'

Her niece thought it perfectly reasonable. She rated her own claims to comfort as low even as Mrs Norris could; and when Sir Thomas, soon afterwards, just opening the door, said, 'Fanny, at what time would you have the carriage come round?' she felt a degree of astonishment which made it impossible for her to speak.

'My dear Sir Thomas!' cried Mrs Norris, red with anger, 'Fanny can walk.'

'Walk!' repeated Sir Thomas, in a tone of most unanswerable dignity, and coming farther into the room. 'My niece walk to a dinner engagement at this time of the year! Will twenty minutes after four suit you?'

'Yes, sir,' was Fanny's humble answer, given with the feelings almost of a

'My dear Sir Thomas, Fanny can walk'

criminal towards Mrs Norris; and not bearing to remain with her in what might seem a state of triumph, she followed her uncle out of the room, having stayed behind him only long enough to hear these words spoken in angry agitation:—

'Quite unnecessary! a great deal too kind! But Edmund goes; true, it is upon Edmund's account. I observed he was hoarse on Thursday night.'

But this could not impose on Fanny. She felt that the carriage was for herself alone; and her uncle's consideration of her, coming immediately after such representations from her aunt, cost her some tears of gratitude when she was alone.

The coachman drove round to a minute; another minute brought down the gentleman; and as the lady had, with a most scrupulous fear of being late, been many minutes seated in the drawing-room, Sir Thomas saw them off in as good time as his own correctly punctual habits required.

'Now I must look at you, Fanny,' said Edmund, with the kind smile of an affectionate brother, 'and tell you how I like you; and as well as I can judge by this light, you look very nicely indeed. What have you got on?'

'The new dress that my uncle was so good as to give me on my cousin's marriage. I hope it is not too fine; but I thought I ought to wear it as soon as I could, and that I might not have such another opportunity all the winter. I hope you do not think me too fine.'

'A woman can never be too fine while she is all in white. No, I see no finery about you; nothing but what is perfectly proper. Your gown seems very pretty. I like these glossy spots. Has not Miss Crawford a gown something the same?'

In approaching the Parsonage they passed close by the stable-yard and coach-house.

'Hey-day!' said Edmund, 'here's company, here's a carriage! who have they got to meet us?' And letting down the side-glass to distinguish, ''Tis Crawford's, Crawford's barouche, I protest! There are his own two men pushing it back into its old quarters. He is here, of course. This is quite a surprise, Fanny. I shall be very glad to see him.'

There was no occasion, there was no time for Fanny to say how very differently she felt; but the idea of having such another to observe her, was a great increase of the trepidation with which she performed the very aweful ceremony of walking into the drawing-room.

In the drawing-room Mr Crawford certainly was; having been just long enough arrived to be ready for dinner; and the smiles and pleased looks of the three others standing round him, showed how welcome was his sudden resolution of coming to them for a few days on leaving Bath. A very cordial meeting passed between him and Edmund; and with the exception of Fanny, the pleasure was general; and even to *her*, there might be some advantage in his presence, since every addition to the party must rather forward her favourite indulgence of being suffered to sit silent and unattended to. She was soon aware of this herself; for though she must submit, as her own propriety of mind directed, in spite of her Aunt Norris's opinion, to being the principal lady in company, and to all the little distinctions consequent thereon, she found, while they were at table, such a happy flow of conversation prevailing in which she was not required to take any part – there was so much to be said between the brother and sister about Bath, so much between the two young men about hunting, so much of politics between Mr Crawford and Dr Grant, and of every thing and all together between Mr Crawford and Mrs Grant, as to leave her the fairest prospect of having only to listen in quiet, and of passing a very agreeable day. She could not compliment the newly-arrived gentleman, however, with any appearance of interest in a scheme for extending his stay at Mansfield, and sending for his hunters from Norfolk, which, suggested by Dr

Grant, advised by Edmund, and warmly urged by the two sisters, was soon in possession of his mind, and which he seemed to want to be encouraged even by her to resolve on. Her opinion was sought as to the probable continuance of the open weather, but her answers were as short and indifferent as civility allowed. She could not wish him to stay, and would much rather not have him speak to her.

Her two absent cousins, especially Maria, were much in her thoughts on seeing him; but no embarrassing remembrance affected *his* spirits. Here he was again on the same ground where all had passed before, and apparently as willing to stay and be happy without the Miss Bertrams, as if he had never known Mansfield in any other state. She heard them spoken of by him only in a general way, till they were all re-assembled in the drawing-room, when Edmund, being engaged apart in some matter of business with Dr Grant, which seemed entirely to engross them, and Mrs Grant occupied at the tea-table, he began talking of them with more particularity to his other sister. With a significant smile, which made Fanny quite hate him, he said, 'So Rushworth and his fair bride are at Brighton, I understand; happy man!'

'Yes, they have been there about a fortnight, Miss Price, have they not? And Julia is with them.'

'And Mr Yates, I presume, is not far off.'

'Mr Yates! Oh! we hear nothing of Mr Yates. I do not imagine he figures much in the letters to Mansfield Park; do you, Miss Price? I think my friend Julia knows better than to entertain her father with Mr Yates.'

'Poor Rushworth and his two-and-forty speeches!' continued Crawford. 'Nobody can ever forget them. Poor fellow! I see him now – his toil and his despair. Well, I am much mistaken if his lovely Maria will ever want him to make two-and-forty speeches to her;' adding, with a momentary seriousness, 'She is too good for him – much too good.' And then changing his tone again to one of gentle gallantry, and addressing Fanny, he said, 'You were Mr Rushworth's best friend. Your kindness and patience can never be forgotten, your indefatigable patience in trying to make it possible for him to learn his part – in trying to give him a brain which nature had denied – to mix up an understanding for him out of the superfluity of your own! *He* might not have sense enough himself to estimate your kindness, but I may venture to say that it had honour from all the rest of the party.'

Fanny coloured, and said nothing.

'It is as a dream, a pleasant dream!' he exclaimed, breaking forth again, after a few minutes' musing. 'I shall always look back on our theatricals with exquisite pleasure. There was such an interest, such an animation, such a spirit diffused. Every body felt it. We were all alive. There was employment, hope, solicitude, bustle, for every hour of the day. Always some little objection, some little doubt, some little anxiety to be got over. I never was happier.'

With silent indignation Fanny repeated to herself, 'Never happier! – never happier than when doing what you must know was not justifiable! – never happier than when behaving so dishonourably and unfeelingly! Oh! what a corrupted mind!'

'We were unlucky, Miss Price,' he continued, in a lower tone, to avoid the possibility of being heard by Edmund, and not at all aware of her feelings, 'we certainly were very unlucky. Another week, only one other week, would have been enough for us. I think if we had had the disposal of events – if Mansfield Park had had the government of the winds just for a week or two, about the equinox, there would have been a difference. Not that we would have endangered his safety by any tremendous weather – but only by a steady contrary wind, or a calm. I think, Miss Price, we would have indulged ourselves with a week's calm in the Atlantic at that season.'

He seemed determined to be answered; and Fanny, averting her face, said with a firmer tone than usual, 'As far as *I* am concerned, sir, I would not have delayed his return for a day. My uncle disapproved it all so entirely when he did arrive, that in my opinion every thing had gone quite far enough.'

She had never spoken so much at once to him in her life before, and never so angrily to anyone; and when her speech was over, she trembled and blushed at her own daring. He was surprised; but after a few moments' silent consideration of her, replied in a calmer, graver tone, and as if the candid result of conviction, 'I believe you are right. It was more pleasant than prudent. We were getting too noisy.' And then turning the conversation, he would have engaged her on some other subject, but her answers were so shy and reluctant that he could not advance in any.

Miss Crawford, who had been repeatedly eyeing Dr Grant and Edmund, now observed: 'Those gentlemen must have some very interesting point to discuss.'

'The most interesting in the world,' replied her brother – 'how to make money; how to turn a good income into a better. Dr Grant is giving Bertram instructions about the living he is to step into so soon. I find he takes orders in a few weeks. They were at it in the dining-parlour. I am glad to heart Bertram will be so well off. He will have a very pretty income to make ducks and drakes with, and earned without much trouble. I apprehend he will not have less than seven hundred a year. Seven hundred a year is a fine thing for a younger brother; and as of course he will still live at home, it will be all his for *menus plaisirs*; and a sermon at Christmas and Easter, I suppose, will be the sum total of sacrifice.'

His sister tried to laugh off her feelings by saying, 'Nothing amuses me more than the easy manner with which every body settles the abundance of those who have a great deal less than ourselves. You would look rather blank, Henry, if your *menus plaisirs* were to be limited to seven hundred a year.'

'Perhaps I might; but all *that* you know is entirely comparative. Birthright and habit must settle the business. Bertram is certainly well off for a cadet of even a baronet's family. By the time he is four or five and twenty he will have seven hundred a year, and nothing to do for it.'

Miss Crawford *could* have said that there would be a something to do and to suffer for it, which she could not think lightly of; but she checked herself and let it pass; and tried to look calm and unconcerned when the two gentlemen shortly afterwards joined them.

'Bertram,' said Henry Crawford, 'I shall make a point of coming to Mansfield to hear you preach your first sermon. I shall come on purpose to encourage a young beginner. When is it to be? Miss Price, will not you join me in encouraging your cousin? Will not you engage to attend with your eyes steadily fixed on him the whole time – as I shall do – not to lose a word; or only looking off just to note down any sentence preeminently beautiful? We will provide ourselves with tablets and a pencil. When will it be? You must preach at Mansfield, you know, that Sir Thomas and Lady Bertram may hear you.'

'I shall keep clear of you, Crawford, as long as I can,' said Edmund; 'for you would be more likely to disconcert me, and I should be more sorry to see you trying at it than almost any other man.'

'Will he not feel this?' thought Fanny. 'No, he can feel nothing as he ought.'

The party being now all united, and the chief talkers attracting each other, she remained in tranquillity; and as a whist table was formed after tea – formed really for the amusement of Dr Grant, by his attentive wife, though it was not to be supposed so – and Miss Crawford took her harp, she had nothing to do but to listen; and her tranquillity remained undisturbed the rest of the evening, except when Mr Crawford now and then addressed to her a question or observation, which she could not avoid answering. Miss Crawford was too much vexed by what had passed to be in a humour for anything but music. With that she soothed herself and amused her friend.

The assurance of Edmund's being so soon to take orders, coming upon her like a blow that had been suspended, and still hoped uncertain and at a distance, was felt with resentment and mortification. She was very angry with him. She had thought her influence more. She *had* begun to think of him; she felt that she had, with great regard, with almost decided intentions; but she would now meet him with his own cool feelings. It was plain that he could have no serious views, no true attachment, by fixing himself in a situation which he must know she would never stoop to. She would learn to match him in his indifference. She would henceforth admit his attentions without any idea beyond immediate amusement. If *he* could so command his affections, *hers* should do her no harm.

CHAPTER TWENTY FOUR

HENRY CRAWFORD HAD QUITE made up his mind by the next morning to give another fortnight to Mansfield, and having sent for his hunters, and written a few lines of explanation to the Admiral, he looked round at his sister as he sealed and threw the letter from him, and seeing the coast clear of the rest of the family, said, with a smile: 'And how do you think I mean to amuse myself, Mary, on the days that I do not hunt? I am grown too old to go out more than three times a week; but I have a plan for the intermediate days, and what do you think it is?'

'To walk and ride with me, to be sure.'

'Not exactly, though I shall be happy to do both, but *that* would be exercise only to my body, and I must take care of my mind. Besides, *that* would be all recreation and indulgence, without the wholesome alloy of labour, and I do not like to eat the bread of idleness. No, my plan is to make Fanny Price in love with me.'

'Fanny Price! Nonsense! No, no. You ought to be satisfied with her two cousins.'

'But I cannot be satisfied without Fanny Price, without making a small hole in Fanny Price's heart. You do not seem properly aware of her claims to notice. When we talked of her last night, you none of you seemed sensible of the wonderful improvement that has taken place in her looks within the last six weeks. You see her every day, and therefore do not notice it; but I assure you she is quite a different creature from what she was in the autumn. She was then merely a quiet, modest, not plain-looking girl, but she is now absolutely pretty. I used to think she had neither complexion nor countenance; but in that soft skin of hers, so frequently tinged with a blush as it was yesterday, there is decided beauty; and from what I observed of her eyes and mouth I do not despair of their being capable of expression enough when she has anything to express. And then, her air, her manner, her *tout ensemble*, is so indescribably improved! She must be grown two inches, at least, since October.'

'Phoo! phoo! This is only because there were no tall women to compare her with, and because she has got a new gown, and you never saw her so well dressed before. She is just what she was in October, believe me. The truth is, that she was the only girl in company for you to notice, and you must have a some body. I have always thought her pretty – not strikingly pretty – but "pretty enough," as people say; a sort of beauty that grows on one. Her eyes should be darker, but she has a sweet smile; but as for this wonderful degree of improvement, I am sure it may all be resolved into a better style of dress, and your having nobody else to look at; and therefore, if you do set about a flirtation with her, you never will persuade me that it is in compliment to her beauty, or that it proceeds from any thing but your own idleness and folly.'

'And how do you think I mean to amuse myself, Mary, on the days that I do not hunt?'

Her brother gave only a smile to this accusation, and soon afterwards said, 'I do not quite know what to make of Miss Fanny. I do not understand her. I could not tell what she would be at yesterday. What is her character? Is she solemn? Is she queer? Is she prudish? Why did she draw back and look so grave at me? I could hardly get her to speak. I never was so long in company with a girl in my life, trying to entertain her, and succeed so ill! Never met with a girl who looked so grave on me! I must try to get the better of this. Her looks say, "I will not like you, I am determined not to like you"; and I say she shall.'

'Foolish fellow! And so this is her attraction after all! This it is, her not caring about you, which gives her such a soft skin, and makes her so much taller, and produces all these charms and graces! I do desire that you will not be making her really unhappy; a *little* love, perhaps, may animate and do her good, but I will not have you plunge her deep, for she is as good a little creature as ever lived, and has a great deal of feeling.'

'It can be but for a fortnight,' said Henry; 'and if a fortnight can kill her, she must have a constitution which nothing could save. No, I will not do her any harm, dear little soul! I only want her to look kindly on me, to give me smiles as well as blushes, to keep a chair for me by herself wherever we are, and be all animation when I take it and talk to her; to think as I think, be interested in all my possessions and pleasures, try to keep me longer at Mansfield, and feel when I go away that she shall be never happy again. I want nothing more.'

'Moderation itself!' said Mary. 'I can have no scruples now. Well, you will have opportunities enough of endeavouring to recommend yourself, for we are a great deal together.'

And without attempting any further remonstrance, she left Fanny to her fate, a fate which, had not Fanny's heart been guarded in a way unsuspected by Miss Crawford, might have been a little harder than she deserved; for although there doubtless are such unconquerable young ladies of eighteen (or one should not read about them) as are never to be persuaded into love against their judgment by all that talent, manner, attention, and flattery can do, I have no inclination to believe Fanny one of them, or to think that with so much tenderness of disposition, and so much taste as belonged to her, she could have escaped heartwhole from the courtship (though the courtship only of a fortnight) of such a man as Crawford, in spite of there being some previous ill opinion of him to be overcome, had not her affection been engaged elsewhere. With all the security which love of another and dis-esteem of him could give to the peace of mind he was attacking, his continued attentions – continued, but not obtrusive, and adapting themselves more and more to the gentleness and delicacy of her character – obliged her very soon to dislike him less than formerly. She had by no means forgotten the past, and she thought as ill of him as ever; but she felt his powers: he was entertaining; and his manners were so improved, so polite, so seriously and blamelessly polite, that it was impossible not to be civil to him in return.

A very few days were enough to effect this; and at the end of those few days, circumstances arose which had a tendency rather to forward his views of pleasing her, inasmuch as they gave her a degree of happiness which must dispose her to be pleased with every body. William, her brother, the so long absent and dearly loved brother, was in England again. She had a letter from him herself, a few hurried happy lines, written as the ship came up Channel, and sent into Portsmouth with the first boat that left the *Antwerp* at anchor in Spithead; and when Crawford walked up with the newspaper in his hand, which he had hoped would bring the first tidings, he found her trembling with joy over this letter, and listening with a glowing, grateful countenance to the kind invitation which her uncle was most collectedly dictating in reply.

It was but the day before that Crawford had made himself thoroughly master of the subject, or had in fact become at all aware of her having such a brother, or his being in such a ship, but the interest then excited had been very properly lively, determining him on his return to town to apply for information as to the probable period of the *Antwerp*'s return from the Mediterranean, etc.; and the good luck which attended his early examination of ship news the first morning, seemed the reward of his ingenuity in finding out such a method of pleasing her, as well as of his dutiful attention to the Admiral, in having for many years taken in the paper esteemed to have the earliest naval intelligence. He proved, however, to be too late. All those fine first feelings, of which he had hoped to be the exciter, were already given. But his intention, the kindness of this intention, was thankfully acknowleged: quite thankfully and warmly, for she was elevated beyond the common timidity of her mind by the flow of her love for William.

This dear William would soon be amongst them. There could be no doubt of his obtaining leave of absence immediately, for he was still only a midshipman; and as his parents, from living on the spot, must already have seen him, and be seeing him perhaps daily, his direct holidays might with justice be instantly given to the sister who had been his best correspondent through a period of seven years, and the uncle who had done most for his support and advancement; and accordingly the reply to her reply, fixing a very early day for his arrival, came as soon as possible; and scarcely ten days had passed since Fanny had been in the agitation of a higher nature, watching in the hall, in the lobby, on the stairs, for the first sound of the carriage which was to bring her a brother.

It came happily while she was thus waiting; and there being neither ceremony nor fearfulness to delay the moment of meeting, she was with him as he entered the house, and the first minutes of exquisite feeling had no interruption and no witnesses, unless the servants chiefly intent upon opening the proper doors could be called such. This was exactly what Sir Thomas and Edmund had been conniving at, as each proved to the other by the sympathetic alacrity with which they both advised Mrs Norris's continuing where she was, instead of rushing out into the hall as soon as the noises of the arrival reached them.

William and Fanny soon showed themselves; and Sir Thomas had the

Both advised Mrs Norris's continuing where she was

pleasure of receiving, in his protégé, certainly a very different person from the one he had equipped seven years ago, but a young man of an open, pleasant countenance, and frank, unstudied, but feeling and respectful manners, and such as confirmed him his friend.

It was long before Fanny could recover from the agitated happiness of such an hour as was formed by the last thirty minutes of expectation, and the first of fruition; it was some time even before her happiness could be said to make her happy, before the disappointment inseparable from the alteration of person had vanished, and she could see in him the same William as before, and talk to him, as her heart had been yearning to do, through many a past year. That time, however, did gradually come, forwarded by an affection on his side as warm as her own, and much less encumbered by refinement or self-distrust. She was the first object of his love, but it was a love which his stronger spirits and bolder temper made it as natural for him to express as to feel. On the morrow, they were walking about together with true enjoyment, and every succeeding morrow renewed a *tête-à-tête*, which Sir Thomas could not but observe with complacency, even before Edmund had pointed it out to him.

Excepting the moments of peculiar delight, which any marked or unlooked-for instance of Edmund's consideration of her in the last few months had excited, Fanny had never known so much felicity in her life, as in this unchecked, equal, fearless intercourse with the brother and friend, who was opening all his heart to her, telling her all his hopes and fears, plans, and solicitudes respecting that long thought of, dearly earned, and justly valued blessing of promotion; who could give her direct and minute information of the father and mother, brothers and sisters, of whom she very seldom heard; who was interested in all the comforts and all the little hardships of her home, at Mansfield; ready to think of every member of that home as she directed, or differing only by a less scrupulous opinion, and more noisy abuse of their Aunt Norris, and with whom (perhaps the dearest indulgence of the whole) all the evil and good of their earliest years could be gone over again, and every former united pain and pleasure retraced with the fondest recollection. An advantage this, a strengthener of love, in which even the conjugal tie is beneath the fraternal. Children of the same family, the same blood, with the same first associations and habits, having some means of enjoyment in their power, which no subsequent connections can supply; and it must be by a long and unnatural estrangement, by a divorce which no subsequent connection can justify, if such precious remains of the earliest attachments are ever entirely outlived. Too often, alas! it is so. Fraternal love, sometimes almost every thing, is at others worse than nothing. But with William and Fanny Price it was still a sentiment in all its prime and freshness, wounded by no opposition of interest, cooled by no separate attachment, and feeling the influence of time and absence only in its increase.

An affection so amiable was advancing each in the opinion of all who had hearts to value anything good. Henry Crawford was as much struck with it as any. He honoured the warm-hearted, blunt fondness of the young sailor, which led him to say, with his hands stretched towards Fanny's head: 'Do you know, I begin to like that queer fashion already, though when I first heard of such things being done in England, I could not believe it, and when Mrs Brown, and the other women at the Commissioner's at Gibraltar, appeared in the same trim, I thought they were mad; but Fanny can reconcile me to any thing'; and saw, with lively admiration, the glow of Fanny's cheek, the brightness of her eye, the deep interest, the absorbed attention, while her brother was describing any of the imminent hazards, or terrific scenes, which such a period at sea must supply.

It was a picture which Henry Crawford had moral taste enough to value. Fanny's attractions increased – increased twofold; for the sensibility which beautified her complexion and illumined her countenance was an attraction in itself. He was no longer in doubt of the capabilities of her heart. She had feeling, genuine feeling. It would be something to be loved by such a girl, to excite the first ardours of her young, unsophisticated mind! She interested him more than he had foreseen. A fortnight was not enough. His stay became indefinite.

William was often called on by his uncle to be the talker. His recitals were amusing in themselves to Sir Thomas, but the chief object in seeking them was to understand the reciter, to know the young man by his histories; and he listened to his clear, simple, spirited details with full satisfaction, seeing in them the proof of good principles, professional knowledge, energy, courage and cheerfulness, everything that could deserve or promise well. Young as he was, William had already seen a great deal. He had been in the Mediterranean; in the West Indies; in the Mediterranean again; had been often taken on shore by the favour of his captain, and in the course of seven years had known every variety of danger which sea and war together could offer. With such means in his power he had a right to be listened to; and though Mrs Norris could fidget about the room, and disturb everybody in quest of two needlefuls of thread or a second-hand shirt button, in the midst of her nephew's account of a shipwreck or an engagement, every body else was attentive; and even Lady Bertram could not hear of such horrors unmoved, or without sometimes lifting her eyes from her work to say, 'Dear me! how disagreeable! I wonder any body can ever go to sea.'

To Henry Crawford they gave a different feeling. He longed to have been at sea, and seen and done and suffered as much. His heart was warmed, his fancy fired, and he felt the highest respect for a lad who, before he was twenty, had gone through such bodily hardships, and given such proofs of mind. The glory of heroism, of usefulness, of exertion, of endurance, made his own habits of selfish indulgence appear in shameful contrast and he wished he had been a William Price, distinguishing himself and working his way to fortune and consequence with so much self-respect and happy ardour, instead of what he was!

The wish was rather eager than lasting. He was roused from the reverie of retrospection and regret produced by it, by some enquiry from Edmund as to his plans for the next day's hunting; and he found it was as well to be a man of fortune at once with horses and grooms at his command. In one respect it was better, as it gave him means of conferring a kindness where he wished to oblige. With spirits, courage and curiosity up to any thing, William expressed an inclination to hunt and Crawford could mount him without the slightest inconvenience to himself, and with only some scruples to obviate in Sir Thomas, who knew better than his nephew the value of such a loan, and some alarms to reason away in Fanny. She feared for William; by no means convinced by all that he could relate of his own horsemanship in various countries, of the scrambling parties in which he has been engaged, the rough horses and mules he had ridden, or his many narrow escapes from dreadful falls, that he was at all equal to the management of a high-fed hunter in an English fox-chase; nor till he returned safe and well, without accident or discredit, could she be reconciled to the risk, or feel any of that obligation to Mr Crawford for lending the horse, which he had fully intended it should produce. When it was proved, however, to have done William no harm, she could allow it to be a kindness, and even reward the owner with a smile when the animal was one minute tendered to his use again; and the next, with the greatest cordiality, and in a manner not to be resisted, made over to his use entirely so long as he remained in Northamptonshire.

CHAPTER TWENTY FIVE

THE INTERCOURSE OF THE two families was at this period more nearly restored to what it had been in the autumn, than any member of the old intimacy had thought ever likely to be again. The return of Henry Crawford, and the arrival of William Price, had much to do with it, but much was still owing to Sir Thomas's more than toleration of the neighbourly attempts at the Parsonage. His mind, now disengaged from the cares which had pressed on him at first, was at leisure to find the Grants and their young inmates really worth visiting; and though infinitely above scheming or contriving for any the most advantageous matrimonial establishment that could be among the apparent possibilities of anyone most dear to him, and disdaining even as a littleness the being quick-sighted on such points, he could not avoid perceiving, in a grand and careless way, that Mr Crawford was somewhat distinguishing his niece – nor perhaps refrain (though unconsciously) from giving a more willing assent to invitations on that account.

His readiness, however, in agreeing to dine at the Parsonage, when the general invitation was at last hazarded, after many debates and many doubts as to whether it were worth while, 'because Sir Thomas seemed so ill inclined, and Lady Bertram was so indolent!' proceeded from good breeding and good will alone, and had nothing to do with Mr Crawford, but as being one in an agreeable group; for it was in the course of that very visit, that he first began to think, that anyone in the habit of such idle observations *would have thought* that Mr Crawford was the admirer of Fanny Price.

The meeting was generally felt to be a pleasant one, being composed in a good proportion of those who would talk and those who would listen; and the dinner itself was elegant and plentiful, according to the usual style of the Grants, and too much according to the usual habits of all to raise any emotion except in Mrs Norris, who could never behold either the wide table or the number of dishes on it with patience, and who did always contrive to experience some evil from the passing of the servants behind her chair, and to bring away some fresh conviction of its being impossible among so many dishes but that some must be cold.

In the evening it was found, according to the predetermination of Mrs Grant and her sister, that after making up the whist table there would remain sufficient for a round game, and everybody being as perfectly complying and without a choice as on such occasions they always are, speculation was decided on almost as soon as whist; and Lady Bertram soon found herself in the critical situation of being applied to for her own choice between the games, and being required either to draw a card for whist or not. She hesitated. Luckily Sir Thomas was at hand.

'What shall I do, Sir Thomas? Whist and speculation; which will amuse me most?'

Sir Thomas, after a moment's thought, recommended speculation. He was a whist player himself, and perhaps might feel that it would not much amuse him to have her for a partner.

'Very well,' was her ladyship's contented answer; 'then speculation, if you please, Mrs Grant. I know nothing about it, but Fanny must teach me.'

Here Fanny interposed, however, with anxious protestations of her own equal ignorance; she had never played the game nor seen it played in her life; and Lady Bertram felt a moment's indecision again; but upon every body's assuring her that nothing could be so easy, that it was the easiest game on the cards, and Henry Crawford's stepping forward with a most earnest request to be allowed to sit between her ladyship and Miss Price, and teach them both, it was so settled; and Sir Thomas, Mrs Norris and Dr and Mrs Grant being seated at the table of prime intellectual state and dignity, the remaining six, under Miss Crawford's direction, were arranged round the other. It was a fine arrangement for Henry Crawford, who was close to Fanny, and with his hands full of business, having two persons' cards to manage as well as his own; for though it was impossible for Fanny not to feel herself mistress of the rules of the game in three minutes, he had yet to inspirit her play, sharpen her avarice, and harden her heart, which, especially in any competition with William, was a work of some difficulty; and as for Lady Bertram, he must continue in charge of all her fame and fortune through the whole evening; and if quick enough to keep her from looking at her cards when the deal began, must direct her in whatever was to be done with them to the end of it.

He was in high spirits, doing everything with happy ease, and preeminent in all the lively turns, quick resources, and playful impudence that could do honour to the game; and the round table was altogether a very comfortable contrast to the steady sobriety and orderly silence of the other.

Twice had Sir Thomas enquired into the enjoyment and success of his lady, but in vain; no pause was long enough for the time his measured manner needed; and very little of her state could be known till Mrs Grant was able, at the end of the first rubber, to go to her and pay her compliments.

'I hope your ladyship is pleased with the game.'

'Oh dear, yes! Very entertaining, indeed. A very odd game. I do not know what it is all about. I am never to see my cards; and Mr Crawford does all the rest.'

'Bertram,' said Crawford, some time afterwards, taking the opportunity of a little languor in the game, 'I have never told you what happened to me yesterday in my ride home.' They had been hunting together, and were in the midst of a good run, and at some distance from Mansfield when his horse being found to have flung a shoe, Henry Crawford had been obliged to give up, and make the best of his way back. 'I told you I lost my way after passing that old farmhouse, with the yew-trees, because I can never bear to ask; but I have not told you that, with my usual luck – for I never do wrong without gaining by it – I found myself in due time in the very place which I had a curiosity to see. I was suddenly, upon turning the corner of a steepish downy field, in the midst of a retired little village between gently rising hills; a small stream before me to be forded, a church standing on a sort of knoll to my right – which church was strikingly large and handsome for the place, and not a gentleman or half a gentleman's house to be seen excepting one – to be presumed the Parsonage – within a stone's throw of the said knoll and church. I found myself, in short, in Thornton Lacey.'

'It sounds like it,' said Edmund; 'but which way did you turn after passing Sewell's farm?'

'I answer no such irrelevant and insidious questions; though were I to answer all that you could put in the course of an hour, you would never be able to prove that it was *not* Thornton Lacey – for such it certainly was.'

'You enquired, then?'

'No, I never enquire. But I *told* a man mending a hedge that it was Thornton Lacey, and he agreed to it.'

It was Thornton Lacey

'You have a good memory. I had forgotten having ever told you half so much of the place.'

Thornton Lacey was the name of his impending living, as Miss Crawford well knew; and her interest in a negotiation for William Price's knave increased.

'Well,' continued Edmund, 'and how did you like what you saw?'

'Very much, indeed. You are a lucky fellow. There will be work for five summers at least before the place is livable.'

'No, no, not so bad as that. The farmyard must be moved, I grant you; but I am not aware of any thing else. The house is by no means bad, and when the yard is removed, there may be a very tolerable approach to it.'

'The farmyard must be cleared away entirely, and planted up to shut out the blacksmith's shop. The house must be turned to front the east instead of the north; the entrance and principal rooms, I mean, must be on that side, where the view is really very pretty; I am sure it may be done. And *there* must be your approach, through what is at present the garden. You must make a new garden at what is now the back of the house; which will be giving it the best aspect in the world, sloping to the south-east. The ground seems precisely formed for it. I rode fifty yards up the lane, between the church and the house, in order to look about me; and saw how it might all be. Nothing can be easier. The meadows beyond what *will be* the garden, as well as what now *is*, sweeping round from the lane I stood in to the north-east, that is, to the principal road through the village, must be all laid together of course; very pretty meadows they are, finely sprinkled with timber. They belong to the living, I suppose; if not, you must purchase them. Then the stream – some thing must be done with the stream; but I could not quite determine what. I had two or three ideas.'

'And I have two or three ideas also,' said Edmund, 'and one of them is, that very little of your plan for Thornton Lacey will ever be put in practice. I must be satisfied with rather less ornament and beauty. I think the house and premises may be made comfortable, and given the air of a gentleman's residence without any very heavy expense, and that must suffice me; and, I hope, may suffice all who care about me.'

Miss Crawford, a little suspicious and resentful of a certain tone of voice, and a certain half-look attending the last expression of his hope, made a hasty finish of her dealings with William Price; and securing his knave at an exorbitant rate, exclaimed, 'There, I will stake my last like a woman of spirit. No cold prudence for me. I am not born to sit still and do nothing. If I lose the game, it shall not be from not striving for it.'

The game was hers, and only did not pay her for what she had given to secure it. Another deal proceeded, and Crawford began again about Thornton Lacey.

'My plan may not be the best possible; I had not many minutes to form it in; but you must do a good deal. The place deserves it, and you will find yourself not satisfied with much less than it is capable of. (Excuse me, your ladyship must not see your cards. There, let them lie just before you.) The place deserves it, Bertram. You talk of giving it the air of a gentleman's residence. *That* will be done by the removal of the farmyard; for, independent of that terrible nuisance, I never saw a house of the kind which had in itself so much the air of a gentleman's residence, so much the look of a something above a mere parsonage house; above the expenditure of a few hundreds a year. It is not a scrambling collection of low single rooms, with as many roofs as windows; it is not cramped into the vulgar compactness of a square farmhouse; it is a solid, roomy, mansion-like looking house, such as one might suppose a respectable old country family had lived in from generation to generation, through two centuries at least, and were now spending from two to three thousand a year in.' Miss Crawford listened, and Edmund agreed to this. 'The air of a gentleman's residence, therefore, you cannot but give it, if you do anything. But it is capable of much more. (Let me see, Mary; Lady Bertram bids a dozen for that queen; no, no, a dozen is more than it is worth. Lady Bertram does *not* bid a dozen. She will have nothing to say to it. Go on, go on.) By some such improvements as I have suggested (I do not really require you to proceed upon my plan, though, by the by, I doubt any body's striking out a better) – you may give it a higher character. You may raise it into a *place*. From being the mere gentleman's residence, it becomes, by judicious improvement, the residence of a man of education, taste, modern manners, good connections. All this may be stamped on it; and that house receive such an air as to make its owner be set down as the great landholder of the parish, by every creature travelling the road; especially as there is no real squire's house to dispute the point; a circumstance, between ourselves, to enhance the value of such a situation in point of privilege and independence beyond all calculation. *You* think with me, I hope – (turning with a softened voice to Fanny). Have you ever seen the place?'

Fanny gave a quick negative, and tried to hide her interest in the subject by an eager attention to her brother, who was driving as hard a bargain, and imposing on her as much as he could; but Crawford pursued with, 'No, no, you must not part with the queen. You have bought her too dearly, and your brother does not offer half her value. No, no, sir, hands off, hands off. Your sister does not part with the queen. She is quite determined. The game will be yours,' turning to her again – 'it will certainly be yours.'

'And Fanny had much rather it were William's,' said Edmund, smiling at her. 'Poor Fanny! Not allowed to cheat herself as she wishes!'

'Mr Bertram,' said Miss Crawford, a few minutes afterwards, 'you know

Henry to be such a capital improver, that you cannot possibly engage in any thing of the sort at Thornton Lacey without accepting his help. Only think how useful he was at Sotherton! Only think what grand things were produced there by our all going with him one hot day in August to drive about the grounds, and see his genius take fire. There we went, and there we came home home again; and what was done there is not to be told!'

Fanny's eyes were turned on Crawford for a moment with an expression more than grave – even reproachful; but on catching his, were instantly withdrawn. With something of consciousness, he shook his head at his sister, and laughingly replied, 'I cannot say there was much done at Sotherton; but it was a hot day, and we were all walking after each other, and bewildered.' As soon as a general buzz gave him shelter, he added, in a low voice, directed solely at Fanny, 'I should be sorry to have my powers of *planning* judged of by the day at Sotherton. I see things very differently now. Do not think of me as I appeared then.'

Sotherton was a word to catch Mrs Norris, and being just then in the happy leisure which followed securing the odd trick by Sir Thomas's capital play and her own, against Dr and Mrs Grant's great hands, she called out, in high good humour, 'Sotherton! Yes, that is a place, indeed, and we had a charming day there. William, you are quite out of luck; but the next time you come, I hope dear Mr and Mrs Rushworth will be at home, and I am sure I can answer for your being kindly received by both. Your cousins are not of a sort to forget their relations, and Mr Rushworth is a most amiable man. They are at Brighton now, you know; in one of the best houses there, as Mr Rushworth's fine fortune gives them a right to be. I do not exactly know the distance, but when you get back to Portsmouth, if it is not very far off, you ought to go over, and pay your respects to them; and I could send a little parcel by you that I want to get conveyed to your cousins.'

'I should be very happy, aunt; but Brighton is almost by Beachy Head; and if I could get so far, I could not expect to be welcome in such a smart place as that – poor scrubby midshipman as I am.'

Mrs Norris was beginning an eager assurance of the affability he might depend on, when she was stopped by Sir Thomas's saying with authority, 'I do not advise your going to Brighton, William, as I trust you may soon have more convenient opportunities of meeting; but my daughters would be happy to see their cousins anywhere; and you will find Mr Rushworth most sincerely disposed to regard all the connections of our family as his own.'

'I would rather find him private secretary to the First Lord than anything else,' was William's only answer, in an under voice, not meant to reach far, and the subject dropped.

As yet Sir Thomas had seen nothing to remark in Mr Crawford's behaviour; but when the whist table broke up at the end of the second rubber, and leaving Dr Grant and Mrs Norris to dispute over their last play, he became a looker-on at the other, he found his niece the object of attentions, or rather of professions, of a somewhat pointed character.

Henry Crawford was in the first glow of another scheme about Thornton Lacey; and not being able to catch Edmund's ear, was detailing it to his fair neighbour with a look of considerable earnestness. His scheme was to rent the house himself the following winter, that he might have a home of his own in that neighbourhood; and it was not merely for the use of it in the hunting season (as he was then telling her), though *that* consideration had certainly some weight, feeling as he did that, in spite of all Dr Grant's very great kindness, it was impossible for him and his horses to be accommodated where they now were without material inconvenience; but his attachment to that neighbourhood did not depend upon one amusement or one season of the year; he had set his heart upon having a something there that he could come to at any time, a little homestall at his command, where all the holidays of his year might be spent, and he might find himself continuing, improving, and *perfecting* that friendship and intimacy with the Mansfield Park family which was increasing in value to him every day. Sir Thomas heard and was not offended. There was no want of respect in the young man's address; and Fanny's reception of it was so proper and modest, so calm and uninviting, that he had nothing to censure in her. She said little, assented only here and there, and betrayed no inclination either of appropriating any part of the compliment to herself, or of strengthening his views in favour of Northamptonshire. Finding by whom he was observed, Henry Crawford addressed himself on the same subject to Sir Thomas, in a more everyday tone, but still with feeling.

'I want to be your neighbour, Sir Thomas, as you have, perhaps, heard me telling Miss Price. May I hope for your acquiescence, and for your not influencing your son against such a tenant?'

Sir Thomas, politely bowing, replied: 'It is the only way, sir, in which I could *not* wish you established as a permanent neighbour; but I hope, and believe, that Edmund will occupy his own house at Thornton Lacey. Edmund, am I saying too much?'

Edmund, on this appeal, had first to hear what was going on; but, on understanding the question, was at no loss for an answer.

'Certainly, sir, I have no idea but of residence. But, Crawford, though I refuse you as a tenant, come to me as a friend. Consider the house as half your own every winter; and we will add to the stables on your own improved plan, and with all the improvements of your improved plan that may occur to you this spring.'

'We shall be the losers,' continued Sir Thomas. 'His going, though only eight miles, will be an unwelcome contraction of our family circle; but I should have been deeply mortified if any son of mine could reconcile himself to doing less. It is perfectly natural that you should not have thought much on the subject, Mr Crawford. But a parish has wants and claims which can be known only by a clergyman constantly resident, and which no proxy can be capable of satisfying to the same extent. Edmund might, in the common phrase, do the duty of Thornton, that is, he might read prayers and preach, without giving up Mansfield Park; he might ride over every Sunday, to a house nominally inhabited, and go through divine service; he might be the clergyman of Thornton Lacey every seventh day, for three or four hours, if that would content him. But it will not. He knows that human nature needs more lessons than a weekly sermon can convey; and that if he does not live among his parishioners, and prove himself, by constant attention, their well-wisher and friend, he does very little either for their good or his own.'

Mr Crawford bowed his acquiescence.

'I repeat again,' added Sir Thomas, 'that Thornton Lacey is the only house in the neighbourhood in which I should not be happy to wait on Mr Crawford as occupier.'

Mr Crawford bowed his thanks.

'Sir Thomas,' said Edmund, 'undoubtedly understands the duty of a parish priest. We must hope his son may prove that *he* knows it too.'

Whatever effect Sir Thomas's little harangue might really produce on Mr Crawford, it raised some awkward sensations in two of the others, two of his most attentive listeners – Miss Crawford and Fanny. One of whom, having never before understood that Thornton was so soon and so completely to be his home, was pondering with downcast eyes on what it would be *not* to see Edmund every day; and the other, startled from the agreeable fancies she had been previously indulging on the strength of her brother's description, no longer able, in the picture she had been forming of a future Thornton, to shut out the church, sink the clergyman, and see only the respectable, elegant, modernised and occasional residence of a man of independent fortune, was considering Sir Thomas, with decided ill-will, as the destroyer of all this, and suffering the more from that involuntary forbearance which his character and manner commanded, and from not daring to relieve herself by a single attempt at throwing ridicule on his cause.

All the agreeable of *her* speculation was over for that hour. It was time to have done with cards, if sermons prevailed; and she was glad to find it necessary to come to a conclusion, and be able to refresh her spirits by a change of place and neighbour.

The chief of the party were now collected irregularly round the fire, and waiting the final break-up. William and Fanny were the most detached. They remained together at the otherwise deserted card-table, talking very comfortably, and not thinking of the rest, till some of the rest began to think of them. Henry Crawford's chair was the first to be given a direction towards them, and he sat silently observing them for a few minutes; himself, in the meanwhile, observed by Sir Thomas, who was standing in chat with Dr Grant.

'This is the assembly night,' said William. 'If I were at Portsmouth I should be at it, perhaps.'

'But you do not wish yourself at Portsmouth, William.'

'No, Fanny, that I do not. I shall have enough of Portsmouth and of dancing, too, when I cannot have you. And I do not know that there would be any good in going to the assembly, for I might not get a partner. The Portsmouth girls turn up their noses at any body who has not a commission. One might as well be nothing as a midshipman. One *is* nothing, indeed. You remember the Gregorys; they are grown up amazing fine girls, but they will hardly speak to *me*, because Lucy is courted by a lieutenant.'

'Oh! shame, shame! But never mind it, William (her own cheeks in a glow of indignation as she spoke). It is not worth minding. It is no reflection on *you*; it is no more than what the greatest admirals have all experienced, more or less, in their time. You must think of that, you must try to make up your mind to it as one of the hardships which fall to every sailor's share, like bad weather and hard living, only with this advantage, that there will be an end to it, and there will come a time when you will have nothing of that sort to endure. When you are a lieutenant! Only think, William, when you are a lieutenant! how little you will care for any nonsense of this kind.'

'I begin to think I shall never be a lieutenant, Fanny. Every body gets made but me.'

'Oh! my dear William, do not talk so; do not be so desponding. My uncle says nothing, but I am sure he will do everything in his power to get you made. He knows, as well as you do, of what consequence it is.'

She was checked by the sight of her uncle much nearer to them than she had any suspicion of, and each found it necessary to talk of some thing else.

'Are you fond of dancing, Fanny?'

'Yes, very; only I am soon tired.'

'I should like to go to a ball with you and see you dance. Have you never any balls at Northampton? I should like to see you dance, and I'd dance with you if you *would*, for nobody would know who I was here, and I should like to be your partner once more. We used to jump about together many a time, did not we? When the hand-organ was in the street? I am a pretty good dancer in my way, but I dare say you are a better.' And turning to his uncle, who was now close to them, 'Is not Fanny a very good dancer, sir?'

Fanny, in dismay at such an unprecedented question, did not know which way to look, or how to be prepared for the answer. Some very grave reproof, or at least the coldest expression of indifference, must be coming to distress her brother, and sink her to the ground. But, on the contrary, it was no worse than, 'I am sorry to say that I am unable to answer your question. I have never seen Fanny dance since she was a little girl; but I trust we shall both think she acquits herself like a gentlewoman when we do see her, which, perhaps, we may have an opportunity of doing ere long.'

'I have had the pleasure of seeing your sister dance, Mr Price,' said Henry Crawford, leaning forward, 'and will engage to answer every enquiry which you can make on the subject, to your entire satisfaction. But I believe' (seeing Fanny looked distressed) 'it must be at some other time. There is *one* person in company who does not like to have Miss Price spoken of.'

True enough, he had once seen Fanny dance; and it was equally true that he would now have answered for her gliding about with quiet, light elegance, and in admirable time; but in fact he could not for the life of him recall what her dancing had been, and rather took it for granted that she had been present than remembered any thing about her.

He passed, however, for an admirer of her dancing; and Sir Thomas, by no means displeased, prolonged the conversation on dancing in general, and was so well engaged in describing the balls of Antigua, and listening to what his nephew could relate of the different modes of dancing which had fallen within his observation, that he had not heard his carriage announced, and was first called to the knowledge of it by the bustle of Mrs Norris.

'Come, Fanny, Fanny, what are you about? We are going. Do not you see your aunt is going? Quick, quick! I cannot bear to keep good old Wilcox waiting. You should always remember the coachman and horses. My dear Sir Thomas, we have settled it that the carriage should come back for you and Edmund and William.'

Sir Thomas could not dissent, as it had been his own arrangement, previously communicated to his wife and sister; but *that* seemed forgotten by Mrs Norris, who must fancy that she settled it all herself.

Fanny's last feeling in the visit was disappointment: for the shawl which Edmund was quietly taking from the servant to bring and put round her shoulders was seized by Mr Crawford's quicker hand, and she was obliged to be indebted to his more prominent attention.

CHAPTER TWENTY SIX

WILLIAM'S DESIRE OF SEEING Fanny dance made more than a momentary impression on his uncle. The hope of an opportunity, which Sir Thomas had then given, was not given to be thought of no more. He remained steadily inclined to gratify so amiable a feeling; to gratify any body else who might wish to see Fanny dance, and to give pleasure to the young people in general; and having thought the matter over, and taken his resolution in quiet independence, the result of it appeared the next morning at breakfast, when, after recalling and commending what his nephew had said, he added, 'I do not like, William, that you should leave Northamptonshire without this indulgence. It would give me pleasure to see you both dance. You spoke of the balls at Northampton. Your cousins have occasionally attended them: but they would not altogether suit us now. The fatigue would be too much for your aunt. I believe we must not think of a Northampton ball. A dance at home would be more eligible; and if—'.

'Ah, my dear Sir Thomas!' interrupted Mrs Norris, 'I knew what was coming. I knew what you were going to say. If dear Julia were at home, or dearest Mrs Rushworth at Sotherton, to afford a reason, an occasion for such a thing, you would be tempted to give the young people a dance at Mansfield. I knew you would. If *they* were at home to grace the ball, a ball you would have this very Christmas. Thank your uncle, William, thank you uncle!'

'My daughters,' replied Sir Thomas, gravely interposing, 'have their pleasures at Brighton, and I hope are very happy; but the dance which I think of giving at Mansfield will be for their cousins. Could we be all assembled, our satisfaction would undoubtedly be more complete, but the absence of some is not to debar the others of amusement.'

Mrs Norris had not another word to say. She saw decision in his looks, and her surprise and vexation required some minutes' silence to be settled into composure. A ball at such a time! His daughters absent and herself not consulted! There was comfort, however, soon at hand. *She* must be the doer of every thing: Lady Bertram would of course be spared all thought and exertion, and it would all fall upon *her*. She should have to do the honours of the evening; and this reflection quickly restored so much of her good humour as enabled her to join in with the others, before their happiness and thanks were all expressed.

Edmund, William and Fanny did, in their different ways, look and speak as much grateful pleasure in the promised ball as Sir Thomas could desire. Edmund's feelings were for the other two. His father had never conferred a favour or shown a kindness more to his satisfaction.

Lady Bertram was perfectly quiescent and contented, and had no objections to make. Sir Thomas engaged for its giving her very little trouble; and she assured him 'that she was not at all afraid of the trouble; indeed, she could not imagine there would be any.'

Mrs Norris was ready with her suggestions as to the rooms he would think fittest to be used, but found it all prearranged; and when she would have conjectured and hinted about the day, it appeared that the day was settled too. Sir Thomas had been amusing himself with shaping a very complete outline of the business; and as soon as she would listen quietly, could read his list of the families to be invited, from whom he calculated, with all necessary allowance for the shortness of the notice, to collect young people enough to form twelve or fourteen couple: and could detail the considerations which had induced him to fix on the 22nd as the most eligible day. William was required to be at Portsmouth on the 24th; the 22nd would therefore be the last day of his visit; but where the days were so few it would be unwise to fix on any earlier. Mrs Norris was obliged to be satisfied with thinking just the same, and with having been on the point of proposing the 22nd herself, as by far the best day for the purpose.

The ball was now a settled thing, and before the evening a proclaimed thing to all whom it concerned. Invitations were sent with despatch, and many a young lady went to bed that night with her head full of happy cares as well as Fanny. To her, the cares were sometimes almost beyond the happiness; for young and inexperienced, with small means of choice, and no confidence in her own taste, the 'how she should be dressed,' was a point of painful solicitude; and the almost solitary ornament in her possession, a very pretty amber cross which William had brought her from Sicily, was the greatest distress of all, for she had nothing but a bit of ribbon to fasten it to; and though she had worn it in that manner once, would it be allowable at such a time, in the midst of all the rich ornaments which she supposed all the other young ladies would appear in? And yet not to wear it! William had wanted to buy her a gold chain too, but the purchase had been beyond his means, and therefore not to wear the cross might be mortifying him. These were anxious considerations; enough to sober her spirits even under the prospect of a ball given principally for her gratification.

The preparations meanwhile went on, and Lady Bertram continued to sit on her sofa without any inconvenience from them. She had some extra visits from the housekeeper, and her maid was rather hurried in making up a new dress for her: Sir Thomas gave orders, and Mrs Norris ran about; but all this gave *her* no trouble, and as she had foreseen, 'there was, in fact, no trouble in the business.'

Edmund was at this time particularly full of cares; his mind being deeply occupied in the consideration of two important events now at hand, which were to fix his fate in life – ordination and matrimony – events of such a serious character as to make the ball, which would be very quickly followed by one of them, appear of less moment in his eyes than in those of any other person in the house. On the 23rd he was going to a friend near Peterborough, in the same situation as himself, and they were to receive ordination in the course of the Christmas week. Half his destiny would then be determined, but the other half might not be so very smoothly wooed. His duties would be established, but the wife who was to share, and animate, and reward those duties, might yet be unattainable. He knew his own mind, but he was not always perfectly assured of knowing Miss Crawford's. There were points on which they did not quite agree; there were moments in which she did not seem propitious; and though trusting altogether to her affection, so far as to be resolved (almost resolved) on bringing it to a decision within a very short time as soon as the variety of business before him were arranged, and he knew what he had to offer her, he had many anxious feelings, many doubting hours as to the result. His conviction of her regard for him was sometimes very strong; he could look back on a long course of encouragement, and she was as perfect in disinterested attachment as in everything else. But at other times doubt and alarm intermingled with his hopes; and when he thought of her acknowledged disinclination for privacy and retirement, her decided preference of a London life, what could he expect but a determined rejection? Unless it were an acceptance even more to be deprecated, demanding such sacrifices of situation and employment on his side as conscience must forbid.

The issue of all depended on one question. Did she love him well enough to forgo what had used to be essential points? Did she love him well enough to make them no longer essential? And this question, which he was continually repeating to himself, though oftenest answered with a 'Yes,' had sometimes its 'No.'

Miss Crawford was soon to leave Mansfield, and on this circumstance the 'no' and the 'yes' had been very recently in alternation. He had seen her eyes sparkle as she spoke of the dear friend's letter, which claimed a long visit from her in London, and of the kindness of Henry, in engaging to remain where he was till January, that he might convey her thither; he had heard her speak of the pleasure of such a journey with an animation which had 'no' in every tone. But this had occurred on the first day of its being settled, within the first hour of the burst of such enjoyment, when nothing but the friends she was to visit was before her. He had since heard her express herself differently, with other feelings, more checkered feeling; he had heard her tell Mrs Grant that she should leave her with regret; that she began to believe neither the friends nor the pleasures she was going to were worth those she left behind; and that though she felt she must go, and knew she should enjoy herself when once away, she was already looking forward to being at Mansfield again. Was there not a 'yes' in all this?

With such matters to ponder over, and arrange, and rearrange, Edmund could not, on his own account, think very much of the evening which the rest of the family were looking forward to with a more equal degree of strong interest. Independent of his two cousins' enjoyment in it, the evening was to him of no higher value than any other appointed meeting of the two families might be. In every meeting there was a hope of receiving further confirmation of Miss Crawford's attachment; but the whirl of a ballroom, perhaps, was not particularly favourable to the excitement or expression of serious feelings. To engage her early for the two first dances, was all the command of individual happiness which he felt in his power, and the only preparation for the ball which he could enter into, in spite of all that was passing around him on the subject, from morning till night.

Thursday was the day of the ball, and on Wednesday morning Fanny, still unable to satisfy herself as to what she ought to wear, determined to seek the counsel of the more enlightened, and apply to Mrs Grant and her sister, whose acknowledged taste would certainly bear her blameless; and as Edmund and William were gone to Northampton, and she had reason to think Mr Crawford likewise out, she walked down to the Parsonage without much fear of wanting an opportunity for private discussion; and the privacy of such a discussion was a most important part of it to Fanny, being more than half ashamed of her own solicitude.

She met Miss Crawford within a few yards of the Parsonage, just setting out to call on her, and as it seemed to her that her friend, though obliged to insist on turning back, was unwilling to lose her walk, she explained her business at once, and observed that if she would be so kind as to give her opinion, it might be all talked over as well without doors as within. Miss Crawford appeared gratified by the application, and after a moment's thought urged Fanny's returning with her in a much more cordial manner than before, and proposed their going up into her room, where they might have a comfortable cose, without disturbing Dr and Mrs Grant, who were together in the drawing-room. It was just the plan to suit Fanny; and with a great deal of gratitude on her side for such ready and kind attention, they proceeded indoors, and upstairs, and were soon deep in the interesting subject. Miss Crawford, pleased with the appeal, gave her all her best judgment and taste, made every thing easy by her suggestions, and tried to make every thing agreeable by her encouragement. The dress being settled in all its grander parts – 'But what shall you have by way of necklace?' said Miss Crawford. 'Shall not you wear your brother's cross?' And as she spoke she was undoing a small parcel, which Fanny had observed in her hand when they met. Fanny acknowledged her wishes and doubts on this point; she did not know how either to wear the cross, or to refrain from wearing it. She was answered by having a small trinket-box placed before her, and being requested to choose from among several gold chains and necklaces. Such had been the parcel with which Miss Crawford was provided, and such the object of her intended visit: and in the kindest manner she now urged Fanny's taking one for the cross and to keep for her sake, saying every thing she could think of to obviate the scruples which were making Fanny start back at first with a look of horror at the proposal.

'You see what a collection I have,' said she, 'more by half than I ever use or think of. I do not offer them as new. I offer nothing but an old necklace. You must forgive the liberty, and oblige me.'

Fanny still resisted, and from her heart. The gift was too valuable. But Miss Crawford persevered, and argued the case with so much affectionate earnestness through all the heads of William and the cross, and the ball, and herself, as to be finally successful. Fanny found herself obliged to yield, that she might not be accused of pride or indifference, or some other littleness; and having with modest reluctance given consent, proceeded to make the selection. She looked and looked, longing to know which might be least valuable; and was determined in her choice at last, by fancying there was one necklace more frequently placed before her eyes than the rest. It was of gold, prettily worked; and though Fanny would have preferred a longer and a plainer chain as more adapted for her purpose, she hoped, in fixing on this, to be choosing what Miss Crawford least wished to keep. Miss Crawford smiled her perfect approbation; and hastened to complete the gift by putting the necklace round her, and making her see how well it looked. Fanny had not a word to say against its becomingness, and excepting what remained of her scruples, was exceedingly pleased with an acquisition so very apropos. She would rather perhaps have been obliged to some other person. But this was an unworthy feeling. Miss Crawford had anticipated her wants with a kindness which proved her a real friend. 'When I wear this necklace I shall always think of you,' said she, 'and feel how very kind you were.'

'You must think of some body else, too, when you wear that necklace,' replied Miss Crawford. 'You must think of Henry, for it was his choice in the first place. He gave it to me, and with the necklace I make over to you all the duty of remembering the original giver. It is to be a family remembrancer. The sister is not to be in your mind without bringing the brother too.'

Fanny, in great astonishment and confusion, would have returned the present instantly. To take what had been the gift of another person, of a brother too, impossible! It must not be! And with an eagerness and

Making her see how well it looked

embarrassment quite diverting to her companion, she laid down the necklace again on its cotton, and seemed resolved either to take another or none at all. Miss Crawford thought she had never seen a prettier consciousness. 'My dear child,' said she, laughing, 'what are you afraid of? Do you think Henry will claim the necklace as mine, and fancy you did not come honestly by it? Or are you imagining he would be too much flattered by seeing round your lovely throat an ornament which his money purchased three years ago, before he knew there was such a throat in the world? Or perhaps – looking archly – you suspect a confederacy between us, and that what I am now doing is with his knowledge and at his desire?'

With the deepest blushes Fanny protested against such a thought.

'Well, then,' replied Miss Crawford more seriously, but without at all believing her, 'to convince me that you suspect no trick, and are as unsuspicious of compliment as I have always found you, take the necklace and say no more about it. Its being a gift of my brother's need not make the smallest difference in your accepting it, as I assure you it makes none in my willingness to part with it. He is always giving me some thing or other. I have such innumerable presents from him that it is quite impossible for me to value, or for him to remember half. And as for this necklace, I do not suppose I have worn it six times; it is very pretty, but I never think of it; and though you would be most heartily welcome to any other in my trinket-box, you have happened to fix on the very one which, if I have a choice, I would rather part with and see in your possession than any other. Say no more against it, I entreat you. Such a trifle is not worth half so many words.'

Fanny dared not make any further opposition; and with renewed but less happy thanks accepted the necklace again, for there was an expression in Miss Crawford's eyes which she could not be satisfied with.

It was impossible for her to be insensible of Mr Crawford's change of manners. She had long seen it. He evidently tried to please her; he was gallant, he was attentive, he was something like what he had been to her cousins: he wanted, she supposed, to cheat her of her tranquillity as he had cheated them; and whether he might not have some concern in this necklace? She could not be convinced that he had not, for Miss Crawford, complaisant as a sister, was careless as a woman and a friend.

Reflecting and doubting, and feeling that the possession of what she had so much wished for did not bring much satisfaction, she now walked home again, with a change rather than a diminution of cares since her treading that path before.

CHAPTER TWENTY SEVEN

ON REACHING HOME, Fanny went immediately upstairs to deposit this unexpected acquisition, this doubtful good of a necklace, in some favourite box in the East Room, which held all her smaller treasures; but on opening the door, what was her surprise to find her cousin Edmund there writing at the table! Such a sight having never occurred before, was almost as wonderful as it was welcome.

'Fanny,' said he directly, leaving his seat and his pen, and meeting her with some thing in his hand, 'I beg your pardon for being here. I came to look for you, and after waiting a little while in hope of your coming in, was making use of your inkstand to explain my errand. You will find the beginning of a note to yourself; but I can now speak my business, which is merely to beg your acceptance of this little trifle: a chain for William's cross. You ought to have had it a week ago, but there has been a delay from my brother's not being in town by several days so soon as I expected; and I have only just now received it at Northampton. I hope you will like the chain itself, Fanny. I endeavoured to consult the simplicity of your taste; but at any rate I know you will be kind to my intentions, and consider it, as it really is, a token of the love of one of your oldest friends.'

And so saying, he was hurrying away, before Fanny, overpowered by a thousand feelings of pain and pleasure, could attempt to speak; but quickened by one sovereign wish she then called out, 'Oh! cousin, stop a moment, pray stop!'

He turned back.

'I cannot attempt to thank you,' she continued, in a very agitated manner; 'thanks are out of the question. I feel much more than I can possibly express. Your goodness in thinking of me in such a way is beyond—'

'If that is all you have to say, Fanny—' smiling, and turning away again.

'No, no, it is not. I want to consult you.'

Almost unconsciously she had now undone the parcel he had just put into her hand, and seeing before her, in all the niceness of jewellers' packing, a plain gold chain, perfectly simple and neat, she could not help bursting forth again, 'Oh, this is beautiful, indeed! This is the very thing, precisely what I wished for! This is the only ornament I have ever had a desire to possess. It will exactly suit my cross. They must and shall be worn together. It comes, too, in such an acceptable moment. Oh, cousin, you do not know how acceptable it is.'

'My dear Fanny, you feel these things a great deal too much. I am most happy that you like the chain, and that it should be here in time for to-morrow; but your thanks are far beyond the occasion. Believe me, I have no pleasure in the world superior to that of contributing to yours. No, I can safely say, I have no pleasure so complete, so unalloyed. It is without a drawback.'

Upon such expressions of affection, Fanny could have lived an hour without saying another word; but Edmund, after waiting a moment, obliged her to bring down her mind from its heavenly flight, by saying, 'But what is it that you want to consult me about?'

It was about the necklace, which she was now most earnestly longing to return, and hoped to obtain his approbation of her doing. She gave the history of her recent visit, and now her raptures might well be over; for Edmund was so struck with the circumstance, so delighted with what Miss

Crawford had done, so gratified by such a coincidence of conduct between them, that Fanny could not but admit the superior power of *one* pleasure over his own mind, though it might have its drawback. It was some time before she could get his attention to her plan, or any answer to her demand of his opinion: he was in a reverie of fond reflection, uttering only now and then a few half sentences of praise; but when he did awake and understand, he was very decided in opposing what she wished.

'Return the necklace! No, my dear Fanny, upon no account. It would be mortifying her severely. There can hardly be a more unpleasant sensation than the having any thing returned on our hands which we have given with a reasonable hope of its contributing to the comfort of a friend. Why should she lose a pleasure which she has shown herself so deserving of?'

'If it had been given to me in the first instance,' said Fanny, 'I should not have thought of returning it; but being her brother's present, is not it fair to suppose that she would rather not part with it, when it is not wanted?'

'She must not suppose it not wanted, not acceptable, at least; and its having been originally her brother's gift makes no difference; for as she was not prevented from offering, nor you from taking it on that account, it ought not to prevent you from keeping it. No doubt it is handsomer than mine, and fitter for a ball-room.'

'No, it is not handsomer, not at all handsomer in its way, and, for my purpose, not half so fit. The chain will agree with William's cross beyond all comparison better than the necklace.'

'For one night, Fanny, for only one night, if it *be* a sacrifice – I am sure you will, upon consideration, make that sacrifice rather than give pain to one who has been so studious of your comfort. Miss Crawford's attentions to you have been – not more than you were justly entitled to – I am the last person to think that *could be*, but they have been invariable; and to be returning them with what must have something the *air* of ingratitude, though I know it could never have the *meaning*, is not in your nature, I am sure. Wear the necklace, as you are engaged to do, to-morrow evening, and let the chain, which was not ordered with any reference to the ball, be kept for commoner occasions. This is my advice. I would not have the shadow of a coolness between the two whose intimacy I have been observing with the greatest pleasure, and whose characters there is so much general resemblance in true generosity and natural delicacy as to make the few slight differences, resulting principally from situation, no reasonable hindrance to a perfect friendship. I would not have the shadow of a coolness arise,' he repeated, his voice sinking a little, 'between the two dearest objects I have on earth.'

He was gone as he spoke; and Fanny remained to tranquillise herself as she could. She was one of his two dearest – that must support her. But the other:

the first! She had never heard him speak so openly before, and though it told her no more than what she had long perceived, it was a stab, for it told of his own convictions and views. They were decided. He would marry Miss Crawford. It was a stab, in spite of every long-standing expectation; and she was obliged to repeat again and again, that she was one of his two dearest, before the words gave her any sensation. Could she believe Miss Crawford to deserve him, it would be – oh, how different would it be – how far more tolerable! But he was deceived in her; he gave her merits which she had not; her faults were what they had ever been, but he saw them no longer. Till she had shed many tears over this deception, Fanny could not subdue her agitation; and the dejection which followed could only be relieved by the influence of fervent prayers for his happiness.

It was her intention, as she felt it to be her duty, to try to overcome all that was excessive, all that bordered on selfishness, in her affection for Edmund. To call or to fancy it a loss, a disappointment, would be a presumption for which she had not words strong enough to satisfy her own humility. To think of him as Miss Crawford might be justified in thinking would in her be insanity. To her he could be nothing under any circumstances; nothing dearer than a friend. Why did such an idea occur to her even enough to be reprobated and forbidden? It ought not to have touched on the confines of her imagination. She would endeavour to be rational, and to deserve the right of judging of Miss Crawford's character, and the privilege of true solicitude for him by a sound intellect and an honest heart.

She had all the heroism of principle, and was determined to do her duty; but having also many of the feelings of youth and nature, let her not be much wondered at, if, after making all these good resolutions on the side of self-government, she seized the scrap of paper on which Edmund had begun writing to her, as a treasure beyond all her hopes, and reading with the tenderest emotion these words, 'My very dear Fanny, you must do me the favour to accept—' locked it up with the chain, as the dearest part of the gift. It was the only thing approaching to a letter which she had ever received from him; she might never receive another; it was impossible that she ever should receive another so perfectly gratifying in the occasion and the style. Two lines more prized had never fallen from the pen of the most distinguished author – never more completely blessed the researches of the fondest biographer. The enthusiasm of a woman's love is even beyond the biographer's. To her, the hand-writing itself, independent of any thing it may convey, is a blessedness. Never were such characters cut by any other human being, as Edmund's commonest hand-writing gave! This specimen, written in haste as it was, had not a fault; and there was a felicity in the flow of the first four words, in the arrangement of 'My very dear Fanny,' which she could have looked at for ever.

Having regulated her thoughts and comforted her feelings by this happy mixture of reason and weakness, she was able, in due time, to go down and resume her usual employments near her Aunt Bertram, and pay her the usual observances without any apparent want of spirits.

Thursday, predestined to hope and enjoyment, came; and opened with more kindness to Fanny than such self-willed, unmanageable days often volunteer, for soon after breakfast a very friendly note was brought from Mr Crawford to William, stating that as he found himself obliged to go to London on the morrow for a few days, he could not help trying to procure a companion; and therefore hoped that if William could make up his mind to leave Mansfield half a day earlier than had been proposed, he would accept a place in his carriage. Mr Crawford meant to be in town by his uncle's accustomary late dinner hour, and William was invited to dine with him at the Admiral's. The proposal was a very pleasant one to William himself, who enjoyed the idea of travelling post with four horses, and such a good-humoured, agreeable friend; and, in likening it to going up with dispatches, was saying at once every thing in favour of its happiness and dignity which his imagination could suggest; and Fanny, from a different motive, was exceedingly pleased; for the original plan was that William should go up by the mail from Northampton the following night, which would not have allowed him an hour's rest before he must have got into a Portsmouth coach; and though this offer of Mr Crawford's would rob her of many hours of his company, she was too happy in having William spared from the fatigue of such a journey, to think of any thing else. Sir Thomas approved of it for another reason. His nephew's introduction to Admiral Crawford might be of service. The Admiral, he believed, had interest. Upon the whole, it was a very joyous note. Fanny's spirits lived on it half the morning, deriving some accession of pleasure from its writer being himself to go away.

As for the ball, so near at hand, she had too many agitations and fears to have half the enjoyment in anticipation which she ought to have had, or must have been supposed to have, by the many young ladies looking forward to the same event in situations more at ease, but under circumstances of less novelty, less interest, less peculiar gratification, than would be attributed to her. Miss Price, known only by name to half the people invited, was now to make her first appearance, and must be regarded as the queen of the evening. Who could be happier than Miss Price? But Miss Price had not been brought up to the trade of *coming out*; and had she known in what light this ball was, in general considered respecting her, it would very much have lessened her comfort by increasing the fears she already had of doing wrong and being looked at. To dance without much observation or any extraordinary fatigue, to have strength and partners for about half the evening, to dance a little with Edmund, and not a great deal with Mr Crawford, to see William enjoy himself, and be able to keep away from her Aunt Norris, was the height of her ambition, and seemed to comprehend her greatest possibility of happiness. As these were the best of her hopes, they could not always prevail; and in the course of a long morning, spent principally with her two aunts, she was often under the influence of much less sanguine views. William, determined to make this last day a day of thorough enjoyment, was out snipe-shooting; Edmund, she had too much reason to suppose, was at the Parsonage; and left alone to bear the worrying of Mrs Norris, who was cross because the housekeeper would have her own way with the supper, and whom *she* could not avoid though the housekeeper might, Fanny was worn down at last to think every thing an evil belonging to the ball, and when sent off with a parting worry to dress, moved as languidly towards her own room, and felt as incapable of happiness as if she had been allowed no share in it.

As she walked slowly upstairs she thought of yesterday; it had been about the same hour that she had returned from the Parsonage, and found Edmund in the East Room. 'Suppose I were to find him there again to-day!' said she to herself, in a fond indulgence of fancy.

'Fanny,' said a voice at that moment near her. Starting and looking up, she saw across the lobby she had just reached, Edmund himself, standing at the head of a different staircase. He came towards her. 'You look tired and fagged, Fanny. You have been walking too far.'

'No, I have not been out at all.'

'Then you have had fatigues within doors, which are worse. You had better have gone out.'

Fanny, not liking to complain, found it easiest to make no answer; and though he looked at her with his usual kindness, she believed he had soon ceased to think of her countenance. He did not appear in spirits; something unconnected with her was probably amiss. They proceeded upstairs together, their rooms being on the same floor above.

'I come from Dr Grant's,' said Edmund, presently. 'You may guess my errand there, Fanny.' And he looked so conscious, that Fanny could think but of one errand, which turned her too sick for speech. 'I wished to engage Miss Crawford for the first two dances,' was the explanation that followed, and brought Fanny to life again, enabling her, as she found she was expected to speak, to utter something like an enquiry as to the result.

'Yes,' he answered, 'she is engaged to me; but (with a smile that did not sit easy) she says it is to be the last time that she ever will dance with me. She is not serious. I think, I hope, I am sure she is not serious; but I would rather not hear it. She never has danced with a clergyman, she says, and she never *will*. For my own sake, I could wish there had been no ball just at – I mean not this very week, this very day; to-morrow I leave home.'

Fanny struggled for speech, and said, 'I am very sorry that any thing has occurred to distress you. This ought to be a day of pleasure. My uncle meant it so.'

'Oh yes, yes! and it will be a day of pleasure. It will all end right. I'm only vexed for a moment. In fact, it is not that I consider the ball as ill-timed; what does it signify? But, Fanny,' stopping her, by taking her hand, and speaking low and seriously, 'you know what all this means. You see how it is; and could tell me, perhaps better than I could tell you, how and why I am vexed. Let me talk to you a little. You are a kind, kind listener. I have been pained by her manner this morning, and cannot get the better of it. I know her disposition to be as sweet and faultless as your own, but the influence of her former companions makes her seem – gives to her conversation, to her professed opinions, sometimes a tinge of wrong. She does not *think* evil, but she speaks it, speaks it in playfulness; and though I know it to be playfulness, it grieves me to the soul.'

'The effect of education,' said Fanny gently.

Edmund could not but agree to it. 'Yes, that uncle and aunt! They have injured the finest mind; for sometimes, Fanny, I own to you, it does appear more than manner; it appears as if the mind itself was tainted.'

Fanny imagined this to be an appeal to her judgment, and therefore, after a moment's consideration, said, 'If you only want me as a listener, cousin, I will be as useful as I can; but I am not qualified for an adviser. Do not ask advice of *me*. I am not competent.'

'You are right, Fanny, to protest against such an office, but you need not be afraid. It is a subject on which I should never ask advice; it is the sort of subject on which it had better never be asked; and few, I imagine, do ask it, but when they want to be influenced against their conscience. I only want to talk to you.'

'One thing more. Excuse the liberty; but take care *how* you talk to me. Do not tell me any thing now, which hereafter you may be sorry for. The time may come—'

The colour rushed into her cheeks as she spoke.

'Dearest Fanny!' cried Edmund, pressing her hand to his lips with almost as much warmth as if it had been Miss Crawford's, 'you are all considerate thought! But it is unnecessary here. The time will never come. No such time as you allude to will ever come. I begin to think it most improbable; the chances grow less and less; and even if it should there will be nothing to be remembered by either you or me that we need be afraid of, for I can never be ashamed of my own scruples; and if they are removed, it must be by changes that will only raise her character the more by the recollection of the faults she once had. You are the only being upon earth to whom I should say what I have said; but you have always known my opinion of her; you can bear me witness, Fanny, that I have never been blinded. How many a time have we talked over her little errors! You need not fear me; I have almost given up every serious idea of her; but I must be a blockhead indeed, if, whatever befell me, I could think of your kindness and sympathy without the sincerest gratitude.'

He had said enough to shake the experience of eighteen. He had said enough to give Fanny some happier feelings than she had lately known, and with a brighter look, she answered, 'Yes, cousin, I am convinced that *you* would be incapable of any thing else, though perhaps some might not. I cannot be afraid of hearing any thing you wish to say. Do not check yourself. Tell me whatever you like.'

They were now on the second floor, and the appearance of a housemaid prevented any further conversation. For Fanny's present comfort it was concluded, perhaps, at the happiest moment: had he been able to talk another five minutes, there is no saying that he might not have talked away all Miss Crawford's faults and his own despondence. But as it was, they parted with looks on his side of grateful affection, and with some very precious sensations on hers. She had felt nothing like it for hours. Since the first joy from Mr Crawford's note to William had worn away, she had been in a state absolutely the reverse; there had been no comfort around, no hope within her. Now every thing was smiling. William's good fortune returned again upon her mind, and seemed of greater value than at first. The ball, too – such an evening of pleasure before her! It was now a real animation; and she began to dress for it with much of the happy flutter which belongs to a ball. All went well; she did not dislike her own looks; and when she came to the necklaces again, her good fortune seemed complete, for upon trial the one given her by Miss Crawford would by no means go through the ring of the cross. She had, to oblige Edmund, resolved to wear it; but it was too large for the purpose. His, therefore, must be worn; and having, with delightful feelings, joined the chain and the cross – those memorials of the two most beloved of her heart, those dearest tokens so formed for each other by everything real and imaginary – and put them round her neck, and seen and felt how full of William and Edmund they were, she was able, without an effort, to resolve on wearing Miss Crawford's necklace too. She acknowledged it to be right. Miss Crawford had a claim; and when it was no longer to encroach on, to interfere with the stronger claims, the truer kindness of another, she could do her justice even with pleasure to herself. The necklace really looked very well; and Fanny left her room at last, comfortably satisfied with herself and all about her.

Her Aunt Bertram had recollected her on this occasion with an unusual degree of wakefulness. It had really occurred to her, unprompted, that Fanny, preparing for a ball, might be glad of better help than the upper housemaid's, and when dressed herself, she actually sent her own maid to assist her; too late, of course, to be of any use. Mrs Chapman had just reached the attic floor, when Miss Price came out of her room completely dressed, and only civilities were necessary; but Fanny felt her aunt's attention almost as much as Lady Bertram or Mrs Chapman could do themselves.

CHAPTER TWENTY EIGHT

HER UNCLE AND BOTH her aunts were in the drawing-room when Fanny went down. To the former she was an interesting object, and he saw with pleasure the general elegance of her appearance, and her being in remarkably good looks. The neatness and propriety of her dress was all that he would allow himself to commend in her presence, but upon her leaving the room again soon afterwards, he spoke of her beauty with very decided praise.

'Yes,' said Lady Bertram, 'she looks very well. I sent Chapman to her.'

'Look well! Oh, yes!' cried Mrs Norris, 'she has good reason to look well with all her advantages; brought up in this family as she has been, with all the benefit of her cousins' manners before her. Only think, my dear Sir Thomas, what extraordinary advantages you and I have been the means of giving her. The very gown you have been taking notice of is your own generous present to her when dear Mrs Rushworth married. What would she have been if we had not taken her in hand?'

Sir Thomas said no more; but when they sat down to table the eyes of the two young men assured him that the subject might be gently touched again when the ladies withdrew, with more success. Fanny saw that she was approved; and the consciousness of looking well made her look still better. From a variety of causes she was happy, and she soon was made still happier; for in following her aunts out of the room, Edmund, who was holding open the door, said, as she passed him, 'you must dance with me, Fanny; you must keep two dances for me; any two that you like, except the first.' She had nothing more to wish for. She had hardly ever been in a state so nearly approaching high spirits in her life. Her cousins' former gaiety on the day of a ball was no longer surprising to her; she felt it to be indeed very charming, and was actually practising her steps about the drawing-room as long as she could be safe from the notice of her Aunt Norris, who was entirely taken up in fresh arranging and injuring the noble fire which the butler had prepared.

Half an hour followed, that would have been at least languid under any other circumstances, but Fanny's happiness still prevailed. It was but to think of her conversation with Edmund; and what was the restlessness of Mrs Norris? What were the yawns of Lady Bertram?

The gentlemen joined them; and soon after began the sweet expectation of a carriage, when a general spirit of ease and enjoyment seemed diffused and they all stood about and talked and laughed, and every moment had its pleasure and its hope. Fanny felt that there must be a struggle in Edmund's cheerfulness, but it was delightful to see the effort so successfully made.

When the carriages were really heard, when the guests began really to assemble, her own gaiety of heart was much subdued: the sight of so many strangers threw her back into herself; and besides the gravity and formality of the first great circle, which the manners of neither Sir Thomas nor Lady Bertram were of a kind to do away, she found herself occasionally called on to endure something worse. She was introduced here and there by her uncle, and forced to be spoken to, and to curtsey, and speak again. This was a hard duty, and she was never summoned to it without looking at William, as he walked about at his ease in the background of the scene, and longing to be with him.

The entrance of the Grants and Crawfords was a favourable epoch. The stiffness of the meeting soon gave way before their popular manners and more diffuse intimacies: little groups were formed, and everybody grew comfortable. Fanny felt the advantage; and, drawing back from the toils of civility, would have been again most happy, could she have kept her eyes from wandering between Edmund and Mary Crawford. *She* looked all loveliness – and what might not be the end of it? Her own musings were brought to an end on perceiving Mr Crawford before her, and her thoughts were put into another channel by his engaging her almost instantly for the two first dances. Her happiness on this occasion was very much à-la-mortal, finely chequered. To be secure of a partner at first was a most essential good – for the moment of beginning was now growing seriously near; and she so little understood her own claims as to think that if Mr Crawford had not asked her; she must have been the last to be sought after, and should have received a partner only through a series of enquiry, and bustle, and interference, which would have been terrible; but at the same time there was a pointedness in his manner of asking her which she did not like, and she saw his eye glancing for a moment at her necklace, with a smile – she thought there was a smile – which made her blush and feel wretched. And though there was no second glance to disturb her, though his object seemed then to be only quietly agreeable, she could not get the better of her embarrassment, heightened as it was by the idea of his perceiving it, and had no composure till he turned away to some one else. Then she could gradually rise up to the genuine satisfaction of having a partner, a voluntary partner, secured against the dancing began.

When the company were moving into the ball-room, she found herself for the first time near Miss Crawford, whose eyes and smiles were immediately and more unequivocally directed, as her brother's had been, and who was beginning to speak on the subject, when Fanny, anxious to get the story over, hastened to give the explanation of the second necklace: the real chain. Miss Crawford listened; and all her intended compliments and insinuations to Fanny were forgotten: she felt only one thing; and her eyes,

Conducted to the top of the room

bright as they had been before, showing they could yet be brighter, she exclaimed with eager pleasure, 'Did he? Did Edmund? That was like himself. No other man would have thought of it. I honour him beyond expression.' And she looked around as if longing to tell him so. He was not near, he was attending a party of ladies out of the room; and Mrs Grant coming up to the two girls, and taking an arm of each, they followed with the rest.

Fanny's heart sunk, but there was no leisure for thinking long even of Miss Crawford's feelings. They were in the ball-room, the violins were playing, and her mind was in a flutter that forbade its fixing on any thing serious. She must watch the general arrangements, and see how every thing was done.

In a few minutes Sir Thomas came to her, and asked if she were engaged: and the 'Yes, sir; to Mr Crawford,' was exactly what he had intended to hear. Mr Crawford was not far off; Sir Thomas brought him to her, saying something which discovered to Fanny that *she* was to lead the way and open the ball; an idea that had never occurred to her before. Whenever she had thought of the minutiæ of the evening, it had been as a matter of course that Edmund would begin with Miss Crawford; and the impression was so strong, that though *her uncle* spoke the contrary, she could not help an exclamation of surprise, a hint of her unfitness, an entreaty even to be excused. To be urging her opinion against Sir Thomas's, was a proof of the extremity of the case; but such was her horror at the first suggestion, that she could actually look him in the face and say that she hoped it might be settled otherwise; in vain, however; Sir Thomas smiled, tried to encourage her, and then looked too serious, and said too decidedly – 'It must be so, my dear,' for her to hazard another word; and she found herself the next moment conducted by Mr Crawford to the top of the room, and standing there to be joined by the rest of the dancers, couple after couple as they were formed.

She could hardly believe it. To be placed above so many elegant young women! The distinction was too great. It was treating her like her cousins! And her thoughts flew to those absent cousins with most unfeigned and truly tender regret, that they were not at home to take their own place in the room, and have their share of a pleasure which would have been so very delightful to them. So often as she had heard them wish for a ball at home as the greatest of all felicities! And to have them away when it was given – and for *her* to be opening the ball – and with Mr Crawford too! She hoped they would not envy her that distinction *now*; but when she looked back to the state of things in the autumn, to what they had all been to each other when once dancing in that house before, the present arrangement was almost more than she could understand herself.

The ball began. It was rather honour than happiness to Fanny, for the first dance at least: her partner was in excellent spirits, and tried to impart them to her; but she was a great deal too much frightened to have any enjoyment, till she could suppose herself no longer looked at. Young, pretty, and gentle, however, she had no awkwardnesses that were not as good as graces, and there were few persons present that were not disposed to praise her. She was attractive, she was modest, she was Sir Thomas's niece, and she was soon said to be admired by Mr Crawford. It was enough to give her general favour. Sir Thomas himself was watching her progress down the dance with much complacency; he was proud of his niece; and without attributing all her personal beauty, as Mrs Norris seemed to do, to her transplantation to Mansfield, he was pleased with himself for having supplied every thing else: education and manners she owed to him.

Miss Crawford saw much of Sir Thomas's thoughts as he stood and, having in spite of all his wrongs towards her, a general prevailing desire of recommending herself to him, took an opportunity of stepping aside to say something agreeable of Fanny. Her praise was warm, and he received it as she could wish, joining in it as far as discretion, and politeness, and slowness of speech would allow, and certainly appearing to greater advantage on the subject than his lady did soon afterwards, when Mary, perceiving her on a sofa very near, turned round before she began to dance, to compliment her on Miss Price's looks.

'Yes, she does look very well,' was Lady Bertram's placid reply. 'Chapman helped her to dress. I sent Chapman to her.' Not but that she was really pleased to have Fanny admired; but she was so much more struck with her own kindness in sending Chapman to her, that she could not get it out of her head.

Miss Crawford knew Mrs Norris too well to think of gratifying *her* by commendations of Fanny; to her, it was as the occasion offered – 'Ah! ma'am, how much we want dear Mrs Rushworth and Julia to-night!' and Mrs Norris paid her with as many smiles and courteous words as she had time for, amid so much occupation as she found for herself in making up card-tables, giving hints to Sir Thomas, and trying to move all the chaperons to a better part of the room.

Miss Crawford blundered most towards Fanny herself in her intentions to please. She meant to be giving her little heart a happy flutter, and filling her with sensations of delightful self-consequence; and misinterpreting Fanny's blushes, still thought she must be doing so, when she went to her after the two first dances, and said, with a significant look, 'Perhaps *you* can tell me why my brother goes to town to-morrow? He says he has business there, but will not tell me what. The first time he ever denied me his confidence! But this is what we all come to. All are supplanted sooner or later. Now, I must apply to you for information. Pray, what is Henry going for?'

Fanny protested her ignorance as steadily as her embarrassment allowed.

'Well, then,' replied Miss Crawford, laughing, 'I must suppose it to be purely for the pleasure of conveying your brother, and of talking of you by the way.'

Fanny was confused, but it was the confusion of discontent; while Miss Crawford wondered she did not smile, and thought her over-anxious, or thought her odd, or thought her anything rather than insensible of pleasure in Henry's attentions. Fanny had a good deal of enjoyment in the course of the evening; but Henry's attentions had very little to do with it. She would much rather *not* have been asked by him again so very soon, and she wished she had not been obliged to suspect that his previous enquiries of Mrs Norris about the supper hour, were all for the sake of securing her at that part of the evening. But it was not to be avoided: he made her feel that she was the object of all; though she could not say it was unpleasantly done, that there was indelicacy or ostentation in his manner; and sometimes, when he talked of William, he was really not unagreeable, and showed even a warmth of heart which did him credit. But still his attentions made no part of her satisfaction. She was happy whenever she looked at William, and saw how perfectly he was enjoying himself, in every five minutes that she could walk about with him, and hear his account of his partners; she was happy in knowing herself admired; and she was happy in having the two dances with Edmund still to look forward to, during the greatest part of the evening, her hand being so eagerly sought after, that her indefinite engagement with *him* was in continual perspective. She was happy even when they did take place; but not from any flow of spirits on his side, or any such expressions of tender gallantry as had blessed the morning. His mind was fagged, and her happiness sprung from being the friend with whom he could find repose. 'I am worn out with civility,' said he. 'I have been talking incessantly all night, and with nothing to say. But with *you*, Fanny, there may be peace. You will not want to be talked to. Let us have the luxury of silence.' Fanny would hardly even speak her agreement. A weariness, arising probably, in great measure, from the same feelings which he had acknowledged in the morning, was peculiarly to be respected, and they went down their two dances together with such sober tranquillity as might satisfy any looker-on that Sir Thomas had been bringing up no wife for his younger son.

The evening had afforded Edmund little pleasure. Miss Crawford had been in gay spirits when they first danced together, but it was not her gaiety that could do him good; it rather sank than raised his comfort; and afterwards, for he found himself still impelled to seek her again, she had absolutely pained him by her manner of speaking of the profession to which he was now on the point of belonging. They had talked, and they had been silent; he had reasoned, she had ridiculed; and they had parted at last with mutual vexation. Fanny, not able to refrain entirely from observing them, had seen enough to be tolerably satisfied. It was barbarous to be happy when Edmund was suffering. Yet some happiness must and would arise from the very conviction that he did suffer.

When her two dances with him were over, her inclination and strength for more were pretty well at an end; and Sir Thomas, having seen her walk rather than dance down the shortening set, breathless, and with her hand at her side, gave his orders for her sitting down entirely. From that time Mr Crawford sat down likewise.

'Poor Fanny!' cried William, coming for a moment to visit her, and working away his partner's fan as if for life, 'how soon she is knocked up! Why, the sport is but just begun. I hope we shall keep it up these two hours. How can you be tired so soon?'

'So soon! my good friend,' said Sir Thomas, producing his watch with all necessary caution; 'it is three o'clock, and your sister is not used to these sort of hours.'

'Well, then, Fanny, you shall not get up to-morrow before I go. Sleep as long as you can, and never mind me.'

'Oh! William.'

'What! Did she think of being up before you set off?'

'Oh! yes, sir,' cried Fanny, rising eagerly from her seat to be nearer her uncle; 'I must get up and breakfast with him. It will be the last time, you know; the last morning.'

'You had better not. He is to have breakfasted and be gone by half-past nine. Mr Crawford, I think you call for him at half-past nine?'

Fanny was too urgent, however, and had too many tears in her eyes for denial; and it ended in a gracious 'Well, well!' which was permission.

'Yes, half-past nine,' said Crawford to William, as the latter was leaving them, 'and I shall be punctual for there will be no kind sister to get up for *me*.' And in a lower tone to Fanny, 'I shall have only a desolate house to hurry from. Your brother will find my ideas of time and his own very different to-morrow.'

After a short consideration, Sir Thomas asked Crawford to join the early breakfast party in that house instead of eating alone; he should himself be of it; and the readiness with which his invitation was accepted convinced him that the suspicions whence, he must confess to himself, this very ball had in great measure sprung, were well founded. Mr Crawford was in love with Fanny. He had a pleasing anticipation of what would be. His niece, meanwhile, did not thank him for what he had just done. She had hoped to have William all to herself the last morning. It would have been an

'Poor Fanny!' cried William

unspeakable indulgence. But though her wishes were overthrown, there was no spirit of murmuring within her. On the contrary, she was so totally unused to have her pleasure consulted, or to have any thing take place at all in the way she could desire, that she was more disposed to wonder and rejoice in having carried her point so far, than to repine at the counter-action which followed.

Shortly afterward, Sir Thomas was again interfering a little with her inclination, by advising her to go immediately to bed. 'Advise' was his word, but it was the advice of absolute power, and she had only to rise, and with Mr Crawford's very cordial adieus, pass quietly away; stopping at the entrance door, like the Lady of Branxholm Hall, 'one moment and no more,' to view the happy scene, and take a last look at the five or six determined couple, who were still hard at work; and then, creeping slowly up the principal staircase, pursued by the ceaseless country-dance, feverish with hopes and fears, soup and negus, sore-footed and fatigued, restless and agitated, yet feeling, in spite of everything, that a ball was indeed delightful.

In thus sending her away, Sir Thomas perhaps might not be thinking merely of her health. It might occur to him that Mr Crawford had been sitting by her long enough, or he might mean to recommend her as a wife by showing her persuadableness.

CHAPTER TWENTY NINE

THE BALL WAS OVER, and the breakfast was soon over too; the last kiss was given, and William was gone. Mr Crawford had, as he foretold, been very punctual, and short and pleasant had been the meal.

After seeing William to the last moment, Fanny walked back to the breakfast-room with a very saddened heart to grieve over the melancholy change; and there her uncle kindly left her to cry in peace, conceiving, perhaps, that the deserted chair of each young man might exercise her tender enthusiasm, and that the remaining cold pork bones and mustard in William's plate, might but divide her feelings with the broken egg-shells in Mr Crawford's. She sat and cried con amore as her uncle intended, but it was con amore fraternal and no other. William was gone, and she now felt as if she had wasted half his visit in idle cares and selfish solicitudes unconnected with him.

Fanny's disposition was such that she could never even think of her Aunt Norris in the meagreness and cheerlessness of her own small house, without reproaching herself for some little want of attention to her when they had been last together; much less could her feelings acquit her of having done and said and thought every thing by William, that was due to him for a whole fortnight.

It was a heavy, melancholy day. Soon after the second breakfast, Edmund bade them good-bye for a week, and mounted his horse for Peterborough, and then all were gone. Nothing remained of last night but remembrances, which she had nobody to share in. She talked to her Aunt Bertram; she must talk to some body of the ball; but her aunt had seen so little of what had passed, and had so little curiosity, that it was heavy work. Lady Bertram was not certain of any body's dress or any body's place at supper, but her own. 'She could not recollect what it was that she had heard about one of the Miss Maddoxes, or what it was that Lady Prescott had noticed in Fanny; she was not sure whether Colonel Harrison had been talking of Mr Crawford or of William, when he said he was the finest young man in the room; some body had whispered some thing to her; she had forgot to ask Sir Thomas what it could be.' And these were her longest speeches and clearest communications: the rest was only a languid 'Yes, yes; very well; did you? Did he? I did not see *that*; I should not know one from the other.' This was very bad. It was only better than Mrs Norris's sharp answers would have been; but she being gone home with all the supernumerary jellies to nurse a sick maid, there was peace and good humour in their little party, though it could not boast much beside.

The evening was heavy like the day: 'I cannot think what is the matter with me,' said Lady Bertram, when the tea-things were removed. 'I feel quite stupid. It must be sitting up so late last night. Fanny, you must do some thing to keep me awake. I cannot work. Fetch the cards; I feel so very stupid.'

The cards were brought, and Fanny played at cribbage with her aunt till bedtime; and as Sir Thomas was reading to himself, no sounds were heard in the room for the next two hours beyond the reckonings of the game: – 'And *that* makes thirty-one; four in hand and eight in crib. You are to deal, ma'am; shall I deal for you?' Fanny thought and thought again of the difference which twenty-four hours had made in that room and all that part of the house. Last night it had been hope and smiles, bustle and motion, noise and brilliancy, in the drawing-room, and out of the drawing-room and every where. Now it was languor, and all but solitude.

A good night's rest improved her spirits. She could think of William the next day more cheerfully; and as the morning afforded her an opportunity of talking over Thursday night with Mrs Grant and Miss Crawford, in a very handsome style, with all the heightenings of imagination and all the laughs of playfulness, which are so essential to the shade of a departed ball, she could afterwards bring her mind without much effort into its everyday state, and easily conform to the tranquillity of the present quiet week.

They were indeed a smaller party than she had ever known there for a whole day together, and *he* was gone on whom the comfort and cheerfulness of every family meeting and every meal chiefly depended. But this must be learned to be endured. He would soon be always gone; and she was thankful that she could now sit in the same room with her uncle, hear his voice, receive his questions, and even answer them without such wretched feelings as she had formerly known.

'We miss our two young men,' was Sir Thomas's observation on both the first and second day, as they formed the very reduced circle after dinner; and in consideration of Fanny's swimming eyes, nothing more was said on the first day than to drink their good health; but on the second it led to some thing further. William was kindly commended and his promotion hoped for. 'And there is no reason to suppose,' added Sir Thomas, 'but that his visits to us may now be tolerably frequent. As to Edmund, we must learn

Talking over Thursday night

to do without him. This will be the last winter of his belonging to us, as he has done.'

'Yes,' said Lady Bertram, 'but I wish he was not going away. They are all going away, I think. I wish they would stay at home.'

This wish was levelled principally at Julia, who had just applied for permission to go to town with Maria; and as Sir Thomas thought it best for each daughter that the permission should be granted, Lady Bertram, though in her own good nature she would not have prevented it, was lamenting the change it made in the prospect of Julia's return, which would otherwise have taken place about this time. A great deal of good sense followed on Sir Thomas's side, tending to reconcile his wife to the arrangements. Every thing that a considerate parent *ought* to feel was advanced for her use, and every thing that an affectionate mother *must* feel in promoting her children's enjoyment was attributed to her nature. Lady Bertram agreed to it all with a calm 'Yes;' and at the end of a quarter of an hour's silent consideration spontaneously observed, 'Sir Thomas, I have been thinking – and I am very glad we took Fanny as we did, for now the others are away we feel the good of it.'

Sir Thomas immediately improved this compliment by adding, 'Very true. We show Fanny what a good girl we think her by praising her to her face; she is now a very valuable companion. If we have been kind to *her*, she is now quite as necessary to *us*.'

'Yes,' said Lady Bertram, presently; 'and it is a comfort to think that we shall always have *her*.'

Sir Thomas paused, half smiled, glanced at his niece, and then gravely replied, 'She will never leave us, I hope, till invited to some other home that may reasonably promise her greater happiness than she knows here.'

'And *that* is not very likely to be, Sir Thomas. Who should invite her? Maria might be very glad to see her at Sotherton now and then, but she would not think of asking her to live there; and I am sure she is better off here; and besides, I cannot do without her.'

The week which passed so quietly and peaceably at the great house in Mansfield had a very different character at the Parsonage. To the young lady, at least, in each family, it brought very different feelings. What was tranquillity and comfort to Fanny was tediousness and vexation to Mary. Something arose from difference of disposition and habit: one so easily satisfied, the other so unused to endure; but still more might be imputed to difference of circumstances. In some points of interest they were exactly opposed to each other. To Fanny's mind, Edmund's absence was really in its cause and its tendency a relief. To Mary it was every way painful. She felt the want of his society every day, almost every hour, and was too much in want of it to derive anything but irritation from considering the object for which he went. He could not have devised any thing more likely to raise his consequence than this week's absence, occurring as it did at the very time of her brother's going away, of William Price's going too, and completing the sort of general break-up of a party which had been so animated. She felt it keenly. They were now a miserable trio, confined within doors by a series of rain and snow, with nothing to do and no variety to hope for. Angry as she was with Edmund for adhering to his own notions, and acting on them in defiance of her (and she had been so angry that they had hardly parted friends at the hall), she could not help thinking of him continually when absent, dwelling on his merits and affection, and longing again for the almost daily meetings they lately had. His absence was unnecessarily long. He should not have planned such an absence; he should not have left home for a week, when her own departure from Mansfield was so near. Then she began to blame herself. She wished she had not spoken so warmly in their last conversation. She was afraid she had used some strong, some contemptuous expressions in speaking of the clergy, and *that* should not have been. It was ill-bred; it was wrong. She wished such words unsaid with all her heart.

Her vexation did not end with the week. All this was bad, but she had still more to feel when Friday came round again and brought no Edmund; when Saturday came and still no Edmund; and when, through the slight communication with the other family which Sunday produced, she learned that he had actually written home to defer his return, having promised to remain some days longer with his friend.

If she had felt impatience and regret before – if she had been sorry for what she said, and feared its too strong effect on him – she now felt and feared it all tenfold more. She had, moreover, to contend with one disagreeable emotion entirely new to her – jealousy. His friend Mr Owen had sisters; he might find them attractive. But at any rate his staying away at a time when, according to all preceding plans, she was to remove to London, meant some thing that she could not bear. Had Henry returned, as he talked of doing, at the end of three or four days, she should now have been leaving Mansfield. It became absolutely necessary for her to get to Fanny and try to learn some thing more. She could not live any longer in such solitary wretchedness; and she made her way to the Park, through difficulties of walking which she had deemed unconquerable a week before, for the chance of hearing a little in addition, for the sake of at least hearing his name.

The first half hour was lost, for Fanny and Lady Bertram were together, and unless she had Fanny to herself she could hope for nothing. But at last Lady Bertram left the room, and then almost immediately Miss Crawford thus began, with a voice as well regulated as she could:—

'And how do *you* like your cousin Edmund's staying away so long! Being the only young person at home, I consider *you* as the greatest sufferer. You must miss him. Does his staying longer surprise you?'

'I do not know,' Fanny said hesitatingly. 'Yes; I had not particularly expected it.'

'Perhaps he will always stay longer than he talks of. It is the general way all young men do.'

'He did not, the only time he went to see Mr Owen before.'

'He finds the house more agreeable *now*. He is a very – a very pleasing young man himself, and I cannot help being rather concerned at not seeing him again before I go to London, as will now undoubtedly be the case. I am looking for Henry every day, and as soon as he comes there will be nothing to detain me at Mansfield. I should like to have seen him once more, I confess. But you must give my compliments to him. Yes; I think it must be compliments. Is not there a something wanted, Miss Price, in our language – a something between compliments and – and love – to suit the sort of friendly acquaintance we have had together? So many months' acquaintance! But compliments may be sufficient here. Was his letter a long one? Does he give you much account of what he is doing? Is it Christmas gaieties that he is staying for?'

'I only heard a part of the letter; it was to my uncle; but I believe it was very short; indeed I am sure it was but a few lines. All that I heard was that his friend had pressed him to stay longer, and that he had agreed to do so. A *few* days longer, or *some* days longer; I am not quite sure which.'

'Oh! if he wrote to his father – but I thought it might have been to Lady Bertram or you. But if he wrote to his father, no wonder he was concise. Who could write chat to Sir Thomas? If he had written to you, there would have been more particulars. You would have heard of balls and parties. He would have sent you a description of every thing and every body. How many Miss Owens are there?'

'Three grown up.'

'Are they musical?'

'I do not at all know. I never heard.'

'That is the first question, you know,' said Miss Crawford, trying to appear gay and unconcerned, 'which every woman who plays herself is sure to ask about another. But it is very foolish to ask questions about any young ladies – about any three sisters just grown up; for one knows, without being told, exactly what they are: all very accomplished and pleasing, and *one* very pretty. There is a beauty in every family; it is a regular thing. Two play on the pianoforte, and one on the harp; and all sing, or would sing if they were taught, or sing all the better for not being taught; or some thing like it.'

'I know nothing of the Miss Owens,' said Fanny calmly.

'You know nothing and you care less as people say. Never did tone express indifference plainer. Indeed, how can one care for those one has never seen? Well, when your cousin comes back, he will find Mansfield very quiet; all the noisy ones gone, your brother and mine and myself. I do not like the idea of leaving Mrs Grant now the time draws near. She does not like my going.'

Fanny felt obliged to speak. 'You cannot doubt your being missed by many,' said she. 'You will be very much missed.'

Miss Crawford turned her eye on her, as if wanting to hear or see more, and then laughingly said, 'Oh yes! missed as every noisy evil is missed when it is taken away; that is, there is a great difference felt. But I am not fishing: don't compliment me. If I *am* missed, it will appear. I may be discovered by those who want to see me. I shall not be in any doubtful, or distant, or unapproachable region.'

Now Fanny could not bring herself to speak, and Miss Crawford was disappointed; for she had hoped to hear some pleasant assurance of her power, from one who she thought must know, and her spirits were clouded again.

'The Miss Owens,' said she, soon afterwards; 'suppose you were to have one of the Miss Owens settled at Thornton Lacey, how should you like it? Stranger things have happened. I dare say they are trying for it. And they are quite in the right, for it would be a very pretty establishment for them. I do not at all wonder or blame them. It is every body's duty to do as well for themselves as they can. Sir Thomas Bertram's son is some body; and now he is in their own line. Their father is a clergyman, and their brother is a clergyman, and they are all clergymen together. He is their lawful property; he fairly belongs to them. You don't speak, Fanny; Miss Price, you don't speak. But honestly now, do not you rather expect it than otherwise?'

'No,' said Fanny stoutly, 'I do not expect it at all.'

'Not at all!' cried Miss Crawford, with alacrity. 'I wonder at that. But I dare say you know exactly – I always imagine you are – perhaps you do not think him likely to marry at all – or not at present.'

'No, I do not,' said Fanny softly, hoping she did not err either in the belief or the acknowledgement of it.

Her companion looked at her keenly; and gathering greater spirit from the blush soon produced from such a look, only said, 'He is best off as he is,' and turned the subject.

CHAPTER THIRTY

MISS CRAWFORD'S UNEASINESS was much lightened by this conversation, and she walked home again in spirits which might have defied almost another week of the same small party in the same bad weather, had they been put to the proof; but as that very evening brought her brother down from London again in quite, or more than quite, his usual cheerfulness, she had nothing further to try her own. His still refusing to tell her what he had gone for was but the promotion of gaiety; a day before it might have irritated, but now it was a pleasant joke; suspected only of concealing some thing planned as a pleasant surprise to herself. And the next day *did* bring a surprise to her. Henry had said he should just go and ask the Bertrams how they did, and be back in ten minutes, but he was gone above an hour; and when his sister, who had been waiting for him to walk with her in the garden, met him at last most impatiently in the sweep, and cried out, 'My dear Henry, where can you have been all this time?' he had only to say that he had been sitting with Lady Bertram and Fanny.

'Sitting with them an hour and a half!' exclaimed Mary.

But this was only the beginning of her surprise.

'Yes, Mary,' said he, drawing her arm within his, and walking along the sweep as if not knowing where he was: 'I could not get away sooner; Fanny looked so lovely! I am quite determined, Mary. My mind is entirely made up. Will it astonish you? No: you must be aware that I am quite determined to marry Fanny Price.'

The surprise was now complete; for, in spite of whatever his consciousness might suggest, a suspicion of his having any such views had never entered his sister's imagination; and she looked so truly the astonishment she felt, that he was obliged to repeat what he had said and more fully and more solemnly. The conviction of his determination once admitted, it was not unwelcome. There was even pleasure with the surprise. Mary was in a state of mind to rejoice in a connection with the Bertram family, and to be not displeased with her brother's marrying a little beneath him.

'Yes, Mary,' was Henry's concluding assurance. 'I am fairly caught. You know with what idle designs I began; but this is the end of them. I have (I flatter myself) made no inconsiderable progress in her affections; but my own are entirely fixed.'

'Lucky, lucky girl!' cried Mary, as soon as she could speak; 'what a match for her! My dearest Henry, this must be my *first* feeling; but my *second*, which you shall have as sincerely, is, that I approve your choice from my soul, and foresee your happiness as heartily as I wish and desire it. You will have a sweet little wife; all gratitude and devotion. Exactly what you deserve. What an amazing match for her! Mrs Norris often talks of her luck; what will she say now? The delight of all the family, indeed! And she has some *true* friends in it! How *they* will rejoice! But tell me all about it! Talk to me for ever. When did you begin to think seriously about her?'

Nothing could be more impossible than to answer such a question, though nothing could be more agreeable than to have it asked. 'How the pleasing plague had stolen on him' he could not say; and before he had expressed the same sentiment with a little variation of words three times over, his sister eagerly interrupted him with 'Ah, my dear Henry, and this is what took you to London! This was your business! You chose to consult the Admiral before you made up your mind.'

But this he stoutly denied. He knew his uncle too well to consult him on any matrimonial scheme. The Admiral hated marriage, and thought it never pardonable in a young man of independent fortune.

'When Fanny is known to him,' continued Henry, 'he will dote on her. She is exactly the woman to do away every prejudice of such a man as the Admiral, for she is exactly such a woman as he thinks does not exist in the world. She is the very impossibility he would describe, if indeed he has now delicacy of language enough to embody his own ideas. But till it is absolutely settled – settled beyond all interference – he shall know nothing of the matter. No, Mary, you are quite mistaken. You have not discovered my business yet.'

'Well, well, I am satisfied. I know now to whom it must relate, and am in no hurry for the rest. Fanny Price! wonderful, quite wonderful! That Mansfield should have done so much for – that *you* should have found your fate in Mansfield! But you are quite right; you could not have chosen better. There is not a better girl in the world, and you do not want for fortune; and as to her connections, they are more than good. The Bertrams are undoubtedly some of the first people in this country. She is niece to Sir Thomas Bertram; that will be enough for the world. But go on, go on. Tell me more. What are your plans? Does she know her own happiness?'

'No.'

'What are you waiting for?'

'For – for very little more than opportunity. Mary, she is not like her cousins; but I think I shall not ask in vain.'

'Oh no! you cannot. Were you even less pleasing – supposing her not to love you already (of which, however, I can have little doubt) – you would be safe. The gentleness and gratitude of her disposition would secure her all your own immediately. From my soul I do not think she would marry you *without* love; that is, if there is a girl in the world capable of being uninfluenced by ambition, I can suppose it her; but ask her to love you, and she will never have the heart to refuse.'

As soon as her eagerness could rest in silence, he was as happy to tell as she could be to listen; and a conversation followed almost as deeply interesting to her as to himself, though he had in fact nothing to relate but his own sensations, nothing to dwell on but Fanny's charms. Fanny's beauty of face and figure, Fanny's graces of manner and goodness of heart, were the exhaustless theme. The gentleness, modesty, and sweetness of her character were warmly expatiated on; that sweetness which makes so essential a part of every woman's worth in the judgment of man, that though he some times loves where it is not, he can never believe it absent. Her temper he had good reason to depend on and to praise. He had often seen it tried. Was there one of the family, excepting Edmund, who had not in some way or other continually exercised her patience and forbearance? Her affections were evidently strong. To see her with her brother! What could more delightfully prove that the warmth of her heart was equal to its gentleness? What could be more encouraging to a man who had her love in view? Then, her understanding was beyond every suspicion, quick and clear: and her manners were the mirror of her own modest and elegant mind. Nor was this all. Henry Crawford had too much sense not to feel the worth of good principles in a wife, though he was too little accustomed to serious reflection to know them by their proper name; but when he talked of her having such a steadiness and regularity of conduct, such a high notion of honour, and such an observance of decorum as might warrant any man in the fullest dependence on her faith and integrity, he expressed what was inspired by the knowledge of her being well principled and religious.

'I could so wholly and absolutely confide in her,' said he, 'and *that* is what I want.'

Well might his sister, believing as she really did that his opinion of Fanny Price was scarcely beyond her merits, rejoice in her prospects.

'The more I think of it,' she cried, 'the more am I convinced that you are doing quite right; and though I should never have selected Fanny Price as the girl most likely to attach you, I am now persuaded she is the very one to make you happy. Your wicked project upon her peace turns out a clever thought indeed. You will both find your good in it.'

'It was bad, very bad in me against such a creature; but I did not know her then; and she shall have no reason to lament the hour that first put it into my head. I will make her very happy, Mary; happier than she has ever yet been herself, or ever seen anybody else. I will not take her from Northamptonshire. I shall let Everingham, and rent a place in this neighbourhood; perhaps Stanwix Lodge. I shall let a seven years' lease of

Everingham. I am sure of an excellent tenant at half a word. I could name three people now, who would give me my own terms and thank me.'

'Ha!' cried Mary; 'settle in Northamptonshire! That is pleasant! Then we shall be all together.'

When she had spoken it, she recollected herself, and wished it unsaid; but there was no need of confusion; for her brother saw her only as the supposed inmate of Mansfield Parsonage, and replied but to invite her in the kindest manner to his own house, and to claim the best right in her.

'You must give us more than half your time,' said he, 'I cannot admit Mrs Grant to have an equal claim with Fanny and myself, for we shall both have a right in you. Fanny will be so truly your sister!'

Mary had only to be grateful and give general assurances; but she was now very fully purposed to be the guest of neither brother nor sister many months longer.

'You will divide your year between London and Northamptonshire?'

'Yes.'

'That's right; and in London, of course, a house of your own; no longer with the Admiral. My dearest Henry, the advantage to you of getting away from the Admiral before your manners are hurt by the contagion of his, before you have contracted any of his foolish opinions, or learned to sit over your dinner, as if it were the best blessing of life! *You* are not sensible of the gain, for your regard for him has blinded you; but, in my estimation, your marrying early may be the saving of you. To have seen you grow like the Admiral in word or deed, look or gesture, would have broken my heart.'

'Well, well, we do not think quite alike here. The Admiral has his faults, but he is a very good man, and has been more than a father to me. Few fathers would have let me have my own way half so much. You must not prejudice Fanny against him. I must have them love one another.'

Mary refrained from saying what she felt, that there could not be two persons in existence whose characters and manners were less accordant: time would discover it to him; but she could not help *this* reflection on the Admiral. 'Henry, I think so highly of Fanny Price that if I could suppose the next Mrs Crawford would have half the reason which my poor ill-used aunt had to abhor the very name, I would prevent the marriage, if possible; but I know that a wife you *loved* would be the happiest of women, and that even when you ceased to love, she would yet find in you the liberality and good-breeding of a gentleman.'

The impossibility of not doing every thing in the world to make Fanny Price happy, or of ceasing to love Fanny Price, was of course the ground-work of his eloquent answer.

'Had you seen her this morning, Mary,' he continued, 'attending with such ineffable sweetness and patience to all the demands of her aunt's stupidity, working with her, and for her, her colour beautifully heightened as she leant over the work, then returning to her seat to finish a note which she was previously engaged in writing for that stupid woman's service, and all this with such unpretending gentleness, so much as if it were a matter of course that she was not to have a moment at her own command, her hair arranged as neatly as it always is, and one little curl falling forward as she wrote, which she now and then shook back, and in the midst of all this, still speaking at intervals to *me*, or listening, and as if she liked to listen, to what I said. Had you seen her so, Mary, you would not have implied the possibility of her power over my heart ever ceasing.'

'My dearest Henry,' cried Mary, stopping short, and smiling in his face, 'how glad I am to see you so much in love! It quite delights me. But what will Mrs Rushworth and Julia say?'

'I care neither what they say nor what they feel. They will now see what sort of woman it is that can attach me, that can attach a man of sense. I wish the discovery may do them any good. And they will now see their cousin treated as she ought to be, and I wish they may be heartily ashamed of their own abominable neglect and unkindness. They will be angry,' he added, after a moment's silence, and in a cooler tone: 'Mrs Rushworth will be very angry. It will be a bitter pill to her; that is, like other bitter pills, it will have two moments' ill flavour, and then be swallowed and forgotten; for I am not such a coxcomb as to suppose her feelings more lasting than other women's, though *I* was the object of them. Yes, Mary, my Fanny will feel a difference, indeed; a daily, hourly difference, in the behaviour of every being who approaches her; and it will be the completion of my happiness to know that I am the doer of it; that I am the person to give the consequence so justly her due. Now she is dependent, helpless, friendless, neglected, forgotten.'

'Nay, Henry, not by all; not forgotten by all; not friendless, or forgotten. Her cousin Edmund never forgets her.'

'Edmund! True, I believe he is, generally speaking, kind to her, and so is Sir Thomas in his way; but it is the way of a rich, superior, long-worded, arbitrary uncle. What can Sir Thomas and Edmund together do, what *do* they do for her happiness, comfort, honour, and dignity in the world, to what I *shall* do?'

CHAPTER THIRTY ONE

HENRY CRAWFORD WAS AT Mansfield Park again the next morning, and at an earlier hour than common visiting warrants. The two ladies were together in the breakfast-room, and, fortunately for him, Lady Bertram was on the very point of quitting it as he entered. She was almost at the door, and not choosing by any means to take so much trouble in vain, she still went on, after a civil reception, a short sentence about being waited for, and a 'Let Sir Thomas know,' to the servant.

Henry, overjoyed to have her go, bowed and watched her off, and without losing another moment, turned instantly to Fanny, and, taking out some letters, said, with a most animated look, 'I must acknowledge myself infinitely obliged to any creature who gives me such an opportunity of seeing you alone: I have been wishing it more than you can have any idea. Knowing as I do what your feelings as a sister are, I could hardly have borne that any one in the house should share with you in the first knowledge of the news I now bring. He is made. Your brother is a lieutenant. I have the infinite satisfaction of congratulating you on your brother's promotion. Here are the letters which announce it, this moment come to hand. You will perhaps, like to see them.'

Fanny could not speak, but he did not want her to speak. To see the expression of her eyes, the change of her complexion, the progress of her feelings, their doubt, confusion, and felicity was enough. She took the letters as he gave them. The first was from the Admiral to inform his nephew, in a few words, of his having succeeded in the object he had undertaken, the promotion of young Price, and enclosing two more, one from the Secretary of the First Lord to a friend, whom the Admiral had set to work in the business; the other from that friend to himself, by which it appeared that his lordship had the very great happiness of attending to the recommendation of Sir Charles; that Sir Charles was much delighted in having such an opportunity of proving his regard for Admiral Crawford, and that the circumstance of Mr William Price's commission as Second Lieutenant of H.M. Sloop Thrush, being made out, was spreading general joy through a wide circle of great people.

While her hand was trembling under these letters, her eye running from one to the other, and her heart swelling with emotion, Crawford thus continued, with unfeigned eagerness, to express his interest in the event:—

'I will not talk of my own happiness,' said he, 'great as it is, for I think only

She still went on, after a civil reception

of yours. Compared with you, who has a right to be happy? I have almost grudged myself my own prior knowledge of what you ought to have known before all the world. I have not lost a moment, however. The post was late this morning, but there has not been since a moment's delay. How impatient, how anxious, how wild I have been on the subject, I will not attempt to describe; how severely mortified, how cruelly disappointed, in not having it finished while I was in London! I was kept there from day to day in the hope of it, for nothing less dear to me than such an object would have detained me half the time from Mansfield. But though my uncle entered into my wishes with all the warmth I could desire, and exerted himself immediately, there were difficulties from the absence of one friend, and the engagements of another which at last I could no longer bear to stay the end of, and knowing in what good hands I left the cause, I came away on Monday, trusting that many posts would not pass before I should be followed by such very letters as these. My uncle, who is the very best man in the world, has exerted himself, as I knew he would, after seeing your brother. He was delighted with him. I would not allow myself yesterday to say *how* delighted, or to repeat half that the Admiral said in his praise. I deferred it all till his praise should be proved the praise of a friend, as this day *does* prove it. *Now* I may say that *I* could not require William Price to excite a greater interest or be followed by warmer wishes and higher commendation, than were most voluntarily bestowed by my uncle after the evening they had passed together.'

'Has this been all *your* doing, then?' cried Fanny. 'Good heaven! how very, very kind! Have you really – was it by *your* desire? I beg your pardon, but I am bewildered. Did Admiral Crawford apply? How was it? I am stupefied.'

Henry was most happy to make it more intelligible, by beginning at an earlier stage, and explaining very particularly what he had done. His last journey to London had been undertaken with no other view than that of introducing her brother in Hill Street, and prevailing on the Admiral to exert whatever interest he might have for getting him on. This had been his business. He had communicated it to no creature; he had not breathed a syllable of it even to Mary; while uncertain of the issue, he could not have borne any participation of his feelings, but this had been his business; and he spoke with such a glow of what his solicitude had been, and used such strong expressions, was so abounding in the *deepest interest*, in *twofold motives*, in *views and wishes more than could be told*, that Fanny could not have remained insensible of his drift, had she been able to attend; but her heart was so full and her senses still so astonished, that she could listen but imperfectly even to what he told her of William, and saying only when he paused, 'How kind! how very kind! Oh, Mr Crawford, we are infinitely obliged to you! Dearest, dearest William!' She jumped up and moved in haste towards the door, crying out, 'I will go to my uncle. My uncle ought to know it as soon as possible.' But this could not be suffered. The opportunity was too fair, and his feelings too impatient. He was after her immediately. 'She must not go, she must allow him five minutes longer,' and he took her hand and led her back to her seat, and was in the middle of his further explanation, before she had suspected for what she was detained. When she did understand it, however, and found herself expected to believe that *she* had created sensations which his heart had never known before, and that every thing he had done for William was to be placed to the account of his excessive and unequalled attachment to her, she was exceedingly distressed, and for some moments unable to speak. She considered it all as nonsense, as mere trifling and gallantry, which meant only to deceive for the hour; she could not but feel that it was treating her improperly and unworthily, and in such a way as she had not deserved; but it was like himself, and entirely of a piece with what she had seen before; and she would not allow herself to show half the displeasure she felt, because he had been conferring an obligation, which no want of delicacy on his part could make a trifle to her. While her heart was still bounding with joy and gratitude on William's behalf, she could not be severely resentful of anything that injured only herself; and after having twice drawn back her hand, and twice attempted in vain to turn away from him, she got up, and said only, with much agitation, 'Don't, Mr Crawford, pray don't! I beg you would not. This is a sort of talking which is very unpleasant to me. I must go away. I cannot bear it.' But he was still talking on, describing his affection, soliciting a return, and finally, in words so plain as to bear but one meaning even to *her*, offering himself, hand, fortune, everything to her acceptance. It was so; he had said it. Her astonishment and confusion increased; and though still not knowing how to suppose him serious, she could hardly stand. He pressed for an answer.

'No, no, no!' she cried, hiding her face. 'This is all nonsense. Do not distress me. I can hear no more of this. Your kindness to William makes me more obliged to you than words can express; but I do not want, I cannot bear, I must not listen to such – no, no, don't think of me. But you are *not* thinking of me. I know it is all nothing.'

She had burst away from him, and at that moment Sir Thomas was heard speaking to a servant in his way towards the room they were in. It was no time for further assurances or entreaty, though to part with her at a moment when her modesty alone seemed, to his sanguine and pre-assured mind, to stand in the way of the happiness he sought, was a cruel necessity. She rushed out at an opposite door from the one her uncle was approaching, and was walking up and down the East Room in the utmost confusion of contrary feeling, before Sir Thomas's politeness or apologies were over, or he had reached the beginning of the joyful intelligence which his visitor came to communicate.

She was feeling, thinking, trembling, about every thing; agitated, happy, miserable, infinitely obliged, absolutely angry. It was all beyond belief! He was inexcusable, incomprehensible! But such were his habits, that he could do nothing without a mixture of evil. He had previously made her the happiest of human beings, and now he had insulted – she knew not what to say – how to class, or how to regard it. She would not have him be serious, and yet what could excuse the use of such words and offers, if they meant but to trifle?

But William was a lieutenant. *That* was a fact beyond a doubt, and without an alloy. She would think of it for ever and forget all the rest. Mr Crawford would certainly never address her so again; he must have seen how unwelcome it was to her; and in that case, how gratefully she could esteem him for his friendship to William!

She would not stir further from the East Room than the head of the great staircase, till she had satisfied herself of Mr Crawford's having left the house; but when convinced of his being gone, she was eager to go down and be with her uncle, and have all the happiness of his joy as well as her own, and all the benefit of his information or his conjectures as to what would now be William's destination. Sir Thomas was as joyful as she could desire, and very kind and communicative; and she had so comfortable a talk with him about William as to make her feel as if nothing had occurred to vex her, till she found, towards the close, that Mr Crawford was engaged to return and dine there that very day. This was a most unwelcome hearing, for though *he* might think nothing of what had passed, it would be quite distressing to her to see him again so soon.

She tried to get the better of it; tried very hard, as the dinner hour approached, to feel and appear as usual; but it was quite impossible for her not to look most shy and uncomfortable when their visitor entered the room. She could not have supposed it in the power of any concurrence of circumstances to give her so many painful sensations on the first day of hearing of William's promotion.

Mr Crawford was not only in the room – he was soon close to her. He had a note to deliver from his sister. Fanny could not look at him, but there was no consciousness of past folly in his voice. She opened her note immediately, glad to have any thing to do, and happy, as she read it, to feel that the fidgetings of her Aunt Norris, who was also to dine there, screened her a little from view.

> 'MY DEAR FANNY – *for so I may now always call you, to the infinite relief of a tongue that has been stumbling at* Miss Price *for at least the last six weeks: I cannot let my brother go without sending you a few lines of general congratulation, and giving my most joyful consent and approval. Go on, my dear Fanny, and without fear; there can be no difficulties worth naming. I choose to suppose that the assurance of* my *consent will be some thing; so you may smile upon him with your sweetest smiles this afternoon, and send him back to me even happier than he goes. – Yours affectionately,*
>
> *'M. C.'*

These were not expressions to do Fanny any good; for though she read in too much haste and confusion to form the clearest judgment of Miss Crawford's meaning, it was evident that she meant to compliment her on her brother's attachment, and even to *appear* to believe it serious. She did not know what to do, or what to think. There was wretchedness in the idea of its being serious; there was perplexity and agitation every way. She was distressed whenever Mr Crawford spoke to her, and he spoke to her much too often; and she was afraid there was a something in his voice and manner in addressing her very different from what they were when he talked to the others. Her comfort in that day's dinner was quite destroyed: she could hardly eat anything; and when Sir Thomas good-humouredly observed that joy had taken away her appetite she was ready to sink with shame, from the dread of Mr Crawford's interpretation; for though nothing could have tempted her to turn her eyes to the right hand, where he sat, she felt that *his* were immediately directed towards her.

She was more silent than ever. She would hardly join even when William was the subject, for his commission came all from the right hand too, and there was pain in the connection.

She thought Lady Bertram sat longer than ever, and began to be in despair of ever getting away; but at last they were in the drawing-room, and she was able to think as she would, while her aunts finished the subject of William's appointment, in their own style.

Mrs Norris seemed as much delighted with the saving it would be to Sir Thomas as with any part of it. '*Now* William would be able to keep himself, which would make a vast difference to his uncle, for it was unknown how much he had cost his uncle; and, indeed, it would make some difference in *her* presents too. She was very glad that she had given William what she did at parting, very glad, indeed, that it had been in her power, without material inconvenience, just at that time to give him some thing rather considerable; that is, for *her* with *her* limited means, for now it would all be useful in helping to fit up his cabin. She knew he must be at some expense, that he would have many things to buy, though to be sure his father and mother would be able to put him in the way of getting every thing very cheap; but she was very glad she had contributed her mite towards it.'

'I am glad you gave him something considerable,' said Lady Bertram, with most unsuspicious calmness, 'for *I* gave him only £10.'

'Indeed!' cried Mrs Norris, reddening. 'Upon my word, he must have gone off with his pockets well lined, and at no expense for his journey to London either!'

'Sir Thomas told me £10 would be enough.'

Mrs Norris being not at all inclined to question its sufficiency began to take the matter in another point.

'It is amazing,' said she, 'how much young prople cost their friends, what with bringing them up and putting them out in the world! They little think how much it comes to, or what their parents, or their uncles and aunts pay for them in the course of the year. Now, here are my sister Price's children; take them all together, I dare say nobody would believe what a sum they cost Sir Thomas every year, to say nothing of what *I* do for them.'

'Very true, sister, as you say. But poor things! They cannot help it; and you know it makes very little difference to Sir Thomas. Fanny, William must not forget my shawl, if he goes to the East Indies; and I shall give him a commission for any thing else that is worth having. I wish he may go to the East Indies, that I may have my shawl. I think I will have two shawls, Fanny.'

Fanny, meanwhile, speaking only when she could not help it, was very earnestly trying to understand what Mr and Miss Crawford were at. There was every thing in the world *against* their being serious, but his words and manner. Every thing natural, probable, reasonable, was against it; all their habits and ways of thinking, and all her own demerits. How could *she* have excited serious attachment in a man who had seen so many, and been admired by so many, and flirted with so many, infinitely her superiors; who seemed so little open to serious impressions, even where pains had been taken to please him; who thought so slightly, so carelessly, so unfeelingly on all such points; who was every thing to every body, and seemed to find no one essential to him? And further, how could it be supposed that his sister, with all her high and worldly notions of matrimony, would be forwarding anything of a serious nature in such a quarter? Nothing could be more unnatural in either. Fanny was ashamed of her own doubts. Every thing might be possible rather than serious attachment, or serious approbation of it towards her. She had quite convinced herself of this before Sir Thomas and Mr Crawford joined them. The difficulty was in maintaining the conviction quite so absolutely after Mr Crawford was in the room; for once or twice a look seemed forced on her which she did not know how to class among the common meaning; in any other man, at least, she would have said that it meant something very earnest, very pointed. But she still tried to believe it no more than what he might often have expressed towards her cousins and fifty other women.

She thought he was wishing to speak to her unheard by the rest. She fancied he was trying for it the whole evening at intervals, whenever Sir Thomas was out of the room, or at all engaged with Mrs Norris, and she carefully refused him every opportunity.

At last – it seemed an at last to Fanny's nervousness, though not remarkably late – he began to talk of going away; but the comfort of the sound was impaired by his turning to her the next moment, and saying,

'Have you nothing to send to Mary? No answer to her note? She will be disappointed if she receives nothing from you. Pray write to her, if it be only a line.'

'Oh yes! certainly,' cried Fanny, rising in haste, the haste of embarrassment and of wanting to get away. 'I will write directly.'

The note was held out, and must be taken

She went accordingly to the table, where she was in the habit of writing for her aunt, and prepared her materials without knowing what in the world to say. She had read Miss Crawford's note only once, and how to reply to any thing so imperfectly understood was most distressing. Quite unpractised in such sort of notewriting, had there been time for scruples and fears as to style she would have felt them in abundance; but some thing must be instantly written; and with only one decided feeling, that of wishing not to appear to think any thing really intended, she wrote thus, in great trembling both of spirits and hand:—

'I am very much obliged to you, my dear Miss Crawford, for your kind congratulations as far as they relate to my dearest William. The rest of your note, I know, means nothing; but I am so unequal to any thing of the sort, that I hope you will excuse my begging you to take no further notice. I have seen too much of Mr Crawford not to understand his manners; if he understood me as well, he would, I dare say, behave differently. I do not know what I write, but it would be a great favour of you never to mention the subject again. With thanks for the honour of your note, I remain, dear Miss Crawford, etc., etc.'

The conclusion was scarcely intelligible from increasing fright, for she found that Mr Crawford, under pretence of receiving the note, was coming towards her.

'You cannot think I mean to hurry you,' said he, in an under voice, perceiving the amazing trepidation with which she made up the note; 'you cannot think I have any such object. Do not hurry yourself, I entreat.'

'Oh! I thank you; I have quite done, just done; it will be ready in a moment; I am very much obliged to you; if you will be so good as to give *that* to Miss Crawford.'

The note was held out, and must be taken; and as she instantly and with averted eyes walked towards the fireplace, where sat the others, he had nothing to do but to go in good earnest.

Fanny thought she had never known a day of greater agitation, both of pain and pleasure; but happily, the pleasure was not of a sort to die with the day; for every day would restore the knowledge of William's advancement, whereas the pain, she hoped, would return no more. She had no doubt that her note must appear excessively ill-written, that the language would disgrace a child, for her distress had allowed no arrangement; but at least it would assure them both of her being neither imposed on nor gratified by Mr Crawford's attentions.

CHAPTER THIRTY TWO

FANNY HAD BY NO MEANS forgotten Mr Crawford when she awoke the next morning; but she remembered the purport of her note, and was not less sanguine as to its effect than she had been the night before. If Mr Crawford would but go away! That was what she most earnestly desired; go and take his sister with him, as he was to do, and as he returned to Mansfield on purpose to do. And why it was not done already she could not devise, for Miss Crawford certainly wanted no delay. Fanny had hoped, in the course of his yesterday's visit, to hear the day named; but he had only spoken of their journey as what would take place ere long.

Having so satisfactorily settled the conviction her note would convey, she could not but be astonished to see Mr Crawford, as she accidentally did, coming up to the house again, and at an hour as early as the day before. His coming might have nothing to do with her, but she must avoid seeing him if possible; and being then on her way upstairs, she resolved there to remain, during the whole of his visit, unless actually sent for; and as Mrs Norris was still in the house, there seemed little danger of her being wanted.

She sat some time in a good deal of agitation, listening, trembling, and fearing to be sent for every moment; but as no footsteps approached the East Room, she grew gradually composed, could sit down, and be able to employ herself, and able to hope that Mr Crawford had come and would go without her being obliged to know any thing of the matter.

Nearly half an hour had passed, and she was growing very comfortable, when suddenly the sound of a step in regular approach was heard; a heavy step, an unusual step in that part of the house; it was her uncle's; she knew it as well as his voice; she had trembled at it as often, and began to tremble again, at the idea of his coming up to speak to her, whatever might be the subject. It was indeed Sir Thomas, who opened the door and asked if she were there, and if he might come in. The terror of his former occasional visits to that room seemed all renewed, and she felt as if he were going to examine her again in French and English.

She was all attention, however, in placing a chair for him, and trying to appear honoured; and in her agitation, had quite overlooked the deficiencies of her apartment, till he, stopping short as he entered, said, with much surprise, 'Why have you no fire to-day?'

There was snow on the ground, and she was sitting in a shawl. She hesitated.

'I am not cold, sir: I never sit here long at this time of year.'

'But you have a fire in general?'

'No, sir.'

'How comes this about? Here must be some mistake. I understood that you had the use of this room by way of making you perfectly comfortable. In your bedchamber I know you *cannot* have a fire. Here is some great misapprehension which must be rectified. It is highly unfit for you to sit, be it only half an hour a day, without a fire. You are not strong. You are chilly. Your aunt cannot be aware of this.'

Fanny would rather have been silent; but being obliged to speak, she could not forbear, in justice to the aunt she loved best, from saying something in which the words 'my Aunt Norris' were distinguishable.

'I understand,' cried her uncle, recollecting himself, and not wanting to hear more: 'I understand. Your Aunt Norris has always been an advocate, and very judiciously, for young people's being brought up without unnecessary indulgences; but there should be moderation in every thing. She is also very hardy herself, which of course will influence her in her opinion of the wants of others. And on another account, too, I can perfectly comprehend. I know what her sentiments have always been. The principle was good in itself, but it may have been, and I believe *has been*, carried too far in your case. I am aware that there has been sometimes in some points, a misplaced distinction; but I think too well of you, Fanny, to suppose you will ever harbour resentment on that account. You have an understanding which will prevent you from receiving things only in part, and judging partially by the event. You will take in the whole of the past, you will consider times, persons, and probabilities, and you will feel that *they* were not least your friends who were educating and preparing you for that mediocrity of condition which *seemed* to be your lot. Though their caution may prove eventually unnecessary, it was kindly meant; and of this you may be assured, that every advantage of affluence will be doubled by the little privations and restrictions that may have been imposed. I am sure you will not disappoint my opinion of you, by failing at any time to treat your Aunt Norris with the respect and attention that are due to her. But enough of this. Sit down, my dear. I must speak to you for a few minutes, but I will not detain you long.'

Fanny obeyed, with eyes cast down and colour rising. After a moment's pause, Sir Thomas, trying to suppress a smile, went on.

'You are not aware, perhaps, that I have had a visitor this morning. I had not been long in my own room, after breakfast, when Mr Crawford was shown in. His errand you may probably conjecture.'

Fanny's colour grew deeper and deeper; and her uncle, perceiving that she was embarrassed to a degree that made either speaking or looking up quite impossible, turned away his own eyes, and without any further pause proceeded in his account of Mr Crawford's visit.

Mr Crawford's business had been to declare himself the lover of Fanny, make decided proposals for her, and entreat the sanction of the uncle, who seemed to stand in the place of her parents; and he had done it all so well, so openly, so liberally, so properly, that Sir Thomas, feeling, moreover, his own replies, and his own remarks to have been very much to the purpose, was exceedingly happy to give the particulars of their conversation, and, little aware of what was passing in his niece's mind, conceived, that by such details he must be gratifying her far more than himself. He talked, therefore, for several minutes, without Fanny's daring to interrupt him. She had hardly even attained the wish to do it. Her mind was in too much confusion. She had changed her position; and, with her eyes fixed intently on one of the windows, was listening to her uncle in the utmost perturbation and dismay. For a moment he ceased, but she had barely become conscious of it, when, rising from his chair, he said: 'And now, Fanny, having performed one part of my commission, and shown you every thing placed on a basis the most assured and satisfactory, I may execute the remainder by prevailing on you to accompany me downstairs, where, though I cannot but presume on having been no unacceptable companion myself, I must submit to your finding one still better worth listening to. Mr Crawford, as you have perhaps foreseen, is yet in the house. He is in my room, and hoping to see you there.'

There was a look, a start, an exclamation, on hearing this, which astonished Sir Thomas; but what was his increase of astonishment on hearing her exclaim: 'Oh! no, sir, I cannot, indeed I cannot go down to him. Mr Crawford ought to know – he must know that; I told him enough yesterday to convince him; he spoke to me on this subject yesterday, and I told him without disguise that it was very disagreeable to me, and quite out of my power to return his good opinion.'

'I do not catch your meaning,' said Sir Thomas, sitting down again. 'Out of your power to return his good opinion? What is all this? I know he spoke to you yesterday, and (as far as I understand) received as much encouragement to proceed as a well-judging young woman could permit herself to give. I was very much pleased with what I collected to have been your behaviour on the occasion; it showed a discretion highly to be commended. But now, when he has made his overtures so properly, and honourably – what are your scruples *now*?'

'You are mistaken, sir,' cried Fanny, forced by the anxiety of the moment even to tell her uncle that he was wrong; 'you are quite mistaken. How could Mr Crawford say such a thing? I gave him no encouragement yesterday. On the contrary, I told him, I cannot recollect my exact words, but I am sure I told him that I would not listen to him, that it was very unpleasant to me in every respect, and that I begged him never to talk to me in that manner again. I am sure I said as much as that and more; and I should have said still more, if I had been quite certain of his meaning any thing seriously; but I did not like to be, I could not bear to be, imputing more than might be intended. I thought it might all pass for nothing with *him*.'

She could say no more; her breath was almost gone.

'Am I to understand,' said Sir Thomas, after a few moments' silence, that you mean to *refuse* Mr Crawford?'

'Yes, sir.'

'Refuse him?'

'Yes, sir.'

'Refuse Mr Crawford! Upon what plea? For what reason?'

'I – I cannot like him, sir, well enough to marry him.'

'This is very strange!' said Sir Thomas, in a voice of calm displeasure. 'There is something in this which my comprehension does not reach. Here is a young man wishing to pay his addresses to you, with everything to recommend him; not merely situation in life, fortune, and character, but with more than common agreeableness, with address and conversation pleasing to every body. And he is not an acquaintance of to-day; you have now known him some time. His sister, moreover, is your intimate friend and he has been doing *that* for your brother, which I should suppose would have been almost sufficient recommendation to you, had there been no other. It is very uncertain when my interest might have got William on. He has done it already.'

'Yes,' said Fanny, in a faint voice, and looking down with fresh shame; and she did feel almost ashamed of herself, after such a picture as her uncle had drawn, for not liking Mr Crawford.

'You must have been aware,' continued Sir Thomas presently, 'you must have been some time aware of a particularity in Mr Crawford's manners to you. This cannot have taken you by surprise. You must have observed his attentions; and though you always received them very properly (I have no accusation to make on that head), I never perceived them to be unpleasant to you. I am half inclined to think, Fanny, that you do not quite know your own feelings.'

'Oh, yes, sir! indeed I do. His attentions were always – what I did not like.'

Sir Thomas looked at her with deeper surprise. 'This is beyond me,' said he. 'This requires explanation. Young as you are, and having seen scarcely any one, it is hardly possible that your affections—'

He paused and eyed her fixedly. He saw her lips formed into a *no*, though the sound was inarticulate, but her face was like scarlet. That, however, in so modest a girl might be very compatible with innocence; and choosing at least to appear satisfied, he quickly added, 'No, no, I know *that* is quite out of the question; quite impossible. Well, there is nothing more to be said.'

And for a few minutes he did say nothing. He was deep in thought. His niece was deep in thought likewise, trying to harden and prepare herself against further questioning. She would rather die than own the truth; and she hoped by a little reflection to fortify herself beyond betraying it.

'Independently of the interest which Mr Crawford's *choice* seemed to justify,' said Sir Thomas, beginning again, and very composedly, 'his wishing to marry at all so early is recommendatory to me. I am an advocate for early marriages, where there are means in proportion, and would have every young man, with a sufficient income, settle as soon after four-and-twenty as he can. This is so much my opinion, that I am sorry to think how little likely my own eldest son, your cousin, Mr Bertram, is to marry early; but at present, as far as I can judge, matrimony makes no part of his plans or thoughts. I wish he were more likely to fix.' Here was a glance at Fanny. 'Edmund, I consider, from his disposition and habits, as much more likely to marry early than his brother. *He*, indeed, I have lately thought has seen the woman he could love, which, I am convinced, my eldest son has not. Am I right? Do you agree with me, my dear?'

'Yes, sir.'

It was gently, but it was calmly said, and Sir Thomas was easy on the score of the cousins. But the removal of his alarm did his niece no service; as her unaccountableness was confirmed his displeasure increased; and getting up and walking about the room, with a frown, which Fanny could picture to herself, though she dared not lift up her eyes, he shortly afterwards, and in a voice of authority, said, 'Have you any reason, child, to think ill of Mr Crawford's temper?'

'No, sir.'

She longed to add, 'But of his principles I have'; but her heart sank under the appalling prospect of discussion, explanation, and probably non-conviction. Her ill opinion of him was founded chiefly on observations, which, for her cousins' sake, she could scarcely dare mention to their father. Maria and Julia, and especially Maria, were so closely implicated in Mr Crawford's misconduct, that she could not give his character, such as she believed it, without betraying them. She had hoped that, to a man like her uncle, so discerning, so honourable, so good, the simple acknowledgment of settled *dislike* on her side, would have been sufficient. To her infinite grief she found it was not.

Sir Thomas came towards the table where she sat in trembling wretchedness, and with a good deal of cold sternness, said: 'It is of no use, I perceive, to talk to you. We had better put an end to this most mortifying conference. Mr Crawford must not be kept longer waiting. I will, therefore, only add, as thinking it my duty to mark my opinion of your conduct, that you have disappointed every expectation I had formed, and proved yourself of a character the very reverse of what I had supposed. For I *had*, Fanny, as I think my behaviour must have shown, formed a very favourable opinion of you from the period of my return to England. I had thought you peculiarly free from wilfulness of temper, self-conceit, and every tendency to that independence of spirit which prevails so much in modern days, even in young women, and which in young women is offensive and disgusting beyond all common offence. But you have now shown me that you can be wilful and perverse; that you can and will decide for yourself, without any consideration or deference for those who have surely some right to guide you, without even asking their advice. You have shown yourself very, very different from anything that I had imagined. The advantage or disadvantage of your family, of your parents, your brothers and sisters, never seems to have had a moment's share in your thoughts on this occasion. How *they* might be benefited, how *they* must rejoice in such an establishment for you, is nothing to *you*. You think only of yourself, and because you do not feel for Mr Crawford exactly what a young heated fancy imagines to be necessary for happiness, you resolve to refuse him at once, without wishing even for a little time to consider of it, a little more time for cool consideration, and for really examining your own inclinations; and are, in a wild fit of folly, throwing away from you such an opportunity of being settled in life, eligibly, honourably, nobly settled, as will, probably, never occur to you again. Here is a young man of sense, of character, of temper, of manners, and of fortune, exceedingly attached to you, and seeking your hand in the most handsome and disinterested way; and let me tell you, Fanny, that you may live eighteen years longer in the world, without being addressed by a man of half Mr Crawford's estate, or a tenth part of its merits. Gladly would I have bestowed either of my own daughters on him. Maria is nobly married; but had Mr Crawford sought Julia's hand, I should have given it to him with superior and more heartfelt satisfaction than I gave Maria's to Mr Rushworth.' After half a moment's pause: 'And I should have been very much surprised had either of my daughters, on receiving a proposal of marriage at any time, which might carry with it only *half* the eligibility of *this*, immediately and peremptorily, and without paying my opinion or my regard the compliment of any consultation, put a decided negative on it. I should have been much surprised and much hurt, by such a proceeding. I should have thought it a gross violation of duty and respect. *You* are not to be judged by the same rule. You do not owe me the duty of a child. But, Fanny, if your heart can acquit you of *ingratitude*—'

He ceased. Fanny was by this time crying so bitterly, that, angry as he was, he would not press that article further. Her heart was almost broken by such a picture of what she appeared to him; by such accusations, so heavy, so multiplied, so rising in dreadful gradation! Self-willed, obstinate, selfish, and ungrateful. He thought her all this. She had deceived his expectations; she had lost his good opinion. What was to become of her?

'I am very sorry,' said she, inarticulately, through her tears, 'I am very sorry, indeed.'

'Sorry! Yes, I hope you are sorry; and you will probably have reason to be long sorry for this day's transactions.'

'If it were possible for me to do otherwise—' said she, with another strong effort; 'but I am so perfectly convinced that I could never make him happy, and that I should be miserable myself.'

Another burst of tears; but in spite of that burst, and in spite of that great black word *miserable*, which served to introduce it, Sir Thomas began to think a little relenting, a little change of inclination, might have some thing to do with it; and to augur favourably from the personal entreaty of the young man himself. He knew her to be very timid, and exceedingly nervous; and thought it not improbable that her mind might be in such a state as a little time, a little pressing, a little patience, and a little impatience, a judicious mixture of all on the lover's side, might work their usual effect on. If the gentleman would but persevere, if he had but love enough to persevere, Sir Thomas began to have hopes; and these reflections having passed across his mind and cheered it, 'Well,' said he, in a tone of becoming gravity, but of less anger, 'well, child, dry up your tears. There is no use in these tears; they can do no good. You must now come downstairs with me. Mr Crawford has been kept waiting too long already. You must give him your own answer; we cannot expect him to be satisfied with less; and you only can explain to him the grounds of that misconception of your sentiments, which, unfortunately for himself, he certainly has imbibed. I am totally unequal to it.'

But Fanny showed such reluctance, such misery, at the idea of going down to him, that Sir Thomas, after a little consideration, judged it better to indulge her. His hopes from both gentleman and lady suffered a small depression in consequence; but when he looked at his niece, and saw the state of feature and complexion which her crying had brought her into, he thought there might be as much lost as gained by an immediate interview. With a few words, therefore, of no particular meaning, he walked off by himself, leaving his poor niece to sit and cry over what had passed, with very wretched feelings.

Her mind was all disorder. The past, present, future, every thing was terrible. But her uncle's anger gave her the severest pain of all. Selfish and ungrateful! to have appeared so to him! She was miserable for ever. She had no one to take her part, to counsel, or speak for her. Her only friend was absent. He might have softened his father; but all, perhaps all, would think her selfish and ungrateful. She might have to endure the reproach again and again; she might hear it, or see it, or know it to exist for ever in every connection about her. She could not but feel some resentment against Mr Crawford; yet, if he really loved her, and were unhappy too—! It was all wretchedness together.

In about a quarter of an hour her uncle returned; she was almost ready to faint at the sight of him. He spoke calmly, however, without austerity, without reproach, and she revived a little. There was comfort, too, in his words, as well as his manner, for he began with, 'Mr Crawford is gone: he has just left me. I need not repeat what has passed. I do not want to add to any thing you may now be feeling, by an account of what he has felt. Suffice it, that he has behaved in the most gentlemanlike and generous manner, and had confirmed me in a most favourable opinion of his understanding, heart and temper. Upon my representation of what you were suffering, he immediately, and with the greatest delicacy, ceased to urge to see you for the present.'

Here Fanny, who had looked up, looked down again.

'Of course,' continued her uncle, 'it cannot be supposed but that he should request to speak with you alone, be it only for five minutes; a request too natural, a claim too just to be denied. But there is no time fixed; perhaps to-morrow, or whenever your spirits are composed enough. For the present you have only to tranquillise yourself. Check these tears; they do but exhaust you. If, as I am willing to suppose, you wish to show me any observance, you will not give way to these emotions, but endeavour to reason yourself into a stronger frame of mind. I advise you to go out; the air will do you good; go out for an hour on the gravel; you will have the shrubbery to yourself, and will be the better for air and exercise. And, Fanny (turning back again for a moment), I shall make no mention below of what has passed; I shall not even tell your Aunt Bertram. There is no occasion for spreading the disappointment; say nothing about it yourself.'

This was an order to be most joyfully obeyed; this was an act of kindness which Fanny felt at her heart. To be spared from her Aunt Norris's interminable reproaches; he left her in a glow of gratitude. Any thing might be bearable rather than such reproaches. Even to see Mr Crawford would be less overpowering.

She walked out directly as her uncle recommended, and followed his advice throughout, as far as she could; did check her tears; did earnestly try to compose her spirits and strengthen her mind. She wished to prove to him that she did desire his comfort, and sought to regain his favour; and he had given her another strong motive for exertion, in keeping the whole affair from the knowledge of her aunts. Not to excite suspicion by her look or manner, was now an object worth attaining; and she felt equal to almost any thing that might save her from her Aunt Norris.

She was struck, quite struck, when, on returning from her walk and going into the East Room again, the first thing which caught her eye was a fire lighted and burning. A fire! It seemed too much; just at that time to be giving her such an indulgence was exciting even painful gratitude. She wondered that Sir Thomas could have leisure to think of such a trifle again; but she soon found, from the voluntary information of the housemaid, who came in to attend it, that so it was to be every day. Sir Thomas had given orders for it.

'I must be a brute, indeed, if I can be really ungrateful!' said she, in soliloquy. 'Heaven defend me from being ungrateful!'

She saw nothing more of her uncle, nor of her Aunt Norris, till they met at dinner. Her uncle's behaviour to her was then as nearly as possible what it had been before; she was sure he did not mean there should be any change, and that it was only her own conscience that could fancy any; but her aunt was soon quarrelling with her; and when she found how much and how pleasantly her having only walked out without her aunt's knowledge could be dwelt on, she felt all the reason she had to bless the kindness which saved her from the same spirit of reproach, exerted on a more momentous subject.

'If I had known you were going out, I should have got you just to go as far as my house with some orders for Nanny,' said she, 'which I have since, to my very great inconvenience, been obliged to go and carry myself. I could very ill spare the time, and you might have saved me the trouble, if you would only have been so good as to let us know you were going out. It would have made no difference to you, I suppose, whether you had walked in the shrubbery or gone to my house.'

'I recommended the shrubbery to Fanny as the driest place,' said Sir Thomas.

'Oh!' said Mrs Norris, with a moment's check, 'that was very kind of you, Sir Thomas, but you do not know how dry the path is to my house. Fanny would have had quite as good a walk there, I assure you, with the advantage of being of some use, and obliging her aunt: it is all her fault. If she would but have let us know she was going out – but there is a some thing about Fanny, I have often observed it before – she likes to go her own way to work; she does not like to be dictated to; she takes her own independent walk whenever she can; she certainly has a little spirit of secrecy, and

Mrs Norris called out, 'Stay, stay, Fanny! don't be in such a hurry'

independence, and nonsense, about her, which I would advise her to get the better of.'

As a general reflection on Fanny, Sir Thomas thought nothing could be more unjust, though he had been so lately expressing the same sentiments himself, and he tried to turn the conversation: tried repeatedly before he could succeed; for Mrs Norris had not discernment enough to perceive, either now, or at any other time, to what degree he thought well of his niece, or how very far he was from wishing to have his own children's merits set off by the depreciation of hers. She was talking *at* Fanny, and resenting this private walk half through the dinner.

It was over, however, at last; and the evening set in with more composure to Fanny, and more cheerfulness of spirits than she could have hoped for after so stormy a morning; but she trusted, in the first place, that she had done right; that her judgment had not misled her. For the purity of her intentions she could answer; and she was willing to hope, secondly, that her uncle's displeasure was abating, and would abate further as he considered the matter with more impartiality, and felt, as a good man must feel, how wretched, and how unpardonable, how hopeless, and how wicked it was, to marry without affection.

When the meeting with which she was threatened for the morrow was past, she could not but flatter herself that the subject would be finally concluded, and Mr Crawford once gone from Mansfield, that every thing would soon be as if no such subject had existed. She would not, could not believe, that Mr Crawford's affection for her could distress him long; his mind was not of that sort. London would soon bring its cure. In London he would soon learn to wonder at his infatuation, and be thankful for the right reason in her which had saved him from its evil consequences.

While Fanny's mind was engaged in these sort of hopes, her uncle was, soon after tea, called out of the room; an occurrence too common to strike her, and she thought nothing of it till the butler reappeared ten minutes afterwards, and advancing decidedly towards herself, said, 'Sir Thomas wishes to speak with you, ma'am, in his own room.' Then it occurred to her what might be going on; a suspicion rushed over her mind which drove the colour from her cheeks; but instantly rising, she was preparing to obey, when Mrs Norris called out, 'Stay, stay, Fanny! What are you about? Where are you going? Don't be in such a hurry. Depend upon it, it is not you who are wanted; depend upon it, it is me' (looking at the butler) 'but you are so very eager to put yourself forward. What should Sir Thomas want you for? It is me, Baddeley, I am sure; Sir Thomas wants me, not Miss Price.'

But Baddeley was stout. 'No, ma'am, it is Miss Price; I am certain of its being Miss Price.' And there was a half smile with the words, which meant, 'I do not think *you* would answer the purpose at all.'

Mrs Norris, much discontented, was obliged to compose herself to work again; and Fanny, walking off in agitating consciousness, found herself, as she anticipated, in another minute alone with Mr Crawford.

CHAPTER THIRTY THREE

THE CONFERENCE WAS NEITHER so short nor so conclusive as the lady had designed. The gentleman was not so easily satisfied. He had all the disposition to persevere that Sir Thomas could wish him. He had vanity, which strongly inclined him in the first place to think she did love him, though she might not know it herself; and which, secondly, when constrained at last to admit that she did know her own present feelings, convinced him that he should be able in time to make those feelings what he wished.

He was in love, very much in love; and it was a love which, operating on an active, sanguine spirit, of more warmth than delicacy, made her affection appear of greater consequence because it was withheld, and determined him to have the glory, as well as the felicity, of forcing her to love him.

He would not despair: he would not desist. He had every well-grounded reason for solid attachment; he knew her to have all the worth that could justify the warmest hopes of lasting happiness with her; her conduct at this time by speaking the disinterestedness and delicacy of her character (qualities which he believed most rare indeed), was of a sort to heighten all his wishes, and confirm all his resolutions. He knew not that he had a pre-engaged heart to attack. Of *that* he had no suspicion. He considered her rather as one who had never thought on the subject enough to be in danger; who had been guarded by youth, a youth of mind as lovely as of person; whose modesty had prevented her from understanding his attentions, and who was still overpowered by the suddenness of addresses so wholly unexpected, and the novelty of a situation which her fancy had never taken into account.

Must it not follow of course, that, when he was understood, he should succeed? He believed it fully. Love such as his, in a man like himself, must with perseverance secure a return, and at no great distance; and he had so much delight in the idea of obliging her to love him in a very short time, that her not loving him now was scarcely regretted. A little difficulty to be overcome was no evil to Henry Crawford. He rather derived spirits from it. He had been apt to gain hearts too easily. His situation was new and animating.

To Fanny, however, who had known too much opposition all her life to find any charm in it, all this was unintelligible. She found that he did mean to persevere; but how he could, after such language from her as she felt herself obliged to use, was not to be understood. She told him that she did not love him, could not love him, was sure she never should love him; that such a change was quite impossible; that the subject was most painful to her; that she must intreat him never to mention it again, to allow her to leave him at once, and let it be considered as concluded for ever. And when further pressed, had added, that in her opinion their dispositions were so totally dissimilar, as to make mutual affection incompatible; and that they were unfitted for each other by nature, education, and habit. All this she had said, and with the earnestness of sincerity; yet this was not enough, for he immediately denied there being any thing uncongenial in their characters, or any thing unfriendly in their situations; and positively declared that he would still love, and still hope!

Fanny knew her own meaning, but was no judge of her own manner. Her manner was incurably gentle; and she was not aware how much it concealed the sternness of her purpose. Her diffidence, gratitude, and softness made every expression of indifference seem almost an effort of self-denial; seem, at least, to be giving nearly as much pain to herself as to him. Mr Crawford was no longer the Mr Crawford who, as the clandestine, insidious, treacherous admirer of Maria Bertram, had been her abhorrence, whom she had hated to see or to speak to, in whom she could believe no good quality to exist, and whose power, even of being agreeable, she had barely acknowledged. He was now the Mr Crawford who was addressing herself with ardent, disinterested love; whose feelings were apparently become all that was honourable and upright, whose views of happiness were all fixed on a marriage of attachment; who was pouring out his sense of her merits, describing and describing again his affection, proving, as far as words could prove it, and in the language, tone, and spirit of a man of talent, too, that he sought her for her gentleness and her goodness; and to complete the whole, he was now the Mr Crawford who had procured William's promotion!

Here was a change, and here were claims which could not but operate! She might have disdained him in all the dignity of angry virtue in the grounds of Sotherton, or the theatre at Mansfield Park; but he approached her now with rights that demanded different treatment. She must be courteous, and she must be compassionate. She must have a sensation of being honoured, and whether thinking of herself or her brother, she must have a strong feeling of gratitude. The effect of the whole was a manner so pitying and agitated, and words intermingled with her refusal so expressive of obligation and concern, that to a temper of vanity and hope like Crawford's, the truth, or at least the strength of her indifference, might well be questionable; and he was not so irrational as Fanny considered him, in the professions of persevering, assiduous, and not desponding attachment which closed the interview.

It was with reluctance that he suffered her to go; but there was no look of despair in parting to bely his words, or give her hopes of his being less unreasonable than he professed himself.

Now she was angry. Some resentment did arise at a perseverance so selfish and ungenerous. Here was again a want of delicacy and regard for others which had formerly so struck and disgusted her. Here was again a something of the same Mr Crawford whom she had so reprobated before. How evidently was there a gross want of feeling and humanity where his own pleasure was concerned; and alas! how always known, no principle to supply as a duty what the heart was deficient in! Had her own affections been as free as perhaps they ought to have been, he never could have engaged them.

So thought Fanny, in good truth and sober sadness, as she sat musing over that too great indulgence and luxury of a fire upstairs; wondering at the past and present; wondering at what was yet to come, and in a nervous agitation which made nothing clear to her but the persuasion of her being never under any circumstances able to love Mr Crawford, and the felicity of having a fire to sit over and think of it.

Sir Thomas was obliged, or obliged himself, to wait till the morrow for a knowledge of what had passed between the young people. He then saw Mr Crawford, and received his account. The first feeling was disappointment: he had hoped better things; he had thought that an hour's entreaty from a young man like Crawford could not have worked so little change on a gentle-tempered girl like Fanny; but there was speedy comfort in the determined views and sanguine perseverance of the lover; and when seeing such confidence of success in the principal, Sir Thomas was soon able to depend on it himself.

Nothing was omitted, on his side, of civility, compliment, or kindness, that might assist the plan. Mr Crawford's steadiness was honoured, and Fanny was praised, and the connection was still the most desirable in the world. At Mansfield Park Mr Crawford would always be welcome; he had only to consult his own judgment and feelings as to the frequency of his visits, at present or in future. In all his niece's family and friends, there could be but one opinion, one wish on the subject; the influence of all who loved her must incline one way.

Every thing was said that could encourage, every encouragement received with grateful joy, and the gentlemen parted the best of friends.

Satisfied that the cause was now on a footing the most proper and hopeful, Sir Thomas resolved to abstain from all further importunity with his niece, and to show no open inteference. Upon her disposition he believed kindness might be the best way of working. Intreaty should be from one quarter only. The forbearance of her family on a point, respecting which she could be in no doubt of their wishes, might be their surest means of forwarding it. Accordingly, on this principle, Sir Thomas took the first opportunity of saying to her, with a mild gravity, intended to be overcoming, 'Well, Fanny, I have seen Mr Crawford again, and learnt from him exactly how matters stand between you. He is a most extraordinary young man, and whatever be the event, you must feel that you have created an attachment of no common character; though, young as you are, and little acquainted with the transient, varying, unsteady nature of love, as it generally exists, you cannot be struck as I am with all that is wonderful in a perseverance of this sort against discouragement. With him, it is entirely a matter of feeling; he claims no merit in it; perhaps is entitled to none. Yet, having chosen so well, his constancy has a respectable stamp. Had his choice been less unexceptionable, I should have condemned his persevering.'

'Indeed, sir,' said Fanny, 'I am very sorry that Mr Crawford should continue to— I know that it is paying me a very great compliment, and I feel most undeservedly honoured; but I am so perfectly convinced, and I have told him so, that it never will be in my power—'

'My dear,' interrupted Sir Thomas, 'there is no occasion for this. Your feelings are as well known to me as my wishes and regrets must be to you. There is nothing more to be said or done. From this hour, the subject is never to be revived between us. You will have nothing to fear, or to be agitated about. You cannot suppose me capable of trying to persuade you to marry against your inclinations. Your happiness and advantage are all that I have in view, and nothing is required of you but to bear with Mr Crawford's endeavours to convince you that they may not be incompatible with his. He proceeds at his own risk. You are on safe ground. I have engaged for your seeing him whenever he calls, as you might have done had nothing of this sort occurred. You will see him with the rest of us, in the same manner, and, as much as you can, dismissing the recollection of every thing unpleasant. He leaves Northamptonshire so soon, that even this slight sacrifice cannot be often demanded. The future must be very uncertain. And now, my dear Fanny, this subject is closed between us.'

The promised departure was all that Fanny could think of with much satisfaction. Her uncle's kind expressions, however, and forbearing manner were sensibly felt; and when she considered how much of the truth was unknown to him, she believed she had no right to wonder at the line of conduct he pursued. He, who had married a daughter to Mr Rushworth: romantic delicacy was certainly not to be expected from him. She must do her duty, and trust that time might make her duty easier than it now was.

She could not, though only eighteen, suppose Mr Crawford's attachment would hold out for ever; she could not but imagine that steady, unceasing discouragement from herself would put an end to it in time. How much time she might, in her own fancy, allot for its dominion, is another concern. It would not be fair to inquire into a young lady's exact estimate of her own perfections.

In spite of his intended silence, Sir Thomas found himself once more obliged to mention the subject to his niece, to prepare her briefly for its being imparted to her aunts; a measure which he would still have avoided, if possible, but which became necessary from the totally opposite feelings of Mr Crawford, as to any secrecy of proceeding. He had no idea of concealment. It was all known at the Parsonage, where he loved to talk over the future with both his sisters, and it would be rather gratifying to him to have enlightened witnesses of the progress of his success. When Sir Thomas understood this, he felt the necessity of making his own wife and sister-in-law acquainted with the business without delay; though, on Fanny's account, he almost dreaded the effect of the communication to Mrs Norris as much as Fanny herself. He deprecated her mistaken but well-meaning zeal. Sir Thomas, indeed, was, by this time, not very far from classing Mrs Norris as one of those well-meaning people who are always doing mistaken and very disagreeable things.

Mrs Norris, however, relieved him. He pressed for the strictest forbearance and silence towards their niece; she not only promised, but did observe it. She only looked her increased ill-will. Angry she was: bitterly angry; but she was more angry with Fanny for having received such an offer, than for refusing it. It was an injury and affront to Julia, who ought to have been Mr Crawford's choice; and independently of that, she disliked Fanny, because she had neglected her; and she would have grudged such an elevation to one whom she had been always trying to depress.

Sir Thomas gave her more credit for discretion on the occasion than she deserved; and Fanny could have blessed her for allowing her only to see her displeasure, and not to hear it.

Lady Bertram took it differently. She had been a beauty, and a prosperous beauty, all her life; and beauty and wealth were all that excited her respect. To know Fanny to be sought in marriage by a man of fortune, raised her, therefore, very much in her opinion. By convincing her that Fanny *was* very pretty, which she had been doubting about before, and that she would be advantageously married, it made her feel a sort of credit in calling her niece.

'Well, Fanny,' said she, as soon as they were alone together afterwards, and she really had known something like impatience to be alone with her, and her countenance, as she spoke, had extraordinary animation: 'Well, Fanny, I have had a very agreeable surprise this morning. I must just speak of it *once*, and then I shall have done. I give you joy, my dear niece.' And looking at her complacently, she added, 'Humph, we certainly are a handsome family!'

Fanny coloured, and doubted at first what to say; when hoping to assail her on her vulnerable side, she presently answered –

'My dear aunt, *you* cannot wish me to do differently from what I have done, I am sure. *You* cannot wish me to marry; for you would miss me, should not you? Yes, I am sure you would miss me too much for that.'

'No, my dear, I should not think of missing you, when such an offer as this comes in your way. I could do very well without you, if you were married to a man of such good estate as Mr Crawford. And you must be aware, Fanny, that it is every young woman's duty to accept such a very unexceptionable offer as this.'

This was almost the only rule of conduct, the only piece of advice, which Fanny had ever received from her aunt in the course of eight years and a half. It silenced her. She felt how unprofitable contention would be. If her aunt's feelings were against her, nothing could be hoped from attacking her understanding. Lady Bertram was quite talkative.

'I will tell you what, Fanny,' said she, 'I am sure he fell in love with you at the ball; I am sure the mischief was done that evening. You did look remarkably well. Every body said so. Sir Thomas said so. And you know you had Chapman to help you to dress. I am very glad I sent Chapman to you. I shall tell Sir Thomas that I am sure it was done that evening.' And still pursuing the same cheerful thoughts, she soon afterwards added, 'And I will tell you what, Fanny, which is more than I did for Maria, the next time pug has a litter you shall have a puppy.'

CHAPTER THIRTY FOUR

EDMUND HAD GREAT THINGS to hear on his return. Many surprises were awaiting him. The first that occurred was not least in interest: the appearance of Henry Crawford and his sister walking together through the village as he rode into it. He had concluded – he had meant them to be far distant. His absence had been extended beyond a fortnight purposely to avoid Miss Crawford. He was returning to Mansfield with spirits ready to feed on melancholy remembrances, and tender associations, when her own fair self was before him, leaning on her brother's arm, and he found himself receiving a welcome, unquestionably friendly, from the woman whom, two moments before, he had been thinking of as seventy miles off, and as farther, much farther, from him in inclination than any distance could express.

Her reception of him was of a sort which he could not have hoped for, had he expected to see her. Coming as he did from such a purport fulfilled as had taken him away, he would have expected any thing rather than a look of satisfaction, and words of simple, pleasant meaning. It was enough to set his heart in a glow, and to bring him home in the properest state for feeling the full value of the other joyful surprises at hand.

William's promotion, with all its particulars, he was soon master of; and with such a secret provision of comfort within his own breast to help the joy, he found in it a source of most gratifying sensation, and unvarying cheerfulness all dinner-time.

After dinner, when he and his father were alone, he had Fanny's history; and then all the great events of the last fortnight, and the present situation of matters at Mansfield were known to him.

Fanny suspected what was going on. They sat so much longer than usual in the dining-parlour, that she was sure they must be talking of her; and when tea at last brought them away, and she was to be seen by Edmund again, she felt dreadfully guilty. He came to her, sat down by her, took her

Receiving a welcome

hand, and pressed it kindly; and at that moment she thought that, but for the occupation and the screen which the tea-things afforded, she must have betrayed her emotion in some unpardonable excess.

He was not intending, however, by such action, to be conveying to her that unqualified approbation and encouragement which her hopes drew from it. It was designed only to express his participation in all that interested her, and to tell her that he had been hearing what quickened every feeling of affection. He was, in fact, entirely on his father's side of the question. His surprise was not so great as his father's at her refusing Crawford, because, so far from supposing her to consider him with any thing like a preference, he had always believed it to be rather the reverse, and could imagine her to be taken perfectly unprepared, but Sir Thomas could not regard the connection as more desirable than he did. It had every recommendation to him; and while honouring her for what she had done under the influence of her present indifference, honouring her in rather stronger terms than Sir Thomas could quite echo, he was most earnest in hoping and sanguine in believing, that it would be a match at last, and that, united by mutual affection, it would appear that their dispositions were as exactly fitted to make them blessed in each other, as he was now beginning seriously to consider them. Crawford had been too precipitate. He had not given her time to attach herself. He had begun at the wrong end. With such powers as his, however, and such a disposition as hers, Edmund trusted that everything would work out a happy conclusion. Meanwhile, he saw enough of Fanny's embarrassment to make him scrupulously guard against exciting it a second time, by any word, or look, or movement.

Crawford called the next day, and on the score of Edmund's return, Sir Thomas felt himself more than licensed to ask him to stay to dinner; it was really a necessary compliment. He stayed of course, and Edmund had then ample opportunity for observing how he sped with Fanny, and what degree of immediate encouragement for him might be extracted from her manners; and it was so little, so very very little (every chance, every possibility of it, resting upon her embarrassment only: if there was not hope in her confusion, there was hope in nothing else), that he was almost ready to wonder at his friend's perseverance. Fanny was worth it all; he held her to be worth every effort of patience, every exertion of mind, but he did not think he could have gone on himself with any woman breathing, without something more to warm his courage than his eyes could discern in hers. He was very willing to hope that Crawford saw clearer, and this was the most comfortable conclusion for his friend that he could come to from all that he observed to pass before, and at, and after dinner.

In the evening a few circumstances occurred which he thought more promising. When he and Crawford walked into the drawing-room, his mother and Fanny were sitting as intently and silently at work as if there were nothing else to care for. Edmund could not help noticing their apparently deep tranquillity.

'We have not been so silent all the time,' replied his mother. 'Fanny has been reading to me, and only put the book down upon hearing you coming.' And sure enough there was a book on the table which had the air of being very recently closed: a volume of Shakespeare. 'She often reads to me out of those books; and she was in the middle of a very fine speech of that man's – what's his name, Fanny? – when we heard your footsteps.'

Crawford took the volume. 'Let me have the pleasure of finishing that speech to your ladyship,' said he. 'I shall find it immediately.' And by carefully giving way to the inclination of the leaves, he did find it, or within a page or two, quite near enough to satisfy Lady Bertram, who assured him, as soon as he mentioned the name of Cardinal Wolsey, that he had got the very speech. Not a look, or an offer of help had Fanny given; not a syllable for or against. All her attention was for her work. She seemed determined to be interested by nothing else. But taste was too strong in her. She could not abstract her mind five minutes; she was forced to listen; his reading was capital, and her pleasure in good reading extreme. To *good* reading, however, she had been long used; her uncle read well, her cousins all, Edmund very well, but in Mr Crawford's reading there was a variety of excellence beyond what she had ever met with. The King, the Queen, Buckingham, Wolsey, Cromwell, all were given in turn; for with the happiest knack, the happiest power of jumping and guessing, he could always alight at will on the best scene, or the best speeches of each; and whether it were dignity or pride, or tenderness or remorse, or whatever were to be expressed, he could do it with equal beauty. It was truly dramatic. His acting had first taught Fanny what pleasure a play might give, and his reading brought all his acting before her again; nay, perhaps with greater enjoyment, for it came unexpectedly, and with no such drawback as she had been used to suffer in seeing him on the stage with Miss Bertram.

Edmund watched the progress of her attention, and was amused and gratified by seeing how she gradually slackened in the needlework, which at the beginning, seemed to occupy her totally; how it fell from her hand while she sat motionless over it, and at last, how the eyes which had appeared so studiously to avoid him throughout the day, were turned and fixed on Crawford; fixed on him for minutes, fixed on him, in short, till the attraction drew Crawford's upon her, and the book was closed, and the charm was broken. Then she was shrinking again into herself, and blushing and working as hard as ever; but it had been enough to give Edmund encouragement for his friend, and as he cordially thanked him, he hoped to be expressing Fanny's secret feelings too.

'That play must be a favourite with you,' said he; 'you read as if you knew it well.'

'It will be a favourite, I believe, from this hour,' replied Crawford; 'but I do not think I have had a volume of Shakespeare in my hand before since I was fifteen. I once saw Henry the Eighth acted, or I have heard of it from some body who did, I am not certain which. But Shakespeare one gets acquainted with without knowing how. It is a part of an Englishman's constitution. His thoughts and beauties are so spread abroad that one touches them every where; one is intimate with him by instinct. No man of any brain can open at a good part of one of his plays without falling into the flow of his meaning immediately.'

'No doubt one is familiar with Shakespeare in a degree,' said Edmund, 'from one's earliest years. His celebrated passages are quoted by every body; they are in half the books we open, and we all talk Shakespeare, use his similes, and describe with his descriptions; but this is totally distinct from giving his sense as you gave it. To know him in bits and scraps is common enough; to know him pretty thoroughly is, perhaps, not uncommon; but to read him well aloud is no every-day talent.'

'Sir, you do me honour,' was Crawford's answer, with a bow of mock gravity.

Both gentlemen had a glance at Fanny, to see if a word of accordant praise could be extorted from her; yet both feeling that it could not be. Her praise had been given in her attention; *that* must content them.

Lady Bertram's admiration was expressed, and strongly too. 'It was really like being at a play,' said she. 'I wish Sir Thomas had been here.'

Crawford was excessively pleased. If Lady Bertram, with all her incompetency and languor, could feel this, the inference of what her niece, alive and enlightened as she was, must feel, was elevating.

'You have a great turn for acting, I am sure, Mr Crawford,' said her ladyship soon afterwards; 'and I will tell you what, I think you will have a theatre, some time or other, at your house in Norfolk. I mean when you are settled there. I do, indeed. I think you will fit up a theatre at your house in Norfolk.'

'Do you, ma'am?' cried he, with quickness. 'No, no, that will never be. Your ladyship is quite mistaken. No theatre at Everingham! Oh, no!' And he looked at Fanny with an expressive smile, which evidently meant, 'that lady will never allow a theatre at Everingham.'

Edmund saw it all, and saw Fanny so determined *not* to see it, as to make it clear that the voice was enough to convey the full meaning of the protestation; and such a quick consciousness of compliment, such a ready comprehension of a hint, he thought, was rather favourable than not.

The subject of reading aloud was further discussed. The two young men were the only talkers, but they, standing by the fire, talked over the too common neglect of the qualification, the total inattention to it, in the ordinary school-system for boys, the consequently natural yet in some instances almost unnatural, degree of ignorance and uncouthness of men, of sensible and well-informed men, when suddenly called to the necessity of reading aloud, which had fallen within their notice, giving instances of blunders, and failures with their secondary causes, the want of management of the voice, of proper modulation and emphasis, of foresight and judgment, all proceeding from the first cause: want of early attention and habit; and Fanny was listening again with great entertainment.

'Even in my profession,' said Edmund, with a smile, 'how little the art of reading has been studied! How little a clear manner, and good delivery, have been attended to! I speak rather of the past, however, than the present. There is now a spirit of improvement abroad; but among those who were ordained twenty, thirty, forty years ago, the larger number, to judge by their performance, must have thought reading was reading, and preaching was preaching. It is different now. The subject is more justly considered. It is felt that distinctness and energy may have weight in recommending the most solid truths; and besides there is more general observation and taste, a more critical knowledge diffused than formerly; in every congregation there is a larger proportion who know a little of the matter, and who can judge and criticise.'

Edmund had already gone through the service once since his ordination; and upon this being understood, he had a variety of questions from Crawford as to his feelings and success; questions, which being made, though with the vivacity of friendly interest and quick taste, without any touch of that spirit of banter or air of levity which Edmund knew to be most offensive to Fanny, he had true pleasure in satisfying; and when Crawford proceeded to ask his opinion and give his own as to the properest manner in which particular passages in the service should be delivered, showing it to be a subject on which he had thought before, and thought with judgment, Edmund was still more and more pleased. This would be the way to Fanny's heart. She was not to be won by all that gallantry and wit and good-nature together could do; or at least, she would not be won by them nearly so soon, without the assistance of sentiment and feeling, and seriousness on serious subjects.

'Our liturgy,' observed Crawford, 'has beauties which not even a careless slovenly style of reading can destroy; but it has also redundancies and repetitions which require good reading not to be felt. For myself, at least, I must confess being not always so attentive as I ought to be' (here was a glance at Fanny); 'that nineteen times out of twenty, I am thinking how such a prayer ought to be read, and longing to have it to read myself. Did you speak?' stepping eagerly to Fanny, and addressing her in a softened voice; and upon her saying 'No,' he added, 'Are you sure you did not speak? I saw your lips move. I fancied you might be going to tell me I *ought* to be more attentive, and not *allow* my thoughts to wander. Are not you going to tell me so?'

'No, indeed, you know your duty too well for me to – even supposing—'

She stopped, felt herself getting into a puzzle, and could not be prevailed on to add another word, not by dint of several minutes of supplication and waiting. He then returned to his former station, and went on as if there had been no such tender interruption.

'A sermon, well delivered, is more uncommon even than prayers well read. A sermon, good in itself, is no rare thing. It is more difficult to speak well than to compose well; that is, the rules and trick of composition are often an object of study. A thoroughly good sermon, thoroughly well delivered, is a capital gratification. I can never hear such a one without the greatest admiration and respect, and more than half a mind to take orders and preach myself. There is some thing in the eloquence of the pulpit, when it is really eloquence, which is entitled to the highest praise and honour. The preacher who can touch and affect such a heterogeneous mass of hearers, on subjects limited, and long worn threadbare in all common hands; who can say any thing new or striking, any thing that rouses the attention, without offending the taste, or wearing out the feelings of his hearers, is a man whom one could not in his public capacity honour enough. I should like to be such a man.'

Edmund laughed.

'I should indeed. I never listened to a distinguished preacher in my life without a sort of envy. But then, I must have a London audience. I could not preach but to the educated; to those who were capable of estimating my composition. And I do not know that I should be fond of preaching often; now and then, perhaps, once or twice in the spring, after being anxiously expected for half-a-dozen Sundays together; but not for a constancy; it would not do for a constancy.'

Here Fanny who could not but listen, involuntarily shook her head, and Crawford was instantly by her side again, intreating to know her meaning; and as Edmund perceived, by his drawing in a chair, and sitting down close by her, that it was to be a very thorough attack, that looks and undertones were to be well tried, he sank as quietly as possible into a corner, turned his back, and took up a newspaper, very sincerely wishing that dear little Fanny might be persuaded into explaining away that shake of the head to the satisfaction of her ardent lover; and as earnestly trying to bury every sound of the business from himself in murmurs of his own, over the various advertisements of 'A most desirable Estate in South Wales;' 'To Parents and Guardians;' and a 'Capital season'd Hunter.'

Fanny meanwhile, vexed with herself for not having been as motionless as she was speechless, and grieved to the heart to see Edmund's arrangements, was trying by every thing in the power of her modest, gentle nature, to repulse Mr Crawford, and avoid both his looks and enquiries; and he, unrepulsable, was persisting in both.

'What did that shake of the head mean?' said he. 'What was it meant to express? Disapprobation, I fear. But of what? What had I been saying to displease you? Did you think me speaking improperly, lightly, irreverently on the subject? Only tell me if I was. Only tell me if I was wrong. I want to be set right. Nay, nay, I intreat you; for one moment put down your work. What did that shake of the head mean?'

In vain was her 'Pray, sir, don't; pray, Mr Crawford;' repeated twice over; and in vain did she try to move away. In the same low, eager voice, and the same close neighbourhood, he went on, re-urging the same questions as before. She grew more agitated and displeased.

'How can you, sir? You quite astonish me; I wonder how you can—'

'Do I astonish you?' said he. 'Do you wonder? Is there any thing in my present intreaty that you do not understand? I will explain to you instantly all that makes me urge you in this manner, all that gives me an interest in what you look and do, and excites my present curiosity. I will not leave you to wonder long.'

In spite of herself, she could not help half a smile, but she said nothing.

'You shook your head at my acknowledging that I should not like to engage in the duties of a clergyman always for a constancy. Yes, that was the word. Constancy: I am not afraid of the word. I would spell it, read it, write it with any body. I see nothing alarming in the word. Did you think I ought?'

'Perhaps, sir,' said Fanny, wearied at last into speaking; 'perhaps, sir, I thought it was a pity you did not always know yourself as well as you seemed to do at that moment.'

Crawford, delighted to get her to speak at any rate, was determined to keep it up; and poor Fanny, who had hoped to silence him by such an extremity of reproof, found herself sadly mistaken, and that it was only a change from one object of curiosity and one set of words to another. He had always something to intreat the explanation of. The opportunity was too fair. None such had occurred since his seeing her in her uncle's room, none such might occur again before his leaving Mansfield. Lady Bertram's being just on the other side of the table was a trifle, for she might always be considered as only half awake, and Edmund's advertisements were still of the first utility.

'Well,' said Crawford, after a course of rapid questions and reluctant answers; 'I am happier than I was, because I now understand more clearly your opinion of me. You think me unsteady; easily swayed by the whim of the moment, easily tempted, easily put aside. With such an opinion, no wonder that—But we shall see. It is not by protestations that I shall endeavour to convince you I am wronged; it is not by telling you that my affections are steady. My conduct shall speak for me; absence, distance, time shall speak for me. *They* shall prove that, as far as you can be deserved by any body, I do deserve you. You are infinitely my superior in merit; all *that* I know. You have qualities which I had not before supposed to exist in such a degree in any human creature. You have some touches of the angel in you beyond what – not merely beyond what one sees, because one never sees any thing like it – but beyond what one fancies might be. But still I am not frightened. It is not by equality of merit that you can be won. That is out of the question. It is he who sees and worships your merit the strongest, who loves you most devotedly, that has the best right to a return. There I build my confidence. By that right I do and will deserve you; and when once convinced that my attachment is what I declare it, I know you too well not to entertain the warmest hopes. Yes, dearest, sweetest Fanny. Nay –' (seeing her draw back displeased) – 'forgive me. Perhaps I have as yet no right; but by what other name can I call you? Do you suppose you are ever present to my imagination under any other? No, it is "Fanny" that I think of all day, and dream of all night. You have given the name such reality of sweetness, that nothing else can now be descriptive of you.'

Fanny could hardly have kept her seat any longer, or have refrained from at least trying to get away in spite of all the too public opposition she foresaw to it, had it not been for the sound of approaching relief, the very sound which she had been long watching for, and long thinking strangely delayed.

The solemn procession, headed by Baddeley, of teaboard, urn, and cake-bearers, made its appearance, and delivered her from a grievous imprisonment of body and mind. Mr Crawford was obliged to move. She was at liberty, she was busy, she was protected.

Edmund was not sorry to be admitted again among the number of those who might speak and hear. But though the conference had seemed full long to him, and though on looking at Fanny he saw rather a flush of vexation, he inclined to hope that so much could not have been said and listened to, without some profit to the speaker.

CHAPTER THIRTY FIVE

EDMUND HAD DETERMINED that it belonged entirely to Fanny to choose whether her situation with regard to Crawford should be mentioned between them or not; and that if she did not lead the way, it should never be touched on by him; but after a day or two of mutual reserve, he was induced by his father to change his mind, and try what his influence might do for his friend.

A day, and very early day, was actually fixed for the Crawford's departure; and Sir Thomas thought it might be as well to make one more effort for the young man before he left Mansfield, that all his professions and vows of unshaken attachment might have as much hope to sustain them as possible.

Sir Thomas was most cordially anxious for the perfection of Mr Crawford's character in that point. He wished him to be a model of constancy; and fancied the best means of effecting it would be by not trying him too long.

Edmund was not unwilling to be persuaded to engage in the business; he wanted to know Fanny's feelings. She had been used to consult him in every difficulty, and he loved her too well to bear to be denied her confidence now; he hoped to be of service to her, he thought he must be of service to her; whom else had she to open her heart to? If she did not need counsel, she must need the comfort of communication. Fanny estranged from him, silent, and reserved, was an unnatural state of things; a state which he must break through, and which he could easily learn to think she was wanting him to break through.

'I will speak to her, sir: I will take the first opportunity of speaking to her alone,' was the result of such thoughts as these; and upon Sir Thomas's information of her being at that very time walking alone in the shrubbery, he instantly joined her.

'I am come to walk with you, Fanny,' said he. 'Shall I?' Drawing her arm within his. 'It is a long while since we have had a comfortable walk together.'

She assented to it all rather by look than word. Her spirits were low.

'But, Fanny,' he presently added, 'in order to have a comfortable walk, something more is necessary than merely pacing this gravel together. You must talk to me. I know you have some thing on your mind. I know what you are thinking of. You cannot suppose me uninformed. Am I to hear of it from every body but Fanny herself?'

Fanny, at once agitated and dejected, replied, 'If you hear of it from every body, cousin, there can be nothing for me to tell.'

'Not of facts, perhaps; but of feelings, Fanny. No one but you can tell me them. I do not mean to press you, however. If it is not what you wish yourself, I have done. I had thought it might be a relief.'

'I am afraid we think too differently, for me to find any relief in talking of what I feel.'

'Do you suppose that we think differently? I have no idea of it. I dare say that on a comparison of our opinions, they would be found as much alike as they have been used to be: to the point – I consider Crawford's proposals as most advantageous and desirable, if you could return his affection. I consider it as most natural that all your family should wish you could return it; but that as you cannot, you have done exactly as you ought in refusing him. Can there be any disagreement between us here?'

'Oh, no! But I thought you blamed me. I thought you were against me. This is such a comfort!'

'This comfort you might have had sooner, Fanny, had you sought it. But how could you possibly suppose me against you? How could you imagine me an advocate for marriage without love? Were I even careless in general on such matters, how could you imagine me so where *your* happiness was at stake?'

'My uncle thought me wrong, and I knew he had been talking to you.'

'As far as you have gone, Fanny, I think you perfectly right. I may be sorry, I may be surprised: though hardly *that*, for you had not had time to attach yourself: but I think you perfectly right. Can it admit of a question? It is disgraceful to us if it does. You did not love him; nothing could have justified you accepting him.'

Fanny had not felt so comfortable for days and days.

'So far your conduct has been faultless, and they were quite mistaken who wished you to do otherwise. But the matter does not end here. Crawford's is no common attachment; he perseveres, with the hope of creating that regard which had not been created before. This, we know, must be a work of time. But' (with an affectionate smile) 'let him succeed at last, Fanny, let him succeed at last. You have proved yourself upright and disinterested, prove yourself grateful and tender-hearted; and then you will be the perfect model of a woman, which I have always believed you born for.'

'Oh! never, never, never! he never will succeed with me.' And as she spoke with a warmth which quite astonished Edmund, and which she blushed at the recollection of herself, when she saw his look, and heard him reply, 'Never! Fanny! so very determined and positive! This is not like yourself, your rational self.'

'I mean,' she cried, sorrowfully correcting herself, 'that I *think* I never shall, as far as the future can be answered for; I think I never shall return his regard.'

'I must hope better things. I am aware, more aware than Crawford can be, that the man who means to make you love him (you having due notice of his intentions) must have very up-hill work, for there are all your early attachments and habits in battle-array; and before he can get your heart for his own use he has to unfasten it from all the holds upon things animate and inanimate, which so many years' growth have confirmed, and which are considerably tightened for the moment by the very idea of separation. I know that the apprehension of being forced to quit Mansfield will for a time be arming you against him. I wish he had not been obliged to tell you what he was trying for. I wish he had known you as well as I do, Fanny. Between us, I think we should have won you. My theoretical and his practical knowledge together, could not have failed. He should have worked upon my plans. I must hope, however, that time proving him (as I firmly believe it will), to deserve you by his steady affection, will give him his reward. I cannot suppose that you have not the *wish* to love him – the natural wish of gratitude. You must have some feeling of that sort. You must be sorry for your own indifference.'

'We are so totally unlike,' said Fanny, avoiding a direct answer, 'we are so very, very different in all our inclinations and ways, that I consider it as quite impossible we should ever be tolerably happy together, even if I *could* like him. There never were two people more dissimilar. We have not one taste in common. We should be miserable.'

'You are mistaken, Fanny. The dissimilarity is not so strong. You are quite enough alike. You *have* tastes in common. You have moral and literary tastes in common. You have both warm hearts and benevolent feelings; and, Fanny, who that heard him read, and saw you listen to Shakespeare the other night, will think you unfitted as companions? You forget yourself: there is a decided difference in your tempers, I allow. He is lively, you are serious; but so much the better; his spirits will support yours. It is your disposition to be easily dejected and to fancy difficulties greater than they are. His cheerfulness will counteract this. He sees difficulties nowhere: and his pleasantness and gaiety will be a constant support to you. Your being so far unlike, Fanny, does not in the smallest degree make against the probability of your happiness together: do not imagine it. I am myself convinced that it is rather a favourable circumstance. I am perfectly persuaded that the tempers had better be unlike: I mean unlike in the flow of the spirits, in the manners, in the inclination for much or little company, in the propensity to talk or to be silent, to be grave or to be gay. Some opposition here is, I am thoroughly convinced, friendly to matrimonial happiness. I exclude extremes, of course; and a very close resemblance in all those points would be the likeliest way to produce an extreme. A counteraction, gentle and continual, is the best safeguard of manners and conduct.'

Full well could Fanny guess where his thoughts were now, Miss Crawford's power was all returning. He had been speaking of her cheerfully from the hour of his coming home. His avoiding her was quite at an end. He had dined at the Parsonage only the preceding day.

After leaving him to his happier thoughts for some minutes, Fanny, feeling it due to herself, returned to Mr Crawford, and said, 'It is not merely in *temper* that I consider him as totally unsuited to myself, though, in *that* respect, I think the difference between us too great, infinitely too great; his spirits often oppress me: but there is some thing in him which I object to still more. I must say, cousin, that I cannot approve his character. I have not thought well of him from the time of the play. I then saw him behaving, as it appeared to me, so very improperly and unfeelingly – I may speak of it now because it is all over – so improperly by poor Mr Rushworth, not seeming to care how he exposed or hurt him, and paying attentions to my cousin Maria, which – in short, at the time of the play, I received an impression which will never be got over.'

'My dear Fanny,' replied Edmund, scarcely hearing her to the end, 'let us not, any of us, be judged by what we appeared at that period of general folly. The time of the play is a time which I hate to recollect. Maria was wrong, Crawford was wrong, we were all wrong together; but none so wrong as myself. Compared with me, all the rest were blameless. I was playing the fool with my eyes open.'

'As a bystander,' said Fanny, 'perhaps I saw more than you did; and I do think that Mr Rushworth was sometimes very jealous.'

'Very possibly. No wonder. Nothing could be more improper than the whole business. I am shocked whenever I think that Maria could be capable of it; but, if she could undertake the part, we must not be surprised at the rest.'

'Before the play, I am much mistaken, if *Julia* did not think he was paying her attentions.'

'Julia! I have heard before from some one of his being in love with Julia; but I could never see any thing of it. And, Fanny, though I hope I do justice to my sisters' good qualities, I think it very possible that they might, one or both, be more desirous of being admired by Crawford, and might show that desire rather more unguardedly than was perfectly prudent. I can remember that they were evidently fond of his society; and with such encouragement, a man like Crawford, lively, and it may be, a little unthinking, might be led on to – There could be nothing very striking, because it is clear that he had no pretensions: his heart was reserved for you.

And I must say, that its being for you has raised him inconceivably in my opinion. It does him the highest honour; it shows his proper estimation of the blessing of domestic happiness and pure attachment. It proves him unspoilt by his uncle. It proves him, in short, every thing that I had been used to wish to believe him and feared he was not.'

'I am persuaded that he does not think, as he ought, on serious subjects.'

'Say, rather, that he has not thought at all upon serious subjects, which I believe to be a good deal the case. How could it be otherwise, with such an education and adviser? Under the disadvantages, indeed, which both have had, is it not wonderful that they should be what they are? Crawford's *feelings*, I am ready to acknowledge, have hitherto been too much his guides. Happily, those feelings have generally been good. You will supply the rest; and a most fortunate man he is to attach himself to such a creature – to a woman, who, firm as a rock in her own principles, has a gentleness of character so well adapted to recommend them. He has chosen his partner, indeed, with rare felicity; he will make you happy, Fanny; I know he will make you happy; but you will make him every thing.'

'I would not engage in such a charge,' cried Fanny, in a shrinking accent; 'in such an office of high responsibility!'

'As usual, believing yourself unequal to anything! fancying every thing too much for you! Well, though I may not be able to persuade you into different feelings, you will be persuaded into them, I trust. I confess myself sincerely anxious that you may. I have no common interest in Crawford's well-doing. Next to your happiness, Fanny, his has the first claim on me. You are aware of my having no common interest in Crawford.'

Fanny was too well aware of it to have any thing to say; and they walked on together some fifty yards in mutual silence and abstraction. Edmund first began again:—

'I was very much pleased by her manner of speaking of it yesterday, particularly pleased, because I had not depended upon her seeing every thing in so just a light. I knew she was very fond of you; but yet I was afraid of her not estimating your worth to her brother quite as it deserved, and of her regretting that he had not rather fixed on some woman of distinction or fortune. I was afraid of the bias of those worldly maxims which she has been too much used to hear. But it was very different. She spoke of you, Fanny, just as she ought. She desires the connection as warmly as your uncle or myself. We had a long talk about it. I should not have mentioned the subject, though very anxious to know her sentiments, but I had not been in the room five minutes before she began introducing it with all that openness of heart, and sweet peculiarity of manner, that spirit of ingenuousness which are so much a part of herself. Mrs Grant laughed at her for her rapidity.'

'Was Mrs Grant in the room, then?'

'Yes, when I reached the house I found the two sisters together by themselves; and when once we had begun, we had not done with you, Fanny, till Crawford and Dr Grant came in.'

'It is above a week since I saw Miss Crawford.'

'Yes, she laments it; yet owns it may have been best. You will see her, however, before she goes. She is very angry with you, Fanny; you must be prepared for that. She calls herself very angry, but you can imagine her anger. It is the regret and disappointment of a sister, who thinks her brother has a right to every thing he may wish for, at the first moment. She is hurt, as you would be for William; but she loves and esteems you with all her heart.'

'I knew she would be very angry with me.'

'My dearest Fanny,' cried Edmund, pressing her arm closer to him, 'do not let the idea of her anger distress you. It is anger to be talked of rather than felt. Her heart is made for love and kindness, not for resentment. I wish you could have overheard her tribute of praise; I wish you could have seen her countenance, when she said that you *should* be Henry's wife. And I observed that she always spoke of you as "Fanny," which she was never used to do; and it had a sound of most sisterly cordiality.'

'And Mrs Grant did she say – did she speak; was she there all the time?'

'Yes, she was agreeing exactly with her sister. The surprise of your refusal, Fanny, seems to have been unbounded. That you could refuse such a man as Henry Crawford, seems more than they can understand. I said what I could for you; but in good truth, as they stated the case – you must prove yourself to be in your senses as soon as you can, by a different conduct; nothing else will satisfy them. But this is teasing you. I have done. Do not turn away from me.'

'I *should* have thought,' said Fanny, after a pause of recollection and exertion, 'that every woman must have felt the possibility of a man's not being approved, not being loved by some one of her sex, at least, let him be ever so generally agreeable. Let him have all the perfections in the world, I think it ought not to be set down as certain that a man must be acceptable to every woman he may happen to like himself. But, even supposing it is so, allowing Mr Crawford to have all the claims which his sisters think he has, how was I to be prepared to meet him with any feeling answerable to his own? He took me wholly by surprise. I had not an idea that his behaviour to me before had any meaning; and surely I was not to be teaching myself to like him only because he was taking what seemed very idle notice of me. In my situation, it would have been the extreme of vanity to be forming expectations on Mr Crawford. I am sure his sisters, rating him as they do, must have thought it so, supposing he had meant nothing. How, then, was I to be – to be in love with him the moment he said he was with me? How was I to have an attachment at his service, as soon as it was asked for? His sisters should consider me as well as him. The higher his deserts, the more improper for me ever to have thought of him. And, and – we think very differently of the nature of women, if they can imagine a woman so very soon capable of returning an affection, as this seems to imply.'

'My dear, dear Fanny, now I have the truth. I know this to be the truth; and most worthy of you are such feelings. I had attributed them to you before. I thought I could understand you. You have now given exactly the explanation which I ventured to make for you to your friend and Mrs Grant, and they were both better satisfied, though your warm-hearted friend was still run away with a little by the enthusiasm of her fondness for Henry. I told them, that you were of all human creatures the one over whom habit had most power and novelty least; and that the very circumstance of the novelty of Crawford's addresses was against him. Their being so new and so recent was all in their disfavour; that you could tolerate nothing that you were not used to; and a great deal more to the same purpose, to give them a knowledge of your character. Miss Crawford made us laugh by her plans of encouragement for her brother. She meant to urge him to persevere in the hope of being loved in time, and of having his addresses most kindly received at the end of about ten years' happy marriage.'

Fanny could with difficulty give the smile that was here asked for. Her feelings were all in revolt. She feared she had been doing wrong: saying too much, overacting the caution which she had been fancying necessary; in guarding against one evil, laying herself open to another; and to have Miss Crawford's liveliness repeated to her at such a moment, and on such a subject, was a bitter aggravation.

Edmund saw weariness and distress in her face, and immediately resolved to forbear all further discussion; and not even to mention the name of Crawford again, except as it might be connected with what *must* be agreeable to her. On this principle, he soon afterwards observed—

'They go on Monday. You are sure, therefore, of seeing your friend either to-morrow or Sunday. They really go on Monday; and I was within a trifle of being persuaded to stay at Lessingby till that very day! I had almost promised it. What a difference it might have made! Those five or six days more at Lessingby might have been felt all my life.'

'You were near staying there?'

'Very. I was most kindly pressed, and had nearly consented. Had I received any letter from Mansfield, to tell me how you were all going on, I believe I should certainly have stayed; but I knew nothing that had happened here for a fortnight, and felt that I had been away long enough.'

'You spent your time pleasantly there?'

'Yes; that is, it was the fault of my own mind if I did not. They were all very pleasant. I doubt their finding me so. I took uneasiness with me, and there was no getting rid of it till I was in Mansfield again.'

'The Miss Owens – you liked them, did not you?'

'Yes, very well. Pleasant, good-humoured, unaffected girls. But I am spoilt, Fanny, for common female society. Good-humoured, unaffected girls will not do for a man who has been used to sensible women. They are two distinct orders of being. You and Miss Crawford have made me too nice.'

Still, however, Fanny was oppressed and wearied; he saw it in her looks, it could not be talked away; and in attempting it no more, he led her directly, with the kind authority of a privileged guardian, into the house.

CHAPTER THIRTY SIX

EDMUND NOW BELIEVED himself perfectly acquainted with all that Fanny could tell, or could leave to be conjectured of her sentiments, and he was satisfied. It had been, as he before presumed, too hasty a measure on Crawford's side, and time must be given to make the idea first familiar, and then agreeable to her. She must be used to the consideration of his being in love with her, and then a return of affection might not be very distant.

He gave this opinion as the result of the conversation to his father; and recommended there being nothing more said to her: no further attempts to influence or persuade; but that every thing should be left to Crawford's assiduities, and the natural workings of her own mind.

Sir Thomas promised that it should be so. Edmund's account of Fanny's disposition he could believe to be just; he supposed she had all those feelings, but he must consider it as very unfortunate that she *had*; for, less willing than his son to trust to the future, he could not help fearing that if such very long allowances of time and habit were necessary for her, she might not have persuaded herself into receiving his addresses properly, before the young man's inclination for paying them were over. There was nothing to be done, however, but to submit quietly and hope the best.

The promised visit from 'her friend,' as Edmund called Miss Crawford, was a formidable threat to Fanny, and she lived in continual terror of it. As a sister, so partial and so angry, and so little scrupulous of what she said, and in another light so triumphant and secure, she was in every way an object of painful alarm. Her displeasure, her penetration and her happiness were all fearful to encounter; and the dependence of having others present when they met, was Fanny's only support in looking forward to it. She absented herself as little as possible from Lady Bertram, kept away from the East Room, and took no solitary walk in the shrubbery, in her caution to avoid any sudden attack.

She succeeded. She was safe in the breakfast-room, with her aunt, when Miss Crawford did come; and the first misery over, and Miss Crawford looking and speaking with much less particularity of expression than she had anticipated, Fanny began to hope there would be nothing worse to be endured than an half hour of moderate agitation. But here she hoped too much; Miss Crawford was not the slave of opportunity. She was determined to see Fanny alone, and therefore said to her tolerably soon, in a low voice, 'I must speak to you for a few minutes some where;' words that Fanny felt all over her, in all her pulses and all her nerves. Denial was impossible. Her habits of ready submission, on the contrary, made her almost instantly rise and lead the way out of the room. She did it with wretched feelings, but it was inevitable.

They were no sooner in the hall than all restraint of countenance was over on Miss Crawford's side. She immediately shook her head at Fanny with arch, yet affectionate reproach, and taking her hand, seemed hardly able to help beginning directly. She said nothing, however, but, 'Sad, sad, girl! I do not know when I shall have done scolding you,' and had discretion enough to reserve the rest till they might be secure of having four walls to themselves. Fanny naturally turned upstairs, and took her guest to the apartment which was now always fit for comfortable use; opening the door, however, with a most aching heart, and feeling that she had a more distressing scene before her than ever that spot had yet witnessed. But the evil ready to burst on her, was at least delayed by the sudden change in Miss Crawford's ideas; by the strong effect on her mind which the finding herself in the East Room again produced.

'Ha!' she cried, with instant animation, 'am I here again? The East Room! Once only was I in this room before;' and after stopping to look about her, and seemingly to retrace all that had then passed, she added, 'once only before. Do you remember it? I came to rehearse. Your cousin came too; and we had a rehearsal. You were our audience and prompter. A delightful rehearsal. I shall never forget it. Here we were, just in this part of the room; here was your cousin, here was I, here were the chairs. Oh! why will such things ever pass away?'

Happily for her companion, she wanted no answer. Her mind was entirely self-engrossed. She was in a reverie of sweet remembrances.

'The scene we were rehearsing was so very remarkable! The subject of it so very – very – what shall I say? He was to be describing and recommending matrimony to me. I think I see him now, trying to be as demure and composed as Anhalt ought, through the two long speeches. "When

She said nothing but, 'Sad, sad, girl'

two sympathetic hearts meet in the marriage state, matrimony may be called a happy life." I suppose no time can ever wear out the impression I have of his looks and voice as he said those words. It was curious, very curious that we should have such a scene to play! If I had the power of recalling any one week of my existence, it should be that week – that acting week. Say what you would, Fanny, it should be *that*; for I never knew such exquisite happiness in any other. His sturdy spirit to bend as it did! Oh! it was sweet beyond expression. But alas, that very evening destroyed it all. That very evening brought your most unwelcome uncle. Poor Sir Thomas, who was glad to see you? Yet, Fanny, do not imagine I would now speak disrespectfully of Sir Thomas, though I certainly did hate him for many a week. No, I do him justice now. He is just what the head of such a family should be. Nay, in sober sadness, I believe I now love you all.' And having said so, with a degree of tenderness and consciousness which Fanny had never seen in her before, and now thought only too becoming, she turned away for a moment to recover herself. 'I have had a little fit since I came into this room, as you may perceive,' said she presently, with a playful smile, 'but it is over now; so let us sit down and be comfortable; for as to scolding you, Fanny, which I came fully intending to do, I have not the heart for it when it comes to the point.' And embracing her very affectionately, 'Good, gentle Fanny! when I think of this being the last time of seeing you for I do not know how long, I feel it quite impossible to do any thing but love you.'

Fanny was affected. She had not foreseen any thing of this, and her feelings could seldom withstand the melancholy influence of the word 'last.' She cried as if she had loved Miss Crawford more than she possibly could; and Miss Crawford, yet further softened by the sight of such emotion, hung about her with fondness, and said, 'I hate to leave you. I shall see no one half so amiable where I am going. Who says we shall not be sisters? I know we shall. I feel that we are born to be connected; and those tears convince me that you feel it too, dear Fanny.'

Fanny roused herself, and replying only in part, said, 'But you are only going from one set of friends to another. You are going to a very particular friend.'

'Yes, very true. Mrs Fraser has been my intimate friend for years. But I have not the least inclination to go near her. I can think only of the friends I am leaving; my excellent sister, yourself, and the Bertrams in general. You have all so much more *heart* among you than one finds in the world at large. You all give me a feeling of being able to trust and confide in you, which in common intercourse one knows nothing of. I wish I had settled with Mrs Fraser not to go to her till after Easter, a much better time for the visit, but now I cannot put her off. And when I have done with her, I must go to her sister, Lady Stornaway, because *she* was rather my most particular friend of the two, but I have not cared much for *her* these three years.'

After this speech the two girls sat many minutes silent, each thoughtful; Fanny meditating on the different sorts of friendship in the world, Mary on something of less philosophic tendency. *She* first spoke again.

'How perfectly I remember my resolving to look for you upstairs, and setting off to find my way to the East Room, without having an idea whereabouts it was! How well I remember what I was thinking of as I came along, and my looking in and seeing you here sitting at this table at work; and then your cousin's astonishment, when he opened the door, at seeing me here! To be sure, your uncle's returning that very evening! there never was any thing quite like it.'

Another short fit of abstraction followed, when, shaking it off, she thus attacked her companion.

'Why, Fanny, you are absolutely in a reverie. Thinking, I hope, of one who is always thinking of you. Oh! that I could transport you for a short time into our circle in town, that you might understand how your power over Henry is thought of there! Oh! the envyings and heart-burnings of dozens and dozens; the wonder, the incredulity that will be felt at hearing what you have done! For as to secrecy, Henry is quite the hero of an old romance, and glories in his chains. You should come to London to know how to estimate your conquest. If you were to see how he is courted, and how I am courted for his sake! Now, I am well aware that I shall not be half so welcome to Mrs Fraser in consequence of his situation with you. When she comes to know the truth she will, very likely, wish me in Northamptonshire again; for there is a daughter of Mr Fraser, by a first wife, whom she is wild to get married, and wants Henry to take. Oh! she has been trying for him to such a degree. Innocent and quiet as you sit here you cannot have an idea of the *sensation* that you will be occasioning, of the curiosity there will be to see you, of the endless questions I shall have to answer! Poor Margaret Fraser will be at me for ever about your eyes and your teeth, and how you do your hair, and who makes your shoes. I wish Margaret were married, for my poor friend's sake, for I look upon the Frasers to be about as unhappy as most other married people. And yet it was a most desirable match for Janet at the time. We were all delighted. She could not do otherwise than accept him, for he was rich, and she had nothing; but he turns out ill-tempered and exigeant, and wants a young woman, a beautiful young woman of five-and twenty, to be as steady as himself. And my friend does not manage him well; she does not seem to know how to make the best of it. There is a spirit of irritation which, to say nothing worse, is certainly very ill-bred. In their house I shall call to mind the conjugal manners of Mansfield Parsonage with respect. Even Dr Grant does show a thorough confidence in my sister, and a certain consideration for her judgment, which makes one feel there *is* attachment; but of that I shall see nothing with the Frasers. I shall be at Mansfield for ever, Fanny. My own sister as a wife, Sir Thomas Bertram as a husband, are my standards of perfection. Poor Janet has been sadly taken in, and yet there was nothing improper on her side; she did not run into the match inconsiderately; there was no want of foresight. She took three days to consider of his proposals, and during those three days asked the advice of every body connected with her whose opinion was worth having, and especially applied to my late dear aunt, whose knowledge of the world made her judgment very generally and deservedly looked up to by all the young people of her acquaintance, and she was decidedly in favour of Mr Fraser. This seems as if nothing were a security for matrimonial comfort. I have not so much to say for my friend Flora, who jilted a very nice young man in the Blues for the sake of that horrid Lord Stornaway, who has about as much sense, Fanny, as Mr Rushworth, but much worse looking, and with a blackguard character. I *had* my doubts at the time about her being right, for he has not even the air of a gentleman, and now I am sure she was wrong. By-the-bye, Flora Ross was dying for Henry the first winter she came out. But were I to attempt to tell you of all the women whom I have known to be in love with him, I should never have done. It is you, only you, insensible Fanny, who can think of him with any thing like indifference. But are you so insensible as you profess yourself? No, no, I see you are not.'

There was indeed so deep a blush over Fanny's face at that moment, as might warrant strong suspicion in a predisposed mind.

'Excellent creature! I will not tease you. Every thing shall take its course. But, dear Fanny, you must allow that you were not so absolutely unprepared to have the question asked as your cousin fancies. It is not possible but that you must have had some thoughts on the subject, some surmises as to what might be. You must have seen that he was trying to please you by every attention in his power. Was not he devoted to you at the ball? And then before the ball, the necklace! Oh! you received it just as it was meant. You were as conscious as heart could desire. I remember it perfectly.'

'Do you mean, then, that your brother knew of the necklace beforehand? Oh! Miss Crawford, *that* was not fair.'

'Knew of it! It was his own doing entirely, his own thought. I am ashamed to say that it had never entered my head, but I was delighted to act on his proposal for both your sakes.'

'I will not say,' replied Fanny, 'that I was not half afraid at the time of its being so, for there was some thing in your look that frightened me – but not at first – I was as unsuspicious of it at first – indeed, indeed I was. It is as true as that I sit here. And had I had an idea of it, nothing should have induced me to accept the necklace. As to your brother's behaviour, certainly I was sensible of a particularity; I had been sensible of it some little time, perhaps two or three weeks, but then I considered it as meaning nothing; I put it down as simply being his way, and was as far from supposing as from wishing him to have any serious thoughts of me. I had not, Miss Crawford, been an inattentive observer of what was passing between him and some part of this family in the summer and autumn. I was quiet, but I was not blind. I could not but see that Mr Crawford allowed himself in gallantries which did mean nothing.'

'Ah! I cannot deny it. He has now and then been a sad flirt, and cared very little for the havoc he might be making in young ladies' affections. I have often scolded him for it, but it is his only fault; and there is this to be said, that very few young ladies have any affections worth caring for. And then, Fanny, the glory of fixing one who has been shot at by so many; of having it in one's power to pay off the debts of one's sex! Oh! I am sure it is not in woman's nature to refuse such a triumph.'

Fanny shook her head. 'I cannot think well of a man who sports with any woman's feelings; and there may often be a great deal more suffered than a stander-by can judge of.'

'I do not defend him. I leave him entirely to your mercy, and when he has got you at Everingham I do not care how much you lecture him. But this I will say, that his fault, the liking to make girls a little in love with him, is not half so dangerous to a wife's happiness, as a tendency to fall in love himself, which he has never been addicted to. And I do seriously and truly believe that he is attached to you in a way that he never was to any woman before; that he loves you with all his heart, and will love you as nearly for ever as possible. If any man ever loved a woman for ever, I think Henry will do so much for you.'

Fanny could not avoid a faint smile, but had nothing to say.

'I cannot imagine Henry ever to have been happier,' continued Mary, presently, 'than when he had succeeded in getting your brother's commission.'

She had made a sure push at Fanny's feelings here.

'Oh! yes. How very, very kind of him.'

'I know he must have exerted himself very much, for I know the parties he had to move. The Admiral hates trouble, and scorns asking favours; and there are so many young men's claims to be attended to in the same way, that a friendship and energy, not very determined, is easily put by. What a happy creature William must be! I wish we could see him.'

Poor Fanny's mind was thrown into the most distressing of all its varieties. The recollection of what had been done for William was always the most powerful disturber of every decision against Mr Crawford; and she sat thinking deeply of it till Mary, who had been first watching her complacently, and then musing on some thing else, suddenly called her attention by saying: 'I should like to sit talking with you here all day, but we must not forget the ladies below, and so good-bye, my dear, my amiable, my excellent Fanny, for though we shall nominally part in the breakfast parlour, I must take leave of you here. And I do take leave, longing for a happy re-union, and trusting that when we meet again it will be under circumstances which may open our hearts to each other, without any remnant or shadow of reserve.'

A very, very kind embrace, and some agitation of manner, accompanied these words.

'I shall see your cousin in town soon: he talks of being there tolerably soon; and Sir Thomas, I dare say, in the course of the spring; and your eldest cousin, and the Rushworths, and Julia, I am sure of meeting again and again, and all but you. I have two favours to ask, Fanny: one is your correspondence. You must write to me. And the other, that you will often call on Mrs Grant, and make her amends for my being gone.'

The first, at least, of these favours Fanny would rather not have been asked; but it was impossible for her to refuse the correspondence; it was impossible for her even not to accede to it more readily than her own judgment authorised. There was no resisting so much apparent affection. Her disposition was peculiarly calculated to value a fond treatment, and from having hitherto known so little of it, she was the more overcome by Miss Crawford's. Besides, there was gratitude towards her, for having made their *tête-à-tête* so much less painful than her fears had predicted.

It was over, and she had escaped without reproaches and without detection. Her secret was still her own; and while that was the case, she thought she could resign herself to almost every thing.

In the evening there was another parting. Henry Crawford came and sat some time with them; and her spirits not being previously in the strongest state, her heart was softened for a while towards him, because he really seemed to feel. Quite unlike his usual self, he scarcely said any thing. He was evidently oppressed, and Fanny must grieve for him, though hoping she might never see him again, till he were the husband of some other woman.

When it came to the moment of parting, he would take her hand, he would not be denied it; he said nothing, however, or nothing that she heard, and when he had left the room, she was better pleased that such a token of friendship had passed.

On the morrow the Crawfords were gone.

CHAPTER THIRTY SEVEN

MR CRAWFORD GONE, SIR THOMAS'S next object was that he should be missed; and he entertained great hope that his niece would find a blank in the loss of those attentions which at the time she had felt, or fancied, an evil. She had tasted of consequence in its most flattering form; and he did hope that the loss of it, the sinking again into nothing, would awaken very wholesome regrets in her mind. He watched her with this idea; but he could hardly tell with what success. He hardly knew whether there were any difference in her spirits or not. She was always so gentle and retiring, that her emotions were beyond his discrimination. He did not understand her; he felt that he did not; and therefore applied to Edmund to tell him how she stood affected on the present occasion, and whether she were more or less happy than she had been.

Edmund did not discern any symptoms of regret, and thought his father a little unreasonable in supposing the first three or four days could produce any.

What chiefly surprised Edmund was, that Crawford's sister, the friend and companion, who had been so much to her, should not be more visibly regretted. He wondered that Fanny spoke so seldom of *her*, and had so little voluntarily to say of her concern at this separation.

Alas! it was this sister, this friend and companion, who was now the chief bane of Fanny's comfort. If she could have believed Mary's future fate as unconnected with Mansfield as she was determined the brother's should be, if she could have hoped her return thither to be as distant as she was much inclined to think his, she would have been light of heart indeed; but the more she recollected and observed, the more deeply was she convinced that every thing was now in a fairer train for Miss Crawford's marrying Edmund than it had ever been before. On his side the inclination was stronger, on hers less equivocal. His objections, the scruples of his integrity, seemed all done away, nobody could tell how, and the doubts and hesitations of her ambition were equally got over; and equally without apparent reason. It could only be imputed to increasing attachment. His good and her bad feelings yielded to love, and such love must unite them. He was to go to town, as soon as some business relative to Thornton Lacey were completed, perhaps within a fortnight; he talked of going, he loved to talk of it; and when once with her again, Fanny could not doubt the rest. Her acceptance must be as certain as his offer; and yet there were bad feelings still remaining which made the prospect of it most sorrowful to her, independently, she believed, independently of self.

In their very last conversation, Miss Crawford, in spite of some amiable sensations, and much personal kindness, had still been Miss Crawford; still shown a mind led astray and bewildered, and without any suspicion of being so, darkened, yet fancying itself light. She might love, but she did not deserve Edmund by any other sentiment. Fanny believed there was scarcely a second feeling in common between them; and she may be forgiven by older sages for looking on the chance of Miss Crawford's future improvement as nearly desperate, for thinking that if Edmund's influence in this season of love had already done so little in clearing her judgment, and regulating her notions, his worth would be finally wasted on her even in years of matrimony.

Experience might have hoped more for any young people so circumstanced, and impartiality would not have denied to Miss Crawford's nature that participation of the general nature of women which would lead her to adopt the opinions of the man she loved and respected as her own. But as such were Fanny's persuasions, she suffered very much from them, and could never speak of Miss Crawford without pain.

Sir Thomas, meanwhile, went on with his own hopes, and his own observations, still feeling a right, by all his knowledge of human nature, to expect to see the effect of the loss of power and consequence on his niece's spirits, and the past attentions of the lover producing a craving for their return; and he was soon afterwards able to account for his not yet completely and indubitably seeing all this, by the prospect of another visitor, whose approach he could allow to be quite enough to support the spirits he was watching. William had obtained a ten days' leave of absence, to be given to Northamptonshire, and was coming, the happiest of lieutenants, because the latest made, to show his happiness and describe his uniform.

He came; and he would have been delighted to show his uniform there too, had not cruel custom prohibited its appearance except on duty. So the uniform remained at Portsmouth, and Edmund conjectured that before Fanny had any chance of seeing it, all its own freshness and all the freshness of its wearer's feelings must be worn away. It would be sunk into a badge of disgrace; for what can be more unbecoming, or more worthless, than the uniform of a lieutenant, who has been a lieutenant a year or two, and sees others made commanders before him? So reasoned Edmund, till his father made him the confidant of a scheme which placed Fanny's chance of seeing the second lieutenant of H.M.S. 'Thrush' in all his glory in another light.

This scheme was that she should accompany her brother back to Portsmouth, and spend a little time with her own family. It had occurred to Sir Thomas, in one of his dignified musings, as a right and desirable measure; but before he absolutely made up his mind, he consulted his son. Edmund considered it every way, and saw nothing but what was right. The thing was good in itself, and could not be done at a better time; and he had no doubt of it being highly agreeable to Fanny. This was enough to determine Sir Thomas; and a decisive 'then so it shall be' closed that stage of the business; Sir Thomas retiring from it with some feelings of satisfaction, and views of good over and above what he had communicated to his son; for his prime motive in sending her away had very little to do with the propriety of her seeing her parents again, and nothing at all with any idea of making her happy. He certainly wished her to go willingly, but he as certainly wished her to be heartily sick of home before her visit ended; and that a little abstinence from the elegancies and luxuries of Mansfield Park would bring her mind into a sober state, and incline her to a juster estimate of the value of that home of greater permanence, and equal comfort, of which she had the offer.

It was a medicinal project upon his niece's understanding, which he must consider as at present diseased. A residence of eight or nine years in the abode of wealth and plenty had a little disordered her powers of comparing and judging. Her father's house would, in all probability, teach her the value of a good income; and he trusted that she would be the wiser and happier woman, all her life, for the experiment he had devised.

Had Fanny been at all addicted to raptures, she must have had a strong attack of them when she first understood what was intended, when her uncle first made her the offer of visiting the parents, and brothers, and sisters, from whom she had been divided, almost half her life; of returning for a couple of months to the scenes of her infancy, with William for the protector and companion of her journey, and the certainty of continuing to see William to the last hour of his remaining on land. Had she ever given way to bursts of delight, it must have been then, for she was delighted, but her happiness was of a quiet, deep, heart-swelling sort, and though never a great talker, she was always more inclined to silence when feeling most strongly. At the moment she could only thank and accept. Afterwards, when familiarised with the visions of enjoyment so suddenly opened, she could speak more largely to William and Edmund of what she felt; but still there were emotions of tenderness that could not be clothed in words. The remembrance of all her earliest pleasures, and of what she had suffered in being torn from them, came over her with renewed strength, and it seemed as if to be at home again would heal every pain that had since grown out of the separation. To be in the centre of such a circle, loved by so many, and more loved by all than she had ever been before; to feel affection without fear or restraint; to feel herself the equal of those who surrounded her; to be at peace from all mention of the Crawfords, safe from every look which could be fancied a reproach on their account – this was a prospect to be dwelt on with a fondness that could be but half acknowledged.

Edmund, too – to be two months from *him*, and perhaps, she might be allowed to make her absence three, must do her good. At a distance, unassailed by his looks or his kindness, and safe from the perpetual irritation of knowing his heart, and striving to avoid his confidence, she should be able to reason herself into a proper state; she should be able to think of him as in London, and arranging every thing there, without wretchedness. What might have been hard to bear at Mansfield was to become a slight evil at Portsmouth.

The only drawback was the doubt of her Aunt Bertram's being comfortable without her. She was of use to no one else; but *there* she might be missed to a degree that she did not like to think of; and that part of the arrangement was, indeed, the hardest for Sir Thomas to accomplish, and what only *he* could have accomplished at all.

But he was master at Mansfield Park. When he had really resolved on any measure, he could always carry it through; and now by dint of long talking on the subject, explaining and dwelling on the duty of Fanny's some times seeing her family, he did induce his wife to let her go; obtaining it rather from submission, however, than conviction, for Lady Bertram was convinced of very little more than that Sir Thomas thought Fanny ought to go, and therefore that she must. In the calmness of her own dressing-room, in the impartial flow of her own meditations, unbiassed by his bewildering statements, she could not acknowledge any necessity for Fanny's ever going near a father and mother who had done without her so long, while she was so useful to herself. And as to the not missing her, which under Mrs Norris's discussion was the point attempted to be proved, she set herself very steadily against admitting any such thing.

Sir Thomas had appealed to her reason, conscience and dignity. He called it a sacrifice, and demanded it of her goodness and self-command as such. But Mrs Norris wanted to persuade her that Fanny could be very well spared (*she* being ready to give up all her own time to her as requested) and in short, could not really be wanted or missed.

'That may be, sister,' was all Lady Bertram's reply. 'I dare say you are very right; but I am sure I shall miss her very much.'

The next step was to communicate with Portsmouth. Fanny wrote to offer herself; and her mother's answer, though short, was so kind – a few simple lines expressed so natural and motherly a joy in the prospect of seeing her child again, as to confirm all the daughter's views of happiness in being with her – convincing her that she should now find a warm and affectionate friend in the 'mamma' who had certainly shown no remarkable fondness for her formerly; but this she could easily suppose to have been her own fault or her own fancy. She had probably alienated love by the helplessness and fretfulness of a fearful temper, or been unreasonable in wanting a larger share than any one among so many could deserve. Now, when she knew better how to be useful, and how to forbear, and when her mother could be no longer occupied by the incessant demands of a house full of little children, there would be leisure and inclination for every comfort, and they should soon be what mother and daughter ought to be to each other.

William was almost as happy in the plan as his sister. It would be the greatest pleasure to him to have her there to the last moment before he sailed, and perhaps find her there still when he came in from his first cruise. And besides, he wanted her so very much to see the 'Thrush' before she went out of harbour (the 'Thrush' was certainly the finest sloop in the service); and there were several improvements in the dockyard, too, which he quite longed to show her.

He did not scruple to add, that her being at home for a while would be a great advantage to every body.

'I do not know how it is,' said he; 'but we seem to want some of your nice ways and orderliness at my father's. The house is always in confusion. You will set things going in a better way, I am sure. You will tell my mother how it all ought to be, and you will be so useful to Susan, and you will teach Betsey, and make the boys love and mind you. How right and comfortable it will all be!'

By the time Mrs Price's answer arrived, there remained but a very few days more to be spent at Mansfield; and for part of one of those days, the young travellers were in a good deal of alarm on the subject of their journey, for when the mode of it came to be talked of, and Mrs Norris found that all her anxiety to save her brother-in-law's money was vain, and that in spite of her wishes and hints for a less expensive conveyance of Fanny, they were to travel post; when she saw Sir Thomas actually give William notes for the purpose, she was struck with the idea of there being room for a third in the carriage, and suddenly seized with a strong inclination to go with them, to go and see her poor dear sister Price. She proclaimed her thoughts. She must say that she had more than half a mind to go with the young people; it would be such an indulgence to her; she had not seen her poor dear sister Price for more than twenty years; and it would be a help to the young people in their journey to have her older head to manage for them; and she could not help thinking her poor dear sister Price would feel it very unkind of her not to come by such an opportunity.

William and Fanny were horror-struck at the idea.

All the comfort of their comfortable journey would be destroyed at once. With woeful countenances they looked at each other. Their suspense lasted an hour or two. No one interfered to encourage or dissuade. Mrs Norris was left to settle the matter by herself; and it ended, to the infinite joy of her nephew and niece, in the recollection that she could not possibly be spared from Mansfield Park at present; that she was a great deal too necessary to Sir Thomas and Lady Bertram for her to be able to answer it to herself to leave them even for a week, and therefore must certainly sacrifice every other pleasure to that of being useful to them.

It had, in fact, occurred to her, that though taken to Portsmouth for nothing, it would be hardly possible for her to avoid paying her own expenses back again. So her poor dear sister Price was left to all the disappointment of her missing such an opportunity, and another twenty years' absence, perhaps, begun.

Edmund's plans were affected by this Portsmouth journey, this absence of Fanny's. He, too, had a sacrifice to make to Mansfield Park as well as his aunt. He had intended, about this time, to be going to London; but he could not leave his father and mother just when every body else of most importance to their comfort was leaving them; and with an effort, felt but

William and Fanny were horror-struck at the idea

not boasted of, he delayed for a week or two longer a journey which he was looking forward to with the hope of its fixing his happiness for ever.

He told Fanny of it. She knew so much already, that she must know every thing. It made the substance of one other confidential discourse about Miss Crawford; and Fanny was the more affected from feeling it to be the last time in which Miss Crawford's name would ever be mentioned between them with any remains of liberty. Once afterwards she was alluded to by him. Lady Bertram had been telling her niece in the evening to write to her soon and often, and promising to be a good correspondent herself; and Edmund, at a convenient moment, then added in a whisper, 'And *I* shall write to you, Fanny, when I have any thing worth writing about, any thing to say that I think you will like to hear, and that you will not hear so soon from any other quarter.' Had she doubted his meaning while she listened, the glow in his face, when she looked up at him, would have been decisive.

For this letter she must try to arm herself. That a letter from Edmund should be a subject of terror! She began to feel that she had not yet gone through all the changes of opinion and sentiment which the progress of time and variation of circumstances occasion in this world of changes. The vicissitudes of the human mind had not yet been exhausted by her.

Poor Fanny! Though going as she did willingly and eagerly, the last evening at Mansfield Park must still be wretchedness. Her heart was completely sad at parting. She had tears for every room in the house, much more for every beloved inhabitant. She clung to her aunt, because she would miss her; she kissed the hand of her uncle with struggling sobs, because she had displeased him; and as for Edmund, she could neither speak, nor look, nor think, when the last moment came with *him*; and it was not till it was over that she knew he was giving her the affectionate farewell of a brother.

All this passed overnight, for the journey was to begin very early in the morning; and when the small, diminished party met at breakfast, William and Fanny were talked of as already advanced one stage.

CHAPTER THIRTY EIGHT

THE NOVELTY OF TRAVELLING, and the happiness of being with William, soon produced their natural effect on Fanny's spirits, when Mansfield Park was fairly left behind; and by the time their first stage was ended, and they were to quit Sir Thomas's carriage, she was able to take leave of the old coachman, and send back proper messages, with cheerful looks.

Of pleasant talk between the brother and sister there was no end.

Every thing supplied an amusement to the high glee of William's mind, and he was full of frolic and joke in the intervals of their higher-toned subjects, all of which ended, if they did not begin, in praise of the 'Thrush,' conjectures how she would be employed, schemes for an action with some superior force, which (supposing the first lieutenant out of the way, and William was not very merciful to the first lieutenant) was to give himself the next step as soon as possible, or speculations upon prize-money, which was to be generously distributed at home, with only the reservation of enough to make the little cottage comfortable, in which he and Fanny were to pass all their middle and later life together.

Fanny's immediate concerns, as far as they involved Mr Crawford, made no part of their conversation. William knew what had passed, and from his heart lamented that his sister's feelings should be so cold towards a man whom he must consider as the first of human characters; but he was of an age to be all for love, and therefore unable to blame; and knowing her wish on the subject, he would not distress her by the slightest allusion.

She had reason to suppose herself not yet forgotten by Mr Crawford. She had heard repeatedly from his sister within the three weeks which had passed since their leaving Mansfield, and in each letter there had been a few lines from himself, warm and determined like his speeches. It was a correspondence which Fanny found quite as unpleasant as she had feared. Miss Crawford's style of writing, lively and affectionate, was itself an evil, independent of what she was thus forced into reading from the brother's pen, for Edmund would never rest till she had read the chief of the letter to him; and then she had to listen to his admiration of her language, and the warmth of her attachments. There had, in fact, been so much of message, of allusion, of recollection, so much of Mansfield in every letter, that Fanny could not but suppose it meant for him to hear; and to find herself forced into a purpose of that kind, compelled into a correspondence which was bringing her the addresses of the man she did not love, and obliging her to administer to the adverse passion of the man she did, was cruelly mortifying. Here, too, her present removal promised advantage. When no longer under the same roof with Edmund, she trusted that Miss Crawford would have no motive for writing strong enough to overcome the trouble, and that at Portsmouth their correspondence would dwindle into nothing.

With such thoughts as these, among ten hundred others, Fanny proceeded in her journey safely and cheerfully, and as expeditiously as could rationally be hoped in the dirty month of February. They entered Oxford, but she could take only a hasty glimpse of Edmund's college as they passed along, and made no stop any where, till they reached Newbury, where a comfortable meal uniting dinner and supper, wound up the enjoyments and fatigues of the day.

The next morning saw them off again at an early hour; and with no events, and no delays, they regularly advanced, and were in the environs of Portsmouth while there was yet daylight for Fanny to look around her, and wonder at the new buildings. They passed the drawbridge, and entered the town; and the light was only beginning to fail, as, guided by William's powerful voice, they were rattled into a narrow street, leading from the High Street, and drawn up before the door of a small house now inhabited by Mr Price.

Fanny was all agitation and flutter; all hope and apprehension. The moment they stopped, a trollopy-looking maidservant, seemingly in waiting for them at the door, stepped forward, and more intent on telling the news than giving them any help, immediately began with 'The "Thrush" is gone out of harbour, please, sir, and one of the officers has been here to—' She was interrupted by a fine tall boy of eleven years old, who, rushing out of the house, pushed the maid aside, and while William was opening the chaise-door himself, called out, 'You are just in time. We have been looking for you this half-hour. The "Thrush" went out of harbour this morning. I saw her. It was a beautiful sight. And they think she will have her orders in a day or two. And Mr Campbell was here at four o'clock to ask for you: he has got one of the "Thrush's" boats, and is going off to her at six, and hoped you would be here in time to go with him.'

A stare or two at Fanny, as William helped her out of the carriage, was all the voluntary notice which this brother bestowed: but he made no objection to her kissing him, though still entirely engaged in detailing further particulars of the 'Thrush's' going out of harbour, in which he had a strong right of interest, being to commence his career of seamanship in her at this very time.

Another moment and Fanny was in the narrow entrance passage of the house, and in her mother's arms, who met her there with looks of true kindness, and with features which Fanny loved the more, because they brought her Aunt Bertram's before her; and there were her two sisters, Susan, a well-grown, fine girl of fourteen, and Betsey, the youngest of the family, about five – both glad to see her in their way, though with no advantage of manner in receiving her. But manner Fanny did not want. Would they but love her, she should be satisfied.

She was then taken into a parlour, so small that her first conviction was of its being only a passage-room to something better, and she stood for a moment expecting to be invited on; but when she saw there was no other door, and that there were signs of habitation before her, she called back her thoughts, reproved herself, and grieved lest they should have been suspected. Her mother, however, could not stay long enough to suspect any thing. She was gone again to the street-door to welcome William. 'Oh! my dear William, how glad I am to see you. But have you heard about the "Thrush"? She is gone out of harbour already; three days before we had any thought of it; and I do not know what I am to do about Sam's things, they will never be ready in time; for she may have her orders to-morrow, perhaps. It takes me quite unawares. And now you must be off for Spithead too. Campbell has been here, quite in a worry about you; and now what shall we do? I thought to have had such a comfortable evening with you, and here every thing comes upon me at once.'

Her son answered cheerfully, telling her that every thing was always for the best; and making light of his own inconvenience, in being obliged to hurry away so soon.

'To be sure, I had much rather she had stayed in harbour, that I might have sat a few hours with you in comfort; but as there is a boat ashore I had better go off at once, and there is no help for it. Whereabouts does the "Thrush" lie at Spithead? Near the "Canopus"? But no matter; here's Fanny in the parlour, and why should we stay in the passage? Come, mother, you have hardly looked at your own dear Fanny yet.'

In they both came, and Mrs Price having kindly kissed her daughter again, and commented a little on her growth, began with very natural solicitude to feel for their fatigues and wants as travellers.

'Poor dears! How tired you must both be! And now, what will you have? I began to think you would never come. Betsey and I have been watching for you this half hour. And when did you get anything to eat? And what would you like to have now? I could not tell whether you would be for some meat, or only a dish of tea after your journey, or else I would have got something ready. And now I am afraid Campbell will be here before there is time to dress a steak, and we have no butcher at hand. It is very inconvenient to have no butcher in the street. We were better off in our last house. Perhaps you would like some tea as soon as it can be got.'

They both declared they should prefer it to any thing. 'Then, Betsey my dear, run into the kitchen, and see if Rebecca has put the water on; and tell her to bring in the tea-things as soon as she can. I wish we could get the bell mended; but Betsey is a very handy little messenger.'

Betsey went with alacrity, proud to show her abilities before her fine new sister.

'Dear me!' continued the anxious mother, 'what a sad fire we have got, and I dare say you are both starved with cold. Draw your chair nearer, my dear. I cannot think what Rebecca has been about. I am sure I told her to bring some coals half an hour ago. Susan, *you* should have taken care of the fire.'

'I was upstairs, mamma, moving my things,' said Susan, in a fearless, self-defending tone, which startled Fanny. 'You know you had but just settled that my sister Fanny and I should have the other room; and I could not get Rebecca to give me any help.'

Further discussion was prevented by various bustles; first, the driver came

Mr Price kicked away his son's portmanteau and his daughter's band-box

to be paid; then there was a squabble between Sam and Rebecca about the manner of carrying up his sister's trunk, which he would manage all his own way; and lastly in walked Mr Price himself, his own loud voice preceding him, as with some thing of the oath kind he kicked away his son's portmanteau and his daughter's band-box in the passage, and called out for a candle; no candle was brought, however, and he walked into the room.

Fanny with doubting feelings had risen to meet him, but sank down again on finding herself undistinguished in the dusk, and unthought of. With a friendly shake of his son's hand, and eager voice, he instantly began: 'Ha! welcome back, my boy. Glad to see you. Have you heard the news? The "Thrush" went out of harbour this morning. Sharp is the word, you see! By G——, you are just in time! The doctor has been here enquiring for you: he has got one of the boats, and is to be off for Spithead by six, so you had better go with him. I have been to Turner's about your mess; it is all in a way to be done. I should not wonder if you had your orders to-morrow; but you cannot sail with this wind, if you are to cruise to the westward; and Captain Walsh thinks you will certainly have a cruise to the westward, with the "Elephant." By G——, I wish you may! But old Scholey was saying, just now, that he thought you would be sent first to the "Texel." Well, well, we are ready, whatever happens. But by G——, you lost a fine sight by not being here in the morning to see the "Thrush" go out of harbour! I would not have been out of the way for a thousand pounds. Old Scholey ran in at breakfast-time, to say she had slipped her moorings and was coming out. I jumped up, and made but two steps to the platform. If ever there was a perfect beauty afloat, she is one; and there she lays at Spithead and any body in England would take her for an eight-and-twenty. I was upon the platform two hours this afternoon looking at her. She lays close to the "Endymion," between her and the "Cleopatra," just to the eastward of the sheer hulk.'

'Ha!' cried William, '*that's* just where I should have put her myself. It's the best berth at Spithead. But here is my sister, sir; here is Fanny,' turning and leading her forward; 'it is so dark you do not see her.'

With an acknowledgment that he had quite forgot her, Mr Price now received his daughter; and having given her a cordial hug, and observed that she was grown into a woman, and he supposed would be wanting a husband soon, seemed very much inclined to forget her again.

Fanny shrunk back to her seat, with feelings sadly pained by his language and his smell of spirits; and he talked on only to his son, and only of the 'Thrush,' though William, warmly interested as he was in that subject, more than once tried to make his father think of Fanny, and her long absence and long journey.

After sitting some time longer, a candle was obtained; but as there was still no appearance of tea, nor, from Betsey's reports from the kitchen, much hope of any under a considerable period, William determined to go and change his dress, and made the necessary preparations for his removal on board directly, that he might have his tea in comfort afterwards.

As he left the room, two rosy-faced boys, ragged and dirty, about eight and nine years old, rushed into it just released from school, and coming eagerly to see their sister, and tell that the 'Thrush' was gone out of harbour; Tom and Charles. Charles had been born since Fanny's going away, but Tom she had often helped to nurse, and now felt a particular pleasure in seeing again. Both were kissed very tenderly, but Tom she wanted to keep by her, to try to trace the features of the baby she had loved, and talked to, of his infant preference of herself. Tom, however, had no mind for such treatment: he came home not to stand and be talked to, but to run about and make a noise; and both boys had soon burst from her, and slammed the parlour door till her temples ached.

She had now seen all that were at home; there remained only two brothers between herself and Susan, one of whom was a clerk in a public office in London, and the other midshipman on board an Indiaman. But though she had *seen* all the members of the family, she had not yet *heard* all the noise they could make. Another quarter of an hour brought her a great deal more. William was soon calling out, from the landing-place of the second story, for his mother and for Rebecca. He was in distress for something that he had left there, and did not find again. A key was mislaid, Betsey accused of having got at his new hat, and some slight, but essential alteration of his uniform waistcoat, which he had been promised to have done for him, entirely neglected.

Mrs Price, Rebecca, and Betsey, all went up to defend themselves, all talking together, but Rebecca loudest, and the job was to be done, as well as it could, in a great hurry; William trying in vain to send Betsey down again, or keep her from being troublesome where she was; the whole of which, as almost every door in the house was open, could be plainly distinguished in the parlour, except when drowned at intervals by the superior noise of Sam, Tom and Charles chasing each other up and down stairs, and tumbling about and hallooing.

Fanny was almost stunned. The smallness of the house and thinness of the walls brought every thing so close to her, that, added to the fatigue of her journey, and all her recent agitation, she hardly knew how to bear it. *Within* the room all was tranquil enough, for Susan having disappeared with the others, there were soon only her father and herself remaining; and he taking out a newspaper, the accustomary loan of a neighbour, applied himself to studying it, without seeming to recollect her existence. The solitary candle was held between himself and the paper, without any reference to her possible convenience; but she had nothing to do, and was glad to have the light screened from her aching head, as she sat in bewildered, broken, sorrowful contemplation.

She was at home. But, alas! it was not such a home, she had not such a welcome, as – she checked herself; she was unreasonable. What right had she to be of importance to her family? She could have none, so long lost sight of!

William's concerns must be dearest, they always had been, and he had every right. Yet to have so little said or asked about herself, to have scarcely an enquiry made after Mansfield! It did pain her to have Mansfield forgotten; the friends who had done so much; the dear, dear friends! But here, one subject swallowed up all the rest. Perhaps it must be so. The destination of the 'Thrush' must be now pre-eminently interesting. A day or two might show the difference. *She* only was to blame. Yet she thought it would not have been so at Mansfield's. No, in her uncle's house there would have been a consideration of times and seasons, a regulation of subject, a propriety, an attention towards every body which there was not here.

The only interruption which thoughts like these received for nearly half

Mrs Price, Rebecca, and Betsey all went up to defend themselves, all talking together

an hour was from a sudden burst of her father's, not at all calculated to compose them. At a more than ordinary pitch of thumping and hallooing in the passage, he exclaimed, 'Devil take those young dogs! How they are singing out! Ay, Sam's voice louder than all the rest! That boy is fit for a boatswain. Halloa you there! Sam, stop your confounded pipe, or I shall be after you.'

This threat was so palpably disregarded, that though within five minutes afterwards the three boys all burst into the room together and sat down, Fanny could not consider it as a proof of any thing more than their being for the time thoroughly fagged, which their hot faces and panting breaths seemed to prove, especially as they were still kicking each other's shins, and hallooing out at sudden starts immediately under their father's eye.

The next opening of the door brought some thing more welcome; it was for the tea-things, which she had begun almost to despair of seeing that evening. Susan and an attendant girl, whose inferior appearance informed Fanny, to her great surprise, that she had previously seen the upper servant, brought in every thing necessary for the meal: Susan looking, as she put the kettle on the fire and glanced at her sister, as if divided between the agreeable triumph of showing her activity and usefulness, and the dread of being thought to demean herself by such an office. 'She had been into the kitchen,' she said, 'to hurry Sally and help make the toast, and spread the bread and butter, or she did not know when they should have got tea, and she was sure her sister must want some thing after her journey.'

Fanny was very thankful. She could not but own that she should be very glad of a little tea, and Susan immediately set about making it, as if pleased to have the employment all to herself; and with only a little unnecessary bustle, and some few injudicious attempts at keeping her brothers in better order than she could, acquitted herself very well. Fanny's spirit was as much refreshed as her body; her head and heart were soon the better for such well-timed kindness. Susan had an open, sensible countenance; she was like William, and Fanny hoped to find her like him in disposition and good will towards herself.

In this more placid state of things William re-entered, followed not far behind by his mother and Betsey. He, complete in his lieutenant's uniform, looking and moving all the taller, firmer and more graceful for it, and with the happiest smile over his face, walked up directly to Fanny, who, rising from her seat, looked at him for a moment in speechless admiration, and then threw her arms round his neck to sob out her various emotions of pain and pleasure.

Anxious not to appear unhappy, she soon recovered herself; and wiping away her tears, was able to notice and admire all the striking parts of his dress; listening with reviving spirits to his cheerful hopes of being on shore some part of every day before they sailed, and even of getting her to Spithead to see the sloop.

The next bustle brought in Mr Campbell, the surgeon of the 'Thrush,' a very well-behaved young man, who came to call for his friend, and for whom there was with some contrivance found a chair, and with some hasty washing of the young tea-maker's, a cup and saucer; and after another quarter of an hour of earnest talk between the gentlemen, noise rising upon noise, and bustle upon bustle, men and boys at last all in motion together, the moment came for setting off; every thing was ready, William took leave, and all of them were gone; for the three boys, in spite of their mother's entreaty, determined to see their brother and Mr Campbell to the sally-port; and Mr Price walked off at the same time to carry back his neighbour's newspaper.

Something like tranquillity might now be hoped for; and accordingly, when Rebecca had been prevailed on to carry away the tea-things, and Mrs Price had walked about the room some time looking for a shirt-sleeve, which Betsey at last hunted out from a drawer in the kitchen, the small party of females were pretty well composed, and the mother having lamented again over the impossibility of getting Sam ready in time, was at leisure to think of her eldest daughter and the friends she had come from.

A few enquiries began; but one of the earliest – How did her sister Bertram manage about her servants? Was she as much plagued as herself to get tolerable servants? – soon led her mind away from Northamptonshire, and fixed it on her own domestic grievances, and the shocking character of all the Portsmouth servants, of whom she believed her own two were the very worst, engrossed her completely. The Bertrams were all forgotten in detailing the faults of Rebecca, against whom Susan had also much to depose, and little Betsey a great deal more, and who did seem so thoroughly without a single recommendation, that Fanny could not help modestly presuming that her mother meant to part with her when her year was up.

'Her year!' cried Mrs Price; 'I am sure I hope I shall be rid of her before she has stayed a year, for that will not be up till November. Servants are come to such a pass, my dear, in Portsmouth, that it is quite a miracle if one keeps them more than half a year. I have no hope of ever being settled; and if I was to part with Rebecca, I should only get something worse. And yet I do not think I am a very difficult mistress to please; and I am sure the place is easy enough, for there is always a girl under her, and I often do half the work myself.'

Fanny was silent; but not from being convinced that there might not be a remedy found for some of these evils. As she now sat looking at Betsey, she could not but think particularly of another sister, a very pretty little girl, whom she had left there not much younger when she went into

Northamptonshire, who had died a few years afterwards. There had been something remarkably amiable about her. Fanny in those early days had preferred her to Susan; and when the news of her death had at last reached Mansfield, had for a short time been quite afflicted. The sight of Betsey brought the image of little Mary back again, but she would not have pained her mother by alluding to her for the world. While considering her with these ideas, Betsey, at a small distance, was holding out some thing to catch her eyes, meaning to screen it at the same time from Susan's.

'What have you got there, my love?' said Fanny, 'come and show it to me.'

It was a silver knife. Up jumped Susan, claiming it as her own, and trying to get it away; but the child ran to her mother's protection, and Susan could only reproach, which she did very warmly, and evidently hoping to interest Fanny on her side. 'It was very hard that she was not to have her *own* knife; it was her own knife; little sister Mary had left it to her upon her death-bed, and she ought to have had it to keep herself long ago. But mamma kept it from her, and was always letting Betsey get hold of it; and the end of it would be that Betsey would spoil it, and get it for her own, though mamma had *promised* her that Betsey should not have it in her own hands.'

Fanny was quite shocked. Every feeling of duty, honour, and tenderness, was wounded by her sister's speech and her mother's reply.

'Now, Susan,' cried Mrs Price in a complaining voice, 'now, how can you be so cross? You are always quarrelling about that knife. I wish you would not be so quarrelsome. Poor little Betsey; how cross Susan is to you! But you should not have taken it out, my dear, when I sent you to the drawer. You know I told you not to touch it, because Susan is so cross about it. I must hide it another time, Betsey. Poor Mary little thought it would be such a bone of contention when she gave it me to keep, only two hours before she died. Poor little soul! She could but just speak to be heard, and she said so prettily, "Let sister Susan have my knife, mamma, when I am dead and buried." Poor little dear! She was so fond of it, Fanny, that she would have it lie by her in bed, all through her illness. It was the gift of her good godmother, old Mrs Admiral Maxwell, only six weeks before she was taken for death. Poor little sweet creature! Well, she was taken away from evil to come. My own Betsey (fondling her), *you* have not the luck of such a good godmother. Aunt Norris lives too far off to think of such little people as you.'

Fanny had indeed nothing to convey from Aunt Norris, but a message to say she hoped that her god-daughter was a good girl, and learnt her book. There had been at one moment a slight murmur in the drawing-room at Mansfield Park, about sending her a prayer-book; but no second sound had been heard of such a purpose. Mrs Norris, however, had gone home and taken down two old prayer-books of her husband with that idea; but, upon examination, the ardour of generosity went off. One was found to have too small a print for a child's eyes, and the other to be too cumbersome for her to carry about.

Fanny, fatigued and fatigued again, was thankful to accept the first invitation of going to bed; and before Betsey had finished her cry at being allowed to sit up only one hour extraordinary in honour of sister, she was off, leaving all below in confusion and noise again; the boys begging for toasted cheese, her father calling out for his rum and water, and Rebecca never where she ought to be.

There was nothing to raise her spirits in the confined and scantily-furnished chamber that she was to share with Susan. The smallness of the rooms above and below, indeed, and the narrowness of the passage and staircase, struck her beyond her imagination. She soon learned to think with respect of her own little attic at Mansfield Park, in *that* house reckoned too small for anybody's comfort.

CHAPTER THIRTY NINE

COULD SIR THOMAS HAVE seen all his niece's feelings, when she wrote her first letter to her aunt, he would not have despaired; for though a good night's rest, a pleasant morning, the hope of soon seeing William again, and the comparatively quiet state of the house, from Tom and Charles being gone to school, Sam on some project of his own, and her father on his usual lounges, enabled her to express herself cheerfully on the subject of home, there were still, to her own perfect consciousness, many draw-backs suppressed. Could he have seen only half that she felt before the end of a week, he would have thought Mr Crawford sure of her, and been delighted with his own sagacity.

Before the week ended, it was all disappointment. In the first place, William was gone. The 'Thrush' had had her orders, the wind had changed and he was sailed within four days from their reaching Portsmouth; and during those days she had seen him only twice, in a short and hurried way, when he had come ashore on duty. There had been no free conversation, no walk on the ramparts, no visit to the dockyard, no acquaintance with the 'Thrush,' nothing of all that they had planned and depended on. Every thing in that quarter failed her, except William's affection. His last thought on leaving home was for her. He stepped back again to the door to say, 'Take care of Fanny, mother. She is tender, and not used to rough it like the rest of us. I charge you, take care of Fanny.'

William was gone; and the home he had left her in was, Fanny could not conceal it from herself, in almost every respect the very reverse of what she could have wished. It was the abode of noise, disorder and impropriety. Nobody was in their right place, nothing was done as it ought to be. She could not respect her parents as she had hoped. On her father, her confidence had not been sanguine, but he was more negligent of his family, his habits were worse, and his manners coarser, than she had been prepared for. He did not want abilities; but he had no curiosity, and no information beyond his profession; he read only the newspaper and the navy-list; he talked only of the dockyard, the harbour, Spithead, and the Motherbank; he swore and he drank, he was dirty and gross. She had never been able to recall any thing approaching to tenderness in his former treatment of herself. There had remained only a general impression of roughness and loudness; and now he scarcely ever noticed her, but to make her the object of a coarse joke.

Her disappointment in her mother was greater; *there* she had hoped much, and found almost nothing. Every flattering scheme of being of consequence to her soon fell to the ground. Mrs Price was not unkind; but, instead of gaining on her affection and confidence, and becoming more and more dear, her daughter never met with greater kindness from her than on the first day of her arrival. The instinct of nature was soon satisfied, and Mrs Price's attachment had no other source. Her heart and her time were already quite full; she had neither leisure nor affection to bestow on Fanny. Her daughters never had been much to her. She was fond of her sons, especially William, but Betsey was the first of her girls whom she had ever much regarded. To her she was most injudiciously indulgent. William was her pride; Betsey her darling; and John, Richard, Sam, Tom, and Charles occupied all the rest of her maternal solicitude, alternately her worries and her comforts. These shared her heart: her time was given chiefly to her house and her servants. Her days were spent in a kind of slow bustle; always busy without getting on; always behind hand and lamenting it, without altering her ways; wishing to be an economist, without contrivance or regularity; dissatisfied with her servants, without skill to make them better, and whether helping, or reprimanding, or indulging them, without any power of engaging their respect.

Of her two sisters, Mrs Price very much more resembled Lady Bertram than Mrs Norris. She was a manager by necessity, without any of Mrs Norris's inclination for it, or any of her activity. Her disposition was naturally easy and indolent, like Lady Bertram's; and a situation of similar affluence and do-nothingness would have been much more suited to her capacity than the exertions and self-denials of the one which her imprudent marriage had placed her in. She might have made just as good a woman of consequence as Lady Bertram, but Mrs Norris would have been a more respectable mother of nine children on a small income.

Much of all this Fanny could not but be sensible of. She might scruple to make use of the words, but she must and did feel that her mother was a partial, ill-judging parent, a dawdle, a slattern, who neither taught nor restrained her children, whose house was the scene of mismanagement and discomfort from beginning to end, and who had no talent, no conversation, no affection towards herself; no curiosity to know her better, no desire of her friendship, and no inclination for her company that could lessen her sense of such feelings.

Fanny was very anxious to be useful, and not to appear above her home, or in any way disqualified or disinclined, by her foreign education, from contributing her help to its comforts, and therefore set about working for Sam immediately, and by working early and late, with perseverance and great despatch, did so much that the boy was shipped off at last, with more than half his linen ready. She had great pleasure in feeling her usefulness, but could not conceive how they would have managed without her.

Sam, loud and overbearing as he was, she rather regretted when he went, for he was clever and intelligent, and glad to be employed in any errand in the town; and though spurning the remonstrances of Susan, given as they were, though very reasonable in themselves, with ill-timed and powerless warmth, was beginning to be influenced by Fanny's services and gentle persuasions; and she found that the best of the three younger ones was gone in him; Tom and Charles being at least as many years as they were his juniors distant from that age of feeling and reason, which might suggest the expediency of making friends, and of endeavouring to be less disagreeable. Their sister soon despaired of making the smallest impression on *them*; they were quite untameable by any means of address which she had spirits or time to attempt. Every afternoon brought a return of their riotous games all over the house; and she very early learned to sigh at the approach of Saturday's constant half holiday.

Betsey, too, a spoiled child, trained up to think the alphabet her greatest enemy, left to be with the servants at her pleasure, and then encouraged to report any evil of them, she was almost as ready to despair of being able to love or assist; and of Susan's temper she had many doubts. Her continual disagreements with her mother, her rash squabbles with Tom and Charles, and petulance with Betsey, were at least so distressing to Fanny, that though admitting they were by no means without provocation, she feared the disposition that could push them to such length must be far from amiable, and from affording any repose to herself.

Such was the home which was to put Mansfield out of her head, and teach her to think of her cousin Edmund with moderated feelings. On the contrary, she could think of nothing but Mansfield, its beloved inmates, its happy ways. Every thing where she now was was in full contrast to it. The elegance, propriety, regularity, harmony, and perhaps, above all, the peace and tranquillity of Mansfield, were brought to her remembrance every hour of the day, by the prevalence of everything opposite to them *here*.

The living in incessant noise was, to a frame and temper delicate and nervous like Fanny's, an evil which no super-added elegance or harmony could have entirely atoned for. It was the greatest misery of all. At Mansfield, no sounds of contention, no raised voice, no abrupt bursts, no tread of violence, was ever heard; all proceeded in a regular course of cheerful orderliness; every body had their due importance; every body's feelings were consulted. If tenderness could be ever supposed wanting, good sense and good breeding supplied its place; and as to the little irritations, some times introduced by Aunt Norris, they were short, they were trifling, they were as a drop of water to the ocean, compared with the ceaseless tumult of her present abode. Here, every body was noisy, every voice was loud (excepting, perhaps, her mother's, which resembled the soft monotony of Lady Bertram's, only worn into fretfulness). Whatever was wanted was halloo'd for, and the servants halloo'd out their excuses from the kitchen. The doors were in constant banging, the stairs were never at rest, nothing was done without a clatter, nobody sat still, and nobody could command attention when they spoke.

In a review of the two houses, as they appeared to her before the end of a week, Fanny was tempted to apply to them Dr Johnson's celebrated judgment as to matrimony and celibacy, and say, that though Mansfield Park might have some pains, Portsmouth could have no pleasures.

CHAPTER FORTY

FANNY WAS RIGHT ENOUGH IN not expecting to hear from Miss Crawford now, at the rapid rate in which their correspondence had begun; Mary's next letter was after a decidedly longer interval than the last, but she was not right in supposing that such an interval would be felt a great relief to herself. Here was another strange revolution of mind! She was really glad to receive the letter when it did come. In her present exile from good society, and distance from every thing that had been wont to interest her, a letter from one belonging to the set where her heart lived, written with affection, and some degree of elegance, was thoroughly acceptable. The usual plea of increasing engagements was made in excuse for not having written to her earlier; 'and now that I have begun,' she continued, 'my letter will not be worth your reading, for there will be no little offering of love at the end, no three or four lines passionnées from the most devoted H. C. in the world, for

Henry is in Norfolk; business called him to Everingham ten days ago, or perhaps he only pretended the call, for the sake of being travelling at the same time that you were. But there he is, and, by the bye, his absence may sufficiently account for any remissness of his sister's in writing, for there has been no "Well, Mary, when do you write Fanny? Is not it time for you to write to Fanny?" to spur me on. At last, after various attempts at meeting, I have seen your cousins, "dear Julia and dearest Mrs Rushworth;" they found me at home yesterday and we were glad to see each other again. We *seemed very* glad to see each other, and I do really think we were a little. We had a vast deal to say. Shall I tell you how Mrs Rushworth looked when your name was mentioned? I did not use to think her wanting in self-possession, but she had not quite enough for the demands of yesterday. Upon the whole Julia was in the best looks of the two, at least after you were spoken of. There was no recovering the complexion from the moment that I spoke of "Fanny", and spoke of her as a sister should. But Mrs Rushworth's day of good looks will come; we have cards for her first party on the 28th. Then she will be in beauty, for she will open one of the best houses in Wimpole Street. I was in it two years ago, when it was Lady Lascelles's, and prefer it to almost any I know in London, and certainly she will then feel, to use a vulgar phrase, that she has got her pennyworth for her penny. Henry could not have afforded her such a house. I hope she will recollect it, and be satisfied, as well as she may, with moving the queen of a palace, though the king may appear best in the background; and as I have no desire to tease her, I shall never *force* your name upon her again. She will grow sober by degrees. From all that I hear and guess, Baron Wildenheim's attentions to Julia continue, but I do not know that he has any serious encouragement. She ought to do better. A poor honourable is no catch, and I cannot imagine any liking in the case, for, take away his rants, and the poor baron has nothing. What a difference a vowel makes! If his rents were but equal to his rants! Your cousin Edmund moves slowly; detained, perchance, by parish duties. There may be some old woman at Thornton Lacey to be converted. I am unwilling to fancy myself neglected for a *young* one. Adieu! my dear sweet Fanny, this is a long letter from London: write me a pretty one in reply to gladden Henry's eyes, when he comes back, and send me an account of all the dashing young captains whom you disdain for his sake.'

There was great food for meditation in this letter, and chiefly for unpleasant meditation; and yet, with all the uneasiness it supplied, it connected her with the absent, it told her of people and things about whom she had never felt so much curiosity as now, and she would have been glad to have been sure of such a letter every week. Her correspondence with her Aunt Bertram was her only concern of higher interest.

As for any society in Portsmouth, that could at all make amends for deficiencies at home, there were none within the circle of her father's and mother's acquaintance to afford her the smallest satisfaction; she saw nobody in whose favour she could wish to overcome her own shyness and reserve. The men appeared to her all coarse, the women all pert, every body underbred; and she gave as little contentment as she received from introductions either to old or new acquaintances. The young ladies who approached her at first with some respect, in consideration of her coming from a baronet's family, were soon offended by what they termed 'airs'; for, as she neither played on the pianoforte, nor wore fine pelisses, they could, on farther observation, admit no right of superiority.

The first solid consolation which Fanny received for the evils of home, the first which her judgment could entirely approve, and which gave any promise of durability, was in a better knowledge of Susan, and a hope of being of service to her. Susan had always behaved pleasantly to herself, but the determined character of her general manners had astonished and alarmed her, and it was at least a fortnight before she began to understand a disposition so totally different from her own. Susan saw that much was wrong at home, and wanted to set it right. That a girl of fourteen, acting only on her own unassisted reason, should err in the method of reform, was not wonderful; and Fanny soon became more disposed to admire the natural light of the mind which could so early distinguish justly, than to censure severely the faults of conduct to which it led. Susan was only acting on the same truths, and pursuing the same system, which her own judgment acknowledged, but which her more supine and yielding temper would have shrunk from asserting. Susan tried to be useful, where *she* could only have gone away and cried; and that Susan was useful she could perceive; that things, bad as they were, would have been worse but for such interposition, and that both her mother and Betsey were restrained from some excesses of very offensive indulgence and vulgarity.

In every argument with her mother, Susan had in point of reason the advantage, and never was there any maternal tenderness to buy her off. The blind fondness which was for ever producing evil around her *she* had never known. There was no gratitude for affection past or present to make her better bear with its excesses to the others.

All this became gradually evident, and gradually placed Susan before her sister as an object of mingled compassion and respect. That her manner was wrong, however, at times very wrong, her measures often ill-chosen and ill-timed, and her looks and language very often indefensible, Fanny could not cease to feel; but she began to hope they might be rectified. Susan, she found, looked up to her and wished for her good opinion; and new as any thing like an office of authority was to Fanny, new as it was to imagine herself capable of guiding or informing any one, she did resolve to give occasional hints to Susan, and endeavour to exercise for her advantage the juster notions of what was due to every body, and what would be wisest for herself, which her own more favoured education had fixed in her.

Her influence, or at least the consciousness and use of it, originated in an act of kindness by Susan which, after many hesitations of delicacy, she at last worked herself up to. It had very early occurred to her that a small sum of money might, perhaps, restore peace for ever on the sore subject of the silver knife, canvassed as it now was continually, and the riches which she was in possession of herself, her uncle having given her £10 at parting, made her as able as she was willing to be generous. But she was so wholly unused to confer favours, except on the very poor, so unpractised in removing evils, or bestowing kindnesses among her equals, and so fearful of appearing to elevate herself as a great lady at home, that it took some time to determine that it would not be unbecoming in her to make such a present. It was made, however, at last; a silver knife was bought for Betsey, and accepted with great delight, its newness giving it every advantage over the other that could be desired; Susan was established in the full possession of her own, Betsey handsomely declaring that now she had got one so much prettier herself, she should never want *that* again; and no reproach seemed conveyed to the equally satisfied mother, which Fanny had almost feared to be impossible. The deed thoroughly answered; a source of domestic altercation was entirely done away, and it was the means of opening Susan's heart to her, and giving her some thing more to love and be interested in. Susan showed that she had delicacy; pleased as she was to be mistress of property which she had been struggling for at least two years, she yet feared that her sister's judgment had been against her, and that a reproof was designed for her having so struggled as to make the purchase necessary for the tranquillity of the house.

Her temper was open. She acknowledged her fears, blamed herself for having contended so warmly; and from that hour Fanny, understanding the worth of her disposition, and perceiving how fully she was inclined to seek her good opinion and refer to her judgment, began to feel again the blessing of affection, and to entertain the hope of being useful to a mind so much in need of help, and so much deserving it. She gave advice, advice too sound to be resisted by a good understanding, and given so mildly and considerately as not to irritate an imperfect temper, and she had the happiness of observing its good effects not unfrequently. More was not expected by one who, while seeing all the obligation and expediency of submission and forbearance, saw also with sympathetic acuteness of feeling all that must be hourly grating to a girl like Susan. Her greatest wonder on the subject soon became – not that Susan should have been provoked into disrespect and impatience against her better knowledge – but that so much better knowledge, so many good notions should have been hers at all; and that, brought up in the midst of negligence and error, she should have formed such proper opinions of what ought to be; she, who had had no cousin Edmund to direct her thoughts or fix her principles.

The intimacy thus begun between them was a material advantage to each. By sitting together upstairs, they avoided a great deal of the disturbance of the house; Fanny had peace, and Susan learned to think it no misfortune to be quietly employed. They sat without a fire; but *that* was a privation familiar even to Fanny, and she suffered the less because reminded by it of the East Room. It was the only point of resemblance. In space, light, furniture, and prospect, there was nothing alike in the two apartments; and she often heaved a sigh at the remembrance of all her books and boxes, and various comforts there. By degrees the girls came to spend the chief of the morning upstairs, at first only in working and talking, but after a few days, the remembrance of the said books grew so potent and stimulative, that Fanny found it impossible not to try for books again. There were none in her father's house; but wealth is luxurious and daring, and some of hers found its way to a circulating library. She became a subscriber; amazed at being anything in propria persona, amazed at her own doings in every way, to be a renter, a chooser of books! And to be having any one's improvement in view in her choice! But so it was. Susan had read nothing, and Fanny longed to give her a share in her own first pleasure, and inspire a taste for the biography and poetry which she delighted in herself.

In this occupation she hoped, moreover, to bury some of the recollections of Mansfield, which were too apt to seize her mind if her fingers only were busy; and especially at this time, hoped it might be useful in diverting her thoughts from pursuing Edmund to London, whither, on the authority of her aunt's last letter, she knew he was gone. She had no doubt of what would ensue. The promised notification was hanging over her head. The postman's knock within the neighbourhood was beginning to bring its daily terrors, and if reading could banish the idea for even half an hour, it was something gained.

CHAPTER FORTY ONE

A WEEK WAS GONE SINCE Edmund might be supposed in town, and Fanny had heard nothing of him. There were three different conclusions to be drawn from his silence, between which her mind was in fluctuation; each of them at times being held the most probable. Either his going had been again delayed or he had yet procured no opportunity of seeing Miss Crawford alone, or he was too happy for letter-writing!

One morning, about this time, Fanny having now been nearly four weeks from Mansfield, a point which she never failed to think over and calculate every day, as she and Susan were preparing to remove, as usual, upstairs, they were stopped by the knock of a visitor, whom they felt they could not avoid, from Rebecca's alertness in going to the door, a duty which always interested her beyond any other.

It was a gentleman's voice; it was a voice that Fanny was just turning pale about, when Mr Crawford walked into the room.

Good sense, like hers, will always act when really called upon; and she found that she had been able to name him to her mother, and recall her remembrance of the name, as that of 'William's friend,' though she could not previously have believed herself capable of uttering a syllable at such a moment. The consciousness of his being known there only as William's friend was some support. Having introduced him, however, and being all reseated, the terrors that occurred of what this visit might lead to were overpowering, and she fancied herself on the point of fainting away.

While trying to keep herself alive, their visitor, who had at first approached her with as animated a countenance as ever, was wisely and kindly keeping his eyes away, and giving her time to recover, while he devoted himself entirely to her mother, addressing her, and attending to her with the utmost politeness and propriety, at the same time with a degree of friendliness, of interest, at least, which was making his manner perfect.

Mrs Price's manners were also at their best. Warmed by the sight of such a friend to her son, and regulated by the wish of appearing to advantage before him, she was overflowing with gratitude, artless, maternal gratitude, which could not be unpleasing. Mr Price was out, which she regretted very much. Fanny was just recovered enough to feel that *she* could not regret it; for to her many other sources of uneasiness was added the severe one of shame for the home in which he found her. She might scold herself for the weakness, but there was no scolding it away. She was ashamed, and she would have been yet more ashamed of her father than of all the rest.

They talked of William; a subject on which Mrs Price could never tire; and Mr Crawford was as warm in his commendation as even her heart could wish. She felt that she had never seen so agreeable a man in her life; and was only astonished to find, that so great and so agreeable as he was, he should be come down to Portsmouth neither on a visit to the port-admiral, nor the commissioner, nor yet with the intention of going over to the island, nor of seeing the dockyard. Nothing of all that she had been used to think of as the proof of importance, or the employment of wealth, had brought him to Portsmouth. He had reached it late the night before, was come for a day or two, was staying at the Crown, had accidentally met with a navy officer or two of his acquaintance since his arrival, but had no object of that kind in coming.

By the time he had given all this information, it was not unreasonable to suppose that Fanny might be looked at and spoken to; and she was tolerably able to bear his eye, and hear that he had spent half an hour with his sister the evening before his leaving London; that she had sent her best and kindest love, but had had no time for writing; that he thought himself lucky in seeing Mary for even half an hour, having spent scarcely twenty-four hours in London, after his return from Norfolk, before he set off again; that her cousin Edmund was in town, had been in town, he understood, a few days; that he had not seen him himself, but that he was well, had left them all well at Mansfield, and was to dine, as yesterday, with the Frasers.

Fanny listened collectedly, even to the last-mentioned circumstance; nay, it seemed a relief to her worn mind to be at any certainty; and the words, 'then by this time it is all settled,' passed internally, without more evidence of emotion than a faint blush.

After talking a little more about Mansfield, a subject in which her interest was most apparent, Crawford began to hint at the expediency of an early walk. 'It was a lovely morning, and at that season of the year a fine morning so often turned off, that it was wisest for every body not to delay their exercise;' and such hints producing nothing, he soon proceeded to a positive recommendation to Mrs Price and her daughters, to take their walk without loss of time. Now they came to an understanding. Mrs Price, it appeared, scarcely ever stirred out of doors, except on a Sunday; she owned she could seldom, with her large family, find time for a walk. 'Would she not, then, persuade her daughters to take advantage of such weather, and allow him the pleasure of attending them?' Mrs Price was greatly obliged and very complying. 'Her daughters were very much confined; Portsmouth was a sad place; they did not often get out; and she knew they had some errands in the town, which they would be very glad to do.' And the consequence was that Fanny, strange as it was, strange, awkward, and distressing, found herself and Susan, within ten minutes, walking towards the High Street, with Mr Crawford.

It was soon pain upon pain, confusion upon confusion; for they were hardly in the High Street, before they met her father, whose appearance was not the better from its being Saturday. He stopped, and, ungentlemanlike as he looked, Fanny was obliged to introduce him to Mr Crawford. She could not have a doubt of the manner in which Mr Crawford must be struck. He must be ashamed and disgusted altogether. He must soon give her up, and cease to have the smallest inclination for the match; and yet, though she had been so much wanting his affection to be cured, this was a sort of cure that

Fanny was obliged to introduce him to Mr Crawford

would be almost as bad as the complaint; and I believe there is scarcely a young lady in the United Kingdoms who would not rather put up with the misfortune of being sought by a clever, agreeable man, than have him driven away by the vulgarity of her nearest relations.

Mr Crawford probably could not regard his future father-in-law with any idea of taking him for a model in dress; but (as Fanny instantly, and to her great relief, discerned) her father was a very different man, a very different Mr Price in his behaviour to this most highly respected stranger, from what he was in his own family at home. His manners now, though not polished, were more than passable; they were grateful, animated, manly; his expressions were those of an attached father, and a sensible man; his loud tones did very well in the open air, and there was not a single oath to be heard. Such was his instinctive compliment to the good manners of Mr Crawford; and, be the consequence what it might, Fanny's immediate feelings were infinitely soothed.

The conclusion of the two gentlemen's civilities was an offer of Mr Price's to take Mr Crawford into the dockyard, which Mr Crawford desirous of accepting as a favour what was intended as such, though he had seen the dockyard again and again, and hoping to be so much the longer with Fanny, was very gratefully disposed to avail himself of, if the Miss Prices were not afraid of the fatigue; and as it was somehow or other ascertained or inferred, or at least acted upon, that they were not at all afraid, to the dockyard they were all to go; and but for Mr Crawford, Mr Price would have turned thither directly, without the smallest consideration for his daughters' errands in the High Street. He took care, however, that they should be allowed to go to the shops they came out expressly to visit; and it did not delay them long, for Fanny could so little bear to excite inpatience, or be waited for, that before the gentlemen, as they stood at the door, could do more than begin upon the last naval regulations, or settle the number of three-deckers now in commission, their companions were ready to proceed.

They were then to set forward for the dockyard at once, and the walk would have been conducted (according to Mr Crawford's opinion) in a singular manner, had Mr Price been allowed the entire regulation of it, as the two girls, he found, would have been left to follow, and keep up with them or not, as they could, while they walked on together at their own hasty pace. He was able to introduce some improvement occasionally, though by no means to the extent he wished; he absolutely would not walk away from them; and at any crossing or any crowd, when Mr Price was only calling out, 'Come, girls; come, Fan; come, Sue, take care of yourselves; keep a sharp look out!' he would give them his particular attendance.

Once fairly in the dockyard, he began to reckon upon some happy intercourse with Fanny, as they were very soon joined by a brother lounger of Mr Price's, who was come to take his daily survey of how things went on, and who must prove a far more worthy companion than himself; and after a time the two officers seemed very well satisfied going about together, and discussing matters of equal and never-failing interest, while the young people sat down upon some timbers in the yard, or found a seat on board a vessel in the stocks which they all went to look at. Fanny was most conveniently in want of rest. Crawford could not have wished her more fatigued or more ready to sit down; but he could have wished her sister away. A quick-looking girl of Susan's age was the very worst third in the world: totally different from Lady Bertram, all eyes and ears; and there was no introducing the main point before her. He must content himself with being only generally agreeable, and letting Susan have her share of entertainment, with the indulgence, now and then, of a look or hint for the better informed and conscious Fanny. Norfolk was what he had mostly to talk of: there he had been some time, and everything there was rising in importance from his present schemes. Such a man could come from no place, no society, without importing something to amuse; his journeys and his acquaintances were all of use, and Susan was entertained in a way quite new to her. For Fanny, somewhat more was related than the accidental agreeableness of the parties he had been in. For her approbation, the particular reason of his going into Norfolk at all, at this unusual time of year, was given. It had been real business, relative to the renewal of a lease in which the welfare of a large and (he believed) industrious family was at stake. He had suspected his agent of some underhand dealing; of meaning to bias him against the deserving; and he had determined to go himself, and thoroughly investigate the merits of the case. He had gone, had done even more good than he had foreseen, had been useful to more than his first plan had comprehended, and was now able to congratulate himself upon it, and to feel that, in performing a duty, he had secured agreeable recollections for his own mind. He had introduced himself to some tenants, whom he had never seen before; he had begun making acquaintances with cottages whose very existence, though on his own estate, had been hitherto unknown to him. This was aimed, and well aimed, at Fanny. It was pleasing to hear him speak so properly; here he had been acting as he ought to do. To be the friend of the poor and the oppressed! Nothing could be more grateful to her; and she was on the point of giving him an approving look when it was all frightened off, by his adding a something too pointed of his hoping soon to have an assistant, a friend, a guide in every plan of utility or charity for Everingham; a somebody that would make Everingham and all about it a dearer object than it had ever been yet.

She turned away, and wished he would not say such things. She was willing to allow he might have more good qualities than she had been wont to suppose. She began to feel the possibility of his turning out well at last; but he was and must ever be completely unsuited to her, and ought not to think of her.

He perceived that enough had been said of Everingham, and that it would be as well to talk of something else, and turned to Mansfield. He could not have chosen better; that was a topic to bring back her attention and her looks almost instantly. It was a real indulgence to her to hear or to speak of Mansfield. Now so long divided from every body who knew the place, she felt it quite the voice of a friend when he mentioned it, and led the way to her fond exclamations in praise of its beauties and comforts, and by his honourable tribute to its inhabitants allowed her to gratify her own heart in the warmest eulogium, in speaking of her uncle as all that was clever and good, and her aunt as having the sweetest of all sweet tempers.

He had a great attachment to Mansfield himself; he said so; he looked forward with the hope of spending much, very much, of his time there; always there, or in the neighbourhood. He particularly built upon a very happy summer and autumn there this year; he felt that it would be so; he depended upon it; a summer and autumn infinitely superior to the last. As animated as diversified, as social, but with circumstances of superiority undescribable.

'Mansfield, Sotherton, Thornton Lacey,' he continued, 'what a society will be comprised in those houses! And at Michaelmas, perhaps, a fourth may be added: some small hunting-box in the vicinity of everything so dear; for as to any partnership in Thornton Lacey, as Edmund Bertram once good-humouredly proposed, I hope I foresee two objections: two fair, excellent, irresistible objections to that plan.'

Fanny was doubly silenced here; though when the moment was passed, could regret that she had not forced herself into the acknowledged comprehension of one half of his meaning, and encouraged him to say something more of his sister and Edmund. It was a subject which she must learn to speak of, and the weakness that shrunk from it would soon be quite unpardonable.

When Mr Price and his friend had seen all that they wished, or had time for, the others were ready to return; and in the course of their walk back, Mr Crawford contrived a minute's privacy for telling Fanny that his only business in Portsmouth was to see her; that he was come down for a couple of days on her account and hers only, and because he could not endure a longer total separation. She was sorry, really sorry; and yet in spite of this and the two or three other things which she wished he had not said, she thought him altogether improved since she had seen him; he was much more gentle, obliging, and attentive to other people's feelings than he had ever been at Mansfield; she had never seen him so agreeable – so *near* being agreeable; his behaviour to her father could not offend, and there was something particularly kind and proper in the notice he took of Susan. He was decidedly improved. She wished the next day over, she wished he had come only for one day; but it was not so very bad as she would have expected: the pleasure of talking of Mansfield was so very great.

Before they parted, she had to thank him for another pleasure, and one of no trivial kind. Her father asked him to do them the honour of taking his mutton with them, and Fanny had time for only one thrill of horror, before he declared himself prevented by a prior engagement. He was engaged to dinner already both for that day and the next; he had met with some acquaintance at the Crown who would not be denied; he should have the honour, however, of waiting on them again on the morrow, etc., and so they parted – Fanny in a state of actual felicity from escaping so horrible an evil!

To have had him join their family dinner-party, and see all their deficiencies, would have been dreadful! Rebecca's cookery, and Rebecca's waiting, and Betsey's eating at table without restraint, and pulling every thing about as she chose, were what Fanny herself was not yet enough inured to for her often to make a tolerable meal. *She* was nice only from natural delicacy, but *he* had been brought up in a school of luxury and epicurism.

CHAPTER FORTY TWO

THE PRICES WERE JUST setting off for church the next day when Mr Crawford appeared again. He came, not to stop, but to join them; he was asked to go with them to the Garrison Chapel, which was exactly what he had intended, and they all walked thither together.

The family were now seen to advantage. Nature had given them no inconsiderable share of beauty, and every Sunday dressed them in their cleanest skins and best attire. Sunday always brought this comfort to Fanny, and on this Sunday she felt it more than ever. Her poor mother now did not look so very unworthy of being Lady Bertram's sister as she was but too apt to look. It often grieved her to the heart to think of the contrast between them; to think that where nature had made so little difference, circumstances should have made so much, and that her mother as handsome as Lady Bertram, and some years her junior, should have an appearance so much more worn and faded, so comfortless, so slatternly, so shabby. But Sunday made her a very creditable and tolerably cheerful-looking Mrs Price, coming abroad with a fine family of children, feeling a little respite of her weekly cares, and only discomposed if she saw her boys run into danger, or Rebecca pass by with a flower in her hat.

In chapel they were obliged to divide, but Mr Crawford took care not to be divided from the female branch; and after chapel he still continued with them, and made one in the family party on the ramparts.

Mrs Price took her weekly walk on the ramparts every fine Sunday throughout the year, always going directly after morning service and staying till dinner-time. It was her public place: there she met her acquaintances, heard a little news, talked over the badness of the Portsmouth servants, and wound up her spirits for the six days ensuing.

Thither they now went; Mr Crawford most happy to consider the Miss Prices as his peculiar charge; and before they had been there long, somehow

Only discomposed if she saw Rebecca pass by with a flower in her hat

or other, there was no saying how, Fanny could not have believed it, but he was walking between them with an arm of each under his, and she did not know how to prevent or put an end to it. It made her uncomfortable for a time, but yet there were enjoyments in the day and in the view which would be felt.

The day was uncommonly lovely. It was really March; but it was April in its mild air, brisk soft wind, and bright sun, occasionally clouded for a minute; and every thing looked so beautiful under the influence of such a sky; the effects of the shadows pursuing each other on the ships at Spithead and the island beyond, with the ever-varying hues of the sea, now at high water, dancing in its glee and dashing against the ramparts with so fine a sound, produced altogether such a combination of charms for Fanny, as made her gradually almost careless of the circumstances under which she felt them. Nay, had she been without his arm, she would soon have known that she needed it, for she wanted strength for a two hours' saunter of this kind, coming, as it generally did, upon a week's previous inactivity. Fanny was beginning to feel the effect of being debarred from her usual regular exercise; she had lost ground as to health since her being in Portsmouth; and but for Mr Crawford and the beauty of the weather would soon have been knocked up now.

The loveliness of the day, and of the view, he felt like herself. They often stopped with the same sentiment and taste, leaning against the wall some minutes, to look and admire, and considering he was not Edmund, Fanny could not but allow that he was sufficiently open to the charms of nature, and very well able to express his admiration. She had a few tender reveries now and then, which he could some times take advantage of to look on her face without detection; and the result of these looks was, that though as bewitching as ever, her face was less blooming than it ought to be. She *said* she was very well, and did not like to be supposed otherwise; but take it all in all, he was convinced that her present residence could not be comfortable, and therefore could not be salutary for her, and he was growing anxious for her being again at Mansfield, where her own happiness, and his in seeing her, must be so much greater.

'You have been here a month, I think?' said he.

'No; not quite a month. It is only four weeks to-morrow since I left Mansfield.'

'You are a most accurate and honest reckoner. I should call that a month.'

'I did not arrive here till Tuesday evening.'

'And it is to be a two months' visit, is not it?'

'Yes. My uncle talked of two months. I suppose it will not be less.'

'And how are you to be conveyed back again? Who comes for you?'

'I do not know. I have heard nothing about it yet from my aunt. Perhaps I may be able to stay longer. It may not be convenient for me to be fetched exactly at the two months' end.'

After a moment's reflection Mr Crawford replied, 'I know Mansfield, I know its way, I know its faults towards *you*. I know the danger of your being so far forgotten, as to have your comforts give way to the imaginary convenience of any single being in the family. I am aware that you may be left here week after week, if Sir Thomas cannot settle every thing for coming himself, or sending your aunt's maid for you, without involving the slightest alteration of the arrangements which he may have laid down for the next quarter of a year. This will not do. Two months is an ample allowance; I should think six weeks quite enough. I am considering your sister's health,' said he, addressing himself to Susan, 'which I think the confinement of Portsmouth unfavourable to. She requires constant air and exercise. When you know her as well as I do, I am sure you will agree that she does, and that she ought never to be long banished from the free air and liberty of the country. If, therefore' (turning again to Fanny), 'you find yourself growing unwell, and any difficulties arise about your returning to Mansfield, without waiting for the two months to be ended, *that* must not be regarded as of any consequence, if you feel yourself at all less strong or comfortable than usual, and will only let my sister know it, give her only the slightest hint, she and I will immediately come down, and take you back to Mansfield. You know the ease and the pleasure with which this would be done. You know all that would be felt on the occasion.'

Fanny thanked him, but tried to laugh it off.

'I am perfectly serious,' he replied, 'as you perfectly know. And I hope you will not be cruelly concealing any tendency to indisposition. Indeed, you shall *not*; it shall not be in your power; for so long only as you positively say, in every letter to Mary, "I am well," and I know you cannot speak or write a falsehood, so long only shall you be considered as well.'

Fanny thanked him again, but was affected and distressed to a degree that made it impossible for her to say much, or even to be certain of what she ought to say. This was towards the close of their walk. He attended them to the last, and left them only at the door of their own house, when he knew them to be going to dinner, and therefore pretended to be waited for elsewhere.

'I wish you were not so tired,' said he, still detaining Fanny after all the others were in the house – 'I wish I felt you in stronger health. Is there any thing I can do for you in town? I have half an idea of going into Norfolk again soon. I am not satisfied about Maddison. I am sure he still means to impose on me if possible, and get a cousin of his own into a certain mill, which I design for some body else. I must come to an understanding with him. I must make him know that I will not be tricked on the south side of Everingham, any more than on the north: that I will be master of my own property. I was not explicit enough with him before. The mischief such a man does on an estate, both as to the credit of his employer and the welfare of the poor, is inconceivable. I have a great mind to go back into Norfolk directly, and put every thing at once on such a footing as cannot be afterwards swerved from. Maddison is a clever fellow; I do not wish to displace him, provided he does not try to displace *me*; but it would be simple to be duped by a man who has no right of creditor to dupe me, and worse than simple to let him give me a hard-hearted, griping fellow for a tenant, instead of an honest man, to whom I have given half a promise already. Would it not be worse than simple? Shall I go? Do you advise it?'

'I advise! You know very well what is right.'

'Yes. When you give me your opinion, I always know what is right. Your judgment is my rule of right.'

'Oh, no! do not say so. We have all a better guide in ourselves, if we would attend to it, than any other person can be. Good-bye; I wish you a pleasant journey to-morrow.'

'Is there nothing I can do for you in town?'

'Nothing, I am much obliged to you.'

'Have you no message for any body?'

'My love to your sister, if you please; and when you see my cousin, my cousin Edmund, I wish you would be so good as to say that I suppose I shall soon hear from him.'

'Certainly; and if he is lazy or negligent, I will write his excuses myself.'

He could say no more, for Fanny would be no longer detained. He pressed her hand, looked at her, and was gone. *He* went to while away the next three hours as he could, with his other acquaintance, till the best dinner that a capital inn afforded was ready for their enjoyment, and *she* turned in to her more simple one immediately.

Their general fare bore a very different character; and could he have suspected how many privations, besides that of exercise, she endured in her father's house, he would have wondered that her looks were not much more affected than he found them. She was so little equal to Rebecca's puddings and Rebecca's hashes, brought to table, as they all were, with such accompaniments of half-cleaned plates, and not half-cleaned knives and forks, that she was very often constrained to defer her heartiest meal till she could send her brothers in the evening for biscuits and buns. After being nursed up at Mansfield, it was too late in the day to be hardened at Portsmouth; and though Sir Thomas, had he known all, might have thought his niece in the most promising way of being starved, both mind and body, into a much juster value of Mr Crawford's good company and good fortune, he would probably have feared to push his experiment farther, lest she might die under the cure.

Fanny was out of spirits all the rest of the day. Though tolerably secure of not seeing Mr Crawford again, she could not help being low. It was parting with some body of the nature of a friend; and though, in one light, glad to have him gone, it seemed as if she was now deserted by every body; it was a sort of renewed separation from Mansfield; and she could not think of his returning to town and being frequently with Mary and Edmund, without feelings so near akin to envy as made her hate herself for having them.

Her dejection had no abatement from anything passing around her; a friend or two of her father's, as always happened if he was not with them, spent the long, long evening there; and from six o'clock till half-past nine, there was little intermission of noise or grog. She was very low. The wonderful improvement which she still fancied in Mr Crawford was the nearest to administering comfort of any thing within the current of her thoughts. Not considering in how different a circle she had been just seeing him, nor how much might be owing to contrast, she was quite persuaded of his being astonishingly more gentle and regardful of others than formerly. And, if in little things, must it not be so in great? So anxious for her health and comfort, so very feeling as he now expressed himself, and really seemed, might not it be fairly supposed that he would not much longer persevere in a suit so distressing to her?

CHAPTER FORTY THREE

IT WAS PRESUMED THAT Mr Crawford was travelling back to London, on the morrow, for nothing more was seen of him at Mr Price's; and two days afterwards, it was a fact ascertained to Fanny by the following letter from his sister, opened and read by her, on another account, with the most anxious curiosity:—

'I have to inform you, my dearest Fanny, that Henry has been down to Portsmouth to see you; that he had a delightful walk with you to the dockyard last Saturday, and one still more to be dwelt on the next day, on the ramparts; when the balmy air, the sparkling sea, and your sweet looks and conversation were altogether in the most delicious harmony, and afforded sensations which are to raise ecstasy even in retrospect. This, as well as I understand , is to be the substance of my information. He makes me write, but I do not know what else is to be communicated, except this said visit to Portsmouth, and these two said walks and his introduction to your family, especially to a fair sister of yours, a fine girl of fifteen, who was of the party on the ramparts, taking her first lesson, I presume, in love. I have not time for writing much, but it would be

out of place if I had, for this is to be a mere letter of business, penned for the purpose of conveying necessary information, which could not be delayed without risk of evil. My dear, dear Fanny, if I had you here, how I would talk to you! You should listen to me till you were tired, and advise me till you were still tired more; but it is impossible to put a hundredth part of my great mind on paper, so I will abstain altogether, and leave you to guess what you like. I have no news for you. You have politics, of course; and it would be too bad to plague you with the names of people and parties that fill up my time. I ought to have sent you an account of your cousin's first party, but I was lazy, and now it is too long ago; suffice it, that everything was just as it ought to be, in a style that any of her connections must have been gratified to witness, and that her own dress and manners did her the greatest credit. My friend, Mrs Fraser, is made for such a house, and it would not make me *miserable. I go to Lady Stornaway after Easter; she seems in high spirits, and very happy. I fancy Lord S. is very good-humoured and pleasant in his own family, and I do not think him so very ill-looking as I did – at least, one sees many worse. He will not do by the side of your cousin Edmund. Of the last-mentioned hero, what shall I say? If I avoided his name entirely, it would look suspicious. I will say, then, that we have seen him two or three times, and that my friends here are very much struck with his gentlemanlike appearance. Mrs Fraser (no bad judge) declares she knows but three men in town who have so good a person, height, and air; and I must confess, when he dined here the other day, there were none to compare with him, and we were a party of sixteen. Luckily there is no distinction of dress nowadays to tell tales, but—but—but— Yours affectionately—*

'I had almost forgot (it was Edmund's fault: he gets into my head more than does me good) one very material thing I had to say from Henry and myself – I mean about our taking you back into Northamptonshire. My dear little creature, do not stay at Portsmouth to lose your pretty looks. Those vile sea-breezes are the ruin of beauty and health. My poor aunt always felt affected if within ten miles of the sea, which the Admiral of course never believed, but I know it was so. I am at your service and Henry's, at an hour's notice. I should like the scheme, and we would make a little circuit, and show you Everingham in our way, and perhaps you would not mind passing through London, and seeing the inside of St George's, Hanover Square. Only keep your cousin Edmund from me at such a time: I should not like to be tempted. What a long letter! one word more. Henry, I find, has some idea of going into Norfolk again upon some business that you *approve but this cannot possibly be permitted before the middle of next week; that is, he cannot anyhow be spared till after the* 14th, *for* we *have a party that evening. The value of a man like Henry, on such an occasion, is what you can have no conception of; so you*

must take it upon my word to be inestimable. He will see the Rushworths, which I own I am not sorry for – having a little curiosity, and so I think has he – though he will not acknowledge it.'

This was a letter to be run through eagerly, to be read deliberately, to supply matter for much reflection, and to leave everything in greater suspense than ever. The only certainty to be drawn from it was, that nothing decisive had yet taken place. Edmund had not yet spoken. How Miss Crawford really felt, how she meant to act, or might act without or against her meaning; whether his importance to her were quite what it had been before the last separation; whether, if lessened, it were likely to lessen more, or to recover itself, were subjects for endless conjecture, and to be thought of on that day and many days to come, without producing any conclusion. The idea that returned the oftenest was that Miss Crawford, after proving herself cooled and staggered by a return to London habits, would yet prove herself in the end too much attached to him to give him up. She would try to be more ambitious than her heart would allow. She would hesitate, she would tease, she would condition, she would require a great deal, but she would finally accept.

This was Fanny's most frequent expectation. A house in town, *that*, she thought, must be impossible. Yet there was no saying what Miss Crawford might not ask. The prospect for her cousin grew worse and worse. The woman who could speak of him, and speak only of his appearance! What an unworthy attachment! To be deriving support from the commendations of Mrs Fraser! *She* who had known him intimately half a year! Fanny was ashamed of her. Those parts of the letter which related only to Mr Crawford and herself, touched her, in comparison, slightly. Whether Mr Crawford went into Norfolk before or after the 14th was certainly no concern of hers, though, every thing considered she thought he *would* go without delay. That Miss Crawford should endeavour to secure a meeting between him and Mrs Rushworth was all in her worst line of conduct, and grossly unkind and ill-judged; but she hoped *he* would not be actuated by any such degrading curiosity. He acknowledged no such inducement, and his sister ought to have given him credit for better feelings than her own.

She was yet more impatient for another letter from town after receiving this than she had been before; and for a few days was so unsettled by it altogether, by what had come, and what might come, that her usual readings and conversations with Susan were much suspended. She could not command her attention as she wished. If Mr Crawford remembered her message to her cousin, she thought it very likely, *most* likely, that he would write to her at all events; it would be most consistent with his usual kindness; and till she got rid of this idea, till it gradually wore off, by no letters appearing in the course of three or four days more, she was in a most restless, anxious state.

At length, a something like composure succeeded. Suspense must be submitted to, and must not be allowed to wear her out, and make her useless. Time did something, her own exertions something more, and she resumed her attentions to Susan, and again awakened the same interest in them.

Susan was growing very fond of her, and though without any of the early delight in books, which had been so strong in Fanny, with a disposition much less inclined to sedentary pursuits, or to information for information's sake, she had so strong a desire, of not *appearing* ignorant, as, with a good clear understanding, made her a most attentive, profitable, thankful pupil. Fanny was her oracle. Fanny's explanations and remarks were a most important addition to every essay, or every chapter of history. What Fanny told her of former tomes dwelt more on her mind than the pages of Goldsmith; and she paid her sister the compliment of preferring her style to that of any printed author. The early habit of reading was wanting.

Their conversations, however, were not always on subjects so high as history or morals. Others had their hour; and of lesser matters none returned so often, or remained so long between them, as Mansfield Park, a description of the people, the manners, the amusements, the ways of Mansfield Park. Susan, who had an innate taste for the genteel and well-appointed, was eager to hear, and Fanny could not but indulge herself in dwelling on so beloved a theme. She hoped it was not wrong; though, after a time, Susan's very great admiration of every thing said or done in her uncle's house, and earnest longing to go into Northamptonshire, seemed almost to blame her for exciting feelings which could not be gratified.

Poor Susan was very little better fitted for home than her elder sister; and as Fanny grew thoroughly to understand this, she began to feel that when her own release from Portsmouth came, her happiness would have a material drawback in leaving Susan behind. That a girl so capable of being made every thing good should be left in such hands, distressed her more and more. Were *she* likely to have a home to invite her to, what a blessing it would be! And had it been possible for her to return Mr Crawford's regard, the probability of his being very far from objecting to such a measure would have been the greatest increase of all her own comforts. She thought he was really good-tempered, and could fancy his entering into a plan of that sort most pleasantly.

CHAPTER FORTY FOUR

SEVEN WEEKS OF THE TWO months were very nearly gone, when the one letter, the letter from Edmund, so long expected, was put into Fanny's hands. As she opened, and saw its length, she prepared herself for a minute detail of happiness and a profusion of love and praise towards the fortunate creature who was now mistress of his fate. These were the contents:—

Mansfield Park.

'MY DEAR FANNY,

Excuse me that I have not written before. Crawford told me that you were wishing to hear from me, but I found it impossible to write from London, and persuaded myself that you would understand my silence. Could I have sent a few happy lines, they should not have been wanting, but nothing of that nature was ever in my power. I am returned to Mansfield in a less assured state than when I left it. My hopes are much weaker. You are probably aware of this already. So very fond of you as Miss Crawford is, it is most natural that she should tell you enough of her own feelings to furnish a tolerable guess at mine. I will not be prevented however, from making my own communication. Our confidences in you need not clash. I ask no questions. There is some thing soothing in the idea that we have the same friend, and that whatever unhappy differences of opinion may exist between us, we are united in our love of you. It will be a comfort to me to tell you how things now are, and what are my present plans, if plans I can be said to have. I have been returned since Saturday. I was three weeks in London, and saw her (for London) very often. I had every attention from the Frasers that could be reasonably expected. I dare say I was not *reasonable in carrying with me hopes of an intercourse at all like that of Mansfield. It was her manner, however, rather than any unfrequency of meeting. Had she been different when I did see her, I should have made no complaint, but from the very first she was altered; my first reception was so unlike what I had hoped, that I had almost resolved on leaving London again directly. I need not particularise. You know the weak side of her character, and may imagine the sentiments and expressions which were torturing me. She was in high spirits, and surrounded by those who were giving all the support of their own bad sense to her too lively mind. I do not like Mrs Fraser. She is a cold-hearted, vain woman, who has married entirely from convenience, and though evidently unhappy in her marriage, places her disappointment not to faults of judgment, or temper, or disproportion of age, but to her being, after all, less affluent than many of her acquaintance, especially than her sister, Lady Stornaway, and is the determined supporter of everything mercenary and ambitious, provided it be only mercenary and ambitious enough. I look upon her intimacy with those two sisters as the greatest misfortune of her life and mine. They have been leading her astray for years. Could she be detached from them! – and sometimes I do not despair of it, for the affection appears to me principally on their side. They are very fond of her; but I am sure she does not love them as she loves you. When I think of her great attachment to you, indeed, and the whole of her judicious, upright conduct as a sister, she appears a very different creature, capable of every thing noble, and I am ready to blame myself for a too harsh construction of a playful manner. I cannot give her up, Fanny. She is the only woman in the world whom I could ever think of as a wife. If I did not believe that she had some regard for me, of course I should not say this, but I do believe it. I am convinced that she is not without a decided preference. I have no jealousy of any individual. It is the influence of the fashionable world altogether that I am jealous of. It is the habits of wealth that I fear. Her ideas are not higher than her own fortune may warrant, but they are beyond what our incomes united could authorise. There is comfort, however, even here. I could better bear to lose her, because not rich enough, than because of my profession. That would only prove her affection not equal to sacrifices, which, in fact, I am scarcely justified in asking; and, if I am refused,* that, *I think, will be the honest motive. Her prejudices, I trust, are not so strong as they were. You have my thoughts exactly as they arise, my dear Fanny; perhaps they are sometimes contradictory, but it will not be a less faithful picture of my mind. Having once begun, it is a pleasure to me to tell you all I feel. I cannot give her up. Connected as we already are, and, I hope, are to be, to give up Mary Crawford would be to give up the society of some of those most dear to me; to banish myself from the very houses and friends whom, under any other distress, I should turn to for consolation. The loss of Mary I must consider as comprehending the loss of Crawford and of Fanny. Were it a decided thing, an actual refusal, I hope I should know how to bear it, and how to endeavour to weaken her hold on my heart, and in the course of a few years – but I am writing nonsense. Were I refused, I must bear it; and till I am, I can never cease to try for her. This is the truth. The only question is* how? *What may be the likeliest means? I have sometimes thought of going to London again after Easter, and sometimes resolved on doing nothing till she returns to Mansfield. Even now, she speaks with pleasure of being in Mansfield in June; but June is at a great distance, and I believe I shall write to her. I have nearly determined on explaining myself by letter. To be at an early certainty is a material object. My present state is miserably irksome. Considering every thing, I think a letter will be decidedly the best method of explanation. I shall be able to write much that I could not say, and shall be giving her time for reflection before she resolves on her answer, and I am less afraid of the result of reflection than of an immediate hasty impulse; I think I am. My greatest danger would lie in her consulting Mrs Fraser, and I at a distance unable to help my own cause. A letter exposes to all the evil of consultation, and where the mind is anything short of perfect decision, an adviser may, in an unlucky moment, lead it to do what it may afterwards regret. I must think this matter over a little. This long letter, full of my own concerns alone, will be enough to tire even the friendship of a Fanny. The last time I saw Crawford was at Mrs Fraser's party. I am more and more satisfied with all that I see and hear of him. There is not a shadow of wavering. He thoroughly knows his own mind, and acts up to his resolutions: an inestimable quality. I could not see him and my eldest sister in the same room, without recollecting what you once told me, and I acknowledge that they did not meet as friends. There was marked coolness on her side. They scarcely spoke. I saw him draw back surprised, and I was sorry that Mrs Rushworth should resent any former supposed slight to Miss Bertram. You will wish to hear my opinion of Maria's degree of comfort as a wife. There is no appearance of unhappiness. I hope they get on pretty well together. I dined twice in Wimpole Street, and might have been there oftener, but it is mortifying to be with Rushworth as a brother. Julia seems to enjoy London exceedingly. I had little enjoyment there, but have less here. We are not a lively party. You are very much wanted. I miss you more than I can express. My mother desires her best love, and hopes to hear from you soon. She talks of you almost every hour, and I am sorry to find how many weeks more she is likely to be without you. My father means to fetch you himself, but it will not be till after Easter, when he has business in town. You are happy at Portsmouth, I hope, but this must not be a yearly visit. I want you at home, that I may have your opinion about Thornton Lacey. I have little heart for extensive improvements till I know that it will ever have a mistress. I think I shall certainly write. It is quite settled that the Grants go to Bath; they leave Mansfield on Monday. I am glad of it. I am not comfortable enough to be fit for any body; but your aunt seems to feel out of luck that such an article of Mansfield news should fall to my pen instead of hers. Yours ever, my dearest Fanny—'*

'I never will, no, I certainly never will wish for a letter again,' was Fanny's secret declaration as she finished this. 'What do they bring but disappointment and sorrow? Not till after Easter! How shall I bear it? And my poor aunt talking of me every hour!'

Fanny checked the tendency of these thoughts as well as she could, but she was within half a minute of starting the idea that Sir Thomas was quite unkind, both to her aunt and to herself. As for the main subject of the letter, there was nothing in that to soothe irritation. She was almost vexed into displeasure and anger against Edmund. 'There is no good in this delay,' said she. 'Why is not it settled? He is blinded, and nothing will open his eyes; nothing can, after having had truths before him so long in vain. He will marry her, and be poor and miserable. God grant that her influence does not make him cease to be respectable!' She looked over the letter again. '"So very fond of me!" 'tis nonsense all. She loves nobody but herself and her brother. "Her friends leading her astray for years!" She is quite as likely to have led *them* astray. They have all, perhaps, been corrupting one another; but if they are so much fonder of her than she is of them, she is the less likely to have been hurt, except by their flattery. "The only woman in the world whom he could ever think of as a wife." I firmly believe it. It is an attachment to govern his whole life. Accepted or refused, his heart is wedded to her for ever. "The loss of Mary I must consider as comprehending the loss of Crawford and Fanny." Edmund, you do not know *me*. The families would never be connected if you did not connect them! Oh! write, write. Finish it at once. Let there be an end of this suspense. Fix, commit, condemn yourself.'

Such sensations, however, were too near akin to resentment to be long guiding Fanny's soliloquies. She was soon more softened and sorrowful. His warm regard, his kind expression, his confidential treatment, touched her strongly. He was only too good to every body. It was a letter, in short, which she would not but have had for the world, and which could never be valued enough. This was the end of it.

Every body at all addicted to letter-writing, without having much to say, which will include a large proportion of the female world, at least, must feel with Lady Bertram that she was out of luck in having such a capital piece of Mansfield news as the certainty of the Grants going to Bath, occur at a time when she could make no advantage of it, and will admit that it must have been very mortifying to her to see it fall to the share of her thankless son, and treated as concisely as possible at the end of a long letter, instead of having it to spread over the largest part of a page of her own. For though Lady Bertram rather shone in the epistolary line, having early in her marriage, from the want of other employment, and the circumstance of Sir Thomas's being in Parliament, got into the way of making and keeping correspondents and formed for herself a very creditable, commonplace, amplifying style, so that very little matter was enough for her: she could not do entirely without any; she must have some thing to write about, even to her niece; and being so soon to lose all the benefit of Dr Grant's gouty symptoms and Mrs Grant's morning calls, it was very hard upon her to be deprived of one of the last epistolary uses she could put them to.

There was a rich amends, however, preparing for her. Lady Bertram's hour of good luck came. Within a few days from the receipt of Edmund's letter, Fanny had one from her aunt, beginning thus:—

'My Dear Fanny,

I take up my pen to communicate some very alarming intelligence, which I make no doubt will give you much concern.'

This was a great deal better than to have to take up the pen to acquaint her with all the particulars of the Grants' intended journey, for the present intelligence was of a nature to promise occupation for the pen for many days to come, being no less than the dangerous illness of her eldest son, of which they had received notice by express a few hours before.

Tom had gone from London with a party of young men to Newmarket, where a neglected fall and a good deal of drinking had brought on a fever; and when the party broke up, being unable to move, had been left by himself at the house of one of these young men to the comforts of sickness and solitude, and the attendance only of servants. Instead of being soon well enough to follow his friends, as he had then hoped, his disorder increased considerably, and it was not long before he thought so ill of himself, as to be as ready as his physician to have a letter dispatched to Mansfield.

'*This distressing intelligence, as you may suppose,*' observed her ladyship, after giving the substance of it, '*has agitated us exceedingly and we cannot prevent ourselves from being greatly alarmed and apprehensive for the poor invalid, whose state Sir Thomas fears may be very critical; and Edmund kindly proposes attending his brother immediately, but I am happy to add that Sir Thomas will not leave me on this distressing occasion, as it would be too trying for me. We shall greatly miss Edmund in our small circle, but I trust and hope he will find the poor invalid in a less alarming state than might be apprehended, and that he will be able to bring him to Mansfield shortly, which Sir Thomas proposes should be done, and thinks best on every account, and I flatter myself the poor sufferer will soon be able to bear the removal without material inconvenience or injury. As I have little doubt of your feeling for us, my dear Fanny, under these distressing circumstances, I will write again very soon.*'

Fanny's feelings on the occasion were indeed considerably more warm and genuine than her aunt's style of writing. She felt truly for them all. Tom dangerously ill, Edmund gone to attend him, and the sadly small party remaining at Mansfield, were cares to shut out every other care, or almost every other. She could just find selfishness enough to wonder whether

Edmund *had* written to Miss Crawford before this summons came, but no sentiment dwelt long with her that was not purely affectionate and disinterestedly anxious. Her aunt did not neglect her; she wrote again and again; they were receiving frequent accounts from Edmund, and these accounts were as regularly transmitted to Fanny, in the same diffuse style, and the same medley of trusts, hopes, and fears, all following and producing each other at haphazard. It was a sort of playing at being frightened. The sufferings which Lady Bertram did not see had little power over her fancy; and she wrote very comfortably about agitation, and anxiety, and poor invalids, till Tom was actually conveyed to Mansfield, and her own eyes had beheld his altered appearance. Then a letter which she had been previously preparing for Fanny was finished in a different style, in the language of real feeling and alarm; then she wrote as she might have spoken. 'He is just come, my dear Fanny, and is taken upstairs; and I am so shocked to see him, that I do not know what to do. I am sure he has been very ill. Poor Tom! I am quite grieved for him, and very much frightened, and so is Sir Thomas; and how glad I should be if you were here to comfort me. But Sir Thomas hopes he will be better to-morrow, and says we must consider his journey.'

The real solicitude now awakened in the maternal bosom was not soon over. Tom's extreme impatience to be removed to Mansfield, and experience those comforts of home and family which had been little thought of in uninterrupted health, had probably induced his being conveyed thither too early, as a return of fever came on, and for a week he was in a more alarming state than ever. They were all very seriously frightened. Lady Bertram wrote her daily terrors to her niece, who might now be said to live upon letters, and pass all her time between suffering from that of to-day and looking forward to to-morrow's. Without any particular affection for her eldest cousin, her tenderness of heart made her feel that she could not spare him, and the purity of her principles added yet a keener solicitude, when she considered how little useful, how little self-denying his life had (apparently) been.

Susan was her only companion and listener on this, as on more common occasions. Susan was always ready to hear and to sympathise. Nobody else could be interested in so remote an evil as illness in a family above a hundred miles off; not even Mrs Price, beyond a brief question or two, if she saw her daughter with a letter in her hand, and now and then the quiet observation of – 'My poor sister Bertram must be in a great deal of trouble.'

So long divided and so differently situated, the ties of blood were little more than nothing. An attachment, originally as tranquil as their tempers, was now become a mere name. Mrs Price did quite as much for Lady Bertram as Lady Bertram would have done for Mrs Price. Three or four

Prices might have been swept away, any or all except Fanny and William, and Lady Bertram would have thought little about it; or perhaps might have caught from Mrs Norris's lips the cant of its being a very happy thing and a great blessing to their poor dear sister Price to have them so well provided for.

CHAPTER FORTY FIVE

AT ABOUT THE WEEK'S END from his return to Mansfield, Tom's immediate danger was over, and he was so far pronounced safe as to make his mother perfectly easy; for being now used to the sight of him in his suffering, helpless state, and hearing only the best, and never thinking beyond what she heard, with no disposition for alarm and no aptitude at a hint, Lady Bertram was the happiest subject in the world for a little medical imposition. The fever was subdued; the fever had been his complaint; of course he would soon be well again. Lady Bertram could think nothing less, and Fanny shared her aunt's security, till she received a few lines from Edmund, written purposely to give her a clearer idea of his brother's situation, and acquaint her with the apprehensions which he and his father had imbibed from the physician with respect to some strong hectic symptoms, which seemed to seize the frame on the departure of the fever. They judged it best that Lady Bertram should not be harassed by alarms which, it was to be hoped, would prove unfounded; but there was no reason why Fanny should not know the truth. They were apprehensive for his lungs.

A very few lines from Edmund showed her the patient and the sick room in a juster and stronger light than all Lady Bertram's sheets of paper could do. There was hardly any one in the house who might not have described, from personal observation, better than herself; not one who was not more useful at times to her son. She could do nothing but glide in quietly and look at him; but when able to talk or be talked to, or read to, Edmund was the companion he preferred. His aunt worried him by her cares, and Sir Thomas knew not how to bring down his conversation or his voice to the level of irritation and feebleness. Edmund was all in all. Fanny would certainly believe him so at least, and must find that her estimation of him was higher than ever when he appeared as the attendant, supporter, cheerer of a suffering brother. There was not only the debility of recent illness to assist; there was also, as she now learnt, nerves much affected, spirits much depressed to calm and raise, and her own imagination added that there must be a mind to be properly guided.

The family were not consumptive, and she was more inclined to hope than fear for her cousin, except when she thought of Miss Crawford; but Miss Crawford gave her the idea of being the child of good luck, and to her selfishness and vanity it would be good luck to have Edmund the only son.

Even in the sick chamber the fortunate Mary was not forgotten. Edmund's letter had this postscript. 'On the subject of my last, I had actually begun a letter when called away by Tom's illness, but I have now changed my mind, and fear to trust the influence of friends. When Tom is better, I shall go.'

Such was the state of Mansfield, and so it continued with scarcely any change till Easter. A line occasionally added by Edmund to his mother's letter was enough for Fanny's information. Tom's amendment was alarmingly slow.

Easter came particularly late this year, as Fanny had most sorrowfully considered on first learning that she had no chance of leaving Portsmouth till after it. It came, and she had yet heard nothing of her return, nothing even of the going to London, which was to precede her return. Her aunt often expressed a wish for her, but there was no notice, no message from the uncle on whom all depended. She supposed he could not yet leave his son, but it was a cruel, a terrible delay to her. The end of April was coming on; it would soon be almost three months, instead of two, that she had been absent from them all and that her days had been passing in a state of penance, which she loved them too well to hope they would thoroughly understand; and who could say when there might be leisure to think of or fetch her?

Her eagerness, her impatience, her longings to be with them, were such as to bring a line or two of Cowper's Tirocinium for ever before her. 'With what intense desire she wants her home,' was continually on her tongue, as the truest description of a yearning which she could not suppose any schoolboy's bosom to feel more keenly.

When she had been coming to Portsmouth, she had loved to call it her home, had been fond of saying that she was going home; the word had been very dear to her, and so it still was, but it must be applied to Mansfield. *That* was now the home. Portsmouth was Portsmouth; Mansfield was home. They had been long so arranged in the indulgence of her secret meditations, and nothing was more consolatory to her than to find her aunt using the same language; 'I cannot but say I much regret your being from home at this distressing time, so very trying to my spirits. I trust and hope, and sincerely wish you may never be absent from home so long again,' were most delightful sentences to her. Still, however, it was her private regale. Delicacy to her parents made her careful not to betray such a preference for her uncle's house. It was always: 'When I go back into Northamptonshire,' or 'when I return to Mansfield, I shall do so and so.' For a great while it was so, but at last the longing grew stronger, it overthrew caution, and she found herself talking of what she should do when she went home, before she was aware. She reproached herself, coloured, and looked fearfully towards her father and mother. She need not have been uneasy. There was no sign of displeasure, or even of hearing her. They were perfectly free from any jealousy of Mansfield. She was as welcome to wish herself there as to be there.

It was sad to Fanny to lose all the pleasures of spring. She had not known before what pleasures she *had* to lose in passing March and April in a town. She had not known before how much the beginnings and progress of vegetation had delighted her. What animation, both of body and mind, she had derived from watching the advance of that season which cannot, in spite of its capriciousness, be unlovely, and seeing its increasing beauties from the earliest flowers in the warmest divisions of her aunt's garden, to the opening of leaves of her uncle's plantations and the glory of his woods. To be losing such pleasures was no trifle; to be losing them because she was in the midst of closeness and noise, to have confinement, bad air, bad smells, substituted for liberty, freshness, fragrance, and verdure, was infinitely worse: but even these incitements to regret were feeble, compared with what arose from the conviction of being missed by her best friends, and the longing to be useful to those who were wanting her!

Could she have been at home, she might have been of service to every creature in the house. She felt that she must have been of use to all. To all she must have saved some trouble of head or hand; and were it only in supporting the spirits of her Aunt Bertram, keeping her from the evil of solitude, or the still greater evil of a restless, officious companion, too apt to be heightening danger in order to enhance her own importance, her being there would have been a general good. She loved to fancy how she could have read to her aunt, how she could have talked to her, and tried at once to make her feel the blessing of what was, and prepare her mind for what might be; and how many walks up and down stairs she might have saved her, and how many messages she might have carried.

It astonished her that Tom's sisters could be satisfied with remaining in London at such a time, through an illness which had now, under different degrees of danger, lasted several weeks. *They* might return to Mansfield when they chose; travelling could be no difficulty to *them*, and she could not comprehend how both could still keep away. If Mrs Rushworth could imagine any interfering obligations, Julia was certainly able to quit London whenever she chose. It appeared from one of her aunt's letters that Julia had offered to return if wanted, but this was all. It was evident that she would rather remain where she was.

Fanny was disposed to think the influence of London very much at war with all respectable attachments. She saw the proof of it in Miss Crawford, as well as in her cousins; *her* attachment to Edmund had been respectable, the most respectable part of her character; her friendship for herself had at least been blameless. Where was either sentiment now? It was so long since Fanny had had any letter from her, that she had some reason to think lightly of the friendship which had been so dwelt on. It was weeks since she had heard any thing of Miss Crawford or of her other connections in town, except through Mansfield, and she was beginning to suppose that she might never know whether Mr Crawford had gone into Norfolk again or not till they met, and might never hear from his sister any more this spring, when the following letter was received to revive old and create some new sensations:—

'Forgive me, my dear Fanny, as soon as you can, for my long silence, and behave as if you could forgive me directly. This is my modest request and expectation, for you are so good, that I depend upon being treated better than I deserve, and I write now to beg an immediate answer. I want to know the state of things at Mansfield Park, and you, no doubt, are perfectly able to give it. One should be a brute not to feel for the distress they are in; and from what I hear, poor Mr Bertram has a bad chance of ultimate recovery. I thought little of his illness at first. I looked upon him as the sort of person to be made a fuss with, and to make a fuss himself in any trifling disorder, and was chiefly concerned for those who had to nurse him; but now it is confidently asserted that he is really in a decline, that the symptoms are most alarming, and that part of the family, at least, are aware of it. If it be so, I am sure you must be included in that part, that discerning part, and therefore entreat you to let me know how far I have been rightly informed. I need not say how rejoiced I shall be to hear there has been any mistake, but the report is so prevalent, that I confess I cannot help trembling. To have such a fine young man cut off in the flower of his days, is most melancholy. Poor Sir Thomas will feel it dreadfully. I really am quite agitated on the subject. Fanny, Fanny, I see you smile and look cunning, but upon my honour I never bribed a physician in my life. Poor young man! If he is to die, there will be two *poor young men less in the world; and with a fearless face and bold voice would I say to anyone, that wealth and consequence could fall into no hands more deserving of them. It was a foolish precipitation last Christmas, but the evil of a few days may be blotted out in part. Varnish and gilding hide many stains. It will be but the loss of the Esquire after his name. With real affection, Fanny, like mine, more might be overlooked. Write to me by return of post, judge of my anxiety, and do not trifle with it. Tell me the real truth, as you have it from the fountain-head. And now do not trouble yourself to be ashamed of either my feelings or your own. Believe me, they are not only natural, they are philanthropic and virtuous. I put it to your conscience, whether "Sir*

Edmund" would not do more good with all the Bertram property than any other possible "Sir." Had the Grants been at home I would not have troubled you, but you are now the only one I can apply to for the truth, his sisters not being within my reach. Mrs R. has been spending the Easter with the Aylmers at Twickenham (as to be sure you know), and is not yet returned; and Julia is with the cousins who live near Bedford Square, but I forget their name and street. Could I immediately apply to either, however, I should still prefer you because it strikes me that they have all along been so unwilling to have their own amusements cut up, as to shut their eyes to the truth. I suppose Mrs R.'s Easter holidays will not last much longer; no doubt they are thorough holidays to her. The Aylmers are pleasant people; and her husband away, she can have nothing but enjoyment, I give her credit for promoting his going dutifully down to Bath, to fetch his mother; but how will she and the dowager agree in one house? Henry is not at hand, so I have nothing to say from him. Do not you think Edmund would have been in town again long ago, but for this illness? – Yours ever,

MARY.

'I had actually began folding my letter when Henry walked in, but he brings no intelligence to prevent my sending it. Mrs R. knows a decline is apprehended; he saw her this morning; she returns to Wimpole Street to-day; the old lady is come. Now do not make yourself uneasy with any queer fancies, because he has been spending a few days at Richmond. He does it every spring. Be assured he cares for nobody but you. At this very moment he is wild to see you, and occupied only in contriving the means for doing so, and for making his pleasure conduce to yours. In proof, he repeats, and more eagerly, what he said at Portsmouth, about our conveying you home, and I join him in it with all my soul. Dear Fanny, write directly, and tell us to come. It will do us all good. He and I can go to the Parsonage, you know, and be no trouble to our friends at Mansfield Park. It would really be gratifying to see them all again, and a little addition of society might be of infinite use to them, and as to yourself, you must feel yourself to be so wanted there, that you cannot in conscience (conscientious as you are) keep away, when you have the means of returning. I have not time or patience to give half Henry's messages; be satisfied that the spirit of each and every one is unalterable affection.'

Fanny's disgust at the greater part of this letter, with her extreme reluctance to bring the writer of it and her cousin Edmund together, would have made her (as she felt) incapable of judging impartially whether the concluding offer might be accepted or not. To herself, individually, it was most tempting. To be finding herself perhaps within three days transported to Mansfield, was an image of the greatest felicity, but it would have been a material drawback to be owing such felicity to persons on whose feeling and conduct, at the present moment, she saw so much to condemn; the sister's feelings, the brother's conduct, *her* coldhearted ambition, *his* thoughtless vanity. To have him still the acquaintance, the flirt, perhaps, of Mrs Rushworth! She was mortified. She had thought better of him. Happily, however, she was not left to weigh and decide between opposite inclinations and doubtful notions of right; there was no occasion to determine whether she ought to keep Edmund and Mary asunder or not. She had a rule to apply to, which settled every thing. Her awe of her uncle, and her dread of taking a liberty with him, made it instantly plain to her what she had to do. She must absolutely decline the proposal. If he wanted, he would send for her; and even to offer an early return was a presumption which hardly any thing would have seemed to justify. She thanked Miss Crawford, but gave a decided negative. 'Her uncle, she understood, meant to fetch her; and as her cousin's illness had continued so many weeks without her being thought at all necessary, she must suppose her return would be unwelcome at present, and that she should be felt an encumbrance.'

Her representation of her cousin's state at this time was exactly according to her own belief of it, and such as she supposed would convey to the sanguine mind of her correspondent the hope of every thing she was wishing for. Edmund would be forgiven for being a clergyman, it seemed, under certain conditions of wealth; and this, she suspected, was all the conquest of prejudice which he was so ready to congratulate himself upon. She had only learnt to think nothing of consequence but money.

CHAPTER FORTY SIX

AS FANNY COULD NOT doubt that her answer was conveying. a real disappointment, she was rather in expectation, from her knowledge of Miss Crawford's temper, of being urged again; and though no second letter arrived for the space of a week, she had still the same feeling when it did come.

On receiving it, she could instantly decide on its containing little writing, and was persuaded of its having the air of a letter of haste and business. Its object was unquestionable; and two moments were enough to start the probability of its being merely to give her notice that they should be in Portsmouth that very day, and to throw her into all the agitation of doubting what she ought to do in such a case. If two moments, however, can surround with difficulties, a third can disperse them; and before she had opened the letter, the possibility of Mr and Miss Crawford's having applied to her uncle and obtained his permission, was giving her ease. This was the letter:

> *'A most scandalous, ill-natured rumour has just reached me, and I write, dear Fanny, to warn you against giving the least credit to it, should it spread into the country. Depend upon it, there is some mistake, and that a day or two will clear it up; at any rate, that Henry is blameless, and in spite of a moment's* étourderie, *thinks of nobody but you. Say not a word of it; hear nothing, surmise nothing, whisper nothing, till I write again. I am sure it will be all hushed up, and nothing proved but Rushworth's folly. If they are gone, I would lay my life they are only gone to Mansfield Park, and Julia with them. But why would not you let us come for you? I wish you may not repent it.—Yours, etc.'*

Fanny stood aghast. As no scandalous, ill-natured rumour had reached her, it was impossible for her to understand much of this strange letter. She could only perceive that it must relate to Wimpole Street and Mr Crawford, and only conjecture that something very imprudent had just occurred in that quarter to draw the notice of the world, and excite her jealousy, in Miss Crawford's apprehension, if she heard it. Miss Crawford need not be alarmed for her. She was only sorry for the parties concerned and for Mansfield, if the report should spread so far; but she hoped it might not. If the Rushworths were gone themselves to Mansfield, as was to be inferred from what Miss Crawford said, it was not likely that anything unpleasant should have preceded them, or at least should make any impression.

As to Mr Crawford, she hoped it might give him a knowledge of his own disposition, convince him that he was not capable of being steadily attached to any one woman in the world, and shame him from persisting any longer in addressing herself.

It was very strange! She had begun to think he really loved her, and to fancy his affection for her some thing more than common; and his sister still said that he cared for nobody else. Yet there must have been some marked display of attentions to her cousin, there must have been some strong indiscretion, since her correspondent was not of a sort to regard a slight one.

Very uncomfortable she was, and must continue, till she heard from Miss Crawford again. It was impossible to banish the letter from her thoughts, and she could not relieve herself by speaking of it to any human being. Miss Crawford need not have urged secrecy with so much warmth; she might have trusted to her sense of what was due to her cousin.

The next day came and brought no second letter. Fanny was disappointed. She could still think of little else all the morning; but, when her father came back in the afternoon with the daily newspaper as usual, she was so far from expecting any elucidation through such a channel that the subject was for a moment out of her head.

She was deep in other musing. The remembrance of her first evening in that room, of her father and his newspaper, came across her. No candle was *now* wanted. The sun was yet an hour and a half above the horizon. She felt that she had, indeed, been three months there; and the sun's rays falling strongly into the parlour, instead of cheering, made her still more melancholy, for sunshine appeared to her a totally different thing in a town and in the country. Here its power was only a glare: a stifling, sickly glare, serving but to bring forward stains and dirt that might otherwise have slept. There was neither health nor gaiety in sunshine in a town. She sat in a blaze of oppressive heat, in a cloud of moving dust, and her eyes could only wander from the walls, marked by her father's head, to the table cut and notched by her brothers, where stood the tea-board never thoroughly cleaned, the cups and saucers wiped in streaks, the milk a mixture of motes floating in thin blue, and the bread and butter growing every minute more greasy than even Rebecca's hands had first produced it. Her father read his newspaper, and her mother lamented over the ragged carpet as usual, while the tea was in preparation, and wished Rebecca would mend it; and Fanny was first roused by his calling out to her, after humphing and considering over a particular paragraph: 'What's the name of your great cousins in town, Fan?'

A moment's recollection enabled her to say, 'Rushworth, sir.'

'And don't they live in Wimpole Street?'

'Yes, sir.'

'Then, there's the devil to pay among them, that's all! There' (holding out the paper to her); 'much good may such fine relations do you. I don't know what Sir Thomas may think of such matters; he may be too much of the courtier and fine gentleman to like his daughter the less. But, by G—! if she belonged to *me*, I'd give her the rope's end as long as I could stand over her. A little flogging for man and woman, too, would be the best way of preventing such things.'

Fanny read to herself that 'it was with infinite concern the newspaper had to announce to the world a matrimonial fracas in the family of Mr R. of Wimpole Street; the beautiful Mrs R., whose name had not long been enrolled in the lists of Hymen, and who had promised to become so brilliant a leader in the fashionable world, having quitted her husband's roof in company with the well-known and captivating Mr C., the intimate friend and associate of Mr R., and it was not known, even to the editor of the

'There (holding out the paper to her)—much good may such fine relations do you'

newspaper, whither they were gone.'

'It is a mistake, sir,' said Fanny, instantly; 'it must be a mistake, it cannot be true; it must mean some other people.'

She spoke from the instinctive wish of delaying shame; she spoke with a resolution which sprung from despair, for she spoke what she did not, could not believe herself. It had been the shock of conviction as she read. The truth rushed on her; and how she could have spoken at all, how she could even have breathed, was afterwards matter of wonder to herself.

Mr Price cared too little about the report to make her much answer. 'It might be all a lie,' he acknowledged, 'but so many fine ladies were going to the devil nowadays that way, that there was no answering for any body.'

'Indeed, I hope it is not true,' said Mrs Price, plaintively; 'it would be so very shocking! If I have spoken once to Rebecca about that carpet, I am sure I have spoken at least a dozen times; have not I, Betsey? And it would not be ten minutes' work.'

The horror of a mind like Fanny's, as it received the conviction of such guilt, and began to take in some part of the misery that must ensue, can hardly be described. At first, it was a sort of stupefaction; but every moment was quickening her perception of the horrible evil. She could not doubt, she dared not indulge a hope, of the paragraph being false. Miss Crawford's letter, which she had read so often as to make every line her own, was in frightful conformity with it. Her eager defence of her brother, her hope of its being *hushed up*, her evident agitation, were all of a piece with something very bad; and if there was a woman of character in existence, who could treat as a trifle this sin of the first magnitude, who would try to gloss it over, and desire to have it unpunished, she could believe Miss Crawford to be the woman! Now she could see her own mistake as to *who* were gone, or *said* to be gone. It was not Mr and Mrs Rushworth; it was Mrs Rushworth and Mr Crawford.

Fanny seemed to herself never to have been shocked before. There was no possibility of rest. The evening passed without a pause of misery, the night was totally sleepless. She passed only from feelings of sickness to shudderings of horror; and from hot fits of fever to cold. The event was so shocking that there were moments even when her heart revolted from it as impossible; when she thought it could not be. A woman married only six months ago; a man professing himself devoted, even *engaged* to another; that other her near relation; the whole family, both families connected as they were by tie upon tie; all friends, all intimate together! It was too horrible a confusion of guilt, too gross a complication of evil, for human nature, not in a state of utter barbarism, to be capable of! Yet her judgment told her it was so. *His* unsettled affections, wavering with his vanity. *Maria's* decided attachment, and no sufficient principle on either side, gave it possibility: Miss Crawford's letter stamped it a fact.

What would be the consequence? Whom would it not injure? Whose views might it not affect? Whose peace would it not cut up for ever? Miss Crawford, herself, Edmund; but it was dangerous, perhaps, to tread such ground. She confined herself, or tried to confine herself, to the simple, indubitable family misery which must envelop all, if it were indeed a matter of certified guilt and public exposure. The mother's sufferings, the father's; there she paused. Julia's, Tom's, Edmund's; there a yet longer pause. They were the two on whom it would fall most horribly. Sir Thomas's parental solicitude and high sense of honour and decorum, Edmund's upright principles, unsuspicious temper, and genuine strength of feeling, made her think it scarcely possible for them to support life and reason under such disgrace; and it appeared to her, that, as far as this world alone was concerned, the greatest blessing to every one of kindred with Mrs Rushworth would be instant annihilation.

Nothing happened the next day, or the next, to weaken her terrors. Two posts came in, and brought no refutation, public or private. There was no second letter to explain away the first from Miss Crawford; there was no intelligence from Mansfield, though it was now full time for her to hear again from her aunt. This was an evil omen. She had, indeed, scarcely the shadow of a hope to soothe her mind, and was reduced to so low and wan and trembling a condition, as no mother, not unkind, except Mrs Price, could have overlooked, when the third day did bring the sickening knock, and a letter was again put into her hands. It bore the London postmark, and came from Edmund.

'DEAR FANNY,

You know our present wretchedness. May God support you under your *share! We have been here two days, but there is nothing to be done. They cannot be traced. You may not have heard of the last blow – Julia's elopement; she is gone to Scotland with Yates. She left London a few hours before we entered it. At any other time this would have been felt dreadfully. Now it seems nothing; yet it is a heavy aggravation. My father is not overpowered. More cannot be hoped. He is still able to think and act; and I write, by his desire, to propose your returning home. He is anxious to get you there for my mother's sake. I shall be at Portsmouth the morning after you receive this, and I hope to find you ready to set off for Mansfield. My father wishes you to invite Susan to go with you for a few months. Settle it as you like; say what is proper; I am sure you will feel such an instance of his kindness at such a moment! Do justice to his meaning, however I may confuse it. You may imagine some thing of my present state. There is no end of the evil let loose upon us. You will see me early by the mail.—Yours, etc.*'

Never had Fanny more wanted a cordial. Never had she felt such a one as this letter contained. To-morrow! To leave Portsmouth to-morrow! She was, she felt she was, in the greatest danger of being exquisitely happy, while so many were miserable. The evil which brought such good to her! She dreaded lest she should learn to be insensible to it. To be going so soon, sent for so kindly, sent for as a comfort, and with leave to take Susan, was altogether such a combination of blessings as set her heart in a glow, and for a time seemed to distance every pain, and make her incapable of suitably sharing the distress even of those whose distress she thought of most. Julia's elopement could affect her comparatively but little; she was amazed and shocked; but it could not occupy her, could not dwell on her mind. She was obliged to call herself to think of it, and acknowledge it to be terrible and grievous, or it was escaping her, in the midst of all the agitating pressing joyful cares attending this summons to herself.

There is nothing like employment, active indispensable employment, for relieving sorrow. Employment, even melancholy, may dispel melancholy, and her occupations were hopeful. She had so much to do, that not even the horrible story of Mrs Rushworth (now fixed to the last point of certainty) could affect her as it had done before. She had no time to be miserable. Within twenty-four hours she was hoping to be gone; her father and mother must be spoken to, Susan prepared, every thing got ready. Business followed business; the day was hardly long enough. The happiness she was imparting, too, happiness very little alloyed by the black communication which must briefly precede it – the joyful consent of her father and mother to Susan's going with her – the general satisfaction with which the going of both seemed regarded, and the ecstasy of Susan herself, serving to support her spirits.

The affliction of the Bertrams was little felt in the family. Mrs Price talked of her poor sister for a few minutes, but how to find any thing to hold Susan's clothes, because Rebecca took away all the boxes and spoilt them, was much more in her thoughts: and as for Susan, now unexpectedly gratified in the first wish of her heart, and knowing nothing personally of those who had sinned, or of those who were sorrowing – if she could help rejoicing from beginning to end, it was as much as ought to be expected from human virtue at fourteen.

As nothing was really left for the decision of Mrs Price, or the good offices of Rebecca, every thing was rationally and duly accomplished, and the girls were ready for the morrow. The advantage of much sleep to prepare them for their journey was impossible. The cousin who was travelling towards them could hardly have less than visited their agitated spirits, one all happiness, the other all varying and indescribable perturbation.

By eight in the morning Edmund was in the house. The girls heard his entrance from above, and Fanny went down. The idea of immediately seeing him, with the knowledge of what he must be suffering, brought back all her own first feelings. He so near her, and in misery. She was ready to sink as she entered the parlour. He was alone, and met her instantly; and found herself pressed to his heart with only these words, just articulate: 'My Fanny, my only sister; my only comfort now!' She could say nothing; nor for some minutes could he say more.

He turned away to recover himself, and when he spoke again, though his voice still faltered, his manner showed the wish of self-command, and the resolution of avoiding any further allusion. 'Have you breakfasted? When shall you be ready? Does Susan go?' were questions following each other rapidly. His great object was to be off as soon as possible. When Mansfield was considered, time was precious; and the state of his own mind made him find relief only in motion. It was settled that he should order the carriage to the door in half an hour. Fanny answered for having breakfasted and being

'No wonder—you must feel it'

quite ready in half an hour. He had already ate, and declined staying for their meal. He would walk round the ramparts, and join them with the carriage. He was gone again; glad to get away even from Fanny.

He looked very ill; evidently suffering under violent emotions, which he was determined to suppress. She knew it must be so, but it was terrible to her.

The carriage came; and he entered the house again at the same moment, just in time to spend a few minutes with the family, and be a witness – but that he saw nothing – of the tranquil manner in which the daughters were parted with, and just in time to prevent their sitting down to the breakfast table, which by dint of much unusual activity, was quite and completely ready as the carriage drove from the door. Fanny's last meal in her father's house was in character with her first; she was dismissed from it as hospitably as she had been welcomed.

How her heart swelled with joy and gratitude as she passed the barriers of Portsmouth, and how Susan's face wore its broadest smiles, may be easily conceived. Sitting forwards, however, and screened by her bonnet, those smiles were unseen.

The journey was likely to be a silent one. Edmund's deep sighs often reached Fanny. Had he been alone with her, his heart must have opened in spite of every resolution; but Susan's presence drove him quite into himself, and his attempts to talk on indifferent subjects could never be long supported.

Fanny watched him with never-failing solicitude, and sometimes catching his eye, revived an affectionate smile, which comforted her; but the first day's journey passed without her hearing a word from him on the subjects that were weighing him down. The next morning produced a little more. Just before their setting out from Oxford, while Susan was stationed at a window, in eager observation of the departure of a large family from the inn, the other two were standing by the fire; and Edmund, particularly struck by the alteration in Fanny's looks, and from his ignorance of the daily evils of her father's house, attributing an undue share of the change, attributing *all* to the recent event, took her hand, and said in a low, but very expressive tone, 'No wonder – you must feel it – you must suffer. How a man who had once loved, could desert you! But *yours* – your regard was new compared with— Fanny, think of *me*!'

The first division of their journey occupied a long day, and brought them, almost knocked up, to Oxford; but the second was over at a much earlier hour. They were in the environs of Mansfield long before the usual dinner-time, and as they approached the beloved place, the hearts of both sisters sank a little. Fanny began to dread the meeting with her aunts and Tom, under so dreadful a humiliation; and Susan to feel with some anxiety, that all her best manners, all her lately acquired knowledge of what was practised here, was on the point of being called into action. Visions of good and ill breeding, of old vulgarisms and new gentilities were before her; and she was meditating much upon silver forks, napkins, and finger glasses. Fanny had been everywhere awake to the difference of the country since February; but when they entered the Park her perceptions and her pleasures were of the keenest sort. It was three months, full three months, since her quitting it, and the change was from winter to summer. Her eye fell everywhere on lawns and plantations of the freshest green; and the trees, though not fully clothed, were in that delightful state when further beauty is known to be at hand, and when, while much is actually given to the sight, more yet remains for the imagination. Her enjoyment, however, was for herself alone. Edmund could not share it. She looked at him, but he was leaning back, sunk in a deeper gloom than ever, and with eyes closed, as if the view of cheerfulness oppressed him, and the lovely scenes of home must be shut out.

It made her melancholy again; and the knowledge of what must be enduring there, invested even the house, modern, airy, and well situated as it was, with a melancholy aspect.

By one of the suffering party within, they were expected with such impatience as she had never known before. Fanny had scarcely passed the solemn-looking servants, when Lady Bertram came from the drawing-room to meet her; came with no indolent step; and falling on her neck, said: 'Dear Fanny! Now I shall be comfortable.'

CHAPTER FORTY SEVEN

IT HAD BEEN A MISERABLE PARTY, each of the three believing themselves most miserable. Mrs Norris, however, as most attached to Maria, was really the greatest sufferer. Maria was her first favourite, the dearest of all; the match had been her own contriving, as she had been wont with such pride of heart to feel and say, and this conclusion of it almost overpowered her.

She was an altered creature, quieted, stupefied, indifferent to every thing that passed. The being left with her sister and nephew, and all the house under her care, had been an advantage entirely thrown away; she had been unable to direct or dictate, or even fancy herself useful. When really touched by affliction, her active powers had been all benumbed, and neither Lady Bertram nor Tom had received from her the smallest support or attempt at support. She had done no more for them than they had done for each other. They had been all solitary, helpless, and forlorn alike; and now the arrival of the others only established her superiority in wretchedness. Her companions were relieved, but there was no good for *her*. Edmund was almost as welcome to his brother as Fanny to her aunt; but Mrs Norris, instead of having comfort from either, was but the more irritated by the sight of the person whom, in the blindness of her anger, she could have charged as the demon of the piece. Had Fanny accepted Mr Crawford this could not have happened.

Susan, too, was a grievance. She had not spirits to notice her in more than a few repulsive looks, but she felt her as a spy, and an intruder, and an indigent niece, and everything most odious. By her other aunt, Susan was received with quiet kindness. Lady Bertram could not give her much time, or many words, but she felt her, as Fanny's sister, to have a claim at Mansfield, and was ready to kiss and like her; and Susan was more than satisfied, for she came perfectly aware that nothing but ill humour was to be expected from Aunt Norris; and was so provided with happiness, so strong in that best of blessings, an escape from many certain evils, that she could have stood against a great deal more indifference than she met with from the others.

She was now left a good deal to herself, to get acquainted with the house and grounds as she could, and spent her days very happily in so doing, while those who might otherwise have attended to her were shut up, or wholly occupied each with the person quite dependent on them, at this time, for everything like comfort; Edmund trying to bury his own feelings in exertions for the relief of his brother's, and Fanny devoted to her Aunt Bertram, returning to every former office with more than former zeal, and thinking she could never do enough for one who seemed so much to want her.

To talk over the dreadful business with Fanny, talk and lament, was all Lady Bertram's consolation. To be listened to and borne with, and hear the voice of kindness and sympathy in return, was every thing that could be done for her. To be otherwise comforted was out of the question. The case admitted of no comfort. Lady Bertram did not think deeply, but, guided by Sir Thomas, she thought justly on all important points; and she saw therefore, in all its enormity, what had happened, and neither endeavoured herself, nor required Fanny to advise her, to think little of guilt and infamy.

Her affections were not acute, nor was her mind tenacious. After a time, Fanny found it not impossible to direct her thoughts to other subjects, and revive some interest in the usual occupations; but whenever Lady Bertram *was* fixed on the event, she could see it only in one light, as comprehending the loss of a daughter, and a disgrace never to be wiped off.

Fanny learned from her all the particulars which had yet transpired. Her aunt was no very methodical narrator, but with the help of some letters to and from Sir Thomas, and what she already knew herself, and could reasonably combine, she was soon able to understand quite as much as she wished of the circumstances attending the story.

Mrs Rushworth had gone, for the Easter holidays, to Twickenham, with a family whom she had just grown intimate with: a family of lively, agreeable manners, and probably of morals and discretion to suit, for to *their* house Mr Crawford had constant access at all times. His having been in the same neighbourhood Fanny already knew. Mr Rushworth had been gone at this time to Bath, to pass a few days with his mother, and bring her back to town, and Maria was with these friends without any restraint, without even Julia; for Julia had removed from Wimpole Street two or three weeks before, on a visit to some relations of Sir Thomas; a removal which her father and mother were now disposed to attribute to some view of convenience on Mr Yates's account. Very soon after the Rushworths' return to Wimpole Street, Sir Thomas had received a letter from an old and most particular friend in London, who hearing and witnessing a good deal to alarm him in that quarter, wrote to recommend Sir Thomas's coming to London himself, and using his influence with his daughter to put an end to the intimacy which was already exposing her to unpleasant remarks, and evidently making Mr Rushworth uneasy.

Sir Thomas was preparing to act upon this letter, without communicating its contents to any creature at Mansfield, when it was followed by another, sent express from the same friend, to break to him the almost desperate situation in which affairs then stood with the young people. Mrs Rushworth had left her husband's house: Mr Rushworth had been in great anger and distress to *him* (Mr Harding) for his advice; Mr Harding feared there had been *at least* very flagrant indiscretion. The maidservant of Mrs Rushworth, senior, threatened alarmingly. He was doing all in his power to quiet every thing, with the hope of Mrs Rushworth's return, but was so much counteracted in Wimpole Street by the influence of Mr Rushworth's mother, that the worst consequences might be apprehended.

This dreadful communication could not be kept from the rest of the family. Sir Thomas set off, Edmund would go with him, and the others had been left in a state of wretchedness, inferior only to what followed the receipt of the next letters from London. Every thing was by that time public beyond a hope. The servant of Mrs Rushworth, the mother, had exposure in her power, and supported by her mistress, was not to be silenced. The two ladies, even in the short time they had been together, had disagreed; and the bitterness of the elder against her daughter-in-law might perhaps arise almost as much from the personal disrespect with which she had herself been treated as from sensibility for her son.

However that might be, she was unmanageable. But had she been less obstinate, or of less weight with her son, who was always guided by the last speaker, by the person who could get hold of and shut him up, the case would still have been hopeless, for Mrs Rushworth did not appear again, and there was every reason to conclude her to be concealed somewhere with Mr Crawford, who had quitted his uncle's house, as for a journey, on the very day of her absenting herself.

Sir Thomas, however, remained yet a little longer in town, in the hope of discovering and snatching her from further vice, though all was lost on the side of character.

His present state Fanny could hardly bear to think of. There was but one of his children who was not at this time a source of misery to him. Tom's complaints had been greatly heightened by the shock of his sister's conduct, and his recovery so much thrown back by it, that even Lady Bertram had been struck by the difference, and all her alarms were regularly sent off to her husband; and Julia's elopement, the additional blow which had met him on his arrival in London, though its force had been deadened at the moment, must, she knew, be sorely felt. She saw that it was. His letters expressed how much he deplored it. Under any circumstances it would have been an unwelcome alliance; but to have it so clandestinely formed, and such a period chosen for its completion, placed Julia's feelings in a most unfavourable light, and severely aggravated the folly of her choice. He called it a bad thing, done in the worst manner, and at the worst time; and though Julia was yet as more pardonable than Maria as folly than vice, he could not but regard the step she had taken as opening the worst probabilities of a conclusion hereafter like her sister's. Such was his opinion of the set into which she had thrown herself.

Fanny felt for him most acutely. He could have no comfort but in Edmund. Every other child must be racking his heart. His displeasure against herself she trusted, reasoning differently from Mrs Norris, would now be done away. *She* should be justified. Mr Crawford would have fully acquitted her conduct in refusing him; but this, though most material to herself, would be poor consolation to Sir Thomas. Her uncle's displeasure was terrible to her; but what could her justification or her gratitude and attachment do for him? His stay must be on Edmund alone.

She was mistaken, however, in supposing that Edmund gave his father no present pain. It was of a much less poignant nature than what the others excited; but Sir Thomas was considering his happiness as very deeply involved in the offence of his sister and friend; cut off by it, as he must be, from the woman whom he had been pursuing with undoubted attachment and strong probability of success; and who, in every thing but this despicable brother, would have been so eligible a connection. He was aware of what

Edmund must be suffering on his own behalf, in addition to all the rest, when they were in town: he had seen or conjectured his feelings; and, having reason to think that *one* interview with Miss Crawford had taken place, from which Edmund derived only increased distress, had been as anxious on that account as on others to get him out of town, and had engaged him in taking Fanny home to her aunt, with a view to his relief and benefit, no less than theirs. Fanny was not in the secret of her uncle's feelings, Sir Thomas not in the secret of Miss Crawford's character. Had he been privy to her conversation with his son, he would not have wished her to belong to him, though her twenty thousand pounds had been forty.

That Edmund must be for ever divided from Miss Crawford did not admit of a doubt with Fanny; and yet, till she knew that he felt the same, her own conviction was insufficient. She thought he did, but she wanted to be assured of it. If he would now speak to her with the unreserve which had sometimes been too much for her before, it would be most consoling; but *that* she found was not to be. She seldom saw him: never alone. He probably avoided being alone with her. What was to be inferred? That his judgment submitted to all his own peculiar and bitter share of this family affliction, but that it was too keenly felt to be a subject of the slightest communication. This must be his state. He yielded, but it was with agonies which did not admit of speech. Long, long would it be ere Miss Crawford's name passed his lips again, or she could hope for a renewal of such confidential intercourse as had been.

It *was* long. They reached Mansfield on Thursday, and it was not till Sunday evening that Edmund began to talk to her on the subject. Sitting with her on Sunday evening – a wet Sunday evening – the very time of all others when, if a friend is at hand, the heart must be opened, and every thing told; no one else in the room, except his mother, who, after hearing an affecting sermon, had cried herself to sleep, it was impossible not to speak; and so, with the usual beginnings, hardly to be traced as to what came first, and the usual declaration that if she would listen to him for a few minutes, he should be very brief, and certainly never tax her kindness in the same way again; she need not fear a repetition; it would be a subject prohibited entirely: he entered upon the luxury of relating circumstances and sensations of the first interest to himself, to one of whose affectionate sympathy he was quite convinced.

How Fanny listened, with what curiosity and concern, what pain and what delight, how the agitation of his voice was watched, and how carefully her own eyes were fixed on any object but himself, may be imagined. The opening was alarming. He had seen Miss Crawford. He had been invited to see her. He had received a note from Lady Stornaway to beg him to call; and regarding it as what was meant to be the last, last interview of friendship, and investing her with all the feelings of shame and wretchedness which Crawford's sister ought to have known, he had gone to her in such a state of mind, so softened, so devoted, as made it for a few moments impossible to Fanny's fears that it should be the last. But as he proceeded in his story, these fears were over. She had met him, he said, with a serious – certainly a serious – even an agitated air; but before he had been able to speak one intelligible sentence, she had introduced the subject in a manner which he owned had shocked him. '"I heard you were in town," said she; "I wanted to see you. Let us talk over this sad business. What can equal the folly of our two relations?" I could not answer, but I believe my looks spoke. She felt reproved. Sometimes how quick to feel! With a graver look and voice she then added, "I do not mean to defend Henry at your sister's expense." So she began, but how she went on, Fanny, is not fit, is hardly fit to be repeated to you. I cannot recall all her words. I would not dwell upon them if I could. Their substance was great anger at the *folly* of each. She reprobated her brother's folly in being drawn on by a woman whom he had never cared for, to do what must lose him the woman he adored; but still more the folly of poor Maria, in sacrificing such a situation, plunging into such difficulties, under the idea of being really loved by a man who had long ago made his indifference clear. Guess what I must have felt. To hear the woman whom— No harsher name than folly given! So voluntarily, so freely, so coolly to canvass it! No reluctance, no horror, no feminine, shall I say, no modest loathings? This is what the world does. For where, Fanny, shall we find a woman whom nature had so richly endowed? Spoilt, spoilt!'

After a little reflection, he went on with a sort of desperate calmness. 'I will tell you every thing, and then have done for ever. She saw it only as folly, and that folly stamped only by exposure. The want of common discretion, of caution; his going down to Richmond for the whole time of her being at Twickenham; her putting herself in the power of a servant; it was the detection, in short – oh, Fanny! it was the detection, not the offence, which she reprobated. It was the imprudence which had brought things to extremity, and obliged her brother to give up every dearer plan in order to fly with her.'

He stopped. 'And what,' said Fanny (believing herself required to speak), 'what could you say?'

'Nothing, nothing to be understood. I was like a man stunned. She went on, began to talk of you; yes, then she began to talk of you, regretting, as well she might, the loss of such a— There she spoke very rationally. But she has always done justice to you. "He has thrown away," said she, "such a woman as he will never see again. She would have fixed him; she would have made him happy for ever." My dearest Fanny, I am giving you, I hope, more pleasure than pain by this retrospect of what might have been – but what never can be now. You do not wish me to be silent? If you do, give me but a look, a word, and I have done.'

No look or word was given.

'Thank God,' said he. 'We were all disposed to wonder, but it seems to have been the merciful appointment of Providence that the heart which knew no guile should not suffer. She spoke of you with high praise and warm affection; yet, even here, there was alloy, a dash of evil; for in the midst of it she could exclaim, "Why would not she have him? It is all her fault. Simple girl! I shall never forgive her. Had she accepted him as she ought, they might now have been on the point of marriage, and Henry would have been too happy and too busy to want any other object. He would have taken no pains to be on terms with Mrs Rushworth again. It would have all ended in a regular standing flirtation, in yearly meetings at Sotherton and Everingham." Could you have believed it possible? But the charm is broken. My eyes are opened.'

'Cruel!' said Fanny, 'quite cruel. At such a moment to give way to gaiety, to speak with lightness, and to you! Absolute cruelty.'

'Cruelty, do you call it? We differ there. No, hers is not a cruel nature. I do not consider her as meaning to wound my feelings. The evil lies yet deeper; in her total ignorance, unsuspiciousness of there being such feelings; in a perversion of mind which made it natural to her to treat the subject as she did. She was speaking only as she had been used to hear others speak, as she imagined every body else would speak. Hers are not faults of temper. She would not voluntarily give unnecessary pain to any one, and though I may deceive myself, I cannot but think that for me, for my feelings, she would – Hers are faults of principle, Fanny; of blunted delicacy and a corrupted, vitiated mind. Perhaps it is best for me, since it leaves me so little to regret. Not so, however. Gladly would I submit to all the increased pain of losing her, rather than have to think of her as I do. I told her so.'

'Did you?'

'Yes; when I left her I told her so.'

'How long were you together?'

'Five-and-twenty minutes. Well, she went on to say that what remained now to be done was to bring about a marriage between them. She spoke of it, Fanny, with a steadier voice than I can.' He was obliged to pause more than once as he continued. '"We must persuade Henry to marry her," said she; "and what with honour, and the certainty of having shut himself out for ever from Fanny, I do not despair of it. Fanny he must give up. I do not think that even *he* could now hope to succeed with one of her stamp, and therefore I hope we may find no insuperable difficulty. My influence, which is not small, shall all go that way; and when once married, and properly supported by her own family, people of respectability as they are, she may recover her footing in society to a certain degree. In some circles, we know, she would never be admitted, but with good dinners, and large parties, there will always be those who will be glad of her acquaintance; and there is, undoubtedly, more liberality and candour on those points than formerly. What I advise is, that your father be quiet. Do not let him injure his own cause by interference. Persuade him to let things take their course. If by any officious exertions of his, she is induced to leave Henry's protection, there will be much less chance of his marrying her than if she remain with him. I know how he is likely to be influenced. Let Sir Thomas trust to his honour and compassion, and it may all end well; but if he gets his daughter away, it will be destroying the chief hold."'

After repeating this, Edmund was so much affected that Fanny, watching him with silent, but most tender concern, was almost sorry that the subject had been entered on at all. It was long before he could speak again. At last, 'Now, Fanny,' said he, 'I shall soon have done. I have told you the substance of all that she said. As soon as I could speak, I replied that I had not supposed it possible, coming in such a state of mind into that house as I have done, that anything could occur to make me suffer more, but that she had been inflicting deeper wounds in almost every sentence. That though I had, in the course of our acquaintance, been often sensible of some difference in our opinions, on points, too, of some moment, it had not entered my imagination to conceive the difference could be such as she had now proved it. That the manner in which she treated the dreadful crime committed by her brother and my sister (with whom lay the greater seduction I pretended not to say), but the manner in which she spoke of the crime itself, giving it every reproach but the right; considering its ill consequences only as they were to be braved or overborne by a defiance of decency and impudence in wrong; and last of all, and above all, recommending to us a compliance, a compromise, an acquiescence, in the continuance of the sin, on the chance of a marriage which, thinking as I now thought of her brother, should rather be prevented than sought; all this together most grievously convinced me that I had never understood her before, and that, as far as related to mind, it had been the creature of my own imagination, not Miss Crawford, that I had been too apt to dwell on for many months past. That, perhaps, it was best for me; I had less to regret in sacrificing a friendship, feelings, hopes which must, at any rate, have been torn from me now. And yet, that I must, and would confess, that, could I have restored her to what she had appeared to me before, I would infinitely prefer any increase of the pain of parting, for the sake of carrying with me the right of tenderness and esteem. This is what I said, the purport of it; but, as you may imagine, not spoken so collectedly or methodically as I have repeated it to you. She was astonished,

'Mr Bertram,' said she, with a smile

exceedingly astonished – more than astonished. I saw her change countenance. She turned extremely red. I imagined I saw a mixture of many feelings: a great, though short struggle; half a wish of yielding to truths, half a sense of shame, but habit, habit carried it. She would have laughed if she could. It was a sort of laugh, as she answered, "A pretty good lecture, upon my word. Was it part of your last sermon? At this rate you will soon reform everybody at Mansfield and Thornton Lacey; and when I hear of you next, it may be as a celebrated preacher in some great society of Methodists, or as a missionary into foreign parts." She tried to speak carelessly, but she was not so careless as she wanted to appear. I only said in reply, that from my heart I wished her well, and earnestly hoped that she might soon learn to think more justly, and not owe the most valuable knowledge we could any of us acquire, the knowledge of ourselves and of our duty, to the lessons of affliction, and immediately left the room. I had gone a few steps, Fanny, when I heard the door open behind me. "Mr Bertram," said she. I looked back. "Mr Bertram," said she, with a smile; but it was a smile ill-suited to the conversation that had passed, a saucy playful smile, seeming to invite in order to subdue me; at least it appeared so to me. I resisted; it was the impulse of the moment to resist, and still walked on. I have since, sometimes, for a moment, regretted that I did not go back, but I know I was right, and such has been the end of our acquaintance. And what an acquaintance has it been! How have I been deceived! Equally in brother and sister deceived! I thank you for your patience, Fanny. This has been the greatest relief, and now we will have done.'

And such was Fanny's dependence on his words, that for five minutes she thought they *had* done. Then, however, it all came on again, or some thing very like it, and nothing less than Lady Bertram's rousing thoroughly up, could really close such a conversation. Till that happened, they continued to talk of Miss Crawford alone, and how she had attached him, and how delightful nature had made her, and how excellent she would have been, had she fallen into good hands earlier. Fanny, now at liberty to speak openly, felt more than justified in adding to his knowledge of her real character, by some hint of what share his brother's state of health might be supposed to have in her wish for a complete reconciliation. This was not an agreeable intimation. Nature resisted it for a while. It would have been a vast deal pleasanter to have had her more disinterested in her attachment; but his vanity was not of a strength to fight long against reason. He submitted to believe that Tom's illness had influenced her, only reserving for himself this consoling thought, that considering the many counteractions of opposing habits, she had certainly been *more* attached to him than could have been expected, and for his sake been more near doing right. Fanny thought exactly the same; and they were also quite agreed in their opinion of the lasting effect, the indelible impression, which such a disappointment must make on his mind. Time would undoubtedly abate somewhat of his sufferings, but still it was a sort of thing which he never could get entirely the better of; and as to his ever meeting with any other woman who could – it was too impossible to be named but with indignation. Fanny's friendship was all that he had to cling to.

CHAPTER FORTY EIGHT

LET OTHER PENS DWELL ON guilt and misery. I quit such odious subjects as soon as I can, impatient to restore every body, not greatly in fault themselves, to tolerable comfort, and to have done with all the rest.

My Fanny, indeed, at this very time, I have the satisfaction of knowing, must have been happy in spite of every thing. She must have been a happy creature in spite of all that she felt, or thought she felt, for the distress of those around her. She had sources of delight that must force their way. She was returned to Mansfield Park, she was useful, she was beloved; she was safe from Mr Crawford; and when Sir Thomas came back she had every proof that could be given in his then melancholy state of spirits, of his perfect approbation and increased regard; and happy as all this must make her, she would still have been happy without any of it, for Edmund was no longer the dupe of Miss Crawford.

It is true that Edmund was very far from happy himself. He was suffering from disappointment and regret, grieving over what was, and wishing for what could never be. She knew it was so, and was sorry; but it was with a sorrow so founded on satisfaction, so tending to ease, and so much in harmony with every dearest sensation, that there are few who might not have been glad to exchange their greatest gaiety for it.

Sir Thomas, poor Sir Thomas, a parent, and conscious of errors in his own conduct as a parent, was the longest to suffer. He felt that he ought not to have allowed the marriage; that his daughter's sentiments had been sufficiently known to him to render him culpable in authorising it; that in so doing he had sacrificed the right to the expedient, and been governed by motives of selfishness and worldly wisdom. These were reflections that required some time to soften; but time will do almost every thing; and though little comfort arose on Mrs Rushworth's side for the misery she had occasioned, comfort was to be found greater than he had supposed in his other children. Julia's match became a less desperate business than he had considered it at first. She was humble, and wishing to be forgiven; and Mr Yates, desirous of being really received into the family, was disposed to look up to him and be guided. He was not very solid; but there was a hope of his becoming less trifling, of his being at least tolerably domestic and quiet; and at any rate, there was comfort in finding his estate rather more, and his debts much less, than he had feared, and in being consulted and treated as the friend best worth attending to. There was comfort also in Tom, who gradually regained his health, without regaining the thoughtlessness and selfishness of his previous habits. He was the better for ever for his illness. He had suffered, and he had learned to think; two advantages that he had never known before; and the self-reproach arising from the deplorable event in Wimpole Street, to which he felt himself accessory by all the dangerous intimacy of his unjustifiable theatre, made an impression on his mind which, at the age of six-and-twenty, with no want of sense or good companions, was durable in its happy effects. He became what he ought to be: useful to his father, steady and quiet, and not living merely for himself.

Sitting under trees with Fanny

Here was comfort indeed! And quite as soon as Sir Thomas could place dependence on such sources of good, Edmund was contributing to his father's ease by improvement in the only point in which *he* had given him pain before: improvement in his spirits. After wandering about and sitting under trees with Fanny all the summer evenings, he had so well talked his mind into submission, as to be very tolerably cheerful again.

These were the circumstances and the hopes which gradually brought their alleviation to Sir Thomas, deadening his sense of what was lost, and in part reconciling him to himself; though the anguish arising from the conviction of his own errors in the education of his daughters was never to be entirely done away.

Too late he became aware how unfavourable to the character of any young people must be the totally opposite treatment which Maria and Julia had been always experiencing at home, where the excessive indulgence and flattery of their aunt had been continually contrasted with his own severity. He saw how ill he had judged, in expecting to counteract what was wrong in Mrs Norris, by its reverse in himself; clearly saw that he had but increased the evil, by teaching them to repress their spirits in his presence so as to make their real disposition unknown to him, and sending them for all their indulgences to a person who had been able to attach them only by the blindness of her affection, and the excess of her praise.

Here had been grievous mismanagement; but, bad as it was, he gradually grew to feel that it had not been the most direful mistake in his plan of education. Some thing must have been wanting *within*, or time would have worn away much of its ill effect. He feared that principle, active principle, had been wanting; that they had never been properly taught to govern their inclinations and tempers by that sense of duty which can alone suffice. They had been instructed theoretically in their religion, but never required to bring it into daily practice. To be distinguished for elegance and accomplishments, the authorised object of their youth, could have had no useful influence that way, no moral effect on the mind. He had meant them to be good, but his cares had been directed to the understanding and manners, not the disposition; and of the necessity of self-denial and humility, he feared they had never heard from any lips that could profit them.

Bitterly did he deplore a deficiency which now he could scarcely comprehend to have been possible. Wretchedly did he feel, that with all the cost and care of an anxious and expensive education, he had brought up his daughters without their understanding their first duties, or his being acquainted with their character and temper.

The high spirit and strong passions of Mrs Rushworth, especially, were made known to him only in their sad result. She was not to be prevailed on to leave Mr Crawford. She hoped to marry him, and they continued together till she was obliged to be convinced that such hope was vain, and till the disappointment and wretchedness arising from the conviction rendered her temper so bad, and her feelings for him so like hatred, as to make them for a while each other's punishment, and then induce a voluntary separation.

She had lived with him to be reproached as the ruin of all his happiness in Fanny, and carried away no better consolation in leaving him, than that she *had* divided them. What can exceed the misery of such a mind in such a situation?

Mr Rushworth had no difficulty in procuring a divorce; and so ended a marriage contracted under such circumstances as to make any better end the effect of good luck not to be reckoned on. She had despised him, and loved another; and he had been very much aware that it was so. The indignities of stupidity, and the disappointments of selfish passion, can excite little pity. His punishment followed his conduct, as did a deeper punishment the deeper guilt of his wife. He was released from the engagement to be mortified and unhappy, till some other pretty girl could attract him into matrimony again, and he might set forward on a second, and it is to be hoped, more prosperous trial of the state: if duped, to be duped at least with good humour and good luck; while *she* must withdraw with infinitely stronger feelings to a retirement and reproach which could allow no second spring of hope or character.

Where she could be placed became a subject of most melancholy and momentous consultation. Mrs Norris, whose attachment seemed to augment with the demerits of her niece, would have had her received at home, and countenanced by them all. Sir Thomas would not hear of it; and Mrs Norris's anger against Fanny was so much the greater, from considering *her* residence there as the motive. She persisted in placing his scruples to *her* account, though Sir Thomas very solemnly assured her that, had there been no young woman in question, had there been no young person of either sex belonging to him, to be endangered by the society or hurt by the character of Mrs Rushworth, he would never have offered so great an insult to the neighbourhood as to expect it to notice her. As a daughter, he hoped a penitent one, she should be protected by him, and secured in every comfort, and supported by every encouragement to do right, which their relative situations admitted; but further than *that* he could not go. Maria had destroyed her own character, and he would not, by a vain attempt to restore what never could be restored by affording his sanction to vice, or in seeking to lessen its disgrace, be anywise accessory to introducing such misery in another man's family, as he had known himself.

It ended in Mrs Norris's resolving to quit Mansfield, and devote herself to her unfortunate Maria, and in an establishment being formed for them in another country, remote and private, where, shut up together with little society, on one side no affection, on the other no judgment, it may be reasonably supposed that their tempers became their mutual punishment. Mrs Norris's removal from Mansfield was the great supplementary comfort of Sir Thomas's life. His opinion of her had been sinking from the day of his return from Antigua: in every transaction together from that period; in their daily intercourse, in business, or in chat, she had been regularly losing ground in his esteem, and convincing him that either time had done her much disservice, or that he had considerably over-rated her sense, and wonderfully borne with her manners before. He had felt her as an hourly evil, which was so much the worse, as there seemed no chance of its ceasing but with life; she seemed a part of himself that must be borne for ever. To be relieved from her, therefore, was so great a felicity that, had she not left bitter remembrances behind her, there might have been danger of his learning almost to approve the evil which produced such a good.

She was regretted by no one at Mansfield. She had never been able to attach even those she loved best, and since Mrs Rushworth's elopement, her temper had been in a state of such irritation as to make her every where tormenting. Not even Fanny had tears for Aunt Norris, not even when she was gone for ever.

That Julia escaped better than Maria was owing, in some measure, to a favourable difference of disposition and circumstance, but in a greater to her having been less the darling of that very aunt, less flattered and less spoilt. Her beauty and acquirements had held but a second place. She had been always used to think herself a little inferior to Maria. Her temper was naturally the easiest of the two; her feelings, though quick, were more controllable, and education had not given her so very hurtful a degree of self-consequence.

She had submitted the best to the disappointment in Henry Crawford. After the first bitterness of the conviction of being slighted was over, she had been tolerably soon in a fair way of not thinking of him again; and when the acquaintance was renewed in town, and Mr Rushworth's house became Crawford's object, she had had the merit of withdrawing herself from it, and of choosing that time to pay a visit to her other friends, in order to secure herself from being again too much attracted. This had been her motive in going to her cousins. Mr Yates's convenience had had nothing to do with it. She had been allowing his attentions some time, but with very little idea of ever accepting him; and had not her sister's conduct burst forth as it did, and her increased dread of her father and of home, on that event, imagining its certain consequence to herself would be greater severity and restraint, made her hastily resolve on avoiding such immediate horrors at all risks, it is probable that Mr Yates would never have succeeded. She had not eloped with any worse feelings than those of selfish alarm. It had appeared to her the only thing to be done. Maria's guilt had induced Julia's folly.

Henry Crawford, ruined by early independence and bad domestic example, indulged in the freaks of a cold-blooded vanity a little too long. Once it had, by an opening undesigned and unmerited, led him into the way of happiness. Could he have been satisfied with the conquest of one amiable woman's affections, could he have found sufficient exultation in overcoming the reluctance, in working himself into the esteem and tenderness of Fanny Price, there would have been every probability of success and felicity for him. His affection had already done some thing. Her influence over him had already given him some influence over her. Would he have deserved more, there can be no doubt that more would have been obtained, especially when that marriage had taken place, which would have given him the assistance of her conscience in subduing her first inclination, and brought them very often together. Would he have persevered, and uprightly, Fanny must have been his reward, and a reward very voluntarily bestowed, within a reasonable period from Edmund's marrying Mary. Had he done as he intended, and as he knew he ought, by going down to Everingham after his return from Portsmouth, he might have been deciding his own happy destiny. But he was pressed to stay for Mrs Fraser's party; his staying was made of flattering consequence, and he was to meet Mrs Rushworth there. Curiosity and vanity were both engaged, and the temptation of immediate pleasure was too strong for a mind unused to make any sacrifice to right: he resolved to defer his Norfolk journey, resolved that writing should answer the purpose of it, or that its purpose was unimportant, and stayed. He saw Mrs Rushworth, was received by her with a coldness which ought to have been repulsive, and have established apparent indifference between them for ever; but he was mortified, he could not bear to be thrown off by the woman whose smiles had been so wholly at his command; he must exert himself to subdue so proud a display of resentment; it was anger on Fanny's account; he must get the better of it, and make Mrs Rushworth Maria Bertram again in her treatment of himself.

In this spirit he began the attack, and by animated perseverance had soon re-established the sort of familiar intercourse of gallantry, of flirtation, which bounded his views; but in triumphing over the discretion which, though beginning in anger, might have saved them both, he had put himself in the power of feelings on her side more strong than he had supposed. She loved him; there was no withdrawing attentions avowedly dear to her. He was entangled by his own vanity, with as little excuse of love as possible, and without the smallest inconstancy of mind towards her cousin. To keep

Fanny and the Bertrams from a knowledge of what was passing became his first object. Secrecy could not have been more desirable for Mrs Rushworth's credit than he felt it for his own. When he returned from Richmond, he would have been glad to see Mrs Rushworth no more. All that followed was the result of her imprudence, and he went off with her at last, because he could not help it, regretting Fanny even at the moment, but regretting her infinitely more when all the bustle of the intrigue was over, and a very few months had taught him, by the force of contrast, to place a yet higher value on the sweetness of her temper, the purity of her mind, and the excellence of her principles.

That punishment, the public punishment of disgrace, should in a just measure attend *his* share of the offence is, we know, not one of the barriers which society gives to virtue. In this world the penalty is less equal than could be wished; but without presuming to look forward to a juster appointment hereafter, we may fairly consider a man of sense, like Henry Crawford, to be providing for himself no small portion of vexation and regret; vexation that must rise sometimes to self-reproach, and regret to wretchedness, in having so requited hospitality, so injured family peace, so forfeited his best, most estimable, and endeared acquaintance, and so lost the woman whom he had rationally as well as passionately loved.

After what had passed to wound and alienate the two families, the continuance of the Bertrams and Grants in such close neighbourhood would have been most distressing; but the absence of the latter, for some months purposely lengthened, ended very fortunately in the necessity, or at least the practicability, of a permanent removal. Dr Grant, through an interest on which he had almost ceased to form hopes, succeeded to a stall in Westminster, which, as affording an occasion for leaving Mansfield, an excuse for residence in London, and an increase of income to answer the expenses of the change, was highly acceptable to those who went and those who stayed.

Mrs Grant, with a temper to love and be loved, must have gone with some regret from the scenes and people she had been used to; but the same happiness of disposition must in any place, and any society, secure her a great deal to enjoy, and she had again a home to offer Mary; and Mary had had enough of her own friends, enough of vanity, ambition, love, and disappointment in the course of the last half-year, to be in need of the true kindness of her sister's heart, and the rational tranquillity of her ways. They lived together; and when Dr Grant had brought on apoplexy and death, by three great institutionary dinners in one week, they still lived together; for Mary, though perfectly resolved against ever attaching herself to a younger brother again, was long in finding among the dashing representatives, or idle heir-apparents, who were at the command of her beauty, and her

£20,000, anyone who could satisfy the better taste she had acquired at Mansfield, whose character and manners could authorise a hope of the domestic happiness she had there learned to estimate, or put Edmund Bertram sufficiently out of her head.

Edmund had greatly the advantage of her in this respect. He had not to wait and wish with vacant affections for an object worthy to succeed her in them. Scarcely had he done regretting Mary Crawford, and observing to Fanny how impossible it was that he should ever meet with such another woman, before it began to strike him whether a very different kind of woman might not do just as well, or a great deal better; whether Fanny herself were not growing as dear, as important to him in all her smiles and all her ways, as Mary Crawford had ever been; and whether it might not be possible, a hopeful undertaking to persuade her that her warm and sisterly regard for him would be foundation enough for wedded love.

I purposely abstain from dates on this occasion, that every one may be at liberty to fix their own, aware that the cure of unconquerable passions, and the transfer of unchanging attachments, must vary much as to time in different people. I only entreat every body to believe that exactly at the time when it was quite natural that it should be so, and not a week earlier, Edmund did cease to care about Miss Crawford, and became as anxious to marry Fanny as Fanny herself could desire.

With such a regard for her, indeed, as his had long been, a regard founded on the most endearing claims of innocence and helplessness, and completed by every recommendation of growing worth, what could be more natural than the change? Loving, guiding, protecting her, as he had been doing ever since her being ten years old, her mind in so great a degree formed by his care, and her comfort depending on his kindness, an object to him of such close and peculiar interest, dearer by all his own importance with her than any one else at Mansfield, what was there now to add, but that he should learn to prefer soft light eyes to sparkling dark ones. And being always with her, and always talking confidentially, and his feelings exactly in that favourable state which a recent disappointment gives, those soft light eyes could not be very long in obtaining the pre-eminence.

Having once set out, and felt that he had done so on this road to happiness, there was nothing on the side of prudence to stop him or make his progress slow; no doubts of her deserving, no fears of opposition of taste, no need of drawing new hopes of happiness from dissimilarity of temper. Her mind, disposition, opinions, and habits wanted no half concealment, no self-deception on the present, no reliance on future improvement. Even in the midst of this late infatuation, he had acknowledged Fanny's mental superiority. What must be his sense of it now, therefore! She was of course only too good for him; but as nobody minds having what is too good for them, he was very steadily earnest in the pursuit of the blessing, and it was not possible that encouragement from her should be long wanting. Timid, anxious, doubting as she was, it was still impossible that such tenderness as hers should not, at times, hold out the strongest hope of success, though it remained for a later period to tell him the whole delightful and astonishing truth. His happiness in knowing himself to have been so long the beloved of such a heart, must have been great enough to warrant any strength of language in which he could clothe it to her or to himself; it must have been a delightful happiness. But there was happiness elsewhere which no description can reach. Let no one presume to give the feelings of a young woman on receiving the assurance of that affection of which she has scarcely allowed herself to entertain a hope.

Their own inclinations ascertained, there were no difficulties behind, no drawback of poverty or parent. It was a match which Sir Thomas's wishes had even forestalled. Sick of ambitious and mercenary connections, prizing more and more the sterling good of principle and temper, and chiefly anxious to bind by the strongest securities all that remained to him of domestic felicity, he had pondered with genuine satisfaction on the more than possibility of the two young friends finding their mutual consolation in each other for all that had occurred of disappointment to either; and the joyful consent which met Edmund's application, the high sense of having realised a great acquisition in the promise of Fanny for a daughter, formed just such a contrast with his early opinion on the subject when the poor little girl's coming had been first agitated, as time is for ever producing between the plans and decisions of mortals, for their own instruction, and their neighbours' entertainment.

Fanny was indeed the daughter that he wanted. His charitable kindness had been rearing a prime comfort for himself. His liberality had a rich repayment, and the general goodness of his intentions by her deserved it. He might have made her childhood happier; but it had been an error of judgment only which had given him the appearance of harshness, and deprived him of her early love; and now, on really knowing each other, their mutual attachment became very strong. After settling her at Thornton Lacey with every kind attention to her comfort, the object of almost every day was to see her there, or to get her away from it.

Selfishly dear as she had long been to Lady Bertram, she could not be parted with willingly by *her*. No happiness of son or niece could make her wish the marriage. But it was possible to part with her, because Susan remained to supply her place. Susan became the stationary niece, delighted to be so; and equally well adapted for it by a readiness of mind, and an inclination for usefulness, as Fanny had been by sweetness of temper and strong feelings of gratitude. Susan could never be spared. First as a comfort to Fanny, then as an auxiliary, and last as her substitute, she was established at Mansfield, with every appearance of equal permanency. Her more fearless disposition and happier nerves made every thing easy to her there. With quickness in understanding the tempers of those she had to deal with, and no natural timidity to restrain any consequent wishes, she was soon welcome and useful to all; and after Fanny's removal succeeded so naturally to her influence over the hourly comfort of her aunt as gradually to become, perhaps, the most beloved of the two. In *her* usefulness, in Fanny's excellence, in William's continued good conduct and rising fame, and in the general well-being and success of the other members of the family, all assisting to advance each other, and doing credit to his countenance and aid, Sir Thomas saw repeated, and for ever repeated reason to rejoice in what he had done for them all, and acknowledge the advantages of early hardship and discipline, and the consciousness of being born to struggle and endure.

With so much true merit and true love, and no want of fortune and friends, the happiness of the married cousins must appear as secure as earthly happiness can be. Equally formed for domestic life, and attached to country pleasures, their home was the home of affection and comfort; and to complete the picture of good, the acquisition of Mansfield living, by the death of Dr Grant, occurred just after they had been married long enough to begin to want an increase of income, and feel their distance from the paternal abode an inconvenience.

On that event they removed to Mansfield; and the Parsonage there, which, under each of its two former owners, Fanny had never been able to approach but with some painful sensation of restraint or alarm, soon grew as dear to her heart, and as thoroughly perfect in her eyes, as everything else within the view and patronage of Mansfield Park had long been.

Persuasion

CHAPTER ONE

SIR WALTER ELLIOT, OF KELLYNCH-HALL, in Somersetshire, was a man who, for his own amusement, never took up any book but the Baronetage; there he found occupation for an idle hour, and consolation in a distressed one; there his faculties were roused into admiration and respect, by contemplating the limited remnant of the earliest patents; there any unwelcome sensations, arising from domestic affairs, changed naturally into pity and contempt, as he turned over the almost endless creations of the last century – and there, if every other leaf were powerless, he could read his own history with an interest which never failed – this was the page at which the favourite volume always opened:

'ELLIOT OF KELLYNCH-HALL.

'Walter Elliot, born March 1, 1760, married, July 15, 1784, Elizabeth, daughter of James Steven, Esq. of South Park, in the county of Gloucester; by which lady (who died 1800) he has issue Elizabeth, born June 1, 1785; Anne, born August 9, 1787; a still-born son, Nov 5, 1789; Mary, born Nov. 20, 1791.

Precisely such had the paragraph originally stood from the printer's hands; but Sir Walter had improved it by adding, for the information of himself and his family, these words, after the date of Mary's birth – 'married, Dec. 16, 1810, Charles, son and heir of Charles Musgrove, Esq. of Uppercross, in the county of Somerset,' – and by inserting most accurately the day of the month on which he had lost his wife.

Then followed the history and rise of the ancient and respectable family, in the usual terms: how it had been first settled in Cheshire; how mentioned in Dugdale – serving the office of High Sheriff, representing a borough in three successive parliaments, exertions of loyalty, and dignity of baronet, in the first year of Charles II., with all the Marys and Elizabeths they had married; forming altogether two handsome duodecimo pages, and concluding with the arms and motto: 'Principal seat, Kellynch Hall, in the county of Somerset,' and Sir Walter's hand-writing again in this finale:

'Heir presumptive, William Walter Elliot, Esq., great grandson of the second Sir Walter.'

Vanity was the beginning and the end of Sir Walter Elliot's character; vanity of person and of situation. He had been remarkably handsome in his youth; and, at fifty-four, was still a very fine man. Few women could think more of their personal appearance than he did; nor could the valet of any new made lord be more delighted with the place he held in society. He considered the blessing of beauty as inferior only to the blessing of a baronetcy; and the Sir Walter Elliot, who united these gifts, was the constant object of his warmest respect and devotion.

His good looks and his rank had one fair claim on his attachment; since to them he must have owed a wife of very superior character to any thing deserved by his own. Lady Elliot had been an excellent woman, sensible and amiable; whose judgment and conduct, if they might be pardoned the youthful infatuation which made her Lady Elliot, had never required indulgence afterwards. – She had humoured, or softened, or concealed his failings, and promoted his real respectability for seventeen years; and though not the very happiest being in the world herself, had found enough in her duties, her friends, and her children, to attach her to life, and make it no matter of indifference to her when she was called on to quit them. – Three girls, the two eldest sixteen and fourteen, was an awful legacy for a mother to bequeath; an awful charge rather, to confide to the authority and guidance of a conceited, silly father. She had, however, one very intimate friend, a sensible, deserving woman, who had been brought, by strong attachment to herself, to settle close by her, in the village of Kellynch; and on her kindness and advice, Lady Elliot mainly relied for the best help and maintenance of the good principles and instruction which she had been anxiously giving her daughters.

This friend, and Sir Walter, did *not* marry, whatever might have been anticipated on that head by their acquaintance. – Thirteen years had passed away since Lady Elliot's death, and they were still near neighbours and intimate friends; and one remained a widower, the other a widow.

That Lady Russell, of steady age and character, and extremely well provided for, should have no thought of a second marriage, needs no apology to the public, which is rather apt to be unreasonably discontented when a woman *does* marry again, than when she does *not*; but Sir Walter's continuing in singleness requires explanation. – Be it known then, that Sir Walter, like a good father, (having met with one or two private disappointments in very unreasonable applications) prided himself on remaining single for his dear daughters' sake. For one daughter, his eldest, he would really have given up any thing, which he had not been very much tempted to do. Elizabeth had succeeded, at sixteen, to all that was possible, of her mother's rights and consequence; and being very handsome, and very like himself, her influence had always been great, and they had gone on together most happily. His two other children were of very inferior value. Mary had acquired a little artificial importance, by becoming Mrs Charles

Musgrove; but Anne, with an elegance of mind and sweetness of character, which must have placed her high with any people of real understanding, was nobody with either father or sister; her word had no weight; her convenience was always to give way; – she was only Anne.

To Lady Russell, indeed, she was a most dear and highly valued god-daughter, favourite and friend. Lady Russell loved them all; but it was only in Anne that she could fancy the mother to revive again.

A few years before, Anne Elliot had been a very pretty girl, but her bloom had vanished early; and as even in its height, her father had found little to admire in her, (so totally different were her delicate features and mild dark eyes from his own); there could be nothing in them now that she was faded and thin, to excite his esteem. He had never indulged much hope, he had now none, of ever reading her name in any other page of his favourite work. All equality of alliance must rest with Elizabeth; for Mary had merely connected herself with an old country family of respectability and large fortune, and had therefore *given* all the honour, and received none: Elizabeth would, one day or other, marry suitably.

It sometimes happens, that a woman is handsomer at twenty-nine than she was ten years before; and, generally speaking, if there has been neither ill health nor anxiety, it is a time of life at which scarcely any charm is lost. It was so with Elizabeth; still the same handsome Miss Elliot that she had begun to be thirteen years ago; and Sir Walter might be excused, therefore, in forgetting her age, or, at least, be deemed only half a fool, for thinking himself and Elizabeth as blooming as ever, amidst the wreck of the good looks of every body else; for he could plainly see how old all the rest of his family and acquaintance were growing. Anne haggard, Mary coarse, every face in the neighbourhood worsting; and the rapid increase of the crow's foot about Lady Russell's temples had long been a distress to him.

Elizabeth did not quite equal her father in personal contentment. Thirteen years had seen her mistress of Kellynch Hall, presiding and directing with a self-possession and decision which could never have given the idea of her being younger than she was. For thirteen years had she been doing the honours, and laying down the domestic law at home, and leading the way to the chaise and four, and walking immediately after Lady Russell out of all the drawing-rooms and dining-rooms in the country. Thirteen winters' revolving frosts had seen her opening every ball of credit which a scanty neighbourhood afforded; and thirteen springs shewn their blossoms, as she travelled up to London with her father, for a few weeks annual enjoyment of the great world. She had the remembrance of all this; she had the consciousness of being nine-and-twenty, to give her some regrets and some apprehensions. She was fully satisfied of being still quite as handsome as ever; but she felt her approach to the years of danger, and would have rejoiced to be certain of being properly solicited by baronet-blood within the next twelvemonth or two. Then might she again take up the book of books with as much enjoyment as in her early youth; but now she liked it not. Always to be presented with the date of her own birth, and see no marriage follow but that of a younger sister, made the book an evil; and more than once, when her father had left it open on the table near her, had she closed it, with averted eyes, and pushed it away.

She had had a disappointment, moreover, which that book and especially the history of her own family, must ever present the remembrance of. The heir presumptive, the very William Walter Elliot, Esq. whose rights had been so generously supported by her father, had disappointed her.

She had, while a very young girl, as soon as she had known him to be, in the event of her having no brother, the future baronet, meant to marry him; and her father had always meant that she should. He had not been known to them as a boy, but soon after Lady Elliot's death Sir Walter had sought the acquaintance, and though his overtures had not been met with any warmth, he had persevered in seeking it, making allowance for the modest drawing back of youth; and in one of their spring excursions to London, when Elizabeth was in her first bloom, Mr Elliot had been forced into the introduction.

He was at that time a very young man, just engaged in the study of the law; and Elizabeth found him extremely agreeable, and every plan in his favour was confirmed. He was invited to Kellynch Hall; he was talked of and expected all the rest of the year; but he never came. The following spring he was seen again in town, found equally agreeable, again encouraged, invited and expected, and again he did not come; and the next tidings were that he was married. Instead of pushing his fortune in the line marked out for the heir of the house of Elliot, he had purchased independence by uniting himself to a rich woman of inferior birth.

Sir Walter had resented it. As the head of the house, he felt that he ought to have been consulted, especially after taking the young man so publicly by the hand: 'For they must have been seen together,' he observed, 'once at Tattersal's, and twice in the lobby of the House of Commons.' His disapprobation was expressed, but apparently very little regarded. Mr Elliot had attempted no apology, and shewn himself as unsolicitous of being longer noticed by the family, as Sir Walter considered him unworthy of it: all acquaintance between them had ceased.

This very awkward history of Mr Elliot, was still, after an interval of several years, felt with anger by Elizabeth, who had liked the man for himself, and still more for being her father's heir, and whose strong family pride could see only in *him*, a proper match for Sir Walter Elliot's eldest daughter. There was not a baronet from A to Z, whom her feelings could have so willingly acknowledged as an equal. Yet so miserably had he conducted himself, that though she was at this present time, (the summer of 1814,) wearing black ribbons for his wife, she could not admit him to be worth thinking of again. The disgrace of his first marriage might, perhaps, as there was no reason to suppose it perpetuated by off-spring, have been got over, had he not done worse; but he had, as by the accustomary intervention of kind friends they had been informed, spoken most disrespectfully of them all, most slightingly and contemptuously of the very blood he belonged to, and the honours which were hereafter to be his own. This could not be pardoned.

Such were Elizabeth Elliot's sentiments and sensations; such the cares to alloy, the agitations to vary, the sameness and the elegance, the prosperity and the nothingness, of her scene of life – such the feelings to give interest to a long, uneventful residence in one country circle, to fill the vacancies which there were no habits of utility abroad, no talents or accomplishments for home, to occupy.

But now, another occupation and solicitude of mind was beginning to be added to these. Her father was growing distressed for money. She knew, that when he now took up the Baronetage, it was to drive the heavy bills of his tradespeople, and the unwelcome hints of Mr Shepherd, his agent, from his thoughts. The Kellynch property was good, but not equal to Sir Walter's apprehension of the state required in its possessor. While Lady Elliot lived, there had been method, moderation, and economy, which had just kept him within his income; but with her had died all such right-mindedness, and from that period he had been constantly exceeding it. It had not been possible for him to spend less; he had done nothing but what Sir Walter Elliot was imperiously called on to do; but blameless as he was, he was not only growing dreadfully in debt, but was hearing of it so often, that it became vain to attempt concealing it longer, even partially, from his daughter. He had given her some hints of it the last spring in town; he had gone so far even as to say, 'Can we retrench? does it occur to you that there is any one article in which we can retrench?' – and Elizabeth, to do her justice, had, in the first ardour of female alarm, set seriously to think what could be done, and had finally proposed these two branches of economy; to cut off some unnecessary charities, and to refrain from new-furnishing the drawing-room; to which expedients she afterwards added the happy thought of their taking no present down to Anne, as had been the usual yearly custom. But these measures, however good in themselves, were insufficient for the real extent of the evil, the whole of which Sir Walter found himself obliged to confess to her soon afterwards. Elizabeth had nothing to propose of deeper efficacy. She felt herself ill-used and unfortunate, as did her father; and they were neither of them able to devise any means of lessening their expenses without compromising their dignity, or relinquishing their comforts in a way not to be borne.

There was only a small part of his estate that Sir Walter could dispose of; but had every acre been alienable, it would have made no difference. He had condescended to mortgage as far as he had the power, but he would never condescend to sell. No; he would never disgrace his name so far. The Kellynch estate should be transmitted whole and entire, as he had received it.

Their two confidential friends, Mr Shepherd, who lived in the neighbouring market town, and Lady Russell, were called on to advise them; and both father and daughter seemed to expect that something should be struck out by one or the other to remove their embarrassments and reduce their expenditure, without involving the loss of any indulgence of taste or pride.

CHAPTER TWO

MR SHEPHERD, A CIVIL, CAUTIOUS lawyer, who, whatever might be his hold or his views on Sir Walter, would rather have the *disagreeable* prompted by any body else, excused himself from offering the slightest hint, and only begged leave to recommend an implicit deference to the excellent judgment of Lady Russell, – from whose known good sense he fully expected to have just such resolute measures advised, as he meant to see finally adopted.

Lady Russell was most anxiously zealous on the subject, and gave it much serious consideration. She was a woman rather of sound than of quick abilities, whose difficulties in coming to any decision in this instance were great, from the opposition of two leading principles. She was of strict integrity herself, with a delicate sense of honour; but she was as desirous of saving Sir Walter's feelings, as solicitous for the credit of the family, as aristocratic in her ideas of what was due to them, as any body of sense and honesty could well be. She was a benevolent, charitable, good woman, and capable of strong attachments; most correct in her conduct, strict in her notions of decorum, and with manners that were held a standard of good-breeding. She had a cultivated mind, and was, generally speaking, rational and consistent – but she had prejudices on the side of ancestry; she had a value for rank and consequence, which blinded her a little to the faults of those who possessed them. Herself, the widow of only a knight, she gave the dignity of a baronet all its due; and Sir Walter, independent of his claims as an old acquaintance, an attentive neighbour, an obliging landlord, the husband of her very dear friend, the father of Anne and her sisters, was, as being Sir Walter, in her apprehension entitled to a great deal of compassion and consideration under his present difficulties.

They must retrench; that did not admit of a doubt. But she was very anxious to have it done with the least possible pain to him and Elizabeth. She drew up plans of economy, she made exact calculations, and she did, what nobody else thought of doing, she consulted Anne, who never seemed considered by the others as having any interest in the question. She consulted, and in a degree was influenced by her, in marking out the scheme of retrenchment, which was at last submitted to Sir Walter. Every emendation of Anne's had been on the side of honesty against importance. She wanted more vigorous measures, a more complete reformation, a quicker release from debt, a much higher tone of indifference for every thing but justice and equity.

'If we can persuade your father to all this,' said Lady Russell, looking over her paper, 'much may be done. If he will adopt these regulations, in seven years he will be clear; and I hope we may be able to convince him and Elizabeth, that Kellynch-hall has a respectability in itself, which cannot be affected by these reductions; and that the true dignity of Sir Walter Elliot will be very far from lessened in the eyes of sensible people, by his acting like a man of principle. What will he be doing, in fact, but what very many of our first families have done – or ought to do? – There will be nothing singular in his case; and it is singularity which often makes the worst part of our suffering, as it always does of our conduct. I have great hope of our prevailing. We must be serious and decided – for, after all, the person who has contracted debts must pay them; and though a great deal is due to the feelings of the gentleman, and the head of a house, like your father, there is still more due to the character of an honest man.'

This was the principle on which Anne wanted her father to be proceeding, his friends to be urging him. She considered it as an act of indispensable duty to clear away the claims of creditors, with all the expedition which the most comprehensive retrenchments could secure, and saw no dignity in any thing short of it. She wanted it to be prescribed, and felt as a duty. She rated Lady Russell's influence highly, and as to the severe degree of self-denial, which her own conscience prompted, she believed there might be little more difficulty in persuading them to a complete, than to half a reformation. Her knowledge of her father and Elizabeth, inclined her to think that the sacrifice of one pair of horses would be hardly less painful than of both, and soon, through the whole list of Lady Russell's too gentle reductions.

How Anne's more rigid requisitions might have been taken, is of little consequence. Lady Russell's had no success at all – could not be put up with – were not to be borne. 'What! Every comfort of life knocked off! Journeys, London, servants, horses, table, – contractions and restrictions every where. To live no longer with the decencies even of a private gentleman! No, he would sooner quit Kellynch-hall at once, than remain in it on such disgraceful terms.'

'Quit Kellynch-hall.' The hint was immediately taken up by Mr Shepherd, whose interest was involved in the reality of Sir Walter's retrenching, and who was perfectly persuaded that nothing would be done without a change of abode. – 'Since the idea had been started in the very quarter which ought to dictate, he had no scruple,' he said, 'in confessing his judgment to be entirely on that side. It did not appear to him that Sir Walter could materially alter his style of living in a house which had such a character of hospitality and ancient dignity to support. – In any other place, Sir Walter might judge for himself; and would be looked up to, as regulating the modes of life, in whatever way he might choose to model his household.'

Sir Walter would quit Kellynch-hall; – and after a very few days more of doubt and indecision, the great question of whither he should go, was settled, and the first outline of this important change made out.

There had been three alternatives, London, Bath, or another house in the country. All Anne's wishes had been for the latter. A small house in their own neighbourhood, where they might still have Lady Russell's society, still be near Mary, and still have the pleasure of sometimes seeing the lawns and groves of Kellynch, was the object of her ambition. But the usual fate of Anne attended her, in having something very opposite from her inclination fixed on. She disliked Bath, and did not think it agreed with her – and Bath was to be her home.

Sir Walter had at first thought more of London, but Mr Shepherd felt that he could not be trusted in London, and had been skilful enough to dissuade him from it, and make Bath preferred. It was a much safer place for a gentleman in his predicament: – he might there be important at comparatively little expense. – Two material advantages of Bath over London had of course been given all their weight, its more convenient distance from Kellynch, only fifty miles, and Lady Russell's spending some part of every winter there; and to the very great satisfaction of Lady Russell, whose first views on the projected change had been for Bath, Sir Walter and Elizabeth were induced to believe that they should lose neither consequence nor enjoyment by settling there.

Lady Russell felt obliged to oppose her dear Anne's known wishes. It would be too much to expect Sir Walter to descend into a small house in his own neighbourhood. Anne herself would have found the mortifications of it more than she foresaw, and to Sir Walter's feelings they must have been dreadful. And with regard to Anne's dislike of Bath, she considered it as a prejudice and mistake, arising first from the circumstance of her having been three years at school there, after her mother's death, and secondly, from her happening to be not in perfectly good spirits, the only winter which she had afterwards spent there with herself.

Lady Russell was fond of Bath in short, and disposed to think it must suit them all; and as to her young friend's health, by passing all the warm months with her at Kellynch-lodge, every danger would be avoided; and it was, in fact, a change which must do both health and spirits good. Anne had been too little from home, too little seen. Her spirits were not high. A larger society would improve them. She wanted her to be more known.

The undesirableness of any other house in the same neighbourhood for Sir Walter, was certainly much strengthened by one part, and a very material part of the scheme, which had been happily engrafted on the beginning. He was not only to quit his home, but to see it in the hands of others; a trial of fortitude, which stronger heads than Sir Walter's have found too much. – Kellynch-hall was to be let. This, however, was a profound secret; not to be breathed beyond their own circle.

Sir Walter could not have borne the degradation of being known to design letting his house. – Mr Shepherd had once mentioned the word 'advertise;' – but never dared approach it again; Sir Walter spurned the idea of its being offered in any manner; forbad the slightest hint being dropped of his having such an intention; and it was only on the supposition of his being spontaneously solicited by some most unexceptionable applicant, on his own terms, and as a great favour, that he would let it at all.

How quick come the reasons for approving what we like! – Lady Russell had another excellent one at hand, for being extremely glad that Sir Walter and his family were to remove from the country. Elizabeth had been lately forming an intimacy, which she wished to see interrupted. It was with a daughter of Mr Shepherd, who had returned, after an unprosperous marriage, to her father's house, with the additional burthen of two children. She was a clever young woman, who understood the art of pleasing; the art of pleasing, at least, at Kellynch-hall; and who had made herself so acceptable to Miss Elliot, as to have been already staying there more than once, in spite of all that Lady Russell, who thought it a friendship quite out of place, could hint of caution and reserve.

Lady Russell, indeed, had scarcely any influence with Elizabeth, and seemed to love her, rather because she would love her, than because Elizabeth deserved it. She had never received from her more than outward attention, nothing beyond the observances of complaisance; had never succeeded in any point which she wanted to carry, against previous inclination. She had been repeatedly very earnest in trying to get Anne included in the visit to London, sensibly open to all the injustice and all the discredit of the selfish arrangements which shut her out, and on many lesser occasions had endeavoured to give Elizabeth the advantage of her own better judgment and experience – but always in vain; Elizabeth would go her own way – and never had she pursued it in more decided opposition to Lady Russell, than in this selection of Mrs Clay; turning from the society of so deserving a sister to bestow her affection and confidence on one who ought to have been nothing to her but the object of distant civility.

From situation, Mrs Clay was, in Lady Russell's estimate, a very unequal, and in her character she believed a very dangerous companion – and a removal that would leave Mrs Clay behind, and bring a choice of more suitable intimates within Miss Elliot's reach, was therefore an object of first-rate importance.

CHAPTER THREE

'I MUST TAKE LEAVE TO OBSERVE, Sir Walter,' said Mr Shepherd one morning at Kellynch, as he laid down the newspaper, 'that the present juncture is much in our favour. This peace will be turning all our rich Navy Officers ashore. They will be all wanting a home. Could not be a better time, Sir Walter, for having a choice of tenants, very responsible tenants. Many a noble fortune has been made during the war. If a rich Admiral were to come in our way, Sir Walter –'

'He would be a very lucky man, Shepherd,' replied Sir Walter, 'that's all I have to remark. A prize indeed would Kellynch Hall be to him; rather the greatest prize of all, let him have taken ever so many before – hey, Shepherd?'

Mr Shepherd laughed, as he knew he must, at this wit, and then added,

'I presume to observe, Sir Walter, that, in the way of business, gentlemen of the navy are well to deal with. I have had a little knowledge of their methods of doing business, and I am free to confess that they have very liberal notions, and are as likely to make desirable tenants as any set of people one should meet with. Therefore, Sir Walter, what I would take leave to suggest is, that if in consequence of any rumours getting abroad of your intention – which must be contemplated as a possible thing, because we know how difficult it is to keep the actions and designs of one part of the world from the notice and curiosity of the other, – consequence has its tax – I, John Shepherd, might conceal any family-matters that I chose, for nobody would think it worth their while to observe me, but Sir Walter Elliot has eyes upon him which it may be very difficult to elude – and therefore, thus much I venture upon, that it will not greatly surprise me if, with all our caution, some rumour of the truth should get abroad – in the supposition of which, as I was going to observe, since applications will unquestionably follow, I should think any from our wealthy naval commanders particularly worth attending to – and beg leave to add, that two hours will bring me over at any time, to save you the trouble of replying.'

Sir Walter only nodded. But soon afterwards, rising and pacing the room, he observed sarcastically,

'There are few among the gentlemen of the navy, I imagine, who would not be surprised to find themselves in a house of this description.'

'They would look around them, no doubt, and bless their good fortune,' said Mrs Clay, for Mrs Clay was present; her father had driven her over, nothing being of so much use to Mrs Clay's health as a drive to Kellynch: 'but I quite agree with my father in thinking a sailor might be a very desirable tenant. I have known a good deal of the profession; and besides their liberality, they are so neat and careful in all their ways! These valuable pictures of yours, Sir Walter, if you chose to leave them, would be perfectly safe. Every thing in and about the house would be taken such excellent care of! the gardens and shrubberies would be kept in almost as high order as they are now. You need not be afraid, Miss Elliot, of your own sweet flower-garden's being neglected.'

'As to all that,' rejoined Sir Walter coolly, 'supposing I were induced to let my house, I have by no means made up my mind as to the privileges to be annexed to it. I am not particularly disposed to favour a tenant. The park would be open to him of course, and few navy officers, or men of any other description, can have had such a range; but what restrictions I might impose on the use of the pleasure-grounds, is another thing. I am not fond of the idea of my shrubberies being always approachable; and I should recommend Miss Elliot to be on her guard with respect to her flower-garden. I am very little disposed to grant a tenant of Kellynch Hall any extraordinary favour, I assure you, be he sailor or soldier.'

After a short pause, Mr Shepherd presumed to say,

'In all these cases, there are established usages which make every thing plain and easy between landlord and tenant. Your interest, Sir Walter, is in pretty safe hands. Depend upon me for taking care that no tenant has more than his just rights. I venture to hint, that Sir Walter Elliot cannot be half so jealous for his own, as John Shepherd will be for him.'

Here Anne spoke, –

'The navy, I think, who have done so much for us, have at least an equal claim with any other set of men, for all the comforts and all the privileges which any home can give. Sailors work hard enough for their comforts, we must all allow.'

'Very true, very true. What Miss Anne says, is very true,' was Mr Shepherd's rejoinder, and 'Oh! certainly,' was his daughter's; but Sir Walter's remark was, soon afterwards –

'The profession has its utility, but I should be sorry to see any friend of mine belonging to it.'

'Indeed!' was the reply, and with a look of surprise.

'Yes; it is in two points offensive to me; I have two strong grounds of objection to it. First, as being the means of bringing persons of obscure birth into undue distinction, and raising men to honours which their fathers and grandfathers never dreamt of; and secondly, as it cuts up a man's youth and vigour most horribly; a sailor grows old sooner than any other man; I have observed it all my life. A man is in greater danger in the navy of being insulted by the rise of one whose father, his father might have disdained to speak to, and of becoming prematurely an object of disgust himself, than in any other line. One day last spring, in town, I was in company with two men, striking instances of what I am talking of, Lord St Ives, whose father we all know to have been a country curate, without bread to eat; I was to give place to Lord St Ives, and a certain Admiral Baldwin, the most deplorable looking personage you can imagine, his face the colour of mahogany, rough and rugged to the last degree, all lines and wrinkles, nine grey hairs of a side, and nothing but a dab of powder at top. – "In the name of heaven, who is that old fellow?" said I, to a friend of mine who was standing near, (Sir Basil Morley.) "Old fellow!" cried Sir Basil, "it is Admiral Baldwin. What do you take his age to be?" "Sixty," said I, "or perhaps sixty-two." "Forty," replied Sir Basil, "forty, and no more." Picture to yourselves my amazement; I shall not easily forget Admiral Baldwin. I never saw quite so wretched an example of what a sea-faring life can do; but to a degree, I know it is the same with them all: they are all knocked about, and exposed to every climate, and every weather, till they are not fit to be seen. It is a pity they are not knocked on the head at once, before they reach Admiral Baldwin's age.'

'Nay, Sir Walter,' cried Mrs Clay, 'this is being severe indeed. Have a little mercy on the poor men. We are not all born to be handsome. The sea is no beautifier, certainly; sailors do grow old betimes; I have often observed it; they soon lose the look of youth. But then, is not it the same with many other professions, perhaps most other? Soldiers, in active service, are not at all better off: and even in the quieter professions, there is a toil and a labour of the mind, if not of the body, which seldom leaves a man's looks to the natural effect of time. The Lawyer plods, quite care-worn; the physician is

'In the name of heaven, who is that old fellow?'

up at all hours, and travelling in all weather; and even the clergyman –' she stopt a moment to consider what might do for the clergyman; – 'and even the clergyman, you know, is obliged to go into infected rooms, and expose his health and looks to all the injury of a poisonous atmosphere. In fact, as I have long been convinced, though every profession is necessary and honourable in its turn, it is only the lot of those who are not obliged to follow any, who can live in a regular way, in the country, choosing their own hours, following their own pursuits, and living on their own property, without the torment of trying for more; it is only *their* lot, I say, to hold the blessings of health and a good appearance to the utmost: I know no other set of men but what lose something of their personableness when they cease to be quite young.'

It seemed as if Mr Shepherd, in this anxiety to bespeak Sir Walter's goodwill towards a naval officer as tenant, had been gifted with foresight; for the very first application for the house was from an Admiral Croft, with whom he shortly afterwards fell into company in attending the quarter sessions at Taunton; and indeed, he had received a hint of the admiral from a London correspondent. By the report which he hastened over to Kellynch to make, Admiral Croft was a native of Somersetshire, who having acquired a very handsome fortune, was wishing to settle in his own country, and had come down to Taunton in order to look at some advertised places in that immediate neighbourhood, which, however, had not suited him; that accidentally hearing – (it was just as he had foretold, Mr Shepherd observed, Sir Walter's concerns could not be kept a secret,) – accidentally hearing of the possibility of Kellynch Hall being to let, and understanding his (Mr Sherherd's) connection with the owner, he had introduced himself to him in order to make particular inquiries, and had, in the course of a pretty long conference, expressed as strong an inclination for the place as man who knew it only by description, could feel; and given Mr Shepherd, in his explicit account of himself, every proof of his being a most responsible, eligible tenant.

'And who is Admiral Croft?' was Sir Walter's cold suspicious inquiry.

Mr Shepherd answered for his being of a gentleman's family, and mentioned a place; and Anne, after the little pause which followed, added –

'He is rear admiral of the white. He was in the Trafalgar action, and has been in the East Indies since; he has been stationed there, I believe, several years.'

'Then I take it for granted,' observed Sir Walter, 'that his face is about as orange as the cuffs and capes of my livery.'

Mr Shepherd hastened to assure him, that Admiral Croft was a very hale, hearty, well-looking man, a little weather-beaten, to be sure, but not much; and quite the gentleman in all his notions and behaviour; – not likely to make the smallest difficulty about terms; – only wanted a comfortable home, and to get into it as soon as possible; – knew he must pay for his convenience; – knew what rent a ready-furnished house of that consequence might fetch; – should not have been surprised if Sir Walter had asked more; – had inquired about the manor; – would be glad of the deputation, certainly, but made no great point of it; – said he sometimes took out a gun, but never killed; – quite the gentleman.

Mr Shepherd was eloquent on the subject; pointing out all the circumstances of the admiral's family, which made him peculiarly desirable as a tenant. He was a married man, and without children; the very state to be wished for. A house was never taken good care of, Mr Shepherd observed, without a lady: he did not know, whether furniture might not be in danger of suffering as much where there was no lady, as where there were many children. A lady, without a family, was the very best preserver of furniture in the world. He had seen Mrs Croft, too; she was at Taunton with the admiral, and had been present almost all the time they were talking the matter over.

'And a very well-spoken, genteel, shrewd lady, she seemed to be,' continued he; 'asked more questions about the house, and terms, and taxes, than the admiral himself, and seemed more conversant with business. And moreover, Sir Walter, I found she was not quite unconnected in this country, any more than her husband; that is to say, she is sister to a gentleman who did live amongst us once; she told me so herself: sister to the gentleman who lived a few years back, at Monkford. Bless me! what was his name, though I have heard it so lately. Penelope, my dear, can you help me to the name of the gentleman who lived at Monkford – Mrs Croft's brother?'

But Mrs Clay was talking so eagerly with Miss Elliot, that she did not hear the appeal.

'I have no conception whom you can mean, Shepherd; I remember no gentleman resident at Monkford since the time of old Governor Trent.'

'Bless me! how very odd! I shall forget my own name soon, I suppose. A name that I am so very well acquainted with; knew the gentleman so well by sight; seen him a hundred times; came to consult me once, I remember, about a trespass of one of his neighbours; farmer's man breaking into his orchard – wall torn down – apples stolen – caught in the fact; and afterwards, contrary to my judgment, submitted to an amicable compromise. Very odd indeed!'

After waiting another moment –

'You mean Mr Wentworth, I suppose,' said Anne.

Mr Shepherd was all gratitude.

'Wentworth was the very name! Mr Wentworth was the very man. He had the curacy of Monkford, you know, Sir Walter, some time back, for two or three years. Came there about the year — 5, I take it. You remember him, I am sure.'

'Wentworth? Oh! ay, – Mr Wentworth, the curate of Monkford. You misled me by the term *gentleman*. I thought you were speaking of some man of property: Mr Wentworth was nobody, I remember; quite unconnected; nothing to do with the Strafford family. One wonders how the names of many of our nobility become so common.'

As Mr Shepherd perceived that this connexion of the Crofts did them no service with Sir Walter, he mentioned it no more; returning, with all his zeal, to dwell on the circumstances more indisputably in their favour; their age, and number, and fortune; the high idea they had formed of Kellynch Hall, and extreme solicitude for the advantage of renting it; making it appear as if they ranked nothing beyond the happiness of being the tenants of Sir Walter Elliot: an extraordinary taste, certainly, could they have been supposed in the secret of Sir Walter's estimate of the dues of a tenant.

It succeeded, however; and though Sir Walter must ever look with an evil eye on any one intending to inhabit that house, and think them infinitely too well off in being permitted to rent it on the highest terms, he was talked into allowing Mr Shepherd to proceed in the treaty, and authorising him to wait on Admiral Croft, who still remained at Taunton, and fix a day for the house being seen.

Sir Walter was not very wise; but still he had experience enough of the world to feel, that a more unobjectionable tenant, in all essentials, than Admiral Croft bid fair to be, could hardly offer. So far went his understanding; and his vanity supplied a little additional soothing, in the admiral's situation in life, which was just high enough, and not too high. 'I have let my house to Admiral Croft,' would sound extremely well; very much better than to any mere *Mr*–; a *Mr* (save, perhaps, some half-dozen in the nation,) always needs a note of explanation. An admiral speaks his own consequence, and, at the same time, can never make a baronet look small. In all their dealings and intercourse, Sir Walter Elliot must ever have the precedence.

Nothing could be done without a reference to Elizabeth; but her inclination was growing so strong for a removal, that she was happy to have it fixed and expedited by a tenant at hand; and not a word to suspend decision was uttered by her.

Mr Shepherd was completely empowered to act; and no sooner had such an end been reached, than Anne, who had been a most attentive listener to the whole, left the room, to seek the comfort of cool air for her flushed cheeks; and as she walked along a favourite grove, said, with a gentle sigh, 'a few months more, and *he*, perhaps, may be walking here.'

CHAPTER FOUR

HE WAS NOT MR WENTWORTH, the former curate of Monkford, however suspicious appearances may be, but a Captain Frederick Wentworth, his brother, who being made commander in consequence of the action off St Domingo, and not immediately employed, had come into Somersetshire, in the summer of 1806; and having no parent living, found a home for half a year, at Monkford. He was, at that time, a remarkably fine young man, with a great deal of intelligence, spirit and brilliancy; and Anne an extremely pretty girl, with gentleness, modesty, taste, and feeling. – Half the sum of attraction, on either side, might have been enough, for he had nothing to do, and she had hardly any body to love; but the encounter of such lavish recommendations could not fail. They were gradually acquainted, and when acquainted, rapidly and deeply in love. It would be difficult to say which had seen highest perfection in the other, or which had been the happiest; she, in receiving his declarations and proposals, or he in having them accepted.

A short period of exquisite felicity followed, and but a short one. – Troubles soon arose. Sir Walter, on being applied to, without actually witholding his consent, or saying it should never be, gave it all the negative of great astonishment, great coldness, great silence, and a professed resolution of doing nothing for his daughter. He thought it a very degrading alliance; and Lady Russell, though with more tempered and pardonable pride, received it as a most unfortunate one.

Anne Elliot, with all her claims of birth, beauty, and mind, to throw herself away at nineteen; involve herself at nineteen in an engagement with a young man, who had nothing but himself to recommend him, and no hopes of attaining affluence, but in the chances of a most uncertain profession, and no connections to secure even his farther rise in that profession; would be, indeed, a throwing away, which she grieved to think of! Anne Elliot, so young; known to so few, to be snatched off by a stranger without alliance or fortune; or rather sunk by him into a state of most wearing, anxious, youth-killing dependence! It must not be, if by any fair interference of friendship, any representations from one who had almost a mother's love, and mother's rights, it would be prevented.

Captain Wentworth had no fortune. He had been lucky in his profession, but spending freely, what had come freely, had realized nothing. But, he was confident that he should soon be rich; – full of life and ardour, he knew that he should soon have a ship, and soon be on a station that would lead to every thing he wanted. He had always been lucky; he knew he should be so still. – Such confidence, powerful in its own warmth, and bewitching in the wit which often expressed it, must have been enough for Anne; but Lady Russell saw it differently. – His sanguine temper, and fearlessness of mind, operated very differently on her. She saw in it but an aggravation of the evil. It only added a dangerous character to himself. He was brilliant, he was headstrong. – Lady Russell had little taste for wit; and of any thing approaching to imprudence a horror. She deprecated the connection in every light.

Such opposition, as these feelings produced, was more than Anne could combat. Young and gentle as she was, it might yet have been possible to withstand her father's ill-will, though unsoftened by one kind word or look on the part of her sister; – but Lady Russell, whom she had always loved and relied on, could not, with such steadiness of opinion, and such tenderness of manner, be continually advising her in vain. She was persuaded to believe the engagement a wrong thing – indiscreet, improper, hardly capable of success, and not deserving it. But it was not a merely selfish caution, under which she acted, in putting an end to it. Had she not imagined herself consulting his good, even more than her own, she could hardly have given him up. – The belief of being prudent, and self-denying principally for *his* advantage, was her chief consolation, under the misery of a parting – a final parting; and every consolation was required, for she had to encounter all the additional pain of opinions, on his side, totally unconvinced and unbending, and of his feeling himself ill-used by so forced a relinquishment. – He had left the country in consequence.

A few months had seen the beginning and the end of their acquaintance; but, not with a few months ended Anne's share of suffering from it. Her attachment and regrets had, for a long time, clouded every enjoyment of youth; and an early loss of bloom and spirits had been their lasting effect.

More than seven years were gone since this little history of sorrowful interest had reached its close; and time had softened down much, perhaps nearly all of peculiar attachment to him, – but she had been too dependant on time alone; no aid had been given in change of place, (except in one visit to Bath soon after the rupture,) or in any novelty or enlargement of society. – No one had ever come within the Kellynch circle, who could bear a comparison with Frederick Wentworth, as he stood in her memory. No second attachment, the only thoroughly natural, happy, and sufficient cure, at her time of life, had been possible to the nice tone of her mind, the fastidiousness of her taste, in the small limits of the society around them. She had been solicited, when about two-and-twenty, to change her name, by the young man, who not long afterwards found a more willing mind in her younger sister; and Lady Russell had lamented her refusal; for Charles Musgrove was the eldest son of a man, whose landed property and general importance, were second, in that country, only to Sir Walter's, and of good character and appearance; and however Lady Russell might have asked yet for something more, while Anne was nineteen, she would have rejoiced to see her at twenty-two, so respectably removed from the partialities and injustice of her father's house, and settled so permanently near herself. But in this case, Anne had left nothing for advice to do; and though Lady Russell, as satisfied as ever with her own discretion, never wished the past undone, she began now to have the anxiety which borders on hopelessness for Anne's being tempted, by some man of talents and independence, to enter a state for which she held her to be peculiarly fitted by her warm affections and domestic habits.

They knew not each other's opinion, either its constancy or its change, on the one leading point of Anne's conduct, for the subject was never alluded to, – but Anne, at seven and twenty, thought very differently from what she had been made to think at nineteen. – She did not blame Lady Russell, she did not blame herself for having been guided by her; but she felt that were any young person, in similar circumstances, to apply to her for counsel, they would never receive any of such certain immediate wretchedness, such uncertain future good. – She was persuaded that under every disadvantage of disapprobation at home, and every anxiety attending his profession, all their probable fears, delays and disappointments, she should yet have been a happier woman in maintaining the engagement, than she had been in the sacrifice of it; and this, she fully believed, had the usual share, had even more than a usual share of all such solicitudes and suspense been theirs, without reference to the actual results of their case, which, as it happened, would have bestowed earlier prosperity than could be reasonably calculated on. All his sanguine expectations, all his confidence had been justified. His genius and ardour had seemed to foresee and to command his prosperous path. He had, very soon after their engagement ceased, got employ; and all that he had told her would follow, had taken place. He had distinguished himself, and early gained the other step in rank – and must now, by successive captures, have made a handsome fortune. She had only navy lists and newspapers for her authority, but she could not doubt his being rich; – and, in favour of his constancy, she had no reason to believe him married.

How eloquent could Anne Elliot have been, – how eloquent, at least, were her wishes on the side of early warm attachment, and a cheerful confidence in futurity, against that over-anxious caution which seems to insult exertion and distrust Providence! – She had been forced into prudence in her youth, she learned romance as she grew older – the natural sequel of an unnatural beginning.

With all these circumstances, recollections and feelings, she could not hear that Captain Wentworth's sister was likely to live at Kellynch, without a revival of former pain; and many a stroll and many a sigh were necessary to dispel the agitation of the idea. She often told herself it was folly, before she could harden her nerves sufficiently to feel the continual discussion of the Crofts and their business no evil. She was assisted, however, by that perfect indifference and apparent unconsciousness, among the only three of her own friends in the secret of the past, which seemed almost to deny any recollection of it. She could do justice to the superiority of Lady Russell's motives in this, over those of her father and Elizabeth; she could honour all the better feelings of her calmness – but the general air of oblivion among them was highly important, from whatever it sprung; and in the event of Admiral Croft's really taking Kellynch-hall, she rejoiced anew over the conviction which had always been most grateful to her, of the past being known to those three only among her connections, by whom no syllable, she believed, would ever be whispered, and in the trust that among his, the brother only with whom he had been residing, had received any information of their short-lived engagement. – That brother had been long removed from the country – and being a sensible man, and, moreover, a single man at the time, she had a fond dependence on no human creature's having heard of it from him.

The sister, Mrs Croft, had then been out of England, accompanying her husband on a foreign station, and her own sister, Mary, had been at school while it all occurred – and never admitted by the pride of some, and the delicacy of others, to the smallest knowledge of it afterwards.

With these supports, she hoped that the acquaintance between herself and the Crofts, which, with Lady Russell still resident in Kellynch, and Mary fixed only three miles off, must be anticipated, need not involve any particular awkwardness.

CHAPTER FIVE

ON THE MORNING APPOINTED for Admiral and Mrs Croft's seeing Kellynch-hall, Anne found it most natural to take her almost daily walk to Lady Russell's, and keep out of the way till all was over; when she found it most natural to be sorry that she had missed the opportunity of seeing them.

This meeting of the two parties proved highly satisfactory, and decided the whole business at once. Each lady was previously well disposed for an agreement, and saw nothing, therefore, but good manners in the other; and, with regard to the gentlemen, there was such an hearty good humour, such an open, trusting liberality on the Admiral's side, as could not but influence Sir Walter, who had besides been flattered into his very best and most polished behaviour by Mr Shepherd's assurances of his being known, by report, to the Admiral, as a model of good breeding.

The house and grounds, and furniture, were approved, the Crofts were approved, terms, time, every thing, and every body, was right; and Mr Shepherd's clerks were set to work, without there having been a single preliminary difference to modify of all that 'This indenture sheweth.'

Sir Walter, without hesitation, declared the Admiral to be the best-looking sailor he had ever met with, and went so far as to say, that, if his own man might have had the arranging of his hair, he should not be ashamed of being seen with him any where; and the Admiral, with sympathetic cordiality, observed to his wife as they drove back through the Park, 'I thought we should soon come to a deal, my dear, in spite of what they told us at Taunton. The baronet will never set the Thames on fire, but there seems no harm in him:' – reciprocal compliments, which would have been esteemed about equal.

The Crofts were to have possession at Michaelmas, and as Sir Walter proposed removing to Bath in the course of the preceding month, there was no time to be lost in making every dependent arrangement.

Lady Russell, convinced that Anne would not be allowed to be of any use, or any importance, in the choice of the house which they were going to secure, was very unwilling to have her hurried away so soon, and wanted to make it possible for her to stay behind, till she might convey her to Bath herself after Christmas; but having engagements of her own, which must take her from Kellynch for several weeks, she was unable to give the full invitation she wished; and Anne, though dreading the possible heats of September in all the white glare of Bath, and grieving to forego all the influence so sweet and so sad of the autumnal months in the country, did not think that, every thing considered, she wished to remain. It would be most right, and most wise, and, therefore, must involve least suffering, to go with the others.

Something occurred, however, to give her a different duty. Mary, often a little unwell, and always thinking a great deal of her own complaints, and always in the habit of claiming Anne when any thing was the matter, was indisposed; and foreseeing that she should not have a day's health all the autumn, entreated, or rather required her, for it was hardly entreaty, to come to Uppercross Cottage, and bear her company as long as she should want her, instead of going to Bath.

'I cannot possibly do without Anne,' was Mary's reasoning; and Elizabeth's reply was, 'Then I am sure Anne had better stay, for nobody will want her in Bath.'

To be claimed as a good, though in an improper style, is at least better than being rejected as no good at all; and Anne, glad to be thought of some use, glad to have any thing marked out as a duty, and certainly not sorry to have the scene of it in the country, and her own dear country, readily agreed to stay.

This invitation of Mary's removed all Lady Russell's difficulties, and it was consequently soon settled that Anne should not go to Bath till Lady Russell took her, and that all the intervening time should be divided between Uppercross Cottage and Kellynch-lodge.

So far all was perfectly right; but Lady Russell was almost startled by the wrong of one part of the Kellynch-hall plan, when it burst on her, which was, Mrs Clay's being engaged to go to Bath with Sir Walter and Elizabeth, as a most important and valuable assistant to the latter in all the business before her. Lady Russell was extremely sorry that such a measure should have been resorted to at all – wondered, grieved, and feared – and the affront it contained to Anne, in Mrs Clay's being of so much use, while Anne could be of none, was a very sore aggravation.

Anne herself was become hardened to such affronts; but she felt the imprudence of the arrangement quite as keenly as Lady Russell. With a great deal of quiet observation, and a knowledge, which she often wished less, of her father's character, she was sensible that results the most serious to his family from the intimacy were more than possible. She did not imagine that her father had at present an idea of the kind. Mrs Clay had freckles, and a projecting tooth, and a clumsy wrist, which he was continually making severe remarks upon, in her absence; but she was young, and certainly altogether well-looking, and possessed, in an acute mind and assiduous pleasing manners, infinitely more dangerous attractions than any merely personal might have been. Anne was so impressed by the degree of their danger, that she could not excuse herself from trying to make it perceptible to her sister. She had little hope of success; but Elizabeth, who in the event of such a reverse would be so much more to be pitied than herself, should never, she thought, have reason to reproach her for giving no warning.

She spoke, and seemed only to offend. Elizabeth could not conceive how such an absurd suspicion should occur to her; and indignantly answered for each party's perfectly knowing their situation.

'Mrs Clay,' she said warmly, 'never forgets who she is; and as I am rather better acquainted with her sentiments than you can be, I can assure you, that upon the subject of marriage they are particularly nice; and that she reprobates all inequality of condition and rank more strongly than most people. And as to my father, I really should not have thought that he, who has kept himself single so long for our sakes, need be suspected now. If Mrs Clay were a very beautiful woman, I grant you, it might be wrong to have her so much with me; not that any thing in the world, I am sure, would induce my father to make a degrading match; but he might be rendered unhappy. But poor Mrs Clay, who, with all her merits, can never have been reckoned tolerably pretty! I really think poor Mrs Clay may be staying here in perfect safety. One would imagine you had never heard my father speak of her personal misfortunes, though I know you must fifty times. That tooth of hers! and those freckles! Freckles do not disgust me so very much as they do him: I have known a face not materially disfigured by a few, but he abominates them. You must have heard him notice Mrs Clay's freckles.'

'There is hardly any personal defect,' replied Anne, 'which an agreeable manner might not gradually reconcile one to.'

'I think very differently,' answered Elizabeth, shortly: 'an agreeable manner may set off handsome features, but can never alter plain ones. However, at any rate, as I have a great deal more at stake on this point than any body else can have, I think it rather unnecessary in you to be advising me.'

Anne had done – glad that it was over, and not absolutely hopeless of doing good. Elizabeth, though resenting the suspicion, might yet be made observant by it.

The last office of the four carriage-horses was to draw Sir Walter, Miss Elliot, and Mrs Clay to Bath. The party drove off on very good spirits; Sir Walter prepared with condescending bows for all the afflicted tenantry and cottagers who might have had a hint to shew themselves: and Anne walked up at the same time, in a sort of desolate tranquillity, to the Lodge, where she was to spend the first week.

Her friend was not in better spirits than herself. Lady Russell felt this break-up of the family exceedingly. Their respectability was as dear to her as her own; and a daily intercourse had become precious by habit. It was painful to look upon their deserted grounds, and still worse to anticipate the new hands they were to fall into; and to escape the solitariness and the melancholy of so altered a village, and be out of the way when Admiral and Mrs Croft first arrived, she had determined to make her own absence from home begin when she must give up Anne. Accordingly their removal was made together, and Anne was set down at Uppercross Cottage, in the first stage of Lady Russell's journey.

Uppercross was a moderate-sized village, which a few years back had been completely in the old English style; containing only two houses superior in appearance to those of the yeomen and labourers, – the mansion of the 'squire, with its high walls, great gates, and old trees, substantial and unmodernized – and the compact, tight parsonage, enclosed in its own neat garden, with a vine and a pear-tree trained round its casements; but upon the marriage of the young 'squire, it had received the improvement of a farmhouse elevated into a cottage for his residence; and Uppercross Cottage, with its veranda, French windows, and other prettiness, was quite as likely to catch the traveller's eye, as the more consistent and considerable aspect and premises of the Great House, about a quarter of a mile farther on.

Here Anne had often been staying. She knew the ways of Uppercross as well as those of Kellynch. The two families were so continually meeting, so much in the habit of running in and out of each other's house at all hours, that it was rather a surprise to her to find Mary alone; but being alone, her being unwell and out of spirits, was almost a matter of course. Though better endowed than the elder sister, Mary had not Anne's understanding or temper. While well, and happy, and properly attended to, she had great good humour and excellent spirits; but any indisposition sunk her completely; she had no resources for solitude; and inheriting a considerable share of the Elliot self-importance, was very prone to add to every other distress that of fancying herself neglected and ill-used. In person, she was inferior to both sisters, and had, even in her bloom, only reached the dignity of being 'a fine girl.' She was now lying on the faded sofa of the pretty little drawing-room, the once elegant furniture of which had been gradually growing shabby, under the influence of four summers and two children; and, on Anne's appearing, greeted her with,

'So, you are come at last! I began to think I should never see you. I am so ill I can hardly speak. I have not seen a creature the whole morning!'

'I am sorry to find you unwell,' replied Anne. 'You sent me such a good account of yourself on Thursday!'

'Yes, I made the best of it; I always do; but I was very far from well at the time; and I do not think I ever was so ill in my life as I have been all this morning – very unfit to be left alone, I am sure. Suppose I were to be seized of a sudden in some dreadful way, and not able to ring the bell! So, Lady Russell would not get out, I do not think she has been in this house three times this summer.'

Anne said what was proper, and enquired after her husband. 'Oh! Charles is out shooting. I have not seen him since seven o'clock. He would go, though I told him how ill I was. He said he should not stay out long; but he has never come back, and now it is almost one. I assure you, I have not seen a soul this whole long morning.'

'You have had your little boys with you?'

'Yes, as long as I could bear their noise; but they are so unmanageable that they do me more harm than good. Little Charles does not mind a word I say, and Walter is growing quite as bad.'

'Well, you will soon be better now,' replied Anne, cheerfully. 'You know I always cure you when I come. How are your neighbours at the Great House?'

'I can give you no account of them. I have not seen one of them to-day, except Mr Musgrove, who just stopped and spoke through the window, but without getting off his horse; and though I told him how ill I was, not one of them have been near me. It did not happen to suit the Miss Musgroves, I suppose, and they never put themselves out of their way.'

'You will see them yet, perhaps, before the morning is gone. It is early.'

'I never want them, I assure you. They talk and laugh a great deal too much for me. O! Anne, I am so very unwell! It is quite unkind of you not to come on Thursday.'

'My dear Mary, recollect what a comfortable account you sent me of yourself! You wrote in the cheerfullest manner, and said you were perfectly well, and in no hurry for me; and that being the case, you must be aware that my wish would be to remain with Lady Russell to the last: and besides what I felt on her account, I have really been so busy, have had so much to do, that I could not very conveniently have left Kellynch sooner.'

'Dear me! what can *you* possibly have to do?'

'A great many things, I assure you. More than I can recollect in a moment: but I can tell you some. I have been making a duplicate of the catalogue of my father's books and pictures. I have been several times in the garden with Mackenzie, trying to understand, and make him understand, which of Elizabeth's plants are for Lady Russell. I have had all my own little concerns to arrange – books and music to divide, and all my trunks to repack, from not having understood in time what was intended as to the waggons. And one thing I have had to do, Mary, of a more trying nature; going to almost every house in the parish, as a sort of take-leave. I was told that they wished it. But all these things took up a great deal of time.'

'Oh! well;' – and after a moment's pause, 'But you have never asked me one word about our dinner at the Pooles yesterday.'

'Did you go then? I have made no enquiries, because I concluded you must have been obliged to give up the party.'

'Oh! yes, I went. I was very well yesterday; nothing at all the matter with me till this morning. It would have been strange if I had not gone.'

'I am very glad you were well enough, and I hope you had a pleasant party.'

'Nothing remarkable. One always knows beforehand what the dinner will be, and who will be there. And it is so very uncomfortable, not having a carriage of one's own. Mr and Mrs Musgrove took me, and we were so crowded! They are both so very large, and take up so much room! And Mr Musgrove always sits forward. So, there was I, crowded into the back seat with Henrietta and Louisa. And I think it very likely that my illness to-day may be owing to it.'

A little farther perseverance in patience, and forced cheerfulness on Anne's side, produced nearly a cure on Mary's. She could soon sit upright on the sofa, and began to hope she might be able to leave it by dinner-time. Then, forgetting to think of it, she was at the other end of the room, beautifying a nosegay; then, she ate her cold meat; and then she was well enough to propose a little walk.

'Where shall we go?' said she, when they were ready. 'I suppose you will not like to call at the Great House before they have been to see you?'

'I have not the smallest objection on that account,' replied Anne. 'I should never think of standing on such ceremony with people I know so well as Mrs and the Miss Musgroves.'

'Oh! but they ought to call upon you as soon as possible. They ought to feel what is due to you as *my* sister. However, we may as well go and sit with them a little while, and when we have got that over, we can enjoy our walk.'

Anne had always thought such a style of intercourse highly imprudent; but she had ceased to endeavour to check it, from believing that, though there were on each side continual subjects of offence, neither family could now do without it. To the Great House accordingly they went, to sit the full half hour in the old-fashioned square parlour, with a small carpet and shining floor, to which the present daughters of the house were gradually giving the proper air of confusion by a grand piano forte and a harp, flower-stands and little tables placed in every direction. Oh! could the originals of the portraits against the wainscot, could the gentlemen in brown velvet and the ladies in blue satin have seen what was going on, have been conscious of such an overthrow of all order and neatness! The portraits themselves seemed to be staring in astonishment.

The Musgroves, like their houses, were in a state of alteration, perhaps of improvement. The father and mother were in the old English style, and the young people in the new. Mr and Mrs Musgrove were a very good sort of people; friendly and hospitable, not much educated, and not at all elegant. Their children had more modern minds and manners. There was a numerous family; but the only two grown up, excepting Charles, were Henrietta and Louisa, young ladies of nineteen and twenty, who had brought from a school at Exeter all the usual stock of accomplishments, and were now, like thousands of other young ladies, living to be fashionable, happy, and merry. Their dress had every advantage, their faces were rather pretty, their spirits extremely good, their manners unembarrassed and pleasant; they were of consequence at home, and favourites abroad. Anne always contemplated them as some of the happiest creatures of her acquaintance; but still, saved as we all are by some comfortable feeling of superiority from wishing for the possibility of exchange, she would not have given up her own more elegant and cultivated mind for all their enjoyments; and envied them nothing but that seemingly perfect good understanding and agreement together, that good-humoured mutual affection, of which she had known so little herself with either of her sisters.

They were received with great cordiality. Nothing seemed amiss on the side of the Great House family, which was generally, as Anne very well knew, the least to blame. The half hour was chatted away pleasantly enough; and she was not at all surprised, at the end of it, to have their walking party joined by both the Miss Musgroves, at Mary's particular invitation.

CHAPTER SIX

ANNE HAD NOT WANTED this visit to Uppercross, to learn that a removal from one set of people to another, though at a distance of only three miles, will often include a total change of conversation, opinion, and idea. She had never been staying there before, without being struck by it, or without wishing that other Elliots could have her advantage in seeing how unknown, or unconsidered there, were the affairs which at Kellynch-hall were treated as of such general publicity and pervading interest; yet, with all this experience, she believed she must now submit to feel that another lesson, in the art of knowing our own nothingness beyond our own circle, was become necessary for her; – for certainly, coming as she did, with a heart full of the subject which had been completely occupying both houses in Kellynch for many weeks, she had expected rather more curiosity and sympathy than she found in the separate, but very similar remark of Mr and Mrs Musgrove – 'So, Miss Anne, Sir Walter and your sister are gone; and what part of Bath do you think they will settle in?' and this, without much waiting for an answer; – or in the young ladies' addition of, 'I hope *we* shall be in Bath in the winter; but remember, papa, if we do go, we must be in a good situation – none of your Queen-squares for us!' or in the anxious supplement from Mary, of 'Upon my word, I shall be pretty well off, when you are all gone away to be happy at Bath!'

She could only resolve to avoid such self-delusion in future, and think with heightened gratitude of the extraordinary blessing of having one such truly sympathizing friend as Lady Russell.

The Mr Musgroves had their own game to guard, and to destroy; their own horses, dogs, and newspapers to engage them; and the females were fully occupied in all the other common subjects of house-keeping, neighbours, dress, dancing, and music. She acknowledged it to be very fitting, that every little social commonwealth should dictate its own matters of discourse; and hoped, ere long, to become a not unworthy member of the one she was now transplanted into. – With the prospect of spending at least two months at Uppercross, it was highly incumbent on her to clothe her imagination, her memory, and all her ideas in as much of Uppercross as possible.

She had no dread of these two months. Mary was not so repulsive and unsisterly as Elizabeth, nor so inaccessible to all influence of hers; neither was there any thing among the other component parts of the cottage inimical to comfort. – She was always on friendly terms with her brother-in-law; and in the children, who loved her nearly as well, and respected her a great deal more than their mother, she had an object of interest, amusement, and wholesome exertion.

Charles Musgrove was civil and agreeable; in sense and temper he was undoubtedly superior to his wife; but not of powers, or conversation, or grace, to make the past, as they were connected together, at all a dangerous contemplation; though, at the same time, Anne could believe, with Lady Russell, that a more equal match might have greatly improved him; and that a woman of real understanding might have given more consequence to his character, and more usefulness, rationality, and elegance to his habits and pursuits. As it was, he did nothing with much zeal, but sport; and his time was otherwise trifled away, without benefit from books, or any thing else. He had very good spirits, which never seemed much affected by his wife's occasional lowness; bore with her unreasonableness sometimes to Anne's admiration; and, upon the whole, though there was very often a little disagreement, (in which she had sometimes more share than she wished, being appealed to by both parties) they might pass for a happy couple. They were always perfectly agreed in the want of more money, and a strong inclination for a handsome present from his father; but here, as on most topics, he had the superiority, for while Mary thought it a great shame that such a present was not made, he always contended for his father's having many other uses for his money, and a right to spend it as he liked.

As to the management of their children, his theory was much better than his wife's, and his practice not so bad. – 'I could manage them very well, if it were not for Mary's interference,' – was what Anne often heard him say, and had a good deal of faith in; but when listening in turn to Mary's reproach of 'Charles spoils the children so that I cannot get them into any order,' – she never had the smallest temptation to say, 'Very true.'

One of the least agreeable circumstances of her residence there, was her being treated with too much confidence by all parties, and being too much in the secret of the complaints of each house. Known to have some influence with her sister, she was continually requested, or at least receiving hints to exert it, beyond what was practicable. 'I wish you could persuade Mary not to be always fancying herself ill,' was Charles's language; and, in an unhappy mood, thus spoke Mary; – 'I do believe if Charles were to see me dying, he would not think there was any thing the matter with me. I am sure, Anne, if you would, you might persuade him that I really am very ill – a great deal worse than I ever own.'

Mary's declaration was, 'I hate sending the children to the Great House, though their grandmamma is always wanting to see them, for she humours and indulges them to such a degree, and gives them so much trash and sweet things, that they are sure to come back sick and cross for the rest of the day.' – And Mrs Musgrove took the first opportunity of being alone with Anne, to say, 'Oh! Miss Anne, I cannot help wishing Mrs Charles had a little of your method with those children. They are quite different creatures with you! But to be sure, in general they are so spoilt! It is a pity you cannot put your sister in the way of managing them. They are as fine healthy children as ever were seen, poor little dears, without partiality; but Mrs Charles knows no more how they should be treated! – Bless me, how troublesome they are

'Charles spoils the children so'

sometimes! – I assure you, Miss Anne, it prevents my wishing to see them at our house so often as I otherwise should. I believe Mrs Charles is not quite pleased with my not inviting them oftener; but you know it is very bad to have children with one, that one is obliged to be checking every moment: "don't do this, and don't do that;" – or that one can only keep in tolerable order by more cake than is good for them.'

She had this communication, moreover, from Mary. 'Mrs Musgrove thinks all her servants so steady, that it would be high treason to call it in question; but I am sure, without exaggeration, that her upper house-maid and laundry-maid, instead of being in their business, are gadding about the village, all day long. I meet them wherever I go; and I declare, I never go twice into my nursery without seeing something of them. If Jemima were not the trustiest, steadiest creature in the world, it would be enough to spoil her; for she tells me, they are always tempting her to take a walk with them.' And on Mrs Musgrove's side, it was, – 'I make a rule of never interfering in any of my daughter-in-law's concerns, for I know it would not do; but I shall tell *you*, Miss Anne, because you may be able to set things to rights, that I have no very good opinion of Mrs Charles's nursery-maid: I hear strange stories of her; she is always upon the gad: and from my own knowledge, I can declare, she is such a fine-dressing lady, that she is enough to ruin any servants she comes near. Mrs Charles quite swears by her, I know; but I just give you this hint, that you may be upon the watch; because, if you see any thing amiss, you need not be afraid of mentioning it.'

Again; it was Mary's complaint, that Mrs Musgrove was very apt not to give her the precedence that was due, when they dined at the Great House with other families; and she did not see any reason why she was to be considered so much at home as to lose her place. And one day, when Anne was walking with only the Miss Musgroves, one of them, after talking of rank, people of rank, and jealousy of rank, said, 'I have no scruple of observing to *you*, how nonsensical some persons are about their place, because, all the world knows how easy and indifferent you are about it; but I wish any body could give Mary a hint that it would be a great deal better if she were not so very tenacious; especially, if she would not be always putting herself forward to take place of mamma. Nobody doubts her right to have precedence of mamma, but it would be more becoming in her not to be always insisting on it. It is not that mamma cares about it the least in the world, but I know it is taken notice of by many persons.'

How was Anne to set all these matters to rights? She could do little more than listen patiently, soften every grievance, and excuse each to the other, give them all hints of the forbearance necessary between such near neighbours, and make those hints broadest which were meant for her sister's benefit.

In all other respects, her visit began and proceeded very well. Her own spirits improved by change of place and subject, by being removed three miles from Kellynch: Mary's ailments lessened by having a constant companion; and their daily intercourse with the other family, since there was neither superior affection, confidence, nor employment in the cottage, to be interrupted by it, was rather an advantage. It was certainly carried nearly as far as possible, for they met every morning, and hardly ever spent an evening asunder; but she believed they should not have done so well without the sight of Mr and Mrs Musgrove's respectable forms in the usual places, or without the talking, laughing, and singing of their daughters.

She played a great deal better than either of the Miss Musgroves; but having no voice, no knowledge of the harp, and no fond parents to sit by and fancy themselves delighted, her performance was little thought of, only out of civility, or to refresh the others, as she was well aware. She knew that when she played she was giving pleasure only to herself; but this was no new sensation: excepting one short period of her life, she had never, since the age of fourteen, never since the loss of her dear mother, known the happiness of being listened to, or encouraged by any just appreciation or real taste. In music she had been always used to feel alone in the world; and Mr and Mrs Musgrove's fond partiality for their own daughters' performance, and total indifference to any other person's, gave her much more pleasure for their sakes, than mortification for her own.

The party at the Great House was sometimes increased by other company. The neighbourhood was not large, but the Musgroves were visited by every body, and had more dinner parties, and more callers, more visitors by invitation and by chance, than any other family. They were more completely popular.

The girls were wild for dancing; and the evenings ended, occasionally, in an unpremeditated little ball. There was a family of cousins within a walk of Uppercross, in less affluent circumstances, who depended on the Musgroves for all their pleasures: they would come at any time, and help play at any thing, or dance any where; and Anne, very much preferring the office of musician to a more active post, played country dances to them by the hour together; a kindness which always recommended her musical powers to the notice of Mr and Mrs Musgrove more than any thing else, and often drew this compliment; – 'Well done, Miss Anne! very well done indeed! Lord bless me! how those little fingers of yours fly about!'

So passed the first three weeks. Michaelmas came; and now Anne's heart must be in Kellynch again. A beloved home made over to others; all the precious rooms and furniture, groves, and prospects, beginning to own other eyes and other limbs! She could not think of much else on the 29th of September; and she had this sympathetic touch in the evening, from Mary, who, on having occasion to note down the day of the month, exclaimed, 'Dear me! is not this the day the Crofts were to come to Kellynch? I am glad I did not think of it before. How low it makes me!'

The Crofts took possession with true naval alertness, and were to be visited. Mary deplored the necessity for herself. 'Nobody knew how much she should suffer. She should put it off as long as she could.' But was not easy till she had talked Charles into driving her over on an early day; and was in a very animated, comfortable state of imaginary agitation, when she came back. Anne had very sincerely rejoiced in there being no means of her going. She wished, however, to see the Crofts, and was glad to be within when the visit was returned. They came; the master of the house was not at home, but the two sisters were together; and as it chanced that Mrs Croft fell to the share of Anne, while the admiral sat by Mary, and made himself very agreeable by his good-humoured notice of her little boys, she was well able to watch for a likeness, and if it failed her in the features, to catch it in the voice, or the turn of sentiment and expression.

Mrs Croft, though neither tall nor fat, had a squareness, uprightness, and vigour of form, which gave importance to her person. She had bright dark eyes, good teeth, and altogether an agreeable face; though her reddened and weather-beaten complexion, the consequence of her having been almost as much at sea as her husband, made her seem to have lived some years longer in the world than her real eight and thirty. Her manners were open, easy, and decided, like one who had no distrust of herself, and no doubts of what to do; without any approach to coarseness, however, or any want of good humour. Anne gave her credit, indeed, for feelings of great consideration towards herself, in all that related to Kellynch; and it pleased her: especially, as she had satisfied herself in the very first half minute, in the instant even of introduction, that there was not the smallest symptom of any knowledge or suspicion on Mrs Croft's side, to give a bias of any sort. She was quite easy on that head, and consequently full of strength and courage, till for a moment electrified by Mrs Croft's suddenly saying, –

'It was you, and not your sister, I find, that my brother had the pleasure of being acquainted with, when he was in this country.'

Anne hoped she had outlived the age of blushing; but the age of emotion she certainly had not.

'Perhaps you may not have heard that he is married,' added Mrs Croft.

She could now answer as she ought; and was happy to feel, when Mrs Croft's next words explained it to be Mr Wentworth of whom she spoke, that she had said nothing which might not do for either brother. She immediately felt how reasonable it was, that Mrs Croft should be thinking and speaking of Edward, and not of Frederick; and with shame at her own forgetfulness, applied herself to the knowledge of their former neighbour's present state, with proper interest.

Declaring he should not go

The rest was all tranquillity; till just as they were moving, she heard the admiral say to Mary,

'We are expecting a brother of Mrs Croft's here soon; I dare say you know him by name.'

He was cut short by the eager attacks of the little boys, clinging to him like an old friend, and declaring he should not go; and being too much engrossed by proposals of carrying them away in his coat pocket, &c. to have another moment for finishing or recollecting what he had begun, Anne was left to persuade herself, as well as she could, that the same brother must still be in question. She could not, however, reach such a degree of certainty, as not to be anxious to hear whether any thing had been said on the subject at the other house, where the Crofts had previously been calling.

The folks of the Great House were to spend the evening of this day at the Cottage; and it being now too late in the year for such visits to be made on foot, the coach was beginning to be listened for, when the youngest Miss Musgrove walked in. That she was coming to apologize, and that they should have to spend the evening by themselves, was the first black idea; and Mary was quite ready to be affronted, when Louisa made all right by saying, that she only came on foot, to leave more room for the harp, which was bringing in the carriage.

'And I will tell you our reason,' she added, 'and all about it. I am come on to give you notice, that papa and mamma are out of spirits this evening, especially mamma; she is thinking so much of poor Richard! and we agreed it would be best to have the harp, for it seems to amuse her more than the piano-forte. I will tell you why she is out of spirits. When the Crofts called this morning, (they called here afterwards, did not they?) they happened to say, that her brother, Captain Wentworth, is just returned to England, or paid off, or something, and is coming to see them almost directly; and most unluckily it came into mamma's head, when they were gone, that Wentworth, or something very like it, was the name of poor Richard's captain, at one time, I do not know when or where, but a great while before he died, poor fellow! And upon looking over his letters and things, she found it was so; and is perfectly sure that this must be the very man, and her head is quite full of it, and of poor Richard! So we must all be as merry as we can, that she may not be dwelling upon such gloomy things.'

The real circumstances of this pathetic piece of family history were, that the Musgroves had had the ill fortune of a very troublesome, hopeless son; and the good fortune to lose him before he reached his twentieth year; that he had been sent to sea, because he was stupid and unmanageable on shore; that he had been very little cared for at any time by his family, though quite as much as he deserved; seldom heard of, and scarcely at all regretted, when the intelligence of his death abroad had worked its way to Uppercross, two years before.

He had, in fact, though his sisters were now doing all they could for him, by calling him 'poor Richard,' been nothing better than a thick-headed, unfeeling, unprofitable Dick Musgrove, who had never done any thing to entitle himself to more than the abbreviation of his name, living or dead.

He had been several years at sea, and had, in the course of those removals to which all midshipmen are liable, and especially such midshipmen as every captain wishes to get rid of, been six months on board Captain Frederick Wentworth's frigate, the Laconia; and from the Laconia he had, under the influence of his captain, written the only two letters which his father and mother had ever received from him during the whole of his absence; that is to say, the only two disinterested letters; all the rest had been mere applications for money.

In each letter he had spoken well of his captain; but yet, so little were they in the habit of attending to such matters, so unobservant and incurious were they as to the names of men or ships, that it had made scarcely any impression at the time; and that Mrs Musgrove should have been suddenly struck, this very day, with a recollection of the name of Wentworth, as connected with her son, seemed one of those extraordinary bursts of mind which do sometimes occur.

She had gone to her letters, and found it all as she supposed; and the reperusal of these letters, after so long an interval, her poor son gone for ever, and all the strength of his faults forgotten, had affected her spirits exceedingly, and thrown her into greater grief for him than she had known on first hearing of his death. Mr Musgrove was, in a lesser degree, affected likewise; and when they reached the cottage, they were evidently in want, first, of being listened to anew on this subject, and afterwards, of all the relief which cheerful companions could give.

To hear them talking so much of Captain Wentworth, repeating his name so often, puzzling over past years, and at last ascertaining that it *might*, that it probably *would*, turn out to be the very same Captain Wentworth whom they recollected meeting, once or twice, after their coming back from Clifton; – a very fine young man; but they could not say whether it was seven or eight years ago, – was a new sort of trial to Anne's nerves. She found, however, that it was one to which she must enure herself. Since he actually was expected in the country, she must teach herself to be insensible on such points. And not only did it appear that he was expected, and speedily, but the Musgroves, in their warm gratitude for the kindness he had shewn poor Dick, and very high respect for his character, stamped as it was by poor Dick's having been six months under his care, and mentioning him in strong, though not perfectly well spelt praise, as 'a fine dashing felow, only two perticular about the school-master,' were bent on introducing themselves, and seeking his acquaintance, as soon as they could hear of his arrival.

The resolution of doing so helped to form the comfort of their evening.

CHAPTER SEVEN

A VERY FEW DAYS MORE, and Captain Wentworth was known to be at Kellynch, and Mr Musgrove had called on him, and come back warm in his praise, and he engaged with the Crofts to dine at Uppercross, by the end of another week. It had been a great disappointment to Mr Musgrove, to find that no earlier day could be fixed, so impatient was he to shew his gratitude, by seeing Captain Wentworth under his own roof, and welcoming him to all that was strongest and best in his cellars. But a week must pass; only a week, in Anne's reckoning, and then, she supposed, they must meet; and soon she began to wish that she could feel secure even for a week.

Captain Wentworth made a very early return to Mr Musgrove's civility, and she was all but calling there in the same half hour! – She and Mary were actually setting forward for the great house, where, as she afterwards learnt, they must inevitably have found him, when they were stopped by the eldest boy's being at that moment brought home in consequence of a bad fall. The child's situation put the visit entirely aside, but she could not hear of her escape with indifference, even in the midst of the serious anxiety which they afterwards felt on his account.

His collar-bone was found to be dislocated, and such injury received in the back, as roused the most alarming ideas. It was an afternoon of distress, and Anne had every thing to do at once – the apothecary to send for – the father to have pursued and informed – the mother to support and keep from hysterics – the servants to control – the youngest child to banish, and the poor suffering one to attend and soothe; – besides sending, as soon as she recollected it, proper notice to the other house, which brought her an accession rather of frightened, enquiring companions, than of very useful assistants.

Her brother's return was the first comfort; he could take best care of his wife, and the second blessing was the arrival of the apothecary. Till he came and had examined the child, their apprehensions were the worse for being vague; – they suspected great injury, but knew not where; but now the collar-bone was soon replaced, and though Mr Robinson felt and felt, and rubbed, and looked grave, and spoke low words both to the father and the aunt, still they were all to hope the best, and to be able to part and eat their dinner in tolerable ease of mind; and then it was just before they parted, that the two young aunts were able so far to digress from their nephew's state, as to give the information of Captain Wentworth's visit: – staying five minutes behind their father and mother, to endeavour to express how perfectly delighted they were with him, how much handsomer, how infinitely more agreeable they thought him than any individual among their male acquaintance, who had been at all a favourite before – how glad they had been to hear papa invite him to stay dinner – how sorry when he said it was quite out of his power – and how glad again, when he had promised in reply to papa and mamma's farther pressing invitations, to come and dine with them on the morrow, actually on the morrow! – And he had promised it in so pleasant a manner, as if he felt all the motive of their attention just as he ought! – And, in short, he had looked and said every thing with such exquisite grace, that they could assure them all, their heads were both turned by him! – And off they ran, quite as full of glee as of love, and apparently more full of Captain Wentworth than of little Charles.

The same story and the same raptures were repeated, when the two girls came with their father, through the gloom of the evening, to make enquiries; and Mr Musgrove, no longer under the first uneasiness about his heir, could add his confirmation and praise, and hope there would be now no occasion for putting Captain Wentworth off, and only be sorry to think that the cottage party, probably, would not like to leave the little boy, to give him the meeting. – 'Oh, no! as to leaving the little boy!' – both father and mother were in much too strong and recent alarm to bear the thought; and Anne, in the joy of the escape, could not help adding her warm protestations to theirs.

Charles Musgrove, indeed, afterwards shewed more of inclination; 'the child was going on so well – and he wished so much to be introduced to Captain Wentworth, that, perhaps, he might join them in the evening; he would not dine from home, but he might walk in for half an hour.' But in this he was eagerly opposed by his wife, with 'Oh, no! indeed, Charles, I cannot bear to have you go away. Only think, if any thing should happen!'

The child had a good night, and was going on well the next day. It must be a work of time to ascertain that no injury had been done to the spine, but Mr Robinson found nothing to increase alarm, and Charles Musgrove began consequently to feel no necessity for longer confinement. The child was to be kept in bed, and amused as quietly as possible; but what was there for a father to do? This was quite a female case, and it would be highly absurd in him, who could be of no use at home, to shut himself up. His father very much wished him to meet Captain Wentworth, and there being no sufficient reason against it, he ought to go; and it ended in his making a bold public declaration, when he came in from shooting, of his meaning to dress directly, and dine in the other house.

'Nothing can be going on better than the child,' said he, 'so I told my father just now that I would come, and he thought me quite right. Your sister being with you, my love, I have no scruple at all. You would not like to leave him yourself, but you see I can be of no use. Anne will send for me if any thing is the matter.'

Husbands and wives generally understand when opposition will be vain. Mary knew, from Charles's manner of speaking, that he was quite determined on going, and that it would be of no use to teaze him. She said nothing, therefore, till he was out of the room, but as soon as there was only Anne to hear,

'So! You and I are to be left to shift by ourselves, with this poor sick child – and not a creature coming near us all the evening! I knew how it would be. This is always my luck! If there is any thing disagreeable going on, men are always sure to get out of it, and Charles is as bad as any of them. Very unfeeling! I must say it is very unfeeling of him, to be running away from his poor little boy; talks of his being going on so well! How does he know that he is going on well, or that there may not be a sudden change half an hour hence? I did not think Charles would have been so unfeeling. So, here he is to go away and enjoy himself, and because I am the poor mother, I am not to be allowed to stir; – and yet, I am sure, I am more unfit than any body else to be about the child. My being the mother is the very reason why my feelings should not be tried. I am not at all equal to it. You saw how hysterical I was yesterday.'

'But that was only the effect of the suddenness of your alarm – of the shock. You will not be hysterical again. I dare say we shall have nothing to distress us. I perfectly understand Mr Robinson's directions, and have no fears; and indeed, Mary, I cannot wonder at your husband. Nursing does not belong to a man, it is not his province. A sick child is always the mother's property, her own feelings generally make it so.'

'I hope I am as fond of my child as any mother – but I do not know that I am of any more use in the sick-room than Charles, for I cannot be always scolding and teazing a poor child when it is ill; and you saw, this morning, that if I told him to keep quiet, he was sure to begin kicking about. I have not nerves for the sort of thing.'

'But, could you be comfortable yourself, to be spending the whole evening away from the poor boy?'

'Yes; you see his papa can, and why should not I? – Jemima is so careful! And she could send us word every hour how he was. I really think Charles might as well have told his father we would all come. I am not more alarmed about little Charles now than he is. I was dreadfully alarmed yesterday, but the case is very different to-day.'

'Well – if you do not think it too late to give notice for yourself, suppose you were to go, as well as your husband. Leave little Charles to my care. Mr and Mrs Musgrove cannot think it wrong, while I remain with him.'

'Are you serious?' cried Mary, her eyes brightening. 'Dear me! that's a very good thought, very good indeed. To be sure I may just as well go as not, for I am of no use at home – am I? and it only harasses me. You, who have not a mother's feelings, are a great deal the properest person. You can make little Charles do any thing; he always minds you at a word. It will be a great deal better than leaving him with only Jemima. Oh! I will certainly go; I am sure I ought if I can, quite as much as Charles, for they want me excessively to be acquainted with Captain Wentworth, and I know you do not mind being left alone. An excellent thought of yours, indeed, Anne! I will go and tell Charles, and get ready directly. You can send for us, you know, at a moment's notice, if any thing is the matter; but I dare say there will be nothing to alarm you. I should not go, you may be sure, if I did not feel quite at ease about my dear child.'

The next moment she was tapping at her husband's dressing-room door, and as Anne followed her up stairs, she was in time for the whole conversation, which began with Mary's saying, in a tone of great exultation,

'I mean to go with you, Charles, for I am of no more use at home than you are. If I were to shut myself up for ever with the child, I should not be able to persuade him to do any thing he did not like. Anne will stay; Anne undertakes to stay at home and take care of him. It is Anne's own proposal, and so I shall go with you, which will be a great deal better, for I have not dined at the other house since Tuesday.'

'This is very kind of Anne,' was her husband's answer, 'and I should be very glad to have you go; but it seems rather hard that she should be left at home by herself, to nurse our sick child.'

Anne was now at hand to take up her own cause, and the sincerity of her manner being soon sufficient to convince him, where conviction was at least very agreeable, he had no farther scruples as to her being left to dine alone, though he still wanted her to join them in the evening, when the child might be at rest for the night, and kindly urged her to let him come and fetch her; but she was quite unpersuadable; and this being the case, she had ere long the pleasure of seeing them set off together in high spirits. They were gone, she hoped, to be happy, however oddly constructed such happiness might seem; as for herself, she was left with as many sensations of comfort, as were, perhaps, ever likely to be hers. She knew herself to be of the first utility to the child; and what was it to her, if Frederick Wentworth were only half a mile distant, making himself agreeable to others!

She would have liked to know how he felt as to a meeting. Perhaps indifferent, if indifference could exist under such circumstances. He must be either indifferent or unwilling. Had he wished ever to see her again, he need not have waited till this time; he would have done what she could not but believe that in his place she should have done long ago, when events had been early giving him the independence which alone had been wanting.

Her brother and sister came back delighted with their new acquaintance, and their visit in general. There had been music, singing, talking, laughing, all that was most agreeable; charming manners in Captain Wentworth, no shyness or reserve; they seemed all to know each other perfectly, and he was coming the very next morning to shoot with Charles. He was to come to breakfast, but not at the Cottage, though that had been proposed at first; but then he had been pressed to come to the Great House instead, and he seemed afraid of being in Mrs Charles Musgrove's way, on account of the child; and therefore, somehow, they hardly knew how, it ended in Charles's being to meet him to breakfast at his father's.

Anne understood it. He wished to avoid seeing her. He had enquired after her, she found, slightly, as might suit a former slight acquaintance, seeming to acknowledge such as she had acknowledged, actuated, perhaps, by the same view of escaping introduction when they were to meet.

The morning hours of the Cottage were always later than those of the other house; and on the morrow the difference was so great, that Mary and Anne were not more than beginning breakfast when Charles came in to say that they were just setting off, that he was come for his dogs, that his sisters were following with Captain Wentworth, his sisters meaning to visit Mary and the child, and Captain Wentworth proposing also to wait on her for a few minutes, if not inconvenient; and though Charles had answered for the child's being in no such state as could make it inconvenient, Captain Wentworth would not be satisfied without his running on to give notice.

Mary, very much gratified by this attention, was delighted to receive him; while a thousand feelings rushed on Anne, of which this was the most consoling, that it would soon be over. And it was soon over. In two minutes after Charles's preparation, the others appeared; they were in the drawing-room. Her eye half met Captain Wentworth's; a bow, a curtsey passed; she heard his voice – he talked to Mary, said all that was right; said something to the Miss Musgroves, enough to mark an easy footing: the room seemed full – full of persons and voices – but a few minutes ended it. Charles shewed himself at the window, all was ready, their visitor had bowed and was gone; the Miss Musgroves were gone too, suddenly resolving to walk to the end of the village with the sportsmen: the room was cleared, and Anne might finish her breakfast as she could.

'It is over! it is over!' she repeated to herself again, and again, in nervous gratitude. 'The worst is over!'

Mary talked, but she could not attend. She had seen him. They had met. They had been once more in the same room!

Soon, however, she began to reason with herself, and try to be feeling less. Eight years, almost eight years had passed, since all had been given up. How absurd to be resuming the agitation which such an interval had banished into distance and indistinctness! What might not eight years do? Events of every description, changes, alienations, removals, – all, all must be comprised in it; and oblivion of the past – how natural, how certain too! It included nearly a third part of her own life.

Alas! with all her reasonings, she found, that to retentive feelings eight years may be little more than nothing.

Now, how were his sentiments to be read? Was this like wishing to avoid her? And the next moment she was hating herself for the folly which asked the question.

On one other question, which perhaps her utmost wisdom might not have prevented, she was soon spared all suspense; for after the Miss Musgroves had returned and finished their visit at the Cottage, she had this spontaneous information from Mary:

'Captain Wentworth is not very gallant by you, Anne, though he was so attentive to me. Henrietta asked him what he thought of you, when they went away; and he said, "You were so altered he should not have known you again."

Mary had no feelings to make her respect her sister's in a common way; but she was perfectly unsuspicious of being inflicting any peculiar wound.

'Altered beyond his knowledge!' Anne fully submitted, in silent, deep mortification. Doubtless it was so; and she could take no revenge, for he was not altered, or not for the worse. She had already acknowledged it to herself, and she could not think differently, let him think of her as he would. No; the years which had destroyed her youth and bloom had only given him a more glowing, manly, open look, in no respect lessening his personal advantages. She had seen the same Frederick Wentworth.

'So altered that he should not have known her again!' These were words which could not but dwell with her. Yet she soon began to rejoice that she had heard them. They were of sobering tendency; they allayed agitation; they composed, and consequently must make her happier.

Frederick Wentworth had used such words, or something like them, but without an idea that they would be carried round to her. He had thought her wretchedly altered, and, in the first moment of appeal, had spoken as he felt. He had not forgiven Anne Elliot. She had used him ill; deserted and disappointed him; and worse, she had shewn a feebleness of character in doing so, which his own decided, confident temper could not endure. She had given him up to oblige others. It had been the effect of over persuasion. It had been weakness and timidity.

He had been most warmly attached to her, and had never seen a woman since whom he thought her equal; but, except from some natural sensation of curiosity, he had no desire of meeting her again. Her power with him was gone for ever.

It was now his object to marry. He was rich, and being turned on shore, fully intended to settle as soon as he could be properly tempted; actually looking round, ready to fall in love with all the speed which a clear head and quick taste could allow. He had a heart for either of the Miss Musgroves, if they could catch it; a heart, in short, for any pleasing young woman who came in his way, excepting Anne Elliot. This was his only secret exception, when he said to his sister, in answer to her suppositions,

'Yes, here I am, Sophia, quite ready to make a foolish match. Any body between fifteen and thirty may have me for asking. A little beauty, and a few smiles, and a few compliments to the navy, and I am a lost man. Should not this be enough for a sailor, who has had no society among women to make him nice?'

He said it, she knew, to be contradicted. His bright, proud eye spoke the conviction that he was nice; and Anne Elliot was not out of his thoughts, when he more seriously described the woman he should wish to meet with. 'A strong mind, with sweetness of manner,' made the first and the last of the description.

'This is the woman I want,' said he. 'Something a little inferior I shall of course put up with, but it must not be much. If I am a fool, I shall be a fool indeed, for I have thought on the subject more than most men.'

CHAPTER EIGHT

FROM THIS TIME CAPTAIN Wentworth and Anne Elliot were repeatedly in the same circle. They were soon dining in company together at Mr Musgrove's, for the little boy's state could no longer supply his aunt with a pretence for absenting herself; and this was but the beginning of other dinings and other meetings.

Whether former feelings were to be renewed, must be brought to the proof; former times must undoubtedly be brought to the recollection of each; *they* could not but be reverted to; the year of their engagement could not but be named by him, in the little narratives or descriptions which conversation called forth. His profession qualified him, his disposition led him, to talk; and '*That* was in the year six;' '*That* happened before I went to sea in the year six,' occurred in the course of the first evening they spent together: and though his voice did not falter, and though she had no reason to suppose his eye wandering towards her while he spoke, Anne felt the utter impossibility, from her knowledge of his mind, that he could be unvisited by remembrance any more than herself. There must be the same immediate association of thought, though she was very far from conceiving it to be of equal pain.

They had no conversation together, no intercourse but what the commonest civility required. Once so much to each other! Now nothing! There *had* been a time, when of all the large party now filling the drawing-room at Uppercross, they would have found it most difficult to cease to speak to one another. With the exception, perhaps, of Admiral and Mrs

Croft, who seemed particularly attached and happy, (Anne could allow no other exception even among the married couples) there could have been no two hearts so open, no tastes so similar, no feelings so in unison, no countenances so beloved. Now they were as strangers: nay, worse than strangers, for they could never become acquainted. It was a perpetual estrangement.

When he talked, she heard the same voice, and discerned the same mind. There was a very general ignorance of all naval matters throughout the party; and he was very much questioned, and especially by the two Miss Musgroves, who seemed hardly to have any eyes but for him, as to the manner of living on board, daily regulations, food, hours, &c.; and their surprise at his accounts, at learning the degree of accommodation and arrangement which was practicable, drew from him some pleasant ridicule, which reminded Anne of the early days when she too had been ignorant, and she too had been accused of supposing sailors to be living on board without any thing to eat, or any cook to dress it if there were, or any servant to wait, or any knife and fork to use.

From thus listening and thinking, she was roused by a whisper of Mrs Musgrove's, who, overcome by fond regrets, could not help saying,

'Ah! Miss Anne, if it had pleased Heaven to spare my poor son, I dare say he would have been just such another by this time.'

Anne suppressed a smile, and listened kindly, while Mrs Musgrove relieved her heart a little more; and for a few minutes, therefore, could not keep pace with the conversation of the others. – When she could let her attention take its natural course again, she found the Miss Musgroves just fetching the navy-list, – (their own navy list, the first that had ever been at Uppercross); and sitting down together to pore over it, with the professed view of finding out the ships which Captain Wentworth had commanded.

'Your first was the Asp, I remember; we will look for the Asp.'

'You will not find her there. – Quite worn out and broken up. I was the last man who commanded her. – Hardly fit for service then. – Reported fit for home service for a year or two, – and so I was sent off to the West Indies.'

The girls looked all amazement.

'The admiralty,' he continued, 'entertain themselves now and then, with sending a few hundred men to sea, in a ship not fit to be employed. But they have a great many to provide for; and among the thousands that may just as well go to the bottom as not, it is impossible for them to distinguish the very set who may be least missed.'

'Phoo! phoo!' cried the admiral, 'what stuff these young fellows talk! Never was a better sloop than the Asp in her day. – For an old built sloop, you would not see her equal. Lucky fellow to get her! – He knows there must have been twenty better men than himself applying for her at the same time. Lucky fellow to get any thing so soon, with no more interest than his.'

'I felt my luck, admiral, I assure you;' replied Captain Wentworth, seriously. – 'I was as well satisfied with my appointment as you can desire. It was a great object with me, at that time, to be at sea, – a very great object. I wanted to be doing some thing.'

'To be sure you did. – What should a young fellow, like you, do ashore, for half a year together? – If a man has not a wife, he soon wants to be afloat again.'

'But, Captain Wentworth,' cried Louisa, 'how vexed you must have been when you came to the Asp, to see what an old thing they had given you.'

'I knew pretty well what she was, before that day;' said he, smiling. 'I had no more discoveries to make, than you would have as to the fashion and strength of any old pelisse, which you had seen lent about among half your acquaintance, ever since you could remember, and which at last, on some very wet day, is lent to yourself. – Ah! she was a dear old Asp to me. She did all that I wanted. I knew she would. – I knew that we should either go to the bottom together, or that she would be the making of me; and I never had two days of foul weather all the time I was at sea in her; and after taking privateers enough to be very entertaining, I had the good luck, in my passage home the next autumn, to fall in with the very French frigate I wanted. – I brought her into Plymouth; and here was another instance of luck. We had not been six hours in the Sound, when a gale came on, which lasted four days and nights, and which would have done for poor old Asp, in half the time; our touch with the Great Nation not having much improved our condition. Four-and-twenty hours later, and I should only have been a gallant Captain Wentworth, in a small paragraph at one corner of the newspapers; and being lost in only a sloop, nobody would have thought about me.'

Anne's shudderings were to herself alone: but the Miss Musgroves could be as open as they were sincere, in their exclamations of pity and horror.

'And so then, I suppose,' said Mrs Musgrove, in a low voice, as if thinking aloud, 'so then he went away to the Laconia, and there he met with our poor boy. – Charles, my dear,' (beckoning him to her), 'do ask Captain Wentworth where it was he first met with your poor brother. I always forget.'

'It was at Gibraltar, mother, I know. Dick had been left ill at Gibraltar, with a recommendation from his former captain to Captain Wentworth.'

'Oh! – but, Charles, tell Captain Wentworth, he need not be afraid of mentioning poor Dick before me, for it would be rather a pleasure to hear him talked of, by such a good friend.'

Charles, being somewhat more mindful of the probabilities of the case, only nodded in reply, and walked away.

The girls were now hunting for the Laconia; and Captain Wentworth could not deny himself the pleasure of taking the precious volume into his own hands to save them the trouble, and once more read aloud the little statement of her name and rate and present non-commissioned class, observing over it, that she too had been one of the best friends man ever had.

'Ah! those were pleasant days when I had the Laconia! How fast I made money in her. – A friend of mine, and I, had such a lovely cruise together off the Western Islands. – Poor Harville, sister! You know how much he wanted money – worse than myself. He had a wife. – Excellent fellow! I shall never forget his happiness. He felt it all, so much for her sake. – I wished for him again the next summer, when I had still the same luck in the Mediterranean.'

'And I am sure, Sir,' said Mrs Musgrove, 'it was a lucky day for *us*, when you were put captain into that ship. *We* shall never forget what you did.'

Her feelings made her speak low; and Captain Wentworth, hearing only in part, and probably not having Dick Musgrove at all near his thoughts, looked rather in suspense, and as if waiting for more.

'My brother,' whispered one of the girls; 'mamma is thinking of poor Richard.'

'Poor dear fellow!' continued Mrs Musgrove; 'he was grown so steady, and such an excellent correspondent, while he was under your care! Ah! it would have been a happy thing, if he had never left you. I assure you, Captain Wentworth, we are very sorry he ever left you.'

There was a momentary expression in Captain Wentworth's face at this speech, a certain glance of his bright eye, and curl of his handsome mouth, which convinced Anne, that instead of sharing in Mrs Musgrove's kind wishes, as to her son, he had probably been at some pains to get rid of him; but it was too transient an indulgence of self-amusement to be detected by any who understood him less than herself; in another moment he was perfectly collected and serious; and almost instantly afterwards coming up to the sofa, on which she and Mrs Musgrove were sitting, took a place by the latter, and entered into conversation with her, in a low voice, about her son, doing it with so much sympathy and natural grace, as shewed the kindest consideration for all that was real and unabsurd in the parent's feelings.

They were actually on the same sofa, for Mrs Musgrove had most readily made room for him; – they were divided only by Mrs Musgrove. It was no insignificant barrier indeed. Mrs Musgrove was of a comfortable substantial size, infinitely more fitted by nature to express good cheer and good humour, than tenderness and sentiment; and while the agitations of Anne's slender form, and pensive face, may be considered as very completely screened, Captain Wentworth should be allowed some credit for the self-command with which he attended to her large fat sighings over the destiny of a son, whom alive nobody had cared for.

Personal size and mental sorrow have certainly no necessary proportions. A large bulky figure has as good a right to be in deep affliction, as the most graceful set of limbs in the world. But, fair or not fair, there are unbecoming conjunctions, which reason will patronize in vain, – which taste cannot tolerate, – which ridicule will seize.

The admiral, after taking two or three refreshing turns about the room with his hands behind him, being called to order by his wife, now came up to Captain Wentworth, and without taking any observation of what he might be interrupting, thinking only of his own thoughts, began with,

'If you had been a week later at Lisbon, last spring, Frederick, you would have been asked to give a passage to Lady Mary Grierson and her daughters.'

'Should I? I am glad I was not a week later then.'

The admiral abused him for his want of gallantry. He defended himself; though professing that he would never willingly admit any ladies on board a ship of his, excepting for a ball, or a visit, which a few hours might comprehend.

'But, if I know myself,' said he, 'this is from no want of gallantry towards them. It is rather from feeling how impossible it is, with all one's efforts, and all one's sacrifices, to make the accommodations on board, such as women ought to have. There can be no want of gallantry, admiral, in rating the claims of women to every personal comfort *high* – and this is what I do. I hate to hear of women on board, or to see them on board; and no ship, under my command, shall ever convey a family of ladies any where, if I can help it.'

This brought his sister upon him.

'Oh Frederick! – But I cannot believe it of you. – All idle refinement! – Women may be as comfortable on board, as in the best house in England. I believe I have lived as much on board as most women, and I know nothing superior to the accommodations of a man of war. I declare I have not a comfort or an indulgence about me, even at Kellynch-hall,' (with a kind bow to Anne) 'beyond what I always had in most of the ships I have lived in; and they have been five altogether.'

'Nothing to the purpose,' replied her brother. 'You were living with your husband; and were the only woman on board.'

'But you, yourself, brought Mrs Harville, her sister, her cousin, and the three children, round from Portsmouth to Plymouth. Where was this super-fine, extraordinary sort of gallantry of yours, then?'

'All merged in my friendship, Sophia. I would assist any brother officer's wife that I could, and I would bring any thing of Harville's from the world's end, if he wanted it. But do not imagine that I did not feel it an evil in itself.'

'Depend upon it they were all perfectly comfortable.'

'I might not like them the better for that, perhaps. Such a number of women and children have no *right* to be comfortable on board.'

'My dear Frederick, you are talking quite idly. Pray, what would become of us poor sailors' wives, who often want to be conveyed to one port or another, after our husbands, if every body had your feelings?'

'My feelings, you see, did not prevent my taking Mrs Harville, and all her family, to Plymouth.'

'But I hate to hear you talking so, like a fine gentleman, and as if women were all fine ladies, instead of rational creatures. We none of us expect to be in smooth water all our days.'

'Ah! my dear,' said the admiral, 'when he has got a wife; he will sing a different tune. When he is married, if we have the good luck to live to another war, we shall see him do as you and I, and a great many others, have

He attended to her large, fat sighings

done. We shall have him very thankful to any body that will bring him his wife.'

'Ay, that we shall.'

'Now I have done,' cried Captain Wentworth – 'When once married people begin to attack me with, "Oh! you will think very differently, when you are married." I can only say, "No, I shall not;" and then they say again, "Yes, you will," and there is an end of it.'

He got up and moved away.

'What a great traveller you must have been, ma'am!' said Mrs Musgrove to Mrs Croft.

'Pretty well, ma'am, in the fifteen years of my marriage; though many women have done more. I have crossed the Atlantic four times, and have been once to the East Indies, and back again; and only once, besides being in different places about home – Cork, and Lisbon, and Gibraltar. But I never went beyond the Streights – and never was in the West Indies. We do not call Bermuda or Bahama, you know, the West Indies.'

Mrs Musgrove had not a word to say in dissent; she could not accuse herself of having ever called them any thing in the whole course of her life.

'And I do assure you, ma'am,' pursued Mrs Croft, 'that nothing can exceed the accommodations of a man of war; I speak, you know, of the higher rates. When you come to a frigate, of course, you are more confined – though any reasonable woman may be perfectly happy in one of them; and I can safely say, that the happiest part of my life has been spent on board a ship. While we were together, you know, there was nothing to be feared. Thank God! I have always been blessed with excellent health, and no climate disagrees with me. A little disordered always the first twenty-four hours of going to sea, but never knew what sickness was afterwards. The only time that I ever really suffered in body or mind, the only time that I ever fancied myself unwell, or had any ideas of danger, was the winter that I passed by myself at Deal, when the Admiral (*Captain* Croft then) was in the North Seas. I lived in perpetual fright at that time, and had all manner of imaginary complaints from not knowing what to do with myself, or when I should hear from him next; but as long as we could be together, nothing ever ailed me, and I never met with the smallest inconvenience.'

'Ay, to be sure. – Yes, indeed, oh yes, I am quite of your opinion, Mrs Croft,' was Mrs Musgrove's hearty answer. 'There is nothing so bad as a separation. I am quite of your opinion. *I* know what it is, for Mr Musgrove always attends the assizes, and I am so glad when they are over, and he is safe back again.'

The evening ended with dancing. On its being proposed, Anne offered her services, as usual, and though her eyes would some times fill with tears as she sat at the instrument, she was extremely glad to be employed, and desired nothing in return but to be unobserved.

It was a merry, joyous party, and no one seemed in higher spirits than Captain Wentworth. She felt that he had every thing to elevate him, which general attention and deference, and especially the attention of all the young women could do. The Miss Hayters, the females of the family of cousins already mentioned, were apparently admitted to the honour of being in love with him; and as for Henrietta and Louisa, they both seemed so entirely occupied by him, that nothing but the continued appearance of the most perfect good-will between themselves, could have made it credible that they were not decided rivals. If he were a little spoilt by such universal, such eager admiration, who could wonder?

These were some of the thoughts which occupied Anne, while her fingers were mechanically at work, proceeding for half an hour together, equally without error, and without consciousness. *Once* she felt that he was looking at herself – observing her altered features, perhaps, trying to trace in them the ruins of the face which had once charmed him; and *once* she knew that he must have spoken of her; – she was hardly aware of it, till she heard the answer; but then she was sure of his having asked his partner whether Miss Elliot never danced? The answer was, 'Oh! no, never; she has quite given up dancing. She had rather play. She is never tired of playing.' Once, too, he spoke to her. She had left the instrument on the dancing being over, and he sat down to try to make out an air which he wished to give the Miss Musgroves an idea of. Unintentionally she returned to that part of the room; he saw her, and, instantly rising, said, with studied politeness,

'I beg your pardon, madam, this is your seat;' and though she immediately drew back with a decided negative, he was not to be induced to sit down again.

Anne did not wish for more of such looks and speeches. His cold politeness, her ceremonious grace, were worse than any thing.

CHAPTER NINE

CAPTAIN WENTWORTH WAS come to Kellynch as to a home, to stay as long as he liked, being as thoroughly the object of the Admiral's fraternal kindness as of his wife's. He had intended, on first arriving, to proceed very soon into Shropshire, and visit the brother settled in that country, but the attractions of Uppercross induced him to put this off. There was so much of friendliness, and of flattery, and of every thing most bewitching in his reception there; the old were so hospitable, the young so agreeable, that he could not but resolve to remain where he was, and take all the charms and perfections of Edward's wife upon credit a little longer.

It was soon Uppercross with him almost every day. The Musgroves could hardly be more ready to invite than he to come, particularly in the morning, when he had no companion at home, for the Admiral and Mrs Croft were generally out of doors together, interesting themselves in their new possessions, their grass, and their sheep, and dawdling about in a way not endurable to a third person, or driving out in a gig, lately added to their establishment.

Hitherto there had been but one opinion of Captain Wentworth, among the Musgroves and their dependencies. It was unvarying, warm admiration every where. But this intimate footing was not more than established, when a certain Charles Hayter returned among them, to be a good deal disturbed by it, and to think Captain Wentworth very much in the way.

Charles Hayter was the eldest of all the cousins, and a very amiable, pleasing young man, between whom and Henrietta there had been a considerable appearance of attachment previous to Captain Wentworth's introduction. He was in orders, and having a curacy in the neighbourhood where residence was not required, lived at his father's house, only two miles from Uppercross. A short absence from home had left his fair one unguarded by his attentions at this critical period, and when he came back he had the pain of finding very altered manners, and of seeing Captain Wentworth.

Mrs Musgrove and Mrs Hayter were sisters. They had each had money, but their marriages had made a material difference in their degree of consequence. Mr Hayter had some property of his own, but it was insignificant compared with Mr Musgrove's; and while the Musgroves were in the first class of society in the country, the young Hayters would, from their parents' inferior, retired, and unpolished way of living, and their own defective education, have been hardly in any class at all, but for their connexion with Uppercross; this eldest son of course excepted, who had chosen to be a scholar and a gentleman, and who was very superior in cultivation and manners to all the rest.

The two families had always been on excellent terms, there being no pride on one side, and no envy on the other, and only such a consciousness of superiority in the Miss Musgroves, as made them pleased to improve their cousins. – Charles's attentions to Henrietta had been observed by her father and mother without any disapprobation. 'It would not be a great match for her; but if Henrietta liked him, – and Henrietta *did* seem to like him.'

Henrietta fully thought so herself, before Captain Wentworth came; but from that time cousin Charles had been very much forgotten.

Which of the two sisters was preferred by Captain Wentworth was as yet quite doubtful, as far as Anne's observation reached. Henrietta was perhaps the prettiest, Louisa had the higher spirits; and she knew not *now*, whether the more gentle or the more lively character were most likely to attract him.

Mr and Mrs Musgrove, either from seeing little, or from an entire confidence in the discretion of both their daughters, and of all the young men who came near them, seemed to leave every thing to take its chance. There was not the smallest appearance of solicitude or remark about them, in the Mansion-house; but it was different at the Cottage; the young couple there were more disposed to speculate and wonder; and Captain Wentworth had not been above four or five times in the Miss Musgroves' company, and Charles Hayter had but just reappeared, when Anne had to listen to the opinions of her brother and sister, as to *which* was the one liked best. Charles gave it for Louisa, Mary for Henrietta, but quite agreeing that to have him marry either would be extremely delightful.

Charles 'had never seen a pleasanter man in his life; and from what he had once heard Captain Wentworth himself say, was very sure that he had not made less than twenty thousand pounds by the war. Here was a fortune at once; besides which, there would be the chance of what might be done in any future war; and he was sure Captain Wentworth was as likely a man to distinguish himself as any officer in the navy. Oh! it would be a capital match for either of his sisters.'

'Upon my word it would,' replied Mary. 'Dear me! If he should rise to any very great honours! If he should ever be made a Baronet! "Lady Wentworth" sounds very well. That would be a noble thing, indeed, for Henrietta! She would take place of me then, and Henrietta would not dislike that. Sir Frederick and Lady Wentworth! It would be but a new creation, however, and I never think much of your new creations.'

It suited Mary best to think Henrietta the one preferred on the very account of Charles Hayter, whose pretensions she wished to see put an end to. She looked down very decidedly upon the Hayters, and thought it would be quite a misfortune to have the existing connection between the families renewed – very sad for herself and her children.

'You know,' said she, 'I cannot think him at all a fit match for Henrietta; and considering the alliances which the Musgroves have made, she has no right to throw herself away. I do not think any young woman has a right to make a choice that may be disagreeable and inconvenient to the *principal* part of her family, and be giving bad connexions to those who have not been used to them. And, pray, who is Charles Hayter? Nothing but a country curate. A most improper match for Miss Musgrove, of Uppercross.'

Her husband, however, would not agree with her here; for besides having a regard for his cousin, Charles Hayter was an eldest son, and he saw things as an eldest son himself.

'Now you are talking nonsense, Mary,' was therefore his answer. 'It would not be a *great* match for Henrietta, but Charles has a very fair chance, through the Spicers of getting something from the Bishop in the course of a year or two; and you will please to remember, that he is the eldest son; whenever my uncle dies, he steps into very pretty property. The estate at Winthrop is not less than two hundred and fifty acres, besides the farm near Taunton, which is some of the best land in the country. I grant you, that any of them but Charles would be a very shocking match for Henrietta, and indeed it could not be; he is the only one that could be possible; but he is a very good-natured, good sort of a fellow; and whenever Winthrop comes into his hands, he will make a different sort of place of it, and live in a very different sort of way; and with that property, he will never be a contemptible man. Good, freehold property. No, no; Henrietta might do worse than marry Charles Hayter; and if she has him, and Louisa can get Captain Wentworth, I shall be very well satisfied.'

'Charles may say what he pleases,' cried Mary to Anne, as soon as he was out of the room, 'but it would be shocking to have Henrietta marry Charles Hayter; a very bad thing for *her*, and still worse for *me*; and therefore it is very much to be wished that Captain Wentworth may soon put him quite out of her head, and I have very little doubt that he has. She took hardly any notice of Charles Hayter yesterday. I wish you had been there to see her behaviour. And as to Captain Wentworth's liking Louisa as well as Henrietta, it is nonsense to say so; for he certainly *does* like Henrietta a great deal the best. But Charles is so positive! I wish you had been with us yesterday, for then you might have decided between us; and I am sure you would have thought as I did, unless you had been determined to give it against me.'

A dinner at Mr Musgrove's had been the occasion, when all these things should have been seen by Anne; but she had staid at home, under the mixed plea of a head-ache of her own, and some return of indisposition in little Charles. She had thought only of avoiding Captain Wentworth; but an escape from being appealed to as umpire, was now added to the advantages of a quiet evening.

As to Captain Wentworth's views, she deemed it of more consequence that he should know his own mind, early enough not to be endangering the happiness of either sister, or impeaching his own honour, than that he should prefer Henrietta to Louisa, or Louisa to Henrietta. Either of them would, in all probability, make him an affectionate, good-humoured wife. With regard to Charles Hayter, she had delicacy which must be pained by any lightness of conduct in a well-meaning young woman, and a heart to sympathize in any of the sufferings it occasioned; but if Henrietta found herself mistaken in the nature of her feelings, the alteration could not be understood too soon.

Charles Hayter had met with much to disquiet and mortify him in his cousin's behaviour. She had too old a regard for him to be so wholly estranged, as might in two meetings extinguish every past hope, and leave him nothing to do but to keep away from Uppercross; but there was such a change as became very alarming, when such a man as Captain Wentworth was to be regarded as the probable cause. He had been absent only two Sundays; and when they parted, had left her interested even to the height of his wishes, in his prospect of soon quitting his present curacy, and obtaining that of Uppercross instead. It had then seemed the object nearest her heart, that Dr Shirley, the rector, who for more than forty years had been zealously discharging all the duties of his office, but was now growing too infirm for many of them, should be quite fixed on engaging a curate; should make his curacy quite as good as he could afford, and should give Charles Hayter the promise of it. The advantage of his having to come only to Uppercross, instead of going six miles another way; of his having, in every respect, a better curacy; of his belonging to their dear Dr Shirley, and of dear, good Dr Shirley's being relieved from the duty which he could no longer get through without most injurious fatigue, had been a great deal, even to Louisa, but had been almost every thing to Henrietta. When he came back, alas! the zeal of the business was gone by. Louisa could not listen at all to his account of a conversation which he had just held with Dr Shirley: she was at window, looking out for Captain Wentworth; and even Henrietta had at best only a divided attention to give, and seemed to have forgotten all the former doubt and solicitude of the negociation.

'Well, I am very glad indeed, but I always thought you would have it; I always thought you sure. It did not appear to me that – In short, you know, Dr Shirley *must* have a curate, and you had secured his promise. Is he coming, Louisa?'

One morning, very soon after the dinner at the Musgroves, at which Anne had not been present, Captain Wentworth walked into the drawing-room at the Cottage, where were only herself and the little invalid Charles, who was lying on the sofa.

The surprise of finding himself almost alone with Anne Elliot, deprived his manners of their usual composure: he started, and could only say, 'I thought the Miss Musgroves had been here – Mrs Musgrove told me I should find them here,' before he walked to the window to recollect himself, and feel how he ought to behave.

'They are up stairs with my sister – they will be down in a few moments, I dare say,' – had been Anne's reply, in all the confusion that was natural; and if the child had not called her to come and do something for him, she would have been out of the room the next moment, and released Captain Wentworth as well as herself.

He continued at the window; and after calmly and politely saying, 'I hope the little boy is better,' was silent.

She was obliged to kneel down by the sofa, and remain there to satisfy her patient; and thus they continued a few minutes, when, to her very great satisfaction, she heard some other person crossing the little vestibule. She hoped, on turning her head, to see the master of the house; but it proved to be one much less calculated for making matters easy – Charles Hayter, probably not at all better pleased by the sight of Captain Wentworth, than Captain Wentworth had been by the sight of Anne.

She only attempted to say, 'How do you do? Will not you sit down? The others will be here presently.'

Captain Wentworth, however, came from his window, apparently not ill-disposed for conversation; but Charles Hayter soon put an end to his attempts, by seating himself near the table, and taking up the newspaper; and Captain Wentworth returned to his window.

Another minute brought another addition. The younger boy, a remarkably stout, forward child, of two years old, having got the door opened for him by some one without, made his determined appearance among them, and went straight to the sofa to see what was going on, and put in his claim to any thing good that might be giving away.

There being nothing to be eat, he could only have some play; and as his aunt would not let him teaze his sick brother, he began to fasten himself upon her, as she knelt, in such a way that, busy as she was about Charles, she could not shake him off. She spoke to him – ordered, intreated, and insisted in vain. Once she did contrive to push him away, but the boy had the greater pleasure in getting upon her back again directly.

'Walter,' said she, 'get down this moment. You are extremely troublesome. I am very angry with you.'

'Walter,' cried Charles Hayter, 'why do you not do as you are bid? Do not you hear your aunt speak? Come to me, Walter, come to cousin Charles.'

But not a bit did Walter stir.

In another moment, however, she found herself in the state of being released from him; some one was taking him from her, though he had bent down her head so much, that his little sturdy hands were unfastened from around her neck, and he was resolutely borne away, before she knew that Captain Wentworth had done it.

Her sensations on the discovery made her perfectly speechless. She could not even thank him. She could only hang over little Charles, with most disordered feelings. His kindness in stepping forward to her relief – the manner – the silence in which it had passed – the little particulars of the circumstance – with the conviction soon forced on her by the noise he was

Some one was taking him from her

studiously making with the child, that he meant to avoid hearing her thanks, and rather sought to testify that her conversation was the last of his wants, produced such a confusion of varying, but very painful agitation, as she could not recover from, till enabled by the entrance of Mary and the Miss Musgroves to make over her little patient to their cares, and leave the room. She could not stay. It might have been an opportunity of watching the loves and jealousies of the four; they were now all together, but she could stay for none of it. It was evident that Charles Hayter was not well inclined towards Captain Wentworth. She had a strong impression of his having said, in a vext tone of voice, after Captain Wentworth's interference, 'You ought to have minded *me*, Walter; I told you not to teaze your aunt;' and could comprehend his regretting that Captain Wentworth should do what he ought to have done himself. But neither Charles Hayter's feelings, nor any body's feelings, could interest her, till she had a little better arranged her own. She was ashamed of herself, quite ashamed of being so nervous, so overcome by such a trifle; but so it was; and it required a long application of solitude and reflection to recover her.

CHAPTER TEN

OTHER OPPORTUNITIES OF making her observations could not fail to occur. Anne had soon been in company with all the four together often enough to have an opinion, though too wise to acknowledge as much at home, where she knew it would have satisfied neither husband nor wife; for while she considered Louisa to be rather the favourite, she could not but think, as far as she might dare to judge from memory and experience, that Captain Wentworth was not in love with either. They were more in love with him; yet there it was not love. It was a little fever of admiration; but it might, probably must, end in love with some. Charles Hayter seemed aware of being slighted, and yet Henrietta had sometimes the air of being divided between them. Anne longed for the power of representing to them all what they were about, and of pointing out some of the evils they were exposing themselves to. She did not attribute guile to any. It was the highest satisfaction to her, to believe Captain Wentworth not in the least aware of the pain he was occasioning. There was no triumph, no pitiful triumph in his manner. He had, probably, never heard, and never thought of any claims of Charles Hayter. He was only wrong in accepting the attentions – (for accepting must be the word) of two young women at once.

After a short struggle, however, Charles Hayter seemed to quit the field. Three days had passed without his coming once to Uppercross; a most decided change. He had even refused one regular invitation to dinner; and having been found on the occasion by Mr Musgrove with some large books before him, Mr and Mrs Musgrove were sure all could not be right, and talked, with grave faces, of his studying himself to death. It was Mary's hope and belief, that he had received a positive dismissal from Henrietta, and her husband lived under the constant dependence of seeing him to-morrow. Anne could only feel that Charles Hayter was wise.

One morning, about this time, Charles Musgrove and Captain Wentworth being gone a shooting together, as the sisters in the cottage were sitting quietly at work, they were visited at the window by the sisters from the mansion-house.

It was a very fine November day, and the Miss Musgroves came through the little grounds, and stopped for no other purpose than to say, that they were going to take a *long* walk, and, therefore, concluded Mary could not like to go with them; and when Mary immediately replied, with some jealousy, at not being supposed a good walker, 'Oh, yes, I should like to join you very much, I am very fond of a long walk,' Anne felt persuaded, by the looks of the two girls, that it was precisely what they did not wish, and admired again the sort of necessity which the family-habits seemed to produce, of every thing being to be communicated, and every thing being to be done together, however undesired and inconvenient. She tried to dissuade Mary from going, but in vain; and that being the case, thought it best to accept the Miss Musgroves' much more cordial invitation to herself to go likewise, as she might be useful in turning back with her sister, and lessening the interference in any plan of their own.

'I cannot imagine why they should suppose I should not like a long walk!' said Mary, as she went up stairs. 'Every body is always supposing that I am not a good walker! And yet they would not have been pleased, if we had refused to join them. When people come in this manner on purpose to ask us, how can one say no?'

Just as they were setting off, the gentlemen returned. They had taken out a young dog, who had spoilt their sport, and sent them back early. Their time and strength, and spirits, were, therefore, exactly ready for this walk, and they entered into it with pleasure. Could Anne have foreseen such a junction, she would have staid at home; but, from some feelings of interest and curiosity, she fancied now that it was too late to retract, and the whole six set forward together in the direction chosen by the Miss Musgroves, who evidently considered the walk as under their guidance.

Anne's object was, not to be in the way of any body, and where the narrow paths across the fields made many separations necessary, to keep with her brother and sister. Her *pleasure* in the walk must arise from the exercise and the day, from the view of the last smiles of the year upon the tawny leaves and withered hedges, and from repeating to herself some few of the thousand poetical descriptions extant of autumn, that season of peculiar and inexhaustible influence on the mind of taste and tenderness, that season which has drawn from every poet, worthy of being read, some attempt at description, or some lines of feeling. She occupied her mind as much as possible in such like musings and quotations; but it was not possible, that when within reach of Captain Wentworth's conversation with either of the Miss Musgroves, she should not try to hear it; yet she caught little very remarkable. It was mere lively chat, – such as any young persons, on an intimate footing, might fall into. He was more engaged with Louisa than with Henrietta. Louisa certainly put more forward for his notice than her sister. This distinction appeared to increase, and there was one speech of Louisa's which struck her. After one of the many praises of the day, which were continually bursting forth, Captain Wentworth added.

'What glorious weather for the Admiral and my sister! They meant to take a long drive this morning; perhaps we may hail them from some of these hills. They talked of coming into this side of the country. I wonder whereabouts they will upset to-day. Oh! it does happen very often, I assure you – but my sister makes nothing of it – she would as lieve be tossed out as not.'

'Ah! You make the most of it, I know,' cried Louisa, 'but if it were really so, I should do just the same in her place. If I loved a man, as she loves the Admiral, I would be always with him, nothing should ever separate us, and I would rather be overturned by him, than driven safely by anybody else.'

It was spoken with enthusiasm.

'Had you?' cried he, catching the same tone; 'I honour you!' And there was silence between them for a little while.

Anne could not immediately fall into a quotation again. The sweet scenes of autumn were for a while put by – unless some tender sonnet, fraught with the apt analogy of the declining year, with declining happiness, and the images of youth and hope, and spring, all gone together, blessed her memory. She roused herself to say, as they struck by order into another path, 'Is not this one of the ways to Winthrop?' But nobody heard, or, at least, nobody answered her.

Winthrop, however, or its environs – for young men are, sometimes, to be met with, strolling about near home, was their destination; and after another half mile of gradual ascent through large enclosures, where the ploughs at work, and the fresh-made path spoke the farmer, counteracting the sweet of poetical despondence, and meaning to have spring again, they gained the summit of the most considerable hill, which parted Uppercross and Winthrop, and soon commanded a full view of the latter, at the foot of the hill on the other side.

Winthrop, without beauty and without dignity, was stretched before them; an indifferent house, standing low, and hemmed in by the barns and buildings of a farm-yard.

Mary exclaimed, 'Bless me! here is Winthrop – I declare I had no idea! – well, now I think we had better turn back; I am excessively tired.'

Henrietta, conscious and ashamed, and seeing no cousin Charles walking along any path, or leaning against any gate, was ready to do as Mary wished;

but 'No, no,' cried Louisa more eagerly, and taking her sister aside, seemed to be arguing the matter warmly.

Charles, in the meanwhile, was very decidedly declaring his resolution of calling on his aunt, now that he was so near; and very evidently, though more fearfully, trying to induce his wife to go too. But this was one of the points on which the lady shewed her strength, and when he recommended the advantage of resting herself a quarter of an hour at Winthrop, as she felt so tired, she resolutely answered, 'Oh! no, indeed! – walking up that hill again would do her more harm than any sitting down could do her good;' – and, in short, her look and manner declared, that go she would not.

After a little succession of these sort of debates and consultations, it was settled between Charles and his two sisters, that he, and Henrietta, should just run down for a few minutes, to see their aunt and cousins, while the rest of the party waited for them at the top of the hill. Louisa seemed the principal arranger of the plan; and, as she went a little way with them, down the hill, still talking to Henrietta, Mary took the opportunity of looking scornfully around her, and saying to Captain Wentworth,

'It is very unpleasant, having such connexions! But I assure you, I have never been in the house above twice in my life.'

She received no other answer, than an artificial, assenting smile, followed by a contemptuous glance, as he turned away, which Anne perfectly knew the meaning of.

The brow of the hill, where they remained, was a cheerful spot; Louisa returned, and Mary finding a comfortable seat for herself, on the step of a stile, was very well satisfied so long as the others all stood about her; but when Louisa drew Captain Wentworth away, to try for a gleaning of nuts in an adjoining hedge-row, and they were gone by degrees quite out of sight and sound, Mary was happy no longer; she quarrelled with her own seat, – was sure Louisa had got a much better somewhere, – and nothing could prevent her from going to look for a better also. She turned through the same gate, – but could not see them. – Anne found a nice seat for her, on a dry sunny bank, under the hedge-row, in which she had no doubt of their still being – in some spot or other. Mary sat down for a moment, but it would not do; she was sure Louisa had found a better seat somewhere else, and she would go on, till she overtook her.

Anne, really tired herself, was glad to sit down; and she very soon heard Captain Wentworth and Louisa in the hedge-row, behind her, as if making their way back, along the rough, wild sort of channel, down the centre. They were speaking as they drew near. Louisa's voice was the first distinguished. She seemed to be in the middle of some eager speech. What Anne first heard was,

'And so, I made her go. I could not bear that she should be frightened from the visit by such nonsense. What! – would I be turned back from doing a thing that I had determined to do, and that I knew to be right, by the airs and interference of such a person? – or, of any person I may say. No, – I have no idea of being so easily persuaded. When I have made up my mind, I have made it. And Henrietta seemed entirely to have made up hers to call at Winthrop to-day – and yet, she was as near giving it up, out of nonsensical complaisance!'

'She would have turned back then, but for you?'

'She would indeed, I am almost ashamed to say it.'

'Happy for her, to have such a mind as yours at hand! – After the hints you gave just now, which did but confirm my own observations, the last time I was in company with him, I need not affect to have no comprehension of what is going on. I see that more than a mere dutiful morning-visit to your aunt was in question; – and woe betide him, and her too, when it comes to things of consequence, when they are placed in circumstances, requiring fortitude and strength of mind, if she have not resolution enough to resist idle interference in such a trifle as this. Your sister is an amiable creature; but *yours* is the character of decision and firmness, I see. If you value her conduct or happiness, infuse as much of your own spirit into her, as you can. But this, no doubt, you have been always doing. It is the worst evil of too yielding and indecisive a character, that no influence over it can be depended on. – You are never sure of a good impression being durable. Every body may sway it; let those who would be happy be firm. – Here is a nut,' said he, catching one down from an upper bough. 'To exemplify, – a beautiful glossy nut, which, blessed with original strength, has outlived all the storms of autumn. Not a puncture, not a weak spot any where. – This nut,' he continued, with playful solemnity, – 'while so many of its brethren have fallen and been trodden under foot, is still in possession of all the happiness that a hazel-nut can be supposed capable of.' Then, returning to his former earnest tone: 'My first wish for all, whom I am interested in, is that they should be firm. If Louisa Musgrove would be beautiful and happy in her November of life, she will cherish all her present powers of mind.'

He had done, – and was unanswered. It would have surprised Anne, if Louisa could have readily answered such a speech – words of such interest, spoken with such serious warmth! – she could imagine what Louisa was feeling. For herself – she feared to move, lest she could be seen. While she remained, a bush of low rambling holly protected her, and they were moving on. Before they were beyond her hearing, however, Louisa spoke again.

'Mary is good-natured enough in many respects,' said she; 'but she does sometimes provoke me excessively, by her nonsense and her pride; the Elliot pride. She has a great deal too much of the Elliot pride. – We do so wish that Charles had married Anne instead. – I suppose you know he wanted to marry Anne?'

After a moment's pause, Captain Wentworth said,

'Do you mean that she refused him?'

'Oh! yes, certainly.'

'When did that happen?'

'I do not exactly know, for Henrietta and I were at school at the time; but I believe about a year before he married Mary. I wish she had accepted him. We should all have liked her a great deal better; and papa and mamma always think it was her great friend Lady Russell's doing, that she did not. – They think Charles might not be learned and bookish enough to please Lady Russell, and that therefore, she persuaded Anne to refuse him.'

The sounds were retreating, and Anne distinguished no more. Her own emotions still kept her fixed. She had much to recover from, before she could move. The listener's proverbial fate was not absolutely hers; she had heard no evil of herself, – but she had heard a great deal of very painful import. She saw how her own character was considered by Captain Wentworth; and there had been just that degree of feeling and curiosity about her in his manner, which must give her extreme agitation.

As soon as she could, she went after Mary, and having found, and walked back with her to their former station, by the stile, felt some comfort in their whole party being immediately afterwards collected, and once more in motion together. Her spirits wanted the solitude and silence which only numbers could give.

Charles and Henrietta returned, bringing, as may be conjectured, Charles Hayter with them. The minutiae of the business Anne could not attempt to understand; even Captain Wentworth did not seem admitted to perfect confidence here; but that there had been a withdrawing on the gentleman's side, and a relenting on the lady's, and that they were now very glad to be together again, did not admit a doubt. Henrietta looked a little ashamed, but very pleased; – Charles Hayter exceedingly happy, and they were devoted to each other almost from the first instant of their all setting forward for Uppercross.

Every thing now marked out Louisa for Captain Wentworth; nothing could be plainer; and where many divisions were necessary, or even where they were not, they walked side by side, nearly as much as the other two. In a long strip of meadow-land, where there was ample space for all, they were thus divided – forming three distinct parties; and to that party of the three which boasted least animation, and least complaisance, Anne necessarily belonged. She joined Charles and Mary, and was tired enough to be very glad of Charles's other arm; – but Charles, though in very good humour with her, was out of temper with his wife. Mary had shewn herself disobliging to him, and was now to reap the consequence, which consequence was his dropping her arm almost every moment, to cut off the heads of some nettles in the hedge with his switch; and when Mary began to complain of it, and lament her being ill-used, according to custom, in being on the hedge side, while Anne was never incommoded on the other, he dropped the arms of both to hunt after a weasel which he had a momentary glance of; and they could hardly get him along at all.

This long meadow bordered a lane, which their footpath, at the end of it, was to cross; and when the party had all reached the gate of exit, the carriage advancing in the same direction, which had been some time heard, was just coming up, and proved to be Admiral Croft's gig. – He and his wife had taken their intended drive, and were returning home. Upon hearing how long a walk the young people had engaged in, they kindly offered a seat to any lady who might be particularly tired; it would save her full a mile, and they were going through Uppercross. The invitation was general, and generally declined. The Miss Musgroves were not at all tired, and Mary was either offended, by not being asked before any of the others, or what Louisa called the Elliot pride could not endure to make a third in a one horse chaise.

The walking-party had crossed the lane, and were surmounting an opposite stile; and the admiral was putting his horse into motion again, when Captain Wentworth cleared the hedge in a moment to say something to his sister. – The something might be guessed by its effects.

'Miss Elliot, I am sure *you* are tired,' cried Mrs Croft. 'Do let us have the pleasure of taking you home. Here is excellent room for three, I assure you. If we were all like you, I believe we might sit four. – You must, indeed, you must.'

Anne was still in the lane; and though instinctively beginning to decline, she was not allowed to proceed. The admiral's kind urgency came in support of his wife's; they would not be refused; they compressed themselves into the smallest possible space to leave her a corner, and Captain Wentworth, without saying a word, turned to her, and quietly obliged her to be assisted into the carriage.

Yes, – he had done it. She was in the carriage, and felt that he had placed her there, that his will and his hands had done it, that she owed it to his perception of her fatigue, and his resolution to give her rest. She was very much affected by the view of his disposition towards her which all these things made apparent. This little circumstance seemed the completion of all that had gone before. She understood him. He could not forgive her, – but he could not be unfeeling. Though condemning her for the past, and considering it with high and unjust resentment, though perfectly careless of her, and though becoming attached to another, still he could not see her suffer, without the desire of giving her relief. It was a remainder of former sentiment; it was an impulse of pure, though unacknowledged friendship; it was a proof of his own warm and amiable heart, which she could not contemplate without emotions so compounded of pleasure and pain, that she knew not which prevailed.

Her answers to the kindness and the remarks of her companions were at first unconsciously given. They had travelled half their way along the rough lane, before she was quite awake to what they said. She then found them talking of 'Frederick.'

'He certainly means to have one or other of those two girls, Sophy,' said the admiral; – 'but there is no saying which. He has been running after them, too, long enough, one would think, to make up his mind. Ay, this comes of the peace. If it were war, now, he would have settled it long ago. – We sailors, Miss Elliot, cannot afford to make long courtships in time of war. How many days was it, my dear, between the first time of my seeing you, and our sitting down together in our lodgings at North Yarmouth?'

'We had better not talk about it, my dear,' replied Mrs Croft, pleasantly; 'for if Miss Elliot were to hear how soon we came to an understanding, she would never be persuaded that we could be happy together. I had known you by character, however, long before.'

'Well, and I had heard of you as a very pretty girl; and what were we to wait for besides? – I do not like having such things so long in hand. I wish Frederick would spread a little more canvas, and bring us home one of these young ladies to Kellynch. Then, there would always be company for them. – And very nice young ladies they both are; I hardly know one from the other.'

'Very good humoured, unaffected girls, indeed,' said Mrs Croft, in a tone of calmer praise, such as made Anne suspect that her keener powers might not consider either of them as quite worthy of her brother; 'and a very respectable family. One could not be connected with better people. – My dear admiral, that post! – we shall certainly take that post.'

But by coolly giving the reins a better direction herself, they happily passed the danger; and by once afterwards judiciously putting out her hand, they neither fell into a rut, nor ran foul of a dung-cart; and Anne, with some amusement at their style of driving, which she imagined no bad representation of the general guidance of their affairs, found herself safely deposited by them at the cottage.

CHAPTER ELEVEN

THE TIME NOW APPROACHED for Lady Russell's return; the day was even fixed, and Anne, being engaged to join her as soon as she was resettled, was looking forward to an early removal to Kellynch, and beginning to think how her own comfort was likely to be affected by it.

It would place her in the same village with Captain Wentworth, within half a mile of him; they would have to frequent the same church, and there must be intercourse between the two families. This was against her; but, on the other hand, he spent so much of his time at Uppercross, that in removing thence she might be considered rather as leaving him behind, than as going towards him; and, upon the whole, she believed she must, on this interesting question, be the gainer, almost as certainly as in her change of domestic society, in leaving poor Mary for Lady Russell.

She wished it might be possible for her to avoid ever seeing Captain Wentworth at the hall; – those rooms had witnessed former meetings which would be brought too painfully before her; but she was yet more anxious for the possibility of Lady Russell and Captain Wentworth never meeting any where. They did not like each other, and no renewal of acquaintance now could do any good; and were Lady Russell to see them together, she might think that he had too much self-possession, and she too little.

These points formed her chief solicitude in anticipating her removal from Uppercross, where she felt she had been stationed quite long enough. Her usefulness to little Charles would always give some sweetness to the memory of her two months visit there, but he was gaining strength apace, and she had nothing else to stay for.

The conclusion of her visit, however, was diversified in a way which she had not at all imagined. Captain Wentworth, after being unseen and unheard of at Uppercross for two whole days, appeared again among them to justify himself by a relation of what had kept him away.

A letter from his friend, Captain Harville, having found him out at last, had brought intelligence of Captain Harville's being settled with his family at Lyme for the winter; of their being therefore, quite unknowingly, within twenty miles of each other. Captain Harville had never been in good health since a severe wound which he received two years before, and Captain Wentworth's anxiety to see him had determined him to go immediately to Lyme. He had been there for four-and-twenty hours. His acquittal was complete, his friendship warmly honoured, a lively interest excited for his friend, and his description of the fine country about Lyme so feelingly attended to by the party, that an earnest desire to see Lyme themselves, and a project for going thither was the consequence.

The young people were all wild to see Lyme. Captain Wentworth talked of going there again himself; it was only seventeen miles from Uppercross; though November, the weather was by no means bad; and, in short, Louisa, who was the most eager of the eager, having formed the resolution to go, and besides the pleasure of doing as she liked, being now armed with the idea of merit in maintaining her own way, bore down all the wishes of her father and mother for putting it off till summer; and to Lyme they were to go – Charles, Mary, Anne, Henrietta, Louisa, and Captain Wentworth.

The first heedless scheme had been to go in the morning and return at night, but to this Mr Musgrove, for the sake of his horses, would not consent; and when it came to be rationally considered, a day in the middle of November would not leave much time for seeing a new place, after deducting seven hours, as the nature of the country required, for going and returning. They were consequently to stay the night there, and not to be expected back till the next day's dinner. This was felt to be a considerable amendment; and though they all met at the Great House at rather an early breakfast hour, and set off very punctually, it was so much past noon before the two carriages, Mr Musgrove's coach containing the four ladies, and Charles's curricle, in which he drove Captain Wentworth, were descending the long hill into Lyme, and entering upon the still steeper street of the town itself, that it was very evident they would not have more than time for looking about them, before the light and warmth of the day were gone.

After securing accommodations, and ordering a dinner at one of the inns, the next thing to be done was unquestionably to walk directly down to the sea. They were come too late in the year for any amusement or variety which Lyme, as a public place, might offer; the rooms were shut up, the lodgers almost all gone, scarcely any family but of the residents left – and, as there is nothing to admire in the buildings themselves, the remarkable situation of the town, the principal street almost hurrying into the water, the walk to the Cobb, skirting round the pleasant little bay, which in the season is animated with bathing machines and company, the Cobb itself, its old wonders and new improvements, with the very beautiful line of cliffs stretching out to the east of the town, are what the stranger's eye will seek; and a very strange stranger it must be, who does not see charms in the immediate environs of Lyme, to make him wish to know it better. The scenes in its neighbourhood, Charmouth, with its high grounds and extensive sweeps of country, and still more its sweet retired bay, backed by dark cliffs, where fragments of low rock among the sands make it the happiest spot for watching the flow of the tide, for sitting in unwearied contemplation; – the woody varieties of the cheerful village of Up Lyme, and, above all, Pinny, with its green chasms between romantic rocks, where the scattered forest trees and orchards of luxuriant growth declare that many a generation must have passed away since the first partial falling of the cliff prepared the ground for such a state, where a scene so wonderful and so lovely is exhibited, as may more than equal any of the resembling scenes of the far-famed Isle of Wight: these places must be visited, and visited again, to make the worth of Lyme understood.

The party from Uppercross passing down by the now deserted and melancholy looking rooms, and still descending, soon found themselves on the sea shore, and lingering only, as all must linger and gaze on a first return to the sea, who ever deserve to look on it at all, proceeded towards the Cobb, equally their object in itself and on Captain Wentworth's account; for in a small house, near the foot of an old pier of unknown date, were the Harvilles settled. Captain Wentworth turned in to call on his friend; the others walked on, and he was to join them on the Cobb.

They were by no means tired of wondering and admiring; and not even Louisa seemed to feel that they had parted with Captain Wentworth long, when they saw him coming after them, with three companions, all well known already by description to be Captain and Mrs Harville, and a Captain Benwick, who was staying with them.

Captain Benwick had some time ago been first lieutenant of the Laconia; and the account which Captain Wentworth had given of him, on his return from Lyme before; his warm praise of him as an excellent young man and an officer, whom he had always valued highly, which must have stamped him well in the esteem of every listener, had been followed by a little history of his private life, which rendered him perfectly interesting in the eyes of all the ladies. He had been engaged to Captain Harville's sister, and was now mourning her loss. They had been a year or two waiting for fortune and promotion. Fortune came, his prize-money as lieutenant being great, – promotion, too, came at *last*; but Fanny Harville did not live to know it. She had died the preceding summer, while he was at sea. Captain Wentworth believed it impossible for man to be more attached to woman than poor Benwick had been to Fanny Harville, or to be more deeply afflicted under the dreadful change. He considered his disposition as of the sort which must suffer heavily, uniting very strong feelings with quiet, serious, and retiring manners, and a decided taste for reading, and sedentary pursuits. To finish the interest of the story, the friendship between him and the Harvilles seemed, if possible, augmented by the event which closed all their views of alliance, and Captain Benwick was now living with them entirely. Captain Harville had taken his present house for half a year, his taste, and his health, and his fortune all directing him to a residence unexpensive, and by the sea;

and the grandeur of the country, and the retirement of Lyme in the winter, appeared exactly adapted to Captain Benwick's state of mind. The sympathy and good-will excited towards Captain Benwick was very great.

'And yet,' said Anne to herself, as they now moved forward to meet the party, 'he has not, perhaps, a more sorrowing heart than I have. I cannot believe his prospects so blighted for ever. He is younger than I am; younger in feeling, if not in fact; younger as a man. He will rally again, and be happy with another.'

They all met, and were introduced. Captain Harville was a tall, dark man, with a sensible, benevolent countenance; a little lame; and from strong features, and want of health, looking much older than Captain Wentworth. Captain Benwick looked and was the youngest of the three, and, compared with either of them, a little man. He had a pleasing face and a melancholy air, just as he ought to have, and drew back from conversation.

Captain Harville, though not equalling Captain Wentworth in manners, was a perfect gentleman, unaffected, warm, and obliging. Mrs Harville, a degree less polished than her husband, seemed however to have the same good feelings; and nothing could be more pleasant than their desire of considering the whole party as friends of their own, because the friends of Captain Wentworth, or more kindly hospitable than their entreaties for their all promising to dine with them. The dinner, already ordered at the inn, was at last, though unwillingly, accepted as an excuse; but they seemed almost hurt that Captain Wentworth should have brought any such party to Lyme, without considering it as a thing of course that they should dine with them.

There was so much attachment to Captain Wentworth in all this, and such a bewitching charm in a degree of hospitality so uncommon, so unlike the usual style of give-and-take invitations, and dinners of formality and display, that Anne felt her spirits not likely to be benefited by an increasing acquaintance among his brother-officers. 'These would have been all my friends,' was her thought; and she had to struggle against a great tendency to lowness.

On quitting the Cobb, they all went indoors with their new friends and found rooms so small as none but those who invite from the heart could think capable of accommodating so many. Anne had a moment's astonishment on the subject herself; but it was soon lost in the pleasanter feelings which sprang from the sight of all the ingenious contrivances and nice arrangements of Captain Harville, to turn the actual space to the best possible account, to supply the deficiencies of lodging-house furniture, and defend the windows and doors against the winter storms to be expected. The varieties in the fitting-up of the rooms, where the common necessaries provided by the owner, in the common indifferent plight, were contrasted with some few articles of a rare species of wood, excellently worked up, and with something curious and valuable from all the distant countries Captain Harville had visited, were more than amusing to Anne: connected as it all was with his profession, the fruit of its labours, the effect of its influence on his habits, the picture of repose and domestic happiness it presented, made it to her a something more, or less, than gratification.

Captain Harville was no reader; but he had contrived excellent accommodations, and fashioned very pretty shelves, for a tolerable collection of well-bound volumes, the property of Captain Benwick. His lameness prevented him from taking much exercise; but a mind of usefulness and ingenuity seemed to furnish him with constant employment within. He drew, he varnished, he carpentered, he glued; he made toys for the children, he fashioned new netting-needles and pins with improvements; and if every thing else was done, sat down to his large fishing-net at one corner of the room.

Anne thought she left great happiness behind her when they quitted the house; and Louisa, by whom she found herself walking, burst forth into raptures of admiration and delight on the character of the navy – their friendliness, their brotherliness, their openness, their uprightness; protesting that she was convinced of sailors having more worth and warmth than any other set of men in England; that they only knew how to live, and they only deserved to be respected and loved.

They went back to dress and dine; and so well had the scheme answered already, that nothing was found amiss; though its being 'so entirely out of season,' and the 'no-thorough-fare of Lyme,' and the 'no expectation of company,' had brought many apologies from the heads of the inn.

Anne found herself by this time growing so much more hardened to being in Captain Wentworth's company than she had at first imagined could ever be, that the sitting down to the same table with him now, and the interchange of the common civilities attending on it – (they never got beyond) was become a mere nothing.

The nights were too dark for the ladies to meet again till the morrow, but Captain Harville had promised them a visit in the evening; and he came, bringing his friend also, which was more than had been expected, it having been agreed that Captain Benwick had all the appearance of being oppressed by the presence of so many strangers. He ventured among them again, however, though his spirits certainly did not seem fit for the mirth of the party in general.

While Captains Wentworth and Harville led the talk on one side of the room, and, by recurring to former days, supplied anecdotes in abundance to occupy and entertain the others, it fell to Anne's lot to be placed rather apart with Captain Benwick; and a very good impulse of her nature obliged her to begin an acquaintance with him. He was shy, and disposed to abstraction; but the engaging mildness of her countenance, and gentleness of her manners, soon had their effect; and Anne was well repaid the first trouble of exertion. He was evidently a young man of considerable taste in reading, though principally in poetry; and besides the persuasion of having given him at least an evening's indulgence in the discussion of subjects, which his

He carpentered

usual companions had probably no concern in, she had the hope of being of real use to him in some suggestions as to the duty and benefit of struggling against affliction, which had naturally grown out of their conversation. For, though shy, he did not seem reserved; it had rather the appearance of feelings glad to burst their usual restraints; and having talked of poetry, the richness of the present age, and gone through a brief comparison of opinion as to the first-rate poets, trying to ascertain whether *Marmion* or *The Lady of the Lake* were to be preferred, and how ranked the *Giaour* and *The Bride of Abydos*; and moreover, how the *Giaour* was to be pronounced, he shewed himself so intimately acquainted with all the tenderest songs of the one poet, and all the impassioned descriptions of hopeless agony of the other; he repeated, with such tremulous feeling, the various lines which imagined a broken heart, or a mind destroyed by wretchedness, and looked so entirely as if he meant to be understood, that she ventured to hope he did not always read only poetry; and to say, that she thought it was the misfortune of poetry, to be seldom safely enjoyed by those who enjoyed it completely; and that the strong feelings which alone could estimate it truly, were the very feelings which ought to taste it but sparingly.

His looks shewing him not pained, but pleased with this allusion to his situation, she was emboldened to go on; and feeling in herself the right of seniority of mind, she ventured to recommend a larger allowance of prose in his daily study; and on being requested to particularize, mentioned such works of our best moralists, such collections of the finest letters, such memoirs of characters of worth and suffering, as occurred to her at the moment as calculated to rouse and fortify the mind by the highest precepts, and the strongest examples of moral and religious endurances.

Captain Benwick listened attentively, and seemed grateful for the interest implied; and though with a shake of the head, and sighs which declared his little faith in the efficacy of any books on grief like his, noted down the names of those she recommended, and promised to procure and read them.

When the evening was over, Anne could not but be amused at the idea of her coming to Lyme, to preach patience and resignation to a young man whom she had never seen before; nor could she help fearing, on more serious reflection, that, like many other great moralists and preachers, she had been eloquent on a point in which her own conduct would ill bear examination.

CHAPTER TWELVE

ANNE AND HENRIETTA, FINDING themselves the earliest of the party the next morning, agreed to stroll down to the sea before breakfast. – They went to the sands, to watch the flowing of the tide, which a fine south-easterly breeze was bringing in with all the grandeur which so flat a shore admitted. They praised the morning; gloried in the sea; sympathized in the delight of the fresh-feeling breeze – and were silent; till Henrietta suddenly began again, with,

'Oh! yes, – I am quite convinced that, with very few exceptions, the sea-air always does good. There can be no doubt of its having been of the greatest service to Dr Shirley, after his illness, last spring twelvemonth. He declares himself, that coming to Lyme for a month, did him more good than all the medicine he took; and, that being by the sea, always makes him feel young again. Now, I cannot help thinking it a pity that he does not live entirely by the sea. I do think he had better leave Uppercross entirely, and fix at Lyme. – Do not you, Anne? – Do not you agree with me, that it is the best thing he could do, both for himself and Mrs Shirley? – She has cousins here, you know, and many acquaintance, which would make it cheerful for her, – and I am sure she would be glad to get to a place where she could have medical attendance at hand, in case of his having another seizure. Indeed I think it quite melancholy to have such excellent people as Dr and Mrs Shirley, who have been doing good all their lives, wearing out their last days in a place like Uppercross, where, excepting our family, they seem shut out from all the world. I wish his friends would propose it to him. I really think they ought. And, as to procuring a dispensation, there could be no difficulty at his time of life, and with his character. My only doubt is, whether any thing could persuade him to leave his parish. He is so very strict and scrupulous in his notions; over-scrupulous, I must say. Do not you think, Anne, it is being over-scrupulous? Do not you think it is quite a mistaken point of conscience, when a clergyman sacrifices his health for the sake of duties, which may be just as well performed by another person? – And at Lyme too, – only seventeen miles off, – he would be near enough to hear, if people thought there was any thing to complain of.'

Anne smiled more than once to herself during this speech, and entered into the subject, as ready to do good by entering into the feelings of a young lady as of a young man, – though here it was good of a lower standard, for what could be offered but general acquiescence? – She said all that was reasonable and proper on the business; felt the claims of Dr Shirley to repose, as she ought; saw how very desirable it was that he should have some active, respectable young man, as a resident curate, and was even courteous enough to hint at the advantage of such resident curate's being married.

'I wish,' said Henrietta, very well pleased with her companion, 'I wish Lady Russell lived at Uppercross, and were intimate with Dr Shirley. I have always heard of Lady Russell, as a woman of the greatest influence with every body! I always look upon her as able to persuade a person to any thing! I am afraid of her, as I have told you before, quite afraid of her, because she is so very clever; but I respect her amazingly, and wish we had such a neighbour at Uppercross.'

Anne was amused by Henrietta's manner of being grateful, and amused also, that the course of events and the new interests of Henrietta's views should have placed her friend at all in favour with any of the Musgrove family; she had only time, however, for a general answer, and a wish that such another woman were at Uppercross, before all subjects suddenly ceased, on seeing Louisa and Captain Wentworth coming towards them. They came also for a stroll till breakfast was likely to be ready; but Louisa recollecting, immediately afterwards, that she had something to procure at a shop, invited them all to go back with her into the town. They were all at her disposal.

When they came to the steps, leading upwards from the beach, a gentleman at the same moment preparing to come down, politely drew back, and stopped to give them way. They ascended and passed him; and as they passed, Anne's face caught his eye, and he looked at her with a degree of earnest admiration, which she could not be insensible of. She was looking remarkably well; her very regular, very pretty features, having the bloom and freshness of youth restored by the fine wind which had been blowing on her complexion, and by the animation of eye which it had also produced. It was evident that the gentleman, (completely a gentleman in manner) admired her exceedingly. Captain Wentworth looked round at her instantly in a way which shewed his noticing of it. He gave her a momentary glance, – a glance of brightness, which seemed to say, 'That man is struck with you, – and even I, at this moment, see something like Anne Elliot again.'

After attending Louisa through her business, and loitering about a little longer, they returned to the inn; and Anne in passing afterwards quickly from her own chamber to their dining-room, had nearly run against the very same gentleman, as he came out of an adjoining apartment. She had before conjectured him to be a stranger like themselves, and determined that a well-looking groom, who was strolling about near the two inns as they came back, should be his servant. Both master and man being in

A gentleman politely drew back

mourning assisted the idea. It was now proved that he belonged to the same inn as themselves; and this second meeting, short as it was, also proved again by the gentleman's looks, that he thought hers very lovely, and by the readiness and propriety of his apologies, that he was a man of exceedingly good manners. He seemed about thirty, and, though not handsome, had an agreeable person. Anne felt that she should like to know who he was.

They had nearly done breakfast, when the sound of a carriage, (almost the first they had heard since entering Lyme) drew half the party to the window. 'It was a gentleman's carriage – a curricle – but only coming round from the stable-yard to the front door – Somebody must be going away. – It was driven by a servant in mourning.'

The word curricle made Charles Musgrove jump up, that he might compare it with his own, the servant in mourning roused Anne's curiosity, and the whole six were collected to look, by the time the owner of the curricle was to be seen issuing from the door amidst the bows and civilities of the household, and taking his seat, to drive off.

'Ah!' cried Captain Wentworth, instantly, and with half a glance at Anne; 'it is the very man we passed.'

The Miss Musgroves agreed to it; and having all kindly watched him as far up the hill as they could, they returned to the breakfast-table. The waiter came into the room soon afterwards.

'Pray,' said Captain Wentworth, immediately, 'can you tell us the name of the gentleman who is just gone away?'

'Yes, Sir, a Mr Elliot; a gentleman of large fortune, – came in last night from Sidmouth, – dare say you heard the carriage, Sir, while you were at dinner; and going on now for Crewkherne, in his way to Bath and London.'

'Elliot!' – Many had looked on each other, and many had repeated the name, before all this had been got through, even by the smart rapidity of a waiter.

'Bless me!' cried Mary; 'it must be our cousin; – it must be our Mr Elliot, it must indeed! – Charles, Anne, must not it? In mourning, you see, just as our Mr Elliot must be. How very extraordinary! In the very same inn with us! Anne, must not it be our Mr Elliot; my father's next heir? Pray Sir,' (turning to the waiter), 'did not you hear, – did not his servant say whether he belonged to the Kellynch family?'

'No, ma'am, – he did not mention no particular family; but he said his master was a very rich gentleman, and would be a baronight some day.'

'There! you see!' cried Mary, in an ecstasy, 'Just as I said! Heir to Sir Walter Elliot! – I was sure that would come out, if it was so. Depend upon it, that is a circumstance which his servants take care to publish wherever he goes. But, Anne, only conceive how extraordinary! I wish I had looked at him more. I wish we had been aware in time, who it was, that he might have been introduced to us. What a pity that we should not have been introduced to each other! – Do you think he had the Elliot countenance? I hardly looked at him, I was looking at the horses; but I think he had something of the Elliot countenance. I wonder the arms did not strike me! Oh! – the great-coat was hanging over the panel, and hid the arms; so it did, otherwise, I am sure, I should have observed them, and the livery too; if the servant had not been in mourning, one should have known him by the livery.'

'Putting all these very extraordinary circumstances together,' said Captain Wentworth, 'we must consider it to be the arrangement of Providence, that you should not be introduced to your cousin.'

When she could command Mary's attention, Anne quietly tried to convince her that their father and Mr Elliot had not, for many years, been on such terms as to make the power of attempting an introduction at all desirable.

At the same time, however, it was a secret gratification to herself to have seen her cousin, and to know that the future owner of Kellynch was undoubtedly a gentleman, and had an air of good sense. She would not, upon any account, mention her having met with him the second time;

luckily Mary did not much attend to their having passed close by him in their early walk, but she would have felt quite ill-used by Anne's having actually run against him in the passage, and received his very polite excuses, while she had never been near him at all; no, that cousinly little interview must remain a perfect secret.

'Of course,' said Mary, 'you will mention our seeing Mr Elliot, the next time you write to Bath. I think my father certainly ought to hear of it; do mention all about him.'

Anne avoided a direct reply, but it was just the circumstance which she considered as not merely unnecessary to be communicated, but as what ought to be suppressed. The offence which had been given her father, many years back, she knew; Elizabeth's particular share in it she suspected; and that Mr Elliot's idea always produced irritation in both, was beyond a doubt. Mary never wrote to Bath herself; all the toil of keeping up a slow and unsatisfactory correspondence with Elizabeth fell on Anne.

Breakfast had not been long over, when they were joined by Captain and Mrs Harville, and Captain Benwick, with whom they had appointed to take their last walk about Lyme. They ought to be setting off for Uppercross by one, and in the meanwhile were to be all together, and out of doors as long as they could.

Anne found Captain Benwick getting near her, as soon as they were all fairly in the street. Their conversation, the preceding evening, did not disincline him to seek her again; and they walked together some time, talking as before of Mr Scott and Lord Byron, and still as unable, as before, and as unable as any other two readers, to think exactly alike of the merits of either, till something occasioned an almost general change amongst their party, and instead of Captain Benwick, she had Captain Harville by her side.

'Miss Elliot,' said he, speaking rather low, 'you have done a good deed in making that poor fellow talk so much. I wish he could have such company oftener. It is bad for him, I know, to be shut up as he is; but what can we do? we cannot part.'

'No,' said Anne, 'that I can easily believe to be impossible; but in time perhaps – we know what time does in every case of affliction, and you must remember, Captain Harville, that your friend may yet be called a young mourner – Only last summer, I understand.'

'Ay, true enough,' (with a deep sigh) 'only June.'

'And not known to him, perhaps, so soon.'

'Not till the first week in August, when he came home from the Cape, – just made into the Grappler. I was at Plymouth, dreading to hear of him; he sent in letters, but the Grappler was under orders for Portsmouth. There the news must follow him, but who was to tell it? not I. I would as soon have been run up to the yard-arm. Nobody could do it, but that good fellow, (pointing to Captain Wentworth.) The Laconia had come into Plymouth the week before; no danger of her being sent to sea again. He stood his chance for the rest – wrote up for leave of absence, but without waiting the return, travelled night and day till he got to Portsmouth, rowed off to the Grappler that instant, and never left the poor fellow for a week; that's what he did, and nobody else could have saved poor James. You may think, Miss Elliot, whether he is dear to us!'

Anne did think on the question with perfect decision, and said as much in reply as her own feelings could accomplish, or as his seemed able to bear, for he was too much affected to renew the subject – and when he spoke again, it was of something totally different.

Mrs Harville's giving it as her opinion that her husband would have quite walking enough by the time he reached home, determined the direction of all the party in what was to be their last walk; they would accompany them to their door, and then return and set off themselves. By all their calculations there was just time for this; but as they drew near the Cobb, there was such a general wish to walk along it once more, all were so inclined, and Louisa soon grew so determined, that the difference of a quarter of an hour, it was found, would be no difference at all, so with all the kind leave-taking, and all the kind interchange of invitations and promises which may be imagined, they parted from Captain and Mrs Harville at their own door, and still accompanied by Captain Benwick, who seemed to cling to them to the last, proceeded to make the proper adieus to the Cobb.

Anne found Captain Benwick again drawing near her. Lord Byron's 'dark blue seas' could not fail of being brought forward by their present view, and she gladly gave him all her attention as long as attention was possible. It was soon drawn per force another way.

There was too much wind to make the high part of the new Cobb pleasant for the ladies, and they agreed to get down the steps to the lower, and all were contented to pass quietly and carefully down the steep flight, excepting Louisa; she must be jumped down them by Captain Wentworth. In all their walks, he had had to jump her from the stiles; the sensation was delightful to her. The hardness of the pavement for her feet, made him less willing upon the present occasion; he did it, however; she was safely down, and instantly, to shew her enjoyment, ran up the steps to be jumped down again. He advised her against it, thought the jar too great; but no, he reasoned and talked in vain; she smiled and said, 'I am determined I will:' he put out his hands; she was too precipitate by half a second, she fell on the pavement on the Lower Cobb, and was taken up lifeless!

There was no wound, no blood, no visible bruise; but her eyes were closed, she breathed not, her face was like death. – The horror of that moment to all who stood around!

Captain Wentworth, who had caught her up, knelt with her in his arms, looking on her with a face as pallid as her own, in an agony of silence. 'She is dead! she is dead!' screamed Mary, catching hold of her husband, and contributing with his own horror to make him immoveable; and in another moment, Henrietta, sinking under the conviction, lost her senses too, and would have fallen on the steps, but for Captain Benwick and Anne, who caught and supported her between them.

'Is there no one to help me?' were the first words which burst from Captain Wentworth, in a tone of despair, and as if all his own strength were gone.

'Go to him, go to him,' cried Anne, 'for heaven's sake go to him. I can support her myself. Leave me, and go to him. Rub her hands, rub her temples; here are salts, – take them, take them.'

Looking on her with a face as pallid as her own

Captain Benwick obeyed, and Charles at the same moment, disengaging himself from his wife, they were both with him; and Louisa was raised up and supported more firmly between them, and every thing was done that Anne had prompted, but in vain; while Captain Wentworth, staggering against the wall for his support, exclaimed in the bitterest agony,

'Oh God! her father and mother!'

'A surgeon!' said Anne.

He caught the word; it seemed to rouse him at once, and saying only 'True, true, a surgeon this instant,' was darting away, when Anne eagerly suggested,

'Captain Benwick, would not it be better for Captain Benwick? He knows where a surgeon is to be found.'

Every one capable of thinking felt the advantage of the idea, and in a moment (it was all done in rapid moments) Captain Benwick had resigned the poor corpse-like figure entirely to the brother's care, and was off for the town with the utmost rapidity.

As to the wretched party left behind, it could scarcely be said which of the three, who were completely rational, was suffering most, Captain Wentworth, Anne, or Charles, who, really a very affectionate brother, hung over Louisa with sobs of grief, and could only turn his eyes from one sister, to see the other in a state as insensible, or to witness the hysterical agitations of his wife, calling on him for help which he could not give.

Anne, attending with all the strength and zeal, and thought, which instinct supplied, to Henrietta, still tried, at intervals, to suggest comfort to the others, tried to quiet Mary, to animate Charles, to assuage the feelings of Captain Wentworth. Both seemed to look to her for directions.

'Anne, Anne,' cried Charles, 'What is to be done next? What, in heaven's name, is to be done next?'

Captain Wentworth's eyes were also turned towards her.

'Had not she better be carried to the inn? Yes, I am sure, carry her gently to the inn.'

'Yes, yes, to the inn,' repeated Captain Wentworth, comparatively collected, and eager to be doing something. 'I will carry her myself. Musgrove, take care of the others.'

By this time the report of the accident had spread among the workmen and boatmen about the Cobb, and many collected near them, to be useful if wanted, at any rate, to enjoy the sight of a dead young lady, nay, two dead young ladies, for it proved twice as fine as the first report. To some of the best-looking of these good people Henrietta was consigned, for, though partially revived, she was quite helpless; and in this manner, Anne walking by her side, and Charles attending to his wife, they set forward, treading back with feelings unutterable, the ground, which so lately, so very lately, and so light of heart, they had passed along.

They were not off the Cobb, before the Harvilles met them. Captain Benwick had been seen flying by their house, with a countenance which shewed something to be wrong; and they had set off immediately, informed and directed, as they passed, toward the spot. Shocked as Captain Harville was, he brought senses and nerves that could be instantly useful; and a look between him and his wife decided what was to be done. She must be taken to their house – all must go to their house – and await the surgeon's arrival there. They would not listen to scruples: he was obeyed; they were all beneath his roof; and while Louisa, under Mrs Harville's direction, was conveyed up stairs, and given possession of her own bed, assistance, cordials, restoratives were supplied by her husband to all who needed them.

Louisa had once opened her eyes but soon closed them again, without apparent consciousness. This had been a proof of life, however, of service to her sister; and Henrietta, though perfectly incapable of being in the same room with Louisa, was kept, by the agitation of hope and fear, from a return of her own insensibility. Mary, too, was growing calmer.

The surgeon was with them almost before it had seemed possible. They were sick with horror while he examined; but he was not hopeless. The head had received a severe contusion, but he had seen greater injuries recovered from: he was by no means hopeless; he spoke cheerfully.

That he did not regard it as a desperate case – that he did not say a few hours must end it – was at first felt, beyond the hope of most; and the ecstasy of such a reprieve, the rejoicing, deep and silent, after a few fervent ejaculations of gratitude to Heaven had been offered, may be conceived.

The tone, the look, with which 'Thank God!' was uttered by Captain Wentworth, Anne was sure could never be forgotten by her; nor the sight of them afterwards, as he sat near a table, leaning over it with folded arms, and face concealed, as if overpowered by the various feelings of his soul, and trying by prayer and reflection to calm them.

Louisa's limbs had escaped. There was no injury but to the head.

It now became necessary for the party to consider what was best to be done, as to their general situation. They were now able to speak to each other, and consult. That Louisa must remain where she was, however distressing to her friends to be involving the Harvilles in such trouble, did not admit a doubt. Her removal was impossible. The Harvilles silenced all scruples; and, as much as they could, all gratitude. They had looked forward and arranged every thing, before the others began to reflect. Captain Benwick must give up his room to them, and get a bed elsewhere – and the whole was settled. They were only concerned that the house could accommodate no more; and yet perhaps by 'putting the children away in the maids' room, or swinging a cot somewhere,' they could hardly bear to think of not finding room for two or three besides, supposing they might wish to stay; though, with regard to any attendance on Miss Musgrove, there need not be the least uneasiness in leaving her to Mrs Harville's care entirely. Mrs Harville was a very experienced nurse; and her nursery-maid, who had lived with her long and gone about with her every where, was just such another. Between those two, she could want no possible attendance by day or night. And all this was said with a truth and sincerity of feeling irresistible.

Charles, Henrietta, and Captain Wentworth were the three in consultation, and for a little while it was only an interchange of perplexity and terror. 'Uppercross, – the necessity of some one's going to Uppercross, – the news to be conveyed – how it could be broken to Mr and Mrs Musgrove – the lateness of the morning, – an hour already gone since they ought to have been off, – the impossibility of being in tolerable time.' At first, they were capable of nothing more to the purpose than such exclamations; but, after a while, Captain Wentworth, exerting himself, said,

'We must be decided, and without the loss of another minute. Every minute is valuable. Some must resolve on being off for Uppercross instantly. Musgrove, either you or I must go.'

Charles agreed; but declared his resolution of not going away. He would be as little incumbrance as possible to Captain and Mrs Harville; but as to leaving his sister in such a state, he neither ought, nor would. So far it was decided; and Henrietta at first declared the same. She, however, was soon persuaded to think differently. The usefulness of her staying! – She, who had not been able to remain in Louisa's room, or to look at her, without sufferings which made her worse than helpless! She was forced to acknowledge that she could do no good; yet was still unwilling to be away, till touched by the thought of her father and mother, she gave it up; she consented, she was anxious to be at home.

The plan had reached this point, when Anne, coming quietly down from Louisa's room, could not but hear what followed, for the parlour door was open.

'Then it is settled, Musgrove,' cried Captain Wentworth, 'that you stay, and that I take care of your sister home. But as to the rest; – as to the others; – If one stays to assist Mrs Harville, I think it need be only one. – Mrs Charles Musgrove will, of course, wish to get back to her children; but, if Anne will stay, no one so proper, so capable as Anne!'

She paused a moment to recover from the emotion of hearing herself so spoken of. The other two warmly agreed to what he said, and she then appeared.

'You will stay, I am sure; you will stay and nurse her;' cried he, turning to her and speaking with a flow, and yet a gentleness, which seemed almost restoring the past. – She coloured deeply; and he recollected himself, and moved away. – She expressed herself most willing, ready, happy to remain.

'It was what she had been thinking of, and wishing to be allowed to do. – A bed on the floor in Louisa's room would be sufficient for her, if Mrs Harville would but think so.'

One thing more, and all seemed arranged. Though it was rather desirable that Mr and Mrs Musgrove should be previously alarmed by some share of delay; yet the time required by the Uppercross horses to take them back, would be a dreadful extension of suspense; and Captain Wentworth proposed, and Charles Musgrove agreed, that it would be much better for him to take a chaise from the inn, and leave Mr Musgrove's carriage and horses to be sent home the next morning early, when there would be the farther advantage of sending an account of Louisa's night.

Captain Wentworth now hurried off to get every thing ready on his part, and to be soon followed by the two ladies. When the plan was made known to Mary, however, there was an end of all peace in it. She was so wretched, and so vehement, complained so much of injustice in being expected to go away, instead of Anne; – Anne, who was nothing to Louisa, while she was her sister, and had the best right to stay in Henrietta's stead! Why was not she to be as useful as Anne? And to go home without Charles, too – without her husband! No, it was too unkind! And, in short, she said more than her husband could long withstand; and as none of the others could oppose when he gave way, there was no help for it: the change of Mary for Anne was inevitable.

Anne had never submitted more reluctantly to the jealous and ill-judging claims of Mary; but so it must be, and they set off for the town, Charles taking care of his sister, and Captain Benwick attending to her. She gave a moment's recollection, as they hurried along, to the little circumstances which the same spots had witnessed earlier in the morning. There she had listened to Henrietta's schemes for Dr Shirley's leaving Uppercross; farther on, she had first seen Mr Elliot; a moment seemed all that could now be given to any one but Louisa, or those who were wrapt up in her welfare.

Captain Benwick was most considerately attentive to her; and, united as they seemed by the distress of the day, she felt an increasing degree of good-will towards him, and a pleasure even in thinking that it might, perhaps, be the occasion of continuing their acquaintance.

Captain Wentworth was on the watch for them, and a chaise and four in waiting, stationed for their convenience in the lowest part of the street; but his evident surprise and vexation, at the substitution of one sister for the other – the change of his countenance – the astonishment – the expressions begun and suppressed, with which Charles was listened to, made but a mortifying reception of Anne; or must at least convince her that she was valued only as she could be useful to Louisa.

She endeavoured to be composed, and to be just. Without emulating the feelings of an Emma towards her Henry, she would have attended on Louisa with a zeal above the common claims of regard, for his sake; and she hoped he would not long be so unjust as to suppose she would shrink unnecessarily from the office of a friend.

In the meantime she was in the carriage. He had handed them both in, and placed himself between them; and in this manner, under these circumstances full of astonishment and emotion to Anne, she quitted Lyme. How the long stage would pass; how it was to affect their manners; what was to be their sort of intercourse, she could not foresee. It was all quite natural, however. He was devoted to Henrietta; always turning towards her; and when he spoke at all, always with the view of supporting her hopes and raising her spirits. In general, his voice and manner were studiously calm. To spare Henrietta from agitation seemed the governing principle. Once only, when she had been grieving over the last ill-judged, ill-fated walk to the Cobb, bitterly lamenting that it ever had been thought of, he burst forth, as if wholly overcome –

'Don't talk of it, don't talk of it,' he cried. 'Oh God! that I had not given way to her at the fatal moment! Had I done as I ought! But so eager and so resolute! Dear, sweet Louisa!'

Anne wondered whether it ever occurred to him now, to question the justness of his own previous opinion as to the universal felicity and advantage of firmness of character; and whether it might not strike him, that, like all other qualities of the mind, it should have its proportions and limits. She thought it could scarcely escape him to feel, that a persuadable temper might sometimes be as much in favour of happiness, as a very resolute character.

They got on fast. Anne was astonished to recognise the same hills and the same objects so soon. Their actual speed, heightened by some dread of the conclusion, made the road appear but half as long as on the day before. It was growing quite dusk, however, before they were in the neighbourhood of Uppercross, and there had been total silence among them for some time, Henrietta leaning back in the corner, with a shawl over her face, giving the hope of her having cried herself to sleep; when, as they were going up their last hill, Anne found herself all at once addressed by Captain Wentworth. In a low, cautious voice, he said,

'I have been considering what we had best do. She must not appear at first. She could not stand it. I have been thinking whether you had not better remain in the carriage with her, while I go in and break it to Mr and Mrs Musgrove. Do you think this a good plan?'

She did: he was satisfied, and said no more. But the remembrance of the appeal remained a pleasure to her – as a proof of friendship, and of deference for her judgment, a great pleasure; and when it became a sort of parting proof, its value did not lessen.

When the distressing communication at Uppercross was over, and he had seen the father and mother quite as composed as could be hoped, and the daughter all the better for being with them, he announced his intention of returning in the same carriage to Lyme; and when the horses were baited, he was off.

CHAPTER THIRTEEN

THE REMAINDER OF ANNE'S time at Uppercross, comprehending only two days, was spent entirely at the mansion-house, and she had the satisfaction of knowing herself extremely useful there, both as an immediate companion, and as assisting in all those arrangements for the future, which, in Mr and Musgrove's distressed state of spirits, would have been difficulties.

They had an early account from Lyme the next morning. Louisa was much the same. No symptoms worse than before had appeared. Charles came a few hours afterwards, to bring a later and more particular account. He was tolerably cheerful. A speedy cure must not be hoped, but every thing was going on as well as the nature of the case admitted. In speaking of the Harvilles, he seemed unable to satisfy his own sense of their kindness, especially of Mrs Harville's exertions as a nurse. 'She really left nothing for Mary to do. He and Mary had been persuaded to go early to their inn last night. Mary had been hysterical again this morning. When he came away, she was going to walk out with Captain Benwick, which, he hoped, would do her good. He almost wished she had been prevailed on to come home the day before; but the truth was, that Mrs Harville left nothing for any body to do.'

Charles was to return to Lyme the same afternoon, and his father had at first half a mind to go with him, but the ladies could not consent. It would be going only to multiply trouble to the others, and increase his own distress; and a much better scheme followed and was acted upon. A chaise was sent for from Crewkherne, and Charles conveyed back a far more useful person in the old nursery-maid of the family, one who having brought up all the children, and seen the very last, the lingering and long-petted master Harry, sent to school after his brothers, was now living in her deserted nursery to mend stockings, and dress all the blains and bruises she could get near her, and who, consequently, was only too happy in being allowed to go and help nurse dear Miss Louisa. Vague wishes of getting Sarah thither, had occurred before to Mrs Musgrove and Henrietta; but without Anne, it would hardly have been resolved on, and found practicable so soon.

They were indebted, the next day, to Charles Hayter for all the minute knowledge of Louisa, which it was so essential to obtain every twenty-four hours. He made it his business to go to Lyme, and his account was still encouraging. The intervals of sense and consciousness were believed to be stronger. Every report agreed in Captain Wentworth's appearing fixed in Lyme.

Anne was to leave them on the morrow, an event which they all dreaded. 'What should they do without her? They were wretched comforters for one another!' And so much was said in this way, that Anne thought she could not do better than impart among them the general inclination to which she was privy, and persuade them all to go to Lyme at once. She had little difficulty; it was soon determined that they would go, go to-morrow, fix themselves at the inn, or get into lodgings, as it suited, and there remain till dear Louisa could be moved. They must be taking off some trouble from the good people she was with; they might at least relieve Mrs Harville from the care of her own children; and in short they were so happy in the decision, that Anne was delighted with what she had done, and felt that she could not spend her last morning at Uppercross better than in assisting their preparations, and sending them off at an early hour, though her being left to the solitary range of the house was the consequence.

She was the last, excepting the little boys at the cottage, she was the very last, the only remaining one of all that had filled and animated both houses, of all that had given Uppercross its cheerful character. A few days had made a change indeed!

If Louisa recovered, it would all be well again. More than former happiness would be restored. There could not be a doubt, to her mind there was none, of what would follow her recovery. A few months hence, and the room now so deserted, occupied but by her silent, pensive self, might be filled again with all that was happy and gay, all that was glowing and bright in prosperous love, all that was most unlike Anne Elliot!

An hour's complete leisure for such reflections as these, on a dark November day, a small thick rain almost blotting out the very few objects ever to be discerned from the windows, was enough to make the sound of Lady Russell's carriage exceedingly welcome; and yet, though desirous to be gone, she could not quit the mansion-house, or look an adieu to the cottage, with its black, dripping, and comfortless veranda, or even notice through the misty glasses the last humble tenements of the village, without a saddened heart. – Scenes had passed in Uppercross, which made it precious. It stood the record of many sensations of pain, once severe, but now softened; and of some instances of relenting feeling, some breathings of friendship and reconciliation, which could never be looked for again, and which could never cease to be dear. She left it all behind her; all but the recollection that such things had been.

Anne had never entered Kellynch since her quitting Lady Russell's house, in September. It had not been necessary, and the few occasions of its being possible for her to go to the hall she had contrived to evade and escape from. Her first return, was to resume her place in the modern and elegant apartments of the lodge, and to gladden the eyes of its mistress.

There was some anxiety mixed with Lady Russell's joy in meeting her. She knew who had been frequenting Uppercross. But happily, either Anne was improved in plumpness and looks, or Lady Russell fancied her so; and Anne, in receiving her compliments on the occasion, had the amusement of connecting them with the silent admiration of her cousin, and of hoping that she was to be blessed with a second spring of youth and beauty.

When they came to converse, she was soon sensible of some mental change. The subjects of which her heart had been full on leaving Kellynch, and which she had felt slighted, and been compelled to smother among the Musgroves, were now become but of secondary interest. She had lately lost sight even of her father and sister and Bath. Their concerns had been sunk under those of Uppercross, and when Lady Russell reverted to their former hopes and fears, and spoke her satisfaction in the house in Camden-place, which had been taken, and her regret that Mrs Clay should still be with them, Anne would have been ashamed to have it known, how much more she was thinking of Lyme, and Louisa Musgrove, and all her acquaintance there; how much more interesting to her was the home and the friendship of the Harvilles and Captain Benwick, than her own father's house in Camden-place, or her own sister's intimacy with Mrs Clay. She was actually forced to exert herself, to meet Lady Russell with any thing like the appearance of equal solicitude, on topics which had by nature the first claim on her.

There was a little awkwardness at first in their discourse on another subject. They must speak of the accident at Lyme. Lady Russell had not been arrived five minutes the day before, when a full account of the whole had burst on her; but still it must be talked of, she must make enquiries, she must regret the imprudence, lament the result, and Captain Wentworth's name must be mentioned by both. Anne was conscious of not doing it so well as Lady Russell. She could not speak the name, and look straight forward to Lady Russell's eye, till she had adopted the expedient of telling her briefly what she thought of the attachment between him and Louisa. When this was told, his name distressed her no longer.

Lady Russell had only to listen composedly, and wish them happy; but internally her heart revelled in angry pleasure, in pleased contempt, that the man who at twenty-three had seemed to understand somewhat of the value of an Anne Elliot, should, eight years afterwards, be charmed by a Louisa Musgrove.

The first three or four days passed most quietly, with no circumstance to mark them excepting the receipt of a note or two from Lyme, which found their way to Anne, she could not tell how, and brought a rather improving account of Louisa. At the end of that period, Lady Russell's politeness could repose no longer, and the fainter self-threatenings of the past, became in a decided tone, 'I must call on Mrs Croft; I really must call upon her soon. Anne, have you courage to go with me, and pay a visit in that house? It will be some trial to us both.'

Anne did not shrink from it; on the contrary, she truly felt as she said, in observing,

'I think you are very likely to suffer the most of the two; your feelings are less reconciled to the change than mine. By remaining in the neighbourhood, I am become inured to it.'

She could have said more on the subject; for she had in fact so high an opinion of the Crofts, and considered her father so very fortunate in his tenants, felt the parish to be so sure of a good example, and the poor of the best attention and relief, that however sorry and ashamed for the necessity of the removal, she could not but in conscience feel that they were gone who deserved not to stay, and that Kellynch-hall had passed into better hands than its owners'. These convictions must unquestionably have their own pain, and severe was its kind; but they precluded that pain which Lady Russell would suffer in entering the house again, and returning through the well-known apartments.

In such moments Anne had no power of saying to herself, 'These rooms ought to belong only to us. Oh, how fallen in their destination! How unworthily occupied! An ancient family to be so driven away! Strangers filling their place!' No, except when she thought of her mother, and remembered where she had been used to sit and preside, she had no sigh of that description to heave.

Mrs Croft always met her with a kindness which gave her the pleasure of fancying herself a favourite; and on the present occasion, receiving her in that house, there was particular attention.

The sad accident at Lyme was soon the prevailing topic; and on comparing their latest accounts of the invalid, it appeared that each lady dated her intelligence from the same hour of yester morn, that Captain Wentworth had been in Kellynch yesterday – (the first time since the accident) had brought Anne the last note, which she had not been able to trace the exact steps of, had staid a few hours and then returned again to Lyme – and without any present intention of quitting it any more. – He had enquired after her, she found, particularly; – had expressed his hope of Miss Elliot's not being the worse for her exertions, and had spoken of those exertions as great. – This was handsome, – and gave her more pleasure than almost any thing else could have done.

As to the sad catastrophe itself, it could be canvassed only in one style by a couple of steady, sensible women, whose judgments had to work on ascertained events; and it was perfectly decided that it had been the consequence of much thoughtlessness and much imprudence; that its effects were most alarming, and that it was frightful to think, how long Miss Musgrove's recovery might yet be doubtful, and how liable she would still remain to suffer from the concussion hereafter! – The Admiral wound it all up summarily by exclaiming,

'Ay, a very bad business indeed. – A new sort of way this, for a young fellow to be making love, by breaking his mistress's head! – is not it, Miss Elliot? – This is breaking a head and giving a plaister truly!'

Admiral Croft's manners were not quite of the tone to suit Lady Russell, but they delighted Anne. His goodness of heart and simplicity of character were irresistible.

'Now, this must be very bad for you,' said he, suddenly rousing from a little reverie, 'to be coming and finding us here. – I had not recollected it before, I declare, – but it must be very bad. – But now, do not stand upon ceremony. – Get up and go over all the rooms in the house if you like it.'

'Another time, Sir, I thank you, not now.'

'Well, whenever it suits you. – You can slip in from the shrubbery at any time. And there you will find we keep our umbrellas, hanging up by that door. A good place, is not it? But' (checking himself) 'you will not think it a good place, for yours were always kept in the butler's room. Ay, so it always is, I believe. One man's ways may be as good as another's, but we all like our own best. And so you must judge for yourself, whether it would be better for you to go about the house or not.'

Anne, finding she might decline it, did so, very gratefully.

'We have made very few changes either!' continued the Admiral, after thinking a moment. 'Very few. – We told you about the laundry-door, at Uppercross. That has been a very great improvement. The wonder was, how any family upon earth could bear with the inconvenience of its opening as it did, so long! – You will tell Sir Walter what we have done, and that Mr Shepherd thinks it the greatest improvement the house ever had. Indeed, I must do ourselves the justice to say, that the few alterations we have made have been all very much for the better. My wife should have the credit of them, however. I have done very little besides sending away some of the large looking-glasses from my dressing-room, which was your father's. A very good man, and very much the gentleman I am sure – but I should think, Miss Elliot' (looking with serious reflection) 'I should think he must be rather a dressy man for his time of life. – Such a number of looking-glasses! oh Lord! there was no getting away from oneself. So I got Sophy to lend me a hand, and we soon shifted their quarters; and now I am quite snug, with my little shaving glass in one corner, and another great thing that I never go near.'

Anne, amused in spite of herself, was rather distressed for an answer, and the Admiral, fearing he might not have been civil enough, took up the subject again, to say,

'The next time you write to your good father, Miss Elliot, pray give him my compliments and Mrs Croft's, and say that we are settled here quite to our liking, and have no fault at all to find with the place. The breakfast-room chimney smokes a little, I grant you, but it is only when the wind is due north and blows hard, which may not happen three times a winter. And take it altogether, now that we have been into most of the houses hereabouts and can judge, there is not one that we like better than this. Pray say so, with my compliments. He will be glad to hear it.'

Lady Russell and Mrs Croft were very well pleased with each other; but the acquaintance which this visit began, was fated not to proceed far at present; for when it was returned, the Crofts announced themselves to be going away for a few weeks, to visit their connexions in the north of the county, and probably might not be at home again before Lady Russell would be removing to Bath.

So ended all danger to Anne of meeting Captain Wentworth at Kellynch-hall, or of seeing him in company with her friend. Every thing was safe enough, and she smiled over the many anxious feelings she had wasted on the subject.

CHAPTER FOURTEEN

THOUGH CHARLES AND MARY had remained at Lyme much longer after Mr and Mrs Musgrove's going, than Anne conceived they could have been at all wanted, they were yet the first of the family to be at home again, and as soon as possible after their return to Uppercross, they drove over to the lodge. – They had left Louisa beginning to sit up; but her head, though clear, was exceedingly weak, and her nerves susceptible to the highest extreme of tenderness; and though she might be pronounced to be altogether doing very well, it was still impossible to say when she might be able to bear the removal home; and her father and mother, who must return in time to receive their younger children for the Christmas holidays, had hardly a hope of being allowed to bring her with them.

They had been all in lodgings together. Mrs Musgrove had got Mrs Harville's children away as much as she could, every possible supply from

Uppercross had been furnished, to lighten the inconvenience to the Harvilles, while the Harvilles had been wanting them to come to dinner every day; and in short, it seemed to have been only a struggle on each side as to which should be most disinterested and hospitable.

Mary had had her evils; but upon the whole, as was evident by her staying so long, she had found more to enjoy than to suffer. – Charles Hayter had been at Lyme oftener than suited her, and when they dined with the Harvilles there had been only a maid-servant to wait, and at first, Mrs Harville had always given Mrs Musgrove precedence; but then, she had received so very handsome an apology from her on finding out whose daughter she was, and there had been so much going on every day, there had been so many walks between their lodgings and the Harvilles, and she had got books from the library and changed them so often, that the balance had certainly been much in favour of Lyme. She had been taken to Charmouth too, and she had bathed, and she had gone to church, and there were a great many more people to look at in the church at Lyme than at Uppercross, – and all this, joined to the sense of being so very useful, had made really an agreeable fortnight.

Anne enquired after Captain Benwick. Mary's face was clouded directly. Charles laughed.

'Oh! Captain Benwick is very well, I believe, but he is a very odd young man. I do not know what he would be at. We asked him to come home with us for a day or two; Charles undertook to give him some shooting, and he seemed quite delighted, and for my part, I thought it was all settled; when behold! on Tuesday night, he made a very awkward sort of excuse; "he never shot" and he had "been quite misunderstood," – and he had promised this and he had promised that, and the end of it was, I found, that he did not mean to come. I suppose he was afraid of finding it dull; but upon my word I should have thought we were lively enough at the Cottage for such a heart-broken man as Captain Benwick.'

Charles laughed again and said, 'Now Mary, you know very well how it really was. – It was all your doing,' (turning to Anne.) 'He fancied that if he went with us, he should find you close by; he fancied every body to be living in Uppercross; and when he discovered that Lady Russell lived three miles off, his heart failed him, and he had not courage to come. That is the fact, upon my honour. Mary knows it is.'

But Mary did not give in to it very graciously; whether from not considering Captain Benwick entitled by birth and situation to be in love with an Elliot, or from not wanting to believe Anne a greater attraction to Uppercross than herself, must be left to be guessed. Anne's good-will, however, was not to be lessened by what she heard. She boldly acknowledged herself flattered, and continued her enquiries.

'Oh! he talks of you,' cried Charles, 'in such terms,' – Mary interrupted him. 'I declare, Charles, I never heard him mention Anne twice all the time I was there. I declare, Anne, he never talks of you at all.'

'No,' admitted Charles, 'I do not know that he ever does, in a general way – but however, it is a very clear thing that he admires you exceedingly. – His head is full of some books that he is reading upon your recommendation, and he wants to talk to you about them; he has found out something or other in one of them which he thinks – Oh! I cannot pretend to remember it, but it was something very fine – I overheard him telling Henrietta all about it – and then "Miss Elliot" was spoken of in the highest terms! – No Mary, I declare it was so, I heard it myself, and you were in the other room. – "Elegance, sweetness, beauty," Oh! there was no end of Miss Elliot's charms.'

'And I am sure,' cried Mary warmly, 'it was very little to his credit, if he did. Miss Harville only died last June. Such a heart is very little worth having; is it, Lady Russell? I am sure you will agree with me.'

'I must see Captain Benwick before I decide,' said Lady Russell, smiling.

'And that you are very likely to do very soon, I can tell you, ma'am,' said Charles. 'Though he had not nerves for coming away with us and setting off again afterwards to pay a formal visit here, he will make his way over to Kellynch one day by himself, you may depend on it. I told him the distance and the road, and I told him of the church's being so very well worth seeing, for as he has a taste for those sort of things, I thought that would be a good excuse, and he listened with all his understanding and soul; and I am sure from his manner that you will have him calling here soon. So, I give you notice, Lady Russell.'

'Any acquaintance of Anne's will always be welcome to me,' was Lady Russell's kind answer.

'Oh! as to being Ann's acquaintance,' said Mary, 'I think he is rather my acquaintance, for I have been seeing him every day this last fortnight.'

'Well, as your joint acquaintance, then, I shall be very happy to see Captain Benwick.'

'You will not find any thing very agreeable in him, I assure you, ma'am. He is one of the dullest young men that ever lived. He has walked with me, sometimes, from one end of the sands to the other, without saying a word. He is not at all a well-bred young man. I am sure you will not like him.'

'There we differ, Mary,' said Anne. 'I think Lady Russell would like him. I think she would be so much pleased with his mind, that she would very soon see no deficiency in his manner.'

'So do I, Anne,' said Charles. 'I am sure Lady Russell would like him. He is just Lady Russell's sort. Give him a book, and he will read all day long.'

'Yes, that he will!' exclaimed Mary, tauntingly. 'He will sit poring over his book, and not know when a person speaks to him, or when one drops one's scissors, or any thing that happens. Do you think Lady Russell would like that?'

Lady Russell could not help laughing. 'Upon my word,' said she, 'I should not have supposed that my opinion of any one could have admitted of such difference of conjecture, steady and matter of fact as I may call myself. I have really a curiosity to see the person who can give occasion to such directly opposite notions. I wish he may be induced to call here. And when he does, Mary, you may depend upon hearing my opinion; but I am determined not to judge him before-hand.'

'You will not like him, I will answer for it.'

Lady Russell began talking of something else. Mary spoke with animation of their meeting with, or rather missing, Mr Elliot so extraordinarily.

'He is a man,' said Lady Russell, 'whom I have no wish to see. His declining to be on cordial terms with the head of his family, has left a very strong impression in his disfavour with me.'

This decision checked Mary's eagerness, and stopped her short in the midst of the Elliot countenance.

With regard to Captain Wentworth, though Anne hazarded no enquiries, there was voluntary communication sufficient. His spirits had been greatly recovering lately, as might be expected. As Louisa improved, he had improved; and he was now quite a different creature from what he had been the first week. He had not seen Louisa; and was so extremely fearful of any ill consequence to her from an interview, that he did not press for it at all; and, on the contrary, seemed to have a plan of going away for a week or ten days, till her head were stronger. He had talked of going down to Plymouth for a week, and wanted to persuade Captain Benwick to go with him; but, as Charles maintained to the last, Captain Benwick seemed much more disposed to ride over to Kellynch.

There can be no doubt that Lady Russell and Anne were both occasionally thinking of Captain Benwick, from this time. Lady Russell could not hear the door-bell without feeling that it might be his herald; nor could Anne return from any stroll of solitary indulgence in her father's grounds, or any visit of charity in the village, without wondering whether she might see him or hear of him. Captain Benwick came not, however. He was either less disposed for it than Charles had imagined, or he was too shy; and after giving him a week's indulgence, Lady Russell determined him to be unworthy of the interest which he had been beginning to excite.

The Musgroves came back to receive their happy boys and girls from school, bringing with them Mrs Harville's little children, to improve the noise of Uppercross, and lessen that of Lyme. Henrietta remained with

Louisa; but all the rest of the family were again in their usual quarters.

Lady Russell and Anne paid their compliments to them once, when Anne could not but feel that Uppercross was already quite alive again. Though neither Henrietta, nor Louisa, nor Charles Hayter, nor Captain Wentworth were there, the room presented as strong a contrast as could be wished, to the last state she had seen it in.

Immediately surrounding Mrs Musgrove were the little Harvilles, whom she was sedulously guarding from the tyranny of the two children from the Cottage, expressly arrived to amuse them. On one side was a table, occupied by some chattering girls, cutting up silk and gold paper; and on the other were tressels and trays, bending under the weight of brawn and cold pies, where riotous boys were holding high revel; the whole completed by a roaring Christmas fire, which seemed determined to be heard, in spite of all the noise of the others. Charles and Mary also came in, of course, during their visit; and Mr Musgrove made a point of paying his respects to Lady Russell, and sat down close to her for ten minutes, talking with a very raised voice, but, from the clamour of the children on his knees, generally in vain. It was a fine family-piece.

Anne, judging from her own temperament, would have deemed such a domestic hurricane a bad restorative of the nerves, which Louisa's illness must have so greatly shaken; but Mrs Musgrove, who got Anne near her on purpose to thank her most cordially, again and again, for all her attentions to them, concluded a short recapitulation of what she had suffered herself, by observing, with a happy glance round the room, that after all she had gone through, nothing was so likely to do her good as a little quiet cheerfulness at home.

Louisa was now recovering apace. Her mother could even think of her being able to join their party at home, before her brothers and sisters went to school again. The Harvilles had promised to come with her and stay at Uppercross, whenever she returned. Captain Wentworth was gone, for the present, to see his brother in Shropshire.

'I hope I shall remember, in future,' said Lady Russell, as soon as they were reseated in the carriage, 'not to call at Uppercross in the Christmas holidays.'

Every body has their taste in noises as well as in other matters; and sounds are quite innoxious, or most distressing, by their sort rather than their quantity. When Lady Russell, not long afterwards, was entering Bath on a wet afternoon, and driving through the long course of streets from the Old Bridge to Camden-place, amidst the dash of other carriages, the heavy rumble of carts and drays, the bawling of newsmen, muffin-men and milk-men, and the ceaseless clink of pattens, she made no complaint. No, these were noises which belonged to the winter pleasures; her spirits rose under

Talking with a very raised voice

their influence; and, like Mrs Musgrove, she was feeling, though not saying, that, after being long in the country, nothing could be so good for her as a little quiet cheerfulness.

Anne did not share these feelings. She persisted in a very determined, though very silent, disinclination for Bath; caught the first dim view of the extensive buildings, smoking in rain, without any wish of seeing them better; felt their progress through the streets to be, however disagreeable, yet too rapid; for who would be glad to see her when she arrived? And looked back, with fond regret, to the bustles of Uppercross and the seclusion of Kellynch.

Elizabeth's last letter had communicated a piece of news of some interest. Mr Elliot was in Bath. He had called in Camden-place; had called a second time, a third; had been pointedly attentive: if Elizabeth and her father did not deceive themselves, had been taking as much pains to seek the acquaintance, and proclaim the value of the connection, as he had formerly taken pains to shew neglect. This was very wonderful, if it were true; and

Lady Russell was in a state of very agreeable curiosity and perplexity about Mr Elliot, already recanting the sentiment she had so lately expressed to Mary, of his being 'a man whom she had no wish to see.' She had a great wish to see him. If he really sought to reconcile himself like a dutiful branch, he must be forgiven for having dismembered himself from the paternal tree.

Anne was not animated to an equal pitch by the circumstance; but she felt that she would rather see Mr Elliot again than not, which was more than she could say for many other persons in Bath.

She was put down in Camden-place; and Lady Russell then drove to her own lodgings, in Rivers-street.

CHAPTER FIFTEEN

SIR WALTER HAD TAKEN a very good house in Camden-place, a lofty, dignified situation, such as becomes a man of consequence; and both he and Elizabeth were settled there, much to their satisfaction.

Anne entered it with a sinking heart, anticipating an imprisonment of many months, and anxiously saying to herself, 'Oh! when shall I leave you again?' A degree of unexpected cordiality, however, in the welcome she received, did her good. Her father and sister were glad to see her, for the sake of shewing her the house and furniture, and met her with kindness. Her making a fourth, when they sat down to dinner, was noticed as an advantage.

Mrs Clay was very pleasant, and very smiling; but her courtesies and smiles were more a matter of course. Anne had always felt that she would pretend what was proper on her arrival; but the complaisance of the others was unlooked for. They were evidently in excellent spirits, and she was soon to listen to the causes. They had no inclination to listen to her. After laying out for some compliments of being deeply regretted in their old neighbourhood, which Anne could not pay, they had only a few faint enquiries to make, before the talk must be all their own. Uppercross excited no interest, Kellynch very little, it was all Bath.

They had the pleasure of assuring her that Bath more than answered their expectations in every respect. Their house was undoubtedly the best in Camden-place; their drawing-rooms had many decided advantages over all the others which they had either seen or heard of; and the superiority was not less in the style of the fitting-up, or the taste of the furniture. Their acquaintance was exceedingly sought after. Every body was wanting to visit them. They had drawn back from many introductions, and still were perpetually having cards left by people of whom they knew nothing.

Here were funds of enjoyment! Could Anne wonder that her father and sister were happy? She might not wonder, but she must sigh that her father should feel no degradation in his change; should see nothing to regret in the duties and dignity of the resident land-holder; should find so much to be vain of in the littleness of a town; and she must sigh, and smile, and wonder too, as Elizabeth threw open the folding-doors, and walked with exultation from one drawing-room to the other, boasting of their space, at the possibility of that woman, who had been mistress of Kellynch Hall, finding extent to be proud of between two walls, perhaps thirty feet asunder.

But this was not all which they had to make them happy. They had Mr Elliot, too. Anne had a great deal to hear of Mr Elliot. He was not only pardoned, they were delighted with him. He had been in Bath about a fortnight; (he had passed through Bath in November, in his way to London, when the intelligence of Sir Walter's being settled there had of course reached him, though only twenty-four hours in the place, but he had not been able to avail himself of it); but he had now been a fortnight in Bath, and his first object, on arriving, had been to leave his card in Camden-place, following it up by such assiduous endeavours to meet, and, when they did meet, by such great openness of conduct, such readiness to apologise for the past, such solicitude to be received as a relation again, that their former good understanding was completely re-established.

They had not a fault to find in him. He had explained away all the appearance of neglect on his own side. It had originated in misapprehension entirely. He had never had an idea of throwing himself off; he had feared that he was thrown off, but knew not why; and delicacy had kept him silent. Upon the hint of having spoken disrespectfully or carelessly of the family, and the family honours, he was quite indignant. He, who had ever boasted of being an Elliot, and whose feelings, as to connection, were only too strict to suit the unfeudal tone of the present day! He was astonished, indeed! But his character and general conduct must refute it. He could refer Sir Walter to all who knew him; and, certainly, the pains he had been taking on this, the first opportunity of reconciliation, to be restored to the footing of a relation and heir-presumptive, was a strong proof of his opinions on the subject.

The circumstances of his marriage too were found to admit of much extenuation. This was an article not to be entered on by himself; but a very intimate friend of his, a Colonel Wallis, a highly respectable man, perfectly the gentleman, (and not an ill-looking man, Sir Walter added) who was living in very good style in Marlborough Buildings, and had, at his own particular request, been admitted to their acquaintance through Mr Elliot, had mentioned one or two things relative to the marriage, which made a material difference in the discredit of it.

Colonel Wallis had known Mr Elliot long, had been well acquainted also with his wife, had perfectly understood the whole story. She was certainly not a woman of family, but well educated, accomplished, rich, and excessively in love with his friend. There had been the charm. She had sought him. Without that attraction, not all her money would have tempted Elliot, and Sir Walter was, moreover, assured of her having been a very fine woman. Here was a great deal to soften the business. A very fine woman, with a large fortune, in love with him! Sir Walter seemed to admit it as complete apology, and though Elizabeth could not see the circumstance in quite so favourable a light, she allowed it be a great extenuation.

Mr Elliot had called repeatedly, had dined with them once, evidently delighted by the distinction of being asked, for they gave no dinners in general; delighted, in short, by every proof of cousinly notice, and placing his whole happiness in being on intimate terms in Camden-place.

Anne listened, but without quite understanding it. Allowances, large allowances, she knew, must be made for the ideas of those who spoke. She heard it all under embellishment. All that sounded extravagant or irrational in the progress of the reconciliation might have no origin but in the language of the relators. Still, however, she had the sensation of there being something more than immediately appeared, in Mr Elliot's wishing, after an interval of so many years, to be well received by them. In a worldly view, he had nothing to gain by being on terms with Sir Walter, nothing to risk by a state of variance. In all probability he was already the richer of the two, and the Kellynch estate would as surely be his hereafter as the title. A sensible man! and he had looked like a *very* sensible man, why should it be an object to him? She could only offer one solution; it was, perhaps, for Elizabeth's sake. There might really have been a liking formerly, though convenience and accident had drawn him a different way, and now that he could afford to please himself, he might mean to pay his addresses to her. Elizabeth was certainly very handsome, with well-bred, elegant manners, and her character might never have been penetrated by Mr Elliot, knowing her but in public, and when very young himself. How her temper and understanding might bear the investigation of his present keener time of life was another concern, and rather a fearful one. Most earnestly did she wish that he might not be too nice, or too observant, if Elizabeth were his object; and that Elizabeth was disposed to believe herself so, and that her friend Mrs Clay was encouraging the idea, seemed apparent by a glance or two between them, while Mr Elliot's frequent visits were talked of.

Anne mentioned the glimpses she had had of him at Lyme, but without being much attended to. 'Oh! yes, perhaps, it had been Mr Elliot. They did not know. It might be him, perhaps.' They could not listen to her description of him. They were discribing him themselves; Sir Walter especially. He did justice to his very gentlemanlike appearance, his air of elegance and fashion, his good shaped face, his sensible eye, but, at the same time, 'must lament his being very much under-hung, a defect which time seemed to have increased; nor could he pretend to say that ten years had not altered almost every feature for the worse. Mr Elliot appeared to think that he (Sir Walter) was looking exactly as he had done when they last parted;' but Sir Walter had 'not been able to return the compliment entirely, which had embarrassed him. He did not mean to complain, however. Mr Elliot was better to look at than most men, and he had no objection to being seen with him any where.'

Mr Elliot, and his friends in Marlborough Buildings, were talked of the whole evening. 'Colonel Wallis had been so impatient to be introduced to them! and Mr Elliot so anxious that he should!' And there was a Mrs Wallis, at present only known to them by description, as she was in daily expectation of her confinement; but Mr Elliot spoke of her as 'a most charming woman, quite worthy of being known in Camden-place,' and as soon as she recovered, they were to be acquainted. Sir Walter thought much of Mrs Wallis; she was said to be an excessively pretty woman, beautiful. 'He longed to see her. He hoped she might make some amends for the many very plain faces he was continually passing in the streets. The worst of Bath was, the number of its plain women. He did not mean to say that there were no pretty women, but the number of the plain was out of all proportion. He had frequently observed, as he walked, that one handsome face would be followed by thirty, or five and thirty frights; and once, as he had stood in a shop in Bond-street he had counted eighty-seven women go by, one after another, without there being a tolerable face among them. It had been a frosty morning, to be sure, a sharp frost, which hardly one woman in a thousand could stand the test of. But still, there certainly were a dreadful multitude of ugly women in Bath; and as for the men! they were infinitely worse. Such scare-crows as the streets were full of! It was evident how little the women were used to the sight of any thing tolerable, by the effect which a man of decent appearance produced. He had never walked any where arm in arm with Colonel Wallis, (who was a fine military figure, though sandy-haired) without observing that every woman's eye was upon him; every woman's eye was sure to be upon Colonel Wallis.' Modest Sir Walter! He was not allowed to escape, however. His daughter and Mrs Clay united in hinting that Colonel Wallis's companion might have as good a figure as Colonel Wallis, and certainly was not sandy-haired.

'How is Mary looking?' said Sir Walter, in the height of his good humour, 'The last time I saw her, she had a red nose, but I hope that may not happen every day.'

'Oh! no, that must have been quite accidental. In general she has been in very good health, and very good looks since Michaelmas.'

'If I thought it would not tempt her to go out in sharp winds, and grow coarse, I would send her a new hat and pelisse.'

Anne was considering whether she should venture to suggest that a gown, or a cap, would not be liable to any such misuse, when a knock at the

Arm-in-arm with Colonel Wallis

door suspended every thing. 'A knock at the door! and so late! It was ten o'clock. Could it be Mr Elliot? They knew he was to dine in Lansdown Crescent. It was possible that he might stop in his way home, to ask them how they did. They could think of no one else. Mrs Clay decidedly thought it Mr Elliot's knock.' Mrs Clay was right. With all the state which a butler and foot-boy could give, Mr Elliot was ushered into the room.

It was the same, the very same man, with no difference but of dress. Anne drew a little back, while the others received his compliments, and her sister his apologies for calling at so unusual an hour, but 'he could not be so near without wishing to know that neither she nor her friend had taken cold the day before, &c. &c.' which was all as politely done, and as politely taken as possible, but her part must follow then. Sir Walter talked of his youngest daughter; 'Mr Elliot must give him leave to present him to his youngest daughter' – (there was no occasion for remembering Mary) and Anne, smiling and blushing, very becomingly shewed to Mr Elliot the pretty features which he had by no means forgotten, and instantly saw, with amusement at his little start of surprise, that he had not been at all aware of who she was. He looked completely astonished, but not more astonished than pleased; his eyes brightened, and with the most perfect alacrity he welcomed the relationship, alluded to the past, and entreated to be received as an acquaintance already. He was quite as good-looking as he had appeared at Lyme, his countenance improved by speaking, and his manners were so exactly what they ought to be, so polished, so easy, so particularly agreeable, that she could compare them in excellence to only one person's manners. They were not the same, but they were, perhaps, equally good.

He sat down with them, and improved their conversation very much. There could be no doubt of his being a sensible man. Ten minutes were enough to certify that. His tone, his expressions, his choice of subject, his knowing where to stop, – it was all the operation of a sensible, discerning mind. As soon as he could, he began to talk to her of Lyme, wanting to compare opinions respecting the place, but especially wanting to speak of the circumstance of their happening to be guests in the same inn at the same time, to give his own route, understand something of hers, and regret that he should have lost such an opportunity of paying his respects to her. She gave him a short account of her party, and business at Lyme. His regret increased as he listened. He had spent his whole solitary evening in the room adjoining theirs; had heard voices – mirth continually; thought they must be a most delightful set of people – longed to be with them; but certainly without the smallest suspicion of his possessing the shadow of a right to introduce himself. If he had but asked who the party were! The name of Musgrove would have told him enough. 'Well, it would serve to cure him of an absurd practice of never asking a question at an inn, which he had adopted, when quite a young man, on the principle of its being very ungenteel to be curious.

'The notions of a young man of one or two and twenty,' said he, 'as to what is necessary in manners to make him quite the thing, are more absurd, I believe, than those of any other set of beings in the world. The folly of the means they often employ is only to be equalled by the folly of what they have in view.'

But he must not be addressing his reflections to Anne alone; he knew it; he was soon diffused again among the others, and it was only at intervals that he could return to Lyme.

His enquiries, however, produced at length an account of the scene she had been engaged in there, soon after his leaving the place. Having alluded to 'an accident,' he must hear the whole. When he questioned, Sir Walter and Elizabeth began to question also; but the difference in their manner of doing it could not be unfelt. She could only compare Mr Elliot to Lady Russell, in the wish of really comprehending what had passed, and in the degree of concern for what she must have suffered in witnessing it.

He staid an hour with them. The elegant little clock on the mantelpiece had struck 'eleven with its silver sounds,' and the watchman was beginning to be heard at a distance telling the same tale, before Mr Elliot or any of them seemed to feel that he had been there long.

Anne could not have supposed it possible that her first evening in Camden-place could have passed so well!

CHAPTER SIXTEEN

THERE WAS ONE POINT WHICH Anne, on returning to her family, would have been more thankful to ascertain, even than Mr Elliot's being in love with Elizabeth, which was, her father's not being in love with Mrs Clay; and she was very far from easy about it, when she had been at home a few hours. On going down to breakfast the next morning, she found there had just been a decent pretence on the lady's side of meaning to leave them. She could imagine Mrs Clay to have said, that 'now Miss Anne was come, she could not suppose herself at all wanted;' for Elizabeth was replying, in a sort of whisper, 'That must not be any reason, indeed. I assure you I feel it none. She is nothing to me, compared with you;' and she was in full time to hear her father say, 'My dear Madam, this must not be. As yet, you have seen nothing of Bath. You have been here only to be useful. You must not run away from us now. You must stay to be acquainted with Mrs Wallis, the beautiful Mrs Wallis. To your fine mind, I well know the sight of beauty is a real gratification.'

He spoke and looked so much in earnest, that Anne was not surprised to see Mrs Clay stealing a glance at Elizabeth and herself. Her countenance, perhaps, might express some watchfulness; but the praise of the fine mind did not appear to excite a thought in her sister. The lady could not but yield to such joint entreaties, and promise to stay.

In the course of the same morning, Anne and her father chancing to be alone together, he began to compliment her on her improved looks; he thought her 'less thin in her person, in her cheeks; her skin, her complexion, greatly improved – clearer, fresher. Had she been using any thing in particular!' 'No, nothing.' 'Merely Gowland,' he supposed. 'No, nothing at all.' 'Ha! he was surprised at that;' and added, 'Certainly you cannot do better than continue as you are; you cannot be better than well; or I should recommend Gowland, the constant use of Gowland, during the spring months. Mrs Clay has been using it at my recommendation, and you see what it has done for her. You see how it has carried away her freckles.'

If Elizabeth could but have heard this! Such personal praise might have struck her, especially as it did not appear to Anne that the freckles were at all lessened. But every thing must take its chance. The evil of the marriage would be much diminished, if Elizabeth were also to marry. As for herself, she might always command a home with Lady Russell.

Lady Russell's composed mind and polite manners were put to some trial on this point, in her intercourse in Camden-place. The sight of Mrs Clay in such favour, and of Anne so overlooked, was a perpetual provocation to her there; and vexed her as much when she was away, as a person in Bath who drinks the water, gets all the new publications, and has a very large acquaintance, has time to be vexed.

As Mr Elliot became known to her, she grew more charitable, or more indifferent, towards the others. His manners were an immediate recommendation; and on conversing with him she found the solid so fully supporting the superficial, that she was at first, as she told Anne, almost ready to exclaim, 'Can this be Mr Elliot?' and could not seriously picture to herself a more agreeable or estimable man. Every thing united in him; good understanding, correct opinions, knowledge of the world, and a warm heart. He had strong feelings of family-attachment and family-honour, without pride or weakness; he lived with the liberality of a man of fortune, without display; he judged for himself in every thing essential, without defying public opinion in any point of worldly decorum. He was steady, observant, moderate, candid; never run away with by spirits or by selfishness, which fancied itself strong feeling; and yet, with a sensibility to what was amiable and lovely, and a value for all the felicities of domestic

He began to compliment her on her improved looks

life, which characters of fancied enthusiasm and violent agitation seldom really possess. She was sure that he had not been happy in marriage. Colonel Wallis said it, and Lady Russell saw it; but it had been no unhappiness to sour his mind, nor (she began pretty soon to suspect) to prevent his thinking of a second choice. Her satisfaction in Mr Elliot outweighed all the plague of Mrs Clay.

It was now some years since Anne had begun to learn that she and her excellent friend could sometimes think differently; and it did not surprise her, therefore, that Lady Russell should see nothing suspicious or inconsistent, nothing to require more motives than appeared, in Mr Elliot's great desire of a reconciliation. In Lady Russell's view, it was perfectly natural that Mr Elliot, at a mature time of life, should feel it a most desirable object, and what would very generally recommend him, among all sensible people, to be on good terms with the head of his family; the simplest process in the world of time upon a head naturally clear, and only erring in the heyday of youth. Anne presumed, however, still to smile about it; and at last to mention 'Elizabeth.' Lady Russell listened, and looked, and made only this cautious reply: 'Elizabeth! Very well. Time will explain.'

It was a reference to the future, which Anne, after a little observation, felt she must submit to. She could determine nothing at present. In that house Elizabeth must be first; and she was in the habit of such general observance as 'Miss Elliot,' that any particularity of attention seemed almost impossible. Mr Elliot, too, it must be remembered, had not been a widower seven months. A little delay on his side might be very excusable. In fact, Anne could never see the crape round his hat, without fearing that she was the inexcusable one, in attributing to him such imaginations; for though his marriage had not been very happy, still it had existed so many years that she could not comprehend a very rapid recovery from the awful impression of its being dissolved.

However it might end, he was without any question their pleasantest acquaintance in Bath; she saw nobody equal to him; and it was a great indulgence now and then to talk to him about Lyme, which he seemed to have as lively a wish to see again, and to see more of, as herself. They went through the particulars of their first meeting a great many times. He gave her to understand that he had looked at her with some earnestness. She knew it well; and she remembered another person's look also.

They did not always think alike. His value for rank and connexion she perceived to be greater than hers. It was not merely complaisance, it must be a liking to the cause, which made him enter warmly into her father and sister's solicitudes on a subject which she thought unworthy to excite them. The Bath paper one morning announced the arrival of the Dowager Viscountess Dalrymple, and her daughter, the Honourable Miss Carteret; and all the comfort of No. – , Camden-place, was swept away for many days; for the Dalrymples (in Anne's opinion, most unfortunately) were cousins of the Elliots; and the agony was, how to introduce themselves properly.

Anne had never seen her father and sister before in contact with nobility, and she must acknowledge herself disappointed. She had hoped better things from their high ideas of their own situation in life, and was reduced to form a wish which she had never foreseen – a wish that they had more pride; for 'our cousins Lady Dalrymple and Miss Carteret;' 'our cousins, the Dalrymples,' sounded in her ears all day long.

Sir Walter had once been in company with the late Viscount, but had never seen any of the rest of the family, and the difficulties of the case arose from there having been a suspension of all intercourse by letters of ceremony, ever since the death of that said late Viscount, when, in consequence of a dangerous illness of Sir Walter's at the same time, there had been an unlucky omission at Kellynch. No letter of condolence had been sent to Ireland. The neglect had been visited on the head of the sinner, for when poor Lady Elliot died herself, no letter of condolence was received at Kellynch, and, consequently, there was but too much reason to apprehend that the Dalrymples considered the relationship as closed. How to have this anxious business set to rights, and be admitted as cousins again, was the question; and it was a question which, in a more rational manner, neither Lady Russell nor Mr Elliot thought unimportant. 'Family connexions were always worth preserving, good company always worth seeking; Lady Dalrymple had taken a house, for three months, in Laura-place, and would be living in style. She had been at Bath the year before, and Lady Russell had heard her spoken of as a charming woman. It was very desirable that the connexion should be renewed, if it could be done, without any compromise of propriety on the side of the Elliots.'

Sir Walter, however, would choose his own means, and at last wrote a very fine letter of ample explanation, regret and entreaty, to his right honourable cousin. Neither Lady Russell nor Mr Elliot could admire the letter; but it did all that was wanted, in bringing three lines of scrawl from the Dowager Viscountess. 'She was very much honoured, and should be happy in their acquaintance.' The toils of the business were over, the sweets began. They visited in Laura-place, they had the cards of Dowager Viscountess Dalrymple, and the Hon. Miss Carteret, to be arranged wherever they might be most visible; and 'Our cousins in Laura-place,' – 'Our cousin, Lady Dalrymple and Miss Carteret,' were talked of to every body.

Anne was ashamed. Had Lady Dalrymple and her daughter even been very agreeable, she would still have been ashamed of the agitation they created, but they were nothing. There was no superiority of manner, accomplishment, or understanding. Lady Dalrymple had acquired the name of 'a charming woman,' because she had a smile and a civil answer for every body. Miss Carteret, with still less to say, was so plain and so awkward, that she would never have been tolerated in Camden-place but for her birth.

Lady Russell confessed that she had expected something better; but yet 'it was an acquaintance worth having,' and when Anne ventured to speak her opinion of them to Mr Elliot, he agreed to their being nothing in themselves, but still maintained that as a family connexion, as good company, as those who would collect good company around them, they had their value. Anne smiled and said,

'My idea of good company, Mr Elliot, is the company of clever, well-informed people, who have a great deal of conversation; that is what I call good company.'

'You are mistaken,' said he gently, 'that is not good company, that is the best. Good company requires only birth, education and manners, and with regard to education is not very nice. Birth and good manners are essential; but a little learning is by no means a dangerous thing in good company, on the contrary, it will do very well. My cousin, Anne, shakes her head. She is not satisfied. She is fastidious. My dear cousin, (sitting down by her) you have a better right to be fastidious than almost any other woman I know; but will it answer? Will it make you happy? Will it not be wiser to accept the society of these good ladies in Laura-place, and enjoy all the advantages of the connexion as far as possible? You may depend upon it, that they will move in the first set in Bath this winter, and as rank is rank, your being known to be related to them will have its use in fixing your family (our family let me say) in that degree of consideration which we must all wish for.'

'Yes,' sighed Anne, 'we shall, indeed, be known to be related to them!' – then recollecting herself, and not wishing to be answered, she added, 'I certainly do think there has been by far too much trouble taken to procure the acquaintance. I suppose (smiling) I have more pride than any of you; but I confess it does vex me, that we should be so solicitous to have the relationship acknowledged, which we may be very sure is a matter of perfect indifference to them.'

'Pardon me, dear cousin, you are unjust to your own claims. In London, perhaps, in your present quiet style of living, it might be as you say: but in Bath, Sir Walter Elliot and his family will always be worth knowing, always acceptable as acquaintance.'

'Well,' said Anne, 'I certainly am proud, too proud to enjoy a welcome which depends so entirely upon place.'

'I love your indignation,' said he; 'it is very natural. But here you are in Bath, and the object is to be established here with all the credit and dignity which ought to belong to Sir Walter Elliot. You talk of being proud, I am called proud I know, and I shall not wish to believe myself otherwise, for our pride, if investigated, would have the same object, I have no doubt, though the kind may seem a little different. In one point, I am sure, my dear cousin, (he continued, speaking lower, though there was no one else in the room) in one point, I am sure, we must feel alike. We must feel that every addition to your father's society, among his equals or superiors, may be of use in diverting his thoughts from those who are beneath him.'

He looked, as he spoke, to the seat which Mrs Clay had been lately occupying, a sufficient explanation of what he particularly meant; and though Anne could not believe in their having the same sort of pride, she was pleased with him for not liking Mrs Clay; and her conscience admitted that his wishing to promote her father's getting great acquaintance, was more than excusable in the view of defeating her.

CHAPTER SEVENTEEN

WHILE SIR WALTER AND Elizabeth were assiduously pushing their good fortune in Laura-place, Anne was renewing an acquaintance of a very different description.

She had called on her former governess, and had heard from her of there being an old school-fellow in Bath, who had the two strong claims on her attention, of past kindness and present suffering. Miss Hamilton, now Mrs Smith, had shewn her kindness in one of those periods of her life when it had been most valuable. Anne had gone unhappy to school, grieving for the loss of a mother whom she had dearly loved, feeling her separation from home, and suffering as a girl of fourteen, of strong sensibility and not high spirits, must suffer at such a time; and Miss Hamilton, three years older than herself, but still from the want of near relations and a settled home, remaining another year at school, had been useful and good to her in a way which had considerably lessened her misery, and could never be remembered with indifference.

Miss Hamilton had left school, and married not long afterwards, was said to have married a man of fortune, and this was all that Anne had known of her, till now that their governess's account brought her situation forward in a more decided but very different form.

She was a widow, and poor. Her husband had been extravagant; and at his death, about two years before, had left his affairs dreadfully involved. She had had difficulties of every sort to contend with, and in addition to these distresses, had been afflicted with a severe rheumatic fever, which finally settling in her legs, had made her for the present a cripple. She had come to Bath on that account, and was now in lodgings near the hot-baths, living in a very humble way, unable even to afford herself the comfort of a servant, and of course almost excluded from society.

Their mutual friend answered for the satisfaction which a visit from Miss Elliot would give Mrs Smith, and Anne therefore lost no time in going. She mentioned nothing of what she had heard, or what she intended, at home. It would excite no proper interest there. She only consulted Lady Russell, who entered thoroughly into her sentiments, and was most happy to convey her as near to Mrs Smith's lodgings in Westgate-buildings, as Anne chose to be taken.

The visit was paid, their acquaintance re-established, their interest in each other more than re-kindled. The first ten minutes had its awkwardness and its emotion. Twelve years were gone since they had parted, and each presented a somewhat different person from what the other had imagined. Twelve years had changed Anne from the blooming, silent, unformed girl of fifteen, to the elegant little woman of seven and twenty, with every beauty excepting bloom, and with manners as consciously right as they were invariably gentle; and twelve years had transformed the fine-looking, well-grown Miss Hamilton, in all the glow of health and confidence of superiority, into a poor, infirm, helpless widow, receiving the visit of her former protegée as a favour; but all that was uncomfortable in the meeting had soon passed away, and left only the interesting charm of remembering former partialities and talking over old times.

Anne found in Mrs Smith the good sense and agreeable manners which she had almost ventured to depend on, and a disposition to converse and be cheerful beyond her expectation. Neither the dissipations of the past – and she had lived very much in the world, nor the restrictions of the present; neither sickness nor sorrow seemed to have closed her heart or ruined her spirits.

In the course of a second visit she talked with great openness, and Anne's astonishment increased. She could scarcely imagine a more cheerless situation in itself than Mrs Smith's. She had been very fond of her husband, – she had buried him. She had been used to affluence, – it was gone. She had no child to connect her with life and happiness again, no relations to assist in the arrangement of perplexed affairs, no health to make all the rest supportable. Her accommodations were limited to a noisy parlour, and a dark bed-room behind, with no possibility of moving from one to the other without assistance, which there was only one servant in the house to afford, and she never quitted the house but to be conveyed into the warm bath. – Yet, in spite of all this, Anne had reason to believe that she had moments only of languor and depression, to hours of occupation and enjoyment. How could it be? – She watched – observed – reflected – and finally determined that this was not a case of fortitude or of resignation only. – A submissive spirit might be patient, a strong understanding would supply resolution, but here was something more: here was that elasticity of mind, that disposition to be comforted, that power of turning readily from evil to good, and of finding employment which carried her out of herself, which was from Nature alone. It was the choicest gift of Heaven; and Anne viewed her friend as one of those instances in which, by a merciful appointment, it seems designed to counterbalance almost every other want.

There had been a time, Mrs Smith told her, when her spirits had nearly failed. She could not call herself an invalid now, compared with her state on first reaching Bath. Then, she had indeed been a pitiable object – for she had caught cold on the journey, and had hardly taken possession of her lodgings, before she was again confined to her bed, and suffering under severe and constant pain; and all this among strangers – with the absolute necessity of having a regular nurse, and finances at that moment paricularly unfit to meet any extraordinary expense. She had weathered it however, and could truly say that it had done her good. It had increased her comforts by making her feel herself to be in good hands. She had seen too much of the world, to expect sudden or disinterested attachment any where, but her illness had proved to her that her landlady had a character to preserve, and would not use her ill; and she had been particularly fortunate in her nurse, as a sister of her landlady, a nurse by profession, and who had always a home in that house when unemployed, chanced to be at liberty just in time to attend her. – 'And she,' said Mrs Smith, 'Besides nursing me most admirably, has really proved an invaluable acquaintance. – As soon as I could use my hands, she taught me to knit, which has been a great amusement; and she put me in the way of making these little thread-cases, pin-cushions and card-racks, which you always find me so busy about, and which supply me with the means of doing a little good to one or two very poor families in this neighbourhood. She has a large acquaintance, of course professionally, among those who can afford to buy, and she disposes of my merchandize. She always takes the right time for applying. Every body's heart is open, you know, when they have recently escaped from severe pain, or are recovering the blessing of health, and nurse Rooke thoroughly understands when to speak. She is a shrewd, intelligent, sensible woman. Hers is a line for seeing human nature; and she has a fund of good sense and observation which, as a companion, make her infinitely superior to thousands of those who having only received "the best education in the world," know nothing worth attending to. Call it gossip if you will; but when nurse Rooke has half an hour's leisure to bestow on me, she is sure to have something to relate that is entertaining and profitable, something that makes one know one's species better. One likes to hear what is going on, to be *au fait* as to the newest modes of being trifling and silly. To me, who live so much alone, her conversation I assure you is a treat.'

Anne, far from wishing to cavil at the pleasure, replied, 'I can easily believe it. Women of that class have great opportunities, and if they are intelligent may be well worth listening to. Such varieties of human nature as they are in the habit of witnessing! And it is not merely in its follies, that they are well read; for they see it occasionally under every circumstance that can be most interesting or affecting. What instances must pass before them of ardent, disinterested, self-denying attachment, of heroism, fortitude, patience, resignation – of all the conflicts and all the sacrifices that ennoble us most. A sick chamber may often furnish the worth of volumes.'

'Yes,' said Mrs Smith more doubtingly, 'sometimes it may, though I fear its lessons are not often in the elevated style you describe. Here and there, human nature may be great in times of trial, but generally speaking it is its weakness and not its strength that appears in a sick chamber; it is selfishness and impatience rather than generosity and fortitude, that one hears of. There is so little real friendship in the world! – and unfortunately' (speaking low and tremulously) 'there are so many who forget to think seriously till it is almost too late.'

Anne saw the misery of such feelings. The husband had not been what he ought, and the wife had been led among that part of mankind which made her think worse of the world, than she hoped it deserved. It was but a passing emotion however with Mrs Smith, she shook it off, and soon added in a different tone,

'I do not suppose the situation my friend Mrs Rooke is in at present, will furnish much either to interest or edify me. – She is only nursing Mrs Wallis of Marlborough-buildings – a mere pretty, silly, expensive, fashionable woman, I believe – and of course will have nothing to report but of lace and finery. – I mean to make my profit of Mrs Wallis, however. She has plenty of money, and I intend she shall buy all the high-priced things I have in hand now.'

Anne had called several times on her friend, before the existence of such a person was known in Camden-place. At last, it became necessary to speak of her. – Sir Walter, Elizabeth and Mrs Clay returned one morning from Laura-place, with a sudden invitation from Lady Dalrymple for the same evening, and Anne was already engaged, to spend that evening in Westgate-buildings. She was not sorry for the excuse. They were only asked, she was sure, because Lady Dalrymple being kept at home by a bad cold, was glad to make use of the relationship which had been so pressed on her, – and she declined on her own account with great alacrity – 'She was engaged to spend the evening with an old schoolfellow.' They were not much interested in any thing relative to Anne, but still there were questions enough asked, to make it understood what this old schoolfellow was; and Elizabeth was disdainful, and Sir Walter severe.

'Westgate-buildings!' said he; 'and who is Miss Anne Elliot to be visiting in Westgate-buildings? – A Mrs Smith. A widow Mrs Smith, – and who was her husband? One of the five thousand Mr Smiths whose names are to be met with every where. And what is her attraction? That she is old and sickly. – Upon my word, Miss Anne Elliot, you have the most extraordinary taste! Every thing that revolts other people, low campany, paltry rooms, foul air, disgusting associations are inviting to you. But surely, you may put off this old lady till to-morrow. She is not so near her end, I presume, but that she may hope to see another day. What is her age? Forty?'

'No, Sir, she is not one and thirty; but I do not think I can put off my engagement, because it is the only evening for some time which will at once suit her and myself. – She goes into the warm bath to-morrow, and for the rest of the week you know we are engaged.'

'But what does Lady Russell think of this acquaintance?' asked Elizabeth.

'She sees nothing to blame in it,' replied Anne; 'on the contrary, she approves it; and has generally taken me, when I have called on Mrs Smith.'

'Westgate-buildings must have been rather surprised by the appearance of a carriage drawn up near its pavement!' observed Sir Walter. – 'Sir Henry Russell's widow, indeed, has no honours to distinguish her arms; but still, it is a handsome equipage, and no doubt is well known to convey a Miss Elliot. – A widow Mrs Smith, lodging in Westgate-buildings! – A poor widow, barely able to live, between thirty and forty – a mere Mrs Smith, an every day Mrs Smith, of all people and all names in the world, to be the chosen friend of Miss Anne Elliot, and to be preferred by her, to her own family connexions among the nobility of England and Ireland! Mrs Smith, such a name!'

Mrs Clay, who had been present while all this passed, now thought it advisable to leave the room, and Anne could have said much and did long to say a little, in defence of *her* friend's not very dissimilar claims to theirs, but her sense of personal respect to her father prevented her. She made no reply. She left it to himself to recollect, that Mrs Smith was not the only widow in Bath between thirty and forty, with little to live on, and no sirname of dignity.

Anne kept her appointment; the others kept theirs, and of course she heard the next morning that they had had a delightful evening. – She had been the only one of the set absent; for Sir Walter and Elizabeth had not only been quite at her ladyship's service themselves, but had actually been happy to be employed by her in collecting others, and had been at the trouble of inviting both Lady Russell and Mr Elliot; and Mr Elliot had made a point of leaving Colonel Wallis early, and Lady Russell had fresh arranged all her evening engagements in order to wait on her. Anne had the whole history of all that such an evening could supply, from Lady Russell. To her, its greatest interest must be, in having been very much talked of between her friend and Mr Elliot, in having been wished for, regretted, and at the same time honoured for staying away in such a cause. – Her kind, compassionate visits to this old schoolfellow, sick and reduced, seemed to have quite delighted Mr Elliot. He thought her a most extraordinary young woman; in her temper, manners, mind, a model of female excellence. He could meet even Lady Russell in a discussion of her merits; and Anne could not be given to understand so much by her friend, could not know herself to be so highly rated by a sensible man, without many of those agreeable sensations which her friend meant to create.

Lady Russell was now perfectly decided in her opinion of Mr Elliot. She was as much convinced of his meaning to gain Anne in time, as of his deserving her; and was beginning to calculate the number of weeks which would free him from all the remaining restraints of widowhood, and leave him at liberty to exert his most open powers of pleasing. She would not speak to Anne with half the certainty she felt on the subject, she would venture on little more than hints of what might be hereafter, of a possible attachment on his side, of the desirableness of the alliance, supposing such attachment to be real, and returned. Anne heard her, and made no violent exclamations. She only smiled, blushed, and gently shook her head.

'I am no match-maker, as you well know,' said Lady Russell, 'being much too well aware of the uncertainty of all human events and calculations. I only mean that if Mr Elliot should some time hence pay his addresses to you, and if you should be disposed to accept him, I think there would be every possibility of your being happy together. A most suitable connection every body must consider it – but I think it might be a very happy one.'

'Mr Elliot is an exceedingly agreeable man, and in many respects I think highly of him,' said Anne; 'but we should not suit.'

Lady Russell let this pass, and only said in rejoinder, 'I own that to be able to regard you as the future mistress of Kellynch, the future Lady Elliot – to look forward and see you occupying your dear mother's place, succeeding to all her rights, and all her popularity, as well as to all her virtues, would be the highest possible gratification to me. – You are your mother's self in countenance and disposition; and if I might be allowed to fancy you such as she was, in situation, and name, and home, presiding and blessing in the same spot, and only superior to her in being more highly valued! My dearest Anne, it would give me more delight than is often felt at my time of life!'

Anne was obliged to turn away, to rise, to walk to a distant table, and, leaning there in pretended employment, try to subdue the feeling this picture excited. For a few moments her imagination and her heart were bewitched. The idea of becoming what her mother had been; of having the precious name of 'Lady Elliot' first revived in herself; of being restored to Kellynch, calling it her home again, her home for ever, was a charm which she could not immediately resist. Lady Russell said not another word, willing to leave the matter to its own operation; and believing that, could Mr Elliot at that moment with propriety have spoken for himself! – She believed, in short, what Anne did not believe. The same image of Mr Elliot speaking for himself, brought Anne to composure again. The charm of Kellynch and of 'Lady Elliot' all faded away. She never could accept him. And it was not only that her feelings were still adverse to any man save one; her judgment, on a serious consideration of the possibilities of such a case, was against Mr Elliot.

Though they had now been acquainted a month, she could not be satisfied that she really knew his character. That he was a sensible man, an agreeable man, – that he talked well, professed good opinions, seemed to judge properly and as a man of principle, – this was all clear enough. He certainly knew what was right, nor could she fix on any one article of moral duty evidently transgressed; but yet she would have been afraid to answer for his conduct. She distrusted the past, if not the present. The names which occasionally dropt of former associates, the allusions to former practices and pursuits, suggested suspicions not favourable of what he had been. She saw that there had been bad habits; that Sunday-travelling had been a common thing; that there had been a period of his life (and probably not a short one) when he had been, at least, careless on all serious matters; and, though he might now think very differently, who could answer for the true sentiments of a clever, cautious man, grown old enough to appreciate a fair character? How could it ever be ascertained that his mind was truly cleansed?

Mr Elliot was rational, discreet, polished, – but he was not open. There was never any burst of feeling, any warmth of indignation or delight, at the evil or good of others. This, to Anne, was decided imperfection. Her early impressions were incurable. She prized the frank, the open-hearted, the eager character beyond all others. Warmth and enthusiasm did captivate her still. She felt that she could so much more depend upon the sincerity of those who sometimes looked or said a careless or a hasty thing, than of those whose presence of mind never varied, whose tongue never slipped.

Mr Elliot was too generally agreeable. Various as were the tempers in her father's house, he pleased them all. He endured too well, – stood too well with everybody. He had spoken to her with some degree of openness of Mrs Clay; had appeared completely to see what Mrs Clay was about, and to hold her in contempt; and yet Mrs Clay found him as agreeable as any body.

Lady Russell saw either less or more than her young friend, for she saw nothing to excite distrust. She could not imagine a man more exactly what he ought to be than Mr Elliot; nor did she ever enjoy a sweeter feeling than the hope of seeing him receive the hand of her beloved Anne in Kellynch church, in the course of the following autumn.

CHAPTER EIGHTEEN

IT WAS THE BEGINNING OF February; and Anne, having been a month in Bath, was growing very eager for news from Uppercross and Lyme. She wanted to hear much more than Mary communicated. It was three weeks since she had heard at all. She only knew that Henrietta was at home again; and that Louisa, though considered to be recovering fast, was still at Lyme; and she was thinking of them all very intently one evening, when a thicker letter than usual from Mary was delivered to her, and, to quicken the pleasure and surprise, with Admiral and Mrs Croft's compliments.

The Crofts must be in Bath! A circumstance to interest her. They were people whom her heart turned to very naturally.

'What is this?' cried Sir Walter. 'The Crofts arrived in Bath? The Crofts who rent Kellynch? What have they brought you?'

'A letter from Uppercross Cottage, Sir.'

'Oh! those letters are convenient passports. They secure an introduction. I should have visited Admiral Croft, however, at any rate. I know what is due to my tenant.'

Anne could listen no longer; she could not even have told how the poor Admiral's complexion escaped; her letter engrossed her. It had been begun several days back.

'February 1st,——

'My dear Anne,

'I make no apology for my silence, because I know how little people think of letters in such a place as Bath. You must be a great deal too happy to care for Uppercross, which, as you well know, affords little to write about. We have had a very dull Christmas; Mr and Mrs Musgrove have not had one dinner-party all the holidays. I do not reckon the Hayters as any body. The holidays, however, are over at last: I believe no children ever had such long ones. I am sure I had not. The house was cleared yesterday, except of the little Harvilles; but you will be surprised to hear they have never gone home. Mrs Harville must be an odd mother to part with them so long. I do not understand it. They are not at all nice children, in my opinion; but Mrs Musgrove seems to like them quite as well, if not better, than her grandchildren. What dreadful weather we have had! It may not be felt in Bath, with your nice pavements; but in the country it is of some consequence. I have not had a creature call on me since the second week in January, except Charles Hayter, who has been calling much oftener than was welcome. Between ourselves, I think it a great

pity Henrietta did not remain at Lyme as long as Louisa; it would have kept her a little out his way. The carriage is gone to-day, to bring Louisa and the Harvilles to-morrow. We are not asked to dine with them, however, till the day after, Mrs Musgrove is so afraid of her being fatigued by the journey, which is not very likely, considering the care that will be taken of her; and it would be much more convenient to me to dine there to-morrow. I am glad you find Mr Elliot so agreeable, and wish I could be acquainted with him too; but I have my usual luck, I am always out of the way when any thing desirable is going on; always the last of my family to be noticed. What an immense time Mrs Clay has been staying with Elizabeth! Does she never mean to go away? But perhaps if she were to leave the room vacant we might now be invited. Let me know what you think of this. I do not expect my children to be asked, you know. I can leave them at the Great House very well, for a month or six weeks. I have this moment heard that the Crofts are going to Bath almost immediately; they think the admiral gouty. Charles heard it quite by chance: they have not had the civility to give me any notice, or offer to take any thing. I do not think they improve at all as neighbours. We see nothing of them, and this is really an instance of gross inattention. Charles joins me in love, and every thing proper.

Yours, affectionately,

'Mary M——.'

'I am sorry to say that I am very far from well; and Jemima has just told me that the butcher says there is a bad sore-throat very much about. I dare say I shall catch it; and my sore-throats, you know, are always worse than anybody's.'

So ended the first part, which had been afterwards put into an envelope, containing nearly as much more.

'I kept my letter open, that I might send you word how Louisa bore her journey, and now I am extremely glad I did, having a great deal to add. In the first place, I had a note from Mrs Croft yesterday, offering to convey any thing to you; a very kind, friendly note indeed, addressed to me, just as it ought; I shall therefore be able to make my letter as long as I like. The admiral does not seem very ill, and I sincerely hope Bath will do him all the good he wants. I shall be truly glad to have them back again. Our neighbourhood cannot spare such a pleasant family. But now for Louisa. I have something to communicate that will astonish you not a little. She and the Harvilles came on Tuesday very safely, and in the evening we went to ask her how she did, when we were rather surprised not to find Captain Benwick of the party, for he had been invited as well as the Harvilles; and what do you think was the reason? Neither more nor less than his being in love with Louisa, and not choosing to

venture to Uppercross till he had had an answer from Mr Musgrove; for it was all settled between him and her before she came away, and he had written to her father by Captain Harville. True, upon my honour. Are not you astonished? I shall be surprised at least if you ever received a hint of it, for I never did. Mrs Musgrove protests solemnly that she knew nothing of the matter. We are all very well pleased, however; for though it is not equal to her marrying Captain Wentworth, it is infinitely better than Charles Hayter; and Mr Musgrove has written his consent, and Captain Benwick is expected to-day. Mrs Harville says her husband feels a good deal on his poor sister's account; but, however, Louisa is a great favourite with both. Indeed Mrs Harville and I quite agree that we love her the better for having nursed her. Charles wonders what Captain Wentworth will say; but if you remember, I never thought him attached to Louisa; I never could see any thing of it. And this is the end, you see, of Captain Benwick's being supposed to be an admirer of yours. How Charles could take such a thing into his head was always incomprehensible to me. I hope he will be more agreeable now. Certainly not a great match for Louisa Musgrove; but a million times better than marrying among the Hayters.'

Mary need not have feared her sister's being in any degree prepared for the news. She had never in her life been more astonished. Captain Benwick and Louisa Musgrove! It was almost too wonderful for belief; and it was with the greatest effort that she could remain in the room, preserve an air of calmness, and answer the common questions of the moment. Happily for her, they were not many. Sir Walter wanted to know whether the Crofts travelled with four horses, and whether they were likely to be situated in such a part of Bath as it might suit Miss Elliot and himself to visit in; but had little curiosity beyond.

'How is Mary?' said Elizabeth; and without waiting for an answer, 'And pray what brings the Crofts to Bath?'

'They come on the Admiral's account. He is thought to be gouty.'

'Gout and decrepitude!' said Sir Walter. 'Poor old gentleman.'

'Have they any acquaintance here?' asked Elizabeth.

'I do not know; but I can hardly suppose that, at Admiral Croft's time of life, and in his profession, he should not have many acquaintance in such a place as this.'

'I suspect,' said Sir Walter coolly, 'that Admiral Croft will be best known in Bath as the renter of Kellynch-hall. Elizabeth, may we venture to present him and his wife in Laura-place?'

'Oh! no, I think not. Situated as we are with Lady Dalrymple, cousins, we ought to be very careful not to embarrass her with acquaintance she might not approve. If we were not related, it would not signify; but as cousins, she would feel scrupulous as to any proposal of ours. We had better leave the

Crofts to find their own level. There are several odd-looking men walking about here, who, I am told, are sailors. The Crofts will associate with them!'

This was Sir Walter and Elizabeth's share of interest in the letter; when Mrs Clay had paid her tribute of more decent attention, in an enquiry after Mrs Charles Musgrove, and her fine little boys, Anne was at liberty.

In her own room she tried to comprehend it. Well might Charles wonder how Captain Wentworth would feel! Perhaps he had quitted the field, had given Louisa up, had ceased to love, had found he did not love her. She could not endure the idea of treachery or levity, or any thing akin to ill-usage between him and his friend. She could not endure that such a friendship as theirs should be severed unfairly.

Captain Benwick and Louisa Musgrove! The high-spirited, joyous, talking Louisa Musgrove, and the dejected, thinking, feeling, reading Captain Benwick, seemed each of them every thing that would not suit the other. Their minds most dissimilar! Where could have been the attraction? The answer soon presented itself. It had been in situation. They had been thrown together several weeks; they had been living in the same small family party; since Henrietta's coming away, they must have been depending almost entirely on each other, and Louisa, just recovering from illness, had been in an interesting state, and Captain Benwick was not inconsolable. That was a point which Anne had not been able to avoid suspecting before; and instead of drawing the same conclusion as Mary, from the present course of events, they served only to confirm the idea of his having felt sone dawning of tenderness towards herself. She did not mean, however, to derive much more from it to gratify her vanity, than Mary might have allowed. She was persuaded that any tolerably pleasing young woman who had listened and seemed to feel for him, would have received the same compliment. He had an affectionate heart. He must love somebody.

She saw no reason against their being happy. Louisa had fine naval fervour to begin with, and they would soon grow more alike. He would gain cheerfulness, and she would learn to be an enthusiast for Scott and Lord Byron; nay, that was probably learnt already; of course they had fallen in love over poetry. The idea of Louisa Musgrove turned into a person of literary taste, and sentimental reflection, was amusing, but she had not doubt of its being so. The day at Lyme, the fall from the Cobb, might influence her health, her nerves, her courage, her character to the end of her life, as thoroughly as it appeared to have influenced her fate.

The conclusion of the whole was, that if the woman who had been sensible of Captain Wentworth's merits could be allowed to prefer another man, there was nothing in the engagement to excite lasting wonder; and if Captain Wentworth lost no friend by it, certainly nothing to be regretted.

No, it was not regret which made Anne's heart beat in spite of herself, and brought the colour into her cheeks when she thought of Captain Wentworth unshackled and free. She had some feelings which she was ashamed to investigate. They were too much like joy, senseless joy!

She longed to see the Crofts, but when the meeting took place, it was evident that no rumour of the news had yet reached them. The visit of ceremony was paid and returned, and Louisa Musgrove was mentioned, and Captain Benwick too, without even half a smile.

The Crofts had placed themselves in lodgings in Gay-street, perfectly to Sir Walter's satisfaction. He was not at all ashamed of the acquaintance, and did, in fact, think and talk a great deal more about the Admiral, than the Admiral ever thought or talked about him.

The Crofts knew quite as many people in Bath as they wished for, and considered their intercourse with the Elliots as a mere matter of form, and not in the least likely to afford them any pleasure. They brought with them their country habit of being almost always together. He was ordered to walk, to keep off the gout, and Mrs Croft seemed to go shares with him in every thing, and to walk for her life, to do him good. Anne saw them wherever she went. Lady Russell took her out in her carriage almost every morning, and she never failed to think of them, and never failed to see them. Knowing their feelings as she did, it was a most attractive picture of happiness to her. She always watched them as long as she could; delighted to fancy she understood what they might be talking of, as they walked along in happy independence, or equally delighted to see the Admiral's hearty shake of the hand when he encountered an old friend, and observe their eagerness of conversation when occasionally forming into a little knot of the navy, Mrs Croft looking as intelligent and keen as any of the officers around her.

Anne was too much engaged with Lady Russell to be often walking herself, but it so happened that one morning, about a week or ten days after the Crofts' arrival, it suited her best to leave her friend, or her friend's carriage, in the lower part of the town, and return alone to Camden-place; and in walking up Milsom-street, she had the good fortune to meet with the Admiral. He was standing by himself, at a printshop window, with his hands behind him, in earnest contemplation of some print, and she not only might have passed him unseen, but was obliged to touch as well as address him before she could catch his notice. When he did perceive and acknowledge her, however, it was done with all his usual frankness and good humour. 'Ha! is it you? Thank you, thank you. This is treating me like a friend. Here I am, you see, staring at a picture. I can never get by this shop without stopping. But what a thing here is, by way of a boat. Do look at it. Did you ever see the like? What queer fellows your fine painters must be, to think that any body would venture their lives in such a shapeless old cockleshell as that. And yet, here are two gentlemen stuck up in it mightily at their ease, and looking about them at the rocks and mountains, as if they were not to be upset the next moment, which they certainly must be. I wonder where that boat was built!' (laughing heartily) 'I would not venture over a horsepond in it. Well,' (turning away) 'now, where are you bound? Can I go any where for you, or with you? Can I be of any use?'

Obliged to touch him before she could catch his notice

'None, I thank you, unless you will give me the pleasure of your company the little way our road lies together. I am going home.'

'That I will, with all my heart, and farther too. Yes, yes, we will have a snug walk together; and I have something to tell you as we go along. There, take my arm; that's right: I do not feel comfortable if I have not a woman there. Lord! what a boat it is!' taking a last look at the picture, as they began to be in motion.

'Did you say that you had something to tell me, sir?'

'Yes, I have. Presently. But here comes a friend, Captain Brigden; I shall only say, "How d'ye do," as we pass, however. I shall not stop. "How d'ye do." Brigden stares to see anybody with me but my wife. She, poor soul, is tied by the leg. She has a blister on one of her heels, as large as a three shilling piece. If you look across the street, you will see Admiral Brand coming down and his brother. Shabby fellows, both of them! I am glad they are not on this side of the way. Sophy cannot bear them. They played me a pitiful trick once – got away some of my best men. I will tell you the whole story another time. There comes old Sir Archibald Drew and his grandson. Look, he sees us; he kisses his hand to you; he takes you for my wife. Ah! the peace has come too soon for that younker. Poor old Sir Archibald! How do you like Bath, Miss Elliot? It suits us very well. We are always meeting with some old friend or other; the streets full of them every morning; sure to have plenty of chat; and then we get away from them all, and shut ourselves into our lodgings, and draw in our chairs, and are as snug as if we were at Kellynch, ay, or as we used to be even at North Yarmouth and Deal. We do not like our lodgings here the worse, I can tell you, for putting us in mind of those we first had at North Yarmouth. The wind blows through one of the cupboards just in the same way.'

When they were got a little farther, Anne ventured to press again for what he had to communicate. She had hoped, when clear of Milsom-street, to have her curiosity gratified; but she was still obliged to wait, for the Admiral had made up his mind not to begin, till they had gained the greater space and quiet of Belmont, and as she was not really Mrs Croft, she must let him have his own way. As soon as they were fairly ascending Belmont, he began,

'Well, now you shall hear something that will surprise you. But first of all, you must tell me the name of the young lady I am going to talk about. That young lady, you know, that we have all been so concerned for. The Miss Musgrove, that all this has been happening to. Her christian name – I always forget her christian name.'

Anne had been ashamed to appear to comprehend so soon as she really did; but now she could safely suggest the name of 'Louisa.'

'Ay, ay, Miss Louisa Misgrove, that is the name. I wish young ladies had

Old Sir Archibald Drew and his grandson

not such a number of fine christian names. I should never be out, if they were all Sophys, or something of that sort. Well, this Miss Louisa, we all thought, you know, was to marry Frederick. He was courting her week after week. The only wonder was, what they could be waiting for, till the business at Lyme came; then, indeed, it was clear enough that they must wait till her brain was set to right. But even then, there was something odd in their way of going on. Instead of staying at Lyme, he went off to Plymouth, and then he went off to see Edward. When we came back from Minehead, he was gone down to Edward's, and there he has been ever since. We have seen nothing of him since November. Even Sophy could not understand it. But now, the matter has taken the strangest turn of all; for this young lady, this same Miss Musgrove, instead of being to marry Frederick, is to marry James Benwick. You know James Benwick.'

'A little. I am a little acquainted with Captain Benwick.'

'Well, she is to marry him. Nay, most likely they are married already, for I do not know what they should wait for.'

'I thought Captain Benwick a very pleasing young man,' said Anne, 'and I understand that he bears an excellent character.'

'Oh! yes, yes, there is not a word to be said against James Benwick. He is only a commander, it is true, made last summer, and these are bad times for getting on, but he has not another fault that I know of. An excellent, good-hearted fellow, I assure you, a very active, zealous officer too, which is more than you would think for, perhaps, for that soft sort of manner does not do him justice.'

'Indeed you are mistaken there, sir. I should never augur want of spirit from Captain Benwick's manners. I thought them particularly pleasing, and I will answer for it they would generally please.'

'Well, well, ladies are the best judges; but James Benwick is rather too piano for me, and though very likely it is all our partiality, Sophy and I cannot help thinking Frederick's manners better than his. There is something about Frederick more to our taste.'

Anne was caught. She had only meant to oppose the too-common idea of spirit and gentleness being incompatible with each other, not at all to represent Captain Benwick's manners as the very best that could possibly be, and, after a little hesitation, she was beginning to say, 'I was not entering into any comparison of the two friends,' but the Admiral interrupted her with,

'And the thing is certainly true. It is not a mere bit of gossip. We have it from Frederick himself. His sister had a letter from him yesterday, in which he tell us of it, and he had just had it in a letter from Harville, written upon the spot, from Uppercross. I fancy they are all at Uppercross.'

This was an opportunity which Anne could not resist; she said, therefore, 'I hope, Admiral, I hope there is nothing in the style of Captain Wentworth's letter to make you and Mrs Croft particulary uneasy. It did certainly seem, last autumn, as if there were an attachment between him and Louisa Musgrove; but I hope it may be understood to have worn out on each side equally, and without violence. I hope his letter does not breathe the spirit of an ill-used man.'

'Not at all, not at all; there is not an oath or a murmur from beginning to end.'

Anne looked down to hide her smile.

'No, no; Frederick is not a man to whine and complain; he has too much spirit for that. If the girl likes another man better, it is very fit she should have him.'

'Certainly. But what I mean is, that I hope there is nothing in Captain Wentworth's manner of writing to make you suppose he thinks himself ill-used by his friend, which might appear, you know, without its being absolutely said. I should be very sorry that such a friendship as has subsisted between him and Captain Benwick should be destroyed, or even wounded, by a circumstance of this sort.'

'Yes, yes, I understand you. But there is nothing at all of that nature in the letter. He does not give the least fling at Benwick; does not so much as say, "I wonder at it, I have a reason of my own for wondering at it." No, you would not guess, from his way of writing, that he had ever thought of this Miss (what's her name?) for himself. He very handsomely hopes they will be happy together, and there is nothing very unforgiving in that, I think.'

Anne did not receive the perfect conviction which the Admiral meant to convey, but it would have been useless to press the enquiry farther. She, therefore, satisfied herself with commonplace remarks, or quiet attention, and the Admiral had it all his own way.

'Poor Frederick!' said he at last. 'Now he must begin all over again with somebody else. I think we must get him to Bath. Sophy must write, and beg him to come to Bath. Here are pretty girls enough, I am sure. It would be of no use to go to Uppercross again, for that other Miss Musgrove, I find, is bespoke by her cousin, the young parson. Do not you think, Miss Elliot, we had better try to get him to Bath?'

CHAPTER NINETEEN

WHILE ADMIRAL CROFT WAS taking this walk with Anne, and expressing his wish of getting Captain Wentworth to Bath, Captain Wentworth was already on his way thither. Before Mrs Croft had written, he was arrived; and the very next time Anne walked out, she saw him.

Mr Elliot was attending his two cousins and Mrs Clay. They were in Milsom-street. It began to rain, not much, but enough to make shelter desirable for women, and quite enough to make it very desirable for Miss Elliot to have the advantage of being conveyed home in Lady Dalrymple's carriage, which was seen waiting at a little distance; she, Anne, and Mrs Clay, therefore, turned into Molland's, while Mr Elliot stepped to Lady Dalrymple, to request her assistance. He soon joined them again, successful, of course; Lady Dalrymple would be most happy to take them home, and would call for them in a few minutes.

Her ladyship's carriage was a barouche, and did not hold more than four with any comfort. Miss Carteret was with her mother; consequently it was not reasonable to expect accommodation for all the three Camden-place ladies. There could be no doubt as to Miss Elliot. Whoever suffered inconvenience, she must suffer none, but it occupied a little time to settle the point of civility between the other two. The rain was a mere trifle, and Anne was most sincere in preferring a walk with Mr Elliot. But the rain was also a mere trifle to Mrs Clay; she would hardly allow it even to drop at all, and her boots were so thick! much thicker than Miss Anne's; and, in short, her civility rendered her quite as anxious to be left to walk with Mr Elliot, as Anne could be, and it was discussed between them with a generosity so polite and so determined, that the others were obliged to settle it for them; Miss Elliot maintaining that Mrs Clay had a little cold already, and Mr Elliot deciding on appeal, that his cousin Anne's boots were rather the thickest.

It was fixed accordingly that Mrs Clay should be of the party in the carriage; and they had just reached this point when Anne, as she sat near the window, descried, most decidedly and distinctly, Captain Wentworth walking down the street.

Her start was perceptible only to herself; but she instantly felt that she was the greatest simpleton in the world, the most unaccountable and absurd! For a few minutes she saw nothing before her. It was all confusion. She was lost; and when she had scolded back her senses, she found the others still waiting for the carriage, and Mr Elliot (always obliging) just setting off for Union-street on a commission of Mrs Clay's.

She now felt a great inclination to go to the outer door; she wanted to see if it rained. Why was she to suspect herself of another motive? Captain Wentworth must be out of sight. She left her seat, she would go, one half of her should not be always so much wiser than the other half, or always suspecting the other of being worse than it was. She would see if it rained. She was sent back, however, in a moment by the entrance of Captain Wentworth himself, among a party of gentlemen and ladies, evidently his acquaintance, and whom he must have joined a little below Milsom-street. He was more obviously struck and confused by the sight of her, than she had ever observed before; he looked quite red. For the first time, since their renewed acquaintance, she felt that she was betraying the least sensibility of the two. She had the advantage of him, in the preparation of the last few moments. All the overpowering, blinding, bewildering, first effects of strong surprise were over with her. Still, however, she had enough to feel! It was agitation, pain, pleasure, a something between delight and misery.

He spoke to her, and then turned away. The character of his manner was embarrassment. She could not have called it either cold or friendly, or any thing so certainly as embarrassed.

After a short interval, however, he came towards her and spoke again. Mutual enquiries on common subjects passed; neither of them, probably, much the wiser for what they heard, and Anne continuing fully sensible of his being less at ease than formerly. They had, by dint of being so very much together, got to speak to each other with a considerable portion of apparent indifference and calmness; but he could not do it now. Time had changed him, or Louisa had changed him. There was consciousness of some sort or other. He looked very well, not as if he had been suffering in health or spirits, and he talked of Uppercross, of the Musgroves, nay, even of Louisa, and had even a momentary look of his own arch significance as he named her; but yet it was Captain Wentworth not comfortable, not easy, not able to feign that he was.

It did not surprise, but it grieved Anne to observe that Elizabeth would not know him. She saw that he saw Elizabeth, that Elizabeth saw him, that there was complete internal recognition on each side; she was convinced that he was ready to be acknowledged as an acquaintance, expecting it, and she had the pain of seeing her sister turn away with unalterable coldness.

Lady Dalrymple's carriage, for which Miss Elliot was growing very impatient, now drew up; the servant came in to announce it. It was beginning to rain again, and altogether there was a delay, and a bustle, and a talking, which must make all the little crowd in the shop understand that Lady Dalrymple was calling to convey Miss Elliot. At last Miss Elliot and her friend, unattended but by the servant, (for there was no cousin returned) were walking off; and Captain Wentworth, watching them, turned again to Anne, and by manner, rather than words, was offering his services to her.

'I am much obliged to you,' was her answer, 'but I am not going with them. The carriage would not accommodate so many. I walk. I prefer walking.'

'But it rains.'

'Oh! very little. Nothing that I regard.'

After a moment's pause he said, 'Though I came only yesterday, I have equipped myself properly for Bath already, you see,' (pointing to a new umbrella) 'I wish you would make use of it, if you are determined to walk; though, I think, it would be more prudent to let me get you a chair.'

She was very much obliged to him, but declined it all, repeating her conviction, that the rain would come to nothing at present, and adding, 'I am only waiting for Mr Elliot. He will be here in a moment, I am sure.'

She had hardly spoken the words, when Mr Elliot walked in. Captain Wentworth recollected him perfectly. There was no difference between him, and the man who had stood on the steps at Lyme, admiring Anne as she passed, except in the air and look and manner of the privileged relation and friend. He came in with eagerness, appeared to see and think only of her, apologised for his stay, was grieved to have kept her waiting, and anxious to get her away without further loss of time, and before the rain increased; and in another moment they walked off together, her arm under his, a gentle

In another moment they walked off

and embarrassed glance, and a 'good morning to you', being all that she had time for, as she passed away.

As soon as they were out of sight, the ladies of Captain Wentworth's party began talking of them.

'Mr Elliot does not dislike his cousin, I fancy?'

'Oh! no, that is clear enough. Once can guess what will happen there. He is always with them; half lives in the family, I believe. What a very good-looking man!'

'Yes, and Miss Atkinson, who dined with him once at the Wallises, says he is the most agreeable man she ever was in company with.'

'She is pretty, I think; Anne Elliot; very pretty, when one comes to look at her. It is not the fashion to say so, but I confess I admire her more than her sister.'

'Oh! so do I.'

'And so do I. No comparison. But the men are all wild after Miss Elliot. Anne is too delicate for them.'

Anne would have been particularly obliged to her cousin, if he would have walked by her side all the way to Camden-place, without saying a word. She had never found it so difficult to listen to him, though nothing could exceed his solicitude and care, and though his subjects were principally such as were wont to be always interesting – praise, warm, just, and discriminating, of Lady Russell, and insinuations highly rational against Mrs Clay. But just now she could think only of Captain Wentworth. She could not understand his present feelings, whether he were really suffering much from disappointment or not; and till that point were settled, she could not be quite herself.

She hoped to be wise and reasonable in time; but alas! alas! she must confess to herself that she was not wise yet.

Another circumstance very essential for her to know, was how long he meant to be in Bath; he had not mentioned it, or she could not recollect it. He might be only passing through. But it was more probable that he should be come to stay. In that case, so liable as every body was to meet every body in Bath, Lady Russell would in all likelihood see him somewhere. – Would she recollect him? How would it all be?

She had already been obliged to tell Lady Russell that Louisa Musgrove was to marry Captain Benwick. It had cost her something to encounter Lady Russell's surprise; and now, if she were by any chance to be thrown into company with Captain Wentworth, her imperfect knowledge of the matter might add another shade of prejudice against him.

The following morning Anne was out with her friend, and for the first hour, in an incessant and fearful sort of watch for him in vain; but at last, in returning down Pulteney-street, she distinguished him on the right hand pavement at such a distance as to have him in view the greater part of the street. There were many other men about him, many groups walking the same way, but there was no mistaking him. She looked instinctively at Lady Russell; but not from any mad idea of her recognising him so soon as she did herself. No, it was not to be supposed that Lady Russell would perceive him till they were nearly opposite. She looked at her however, from time to time, anxiously; and when the moment approached which must point him out, though not daring to look again (for her own countenance she knew was unfit to be seen), she was yet perfectly conscious of Lady Russell's eyes being turned exactly in the direction of him, of her being in short intently observing him. She could throughly comprehend the sort of fascination he must possess over Lady Russell's mind, the difficulty it must be for her to withdraw her eyes, the astonishment she must be feeling that eight or nine years should have passed over him, and in foreign climes and in active service too, without robbing him of one personal grace!

At last, Lady Russell drew back her head. – 'Now, how would she speak of him?'

'You will wonder,' said she 'what has been fixing my eye so long; but I was looking after some window-curtains, which Lady Alicia and Mrs Frankland were telling me of last night. They described the drawing-room window-curtains of one of the houses on this side of the way, and this part of the street, as being the handsomest and best hung of any in Bath, but could not recollect the exact number, and I have been trying to find out which it could be; but I confess I can see no curtains hereabouts that answer their description.'

Anne sighed and blushed and smiled, in pity and disdain, either at her friend or herself. – The part which provoked her most, was that in all this waste of foresight and caution, she should have lost the right moment for seeing whether he saw them.

A day or two passed without producing any thing. – The theatre or the rooms, where he was most likely to be, were not fashionable enough for the Elliots, whose evening amusements were solely in the elegant stupidity of private parties, in which they were getting more and more engaged; and Anne, wearied of such a state of stagnation, sick of knowing nothing, and fancying herself stronger because her strength was not tried, was quite impatient for the concert evening. It was a concert for the benefit of a person patronised by Lady Dalrymple. Of course they must attend. It was really expected to be a good one, and Captain Wentworth was very fond of music. If she could only have a few minutes conversation with him again, she felt all over courage if the opportunity occurred. Elizabeth had turned from him, Lady Russell overlooked him; her nerves were strengthened by these circumstances; she felt that she owed him attention.

She had once partly promised Mrs Smith to spend the evening with her; but in a short hurried call she excused herself and put it off, with the more decided promise of a longer visit on the morrow. Mrs Smith gave a most good-humoured acquiescence.

'By all means,' said she; 'only tell me all about it, when you do come. Who is your party?'

Anne named them all. Mrs Smith made no reply; but when she was leaving her, said, and with an expression half serious, half arch, 'Well, I heartily wish your concert may answer; and do not fail me to-morrow if you can come; for I begin to have a foreboding that I may not have many more visits from you.'

Anne was startled and confused, but after standing in a moment's suspense, was obliged, and not sorry to be obliged, to hurry away.

CHAPTER TWENTY

SIR WALTER, HIS TWO DAUGHTERS, and Mrs Clay, were the earliest of all their party, at the rooms in the evening; and as Lady Dalrymple must be waited for, they took their station by one of the fires in the octagon room. But hardly were they settled, when the door opened again, and Captain Wentworth walked in alone. Anne was the nearest to him, and making yet a little advance, she instantly spoke. He was preparing only to bow and pass on, but her gentle 'How do you do?' brought him out of the straight line to stand near her, and make enquiries in return, in spite of the formidable father and sister in the back ground. Their being in the back ground was a support to Anne; she knew nothing of their looks, and felt equal to every thing which she believed right to be done.

While they were speaking, a whispering between her father and Elizabeth caught her ear. She could not distinguish, but she must guess the subject; and on Captain Wentworth's making a distant bow, she comprehended that her father had judged so well as to give him that simple acknowledgment of acquaintance, and she was just in time by a side glance to see a slight curtsey from Elizabeth herself. This, though late and reluctant and ungracious, was yet better than nothing, and her spirits improved.

After talking however of the weather and Bath and the concert, their conversation began to flag, and so little was said at last, that she was expecting him to go every moment; but he did not; he seemed in no hurry to leave her; and presently with renewed spirit, with a little smile, a little glow, he said,

'I have hardly seen you since our day at Lyme. I am afraid you must have suffered from the shock, and the more from its not overpowering you at the time.'

She assured him that she had not.

'It was a frightful hour,' said he, 'a frightful day!' and he passed his hand across his eyes, as if the remembrance were still too painful; but in a moment half smiling again, added, 'The day has produced some effects however – has had some consequences which must be considered as the very reverse of frightful. – When you had the presence of mind to suggest that Benwick would be the properest person to fetch a surgeon, you could have little idea of his being eventually one of those most concerned in her recovery.'

'Certainly I could have none. But it appears – I should hope it would be a very happy match. There are on both sides good principles and good temper.'

'Yes,' said he, looking not exactly forward – 'but there I think ends the resemblance. With all my soul I wish them happy, and rejoice over every circumstance in favour of it. They have no difficulties to contend with at home, no opposition, no caprice, no delays. – The Musgroves are behaving like themselves, most honourably and kindly, only anxious with true parental hearts to promote their daughter's comfort. All this is much, very much in favour of their happiness; more than perhaps –'

He stopped. A sudden recollection seemed to occur, and to give him some taste of that emotion which was reddening Anne's cheeks and fixing her eyes on the ground. – After clearing his throat, however, he proceeded thus,

'I confess that I do think there is a disparity, too great a disparity, and in a point no less essential than mind. – I regard Louisa Musgrove as a very amiable, sweet-tempered girl, and not deficient in understanding; but Benwick is something more. He is a clever man, a reading man – and I confess that I do consider his attaching himself to her, with some surprise. Had it been the effect of gratitude, had he learnt to love her, because he believed her to be preferring him, it would have been another thing. But I have no reason to suppose it so. It seems, on the contrary, to have been a perfectly spontaneous, untaught feeling on his side, and this surprises me. A man like him, in his situation! With a heart pierced, wounded, almost broken! Fanny Harville was a very superior creature; and his attachment to her was indeed attachment. A man does not recover from such a devotion of the heart to such a woman! – He ought not – he does not.'

Either from the consciousness, however, that his friend had recovered, or from other consciousness, he went no farther; and Anne, who in spite of the agitated voice in which the latter part had been uttered, and in spite of all the various noises of the room, the almost ceaseless slam of the door, and ceaseless buzz of persons walking through, had distinguished every word, was struck, gratified, confused, and beginning to breathe very quick, and feel an hundred things in a moment. It was impossible for her to enter on such a subject; and yet, after a pause, feeling the necessity of speaking, and having not the smallest wish for a total change, she only deviated so far as to say,

'You were a good while at Lyme, I think?'

'About a fortnight. I could not leave it till Louisa's doing well was quite ascertained. I had been too deeply concerned in the mischief to be soon at peace. It had been my doing – solely mine. She would not have been obstinate if I had not been weak. The country round Lyme is very fine. I walked and rode a great deal; and the more I saw, the more I found to admire.'

'I should very much like to see Lyme again,' said Anne.

'Indeed! I should not have supposed that you could have found any thing in Lyme to inspire such a feeling. The horror and distress you were involved in – the stretch of mind, the wear of spirits! – I should have thought your last impressions of Lyme must have been strong disgust.'

'The last few hours were certainly very painful,' replied Anne: 'but when pain is over, the remembrance of it often becomes a pleasure. One does not love a place the less for having suffered in it, unless it has been all suffering, nothing but suffering – which was by no means the case at Lyme. We were only in anxiety and distress during the last two hours; and, previously, there had been a great deal of enjoyment. So much novelty and beauty! I have travelled so little, that every fresh place would be interesting to me – but there is real beauty at Lyme: and in short' (with a faint blush at some recollections) 'altogether my impressions of the place are very agreeable.'

As she ceased, the entrance door opened again, and the very party appeared for whom they were waiting. 'Lady Dalrymple, Lady Dalrymple,' was the rejoicing sound; and with all the eagerness compatible with anxious elegance, Sir Walter and his two ladies stepped forward to meet her. Lady Dalrymple and Miss Carteret, escorted by Mr Elliot and Colonel Wallis, who had happened to arrive nearly at the same instant, advanced into the room. The others joined them, and it was a group in which Anne found herself also necessarily included. She was divided from Captain Wentworth. Their interesting, almost too interesting conversation must be broken up for a time; but slight was the penance compared with the happiness which brought it on! She had learnt, in the last ten minutes, more of his feelings towards Louisa, more of all his feelings, than she dared to think of! and she gave herself up to the demands of the party, to the needful civilities of the moment, with exquisite, though agitated sensations. She was in good humour with all. She had received ideas which disposed her to be

With all the eagerness compatible with anxious elegance

courteous and kind to all, and to pity every one, as being less happy than herself.

The delightful emotions were a little subdued, when, on stepping back from the group, to be joined again by Captain Wentworth, she saw that he was gone. She was just in time to see him turn into the concert room. He was gone – he had disappeared: she felt a moment's regret. But they should meet again. He would look for her – he would find her out long before the evening were over – and at present, perhaps, it was as well to be asunder. She was in need of a little interval for recollection.

Upon Lady Russell's appearance soon afterwards, the whole party was collected, and all that remained, was to marshal themselves, and proceed into the concert room; and be of all the consequence in their power, draw as many eyes, excite as many whispers, and disturb as many people as they could.

Very, very happy were both Elizabeth and Anne Elliot as they walked in. Elizabeth, arm in arm with Miss Carteret, and looking on the broad back of the dowager Viscountess Dalrymple before her, had nothing to wish for which did not seem within her reach; and Anne – but it would be an insult to the nature of Anne's felicity, to draw any comparison between it and her sister's; the origin of one all selfish vanity, of the other all generous attachment.

Anne saw nothing, thought nothing of the brilliancy of the room. Her happiness was from within. Her eyes were bright, and her cheeks glowed, – but she knew nothing about it. She was thinking only of the last half hour, and as they passed to their seats, her mind took a hasty range over it. His choice of subjects, his expressions, and still more his manner and look, had been such as she could see in only one light. His opinion of Louisa Musgrove's inferiority, an opinion which he had seemed solicitous to give, his wonder at Captain Benwick, his feelings as to a first, strong attachment, – sentences begun which he could not finish – his half averted eyes, and more than half expressive glance, – all, all declared that he had a heart returning to her at least; that anger, resentment, avoidance, were no more; and that they were succeeded, not merely by friendship and regard, but by the tenderness of the past, yes, some share of the tenderness of the past. She could not contemplate the change as implying less. – He must love her.

These were thoughts, with their attendant visions, which occupied and flurried her too much to leave her any power of observation; and she passed along the room without having a glimpse of him, without even trying to discern him. When their places were determined on, and they were all properly arranged, she looked round to see if he should happen to be in the same part of the room, but he was not, her eye could not reach him; and the concert being just opening, she must consent for a time to be happy in an humbler way.

The party was divided, and disposed of on two contiguous benches: Anne was among those on the foremost, and Mr Elliot had manoeuvred so well, with the assistance of his friend Colonel Wallis, as to have a seat by her. Miss Elliot, surrounded by her cousins, and the principal object of Colonel Wallis's gallantry, was quite contented.

Anne's mind was in a most favourable state for the entertainment of the evening; it was just occupation enough: she had feelings for the tender, spirits for the gay, attention for the scientific, and patience for the wearisome; and had never liked a concert better, at least during the first act.

Towards the close of it, in the interval succeeding an Italian song, she explained the words of the song to Mr Elliot. – They had a concert bill between them.

'This,' said she, 'is nearly the sense, or rather the meaning of the words, for certainly the sense of an Italian love-song must not be talked of, – but it is as nearly the meaning as I can give; for I do not pretend to understand the language. I am a very poor Italian scholar.'

'Yes, yes, I see you are. I see you know nothing of the matter. You have only knowledge enough of the language, to translate at sight these inverted, transposed, curtailed Italian lines, into clear, comprehensible, elegant English. You need not say anything more of your ignorance. – Here is complete proof.'

'I will not oppose such kind politeness; but I should be sorry to be examined by a real proficient.'

'I have not had the pleasure of visiting in Camden-place so long,' replied he, 'without knowing something of Miss Anne Elliot; and I do regard her as one who is too modest, for the world in general to be aware of half her accomplishments, and too highly accomplished for modesty to be natural in any other woman.'

'For shame! for shame! – this is too much flattery. I forget what we are to have next,' turning to the bill.

'Perhaps,' said Mr Elliot, speaking low, 'I have had a longer acquaintance with your character than you are aware of.'

'Indeed! – How so? You can have been acquainted with it only since I came to Bath, excepting as you might hear me previously spoken of in my own family.'

'I knew you by report long before you came to Bath. I had heard you described by those who knew you intimately. I have been acquainted with you by character many years. Your person, your disposition, accomplishments, manner – they were all present to me.'

Mr Elliot was not disappointed in the interest he hoped to raise. No one can withstand the charm of such a mystery. To have been described long ago to a recent acquaintance, by nameless people, is irresistible; and Anne was all curiosity. She wondered, and questioned him eagerly – but in vain. He delighted in being asked, but he would not tell.

'No, no – some time or other perhaps, but not now. He would mention no names now; but such, he could assure her, had been the fact. He had many years ago received such a description of Miss Anne Elliot, as had inspired him with the highest idea of her merit, and excited the warmest curiosity to know her.'

Anne could think of no one so likely to have spoken with partiality of her many years ago, as the Mr Wentworth, of Monkford, Captain

Wentworth's brother. He might have been in Mr Elliot's company, but she had not courage to ask the question.

'The name of Anne Elliot,' said he, 'has long had an interesting sound to me. Very long has it possessed a charm over my fancy; and, if I dared, I would breathe my wishes that the name might never change.'

Such she believed were his words; but scarcely had she received their sound, than her attention was caught by other sounds immediately behind her, which rendered every thing else trivial. Her father and Lady Dalrymple were speaking.

'A well-looking man,' said Sir Walter, 'a very well-looking man.'

'A very fine young man indeed!' said Lady Dalrymple. 'More air than one often sees in Bath. – Irish, I dare say.'

'No, I just know his name. A bowing acquaintance. Wentworth – Captain Wentworth of the navy. His sister married my tenant in Somersetshire, – the Croft, who rents Kellynch.'

Before Sir Walter had reached this point, Anne's eyes had caught the right direction, and distinguished Captain Wentworth, standing among a cluster of men at a little distance. As her eyes fell on him, his seemed to be withdrawn from her. It had that appearance. It seemed as if she had been one moment too late; and as long as she dared observe, he did not look again: but the performance was re-commencing, and she was forced to seem to restore her attention to the orchestra, and look straight forward.

When she could give another glance, he had moved away. He could not have come nearer to her if he would; she was so surrounded and shut in: but she would rather have caught his eye.

Mr Elliot's speech too distressed her. She had no longer any inclination to talk to him. She wished him not so near her.

The first act was over. Now she hoped for some beneficial change; and, after a period of nothing-saying amongst the party, some of them did decide on going in quest of tea. Anne was one of the few who did not choose to move. She remained in her seat, and so did Lady Russell; but she had the pleasure of getting rid of Mr Elliot; and she did not mean, whatever she might feel on Lady Russell's account, to shrink from conversation with Captain Wentworth, if he gave her the opportunity. She was persuaded by Lady Russell's countenance that she had seen him.

He did not come however. Anne sometimes fancied she discerned him at a distance, but he never came. The anxious interval wore away unproductively. The others returned, the room filled again, benches were reclaimed and re-possessed, and another hour of pleasure or of penance was to be set out, another hour of music was to give delight or the gapes, as real or affected taste for it prevailed. To Anne, it chiefly wore the prospect of an hour of agitation. She could not quit that room in peace without seeing

Captain Wentworth once more, without the interchange of one friendly look.

In re-settling themselves, there were now many changes, the result of which was favourable for her. Colonel Wallis declined sitting down again, and Mr Elliot was invited by Elizabeth and Miss Carteret, in a manner not to be refused, to sit between them; and by some other removals, and a little scheming of her own, Anne was enabled to place herself much nearer the end of the bench than she had been before, much more within reach of a passer-by. She could not do so, without comparing herself with Miss Larolles, the inimitable Miss Larolles, – but still she did it, and not with much happier effect; though by what seemed prosperity in the early abdication in her next neighbours, she found herself at the very end of the bench before the concert closed.

Such was her situation, with a vacant space at hand, when Captain Wentworth was again in sight. She saw him not far off. He saw her too; yet he looked grave, and seemed irresolute, and only by very slow degrees came at last near enough to speak to her. She felt that something must be the matter. The change was indubitable. The difference between his present air and what it had been in the octagon room was strikingly great. – Why was it? She thought of her father – of Lady Russell. Could there have been any unpleasant glances? He began by speaking of the concert, gravely; more like the Captain Wentworth of Uppercross; owned himself disappointed, had expected better singing; and, in short, must confess that he should not be sorry when it was over. Anne replied, and spoke in defence of the performance so well, and yet in allowance for his feelings, so pleasantly, that his countenance improved, and he replied again with almost a smile. They talked for a few minutes more; the improvement held; he even looked down towards the bench, as if he saw a place on it well worth occupying; when, at that moment, a touch on her shoulder obliged Anne to turn round. – It came from Mr Elliot. He begged her pardon, but she must be applied to, to explain Italian again. Miss Carteret was very anxious to have a general idea of what was next to be sung. Anne could not refuse; but never had she sacrificed to politeness with a more suffering spirit.

A few minutes, though as few as possible, were inevitably consumed; and when her own mistress again, when able to turn and look as she had done before, she found herself accosted by Captain Wentworth, in a reserved yet hurried sort of farewell. 'He must wish her good night. He was going – he should get home as fast as he could.'

'Is not this song worth staying for?' said Anne, suddenly struck by an idea which made yet more anxious to be encouraging.

'No!' he replied impressively, 'there is nothing worth my staying for;' and he was gone directly.

Jealousy of Mr Elliot! It was the only intelligible motive. Captain Wentworth jealous of her affection! Could she have believed it a week ago – three hours ago! For a moment the gratification was exquisite. But alas! there were very different thoughts to succeed. How was such jealousy to be quieted? How was the truth to reach him? How, in all the peculiar disadvantages of their respective situations, would he ever learn her real sentiments? It was misery to think of Mr Elliot's attentions. – Their evil was incalculable.

CHAPTER TWENTY ONE

ANNE RECOLLECTED WITH pleasure the next morning her promise of going to Mrs Smith; meaning that it should engage her from home at the time when Mr Elliot would be most likely to call; for to avoid Mr Elliot was almost a first object.

She felt a great deal of good will towards him. In spite of the mischief of his attentions, she owed him gratitude and regard, perhaps compassion. She could not help thinking much of the extraordinary circumstances attending their acquaintance; of the right which he seemed to have to interest her, by every thing in situation, by his own sentiments, by his early prepossession. It was altogether very extraordinary. – Flattering, but painful. How she might have felt, had there been no Captain Wentworth in the case, was not worth enquiry; for there was a Captain Wentworth: and be the conclusion of the present suspense good or bad, her affection would be his for ever. Their union, she believed, could not divide her more from other men, than their final separation.

Prettier musings of high-wrought love and eternal constancy, could never have passed along the streets of Bath, than Anne was sporting with from Camden-place to Westgate-buildings. It was almost enough to spread purification and perfume all the way.

She was sure of a pleasant reception; and her friend seemed this morning particularly obliged to her for coming, seemed hardly to have expected her, though it had been an appointment.

An account of the concert was immediately claimed; and Anne's recollections of the concert were quite happy enough to animate her features, and make her rejoice to talk of it. All that she could tell, she told most gladly; but the all was little for one who had been there, and unsatisfactory for such an enquirer as Mrs Smith, who had already heard, through the short cut of a laundress and a waiter, rather more of the general success and produce of the evening than Anne could relate; and who now asked in vain for several particulars of the company. Every body of any consequence or notoriety in Bath was well known by name to Mrs Smith.

'The little Durands were there, I conclude,' said she, 'with their mouth open to catch the music; like unfledged sparrows ready to be fed. They never miss a concert.'

'Yes. I did not see them myself, but I heard Mr Elliot say they were in the room.'

'The little Durands were there'

'The Ibbotsons – were they there? and the two new beauties, with the tall Irish officer, who is talked of for one of them.'

'I do not know. – I do not think they were.'

'Old Lady Mary Maclean? I need not ask after her. She never misses, I know; and you must have seen her. She must have been in your own circle, for as you went with Lady Dalrymple, you were in the seats of grandeur; round the orchestra, of course.'

'No, that was what I dreaded. It would have been very unpleasant to me in every respect. But happily Lady Dalrymple always chooses to be farther off; and we were exceedingly well placed – that is for hearing; I must not say for seeing, because I appear to have seen very little.'

'Oh! you saw enough for your own amusement. – I can understand. There is a sort of domestic enjoyment to be known even in a crowd, and this you had. You were a large party in yourselves, and you wanted nothing beyond.'

'But I ought to have looked about me more,' said Anne, conscious while she spoke, that there had in fact been no want of looking about; that the object only had been deficient.

'No, no – you were better employed. You need not tell me that you had a pleasant evening. I see it in your eye. I perfectly see how the hours passed – that you had always something agreeable to listen to. In the intervals of the concert, it was conversation.'

Anne half smiled and said, 'Do you see that in my eye?'

'Yes, I do. Your countenance perfectly informs me that you were in company last night with the person, whom you think the most agreeable in the world, the person who interests you at this present time, more than all the rest of the world put together.'

A blush overspread Anne's cheeks. She could say nothing.

'And such being the case,' continued Mrs Smith, after a short pause, 'I hope you believe that I do know how to value your kindness in coming to me this morning. It is really very good of you to come and sit with me, when you must have so many pleasanter demands upon your time.'

Anne heard nothing of this. She was still in the astonishment and confusion excited by her friend's penetration unable to imagine how any report of Captain Wentworth could have reached her. After another short silence –

'Pray,' said Mrs Smith, 'is Mr Elliot aware of your acquaintance with me? Does he know that I am in Bath?'

'Mr Elliot!' repeated Anne, looking up surprised. A moment's reflection shewed her the mistake she had been under. She caught it instantaneously; and, recovering courage with the feeling of safety, soon added, more composedly, 'are you acquainted with Mr Elliot?'

'I have been a good deal acquainted with him,' replied Mrs Smith, gravely, 'but it seems worn out now. It is a great while since we met.'

'I was not at all aware of this. You never mentioned it before. Had I known it, I would have had the pleasure of talking to him about you.'

'To confess the truth,' said Mrs Smith, assuming her usual air of cheerfulness, 'that is exactly the pleasure I want you to have. I want you to talk about me to Mr Elliot. I want your interest with him. He can be of essential service to me; and if you would have the goodness, my dear Miss Elliot, to make it an object to yourself, of course it is done.'

'I should be extremely happy – I hope you cannot doubt my willingness to be of even the slightest use to you,' replied Anne; 'but I suspect that you are considering me as having a higher claim on Mr Elliot – a greater right to influence him, than is really the case. I am sure you have, somehow or other, imbibed such a notion. You must consider me only as Mr Elliot's relation. If in that light, if there is any thing which you suppose his cousin might fairly ask of him, I beg you would not hesitate to employ me.'

Mrs Smith gave her a penetrating glance, and then, smiling, said,

'I have been a little premature, I perceive. I beg your pardon. I ought to have waited for official information. But now, my dear Miss Elliot, as an old friend, do give me a hint as to when I may speak. Next week? To be sure by next week I may be allowed to think it all settled, and build my own selfish schemes on Mr Elliot's good fortune.'

'No,' replied Anne, 'nor next week, nor next, nor next. I assure you that nothing of the sort you are thinking of will be settled any week. I am not going to marry Mr Elliot. I should like to know why you imagine I am.'

Mrs Smith looked at her again, looked earnestly, smiled, shook her head, and exclaimed.

'Now, how I do wish I understood you! How I do wish I knew what you were at! I have a great idea that you do not design to be cruel, when the right moment comes. Till it does come, you know, we women never mean to have any body. It is a thing of course among us, that every man is refused – till he offers. But why should you be cruel? Let me plead for my – present friend I cannot call him – but for my former friend. Where can you look for a more suitable match? Where could you expect a more gentlemanlike, agreeable man? Let me recommend Mr Elliot. I am sure you hear nothing but good of him from Colonel Wallis; and who can know him better than Colonel Wallis?'

'My dear Mrs Smith, Mr Elliot's wife has not been dead much above half a year. He ought not to be supposed to be paying his addresses to any one.'

'Oh, if these are you only objections,' cried Mrs Smith, archly, 'Mr Elliot is safe, and I shall give myself no more trouble about him. Do not forget me when you are married, that's all. Let him know me to be a friend of yours, and then he will think little of the trouble required, which it is very natural for him now, with so many affairs and engagements of his own, to avoid and get rid of as he can – very natural, perhaps. Ninety-nine out of a hundred would do the same. Of course, he cannot be aware of the importance to me. Well, my dear Miss Elliot, I hope and trust you will be very happy. Mr Elliot has sense to understand the value of such a woman. Your peace will not be shipwrecked as mine has been. You are safe in all worldly matters, and safe in his character. He will not be led astray, he will not be misled by others to his ruin.'

'No,' said Anne, 'I can readily believe all that of my cousin. He seems to have a calm, decided temper, not at all open to dangerous impressions. I consider him with great respect. I have no reason, from any thing that has fallen within my observation, to do otherwise. But I have not known him long; and he is not a man, I think, to be known intimately soon. Will not this manner of speaking of him, Mrs Smith, convince you that he is nothing to me? Surely, this must be calm enough. And, upon my word, he is nothing to me. Should he ever propose to me (which I have very little reason to imagine he has any thought of doing), I shall not accept him. I assure you I shall not. I assure you Mr Elliot had not the share which you have been supposing, in whatever pleasure the concert of last night might afford: – not Mr Elliot; it is not Mr Elliot that –'

She stopped regretting with a deep blush that she had implied so much; but less would hardly have been sufficient. Mrs Smith would hardly have believed so soon in Mr Elliot's failure, but from the perception of there being a somebody else. As it was, she instantly submitted, and with all the semblance of seeing nothing beyond; and Anne, eager to escape farther notice, was impatient to know why Mrs Smith should have fancied she was to marry Mr Elliot, where she could have received the idea, or from whom she could have heard it.

'Do tell me how it first came into your head.'

'It first came into my head,' replied Mrs Smith, 'upon finding how much you were together, and feeling it to be the most probable thing in the world to be wished for by everybody belonging to either of you; and you may depend upon it that all your acquaintance have disposed of you in the same way. But I never heard it spoken of till two days ago.'

'And has it indeed been spoken of?'

'Did you observe the woman who opened the door to you, when you called yesterday?'

'No. Was not it Mrs Speed, as usual, or the maid? I observed no one in particular.'

'It was my friend, Mrs Rooke – Nurse Rooke, who, by the by, had a great curiosity to see you, and was delighted to be in the way to let you in. She came away from Marlborough-buildings only on Sunday; and she it was who told me you were to marry Mr Elliot. She had had it from Mrs Wallis herself, which did not seem bad authority. She sat an hour with me on Monday evening, and gave me the whole history.'

'The whole history!' repeated Anne, laughing. 'She could not make a very long history, I think, of one such little article of unfounded news.'

Mrs Smith said nothing.

'But,' continued Anne, presently, 'though there is no truth in my having this claim on Mr Elliot, I should be extremely happy to be of use to you, in any way that I could. Shall I mention to him your being in Bath? Shall I take any message?'

'No, I thank you: no, certainly not. In the warmth of the moment, and under a mistaken impression, I might, perhaps, have endeavoured to interest you in some circumstances. But not now: no, I thank you, I have nothing to trouble you with.'

'I think you spoke of having known Mr Elliot many years?'

'I did.'

'Not before he married, I suppose?'

'Yes; he was not married when I knew him first.'

'And – were you much acquainted?'

'Intimately.'

'Indeed! Then do tell me what he was at that time of life. I have a great curiosity to know what Mr Elliot was as a very young man. Was he at all such as he appears now?'

'I have not seen Mr Elliot these three years,' was Mrs Smith's answer, given so gravely that it was impossible to pursue the subject farther; and Anne felt that she had gained nothing but an increase of curiosity. They were both silent – Mrs Smith very thoughtful. At last,

'I beg your pardon, my dear Miss Elliot,' she cried, in her natural tone of cordiality, 'I beg your pardon for the short answers I have been giving you, but I have been uncertain what I ought to do. I have been doubting and considering as to what I ought to tell you. There were many things to be taken into the account. One hates to be officious, to be giving bad impressions, making mischief. Even the smooth surface of family-union seems worth preserving, though there may be nothing durable beneath. However, I have determined; I think I am right; I think you ought to be made acquainted with Mr Elliot's real character. Though I fully believe that at present you have not the smallest intention of accepting him, there is no saying what may happen. You might, some time or other, be differently affected towards him. Hear the truth, therefore, now, while you are unprejudiced. Mr Elliot is a man without heart or conscience; a designing, wary, cold-blooded being, who thinks only of himself; who, for his own interest or ease, would be guilty of any cruelty, or any treachery, that could be perpetrated without risk of his general character. He has no feeling for others. Those whom he has been the chief cause of leading into ruin, he can neglect and desert without the smallest compunction. He is totally beyond the reach of any sentiment of justice or compassion. Oh! he is black at heart, hollow and black!'

Anne's astonished air, and exclamation of wonder, made her pause, and in a calmer manner she added,

'My expressions startle you. You must allow for an injured angry woman. But I will try to command myself. I will not abuse him. I will only tell you what I have found him. Facts shall speak. He was the intimate friend of my dear husband, who trusted and loved him, and thought him as good as himself. The intimacy had been formed before our marriage. I found them most intimate friends; and I, too, became excessively pleased with Mr Elliot, and entertained the highest opinion of him. At nineteen, you know, one does not think very seriously, but Mr Elliot appeared to me quite as good as others, and much more agreeable than most others, and we were almost always together. We were principally in town, living in very good style. He was then the inferior in circumstances, he was then the poor one; he had chambers in the Temple, and it was as much as he could do to support the appearance of a gentleman. He had always a home with us whenever he chose it; he was always welcome; he was like a brother. My poor Charles, who had the finest, most generous spirit in the world, would have divided his last farthing with him; and I know that his purse was open to him; I know that he often assisted him.'

'This must have been about that very period of Mr Elliot's life,' said Anne, 'which has always excited my particular curiosity. It must have been about the same time that he became known to my father and sister. I never knew him myself, I only heard of him, but there was a something in his conduct then with regard to my father and sister, and afterwards in the circumstances of his marriage, which I never could quite reconcile with present times. It seemed to announce a different sort of man.'

'I know it all, I know it all,' cried Mrs Smith. 'He had been introduced to Sir Walter and your sister before I was acquainted with him, but I heard him speak of them for ever. I know he was invited and encouraged, and I know he did not choose to go. I can satisfy you, perhaps, on points which you would little expect; and as to his marriage, I knew all about it at the time. I was privy to all the fors and againsts, I was the friend to whom he confided his hopes and plans, and though I did not know his wife previously, (her inferior situation in society, indeed, rendered that impossible) yet I knew her all her life afterwards, or, at least, till within the last two years of her life, and can answer any question you wish to put.'

'Nay,' said Anne, 'I have no particular enquiry to make about her. I have always understood they were not a happy couple. But I should like to know why, at that time of his life, he should slight my father's acquaintance as he did. My father was certainly disposed to take very kind and proper notice of him. Why did Mr Elliot draw back?'

'Mr Elliot,' replied Mrs Smith, 'at that period of his life, had one object in view – to make his fortune; and by a rather quicker process than the law. He was determined to make it by marriage. He was determined, at least, not to mar it by an imprudent marriage; and I know it was his belief, (whether justly or not, of course I cannot decide) that your father and sister, in their civilities and invitations, were designing a match between the heir and the young lady; and it was impossible that such a match should have answered his ideas of wealth and independence. That was his motive for drawing back, I can assure you. He told me the whole story. He had no concealments with me. It was curious, that having just left you behind me in Bath, my first and principal acquaintance on marrying, should be your cousin; and that through him, I should be continually hearing of your father and sister. He described one Miss Elliot, and I thought very affectionately of the other.'

'Perhaps,' cried Anne, struck by a sudden idea, 'you sometimes spoke of me to Mr Elliot?'

'To be sure I did, very often. I used to boast of my own Anne Elliot, and vouch for your being a very different creature from –'

She checked herself just in time.

'This accounts for something which Mr Elliot said last night,' cried Anne. 'This explains it. I found he had been used to hear of me. I could not comprehend how. What wild imaginations one forms, where dear self is concerned! How sure to be mistaken! But I beg your pardon; I have interrupted you. Mr Elliot married, then, completely for money? The circumstance, probably, which first opened your eyes to his character.'

Mrs Smith hesitated a little here. 'Oh! those things are too common. When one lives in the world, a man or woman's marrying for money is too common to strike one as it ought. I was very young, and associated only with the young, and we were a thoughtless, gay set, without any strict rules of conduct. We lived for enjoyment. I think differently now; time and sickness, and sorrow, have given me other notions; but, at that period, I must own I saw nothing reprehensible in what Mr Elliot was doing. "To do the best for himself," passed as a duty.'

'But was not she a very low woman?'

'Yes; which I objected to, but he would not regard. Money, money, was all that he wanted. Her father was a grazier, her grandfather had been a butcher, but that was all nothing. She was a fine woman, had had a decent education, was brought forward by some cousins, thrown by chance into Mr Elliot's company, and fell in love with him; and not a difficulty or a scruple was there on his side, with respect to her birth. All his caution was spent in being secured of the real amount of her fortune, before he committed himself. Depend upon it, whatever esteem Mr Elliot may have for his own situation in life now, as a young man he had not the smallest value for it. His chance of the Kellynch estate was something, but all the honour of the family he held as cheap as dirt. I have often heard him declare, that if baronetcies were saleable, any body should have his for fifty pounds, arms and motto, name and livery included; but I will not pretend to repeat half that I used to hear him say on that subject. It would not be fair. And yet you ought to have proof; for what is all this but assertion? and you shall have proof.'

'Indeed, my dear Mrs Smith, I want none,' cried Anne. 'You have asserted nothing contradictory to what Mr Elliot appeared to be some years ago. This is all in confirmation, rather, of what we used to hear and believe. I am more curious to know why he should be so different now?'

'But for my satisfaction; if you will have the goodness to ring for Mary – stay, I am sure you will have the still greater goodness of going yourself into my bed-room, and bringing me the small inlaid box which you will find on the upper shelf of the closet.'

Anne, seeing her friend to be earnestly bent on it, did as she was desired. The box was brought and placed before her, and Mrs Smith, sighing over it as she unlocked it, said,

'This is full of papers belonging to him, to my husband, a small portion only of what I had to look over when I lost him. The letter I am looking for, was one written by Mr Elliot to him before our marriage, and happened to be saved; why, one can hardly imagine. But he was careless and immethodical, like other men, about these things; and when I came to examine his papers, I found it with others still more trivial from different people scattered here and there, while many letters and memorandums of real importance had been destroyed. Here it is. I would not burn it, because being even then very little satisfied with Mr Elliot, I was determined to preserve every document of former intimacy. I have now another motive for being glad that I can produce it.'

This was the letter, directed to 'Charles Smith, Esq. Tunbridge Wells,' and dated from London, as far back as July, 1803.

'Dear Smith,

'I have received yours. Your kindness almost overpowers me. I wish nature had made such hearts as yours common, but I have lived three and twenty years in the world, and have seen none like it. At present, believe me, I have no need of your services, being in cash again. Give me joy: I have got rid of Sir Walter and Miss. They are gone back to Kellynch, and almost made me

swear to visit them this summer, but my first visit to Kellynch will be with a surveyor, to tell me how to bring it with best advantage to the hammer. The baronet, nevertheless, is not unlikely to marry again; he is quite fool enough. If he does, however, they will leave me in peace, which may be a decent equivalent for the reversion. He is worse than last year.

'I wish I had any name but Elliot. I am sick of it. The name of Walter I can drop, thank God! and I desire you will never insult me with my second W. again, meaning, for the rest of my life, to be only yours truly,

'Wm. Elliot.'

Such a letter could not be read without putting Anne in a glow; and Mrs Smith, observing the high colour in her face, said,

'The language, I know, is highly disrespectful. Though I have forgot the exact terms, I have a perfect impression of the general meaning. But it shews you the man. Mark his professions to my poor husband. Can any thing be stronger?'

Anne could not immediately get over the shock and mortification of finding such words applied to her father. She was obliged to recollect that her seeing the letter was a violation of the laws of honour, that no one ought to be judged or to be known by such testimonies, that no private correspondence could bear the eye of others, before she could recover calmness enough to return the letter which she had been meditating over, and say,

'Thank you. This is full proof undoubtedly, proof of every thing you were saying. But why be acquainted with us now?'

'I can explain this too,' cried Mrs Smith, smiling.

'Can you really?'

'Yes, I have shewn you Mr Elliot, as he was a dozen years ago, and I will shew him as he is now. I cannot produce written proof again, but I can give as authentic oral testimony as you can desire, of what he is now wanting, and what he is now doing. He is no hypocrite now. He truly wants to marry you. His present attentions to your family are very sincere, quite from the heart. I will give you my authority; his friend Colonel Wallis.'

'Colonel Wallis! you are acquainted with him?'

'No. It does not come to me in quite so direct a line as that; it takes a bend or two, but nothing of consequence. The stream is as good as at first; the little rubbish it collects in the turnings, is easily moved away. Mr Elliot talks unreservedly to Colonel Wallis of his views on you – which said Colonel Wallis I imagine to be in himself a sensible, careful, discerning sort of character; but Colonel Wallis has a very pretty silly wife, to whom he tells things which he had better not, and he repeats it all to her. She, in the overflowing spirits of her recovery, repeats it all to her nurse; and the nurse, knowing my acquaintance with you, very naturally brings it all to me. On

Monday evening my good friend Mrs Rooke let me thus much into the secrets of Marlborough-buildings. When I talked of a whole history therefore, you see, I was not romancing so much as you supposed.'

'My dear Mrs Smith, your authority is deficient. This will not do. Mr Elliot's having any views on me will not in the least account for the efforts he made towards a reconciliation with my father. That was all prior to my coming to Bath. I found them on the most friendly terms when I arrived.'

'I know you did; I know it all perfectly, but' –

'Indeed, Mrs Smith, we must not expect to get real information in such a line. Facts or opinions which are to pass through the hands of so many, to be misconceived by folly in one, and ignorance in another, can hardly have much truth left.'

'Only give me a hearing. You will soon be able to judge of the general credit due, by listening to some particulars which you can yourself immediately contradict or confirm. Nobody supposes that you were his first inducement. He had seen you indeed, before he came to Bath, and admired you, but without knowing it to be you. So says my historian at least. Is this true? Did he see you last summer or autumn, "somewhere down in the west," to use her own words, without knowing it to be you?'

'He certainly did. So far it is very true. At Lyme; I happened to be at Lyme.'

'Well,' continued Mrs Smith triumphantly, 'grant my friend the credit due to the establishement of the first point asserted. He saw you then at Lyme, and liked you so well as to be exceedingly pleased to meet with you again in Camden-place, as Miss Anne Elliot, and from that moment, I have no doubt, had a double motive in his visits there. But there was another, and an earlier; which I will now explain. If there is any thing in my story which you know to be either false or improbable, stop me. My account states, that your sister's friend, the lady now staying with you, whom I have heard you mention, came to Bath with Miss Elliot and Sir Walter as long ago as September, (in short when they first came themselves) and has been staying there ever since; that she is a clever, insinuating, handsome woman, poor and plausible, and altogether such in situation and manner, as to give a general idea among Sir Walter's acquaintance, of her meaning to be Lady Elliot, and as general a surprise that Miss Elliot should be apparently blind to the danger.'

Here Mrs Smith paused a moment; but Anne had not a word to say, and she continued,

'This was the light in which it appeared to those who knew the family, long before your return to it; and Colonel Wallis had his eye upon your father enough to be sensible of it, though he did not then visit in Camden-place; but his regard for Mr Elliot gave him an interest in watching all that was going on there, and when Mr Elliot came to Bath for a day or two, as he happened to do a little before Christmas, Colonel Wallis made him acquainted with the appearance of things, and the reports beginning to prevail. – Now you are to understand that time had worked a very material change in Mr Elliot's opinions as to the value of a baronetcy. Upon all points of blood and connexion, he is a completely altered man. Having long had as much money as he could spend, nothing to wish for on the side of avarice or indulgence, he has been gradually learning to pin his happiness upon the consequence he is heir to. I thought it coming on, before our acquaintance ceased, but it is now a confirmed feeling. He cannot bear the idea of not being Sir William. You may guess therefore that the news he heard from his friend, could not be very agreeable, and you may guess what it produced; the resolution of coming back to Bath as soon as possible, and of fixing himself here for a time, with the view of renewing his former acquaintance and recovering such a footing in the family, as might give him the means of ascertaining the degree of his danger, and of circumventing the lady if he found it material. This was agreed upon between the two friends, as the only thing to be done; and Colonel Wallis was to assist in every way that he could. He was to be introduced, and Mrs Wallis was to be introduced, and every body was to be introduced. Mr Elliot came back accordingly; and on application was forgiven, as you know, and re-admitted into the family; and there it was his constant object, and his only object (till your arrival added another motive) to watch Sir Walter and Mrs Clay. He omitted no opportunity of being with them, threw himself in their way, called at all hours – but I need not be particular on this subject. You can imagine what an artful man would do; and with this guide, perhaps, may recollect what you have seen him do.'

'Yes,' said Anne, 'you tell me nothing which does not accord with what I have known, or could imagine. There is always something offensive in the details of cunning. The manoeuvres of selfishness and duplicity must ever be revolting, but I have heard nothing which really surprises me. I know those who would be shocked by such a representation of Mr Elliot, who would have difficulty in believing it; but I have never been satisfied. I have always wanted some other motive for his conduct than appeared. – I should like to know his present opinion, as to the probability of the event he has been in dread of; whether he considers the danger to be lessening or not.'

'Lessening, I understand,' replied Mrs Smith. 'He thinks Mrs Clay afraid of him, aware that he sees through her, and not daring to proceed as she might do in his absence. But since he must be absent some time or other, I do not perceive how he can ever be secure, while she holds her present influence. Mrs Wallis has an amusing idea, as nurse tells me, that it is to be put into the marriage articles when you and Mr Elliot marry, that your father is not to marry Mrs Clay. A scheme, worthy of Mrs Wallis's understanding, by all accounts; but my sensible nurse Rooke sees the absurdity of it. – "Why, to be sure, ma'am," said she, "it would not prevent his marrying any body else." And indeed, to own the truth, I do not think nurse in her heart is a very strenuous opposer of Sir Walter's making a second match. She must be allowed to be a favourer of matrimony you know, and (since self will intrude) who can say that she may not have some flying visions of attending the next Lady Elliot, through Mrs Wallis's recommendation?'

'I am very glad to know all this,' said Anne, after a little thoughtfulness. 'It will be more painful to me in some respects to be in company with him, but I shall know better what to do. My line of conduct will be more direct. Mr Elliot is evidently a disingenuous, artificial, worldly man, who has never had any better principle to guide him than selfishness.'

But Mr Elliot was not yet done with. Mrs Smith had been carried away from her first direction, and Anne had forgotten, in the interest of her own family concerns, how much had been originally implied against him; but her attention was now called to the explanation of those first hints, and she listened to a recital which, if it did not perfectly justify the unqualified bitterness of Mrs Smith, proved him to have been very unfeeling in his conduct towards her, very deficient both in justice and compassion.

She learned that (the intimacy between them continuing unimpaired by Mr Elliot's marriage) they had been as before always together, and Mr Elliot had led his friend into expenses much beyond his fortune. Mrs Smith did not want to take blame to herself, and was most tender of throwing any on her husband; but Anne could collect that their income had never been equal to their style of living, and that from the first, there had been a great deal of general and joint extravagance. From his wife's account of him, she could discern Mr Smith to have been a man of warm feelings, easy temper, careless habits, and not strong understanding, much more amiable than his friend, and very unlike him – led by him, and probably despised by him. Mr Elliot, raised by his marriage to great affluence, and disposed to every gratification of pleasure and vanity which could be commanded without involving himself, (for with all his self-indulgence he had become a prudent man) and beginning to be rich, just as his friend ought to have found himself to be poor, seemed to have had no concern at all for that friend's probable finances, but, on the contrary, had been prompting and encouraging expenses, which could only end in ruin. And the Smiths accordingly had been ruined.

The husband had died just in time to be spared the full knowledge of it. They had previously known embarrassments enough to try the friendship of their friends, and to prove that Mr Elliot's had better not be tried; but it was not till his death that the wretched state of his affairs was fully known.

With a confidence in Mr Elliot's regard, more creditable to his feelings than his judgment, Mr Smith had appointed him the executor of his will; but Mr Elliot would not act, and the difficulties and distresses which his refusal had heaped on her, in addition to the inevitable sufferings of her situation, had been such as could not be related without anguish of spirit, or listened to without corresponding indignation.

Anne was shewn some letters of his on the occasion, answers to urgent applications from Mrs Smith, which all breathed the same stern resolution of not engaging in a fruitless trouble, and, under a cold civility, the same hard-hearted indifference to any of the evils it might bring on her. It was a dreadful picture of ingratitude and inhumanity; and Anne felt at some moments, that no flagrant open crime could have been worse. She had a great deal to listen to; all the particulars of the past sad scenes, all the minutiae of distress upon distress, which in former conversations had been merely hinted at, were dwelt on now with a natural indulgence. Anne could perfectly comprehend the exquisite relief, and was only the more inclined to wonder at the composure of her friend's usual state of mind.

There was one circumstance in the history of her grievances of particular irritation. She had good reason to believe that some property of her husband in the West Indies, which had been for many years under a sort of sequestration for the payment of its own incumbrances, might be recoverable by proper measures; and this property, though not large, would be enough to make her comparatively rich. But there was nobody to stir in it. Mr Elliot would do nothing, and she could do nothing herself, equally disabled from personal exertion by her state of bodily weakness, and from employing others by her want of money. She had no natural connexions to assist her even with their counsel, and she could not afford to purchase the assistance of the law. This was a cruel aggravation of actually streightened means. To feel that she ought to be in better circumstances, that a little trouble in the right place might do it, and to fear that delay might be even weakening her claims, was hard to bear!

It was on this point that she had hoped to engage Anne's good offices with Mr Elliot. She had previously, in the anticipation of their marriage, been very apprehensive of losing her friend by it, but on being assured that he could have made no attempt of that nature, since he did not even know her to be in Bath, it immediately occurred, that something might be done in her favour by the influence of the woman he loved, and she had been hastily preparing to interest Anne's feelings, as far as the observances due to Mr Elliot's character would allow, when Anne's refutation of that supposed engagement changed the face of every thing, and while it took from her the new-formed hope of succeeding in the object of her first anxiety, left her at least the comfort of telling the whole story her own way.

After listening to this full description of Mr Elliot, Anne could not but express some surprise at Mrs Smith's having spoken of him so favourably in the beginning of their conversation. 'She had seemed to recommend and praise him!'

'My dear,' was Mrs Smith's reply, 'there was nothing else to be done. I considered your marrying him as certain, though he might not yet have made the offer, and I could no more speak the truth of him, than if he had been your husband. My heart bled for you, as I talked of happiness. And yet, he is sensible, he is agreeable, and with such a woman as you, it was not absolutely hopeless. He was very unkind to his first wife. They were wretched together. But she was too ignorant and giddy for respect, and he had never loved her. I was willing to hope that you must fare better.'

Anne could just acknowledge within herself such a possibility of having been induced to marry him, as made her shudder at the idea of the misery which must have followed. It was just possible that she might have been persuaded by Lady Russell! And under such a supposition, which would have been most miserable, when time had disclosed all, too late?

It was very desirable that Lady Russell should be no longer deceived; and one of the concluding arrangements of this important conference, which carried them through the greater part of the morning, was, that Anne had full liberty to communicate to her friend every thing relative to Mrs Smith, in which his conduct was involved.

CHAPTER TWENTY TWO

ANNE WENT HOME TO THINK over all that she had heard. In one point, her feelings were relieved by this knowledge of Mr Elliot. There was no longer any thing of tenderness due to him. He stood, as opposed to Captain Wentworth, in all his own unwelcome obtrusiveness; and the evil of his attentions last night, the irremediable mischief he might have done, was considered with sensations unqualified, unperplexed. – Pity for him was all over. But this was the only point of relief. In every other respect, in looking around her, or penetrating forward, she saw more to distrust and to apprehend. She was concerned for the disappointment and pain Lady Russell would be feeling, for the mortifications which must be hanging over her father and sister, and had all the distress of foreseeing many evils, without knowing how to avert any one of them. – She was most thankful for her own knowledge of him. She had never considered herself as entitled to reward for not slighting an old friend like Mrs Smith, but here was a reward indeed springing from it! – Mrs Smith had been able to tell her what no one else could have done. Could the knowlege have been extended through her family! – But this was a vain idea. She must talk to Lady Russell, tell her, consult with her, and having done her best, wait the event with as much composure as possible; and after all, her greatest want of composure would be in that quarter of the mind which could not be opened to Lady Russell, in that flow of anxieties and fears which must be all to herself.

She found, on reaching home, that she had, as she intended, escaped seeing Mr Elliot; that he had called and paid them a long morning visit; but hardly had she congratulated herself, and felt safe till to-morrow, when she heard that he was coming again in the evening.

'I had not the smallest intention of asking him,' said Elizabeth, with affected carelessness, 'but he gave so many hints; so Mrs Clay says, at least.'

'Indeed I do say it. I never saw any body in my life spell harder for an invitation. Poor man! I was really in pain for him; for your hard-hearted sister, Miss Anne, seems bent on cruelty.'

'Oh!' cried Elizabeth, 'I have been rather too much used to the game to be soon overcome by a gentleman's hints. However, when I found how excessively he was regretting that he should miss my father this morning, I gave way immediately, for I would never really omit an opportunity of bringing him and Sir Walter together. They appear to so much advantage in company with each other! Each behaving so pleasantly! Mr Elliot looking up with so much respect!'

'Quite delightful!' cried Mrs Clay, not daring, however, to turn her eyes towards Anne. 'Exactly like father and son! Dear Miss Elliot, may I not say father and son?'

'Oh! I lay no embargo on any body's words. If you will have such ideas! But, upon my word, I am scarcely sensible of his attentions being beyond those of other men.'

'My dear Miss Elliot!' exclaimed Mrs Clay, lifting up her hands and eyes, and sinking all the rest of her astonishment in a convenient silence.

'Well, my dear Penelope, you need not be so alarmed about him. I did invite him, you know. I sent him away with smiles. When I found he was really going to his friends at Thornberry-park for the whole day to-morrow, I had compassion on him.'

Anne admired the good acting of the friend, in being able to shew such pleasure as she did, in the expectation, and in the actual arrival of the very person whose presence must really be interfering with her prime object. It was impossible but that Mrs Clay must hate the sight of Mr Elliot; and yet she could assume a most obliging, placid look, and appear quite satisfied with the curtailed license of devoting herself only half as much to Sir Walter as she would have done otherwise.

To Anne herself it was most distressing to see Mr Elliot enter the room; and quite painful to have him approach and speak to her. She had been used before to feel that he could not be always quite sincere, but now she saw insincerity in every thing. His attentive deference to her father, contrasted with his former language, was odious; and when she thought of his cruel conduct towards Mrs Smith, she could hardly bear the sight of his present smiles and mildness, or the sound of his artificial good sentiments. She meant to avoid any such alteration of manners as might provoke a remonstrance on his side. It was a great object with her to escape all enquiry or eclat; but it was her intention to be as decidedly cool to him as might be compatible with their relationship, and to retrace, as quietly as she could, the few steps of unnecessary intimacy she had been gradually led along. She was accordingly more guarded, and more cool, than she had been the night before.

He wanted to animate her curiosity again as to how and where he could have heard her formerly praised; wanted very much to be gratified by more solicitation; but the charm was broken: he found that the heat and animation of a public room were necessary to kindle his modest cousin's vanity; he found, at least, that it was not to be done now, by any of those attempts which he could hazard among the too-commanding claims of the others. He little surmised that it was a subject acting now exactly against his interest, bringing immediately into her thoughts all those parts of his conduct which were least excusable.

She had some satisfaction in finding that he was really going out of Bath the next morning, going early, and that he would be gone the greater part of two days. He was invited again to Camden-place the very evening of his return; but from Thursday to Saturday evening his absence was certain. It was bad enough that a Mrs Clay should be always before her; but that a deeper hypocrite should be added to their party, seemed the destruction of every thing like peace and comfort. It was so humiliating to reflect on the constant deception practised on her father and Elizabeth; to consider the various sources of mortification preparing for them! Mrs Clay's selfishness was not so complicated nor so revolting as his; and Anne would have compounded for the marriage at once, with all its evils, to be clear of Mr Elliot's subtleties, in endeavouring to prevent it.

On Friday morning she meant to go very early to Lady Russell, and accomplish the necessary communication; and she would have gone directly after breakfast but that Mrs Clay was also going out on some obliging purpose of saving her sister trouble, which determined her to wait till she might be safe from such a companion. She saw Mrs Clay fairly off, therefore, before she began to talk of spending the morning in Rivers-street.

'Very well,' said Elizabeth, 'I have nothing to send but my love. Oh! you may as well take back that tiresome book she would lend me, and pretend I have read it through. I really cannot be plaguing myself for ever with all the new poems and states of the nation that come out. Lady Russell quite bores one with her new publications. You need not tell her so, but I thought her dress hideous the other night. I used to think she had some taste in dress, but I was ashamed of her at the concert. Something so formal and *arrangé* in her air! and she sits so upright! My best love, of course.'

'And mine,' added Sir Walter. 'Kindest regards. And you may say, that I mean to call upon her soon. Make a civil message. But I shall only leave my card. Morning visits are never fair by women at her time of life, who make themselves up so little. If she would only wear rouge, she would not be afraid of being seen; but last time I called, I observed the blinds were let down immediately.'

While her father spoke, there was a knock at the door. Who could it be? Anne, remembering the preconcerted visits, at all hours, of Mr Elliot, would have expected him, but for his known engagement seven miles off. After the usual period of suspense, the usual sounds of approach were heard, and 'Mr and Mrs Charles Musgrove' were ushered into the room.

Surprise was the strongest emotion raised by their appearance; but Anne was really glad to see them; and the others were not so sorry but that they could put on a decent air of welcome; and as soon as it became clear that these, their nearest relations, were not arrived with any views of accommodation in that house, Sir Walter and Elizabeth were able to rise in cordiality, and do the honours of it very well. They were come to Bath for a few days with Mrs Musgrove, and were at the White Hart. So much was pretty soon understood; but till Sir Walter and Elizabeth were walking Mary into the other drawing-room, and regaling themselves with her admiration, Anne could not draw upon Charles's brain for a regular history of their coming, or an explanation of some smiling hints of particular business, which had been ostentatiously dropped by Mary, as well as of some apparent confusion as to whom their party consisted of.

She then found that it consisted of Mrs Musgrove, Henrietta, and Captain Harville, beside their two selves. He gave her a very plain, intelligible account of the whole; a narration in which she saw a great deal of most characteristic proceeding. The scheme had received its first impulse by Captain Harville's wanting to come to Bath on business. He had begun to talk of it a week ago; and by way of doing something, as shooting was over, Charles had proposed coming with him, and Mrs Harville had seemed to like the idea of it very much, as an advantage to her husband; but Mary could not bear to be left, and had made herself so unhappy about it that, for a day or two, every thing seemed to be in suspense, or at an end. But then, it had been taken up by his father and mother. His mother had some old friends in Bath, whom she wanted to see; it was thought a good opportunity for Henrietta to come and buy wedding-clothes for herself and her sister; and, in short, it ended in being his mother's party, that every thing might be comfortable and easy to Captain Harville; and he and Mary were included in it, by way of general convenience. They had arrived late the night before. Mrs Harville, her children, and Captain Benwick, remained with Mr Musgrove and Louisa at Uppercross.

Anne's only surprise was, that affairs should be in forwardness enough for Henrietta's wedding-clothes to be talked of: she had imagined such difficulties of fortune to exist there as must prevent the marriage from being near at hand; but she learned from Charles that, very recently, (since Mary's last letter to herself) Charles Hayter had been applied to by a friend to hold a living for a youth who could not possibly claim it under many years; and that, on the strength of his present income, with almost a certainty of something more permanent long before the term in question, the two families had consented to the young people's wishes, and that their marriage was likely to take place in a few months, quite as soon as Louisa's. 'And a very good living it was,' Charles added, 'only five-and-twenty miles from Uppercross, and in a very fine country – fine part of Dorsetshire. In the centre of some of the best preserves in the kingdom, surrounded by three great proprietors, each more careful and jealous than the other; and to two of the three, at least, Charles Hayter might get a special recommendation. Not that he will value it as he ought,' he observed, 'Charles is too cool about sporting. That's the worst of him.'

'I am extremely glad, indeed,' cried Anne, 'particularly glad that this should happen: and that of two sisters, who both deserve equally well, and who have always been such good friends, the pleasant prospects of one should not be dimming those of the other – that they should be so equal in their prosperity and comfort. I hope your father and mother are quite happy with regard to both.'

'Oh! yes. My father would be well pleased if the gentlemen were richer, but he has not other fault to find. Money, you know, coming down with money – two daughters at once – it cannot be a very agreeable operation, and it streightens him as to many things. However, I do not mean to say they have not a right to it. It is very fit they should have daughters' shares; and I am sure he has always been a very kind, liberal father to me. Mary does not above half like Henrietta's match. She never did, you know. But she does not do him justice, nor think enough about Winthrop. I cannot make her attend to the value of the property. It is a very fair match, as times go; and I have liked Charles Hayter all my life, and I shall not leave off now.'

'Such excellent parents as Mr and Mrs Musgrove,' exclaimed Anne,

'Sits at her elbow, reading verses'

'should be happy in their children's marriages. They do every thing to confer happiness, I am sure. What a blessing to young people to be in such hands! Your father and mother seem so totally free from all those ambitious feelings which have led to so much misconduct and misery, both in young and old! I hope you think Louisa perfectly recovered now?'

He answered rather hesitatingly, 'Yes, I believe I do – very much recovered; but she is altered: there is no running or jumping about, no laughing or dancing; it is quite different. If one happens only to shut the door a little hard, she starts and wriggles like a young dab chick in the water; and Benwick sits at her elbow, reading verses, or whispering to her, all day long.'

Anne could not help laughing. 'That cannot be much to your taste, I know,' said she; 'but I do believe him to be an excellent young man.'

'To be sure he is. Nobody doubts it; and I hope you do not think I am so illiberal as to want every man to have the same objects and pleasures as myself. I have a great value for Benwick; and when one can but get him to talk, he has plenty to say. His reading has done him no harm for he has fought as well as read. He is a brave fellow. I got more acquainted with him last Monday than ever I did before. We had a famous set-to at rat-hunting all the morning, in my father's great barns; and he played his part so well, that I have liked him the better ever since.'

Here they were interrupted by the absolute necessity of Charles's following the others to admire mirrors and china; but Anne had heard enough to understand the present state of Uppercross, and rejoice in its happiness; and though she sighed as she rejoiced, her sigh had none of the ill-will of envy in it. She would certainly have risen to their blessings if she could, but she did not want to lessen theirs.

The visit passed off altogether in a high good humour. Mary was in excellent spirits, enjoying the gaiety and the change; and so well satisfied with the journey in her mother-in-law's carriage with four horses, and with her own complete independence of Camden-place, that she was exactly in a temper to admire every thing as she ought, and enter most readily into all the superiorities of the house, as they were detailed to her. She had no demands on her father or sister, and her consequence was just enough increased by their handsome drawing-rooms.

Elizabeth was, for a short time, suffering a good deal. She felt that Mrs Musgrove and all her party ought to be asked to dine with them, but she could not bear to have the difference of style, the reduction of servants, which a dinner must betray, witnessed by those who had been always so inferior to the Elliots of Kellynch. It was a struggle between propriety and vanity; but vanity got the better, and then Elizabeth was happy again. These were her internal persuasions. – 'Old fashioned notions – country hospitality – we do not profess to give dinners – few people in Bath do – Lady Alicia never does; did not even ask her own sister's family, though they were here a month: and I dare say it would be very inconvenient to Mrs Musgrove – put her quite out of her way. I am sure she would rather not come – she cannot feel easy with us. I will ask them all for an evening; that will be much better – that will be a novelty and a treat. They have not seen two such drawing rooms before. They will be delighted to come to-morrow evening. It shall be a regular party – small, but most elegant.' And this satisfied Elizabeth: and when the invitation was given to the two present, and promised for the absent, Mary was as completely satisfied. She was particularly asked to meet Mr Elliot, and be introduced to Lady

Dalrymple and Miss Carteret, who were fortunately already engaged to come; and she could not have received a more gratifying attention. Miss Elliot was to have the honour of calling on Mrs Musgrove in the course of the morning, and Anne walked off with Charles and Mary, to go and see her and Henrietta directly.

Her plan of sitting with Lady Russell must give way for the present. They all three called in Rivers-street for a couple of minutes; but Anne convinced herself that a day's delay of the intended communication could be of no consequence, and hastened forward to the White Hart, to see again the friends and companions of the last autumn, with an eagerness of good will which many associations contributed to form.

They found Mrs Musgrove and her daughter within, and by themselves, and Anne had the kindest welcome from each. Henrietta was exactly in that state of recently-improved views, of fresh-formed happiness, which made her full of regard and interest for every body she had ever liked before at all; and Mrs Musgrove's real affection had been won by her usefulness when they were in distress. It was a heartiness, and a warmth, and a sincerity which Anne delighted in the more, from the sad want of such blessings at home. She was intreated to give them as much of her time as possible, invited for every day and all day long, or rather claimed as a part of the family; and in return, she naturally fell into all her wonted ways of attention and assistance, and on Charles's leaving them together, was listening to Mrs Musgrove's history of Louisa, and to Henrietta's of herself, giving opinions on business, and recommendations to shops; with intervals of every help which Mary required, from altering her ribbon to settling her accounts, from finding her keys, and assorting her trinkets, to trying to convince her that she was not ill used by any body; which Mary, well amused as she generally was in her station, at a window overlooking the entrance to the pump-room, could not but have her moments of imagining.

A morning of thorough confusion was to be expected. A large party in an hotel ensured a quick-changing, unsettled scene. One five minutes brought a note, the next a parcel, and Anne had not been there half an hour, when their dining-room, spacious as it was, seemed more than half filled: a party of steady old friends were seated round Mrs Musgrove, and Charles came back with Captains Harville and Wentworth. The appearance of the latter could not be more than the surprise of the moment. It was impossible for her to have forgotten to feel, that this arrival of their common friends must be soon bringing them together again. Their last meeting had been most important in opening his feelings; she had derived from it a delightful conviction; but she feared from his looks, that the same unfortunate persuasion, which had hastened him away from the concert room, still governed. He did not seem to want to be near enough for conversation.

She tried to be calm, and leave things to take their course; and tried to dwell much on this argument of rational dependence – 'Surely, if there be constant attachment on each side, our hearts must understand each other ere long. We are not boy and girl, to be captiously irritable, misled by every moment's inadvertence, and wantonly playing with our own happiness.' And yet, a few minutes afterwards, she felt as if their present circumstances, could only be exposing them to inadvertencies and misconstructions of the most mischievous kind.

'Anne,' cried Mary, still at her window, 'there is Mrs Clay, I am sure, standing under the colonnade, and a gentleman with her. I saw then turn the corner from Bath-street just now. They seem deep in talk. Who is it? – Come, and tell me. Good heavens! I recollect. – It is Mr Elliot himself.'

'No,' cried Anne quickly, 'it cannot be Mr Elliot, I assure you. He was to leave Bath at nine this morning, and does not come back till to-morrow.'

As she spoke, she felt that Captain Wentworth was looking at her; the consciousness of which vexed and embarrassed her, and made her regret that she had said so much, simple as it was.

Mary, resenting that she should be supposed not to know her own cousin, began talking very warmly about the family features, and protesting still more positively that it was Mr Elliot, calling again upon Anne to come and look herself; but Anne did not mean to stir, and tried to be cool and unconcerned. Her distress returned, however, on perceiving smiles and intelligent glances pass between two or three of the lady visitors, as if they believed themselves quite in the secret. It was evident that the report concerning her had spread; and a short pause succeeded, which seemed to ensure that it would now spread farther.

'Do come, Anne,' cried Mary, 'come and look yourself. You will be too late, if you do not make haste. They are parting, they are shaking hands. He is turning away. Not know Mr Elliot, indeed! – You seem to have forgot all about Lyme.'

To pacify Mary, and perhaps screen her own embarrassment, Anne did move quietly to the window. She was just in time to ascertain that it really was Mr Elliot (which she had never believed), before he disappeared on one side, as Mrs Clay walked quickly off on the other; and checking the surprise which she could not but feel at such an appearance of friendly conference between two persons of totally opposite interests, she calmly said, 'Yes, it is Mr Elliot certainly. He has changed his hour of going, I suppose, that is all – or I may be mistaken; I might not attend;' and walked back to her chair, recomposed, and with the comfortable hope of having acquitted herself well.

The visitors took their leave; and Charles, having civilly seen them off, and then made a face at them, and abused them for coming, began with –

'Well, mother, I have done something for you that you will like. I have been to the theatre, and secured a box for to-morrow night. A'n't I a good boy? I know you love a play; and there is room for us all. It holds nine. I have engaged Captain Wentworth. Anne will not be sorry to join us, I am sure. We all like a play. Have not I done well, mother?'

Mrs Musgrove was good humouredly beginning to express her perfect readiness for the play, if Henrietta and all the others liked, when Mary eagerly interrupted her by exclaiming.

'Good heavens, Charles! how can you think of such a thing? Take a box for to-morrow night! Have you forgot that we are engaged to Camden-place to-morrow night? and that we were most particularly asked on purpose to meet Lady Dalrymple and her daughter, and Mr Elliot – all the principal family connexions – on purpose to be introduced to them? How can you be so forgetful?'

'Phoo! phoo!' replied Charles, 'what's an evening party? Never worth remembering. Your father might have asked us to dinner, I think, if he had wanted to see us. You may do as you like, but I shall go to the play.'

'Oh! Charles, I declare it will be too abominable if you do! when you promised to go.'

'No, I did not promise. I only smirked and bowed, and said the word "happy." There was no promise.'

'But you must go, Charles. It would be unpardonable to fail. We were asked on purpose to be introduced. There was always such a great connexion between the Dalrymples and ourselves. Nothing ever happened on either side that was not announced immediately. We are quite near relations, you know: and Mr Elliot too, whom you ought so particularly to be acquainted with! Every attention is due to Mr Elliot. Consider, my father's heir – the future representative of the family.'

'Don't talk to me about heirs and representatives,' cried Charles. 'I am not one of those who neglect the reigning power to bow to the rising sun. If I would not go for the sake of your father, I should think it scandalous to go for the sake of his heir. What is Mr Elliot to me?'

The careless expression was life to Anne, who saw that Captain Wentworth was all attention, looking and listening with his whole soul; and that the last words brought his enquiring eyes from Charles to herself.

Charles and Mary still talked on in the same style; he, half serious and half jesting, maintaining the scheme for the play; and she, invariably serious, most warmly opposing it, and not omitting to make it known, that however determined to go to Camden-place herself, she should not think herself very well used, if they went to the play without her. Mrs Musgrove interposed.

'We had better put it off. Charles, you had much better go back, and change the box for Tuesday. It would be a pity to be divided, and we should be losing Miss Anne too, if there is a party at her father's; and I am sure neither Henrietta nor I should care at all for the play, if Miss Anne could not be with us.'

Anne felt truly obliged to her for such kindness; and quite as much so, moreover, for the opportunity it gave her of decidedly saying –

'If it depended only on my inclination, ma'am, the party at home (excepting on Mary's account) would not be the smallest impediment. I have no pleasure in the sort of meeting, and should be too happy to change it for a play, and with you. But, it had better not be attempted, perhaps.'

'I only smirked and bowed'

She had spoken it; but she trembled when it was done, conscious that her words were listened to, and daring not even to try to observe their effect.

It was soon generally agreed that Tuesday should be the day, Charles only reserving the advantage of still teasing his wife, by persisting that he would go to the play to-morrow, if nobody else would.

Captain Wentworth left his seat, and walked to the fire-place; probably for the sake of walking away from it soon afterwards, and taking a station, with less bare-faced design, by Anne.

'You have not been long enough in Bath,' said he, 'to enjoy the evening parties of the place.'

'Oh! no. The usual character of them has nothing for me. I am no card-player.'

'You were not formerly, I know. You did not use to like cards; but time makes many changes.'

'I am not yet so much changed,' cried Anne, and stopped, fearing she hardly knew what misconstruction. After waiting a few moments he said – and as if it were the result of immediate feeling – 'It is a period, indeed! Eight years and a half is a period!'

Whether he would have proceeded farther was left to Anne's imagination to ponder over in a calmer hour; for while still hearing the sounds he had uttered, she was startled to other subjects by Henrietta, eager to make use of the present leisure for getting out, and calling on her companions to lose no time, lest somebody else should come in.

They were obliged to move. Anne talked of being perfectly ready, and tried to look it; but she felt that could Henrietta have known the regret and reluctance of her heart in quitting that chair, in preparing to quit the room, she would have found, in all her own sensations for her cousin, in the very security of his affection, wherewith to pity her.

Their preparations, however, were stopped short. Alarming sounds were heard; other visitors approached, and the door was thrown open for Sir Walter and Miss Elliot, whose entrance seemed to give a general chill. Anne felt an instant oppression, and, wherever she looked, saw symptoms of the same. The comfort, the freedom, the gaiety of the room was over, hushed into cold composure, determined silence, or insipid talk, to meet the heartless elegance of her father and sister. How mortifying to feel that it was so!

Her jealous eye was satisfied in one particular. Captain Wentworth was acknowledged again by each, by Elizabeth more graciously than before. She even addressed him once, revolving a great measure. The sequel explained it. After the waste of a few minutes in saying the proper nothings, she began to give the invitation which was to comprise all the remaining dues of the Musgroves. 'To-morrow evening, to meet a few friends, no formal party.' It was all said very gracefully, and the cards with which she had provided herself, the 'Miss Elliot at home,' were laid on the table, with a courteous, comprehensive smile to all; and one smile and one card more decidedly for Captain Wentworth. The truth was, that Elizabeth had been long enough in Bath, to understand the importance of a man of such an air and appearance as his. The past was nothing. The present was that Captain Wentworth would move about well in her drawing-room. The card was pointedly given, and Sir Walter and Elizabeth arose and disappeared.

The interruption had been short, though severe; and ease and animation returned to most of those they left, as the door shut them out, but not to Anne. She could think only of the invitation she had with such astonishment witnessed; and of the manner in which it had been received, a manner of doubtful meaning, of surprise rather than gratification, of polite acknowledgment rather than acceptance. She knew him; she saw disdain in his eye, and could not venture to believe that he had determined to accept such an offering, as atonement for all the insolence of the past. Her spirits sank. He held the card in his hand after they were gone, as if deeply considering it.

'Only think of Elizabeth's including every body!' whispered Mary very audibly. 'I do not wonder Captain Wentworth is delighted! You see he cannot put the card out of his hand.'

Anne caught his eye, saw his cheeks glow, and his mouth form itself in a momentary expression of contempt, and turned away, that she might neither see nor hear more to vex her.

The party separated. The gentlemen had their own pursuits, the ladies proceeded on their own business, and they met no more while Anne belonged to them. She was earnestly begged to return and dine, and give them all the rest of the day; but her spirits had been so long exerted, that at present she felt unequal to more, and fit only for home, where she might be sure of being as silent as she chose.

Promising to be with them the whole of the following morning, therefore, she closed the fatigues of the present, by a toilsome walk to Camden-place, there to spend the evening chiefly in listening to the busy arrangements of Elizabeth and Mrs Clay for the morrow's party, the frequent enumeration of the persons invited, and the continually improving detail of all the embellishments which were to make it the most completely elegant of its kind in Bath, while harassing herself in secret with the never-ending question, of whether Captain Wentworth would come or not? They were reckoning him as certain, but, with her, it was a gnawing solicitude never appeased for five minutes together. She generally thought he would come, because she generally thought he ought; but it was a case which she could not so shape into any positive act of duty or discretion, as inevitably to defy the suggestions of very opposite feelings.

She only roused herself from the broodings of the restless agitation, to let Mrs Clay know that she had been seen with Mr Elliot three hours after his being supposed to be out of Bath; for having watched in vain for some intimation of the interview from the lady herself, she determined to mention it; and it seemed to her that there was guilt in Mrs Clay's face as she listened. It was transient, cleared away in an instant, but Anne could imagine she read there the consciousness of having, by some complication of mutual trick, or some overbearing authority of his, obliged to attend (perhaps for half an hour) to his lectures and restrictions on her designs on Sir Walter. She exclaimed, however, with a very tolerable imitation of nature.

'Oh dear! very true. Only think, Miss Elliot, to my great surprise I met with Mr Elliot in Bath-street! I was never more astonished. He turned back and walked with me to the Pump-yard. He had been prevented setting off for Thornberry, but I really forget by what – for I was in a hurry, and could not much attend, and I can only answer for his being determined not to be delayed in his return. He was full of "to-morrow;" and it is very evident that I have been full of it too ever since I entered the house, and learnt the extension of your plan, and all that had happened, or my seeing him could never have gone so entirely out of my head.'

CHAPTER TWENTY THREE

ONE DAY ONLY HAD PASSED since Anne's conversation with Mrs Smith; but a keener interest had succeeded, and she was now so little touched by Mr Elliot's conduct, except by its effects in one quarter, that it became a matter of course the next morning, still to defer her explanatory visit in Rivers-street. She had promised to be with the Musgroves from breakfast to dinner. Her faith was plighted, and Mr Elliot's character, like the Sultaness Scheherazade's head, must live another day.

She could not keep her appointment punctually, however; the weather was unfavourable, and she had grieved over the rain on her friends' account, and felt it very much on her own, before she was able to attempt the walk. When she reached the White Hart, and made her way to the proper apartment, she found herself neither arriving quite in time, nor the first to arrive. The party before her were Mrs Musgrove, talking to Mrs Croft, and Captain Harville to Captain Wentworth, and she immediately heard that Mary and Henrietta, too impatient to wait, had gone out the moment it had cleared, but would be back again soon, and that the strictest injunctions had been left with Mrs Musgrove, to keep her there till they returned. She had only to submit, sit down, be outwardly composed, and feel herself plunged at once in all the agitations which she had merely laid her account of tasting a little before the morning closed. There was no delay, no waste of time. She was deep in the happiness of such misery, or the misery of such happiness, instantly. Two minutes after her entering the room, Captain Wentworth said,

'We will write the letter we were talking of, Harville, now, if you will give me materials.'

Materials were all at hand, on a separate table; he went to it, and nearly turning his back on them all, was engrossed by writing.

Mrs Musgrove was giving Mrs Croft the history of her eldest daughter's engagement, and just in that inconvenient tone of voice which was perfectly audible while it pretended to be a whisper. Anne felt that she did not belong to the conversation, and yet, as Captain Harville seemed thoughtful and not disposed to talk, she could not avoid hearing many undesirable particulars, such as 'how Mr Musgrove and my brother Hayter had met again and again to talk it over; what my brother Hayter had said one day, and what Mr Musgrove had proposed the next, and what had occurred to my sister Hayter, and what the young people had wished, and what I said at first I never could consent to, but was afterwards persuaded to think might do very well,' and a great deal in the same style of open-hearted communication – Minutiae which, even with every advantage of taste and delicacy which good Mrs Musgrove could not give, could be properly interesting only to the principals. Mrs Croft was attending with great good humour, and whenever she spoke at all, it was very sensibly. Anne hoped the gentlemen might each be too much self-occupied to hear.

'And so, ma'am, all these things considered,' said Mrs Musgrove in her powerful whisper, 'though we could have wished it different, yet altogether we did not think it fair to stand out any longer; for Charles Hayter was quite wild about it, and Henrietta was pretty near as bad; so we thought they had better marry at once, and make the best of it, as many others have done before them. At any rate, said I, it will be better than a long engagement.'

'That is precisely what I was going to observe,' cried Mrs Croft. 'I would rather have young people settle on a small income at once, and have to struggle with a few difficulties together, than be involved in a long engagement. I always think that no mutual –'

'Oh! dear Mrs Croft,' cried Mrs Musgrove, unable to let her finish her speech, 'there is nothing I so abominate for young people as a long engagement. It is what I always protested against for my children. It is all very well, I used to say, for young people to be engaged, if there is a certainty of their being able to marry in six months, or even in twelve, but a long engagement!'

'Yes, dear ma'am,' said Mrs Croft, 'or an uncertain engagement; an engagement which may be long. To begin without knowing that at such a time there will be the means of marrying, I hold to be very unsafe and unwise, and what, I think, all parents should prevent as far as they can.'

Anne found an unexpected interest here. She felt its application to herself, felt it in a nervous thrill all over her, and at the same moment that her eyes instinctively glanced towards the distant table, Captain Wentworth's pen ceased to move, his head was raised, pausing, listening, and he turned round the next instant to give a look – one quick, conscious look at her.

The two ladies continued to talk, to re-urge the same admitted truths, and enforce them with such examples of the ill effect of a contrary practice, as had fallen within their observation, but Anne heard nothing distinctly; it was only a buzz of words in her ear, her mind was in confusion.

Captain Harville, who had in truth been hearing none of it, now left his seat, and moved to a window; and Anne seeming to watch him, though it was from thorough absence of mind, became gradually sensible that he was inviting her to join him where he stood. He looked at her with a smile, and a little motion of the head, which expressed, 'Come to me, I have something to say;' and the unaffected, easy kindness of manner which denoted the feelings of an older acquaintance than he really was, strongly enforced the invitation. She roused herself and went to him. The window at which he stood, was at the other end of the room from where the two ladies were sitting, and though nearer to Captain Wentworth's table, not very near. As she joined him, Captain Harville's countenance reassumed the serious, thoughtful expression which seemed its natural character.

'Look here,' said he, unfolding a parcel in his hand, and displaying a small miniature painting, 'do you know who that is?'

'Certainly, Captain Benwick.'

'Yes, and you may guess who it is for. But (in a deep tone) it was not done for her. Miss Elliot, do you remember our walking together at Lyme, and grieving for him? I little thought then – but no matter. This was drawn at the Cape. He met with a clever young German artist at the Cape, and in compliance with a promise to my poor sister, sat to him, and was bringing it home for her. And I have now the charge of getting it properly set for another! It was a commission to me! But who else was there to employ? I hope I can allow for him. I am not sorry, indeed, to make it over to another. He undertakes it – (looking towards Captain Wentworth) he is writing about it now.' And with a quivering lip he wound up the whole by adding, 'Poor Fanny! she would not have forgotten him so soon!'

'No,' replied Anne, in a low feeling voice. 'That I can easily believe.'

'It was not in her nature. She doated on him.'

'It would not be the nature of any woman who truly loved.'

Captain Harville smiled, as much to say, 'Do you claim that for your sex?' and she answered the question, smiling also, 'Yes. We certainly do not forget you, so soon as you forget us. It is, perhaps, our fate rather than our merit. We cannot help ourselves. We live at home, quiet, confined, and our feelings prey upon us. You are forced on exertion. You have always a profession, pursuits, business of some sort or other, to take you back into the world immediately, and continual occupation and change soon weaken impressions.'

'Granting your assertion that the world does all this so soon for men, (which, however, I do not think I shall grant) it does not apply to Benwick. He has not been forced upon any exertion. The peace turned him on shore at the very moment, and he has been living with us, in our little family-circle ever since.'

'True,' said Anne, 'very true; I did not recollect; but what shall we say now, Captain Harville? If the change be not from outward circumstances, it must be from within; it must be nature, man's nature, which has done the business for Captain Benwick.'

'No, no, it is not man's nature. I will not allow it to be more man's nature than woman's to be inconstant and forget those they do love, or have loved. I believe the reverse. I believe in a true analogy between our bodily frames and our mental; and that as our bodies are the strongest, so are our feelings; capable of bearing most rough usage, and riding out the heaviest weather.'

'Your feelings may be the strongest,' replied Anne, 'but the same spirit of analogy will authorise me to assert that ours are the most tender. Man is more robust than woman, but he is not longer-lived; which exactly explains my view of the nature of their attachments. Nay, it would be too hard upon you, if it were otherwise. You have difficulties, and privations, and dangers enough to struggle with. You are always labouring and toiling, exposed to every risk and hardship. Your home, country, friends, all quitted. Neither time, nor health, nor life, to be called your own. It would be too hard indeed' (with a faltering voice) 'if woman's feelings were to be added to all this.'

'We shall never agree upon this question' – Captain Harville was beginning to say, when a slight noise called their attention to Captain Wentworth's hitherto perfectly quiet division of the room. It was nothing more than that his pen had fallen down, but Anne was startled at finding him nearer than she supposed, and half inclined to suspect that the pen had only fallen, because he had been occupied by them, striving to catch sounds, which yet she did not think he could have caught.

'Have you finished your letter?' said Captain Harville.

'Not quite, a few lines more. I shall have done in five minutes.'

'There is no hurry on my side. I am only ready whenever you are. – I am in very good anchorage here,' (smiling at Anne) 'well supplied, and want for nothing. – No hurry for a signal at all. – Well, Miss Elliot,' (lowering his voice) 'as I was saying, we shall never agree I suppose upon this point. No man and woman would, probably. But let me observe that all histories are against you, all stories, prose and verse. If I had such a memory as Benwick, I could bring you fifty quotations in a moment on my side the argument, and I do not think I ever opened a book in my life which had not something to say upon woman's inconstancy. Songs and proverbs, all talk of woman's fickleness. But perhaps you will say, these were all written by men.'

'Perhaps I shall. – Yes, yes, if you please, no reference to examples in books. Men have had every advantage of us in telling their own story. Education has been theirs in so much higher a degree; the pen has been in their hands. I will not allow books to prove any thing.'

'But how shall we prove any thing?'

'We never shall. We never can expect to prove any thing upon such a point. It is a difference of opinion which does not admit of proof. We each begin probably with a little bias towards our own sex, and upon that bias build every circumstance in favour of it which has occurred within our own circle; many of which circumstances (perhaps those very cases which strike us the most) may be precisely such as cannot be brought forward without betraying a confidence, or in some respect saying what should not be said.'

'Ah!' cried Captain Harville, in a tone of strong feeling, 'if I could but make you comprehend what a man suffers when he takes a last look at his wife and children, and watches the boat that he has sent them off in, as long as it is in sight, and then turns aways and says, "God knows whether we ever meet again!" And then, if I could convey to you the glow of his soul when he does see them again; when, coming back after a twelvemonth's absence perhaps, and obliged to put into another port, he calculates how soon it be possible to get them there, pretending to deceive himself, and saying, "They cannot be here till such a day," but all the while hoping for them twelve hours sooner, and seeing them arrive at last, as if Heaven had given them wings, by many hours sooner still! If I could explain to you all this, and all that a man can bear and do, and glories to do for the sake of these treasures of his existence! I speak, you know, only of such men as have hearts!' pressing his own with emotion.

'Oh!' cried Anne eagerly, 'I hope I do justice to all that is felt by you, and by those who resemble you. God forbid that I should undervalue the warm and faithful feelings of any of my fellow-creatures. I should deserve utter contempt if I dared to suppose that true attachment and constancy were known only by woman. No, I believe you capable of every thing great and good in your married lives. I believe you equal to every important exertion, and to every domestic forbearance, so long as – if I may be allowed the expression, so long as you have an object. I mean, while the woman you love lives, and lives for you. All the privilege I claim for my own sex (it is not a very enviable one, you need not covet it) is that of loving longest, when existence or when hope is gone.'

She could not immediately have uttered another sentence; her heart was too full, her breath too much oppressed.

'You are a good soul,' cried Captain Harville, putting his hand on her arm quite affectionately. 'There is no quarrelling with you. – And when I think of Benwick, my tongue is tied.'

Their attention was called towards the others. – Mrs Croft was taking leave.

'Here, Frederick, you and I part company, I believe,' said she. 'I am going home, and you have an engagement with your friend. – To-night we may have the pleasure of all meeting again, at your party,' (turning to Anne.) 'We had your sister's card yesterday, and I understood Frederick had a card too, though I did not see it – and you are disengaged, Frederick, are you not, as well as ourselves?'

Captain Wentworth was folding up a letter in a great haste, and either could not or would not answer fully.

'Yes,' said he, 'very true; here we separate, but Harville and I shall soon be after you, that is, Harville, if you are ready, I am in half a minute. I know you will not be sorry to be off. I shall be at your service in half a minute.'

Mrs Croft left them, and Captain Wentworth, having sealed his letter with great rapidity, was indeed ready, and had even a hurried, agitated air, which shewed impatience to be gone. Anne knew not how to understand it. She had the kindest 'Good morning, God bless you,' from Captain Harville, but from him not a word, nor a look. He had passed out of the room without a look!

She had only time, however, to move closer to the table where he had been writing, when footsteps were heard returning; the door opened; it was himself. He begged their pardon, but he had forgotten his gloves, and instantly crossing the room to the writing table, and standing with his back towards Mrs Musgrove, he drew out a letter from under the scattered paper, placed it before Anne with eyes of glowing entreaty fixed on her for a moment, and hastily collecting his gloves, was again out of the room, almost before Mrs Musgrove was aware of his being in it – the work of an instant!

The revolution which one instant had made in Anne, was almost beyond expression. The letter, with a direction hardly legible, to 'Miss A.E. –.' was evidently the one which he had been folding so hastily. While supposed to be writing only to Captain Benwick, he had been also addressing her! On the contents of that letter depended all which this world could do for her! Any thing was possible, any thing might be defied rather than suspense. Mrs

Placed it before Anne

Musgrove had little arrangements of her own at her own table; to their protection she must trust, and sinking into the chair which he had occupied, succeeding to the very spot where he had leaned and written, her eyes devoured the following words:

'I can listen no longer in silence. I must speak to you by such means as are within my reach. You pierce my soul. I am half agony, half hope. Tell me not that I am too late, that such precious feelings are gone for ever. I offer myself to you again with a heart even more your own, than when you almost broke it eight years and a half ago. Dare not say that man forgets sooner than woman, that his love has an earlier death. I have loved none but you. Unjust I may have been, weak and resentful I have been, but never inconstant. You alone have brought me to Bath. For you alone I think and plan. – Have you not seen this? Can you fail to have understood my wishes? – I had not waited even these ten days, could I have read your feelings, as I think you must have penetrated mine. I can hardly write. I am

every instant hearing something which overpowers me. You sink your voice, but I can distinguish the tones of that voice, when they would be lost on others. – Too good, too excellent creature! You do us justice indeed. You do believe that there is true attachment and constancy among men. Believe it to be most fervent, most undeviating in

'F.W.

'I must go, uncertain of my fate; but I shall return hither, or follow your party, as soon as possible. A word, a look will be enough to decide whether I enter your father's house this evening or never.'

Such a letter was not to be soon recovered from. Half an hour's solitude and reflection might have tranquillized her; but the ten minutes only, which now passed before she was interrupted, with all the restraints of her situation, could do nothing towards tranquillity. Every moment rather brought fresh agitation. It was an overpowering happiness. And before she was beyond the first stage of full sensation, Charles, Mary, and Henrietta all came in.

The absolute necessity of seeming like herself produced then an immediate struggle; but after a while she could do no more. She began not to understand a word they said, and was obliged to plead indisposition and excuse herself. They could then see that she looked very ill – were shocked and concerned – and would not stir without her for the world. This was dreadful! Would they only have gone away, and left her in the quiet possession of that room, it would have been her cure, but to have them all standing or waiting around her was distracting, and, in desperation, she said she would go home.

'By all means, my dear,' cried Mrs Musgrove, 'go home directly and take care of yourself, that you may be fit for the evening. I wish Sarah was here to doctor you, but I am no doctor myself. Charles, ring and order a chair. She must not walk.'

But the chair would never do. Worse than all! To lose the possibility of speaking two words to Captain Wentworth in the course of her quiet, solitary progress up the town (and she felt almost certain of meeting him) could not be borne. The chair was earnestly protested against; and Mrs Musgrove, who thought only of one sort of illness, having assured herself, with some anxiety, that there had been no fall in the case; that Anne had not, at any time lately, slipped down, and got a blow on her head; that she was perfectly convinced of having had no fall, could part with her cheerfully, and depend on finding her better at night.

Anxious to omit no possible precaution, Anne struggled, and said,

'I am afraid, ma'am, that it is not perfectly understood. Pray be so good as to mention to the other gentlemen that we hope to see your whole party this evening. I am afraid there has been some mistake; and I wish you particularly to assure Captain Harville, and Captain Wentworth, that we hope to see them both.'

'Oh! my dear, it is quite understood, I give you my word. Captain Harville has no thought but of going.'

'Do you think so? But I am afraid; and I should be so very sorry! Will you promise me to mention it, when you see them again? You will see them both again this morning, I dare say. Do promise me.'

'To be sure I will, if you wish it. Charles, if you see Captain Harville any where, remember to give Miss Anne's message. But indeed, my dear, you need not be uneasy. Captain Harville holds himself quite engaged, I'll answer for it; and Captain Wentworth the same, I dare say.'

Anne could do no more; but her heart prophesied some mischance, to damp the perfection of her felicity. It could not be very lasting, however. Even if he did not come to Camden-place himself, it would be in her power to send an intelligible sentence by Captain Harville.

Another momentary vexation occurred. Charles, in his real concern and good-nature, would go home with her; there was no preventing him. This was almost cruel! But she could not be long ungrateful; he was sacrificing an engagement at a gunsmith's to be of use to her; and she set off with him, with no feeling but gratitude apparent.

They were in Union-street, when a quicker step behind, a something of familiar sound, gave her two moments preparation for the sight of Captain Wentworth. He joined them; but, as if irresolute whether to join or to pass on, said nothing – only looked. Anne could command herself enough to receive that look, and not repulsively. The cheeks which had been pale now glowed, and the movements which had hesitated were decided. He walked by her side. Presently, struck by a sudden thought, Charles said,

'Captain Wentworth, which way are you going? only to Gay-street, or farther up the town?'

'I hardly know,' replied Captain Wentworth, surprised.

'Are you going as high as Belmont? Are you going near Camden-place? Because if you are, I shall have no scruple in asking you to take my place, and give Anne your arm to her father's door. She is rather done for this morning, and must not go so far without help. And I ought to be at that fellow's in the market-place. He promised me the sight of a capital gun he is just going to send off; said he would keep it unpacked to the last possible moment, that I might see it; and if I do not turn back now, I have no chance. By his description, a good deal like the second-sized double-barrel of mine, which you shot with one day, round Winthrop.'

There could not be an objection. There could be only a most proper alacrity, a most obliging compliance for public view; and smiles reined in and spirits dancing in private rapture. In half a minute, Charles was at the bottom of Union-street again, and the other two proceeding together; and soon words enough had passed between them to decide their direction towards the comparatively quiet and retired gravel-walk, where the power of conversation would make the present hour a blessing indeed; and prepare it for all the immortality which the happiest recollections of their own future lives could bestow. There they exchanged again those feelings and those promises which had once before seemed to secure every thing, but which had been followed by so many, many years of division and estrangement. There they returned again into the past, more exquisitely happy, perhaps, in their reunion, than when it had been first projected; more tender, more tried, more fixed in a knowledge of each other's character, truth, and attachment; more equal to act, more justified in acting. And there, as they slowly paced the gradual ascent, heedless of every group around them, seeing neither sauntering politicians, bustling house-keepers, flirting girls, nor nursery-maids and children, they could indulge in those retrospections and acknowledgments, and especially in those explanations of what had directly preceded the present moment, which were so poignant and so ceaseless in interest. All the little variations of the last week were gone through; and of yesterday and to-day there could scarcely be an end.

She had not mistaken him. Jealousy of Mr Elliot had been the retarding weight, the doubt, the torment. That had begun to operate in the very hour of first meeting her in Bath; that had returned, after a short suspension, to ruin the concert; and that had influenced him in every thing he had said and done, or omitted to say and do, in the last four-and-twenty hours. It had been gradually yielding to the better hopes which her looks, or words, or actions occasionally encouraged; it had been vanquished at last by those sentiments and those tones which had reached him while she talked with Captain Harville; and under the irresistible governance of which he had seized a sheet of paper, and poured out his feelings.

Of what he had then written, nothing was to be retracted or qualified. He persisted in having loved none but her. She had never been supplanted. He never even believed himself to see her equal. Thus much indeed he was obliged to acknowledge – that he had been constant unconsciously, nay unintentionally; that he had meant to forget her, and believed it to be done. He had imagined himself indifferent, when he had only been angry; and he had been unjust to her merits, because he had been a sufferer from them. Her character was now fixed on his mind as perfection itself, maintaining the loveliest medium of fortitude and gentleness; but he was obliged to acknowledge that only at Uppercross had he learnt to do her justice, and only at Lyme had he begun to understand himself.

At Lyme, he had received lessons of more than one sort. The passing admiration of Mr Elliot had at least roused him, and the scenes on the Cobb, and at Captain Harville's, had fixed her superiority.

In his preceding attempts to attach himself to Louisa Musgrove (the attempts of angry pride), he protested that he had for ever felt it to be impossible; that he had not cared, could not care for Louisa; though, till that day, till the leisure for reflection which followed it, he had not understood the perfect excellence of the mind with which Louisa's could so ill bear a comparison; or the perfect, unrivalled hold it possessed over his own. There, he had learnt to distinguish between the steadiness of principle and the obstinacy of self-will, between the darings of heedlessness and the resolution of a collected mind. There, he had seen every thing to exalt in his estimation the woman he had lost, and there begun to deplore the pride, the folly, the madness of resentment, which had kept him from trying to regain her when thrown in his way.

From that period his penance had become severe. He had no sooner been free from the horror and remorse attending the first few days of Louisa's accident, no sooner begun to feel himself alive again, than he had begun to feel himself, though alive, not at liberty.

'I found,' said he, 'that I was considered by Harville an engaged man! That neither Harville nor his wife entertained a doubt of our mutual attachment. I was startled and shocked. To a degree, I could contradict this instantly; but, when I began to reflect that others might have felt the same – her own family, nay, perhaps herself, I was no longer at my own disposal. I was hers in honour if she wished it. I had been unguarded: I had not thought seriously on this subject before. I had not considered that my excessive intimacy must have its danger of ill consequence in many ways; and that I had no right to be trying whether I could attach myself to either of the girls, at the risk of raising even an unpleasant report, were there no other ill effects. I had been grossly wrong, and must abide the consequences.'

He found too late, in short, that he had entangled himself; and that precisely as he became fully satisfied of his not caring for Louisa at all, he must regard himself as bound to her, if her sentiments for him were what the Harvilles supposed. It determined him to leave Lyme, and await her complete recovery elsewhere. He would gladly weaken, by any fair means, whatever feeling or speculations concerning him might exist; and he went, therefore, to his brother's, meaning after a while to return to Kellynch, and act as circumstances might require.'

'I was six weeks with Edward,' said he, 'and saw him happy. I could have no other pleasure. I deserved none. He enquired after you very particularly; asked even if you were personally altered, little suspecting that to my eye you could never alter.'

Anne smiled, and let it pass. It was too pleasing a blunder for a reproach. It is something for a woman to be assured, in her eight-and-twentieth year, that she has not lost one charm of earlier youth: but the value of such homage was inexpressibly increased to Anne, by comparing it with former words, and feeling it to be the result, not the cause of a revival of his warm attachment.

He had remained in Shropshire, lamenting the blindness of his own pride, and the blunders of his own calculations, till at once released from Louisa by the astonishing and felicitous intelligence of her engagement with Benwick.

'Here,' said he, 'ended the worst of my state; for now I could at least put myself in the way of happiness, I could exert myself, I could do something. But to be waiting so long in inaction, and waiting only for evil, had been dreadful. Within the first five minutes I said, 'I will be at Bath on Wednesday,' and I was. Was in unpardonable to think it worth my while to come? and to arrive with some degree of hope? You were single. It was possible that you might retain the feelings of the past, as I did; and one encouragement happened to be mine. I could never doubt that you would be loved and sought by others, but I knew to a certainty that you had refused one man at least, of better pretensions than myself: and I could not help often saying, Was this for me?'

Their first meeting in Milsom-street afforded much to be said, but the concert still more. That evening seemed to be made up of exquisite moments. The moment of her stepping forward in the octagon-room to speak to him, the moment of Mr Elliot's appearing and tearing her away, and one or two subsequent moments, marked by returning hope or increasing despondence, were dwelt on with energy.

'To see you,' cried he, 'in the midst of those who could not be my well-wishers, to see your cousin close by you, conversing and smiling, and feel all the horrible eligibilities and proprieties of the match! To consider it as the certain wish of every being who could hope to influence you! Even, if your own feelings were reluctant or indifferent, to consider what powerful supports would be his! Was it not enough to make the fool of me which I appeared? How could I look on without agony? Was not the very sight of the friend who sat behind you, was not the recollection of what had been, the knowledge of her influence, the indelible, immoveable impression of what persuasion had once done – was it not all against me?'

'You should have distinguished,' replied Anne. 'You should not have suspected me now; the case so different, and my age so different. If I was wrong in yielding to persuasion once, remember that it was to persuasion exerted on the side of safety, not of risk. When I yielded, I thought it was to duty; but no duty could be called in aid here. In marrying a man indifferent to me, all risk would have been incurred, and all duty violated.'

'Perhaps I ought to have reasoned thus,' he replied, 'but I could not. I could not derive benefit from the late knowledge I had acquired of your character. I could not bring it into play: it was overwhelmed, buried, lost in those earlier feelings which I had been smarting under year after year. I could think of you only as one who had yielded, who had given me up, who had been influenced by any one rather than by me. I saw you with the very person who had guided you in that year of misery. I had no reason to believe her of less authority now. – The force of habit was to be added.'

I should have thought, said Anne, 'that my manner to yourself might have spared you much or all of this.'

'No, no!' your manner might be only the ease which your engagement to another man would give. I left you in this belief; and yet – I was determined to see you again. My spirits rallied with the morning, and I felt that I had still a motive for remaining here.'

At last Anne was at home again, and happier than any one in that house could have conceived. All the surprise and suspense, and every other painful part of the morning dissipated by this conversation, she re-entered the house so happy as to be obliged to find an alloy in some momentary apprehensions of its being impossible to last. An interval of meditation, serious and grateful, was the best corrective of every thing dangerous in such high-wrought felicity; and she went to her room, and grew steadfast and fearless in the thankfulness of her enjoyment.

The evening came, the drawing-rooms were lighted up, the company assembled. It was but a card-party, it was but a mixture of those who had never met before, and those who met too often – a common-place business, too numerous for intimacy, too small for variety; but Anne had never found an evening shorter. Glowing and lovely in sensibility and happiness, and more generally admired than she thought about or cared for, she had cheerful or forbearing feelings for every creature around her. Mr Elliot was there; she avoided, but she could pity him. The Wallises; she had amusement in understanding them. Lady Dalrymple and Miss Carteret; they would soon be innoxious cousins to her. She cared not for Mrs Clay, and had nothing to blush for in the public manners of her father and sister. With the Musgroves, there was the happy chat of perfect ease; with Captain Harville, the kind-hearted intercourse of brother and sister; with Lady Russell, attempts at conversation, which a delicious consciousness cut short; with Admiral and Mrs Croft, every thing of peculiar cordiality and fervent interest, which the same consciousness sought to conceal; – and with Captain Wentworth, some moments of communication continually occurring, and always the hope of more, and always the knowledge of his being there!

It was in one of these short meetings, each apparently occupied in admiring a fine display of green-house plants, that she said –

'I have been thinking over the past, and trying impartially to judge of the right and wrong, I mean with regard to myself; and I must believe that I was right, much as I suffered from it, that I was perfectly right in being guided by the friend whom you will love better than you do now. To me, she was in the place of a parent. Do not mistake me, however. I am not saying that she did not err in her advice. It was, perhaps, one of those cases in which advice is good or bad only as the event decides; and for myself, I certainly never should, in any circumstance of tolerable similiarity, give such advice. But I mean, that I was right in submitting to her, and that if I had done otherwise, I should have suffered more in continuing the engagement than I did even in giving it up, because I should have suffered in my conscience. I have now, as far as such a sentiment is allowable in human nature, nothing to reproach myself with; and if I mistake not, a strong sense of duty is no bad part of a woman's portion.'

He looked at her, looked at Lady Russell, and looking again at her, replied, as if in cool deliberation,

'Not yet. But there are hopes of her being forgiven in time. I trust to being in charity with her soon. But I too have been thinking over the past, and a question has suggested itself, whether there may not have been one person more my enemy even than that lady? My own self. Tell me if, when I returned to England in the year eight, with a few thousand pounds, and was posted into the Laconia, if I had then written to you, would you have answered my letter? would you, in short, have renewed the engagement then?'

'Would I!' was all her answer; but the accent was decisive enough.

'Good God!' he cried, 'you would! It is not that I did not think of it, or desire it, as what could alone crown all my other success. But I was proud, too proud to ask again. I did not understand you. I shut my eyes, and would not understand you, or do you justice. This is a recollection which ought to make me forgive every one sooner than myself. Six years of separation and suffering might have been spared. It is a sort of pain, too, which is new to me. I have been used to the gratification of believing myself to earn every blessing that I enjoyed. I have valued myself on honourable toils and just rewards. Like other great men under reverses,' he added with a smile, 'I must endeavour to subdue my mind to my fortune. I must learn to brook being happier than I deserve.'

CHAPTER TWENTY FOUR

WHO CAN BE IN DOUBT OF what followed? When any two young people take it into their heads to marry, they are pretty sure by perseverance to carry their point, be they ever so poor, or ever so imprudent, or ever so little likely to be necessary to each other's ultimate comfort. This may be bad morality to conclude with, but I believe it to be truth; and if such parties succeed, how should a Captain Wentworth and an Anne Elliot, with the advantage of maturity of mind, consciousness of right, and one independent fortune between them, fail of bearing down every opposition? They might in fact have borne down a great deal more than they met with, for there was little to distress them beyond the want of graciousness and warmth. – Sir Walter made no objection, and Elizabeth did nothing worse than look cold and unconcerned. Captain Wentworth, with five-and-twenty thousand pounds, and as high in his profession as merit and activity could place him, was no longer nobody. He was now esteemed quite worthy to address the daughter of a foolish spendthrift baronet, who had not had principle or sense enough to maintain himself in the situation in which Providence had placed him, and who could give his daughter at present but a small part of the share of ten thousand pounds which must be hers hereafter.

Sir Walter indeed, though he had no affection for Anne, and no vanity flattered, to make him really happy on the occasion, was very far from thinking it a bad match for her. On the contrary, when he saw more of Captain Wentworth, saw him repeatedly by daylight and eyed him well, he was very much struck by his personal claims, and felt that his superiority of appearance might not be unfairly balanced against her superiority of rank; and all this, assisted by his well-sounding name, enabled Sir Walter at last to prepare his pen with a very good grace for the insertion of the marriage in the volume of honour.

The only one among them, whose opposition of feeling could excite any serious anxiety, was Lady Russell. Anne knew that Lady Russell must be suffering some pain in understanding and relinquishing Mr Elliot, and be making some struggles to become truly acquainted with, and do justice to Captain Wentworth. This however was what Lady Russell had now to do. She must learn to feel that she had been mistaken with regard to both; that she had been unfairly influenced by appearances in each; that because Captain Wentworth's manners had not suited her own ideas, she had been too quick in suspecting them to indicate a character of dangerous impetuosity; and that because Mr Elliot's manners had precisely pleased her in their propriety and correctness, their general politeness and suavity, she had been too quick in receiving them as the certain result of the most correct opinions and well regulated mind. There was nothing less for Lady Russell to do, than to admit that she had been pretty completely wrong, and to take up a new set of opinions and of hopes.

There is a quickness of perception in some, a nicety in the discernment of character, a natural penetration, in short, which no experience in others can equal, and Lady Russell had been less gifted in this part of understanding than her young friend. But she was a very good woman, and if her second object was to be sensible and well-judging, her first was to see Anne happy. She loved Anne better than she loved her own abilities; and when the awkwardness of the beginning was over, found little hardship in attaching herself as a mother to the man who was securing the happiness of her other child.

Of all the family, Mary was probably the one most immediately gratified by the circumstance. It was creditable to have a sister married, and she might flatter herself with having been greatly instrumental to the connexion, by keeping Anne with her in the autumn; and as her own sister must be better than her husband's sisters, it was very agreeable that Captain Wentworth should be a richer man than either Captain Benwick or Charles Hayter. – She had something to suffer perhaps when they came into contact again, in seeing Anne restored to the rights of seniority, and the mistress of a very pretty landaulette; but she had a future to look forward to, of powerful consolation. Anne had no Uppercross-hall before her, no landed estate, no headship of a family; and if they could but keep Captain Wentworth from being made a baronet, she would not change situations with Anne.

It would be well for the eldest sister if she were equally satisfied with her situation, for a change is not very probable there. She had soon the mortification of seeing Mr Elliot withdraw; and no one of proper condition has since presented himself to raise even the unfounded hopes which sunk with him.

The news of his cousin Anne's engagement burst on Mr Elliot most unexpectedly. It deranged his best plan of domestic happiness, his best hope of keeping Sir Walter single by the watchfulness which a son-in-law's rights would have given. But, though discomfited and disappointed, he could still do something for his own interest and his own enjoyment. He soon quitted Bath; and on Mrs Clay's quitting it likewise soon afterwards, and being next heard of as established under his protection in London, it was evident how double a game he had been playing, and how determined he was to save himself from being cut out by one artful woman, at least.

Mrs Clay's affections had overpowered her interest, and she had sacrificed, for the young man's sake, the possibility of scheming longer for Sir Walter. She has abilities, however, as well as affections; and it is now a doubtful point whether his cunning, or hers, may finally carry the day; whether, after preventing her from being the wife of Sir Walter, he may not be wheedled and caressed at last into making her the wife of Sir William.

It cannot be doubted that Sir Walter and Elizabeth were shocked and mortified by the loss of their companion, and the discovery of their deception in her. They had their great cousins, to be sure, to resort to for

The mistress of a very pretty landaulette

comfort; but they must long feel that to flatter and follow others, without being flattered and followed in turn, is but a state of half enjoyment.

Anne, satisfied at a very early period of Lady Russell's meaning to love Captain Wentworth as she ought, had no other alloy to the happiness of her prospects than what arose from the consciousness of having no relations to bestow on him which a man of sense could value. There she felt her own inferiority keenly. The disproportion in their fortune was nothing; it did not give her a moment's regret; but to have no family to receive and estimate him properly; nothing of respectability, of harmony, of good-will to offer in return for all the worth and all the prompt welcome which met her in his brothers and sisters, was a source of as lively pain as her mind could well be sensible of, under circumstances of otherwise strong felicity. She had but two friends in the world to add to his list, Lady Russell and Mrs Smith. To those, however, he was very well disposed to attach himself. Lady Russell, in spite of all her former transgressions, he could now value from his heart. While he was not obliged to say that he believed her to have been right in originally dividing them, he was ready to say almost every thing else in her favour; and as for Mrs Smith, she had claims of various kinds to recommend her quickly and permanently.

Her recent good offices by Anne had been enough in themselves; and their marriage, instead of depriving her of one friend, secured her two. She was their earliest visitor in their settled life; and Captain Wentworth, by putting her in the way of recovering her husband's property in the West Indies; by writing for her, acting for her, and seeing her through all the petty difficulties of the case, with the activity and exertion of a fearless man and a determined friend, fully requited the services which she had rendered, or ever meant to render, to his wife.

Mrs Smith's enjoyments were not spoiled by this improvement of income, with some improvement of health, and the acquisition of such friends to be often with, for her cheerfulness and mental alacrity did not fail her; and while these prime supplies of good remained, she might have bid defiance even to greater accessions of worldly prosperity. She might have been absolutely rich and perfectly healthy, and yet be happy. Her spring of felicity was in the glow of her spirits, as her friend Anne's was in the warmth of her heart. Anne was tenderness itself, and she had the full worth of it in Captain Wentworth's affection. His profession was all that could ever make her friends wish that tenderness less; the dread of a future war all that could dim her sunshine. She gloried in being a sailor's wife, but she must pay the tax of quick alarm for belonging to that profession which is, if possible, more distinguished in its domestic virtues than in its national importance.